EMBRACE THE ROMANCE

PETS IN SPACE 2

S.E. SMITH   M.K. EIDEM   SUSAN GRANT

MICHELLE HOWARD   CARA BRISTOL

VERONICA SCOTT   PAULINE BAIRD JONES

LAURIE A. GREEN   SABINE PRIESTLEY

JESSICA E. SUBJECT   CAROL VAN NATTA

ALEXIS GLYNN LATNER

ABOUT EMBRACE THE ROMANCE

The pets are back! Embrace the Romance: Pets in Space 2, featuring twelve of today's leading Science Fiction Romance authors brings you a dozen original stories written just for you! Join in the fun, from the Dragon Lords of Valdier to a trip aboard award-winning author, Veronica Scott's Nebula Zephyr to journeying back to Luda where Grim is King, for stories that will take you out of this world! Join New York Times, USA TODAY, and Award-winning authors S.E. Smith, M.K. Eidem, Susan Grant, Michelle Howard, Cara Bristol, Veronica Scott, Pauline Baird Jones, Laurie A. Green, Sabine Priestley, Jessica E. Subject, Carol Van Natta, and Alexis Glynn Latner as they share stories and help out Hero-Dogs.org, a charity that supports our veterans!

10% of all preorders and the first month's profits go to Hero-Dogs.org. Hero Dogs raises and trains service dogs and places them free of charge with US Veterans to improve quality of life and restore independence.

PEARL'S DRAGON

Dragon Lords of Valdier Story

The single greatest gift for me is to be able to give to others. I am honored to share my talents to bring joy and offer support through the Embrace the Romance: Pets in Space 2 Project. ~ Susan

S.E. Smith is a New York Times/USA TODAY Bestselling Author who encourages readers to reach for the stars and embrace the action, adventure, family, friendship, and true love that is found in the worlds she creates.

http://sesmithfl.com/

PEARL'S RULES FOR LIVING

1. Use your brain - that is why you have one.
2. Safety is something you take seriously, otherwise you end up dead.
3. If you have expressive eyes, keep them covered if you are going to bluff.
4. Give someone enough rope, and they are bound to get tangled and hang themselves.
5. Always carry a roll of quarters, you can do your laundry and knock out bad guys at the same time.
6. There are rules and there are rules, pick which ones work for you.
7. Don't fuck up unless you are willing to make it right.
8. Mistakes are good, learn from them and move on.
9. Always stay alert and don't let your guard down.
10. Ask yourself, 'Am I ready for this?' If the answer is yes, go for it. If the answer is no, run like hell.
11. If you are going to hit someone, make sure they stay down the first time. You might not get a second chance.
12. Don't trust a man, especially a good-looking one who starts out with sweet words. Same goes for a woman, she just wants something.
13. A good book and fresh batteries can make your day tolerable.
14. Your word is your honor, be careful what you promise.
15. Humor solves any problem; think in animation.
16. The only opinion you have to worry about is your own, since *you* have to live with it.

17. Be the best possible you that you can be.
18. Your goal each day is to make it a good one.
19. Words can be as powerful as a fist; be careful how you use them.
20. If you or your family/friends' lives are on the line, ignore all of the above except Rule Number 1.

Unbreakable rule: Family and friends come first. Be loyal, be true, and love them like there is no tomorrow.

PROLOGUE

Present Day:

"The last rule I'm going to share is the Unbreakable Rule," Pearl St. Claire stated in a firm tone. She released a sigh and raised an eyebrow at the scarred warrior sitting in one of the two chairs in the room. He was staring at the board she was pointing to with a mutinous expression. "What is it now, Brogan?"

"I told you when you started. I don't follow anyone's rules but my own," Brogan stated, folding his arms.

"And look where that got you! All I can say is you'd better learn if you want to get out of this room - alive," Pearl snapped in a sharper tone than she originally intended before adding the last word under her breath.

"Pearl," Aslm cautioned in a low voice from where he was sitting on a bench by the door.

Pearl slowly counted to thirty. She'd already bypassed ten and twenty. Why she was chosen for this exasperating task was beyond her. The only thing she could think of was that she had survived raising Riley and Tina without any casualties.

Surely, I can manage a few lessons in humility for the two men sitting in front of me, she thought.

Unfortunately, she felt like she was starting all over again – only this time during the toddler stage. Being over sixty, she'd thought she was finished dealing with stubborn, defiant, and downright ornery kids. Back on Earth, she'd been a surrogate grandmother to the kids in the neighbor-hood. During that time, she had seen and heard a lot. She was well aware that she was the kind of grandmother every kid wanted to have – and the one every parent wished they could hide in the closet.

She didn't dress like a grandmother – she preferred leather and boots to dresses and pearls. She didn't go to church; instead, she owned a bar. She never carried a wooden spoon, but hell if she didn't still have a shotgun loaded with rock salt. Her platinum-white hair was cut short and she stayed in shape by doing Yoga, Zumba, and Weekend Warrior train-ings with her newly adopted great-grandson.

Jabir, Mandra and Ariel's son, had captured her heart as quickly as her own great-grandsons, Roam and Leo, had. Unfortunately, Roam and Leo lived on the Sarafin home world while she lived on Valdier. Living on another planet wasn't much more of a problem than living across town – well, except for having to use a spaceship to visit. Still, Pearl was able to talk with the two boys regularly and they loved visiting her here.

At the moment, she would rather be with the cuddly little dragonling and his menagerie of unusual pets or her great-grandsons. It sure as hell beat resisting the urge to find a baseball bat and knock some sense into two well-seasoned warriors who had an elephant's hair up their asses.

As it was, there were currently only the four of them – her, Asim, and the twin dragon warriors– in the barn's tack room. Her classroom was not much larger than a ten by ten shed back home. There was just enough room for the table and two chairs that Asim had brought in earlier this morning, plus the bench he was sitting on by the door. Harnesses for the Pactors, leashes for the smaller animals, and maintenance tools hung neatly on two of the four walls. The floor was clean and the room smelled of the sweet warm grass that was used as hay for the animals in the outer stalls.

Pearl shot a heated glare at her amused mate when he smothered a chuckle. Asim raised an eyebrow in response and tried to look innocent. With a shake of her head, she slowly turned back to the twin dragons.

She rested one hand on her hip and tapped her fingers against her side. She was really going to have a private talk with Asim later. She needed to remind him that her personality was not conducive to being a teacher.

Pearl studiously observed her two pupils. She had quickly distin-guished the difference between the identical twin dragons known as Barrack and Brogan. Barrack had more patience and control than his brother, Brogan, – by about the width of a human hair.

After hours of trying to explain human culture to the brothers, Pearl decided her patience was fast disintegrating to their level, almost nonexis-tent. While Brogan had questioned or argued every single rule she had tried to explain, Barrack had just released long, drawn-out sighs of impatience.

Raising her chin, Pearl returned Brogan's steely gaze. Time was fast running out for the two men. She was about to open a can of whoop-ass on them if they didn't get their heads out of their asses. She pointed a determined finger at Barrack.

"What is Rule number one?" she snapped.

"Use your brain – that's why we have one," Barrack replied with an uncertain tone in his voice.

Pearl would have felt more confident in Barrack's answer if he hadn't looked doubtful and raised his hand to scratch at his temple. She gave Barrack a firm nod of agreement. Of course, Brogan snorted. She shot the scarred warrior a sharp, reproving look. The fingers of her left hand twitched. Pearl drew in a deep breath. She would not resort to violence!

"Yes, use your brain. You can't use your brain, Brogan, if your head isn't attached to your damn shoulders," she stated.

"Fine, but what has this got to do with our mate? The Curizan takes us to your world, Jaguin and Sara show us where our mate is, and we claim her. Why do we need to learn these… rules?" Brogan demanded with a wave of his hand.

"Because Aikaterina is giving you a second chance at life," a voice dryly replied from the doorway.

Pearl turned to see two tall, lean warriors and a slender, blonde woman standing in the entrance to the tack room. She recognized one of the men and the woman as Jaguin and Sara. For a private meeting, the room was quickly filling up.

"Hi Pearl. Thank you for doing this," Sara said with a sympathetic smile.

"Hi, Sara. I wish I could say teaching these two boneheads was a pleasure, but…." Pearl gave Sara a wink to show she was teasing. "Hi Jaguin, I see you brought a friend. Are you part of this mission, too?" Pearl asked.

Pearl turned her attention to the tall man with the scar running down one side of his face. He positively exuded an air of power and danger. It was a good thing he was obviously a friend because she sure as hell wouldn't want him as an enemy.

"This is Adalard Ha'darra, the captain of our transport to Earth," Jaguin replied.

"Better known as Curizan trash," Brogan added with a heavy dose of disdain.

Pearl had had enough of the twins' attitudes – especially Brogan's. He had a smart retort to just about everything she'd said and an expression of condescension on his face that reminded her of the college-educated Preppies who came into the White Pearl Bar she'd owned back on Earth. He continued to be a pain-in-the-ass from the second he stepped into the classroom. Her patience was on empty.

Pearl decided that some people just needed to learn the hard way and

Brogan was one of those people. She slipped her hand into the pocket of her black pleather jacket she was wearing. She wrapped her fingers around a small but very handy device that she had confiscated from one of her granddaughters. In the background, Pearl heard Asim's loud curse, Jaguin's warning, and Sara's smothered gasp as she stepped forward, pressed the Taser firmly against the dragon warrior's chest, and pushed the button.

"Rule number nine: always stay alert and don't let your guard down," she stated. "That means for everyone," she added with a nod of gratification when he grimaced and hit the floor with a resounding thud.

The grunted curses coming from the two men on the floor finally began to fade. Relaxing back against the wall by the door, Asim patiently waited for the men to recover. Studying the sculpture, he blew off some of the loose scrapings from the small creature he was carving before he lowered the knife and the wood figurine to his lap.

Brogan was the first one to sit up – if you could call scooting back against the wall and propping himself up 'sitting'. Barrack continued to lie on the floor, rubbing his chest. Barrack would have fared much better than his brother if he hadn't growled at Pearl. The second he did, she'd shocked his ass and put him on the floor next to Brogan.

Asim warily studied both men to see if they had calmed down. He had to admit it had been hard not to laugh when Pearl asked if Brogan understood the rule of learning to shut up before it was too late. While the two men lay twitching on the floor, Pearl calmly turned to Sara to ask if she would care for a cup of hot tea and a piece of the freshly baked cake that Ariel brought over the night before.

Pride mixed with exasperation. He probably should have warned Pearl about the possible consequences of enraging Twin Dragon warriors – especially those who already had a history of maiming and killing anyone who got in their way.

"What was that?" Barrack asked in a strained voice.

"*That* was my mate being nice," Asim stated.

"That… was being nice?" Brogan repeated in disbelief. "What happens when she isn't being nice?"

"You don't want to know," Asim assured him with a lopsided grin.

"Why did she react so strongly to Brogan's comment? Is she part Curizan?" Barrack asked, confused.

"Strongly?! She almost killed us! I swear I can still smell my flesh burning," Brogan retorted.

Asim couldn't contain the chuckle that escaped him. He shook his head. He knew exactly what Brogan was talking about. After all, he had been in the same position as the two men on more than one occasion when he finally pushed Pearl too far.

"No, she is fully human," he replied. "She was asked to help you. If you don't listen, expect the consequences," Asim said.

"Are all humans like this? If they are, we need more information about them," Barrack demanded.

"Finally! Some information that will be more useful than a bunch of rules," Brogan retorted under his breath.

"Well, I know enough never to underestimate the powers of a human – be they man or woman. I can't tell you about the others, only those who I have met. You will learn more about them on your journey," he replied.

"Tell us about those you've met then," Barrack insisted.

Asim thought about where to begin and decided that telling his story might help the two warriors. A lot had changed over the centuries and Pearl was a good example of what they could expect, he reasoned. He had heard of the original Twin Dragons. The stories he remembered said they died.

Asim had been shocked when Zoran Reykill, King of the Valdier and ruler of all Dragon Lords, had contacted him requesting Pearl and he help with an urgent matter. The next day, Jaguin and Sara appeared with the legendary and highly volatile warriors who were alive and well. The only thing Jaguin and Sara said was the men needed to be instructed in the ways of the humans, and that a very special person whom they had insisted remain a mystery – much to Asim's annoyance – had requested that Pearl be the one to help the twins understand.

Zoran had been a little more forthcoming. It would appear the Goddess Aikaterina had appeared to both Sara and Jaguin. Worried about Sara after her traumatic experience back on Earth with a group of human men, Zoran had suggested approaching Pearl – after all, he reasoned, Pearl had no problems handling Vox and Viper.

Zoran had felt that Pearl was the only one who could get the twins ready to court their human mate in a timely manner – and teach them a little humility at the same time. Asim didn't know if using that shocking device would count as listening, but it definitely got the men's attention. He just needed to remember to find the damn thing and hide it again – this time in a place where Pearl wasn't likely to find it.

"The story I will tell you will seem incredulous, perhaps no more unbe-lievable than your – second chance – but this species is unlike any that we have encountered before. When Jaguin and Sara told Lord Zoran about your second chance, he decided it was important for you to understand what you will face," Asim explained.

"Surely it cannot be that difficult?" Brogan asked, wiggling his fingers.

"Shut up, Brogan. My chest hurts enough thanks to your comments. I would prefer to keep my head and my nervous system in working order from now on, brother," Barrack retorted.

Asim released a sigh as he remembered his own struggles with the loneliness and despair when he thought he would never find a true mate. He turned the wooden figurine over in his hands, trying to think of what he could tell the men that would help them understand the difference between a Valdier mate and a human one.

The wooden bird in his hand was a creature alien to their world. It was large, flightless, and smart. In a way, his history with the emus reminded him of the humans he had met. Oh, he didn't think of humans as being the actual bird – just that it was easy to misunderstand them, like it had been when he found Jabir's hidden cache of eggs. It was better to have the knowledge before you went into battle – every good warrior knew that.

"Over the last couple of years, my life has become very interesting, more fulfilling than I could ever have hoped – and definitely a lot more complicated. Like you, my dragon felt the emptiness of not having a true mate, but it was my symbiot who grieved the most. It was only my promise to our former king and my sworn duties to Lord Mandra, Lady Ariel, and their young son, Jabir, which gave me the strength to carry on. I never expected to be given the gift of finding my true mate. When I saw Pearl...." Asim shook his head and chuckled. "Shocked would be a mild description of my feelings. To find my mate after so many years... it was a revelation like nothing I could have imagined."

"What do you mean? Your dragon and symbiot would know. The female would immediately recognize what was happening. What could be so surprising?" Barrack asked.

Asim raised an eyebrow. "You assume that Pearl is like a Valdier female, but she is not. Her species do not connect the same way we do. Our dragons and our symbiots recognize our mate even before we do, but we understand what is happening. Humans do not have that same connection. They must be courted," he explained.

Barrack sat up with a confused expression on his face and asked, "Courted? Why should they be forced to go before the council? Are they sentenced to be with another?" he asked.

"No, no. Courted is a term I learned from Lady Ariel. It means you must put your mate first and bring her gifts and spend time with her so that she will accept you and fall in love with you," Asim said.

"Of course, we will put our mate first!" Brogan exclaimed. "As for the rest, once she sees us, she will grow to care for us. How can she resist?" Brogan asked with a skeptical glare.

"Our symbiots will protect her – even from us if necessary," Barrack added, glancing at his brother with a stern expression. "She will not need to fear us. We have learned from our experience before."

Asim shook his head. "You two have a lot to learn about your true mate's species. They are fragile, delicate creatures with a steely will beyond anything you have ever encountered," he replied in exasperation.

"Pearl certainly seems to be," Brogan replied, rubbing his chest. "What is that?" Brogan asked, nodding to the figurine Asim held in his hand.

Asim glanced down and grinned. "This is part of my tale, but first I need to tell you about how I met Pearl," he said, reaching out and handing the odd-looking bird to Barrack. "My story begins just a couple of years ago during a very bizarre Earth ritual called Easter...."

ONE

Three years before:

"No more. You've had enough," Asim Kemark ordered in a stern tone.

Of course, the damn creatures ignored him. The mass of small wiggling bodies turned their heads in unison to gaze up at him with dark, soulful eyes filled with a silent plea for more food. The floor of the barn was covered with furry bodies.

If the colorful Maratts weren't enough to drive him crazy, the Grombots swinging from the makeshift lines and custom playset were doing a pretty good job. He and Mandra Reykill had built dozens of the playsets for the six-legged creatures. At the moment, the Grombots were doing a pretty good job of utilizing them.

No have this problem if you let me eat them, his dragon chortled.

Don't remind me!

"Stop! Get out of there now!" Asim shouted in dismay as he tried to carefully navigate his way to the Grombot reaching into the feed sack he hung on a peg in the wall. The damn thing was using its four hands to sprinkle food onto the floor while handing from by its feet. The Maratts surrounding him turned as one toward the piles of food the Grombot was scattering. His jaw tightened in aggravation when the Grombot looked at him and grinned before it reached into the sack again and dumped not one or two, but four more scoops onto the floor. If he didn't stop the damn beast, it would empty the sack and he would end up nursing several sick baby Maratts!

Lifting his foot, he started to take another step when a stray Maratt darted out from under a bale of freshly cut, warm grass. Asim twisted in an effort to avoid crushing the tiny creature and his arms wildly pinwheeled as he tried to keep his balance. He might have succeeded if another Grombot, hanging upside down from one of the beams above his head, hadn't chosen that exact moment to drop onto his shoulders.

"Ugh!" Asim groaned.

His arms came up to grab the Grombot as he fell. Fortunately, he landed on the warm grass instead of the floor or any critters. If he had landed on the floor, his morning would have ended up going from bad to worse. Some of the little ones were not house-trained yet and the floor was usually a minefield on a good day and a landfill on the bad ones.

Holding the Grombot protectively against his chest, Asim leaned his head back and groaned. Three of the Grombots were now in the upper rafters despite the netting that was fitted across the beams to prevent it. One of the older ones must have figured out how to loosen it.

Asim grimaced when he noticed that one of the three was a juvenile. Lady Ariel would have a fit if she saw them up there, especially the baby. Jabir, on the other hand would probably be sitting up there with them. He had caught the little boy trying to imitate the various creatures on the ranch before. Asim pushed up, still cradling the Grombot against his chest, and gazed down at the mass of Maratts eagerly enjoying their extra breakfast.

"All of you will get sick again and Lady Ariel will be upset," he informed them. Of course, they didn't pay him any attention. He was about to get up when the Grombot in his arms turned its head. "Ouch! *Dragon's Balls*! That is my chest hair you are chewing on. Oh no! You are definitely not trying that! I am not your *Dola*! You need to keep your grubby lips off my man nipples."

The Grombot struggled against his grip, trying to suckle. Asim winced when several of his chest hairs were ripped out. He must remember to wear more than a vest when he fed the animals. Some of them were getting a little too attached – literally! He stood up, placed the Grombot on one of the climbing nets, and rescued the almost empty feedbag. He had no doubt that he was going to have a pile of shit to clean up when he returned this evening. He still needed to take care of the Pactor inherited from Lady Melina. He glanced at his communicator and noticed the time.

"*Bloody Sarafin hairballs*!" Asim cursed. "I'm late and none of you are helping. Pokey, get in here!"

The morning feeding was going about the same as it did every day – complete chaos. He ignored the sniggering of his dragon and waited for his symbiot to come help him. Ever since his dragon learned that none of the tasty treats running under foot and swinging overhead were on the menu, the damn thing was having way too much fun – at his expense.

It better than hurting and being grumpy like Pokey, his dragon pointed out to him.

"I know," Asim snapped before he drew in a deep breath and replied again in a calmer tone. *I know, my friend. I thank you for your control. It is obvious I have very little left.*

True. You also have Grombot escaping, his dragon chuckled.

Asim turned to see the Grombot hatchling slowly crawling toward the opened door of the barn. If Lord Mandra didn't set up another run to these creatures' home planet, they would have to build another barn. It didn't matter how hard he tried to keep the boys and girls apart, they always seemed to get mixed up. It had taken him a month – and almost three dozen new babies – to discover Jabir was sneaking out to play with the creatures after everyone had gone to bed and then returning them to the wrong cages.

"*Dragon's balls!* Don't you care that the Pactor would eat you up if you aren't careful?" Asim demand in exasperation

He was about to pick up the dark gray creature when his symbiot trotted in, snatched it by the back of its neck, and continued past him. Asim turned and raised an eyebrow at his symbiot. The damn thing had been behaving strangely over the last few months.

"What took you so long? You know they get antsy if they don't eat on time," Asim demanded.

His symbiot dropped the Grombot on the bale of warm grass and shook. Its body shimmered for a moment before the glow died. Asim bit back the caustic retort he had been about to direct at the golden creature.

Symbiot like to be called Pokey, his dragon reminded him.

I know, Asim snorted with a shake of his head.

Pokey was the name that Jabir had given Asim's symbiot because he liked a creature his mother told him about called Pokey the Puppy. Of course, his symbiot wasn't the only critter with a name on the vast mountain spread that Lord Mandra, Lady Ariel, and little Jabir retreated to whenever they could. Those visits invariably meant more rescued animals added to the menagerie of creatures now under Asim's care.

"Can you retrieve the three Grombots from the rafters while I take care of the Pactor?" Asim asked.

The symbiot shrugged and began climbing up the thick post. Asim didn't miss that it moved with about as much speed as the Grombots and with a lot less enthusiasm. Concerned, he touched the thin band of gold on his arm to connect with his symbiot. A curse escaped him when the golden creature sent a warning zap of electricity through it. Asim winced and rubbed his arm. It was obvious Pokey wasn't in the mood to communicate.

"How can we help you if you won't let us?" Asim demanded, watching the symbiot climb up onto the rafter.

Asim drew in a swift breath when his symbiot opened to him for a brief moment and showed him the darkness that was dragging it down before it closed their connection again. In that second, it dawned on Asim how much his symbiot and his dragon were hiding from him. While they were all interconnected, the other two had somehow managed to shield awareness of the slender thread of control they were struggling to preserve from him.

"What have I done?" Asim groaned, running his hand over the back of his neck in self-disgust. "I think only of my discomfort without consideration of what I've been doing to you."

You protect us – we protect you, his dragon replied in a solemn tone.

Asim stared out the barn door, lost in thought. Beyond the fences that circled the assorted barns was a long meadow. Tall, purple grass swayed back and forth thanks to the breeze flowing down from the mountains that surrounded the valley. At the far end was a large lake fed by the waterfall and streams coming from the ice capped mountains. A thick forest of trees near the west side of the lake sheltered his modest home.

Perhaps it was time to move on to the next life. It was not as if the prince needed his protection any longer. With Lord Raffvin dead, the threat to the Dragon Lords was vastly reduced to a handful of traitors who were being steadily hunted. There were more than enough warriors to carry on the fight. He was just an old, worn out warrior with little left to give to his king and the rapidly growing royal family.

No! We be alright, his dragon snarled. *We find true mate now.*

The snort from his symbiot told him a different story. He had prolonged the inevitable as long as he possibly could in good conscience. That brief glimpse had shown him that his symbiot was trying to absorb his and his dragon's despair. The negative emotion was slowly killing the creature that fed on their essences.

"We are killing our symbiot, dragon. He can only live on our negative essences for so long before he dies a slow and torturous death. What honor is there in that? Once he dies, so will we. Why should we be so cruel as to push all the weight of our despair on him in the hopes of finding a true mate who does not exist? We are old. What female in her right mind would want a dragon warrior like us? No, it is time to do the honorable thing and acknowledge our time is at an end before we lose control – which *will* happen when our symbiot is no longer with us," he said with a deep sigh.

It not time. We find mate who likes old dragons, his dragon stated stubbornly.

"I need to take care of the Pactor before we can leave," Asim said, ignoring his dragon.

Asim's dragon muttered under his breath before pulling away. Asim had to give his dragon credit for not giving up hope. He wished he could believe there was a true mate out there for them as much as his dragon did.

Unfortunately, now that he knew how sick his dragon and he were making his symbiot, he couldn't deny that they had been deluding themselves and each other. No, tonight he would tell Mandra that it was time for him to move on to the next life. He would order his symbiot to return to the Hive, and he and his dragon would die an honorable death in the ways of the ancient warriors. For now, though, he would enjoy the last of their time here in this world.

"Well, maybe not completely enjoy it," he muttered, staring at the huge piles of Pactor dung in the corral that would need to be shoveled before he could leave.

This is something I will not miss in my next life, he thought as he reached for the large shovel leaning against the fence.

TWO

Pearl St. Claire gazed around her. A part of her wanted to pinch herself again, while the other part remembered that it hurt like hell when you weren't dreaming. There was no denying that she was on an alien world. If the tall purple grass, unusual plants, and even stranger men running around in the shape of dragons and tigers weren't enough to convince her, nothing would.

"Vox, you...!"

Pearl turned in time to see her new grandson-in-law, Vox d'Rojah, King of the Sarafin cat-shifters, pull her oldest granddaughter, Riley, into the large fountain where their son Roam, along with a small burgundy and gold dragonling named Bálint, and he were cavorting. Pearl swore if she tried to say that out loud, either her tongue would get twisted or she would end up in a padded room.

The sound of laughter echoed through the garden. Pearl shook her head and couldn't keep the soft chuckle from escaping her. For the first time in her life, she felt like everything would be alright for her grand-daughters.

"I think they've broken the St. Claire curse," Pearl said in a soft, satis-fied voice.

The St. Claire curse was what her mother had called the St. Claire women's long line of bad relationships. Eloise James St. Claire had blamed the curse on Pearl's great-great-grandmother, who was said to have passed down the curse from one daughter to the next. Pearl had never believed in all the hocus pocus until she had her own daughter. The thought of Teri sent a familiar twist of pain through her. If only....

"Remember rule number eight," Pearl said to herself.

Pearl had developed a list of rules to help remind her when she started to lose her way or forget. Some rules had changed over time, and she had no doubt that more would, but some rules had stayed constant. Rule number eight was a reminder that everyone makes mistakes in their life. Mistakes were okay – as long as you learned from them and moved on. Learning from the past was all right but living in it was not. Pearl had learned that sometimes it was hard to distinguish between the learning and the living, though.

That life lesson occurred when Teri passed away. Pearl had woken in the middle of the night with her heart pounding and tears streaming down her face. The shadowy image of Teri hugging her and smiling before letting her go still burned in her mind. The dream had ripped a cry of denial from her and deeply shaken her.

Unable to go back to sleep, she had slipped out of bed to check on Riley and Tina. Fortunately, both girls were sound asleep, oblivious to her panic. The next morning, the sheriff's office had contacted her. Pearl had quietly made the arrangements for Teri's funeral, unwilling to subject her grand-daughters to the darkness and grief that had been their mother's life.

Deep down, she had always known the girls would find out. She just wanted them to be old enough to understand. She didn't know she had made the right decision until a few years later. Riley had called her and told her that she knew about what had happened to her mom. When Riley thanked her for leaving them with only the good memories of Teri, Pearl had choked up. At the end of their conversation, Riley had quietly asked her not to tell Tina yet.

"She doesn't remember much about mom. I think it would be better to wait until she is older, like me," Riley had suggested.

Pearl had agreed, never really finding a good time or way to tell Tina. Of course, like Riley, Tina had eventually discovered the truth – thanks in part to her biological father. That, of course, opened another can of worms that Pearl didn't want to think about.

While Teri's death initially left a gaping hole inside her heart, having Riley and Tina had quickly filled her life to overflowing. Pearl had sworn she would do everything in her power to give them the home she had struggled to give their mother. It hadn't been easy, but Pearl had trusted her gut and persevered. Oh, she had to learn a lot of hard and painful lessons along the way. In fact, she reckoned that she had done enough self-reflection over the years to fill several volumes in a self-help textbook.

Her early years were complicated. She had fallen like a ton of bricks for Teri's father when she was barely eighteen. A bad boy on leave, Joe had been in the Army and their short time together produced her beautiful daughter. Her mother kicked her out of the house when she found out, but Pearl hadn't cared. She had faced the world with the defiance that only someone as naïve as a young girl in love could.

It wasn't until after her mother's death that Pearl discovered that she was the product of her mother's own youthful indiscretion. It turned out that the man she'd thought was her father had really been her uncle. He had married her mother to protect his older brother who was married to someone else at the time. The hypocrisy of the situation wasn't lost on Pearl, but instead of being angry, she embraced the freedom of the world around her.

That freedom wasn't easy, but she had never asked for easy. She had worked at any and every job she could find to provide a good home for her daughter, but it hadn't been enough. Teri fell in with the wrong crowd when she was fifteen and while Pearl did everything she could to help her daughter, the darkness continued to draw Teri deeper and deeper into a world Pearl struggled to understand.

There were rays of hope that quickly faded with the drugs. The only time Teri remained clean was when she was pregnant. Those were the only two times in her daughter's self-destructive life that Teri had found a reason to fight back. Out of the two girls, Pearl had worried the most about Tina. Riley was too much like herself, a fighter, but Tina was a lot like Teri – quiet, introverted, and smart.

The sounds of Riley's laughter drew her back to the present. The glow on Riley's face and the love in Vox's eyes was enough to send a surge of warmth through Pearl. Viper had that same look in his eyes when he looked at Tina. She chuckled when Riley pushed Vox's head under the water cascading from the top of the fountain. Of course, Vox pulled Riley with him, kissing her with a passion that drew groans of disgust from their young son.

"I hope you aren't expecting me to sit next to wet cat hair on the way home," Pearl called out to Riley before turning to shake her head at the couple who were standing nearby They were kissing as well. "Damn, I swear these have got to be the horniest damn men I've ever seen. How in the hell does anyone get anything done around here?"

Of course, no one answered, not that she was really expecting one. Chuckling under her breath, she walked over to the table where the refreshments were set out. For a brief moment, Pearl wondered if there could be a good-looking, older warrior who might be interested in a more mature woman. With a shake of her head, she pushed the thought aside. Who was she kidding? Even old, these guys looked young enough to be her grandkids!

"What I wouldn't give for a guy with a few lines on his face who spoke to me of fine Kentucky bourbon and messy sheets," she mused.

"Excuse me," a deep voice said from behind her.

THREE

It took Asim longer than he expected to finish the chores scheduled for the day. Two of the baby Grombots had escaped when he was finishing the cleanup of the Pactor's holding pen. They had opened the door to the barn and all the Maratts had run loose. They had frightened the Pactor who, in turn, left him another gift to shovel.

He finally ended up resorting to bribery. A trail of food and the greedy little creatures had followed him, their stomachs practically dragging on the ground because they were so full. Tomorrow morning was not going to be a pleasant day.

He would have to postpone his talk with Mandra tonight. There was no way he would leave the young prince and Lady Ariel with what was bound to be a ton of poop to pick up. He honestly needed to talk to Mandra about shipping the Pactor back to Cree, Calo, and Melina. They had their own spread now. It was about time they shoveled the huge piles of dung.

He was running so late by the time he finished that he almost decided not to attend the function at the palace. It was only his promise to Jabir that he would join the little boy and his parents that compelled Asim to clean up and make the long flight over the mountains. As it was, it was well past the mid-day mark before he soared over the outer wall of the palace grounds.

The guards along the wall raised their hands in a salute of respect for his service and position within the royal family. Asim snapped his tail in response, drawing the attention of some of the young recruits who turned to watch him in awe. He swept past the large towers and curved around to the back gardens.

The sounds of laughter rang out from below. Asim followed the joyous noise, hoping to arrive quietly without Mandra or Ariel realizing how late he was. His gaze skimmed over the families below. Pride and a deep affection swept through him.

Asim understood the feeling of pride. He had been a part of the royal family's lives since the first king, Jalo Reykill, and Lady Morian joined as a mated pair. He had stood guard over each of the princes, but the affection came from the deep bond that he had developed with Mandra.

If anyone had asked, he would have been hard pressed to deny that he thought of Lord Mandra as the son he'd never had. The largest of the Dragon Lords, Mandra had always been self-conscious about his size. It was hard when both the men and women feared you. It was especially difficult for a young dragon coming into his prime.

Asim knew that underneath the huge exterior of the man lay the heart of a true warrior. He was a gentle giant with a tender heart for all creatures large and small. It was one reason the young prince spent so much time at the mountain retreat Asim helped him to build. Asim, lost in the memories of his time with the young lord, was startled when his dragon shouted with excitement.

I find her!

What? Who did you find? Asim asked, focusing on the present again. He tried to concentrate on what his dragon saw. His dragon twisted in the air, narrowly missing the branch of a tree. *What are you doing?*

I find mate! I find her! His dragon excitedly exclaimed.

What are you rambling on about? Have you gone mad? Asim demanded, trying to rein in his dragon when it lunged recklessly toward the garden.

Asim silently swore when he felt another powerful burst of joyful emotion sweep through him. Confusion struck him as to the source until he realized the emotion was coming from his symbiot. It had lagged further and further behind them on their journey here, as if reluctant to be around others, but was now putting on a burst of speed in its excitement. Asim tried to focus on what could have caused such a reaction in his symbiot. A curse ripped through his mind when he saw the vivid mental image of a woman that his dragon was sharing with his symbiot.

The picture of a slender woman flashed through his mind so fast that he barely had time to see more than a glimpse of white hair and what looked like black leather. The confusion he'd felt a second ago was nothing compared to what was hitting him now. He must be mistaken. Perhaps Lady Cara had dyed her hair a different color, or Lady Riley had cut hers. That was it! That color reminded him of the hair color of Lord Vox's mate. He needed to get his dragon under control before the damn thing started another war. With a mental shake of his head, he snapped at his dragon.

Watch out!

His dragon swerved upward and expanded his wings completely at the last second. If Asim hadn't warned the damn thing, they would have made a spectacular exhibition of themselves. Fortunately, they landed on the back side of a large cluster of shrubbery.

Asim shifted into his two-legged form the moment he landed. Irritation flooded him when he stumbled several steps. He hadn't had such an uncoordinated landing since he was a dragonling!

"What is the matter with you?" he snapped.

His dragon was pacing back and forth inside him, trying to escape again. Scales rippled over his body, and he could feel the bands around his wrists heating up almost to the point of burning his skin. He rubbed at the gold bands.

It our mate! I see her, his dragon insisted.

You have lost control, he silently snapped, glancing around the garden. *The only ones here are the princes and their mates.*

I see our mate, his dragon insisted, trying to push him toward the main garden where everyone was.

You need to get under control before we join the others, Asim ordered.

You wait. You see mate, you not be in control no more, his dragon retorted.

Asim shook his head and drew in a deep breath. He glanced over his shoulder when he felt – more than saw – his symbiot land behind him. The large golden body was in the shape of a WereCat with wings. That was a new addition, since Jabir loved WereCats but wanted one that could fly. It shimmered with more colors than Asim had seen in centuries.

"Don't...," he started to warn, lifting a cautioning hand to his symbiot. "Wait here. I don't want to endanger anyone. I am having a hard enough time trying to control my dragon. I don't want to have to try to deal with you as well."

His symbiot snorted and paced back and forth behind him. For a moment, Asim wasn't sure it was going to listen to him. It kept glancing in the direction of the main garden. The huge golden body was shimmering in an ever-changing array of colors, and its ears were moving around like small radars turning to analyze the laughter of each member of the royal family.

Asim studied his symbiot with a wary eye when it froze again. He waited to see if it would follow his orders. He grunted quietly when it shook its head and blinked at him.

"Stay here," he repeated in a firm voice.

He was rewarded with a snort and a light shock to his wrists. Cursing under his breath, Asim glared at his symbiot. Between it and his dragon, he was ready for a drink – or a hundred.

No time to get drunk, we have mate to court, his dragon gleefully retorted.

Court? Asim asked, distracted.

Remember what Ariel say? Mandra court her if he make her mad, his dragon reminded him. *I court my mate. She like me then.*

"We don't have a ma…."

The words died on Asim's lips when he stepped around the bushes and onto the path. He jerked to a stop, his gaze immediately locked on the slender figure of a woman standing near a table laden with food. She was turned slightly away from him so all he could see was her profile.

I told you. I find us mate! His dragon gloated.

Asim swallowed, blinked, and nodded without realizing he was silently agreeing with his dragon. From her profile, he could tell that she was older than the other princesses – a fact that sent a wave of relief through him. She was like finely aged wine that a man could appreciate.

His gaze ran over her short hair that was as white as freshly fallen snow. Her hair was spiked on the top but cut close on the sides. The style showcased her delicate features and made him think of what it would look like after he ran his hands through it.

She was wearing a dark blue, silk blouse tucked into the waist of her black leather trousers and a pair of low cut black boots. His fingers itched to pull the silky fabric free so he could run his hands up under it to caress her skin.

A low curse escaped him when his dragon struggled to get out. Asim acknowledged his dragon was right – they found their mate. Of course, to be absolutely sure, he would need to see if his symbiot agreed. Hope was one thing – all three of them actually agreeing tended to be another. He had met women in the past who he'd thought had the potential to be his mate only to be disappointed when his dragon, his symbiot, or both didn't agree with him.

Where in the vast universe had she come from? He couldn't help but wonder in shock.

He ran a damp palm along his pant leg. He was afraid to test if the Goddess had finally gifted them with a woman who could complete them and fill the empty void gnawing away at them. If the woman wasn't their mate, the disappointment could likely drive all three of them to lose control. But… if she was, he would need to handle this delicately. He would introduce himself, strike up a conversation, and put her at ease so that his dragon, his symbiot and he didn't scare her.

Asim remembered all too well the struggles Mandra and the other Dragon Lords had faced. He decided he would be more controlled, more refined – that should help him in his courting of her. Clearing his throat, Asim took several steps closer to the woman.

"Excuse me," he said in a thick, rasping tone that demonstrated his dragon was close to the surface and he wasn't as in control as he'd hoped.

FOUR

Pearl released a sigh of irritation at being pulled back to reality. She swallowed the sarcastic comment on her lips and turned toward the voice. She needed to watch what she said. After all, she wasn't on Earth anymore.

She had always tended to speak before she thought at times, especially after working at the bar for so many years. That bad habit had gotten her into trouble more than once. Thank goodness for Tiny, her six-foot-five, three-hundred-five-pound bouncer, and her rock salt loaded shotgun. Between the two, she'd seldom been in a situation she couldn't handle. But, that was back on Earth and she needed to remember that she wasn't on her planet any longer.

Still, whenever she heard 'excuse me', a hundred different retorts popped into her mind. Since she was on an alien planet, she decided it was probably best that she didn't say 'Why? Are you about to have a baby explode out of your chest and need someone to catch it?' After all, who knew if it might be true?

Turning to face the man, Pearl couldn't help but suck in a deep, calming breath when her gaze locked on a pair of black booted feet spread apart in a stance that spoke of power. She clenched her fingers into a fist to keep from fanning herself as she ran an appreciative gaze up the man's legs. He was wearing black leather trousers that did nothing to hide his long legs, thick thighs, narrow hips, and....

"Someone crank down the air conditioning, I think I'm having a hot flash. Lordy, but I love a man who can make leather look that good," she said under her breath.

Pearl's gaze paused at the opening of the man's vest. She couldn't stop from licking her bottom lip at the tantalizing view of his rock hard abs. She swallowed and breathed deeply, afraid she might have forgotten how to for a second. Her gaze continued up his muscular frame. She hadn't seen muscles like that in... ever.

Fear of disappointment struck her hard – what if she got to the top and it turned out to be a pimply-faced boy and not a hunk like Sean, Sam, Kurt, Liam, or Denzel? Nothing killed a good fantasy like hearing a rough, sexy voice and finding out it is the kid from down at the Dairy Queen going through puberty and taking steroids.

Her eyes followed the path of exposed tanned skin until she stopped at a set of blazing golden eyes and a face weathered by time and life. The instant attraction hit her hard.

How do you say yummy? Over fifty and single, she thought.

Her delight changed to a scowl of shock at her reaction to him. Hell, she had only made a half-hearted wish, not a full-fledged, certifiable one! It wasn't like she was really in the market for a man in her life! She had been on her own for so long, she wasn't sure she would know what to do with one who had actual working parts. She wouldn't call any of the few serious relationships she ever had in her life earth-shattering. They had all been more like shaking the Jell-O bowl – lots of wobble before they melted into goo. Something told her this guy could make the bed shake like an earthquake!

Asim held his breath when the woman turned to face him. The moment their eyes connected, his dark golden with her vivid blue ones, he knew he was lost. Her expression quickly turned from surprised interest to a dark scowl. Dread swelled inside Asim and a sense of panic began to rise up, threatening to choke him.

"Who the hell are you?" the woman demanded, gazing back at him with an intense look.

"Asim," he automatically replied.

She doesn't like what she sees, he thought in dismay.

You think too much. She like us. She say she love man who make leather look good. You a man and you wearing leather, his dragon sighed in exasperation.

That doesn't mean she likes the rest of me! Asim snapped in irritation.

Pearl was flustered by the way the man was returning her gaze, as if she was part of the brunch buffet. True, she might have been doing a bit of eye-candy sampling, but since she had found herself on an alien world in her sixties, she figured, she deserved to sample all the candy she wanted.

Hell, at her age, she would throw in the whole damn cake with it – in every flavor, along with the ice cream and whipped topping.

The man said something that Pearl wasn't sure she heard correctly. It sounded like a guttural '*Mine!*' The translator thing they had given her must not be working correctly; because there was no way that this man could mean what she thought he said.

"I beg your pardon? What did you say?" she asked with a raised eyebrow.

"You are mine!" the man repeated.

Pearl blinked and took a startled step back when a golden creature suddenly surged from her right to stand between her and the man. The creature was like the other ones she had seen wandering around the gardens – only this one was focused on her like a starving dog eyeing a T-bone steak.

Panic hit her and her hand automatically reached behind her for a weapon to fend off the large, golden cat-shaped creature. Her fingers curled around the handle sticking out of a bowl and she whipped it around, slinging a creamy pudding mixture through the air. Dismay washed through Pearl. The gooey, cream-colored dessert and spoon were no defense against her attacker. In fact, the damn thing opened its mouth and swallowed the flying mixture. Unfortunately, the man standing behind it wasn't quite as agile. Specks of custard dotted his face. The intense expression on his face darkened into one Pearl wasn't sure she could define. The only thing she could think about when the man said '*Mine!*' was he was a dragon and dragons were meat eaters.

"Oh, shit! My old hide is too tough to eat. You'd be better off chewing on your pants," Pearl snapped in exasperation, waving the spoon in front of her.

The symbiot paused for a brief moment, opened its enormous mouth filled with large, impressive razor-sharp teeth, unfolded its tongue, and promptly licked the spoon clean. If that wasn't bad enough, it sat down in front of her, tilted its head sideways, and gave her a silly-ass grin when it was finished.

"Really? You know, that isn't a very intimidating look," Pearl stated dryly, raising an eyebrow.

A reluctant, but amused smile curved her lips. The thing looked so damn proud of itself that it was hard not to be amused by its pleased expression. She was about to drop her arm when the man standing behind the golden creature transformed. One second there was a gorgeous hunk of masculinity in front of her and the next there was a massive, fire-breathing dragon with long claws and sharp teeth. Pearl had to check herself when she started to release a wolf whistle. Even as a dragon, the guy was impressive in a turn-you-on, heat-me-up kind of way.

At least, that was her first thought. Her second one was that she was in deep shit when said gorgeous dragon reached out with his tail and wrapped it around her waist. Pearl released a strangled cry when she felt her feet suddenly leave the ground.

A second later, the golden goofball that had been in front of her transformed. Pearl watched in horrified fascination as long tentacles of gold rose up and reached outward from the creature to form an ornate, adult-size bird cage. If watching the creature transform wasn't disconcerting enough, the thin threads of gold that reached out and wrapped around her wrist was enough send her into panic mode. Pearl released a startled curse and raised her other hand to try to pull away. Before she could break free, new threads wrapped around her right wrist, creating a matching bracelet on each arm.

She had been so focused on the delicate golden bracelets forming around her wrists that she didn't noticed the other change occurring right in front of her until it was too late. Confused by what was happening, she glanced around to see if anyone else was noticing that things were quickly going to hell faster than Satan on a Sunday drive. Her mouth fell open and she stared at the man in front of her in surprise.

Correction – the dragon in front of her was close enough now that she could see every tiny detail of his face. Dark, gun-metal-gray scales lined his face. He had a high brow, long black lashes, and small, white spikes along his cheeks. His eyes had turned to a darker golden color and she swore she could see a bonfire burning in them.

"Oh shit," Pearl whispered in a strangled tone. "To hell with a spoon, I need my fucking gun!"

Lost in his dismal thoughts, it had taken a moment for Asim to realize that his dragon and his symbiot were not suffering from the same self-doubts as he was. If he hadn't been so preoccupied, he would have been aware that the two were silently conspiring against him. He smothered a groan when he saw that his symbiot had ignored his orders to stay and was circling around him from behind. It landed on silent feet a short distance from the woman.

Asim uttered a choked snarl of warning. His symbiot did more than land near the woman; it was now scaring the hell out of her! Asim winced when white globs of creamy dessert flew through the air, splattering tiny dots across his face. He raised a hand to wipe at the food particles while he watched with exasperation as his symbiot licked clean the spoon in the woman's hand. This was not the first impression he wanted to make.

He opened his mouth to protest, but quickly realized something else – his dragon had taken advantage of his distraction to seize control of his body – and this time the damn thing was determined to retain it. Asim understood that none of them wanted to lose the woman now that they discovered her, but there were better ways to do that than by kidnapping her – in front of the entire royal family. He opened his mouth to warn the woman, but promptly made the situation worse, if that was even possible.

"You are *mine!*" slipped from his lips in a barely recognizable voice.

Oh, Pactor's dung, this is not going to end well, he thought as his body shifted to that of a powerful, gray dragon on a mission.

"What the...? Who the hell are you talking about? What the hell is going on? *Riley!*" the woman demanded in a loud voice that held a clear message – she was not happy with her first impression of him.

FIVE

Asim's dragon and symbiot were totally out of control. Since he couldn't fight them both, Asim decided that he might as well focus on damage control. He would concentrate on planning how he would fix this mess once he regained control.

The woman was staring at him with a look of dismay, and with his dragon in control, all he could do was grunt out like some primitive idiot that the woman belonged to him – not that she could understand what he was actually saying since it was his dragon speaking! He could picture Lady Ariel rolling her eyes at him the way she did at Mandra when he tried talking to her in his dragon form. For now, Asim was consigned to watching in despair as his dragon wrapped his tail around the woman and gently lifted her.

The woman's curse echoed through the air, drawing the attention of the others. His dragon carefully deposited the woman in the golden cage his symbiot had become and waited for the bars to seal around her. It was obvious his dragon and symbiot were going to completely ignore everything and everyone around them except the woman.

You know there is going to be hell to pay for this, as Lady Ariel would say, don't you? Asim informed his dragon in a stern voice.

Yes, I know. All be good. We get our mate. You fix trouble, his dragon chuckled.

Asim released a long stream of mental curses, wishing he could say them out loud as his dragon pushed up off the ground. *Correction,* he thought with a grimace. *...His dragon's large battle-scarred body lifting off the ground gripping the cage with a very enraged woman inside.* Asim winced when the woman released a long series of threats.

Yes, they were going to be in big trouble – and most of that trouble looked like it was going to come from the delicate beauty who they just kidnapped. The only saving grace was that none of the royal family appeared to be too concerned about his unusual behavior – especially Lord Vox if the Sarafin king's grinning face was anything to go by.

Correction number two – none of the royal family with perhaps the exception of Lady Riley. She doesn't sound as pleased as her mate, Asim thought with a wince when he heard Riley's frantic yell. *I can just see another Great War about to begin.*

I tell you – you think too much, his dragon replied, releasing a triumphant roar as the small group turned in the air and retraced their flight from a few short minutes before.

"I'm going to cut your wings off and feed them to the buzzards," the woman growled.

Asim snorted in response. She had already threatened that. His least favorite was when she threatened to cut his balls off and use them as a door knocker. Even his dragon grimaced at that promise.

"Where in the hell are you taking me?" the woman demanded.

Asim glanced down. Far below them were the thick forests of Valdier. They would be crossing the North River soon. He turned his gaze to the woman when she muttered under her breath. Concern swept through him when she rubbed her arms. With a swift thought, a section of his symbiot dissolved and formed a thin blanket.

"What...? Oh, thank you," she said with a sigh when the golden blanket wrapped around her. "So, your name is Asim?"

Asim bowed his head and grunted. He mentally ran a hand over his face when his dragon continued to grunt, snort, and speak in *dragon speak.* The damn thing was rambling on about how long they'd been looking for their true mate, how happy they were to find her, how he couldn't wait to share the Dragon's fire with her...

Enough! She can't understand a thing you are saying, Asim said in exasperation.

"What the hell is dragon's fire?" the woman asked before she released a long hiss. "Never mind, I think I get the picture."

Yes, she can. Symbiot showing her, his dragon replied with satisfaction.

You are going to doom us. She will run as far and as fast as she can the moment we release her, Asim groaned.

"My name's Pearl St. Claire, by the way. Not 'woman', 'female', or 'she' if you think anything like Vox and Viper," Pearl dryly replied.

Asim closed his eyes when his dragon continued to talk to the woman – Pearl. Damage control – he kept repeating to himself – just focus on damage control. He didn't even bother to listen to what his dragon was telling Pearl anymore. He had a feeling he was going to be answering a lot of questions anyway, if Pearl was anything like Lady Ariel.

An hour later, they swept through the last mountain pass and into the valley where his home was located. Pearl had grown quieter the closer they got. Normally that would have been a good sign, but the way she was drumming the fingers of her right hand on her knee told him that he needed to be wary.

Take us to the edge of the lake and give me back control, Asim ordered.

Why? What you do if I give control? His dragon asked.

I am going to try to smooth things over. She is sure to be upset about our kidnapping her, Asim replied.

Maybe she not upset. Maybe she like we take her, his dragon suggested in a hopeful tone.

We are about to find out, my friend, Asim dryly retorted.

He wasn't feeling as optimistic. If he wasn't mistaken, her fingers were moving a little faster and the tension in her body was radiating outward. Asim connected with the part of his symbiot wrapped around her wrist and winced.

Yes, she might be just a little upset, Asim thought in resignation.

His dragon circled around and swooped down low over the water. He swerved upward, his powerful wings keeping them airborne while he gently released the cage. His symbiot stretched out, cushioning the cage for a soft landing before it dissolved and reformed in the shape of a large puppy complete with big, pointy ears.

Asim concentrated, focusing on shifting back to his two-legged form. He landed near the edge of the water. His boots sank into the mixture of sand and fine, colorful pebbles. He lifted a hand to run it through his short hair and drew in a deep breath, trying to think of what to say.

"First, I would...."

Asim never had a chance to finish his sentence. The deep breath he had inhaled whooshed from his lungs and he found himself stumbling backwards when a well-placed, booted foot landed squarely in his stomach.

Caught off guard, he lost his balance on the loose gravel under his feet. He barely had time to brace for the icy water that greeted him. He closed his eyes and clamped his lips as the cold water washed over his face. Stunned by the unexpected force of the attack, he lay in the shallow water for a moment before he sat up.

"That is a warning to keep your cotton-picking claws off me unless I tell you that you can touch me. You're lucky I didn't kick you in the balls," she snapped.

Asim blinked up at where Pearl stood on the bank with a large piece of driftwood in her hands. She was pointing the stick at his symbiot and her finger at him in apparent warning not to try anything. Asim ran both hands down his face and shook his head. His symbiot had its butt up in the air, the long tail wagging while its tongue lolled out and its ears twitched. The last time he had seen it behave like this was when he was a dragonling.

"He wants to play," Asim informed her.

Pearl glanced at him and rolled her eyes. "Duh. I think I can figure that out on my own," she retorted, waving the stick.

Yep, just like Lady Ariel, he thought with a grudging smile.

"I guess I deserved this," Asim grimaced, waving his hands at the water he was sitting in. "Though, technically, I did try to stop them from kidnapping you, so I believe my dragon and my symbiot deserve the cold bath more than I do."

Pearl glanced at him again and frowned. "Aren't you all the same thing?" she asked.

Asim pushed up off the ground and stood up. This was his third bath of the day, and it wasn't even late afternoon yet. A shudder of distaste ran through him when he felt the water in his boots as he took a step forward.

"Yes and no," he stated, slowly walking out of the water. "While I can shift to my dragon and we are the same, we still have our own awareness. It is… complicated."

She gazed at him with a skeptical expression. "Obviously," she replied. "So, besides having multiple personalities that can shift into a fire-breathing, mythological beast and having a…." She waved her hand at his symbiot who was now gnawing on the other end of the branch she was holding out. "…whatever in the hell that is, plus a problem with kidnapping the wrong woman, do you have any other psychological issues I should be aware of?" she asked with a raised eyebrow before turning to frown at his symbiot. "Will you knock it off? This is my branch. Go find your own," she ordered in a stern tone.

The symbiot paused and reluctantly released the end of the branch. Asim watched it turn and trot over to several pieces of driftwood. It tested each piece of wood before picking one and returning to sit in front of Pearl with a happy, sloppy grin on its face, a two-meter branch clenched between its jaws. Pearl released a loud huff, threw a hand up in the air in exasperation, and shook her head.

"You are all crazy," she muttered.

Asim didn't bother to hide his amusement. Part of it was because he was beginning to see the humor of the situation and the other part was the joy his dragon, his symbiot, and he were feeling at finding such a perfect woman for him – one with fire! He quickly adjusted his expression when she shot him the same stern look that she had directed at his symbiot.

"May I formally introduce myself? I am Asim Kemark, protector of the royal family, knight of the Valdier, and your true mate," he stated with a deep bow.

Asim waited for several extra seconds when silence greeted his intro-
duction. It wasn't until he heard the soft sound of footsteps against the
loose rocks that he glanced up. Slowly straightening, he stared at the back
of the woman as she walked away from him. He released a deep sigh.

"Well, at least she didn't hit me again," he said with a shake of
his head.

She going wrong way. Home other way, his dragon pointed out to him.

"*Sarafin hair balls*! Well, what are you waiting for? Help me bring her
back!" Asim ordered in aggravation.

He glared at his symbiot who just sat there watching Pearl walk away.
He grimly strode after his mate – loud, squishy boots, chaffing leather, and
low expletives filling the air as he chased her down. He was going to have
a serious man-to-man talk with both his dragon and his symbiot later
tonight.

We still find true mate, his dragon huffed before he yawned and curled
up with a happy sigh. *It exhausting work.*

SIX

"Would you like some hot tea?" Asim asked nearly an hour later.

Pearl turned from where she was standing on the wide deck over-looking the waterfall that flowed from underneath it. She saw a flash of uncertainty flicker through the man's eyes before it was replaced with the same stubborn, determined expression that had brought her to his home. Crossing her arms to keep from reaching out to smooth away the worried expression on his face, she shrugged and nodded.

"You have hot tea?" she asked in surprise.

"Yes. Lady Ariel enjoys it," he replied.

"I would love a cup," she said.

He nodded, turned, and retreated back inside. The moment he was gone, Pearl uncrossed her arms and fanned herself. A snort from the golden creature watching her made her scowl.

"Hot flash," she lied.

The creature shimmered and she could feel the warmth shoot up her arms. It was obvious it knew better. Turning back around, Pearl couldn't prevent the amused grin that crossed her face.

It would appear her later years in life were going to be filled with firsts. The first time she met an alien. The first time she traveled to another planet. And last but not least, the first time she was kidnapped by a horny, dragon-shifting, alien warrior. She wondered what other firsts were in store for her.

"Hopefully, some hot alien sex," she chuckled.

The sound of dishes rattling told her that she hadn't spoken as softly as she thought. She turned to see Asim standing just outside the doorway.

His hands clenched the tray so tightly that Pearl was surprised the metal didn't bend. She lifted her gaze to his face.

Yep, he heard me, she thought with a sigh.

His eyes burned with intensity. He had slipped on a shirt when he changed out of his wet clothes and a pattern of scales was visible under the collar. Vivid images of tangled sheets flooded her with warmth and made her question her sanity. She honestly didn't know if that last thought was hers or his.

"Both," he said in a tight voice. "It has been a long time."

"Honey, if these bands wrapped around my arm are any indication, I'd have to say it has been way too long," she dryly retorted.

"I'm not opposed to correcting that issue," he replied with a grin.

Pearl gazed at Asim for several seconds before she threw her head back and laughed. Damn, but if this man – alien – dragon – warrior – whatever in the hell he was – didn't make her feel young again. Shaking her head, she placed her hands on her hips and grinned.

"I think a cup of hot tea is in order before we jump in the sack," she chuckled.

Asim's face flushed and he returned her grin. "I will hold you to that promise," he said with a matching mischievous grin.

Pearl's eyes widened and she caught herself before she raised her hand again to fan herself. The symbiot knew exactly what she almost did. She shot it a quick glare when it snickered at her.

"Oh, go fetch another stick," she murmured.

Asim's smothered chuckle told her that he'd heard her. It was obvious that these men did not have the same issues with hearing loss that most humans did when they grew older. She would have to remember that – not that it would keep her from speaking her mind.

"So, do you make a habit of kidnapping poor, unsuspecting women with the intentions of ravishing them, or did you just start your nefarious career?" Pearl asked.

"I just started," he admitted with a sheepish grin. "Lady Ariel likes sweet crystals for her tea. Would you care for some?"

"Sweet… oh, sugar. No, thank you," Pearl replied, sliding onto the chair he pulled out at the table. "This is all very impressive. It looks like something out of a Frank Lloyd Wright design. I saw his Falling Water house in Pennsylvania once. Talk about someone having more money than they knew what to do with."

Pearl pursed her lips together. That hadn't come out quite the way she meant it. Luckily, Asim didn't appear to notice her gaffe. He carefully placed a cup of hot tea in front of her before glancing around.

"My home is modest, but comfortable. If you would like something larger, I can build it. I designed and built this home several centuries ago. If you wish a new one, we could design it together," he said.

Pearl lifted her hand to close her mouth after it had dropped open at his first sentence. He thought this was modest? She'd hate to see what he thought of some of the places she and the girls had lived in.

"I've only seen the decking so far, but I'd hardly call this modest. It is… gorgeous," she said, waving her hand at the woods and the small waterfall flowing from under one side of the deck, and continuing its journey on the other side. "How did you manage this?"

Asim's expression relaxed, and he smiled. "I enjoy working with my hands. Before the war, King Jalo gifted me the land in this valley for saving the life of his son, Lord Mandra. It was a gift I could not turn down. I began building this house. I wanted it to blend in with the natural beauty of the forests and mountains. Each plank comes from the trees that grew here and the rocks from the mountains. I planted new trees to replace those I cut down and over time they have grown tall and strong. The flow of the water and the wind in the trees are soothing to an old dragon like me. Over the years, Mandra has helped me add on to the original structure. In time, he asked if he could build a house on the far side of the valley. I was honored to be able to return all the help he had given me," Asim explained, lost in the memories.

Asim described his original home to her. He elaborated on the special features of what could be seen from their vantage point, adding in bits of knowledge about each one. The wall of large, clear windows looked out over the deck to the lake and beyond to the mountains on the far side of the valley. In her mind, she could imagine the winter snow covering the landscape.

She could see the lake that never completely froze solid because of the water flowing from the waterfall. In the distance, she noticed the small hot springs, dotting the valley. Thin wisps of steam rose from them, sending spirals of heated vapor into the air. Her gaze moved to the mountain when he told her of how the animals from the higher elevations would migrate down to the valley for warmth and food in winter. He explained that just before the spring thaw, the herds of wild beasts gave birth.

"That is the hardest time of year for us now," Asim chuckled.

Pearl frowned. "Why? Are they dangerous?" she asked, placing her nearly empty cup down on the table.

"Nothing is more dangerous than a dragon – except a little boy who loves animals," Asim replied. "Jabir has the touch, just like his mother. Animals gravitate to him. He'd have the whole damn lot of them as pets if Mandra didn't put his foot down."

"What you describe reminds me of a place back on Earth called Yellowstone," Pearl shared, fingering her cup. "I took the girls there one summer when we lived in Colorado. Riley thought the buffalo had the mange. We didn't get out of the city much."

"Would you prefer to live in a city? I have a permanent apartment in the palace. If you prefer to live there, we could move," Asim stated.

Pearl shook her head and leaned forward. "Listen, Asim. I'm not sure I understand everything that is going on. Your offer to build a new house, move to the city, yada, yada, is all very impressive, but you don't have to impress me. You do a pretty damn good job of that by just wearing leather. How a guy like you doesn't have some little woman running around catering to your every need is beyond my understanding, but shit happens. Maybe you had someone and she died or discovered she wanted something else. All I can tell you is that I'm not the woman you are looking for. I'm too old, too stubborn, and like my freedom far too much to settle down. Now, saying all that, I'm not opposed to enjoying life either, if you know what I mean."

From the expression on his face, he did understand what she was saying and didn't like it. His face had grown dark, his eyes narrowing with the stubborn glint in them the more she spoke. By the time she finished, his lips were pressed into a firm line and she swore his face looked like it was carved from the same rock as the mountains.

"I understand what you mean, but it is clear you do not understand me. You are my true mate. You are a gift from the Goddess – a perfect match for my dragon, my symbiot, and me. There is only one true mate for a Valdier warrior – and you are mine," he stated in a voice that sounded suspiciously raspy. "I will not let you go. You are not too old, you are perfect. I have no desire for a young female like the princes have. I have lived too long. I wished for a woman who would taste like fine wine."

Pearl slid from her seat when Asim stood up and started walking around the table. The fire was back in his eyes along with the determined look. Scales rippled across his neck and up along his cheeks.

She took several steps back, retreating as he advanced on her. Her eyes grew wary and her hand slipped into her back pocket before she remembered she left her pepper spray in the pocket of her jacket. Great! No gun, no pepper spray, no Taser, and no Tiny. It looked like it was going to be a good, old-fashion form of self-defense if things got rough.

"Asim...," Pearl started to say, stopping and raising her hand.

"I like a mate who is stubborn. She will need to be if she is going to be able to deal with my dragon and me. As for freedom, I will give you all the freedom you desire, as long as it does not endanger you or your dragon," he gritted out.

"Dragon? I don't have a dragon! See, that is another thing, I know that Abby and the other women can somehow change into one now and Riley and Tina can shift into a tiger, but me? I think I'm a little beyond all of that. You know, kind of like going through menopause – no more life changes," Pearl argued.

She froze when Asim lifted his hand and wrapped it around her outstretched one. He pulled her closer, wrapping his other hand around her waist. This was the first time she had felt just how strong he was in his man form. Swallowing, she held back a moan of delight at the feel of his large hand sliding across the thin material of her blouse.

"What... What do you think you are doing?" Pearl asked, pressing her other hand between them.

Asim tugged her forward, his eyes glittering with fire. "Finding out what type of wine you remind me of," he stated before he bent and captured her lips.

Fire swept through Pearl's veins, warming her body as sure as a shot of whiskey. Sliding her hand up his chest and around his neck, she tangled her fingers in the back of his hair. The rush of desire hit her with an unexpected punch.

Forget the wine! This is pure Kentucky bourbon at its finest, Pearl thought, deepening the kiss.

SEVEN

Life was too damn short to risk not embracing the spontaneous moments that were too good to pass up. Pearl knew she was on the other end of the scale when it came to life, so she needed to be extra vigilant. Following her two granddaughters to another world was one adventure she was glad she hadn't passed up. This was going to be another.

Touching her tongue to his lips, she took advantage when he opened for her. She felt him stiffen before a soft groan escaped him and he wrapped both arms around her and tightly pressed her against his body. She tightened her hold on him and settled down to enjoy the kiss. Holy Venus, Goddess of Love, but it had been a long time since she'd felt this kind of arousal.

She pulled back, pressing small kisses to his lips and the corner of his mouth before running them along his jaw. A silent squeal of excitement raced through her when his hands frantically moved from her waist down to cup her buttocks. This was a man who knew what he wanted.

"Say yes," he ordered in a husky voice. "Say you want me as much as I want you."

Pearl chuckled and slid her hand along his neck, down his chest, skimmed the waistband of his trousers, and continued lower. She felt his response to her brazen touch. There was nothing wrong with his packaging. She could tell everything was in working order going by the swelling under the palm of her hand.

"Oh yes," Pearl murmured against his lips. "You bet your sweet ass I want this."

Yes!

Asim could feel his dragon's enthusiastic response reverberating through his body. The fire of his dragon licked through his veins, threatening to scorch him with the heat. His dragon was heating up for his mate just as much as Asim was for his. A soft groan escaped him as his cock throbbed to feel the touch of skin against skin. Behind Pearl, he could see the grinning face of his symbiot, its body shimmering brightly with an assortment of changing colors.

Images flashed through his mind. For a moment, he realized how much pain and anguish his symbiot had endured in order to protect him and his dragon. Reaching out, he sent a wave of warmth and comfort to his symbiot.

We will be whole at last, he assured both his symbiot and his dragon.

I bite? His dragon eagerly asked.

Asim groaned when he felt Pearl pulling his shirt loose from his trousers. He didn't need to answer his dragon. The Dragon's Fire was already driving him to press his lips against her exposed neck.

"I want to share my Dragon's Fire with you, Pearl," he murmured against her throat.

"Dragon's Fire," Pearl gasped as a shiver of need ran through her at his hot breath against her skin. "What… What is Dragon's Fire?"

"Everything I am – everything we can be together," he said.

Asim gazed down into Pearl's eyes. He would give her the choice. He had waited too long for this moment and something told him that Pearl was the type of woman who wouldn't be happy if he didn't. His gut tightened when her eyes narrowed.

"Does this have anything to do with changing me like Riley and Tina?" Pearl suspiciously asked.

Asim scowled and shook his head. "No! You would be a dragon! Not a… not a cat," he firmly stated.

Pearl pulled back in his arms, her hand sliding from his crotch to his chest. She stared back at him with wide eyes, an expression of uncertainty and skepticism in her eyes. Asim could feel his dragon's panic start to rise up, threatening to choke him.

I bite! She say no. I need bite! His dragon groaned.

No, this has to be her decision, Asim grimly replied.

"A dragon… like Abby and the other women?" Pearl repeated in shock.

"Yes."

"Will it hurt?" Pearl asked, her lips curving up as she fingered the buttons on the front of his shirt.

"It… I've heard it can be very intense… sexually. There… there is a chance… a chance that neither of us will survive," Asim choked.

Pearl raised an eyebrow. "Not survive having too much sex? I can think of worse ways to die," she reflected.

That mean yes! His dragon crowed.

No, it does not! Asim growled in exasperation.

"What happens afterwards? So, if we, by chance, survive driving each other to the edge of sexual immolation and all, what does that mean?" Pearl asked.

"More...." Asim cleared his throat. "We... will be true mates. Together.... Pearl, you are driving me crazy. I'm... My dragon isn't helping, either. He wants his mate as much as I want you," he bit out.

The way her fingers kept slipping between the openings of the buttons and teasing his heated flesh was quickly dissolving what little control he was fighting to maintain. His hands had slipped to her waist, unable to completely release her when she pulled back to gaze up at him. His fingers gently kneaded her flesh as he resisted the urge to just pick her up and take her.

"I'm old," she warned.

"I'm older and you are perfect to me," he replied.

"I'm not as quick as I used to be," she stated.

"You knocked me in the water before I knew what happened," he reminded her.

"I may be a little rusty," she admitted.

"We will go as slow as you like. I would prefer to savor you like a glass of fine wine – slowly, so I can enjoy each touch and taste," he countered.

You sip, I gulp. You taking too long! His dragon groaned in frustration.

"You have scales running up your neck," Pearl pointed out.

"My dragon wants to gulp the wine instead of sipping it like a gentleman," Asim admitted in a tight voice.

Asim's eyes widened and his lips parted when Pearl gripped the sides of his shirt and pulled with a lot more force than he expected. The buttons holding his shirt closed popped free, scattering across the polished wood of the deck.

"I love a dragon who knows how to handle his liquor," she said before she captured his lips.

This mean yes! His dragon crowed.

Yes, this means yes, Asim groaned, his hands frantically pulling Pearl's blouse free from her trousers. *Bite, you can bite.*

His dragon didn't need to be told twice. Asim was already moving his lips along Pearl's cheek and down to her neck. He felt his teeth elongate, the Dragon's Fire burning through him like a super-heated torch. Opening his mouth, he sank his teeth into her neck and breathed the fire that would change all their lives.

"*Holy Goddess of Love!*" Pearl hissed, her hands tightening around his waist before her legs gave out under her.

Asim held her close, his hands splayed across the smooth skin of her back while her breasts were pressed against his chest.

The fire licked through both of them, scorching them with its fiery touch. His body was humming with tension. Goddess, he wanted to make love to this woman.

The caress of Asim's lips across her cheek down to her neck made Pearl feel young and beautiful again. The fact that, until a few hours ago, she had never met this man before was a minor technicality to her. She had known men for years without really knowing them. She hadn't felt this surge of instant attraction since Joe – even the faint memories of her infatuation for him paled to the physical and chemical reaction she was having to this old Valdier warrior.

Deep down, she knew that she was playing with a different type of fire – but, hell, life was about grabbing it by the balls and holding on, no matter how hot it got sometimes. She had nothing left to worry about now but her own heart. Riley and Tina were safe and happy. Now it was her time to shine and she was going up like the grand finale at a New Year's Eve fireworks show.

"Asim… You better not burn my heart," Pearl warned.

He reluctantly released her neck. It throbbed where he bit her. Instead of being painful, it pulsed along with the feelings of need burning between her legs. It had been years since she was this aroused.

"Never, Pearl. If you burn, we burn together," he swore. "Let the Dragon's Fire begin."

Pearl's eyes widened and a soft moan escaped her as the first wave hit her. Her arms trembled and she was thankful for his strength to hold her upright. Well, until he scooped her into his arms. She turned her head and buried her face against his neck.

"Damn, that is some powerful shit," she said in a strained voice.

Asim chuckled. "It will be a glorious transformation," he promised.

His burning desire for Pearl was nothing compared to his determination that she survive the changes of the Dragon's Fire. He'd seen her strength when she stood up to his symbiot with nothing more than a custard-covered spoon and when she had knocked him into the lake. This was a woman with the heart of a warrior – and a true match for one as well.

He held her close, sensing the fire burning through her veins. He entered the house, striding through the sitting room and past the kitchen that he designed to take advantage of the view. He rounded the corner and climbed the stairs.

The sound of Pearl's soft moan and the shiver of her slender body in his arms told him that another wave of the Dragon's Fire was breaking through her. He drew in a swift breath when he felt her teeth against his neck. The sharp nip excited him.

She has a lot of fire in her, he thought.

Yes. She perfect mate, his dragon stated, very pleased with himself.

"Damn, but whatever you did has me feeling hotter than a marshmallow on fire. I'm burning up and melting at the same time," she breathed.

"It is the Dragon's Fire. Do not fight it. Let it flow through you and embrace the change," Asim encouraged.

"Lordy, but I'm going to be jumping your bones," Pearl moaned, pressing her lips against his neck.

Pearl had never felt fire like this before. Menopause been quick and painless, a few hot flashes and she was done. This was like an inferno raging inside her. The only difference was instead of wanting a cold shower and a fan; she wanted a hot man and his cock.

Her clothes were driving her crazy. The touch of them against her skin was like sandpaper against silk. She wanted hot flesh and a hairy chest she could tangle her fingers in.

Turning her head, she ran her lips over Asim's neck, nipping, sucking, and leaving a line of tiny hickeys that were bound to multiply over the course of the night. Her fingers searched and found his chest where she had ripped his shirt open. She tangled her fingers in his chest hair, enjoying the coarse feel against her sensitive fingertips.

When Asim set her on her feet again, she pulled back and was surprised to discover they were in a large bedroom. She briefly glanced around, mostly searching for the bed. She turned her head when Asim placed his hand under her chin and gazed mischievously down into her eyes.

"Are you sure the answer is still 'yes'?" he teased. "I have started the fire, but I will not fan it if you ask me not to."

"Honey, unless you want me to bury a dead body, you better do something about this inferno that you started. The answer isn't yes – it is 'hell yes'. You can add as many exclamation points at the end of that as you want. I plan on working my way down your delicious body while you do that," Pearl retorted, reaching up to unbutton her shirt.

Her lips twitched when more buttons went flying, reminiscent of her actions earlier. Their desire for each other was well and truly a wildfire.

Asim growled and finally snapped the front of her bra to free her breasts. Pearl unfastened Asim's pants and buried her hands inside, wrapping them around his cock while her mouth hungrily explored his chest.

She fell backwards, her knees giving way against the bed. Asim took advantage of it and swiftly removed her boots, socks, and pants. Each article of clothing flew in a different direction in their haste.

Asim impatiently kicked his trousers off and wrapped his large hands around her calves. He pulled her to the edge of the bed and stood looking down at her, his cock poised at her moist entrance.

"Are you ready for me?" he asked in a strained voice.

Pearl reached down and felt the moisture between her legs. Hell, she hadn't been this wet without a little help since she could remember. Feeling for his cock, she aligned it with her channel and lifted her hips.

The first touch of his cock entering her coincided with another wave of Dragon's Fire. Asim must have felt the flames overcoming her and the sudden rush of moisture between her legs because he surged forward, impaling her at the same time as the fire peaked. Pearl wrapped her legs around Asim's waist, thanked the goddess of yoga for insisting that she participate, and held on for the ride.

Her sensitive breasts brushed against the coarse hair of his chest, causing her nipples to become taut pebbles. Pearl held onto Asim's shoulders when he bent over her. Her head fell back, exposing her long slender neck. With a smothered oath, he braced his arms on each side of her, sank his teeth into her neck – and breathed.

Silver scales framed by white rippled over Pearl's body and along her arms. Her body felt like it was burning to ash and being reborn. The feel of Asim's stiff cock stroking her channel, his coarse hair teasing her nipples, and the feel and smell of their combined lovemaking tipped the scales and Pearl came harder than she had ever come in her life. Her orgasm rolled on and on, building, peaking and breaking, only to build again.

Asim didn't stop his driving force. Once she came, he pulled out of her, turned her over until she was kneeling on the bed, and climbed up behind her so he could do it again.

The feel of his cock felt hard and delicious as he stroked her. Her fingers curled in the covers and she bowed her head. Her eyes closed as she felt him grow thicker. She could feel the tension building in his body and knew he was going to come.

His fingers tightened on her hips, holding her as his hips rocked back and forth. He continued to slide in and out of her, faster and harder with each movement. Her head came up with she felt him stiffen and groan as he came. His breath hissed and echoed loudly through the room. He held her still, a shudder shaking his large frame as he pulsed.

Pearl was sure they were through and disappointment hit her hard. Bowing her head, she closed her eyes. A soft gasp escaped her when she felt the fire building inside her again. His cock reacted to the muscles along her vagina squeezing him in response. Opening her eyes, she was stunned to feel him begin to move again – his cock thick and full as if he hadn't just emptied himself deep inside her.

"What...? How the hell?" Pearl asked.

Asim pulled out of her and gently rolled her over. Caging her body with his, he pulled her legs up around his waist and sank as far as he could into her once again. His arms wrapped around her and he held her tight as the Dragon's fire flowed through both of their bodies.

"It has been a long, long time," Asim murmured, holding her close as he rocked his hips.

Pearl's eyes widened and the smile on her lips grew. Gripping him with her legs and pushing him, she let him know that she wanted him to roll over. Asim rolled to the side, pulling her with him until she was on top of him.

"Hot damn! I've got my own renewable battery pack," Pearl chuckled. She tilted her head and gazed down at him. "Have you ever been ridden, cowboy?"

Asim's eyes widened when Pearl rose before she sank all the way down on him. The smile on his lips grew when Pearl began to ride him. Pearl didn't miss the way her skin changed, fine silver scales dancing across it – or the new voice in her head, encouraging her to ride as far and as long as she wanted. She decided age must have its advantage, because her dragon wasn't taking its sweet time emerging like Abby and the other women had described.

We ready for mate now! I ride my mate next, the voice whispered. *Dragon style.*

EIGHT

Asim grudgingly rolled out of bed early the next morning. The insistent someone pounding on his door refused to leave when he hadn't answered it. He glanced at Pearl and saw she was watching him with an amused smile.

"I have to answer that," he said, bending over to brush a kiss across her lips.

Pearl chuckled and nodded. "I think I know who it is," she replied, throwing the covers back and sliding out of the bed.

"*Dragon's fire*, but I would be willing to ignore them to keep you in my bed," Asim said.

"Your eyes are flashing with fire again. You'd better answer the door. I have a feeling they aren't going to go away until you do," Pearl chuckled as she grabbed the sheet from the end of the bed, folded and wrapped it around herself like a sarong.

"Surely they will get the message? I swear if it is Mandra, he can shovel the damn Pactor poop by himself today," Asim snapped in frustration.

He reached over and grabbed his trousers from the floor. He looked around for his shirt, but gave up when the pounding increased. With a muttered curse, he turned in time to see Pearl step out of their bedroom.

Hurrying after her, he caught up with her half way down the stairs. His gaze ran appreciatively over her sheet-wrapped body and bare shoulders. At least it wouldn't take long to undress her once he told their unexpected company to get lost or he would bite their heads off. He was a dragon on a mission and that was to mate with Pearl in every way he could. He had a lot of years to make up for and so did his dragon.

They reached the bottom of the stairs and turned toward the front door.

Striding across, he stepped in front of Pearl and opened the door. An irritated Vox stood on the other side, his hand raised to bang on the door again. Vox barely caught himself before he rapped his knuckles between Asim's eyes.

"Where is she?" Vox asked in exasperation.

"None of your business," Asim snapped.

"What the... Grandma?" Riley exclaimed.

Asim glanced over Vox's shoulder and saw Vox's mate staring at Pearl behind him. Riley's eyes were opened wide and her mouth was hanging open. He stepped to the side when he felt Pearl run her hand over his right buttock. He might have been alright if she hadn't pinched it. Of course, his body – still burning with the remains of the Dragon's Fire – ignited.

"Hello, Riley. What brings you here this early? I would have thought you'd still be asleep," Pearl commented.

Asim wrapped his arm protectively around Pearl's waist and drew her close to his side when she stepped up beside him. She shot him a questioning glance and shook her head in amusement before turning her attention back to her stunned granddaughter.

"You look like you've been...," Riley started to say.

The scowl on Asim's face darkened when Riley waved her hand at him before turning back to Pearl. The frown quickly turned to a smothered oath. Pearl's left hand was sliding down the back of his pants and she was kneading his taut butt cheek. If he didn't get rid of Vox and Riley soon, Riley was going to have no doubt as to why her grandmother looked the way she did.

"I have. What have you and Vox been doing? Working on more great-grandbabies for me, I hope. I absolutely adore Roam," Pearl said with an innocent smile.

"I told you she was fine, Riley. Let's go," Vox said, partially turning away.

"Oh, hell no, we are not going! This... this maniac kidnapped my grandmother and you want to just leave her here? She didn't even meet him until yesterday!" Riley stuttered.

"Riley... I really think we should go... now," Vox murmured.

"Would you like some refreshments?" Pearl asked.

"NO!" both men replied at the same time.

"Yes," Riley stubbornly said.

"I really don't think she meant for you to accept her offer, Riley," Vox warned, glancing at Asim's flushed face and the scales rippling up his body.

"Why not?" Riley demanded.

Asim watched Vox bend to whisper in Riley's ear. The younger woman's mouth dropped open again and she blushed. Her gaze darted to him before turning to her grandmother's serene face, then to the front of Asim. Her face turned a bright red.

"Oh!" Riley whispered. "But... She's my grandma!"

Pearl laughed. "I'm also a woman with her hand down the back of a gorgeous man's pants, Riley. I'm old, not dead. I can still appreciate a fine-looking man, a nice bottle of bourbon, and messing up a set of silk sheets," she said with a mischievous grin.

"That's just... too ... TMI, Grandma!" Riley exclaimed.

Asim saw Riley's gaze immediately shift back to his waist. Her face wrinkled into a look of dismay. His hips jerked forward when Pearl ran her nails along his skin. His control was shot.

"Alright, she's safe. It's time to go," Vox said with a determined smile. "Sorry to interrupt, Asim."

"Tell the others to stay away," Asim replied in a strained voice.

"I will," Vox promised.

"But... But... Vox!" Riley started to protest.

Asim released the breath he was holding when Vox wrapped his arm securely around Riley and guided her toward their transport that hovered along the narrow road in front of the house. Reaching around, he wrapped his fingers around Pearl's wrist when she pulled her hand out of the back of his pants. He turned to face her and walked her backwards, barely closing the door before he reached for the sheet around her.

"You...," he started to say before he shook his head and released a long, uneven breath. "All I can say is you better be ready for some serious loving, because my dragon and I are fired up again."

Pearl's fingers were already working on the front of his trousers. "I thought we'd never get rid of them," she laughed. "I want to make love to you in the shower. I've always had a fantasy to try it there. We can work our way through the house after that."

"Goddess, I must have been one good warrior to be rewarded with you as my mate," Asim retorted, kicking his pants to the side and pulling Pearl after him.

"When do we get to try it dragon style?" Pearl asked halfway up the stairs.

Asim stumbled on the step he was about to take and closed his eyes. His dragon was breathing heavily inside him and pacing back and forth. Pearl had noticed the ripple of scales on her arms last night and heard the whisper of her dragon being born. He had hoped to have a few days alone with her, but something told him that wasn't going to happen.

Give me the shower and I'll show her how to shift, Asim practically begged.

She want dragon style. You get shower after, his dragon demanded.

"*Dragon's balls*! He doesn't want to wait now," Asim groaned.

"What does that mean?" Pearl asked, gazing up at him with a hopeful expression.

"We'd better get to the balcony. He's about to call for his mate," Asim replied in resignation.

"Oh, my. I'm going to get some dirty dragon sex!" Pearl laughed, pushing past him and walking up the stairs. "Last one to the deck is on the bottom."

Asim watched Pearl's delightful ass disappear through his bedroom door. It took a moment for her words to sink in. The thought of him being on the bottom with her on top, riding him….

Go! She getting there first! His dragon complained.

I know, Asim calmly replied with a wicked smile.

His eyes glittered with determination and a slow, sly smile curved his lips. If she wanted some dirty dragon sex, she was going to get some dirty dragon sex – in both forms. His dragon had stopped pacing, realizing what Asim was planning.

Yes! I like!

"Pokey!" Asim called to his symbiot. "I think it is time for Pearl to see what happens when she teases a dragon warrior."

His symbiot flowed past him up the stairs. Asim followed at a slightly slower pace. He was going to take his time. His mate wanted to try every spot in the house. Well, he knew of a few places they could start with outside. The smile grew on his face when he heard Pearl's startled curse. He climbed the last few steps and paused in the doorway.

Pearl turned to look at him with an expression of growing anticipation. The gold bracelets on her wrists now wound up her arms. Another band wrapped around her neck while two more formed around her ankles.

"I think it is time an old warrior taught you a few new tricks," Asim stated.

"Thank you, Goddess of Love, I'm got a man who likes to play. I am going to be enjoying this," Pearl chuckled.

NINE

Present Day:

"Stop right there!"

Asim blinked several times and shook his head. He looked at the two men sitting across from him. Both of them had expressions of disbelief on their faces.

"What?" he asked with a frown.

Brogan, the moodier of the two brothers, raised a hand and ran it down his face, looking more perplexed than on edge. He turned to his brother and gestured – as if encouraging Barrack to ask Asim some questions.

"Don't look at me. I'm still trying to scrub the image of dirty dragon sex between Asim and Pearl out of my brain," Barrack stated.

"Perhaps I shouldn't have told you all the details," Asim thoughtfully replied, rubbing his chin.

"Then I will ask." Bewildered, Brogan turned his attention back to Asim. "You kidnapped her and took her as your mate. Why can't we do that?" he asked, turning to raise an eyebrow to encourage his brother to back him up.

Barrack raised his hands and shook his head. "I still want to know how she knocked his ass into the lake – after I wash the dirty dragon sex out of my head first, of course," he added.

"Forget I told you about that part. The point I'm trying to make is that each one of them is different. Pearl was older and more experienced with life. From what Sara told us, Delilah is young and innocent, but that doesn't mean she can't take care of herself. When you find your mate, she needs to be your partner in every way. If you try to control her, you'll lose her for sure. I've seen each of the Dragon Lords learn their lesson with the princesses," Asim explained.

"So, you do not control your mate?" Brogan asked with a skeptical expression.

"*Curizan fireball*! No, Pearl would roast my balls for dinner and serve them to me on a platter if I tried to tell her what to do. She is my mate, my partner, in every sense of the word," Asim insisted.

"Except in battle," Barrack said.

Asim shook his head. "No, especially in battle," he replied in a quieter voice.

"But – how?" Brogan exclaimed with an incredulous expression. "Females are weak! They are not made for fighting."

Asim leaned forward and plucked the sculpture of the bird out of Brogan's hand. He held it up and rotated it between his fingers. He studied it for a moment before he smiled.

"That leads me to my next story.... This one happened just a few months ago. Pearl and I have been together for a couple of years now, but she continues to amaze me in so many ways. During our time together, I have discovered that love and respect is not finite, but continues to grow. And, despite our time together, I learned that I had never really seen what my mate could do when she was truly riled," Asim explained, his voice beginning to fade as the memories rose.

"You hold that as if it means something. What kind of creature is that?" Barrack asked, nodding at the bird.

"This strange creature is part of my story that begins with the dragonlings unexpected adventure to Earth and one little boy's love for all creatures. Lord Mandra and Lady Ariel's son, Jabir, returned home with some very unusual eggs.... Eggs that made me fearful for a little boy, would attract danger to the woman I love, and that would hatch into creatures that would rise up to become the most unlikely army this old Valdier warrior has ever seen. This army was led by none other than a couple of small boys," Asim replied with a chuckle.

"Tell us about this battle," Brogan demanded, leaning forward with his eyes glued to the small, odd-shaped creature made of wood.

"It begins with a story of love...," Asim explained. "This strange creature called an emu is part of the story..."

A few months before...

"You need to keep them covered," Pearl said, smoothing the fresh warm grass over the large, green eggs in the barn a short distance from his parent's house.

"Will they be ables to breathe?" Jabir asked worriedly.

"They should be fine, but I don't know what your Grandpa Paul is going to say when he finds out you took some of the eggs from his ranch," Pearl chuckled and bent to pick up the chubby little boy.

"He would tells me I'm a good hunter! Ruby will keeps them warm. She likes my new eggs," Jabir giggled, watching the chicken settle on top of the mound. Tina and Viper left Ruby at the mountain retreat while they enjoyed their time at the palace. Jabir reached up and wrapped his arms around Pearl's neck. "Ruby promised me that she would take good care of my eggs while I hunts for more."

"Ruby will take very good care of your eggs, I'm sure. Your mom will keep an eye on them as well. We won't be gone long," Pearl promised.

"What happens if Asim finds them?" Jabir asked with a worried frown.

"He'll keep them warm and safe for you. The eggs will be fine. I want to talk to your Grandpa Paul about them before I mention them to Asim. He might be able to help," she chuckled.

"Grandpa Paul knows all about eggs and animals," Jabir replied, happy again.

Pearl watched as Jabir glanced at the small mound of grass in the back stall. Her heart swelled for the little boy who was frantically trying to keep his secret. She and Ariel discovered a week ago that Jabir had done a little exploring and scavenging when he and the other younglings crossed through a portal to Earth created by Phoenix, one of the twin daughters of Creon and Carmen.

The dragonlings' adventure had started with a simple Valentine's Day story and ended with the younglings traveling across the galaxies to find the lonely woman who could heal a dragon whose heart was turning to stone. The dragon, it turned out, was none other than Jarak Draken, the surly Chief Security Officer aboard the *V'ager,* while the lonely woman was Sandy Morrison, the sister of Paul's Grove's childhood friend and attorney, Chad.

The fathers had followed after the younglings. While they were on Earth, the men learned how easy it was to do online shopping and Jabir had discovered the eggs in one of Paul's barns. The return trip had them bringing back a wide range of exciting items – and Jabir's hidden bounty of eggs.

Pearl didn't understand how Phoenix could create a portal that connected the two worlds. There were a lot of things she still didn't understand about this world, even three years later. One thing she did understand was that Phoenix was special – even by alien standards.

She touched by Goddess, her dragon softly murmured.

I already figured that out on my own, Pearl reassured her dragon. *So, how are we going to keep this little secret from Asim? You know we can't lie to him.*

No lie. Just don't tell him, her dragon shrugged. *What he not know, not hurt him. It make Jabir and Ariel happy.*

Pearl chuckled. *I guess we girls do have to stick together.*

Especially if men take Jabir pets away, her dragon snorted.

Yes, well....

Pearl didn't add to that point of view. She and her dragon didn't quite agree that it was time to ship the latest batch of Grombots and Marrats off, but Ariel had grudgingly acknowledged that they were better off on their home world than on Valdier where they were considered a delicacy by the dragons. Of course, the tears flowed down both Ariel and Jabir's cheeks while the men were loading the animals onto the transport.

Mandra and Asim had huffed and puffed, but Pearl noticed that the men secretly kept two pairs of each animal for Ariel and Jabir. The sets included the runts of the group and the ones most unlikely to survive if they were released into the wild. Mandra talked to a local animal doctor who would make sure they couldn't reproduce.

Of course, there were bound to be a collection of more strays from the universe by the time Mandra and Ariel returned from the palace. Pearl came to the conclusion that Mandra must have made a lot of enemies over the years. It seemed like a new creature in need was appearing on the mountain retreat almost weekly.

"Jabir! Time to get ready to go," Ariel called.

"I'm comings," Jabir replied.

Pearl set the little boy down and stood at the door of the barn, watching as he ran across the open area to his mother. She chuckled when he struggled to climb the stairs. He finally gave up, shifted into his dragon form, and used his wings. Her gaze moved to Mandra. The huge Valdier prince had stepped out of the house onto the deck and opened his arms for Jabir.

"When that boy finally has his growing spurt, there are going to be a lot of surprised people," Pearl chuckled, shaking her head in wonder.

She had a lot to do before she and Jabir left to go to the palace in a few minutes. They were leaving a few days early so Jabir could play with his cousins. This would also give her a chance to spend time with Riley, Tina, and her new great-granddaughters, Sacha and Little Pearl, as well as great-grandsons, Roam and Leo.

A smile curved her lips when the small family turned and disappeared inside the house. This world was truly an incredible place compared to Earth and was one that the St. Claire women could call home.

"It is hard to believe I spent most of my life on another world when this one feels more like home," Pearl reflected out loud, gazing around.

Her gaze locked on her mate and she chuckled. Asim was currently arguing with Ariel's newest acquisition, another Pactor. This one had been injured in a mining accident that left it partially blind. It had been abandoned when Ha'ven's brother, Adalard, discovered the poor creature during one of his journeys and shipped it to Mandra as a present.

Pearl had noticed that Mandra and Adalard had a growing competition to outdo each other when it came to gag gifts. Mandra's last gift to Adalard was a pair of Tasiers – a small, round furry creature that could reproduce exponentially if they were not controlled. By the time they arrived at Adalard's home, the two had already multiplied to eight. By the end of the week, Adalard was threatening war against the Valdier again. Of course, the next day the Pactor had arrived to even out the score.

Asim's loud curses floated through the air along with the sound of thuds on the ground coming from behind the animal. The new medicine Asim was giving the Pactor was helping, but it also made it have loose stools. Her heart melted when Asim reached up and stroked the Pactor, murmuring to soothe it, before he walked over to where he left the shovel and pail.

Turning, she returned to her own little bundle of whatever Jabir had brought home. She wasn't an expert, but she suspected the large, avocado-colored eggs were some kind of bird. Since he had retrieved them from Paul's ranch back on Earth, she wasn't too concerned that they would be dangerous. The eggs reminded her of the ostrich eggs she once saw at the Denver zoo.

"Ostriches aren't too bad. Mandra can always have them shipped back to Paul's ranch, though he may have to fight with Ruby over them first," she decided with a laugh.

Checking on the eggs once more, she was satisfied they would be safe. Ruby was sleeping on top of the pile. She chuckled softly as she shut the door to the stall. She could just imagine all of the men's faces if they were to catch a glimpse of the huge eggs that she, Ruby, and Jabir were fretting over. They would go ape-shit over them.

Pearl never could have imagined that a dragon would go nuts over hard-boiled eggs – especially colored ones! She reckoned it was a combination of their competitive nature and their avarice for pretty things. Personally, she just didn't get it.

Pearl closed the door to the barn and looked around for Pokey. The symbiot was sprawled on the house's deck, soaking up the sun. Pokey rolled to his feet when Mandra came out carrying Jabir. Ariel followed with a small suitcase and a backpack in the shape of a dinosaur.

Pokey shook and jumped to the ground. Pearl watched in fascination as the golden body shimmered and transformed. The living metal creature was stretching and curving until a compact, golden transport hovered slightly off the ground waiting for her. She couldn't keep the smile from curling her lips when she thought of what else that living metal could do.

Yes! Her dragon hissed in delight.

You are a horny bitch, you know that, don't you? Pearl silently chuckled.

You the one that likes on top, her dragon retorted.

Yes, I do, Pearl agreed, smiling.

She walked toward where Asim was working. Leaning against the railing, she silently waited for him to finish what he was doing. Even though she was only going to be gone for a few days, she knew that she was going to miss him. While she had spent most of her life alone, she found that she quickly enjoyed having Asim's quiet presence in her life and she missed him when they were apart.

"What are you smiling about?" Asim curiously asked, looking up to catch her smiling at him.

"Sex. On top, on the bottom, dirty dragon style," Pearl quipped, knowing it would start the fire in Asim's eyes.

"Goddess! You mention that to me now when I can't do a thing about it? You are killing me and my dragon, Pearl!" Asim cursed, holding a shovel full of Pactor dung.

Asim dropped the dung into the wagon and walked over to the fence. He propped the shovel up against the rails and pulled his gloves off. Placing them on a post, he leaned forward and brushed a kiss across her lips.

"I'm going to miss you," she said with a sigh.

"I could always fly back and forth each morning and evening," Asim suggested with a smile.

Her eyes glittered with mischief. "With all the kids around…? We'd never have any peace; and you know that I'm talking about the big kids, not the little ones," she chuckled with a shake of her head. "You have enough to do here. It will only be a few days and I'll be spending time with the girls."

"A few days is too long," Asim replied with a mischievous expression. "We could always meet half way."

"Your dragon is stuck on the dirty dragon style, isn't he?" she teased.

"Just a little – so am I," Asim retorted with a wicked grin.

Pearl tilted her head back and laughed. She loved it when they teased each other. It didn't matter what she said, he was able to think of a comeback. Of course, on the few occasions when he couldn't, he used his lips and body instead.

"I'll send you a location for later tonight," she teased, brushing a kiss across his lips with a little suggestive tongue to go along with it.

"Pearl, I ready!" Jabir called out behind her.

"I have to go," she said with a sigh.

"Later tonight," Asim vowed. "Dirty dragon style first."

"You'll have to catch me first," Pearl replied with a wink before she turned and walked away.

TEN

Asim watched his symbiot rise off the ground. Mandra and Ariel were waving to Jabir who was frantically waving back at them. His gaze was fastened on Pearl. She turned and blew him a kiss before Pokey rotated in the air. A moment later, the symbiot transport was just a faint glimmer in the sky.

He blinked when Hobbler, the Pactor he'd threatened to return to Cree and Calo but never did, nudged him. He reached out a hand to calm the beast. He shook his head, retrieved his gloves and the shovel, and finished his chores.

"I swear that woman loves to drive me insane," he told Hobbler as the creature followed him back to the wagon. "So, what do you think of your new friend? Have you accepted him yet?"

Hobbler stretched out her neck and rubbed her forehead against his hand. Asim was going to take that as a yes. He dumped the last shovel-load of poop into the wagon with a sigh. The more he thought about his conversation with Pearl, the funnier it sounded to him. Before long, his shoulders shook with mirth and he had to stop and lean on the shovel.

"Goddess, but I love that woman," he told Hobbler and the new Pactor. "I don't know anyone else who could make me want to laugh while shoveling shit."

Humming under his breath, he finished mucking the corral and lay fresh warm grass in the covered stalls. Hobbler had moved closer to George, Jabir's name for the half-blind beast. Asim nodded in satisfaction when both Pactors stopped at the feed barrels. It would take a few months, but George would fill out like Hobbler had.

He cleaned up the tools and walked to the outer barn. It was empty now that he and Mandra shipped off the majority of the Grombots and Marrats. Pearl had volunteered to clean it up so it would be ready for any new arrivals that would eventually find their way to the mountain refuge for lost, orphaned, and mistreated beasts.

He pushed the small wagon over to the equipment shed and rinsed it out before doing the same with the bucket and shovel. There was a latch on one of the stalls that wasn't working properly and he wanted to check all of them before he forgot. There was nothing worse than having a new beast loose and wreaking havoc.

He opened the door, leaving it slightly ajar to bring in some natural light. Solar powered light panels along the ceiling turned on as he walked along each stall, testing the doors. He frowned when he reached the last one. He could have sworn it was the one that was broken.

Opening the stall door, he tested it several times before he grunted. It looked like it was working now. Glancing around, he noticed that fresh warm grass was piled in the corner instead of spread out. Perhaps Mandra had forgotten to spread it when he fixed the door.

He walked over to the pile and bent to pick up a handful of warm grass. A movement out of the corner of his eye startled him and he jerked back a step. A dry chuckle escaped him when he saw Ruby flap her wings at him.

"I wondered where you moved to. You don't like me gathering all your eggs, do you? Well, I have to say it is your fault. If they weren't so tasty, we dragons wouldn't want to eat them." He yanked his hand back when Ruby pecked at him. "You are lucky you belong to Pearl's granddaughter or you would be in a pot and then into my stomach," he threatened.

Ruby tilted her head and clucked at him before scratching at some loose warm grass near the small dish of feed that was set out for her. Perhaps this was why Jabir kept sneaking out at night. Mandra said he'd caught the little boy more than once trying to sneak out to the barn when he should have been in bed. The little boy had been pestering his father to replicate the chicken. Jabir really wanted to have a pet chicken like Leo. Of course, neither he nor Mandra were opposed to the idea if it meant they had fresh eggs to go along with the bird.

"Go on with you, I have work that needs to be completed," Asim chuckled.

He bent to spread the warm grass, but stiffened in surprise when his fingers touched something hard under the straw. Pulling his hand back, he studied the pile of warm grass for a moment before he gently brushed it aside. Perhaps Ruby left some of her delicious eggs for him and Pearl. His eyes widened and a loud curse exploded from his lips when he saw the shape of a very large, dark green egg. This was *not* one of Ruby's eggs.

He straightened, staring down at the egg with a frown. He had never seen one like it before. Muttering under his breath, he carefully went through the pile of warm grass, counting the eggs he found.

"Six," he said with a shake of his head. "Where in the galaxy did Jabir find these?"

The little boy must have found them somewhere and snuck them into the barn. His eyes widened again as another thought dawned on him – Pearl. She must know about Jabir's stash! She had been adamant about cleaning the barn on her own shortly after the Dragon Lords and the younglings returned from their adventure on Earth. She even insisted that Pokey could help her with the heavy items if she needed it. There was no way she could have cleaned the barn without knowing about the eggs.

Asim quickly covered the eggs again. He would need to research them to see if he could determine what they were. He turned to leave, but paused when he saw the corner of a sack partially hidden behind the handle of a rake. Pulling the rake aside, he saw now the familiar language of Earth's people. He also recognized the symbol of Paul's ranch on the bag. Lady Ariel had shown him the design once.

"Earth…," Asim murmured before his eyes widened. "Jabir! That boy is going to get himself in trouble one of these days."

Asim wrapped his fingers around the top of the bag and stared out of the barn door. Jabir must have recruited Pearl. That would explain why they had been so secretive lately and kept chasing him out of the barn when he asked if they wanted any help.

His gaze moved back to the pile of eggs. They were larger than any he had ever seen – including the Grombot eggs. He would scan one of the eggs and run it through the database, but he would be surprised if they were even listed.

Perhaps Paul would know what they were; after all, they must have come from his ranch. Satisfied that he would get to the bottom of the mysterious eggs, he started to replace the bag on the hook when he realized there was something still in it. Curious, he glanced inside. A frown creased his brow when he saw it was one of Jabir's books.

Asim was surprised the little boy had left the book in the barn. He loved the storybooks his father purchased for him on Earth. Reaching in, he pulled it out and paled.

On the front cover were creatures Ariel called dinosaurs. Several of the beasts were standing by large nests filled with eggs. Asim's gaze moved back to the pile of fresh warm grass. He remembered that Jabir had a fascination with the beasts and wanted something called a Tyrannosaurus Rex for a pet.

"Dragon's balls!" he whispered, his eyes growing wide. He quickly thumbed through the book until he reached the page with the T-Rex, as Ariel and Pearl called the beast. The massive dinosaur was standing over a nest filled with broken shells from at least a half dozen eggs. Under the creature, small miniature versions of herself were snapping at the dead beast hanging from her jaws. "Jabir has found Earth dinosaurs! These T-Rex dinosaurs will eat him!"

Asim looked down at the bag in his hand. He needed to get rid of them, but how? Jabir would be heartbroken and Pearl would kill him for breaking the little boy's heart – not to mention he would also end up upsetting Lady Ariel.

He needed someone who could help him dispose of the eggs quickly and quietly. He could deny any knowledge – no, no, Pearl would know he was lying. He would just say he found them and gave them to one of the princes – but not Mandra.

Who else could he ask? He needed someone who could handle the mission. Someone no one would suspect. Asim glanced down when Ruby strutted over to him and pecked at his boot. A slow smile curved his lips. He knew the perfect accomplice to recruit.

ELEVEN

"You want me to do what?" Vox asked, gaping at Asim on the view screen with a confused frown.

"I need you to dispose of something for me," Asim quietly explained.

"You've done it, haven't you? You've finally killed Riley's grand-mother? I don't blame you, but I'm not touching her dead body. The woman would probably come back to life just to haunt me," Vox warned.

Asim heard Riley's voice calling out to Vox in the background. He needed to keep this as quiet as possible. It wasn't easy when he practically had Vox howling with delight at the thought of Pearl meeting a grievous end.

"Vox, Roam wants you to help with the egg coloring. I need to feed Sacha and change Pearl," Riley called in the background.

"I'll be there in a minute," Vox replied before he leaned closer to the vidcom. "I have to say, I expected you to kill Pearl a lot sooner. You two have been mated for what – almost three years now? I was ready to do the job myself on the first day I met her," he said in a hushed tone so Riley couldn't hear him.

"*No*, I have not killed my mate. I love her. This has nothing to do with killing anyone or hiding dead bodies," Asim growled in frustration.

Vox's expression drooped a little before he looked hopeful again. "Please tell me that you at least ate the damn chicken, then! That crazy feathered beast loves to get in the house and lay eggs when Tina and Viper visit. Roam's been hiding them under my pillow for me. I didn't find the last one until it was too late," he said.

"I have not killed Pearl or eaten Ruby! They are both still alive and healthy. In fact, Pearl should be there any minute. I just want you to take something out and leave it in the woods," Asim snapped before he remembered to lower his voice. "Jabir brought back some eggs from Earth. I want you to take them away and leave them in the forest. I'm hoping that they don't hatch; but if they do, I'm hoping a predator will get them before they grow too large."

"Eggs? Just boil them and eat them," Vox replied with a disappointed expression.

"I can't! I told you, they are Jabir's eggs," Asim growled.

Vox shrugged. "We eat Ruby's eggs all the time, so what is the big deal?" he asked.

"This is the big deal!" Asim growled and held up Jabir's picture book of dinosaurs. "If they hatch, all the dragonlings will want one. Do you want this running around your house?" he demanded.

Vox leaned forward and whistled under his breath. "I know Amber and Jade would love one, but I have enough teeth and poop in my house between Roam and the twins, I don't need any more at the moment," he said, shaking his head. "Are you sure they are these creatures?"

"I am pretty sure they are. Each of the eggs are big, green, and heavy just like the ones in this picture," Asim replied, cupping his hands to demonstrate. "I can't take the chance that they will hatch and eat Jabir or harm my mate."

"I can understand that, but why don't you get rid of them? Why do you want me to do it?" Vox asked with a frown.

"Daddy! I's coloring the eggs on my own!" Roam yelled.

"That's nice. I'll be right there. Make sure you save a few for me," Vox called over his shoulder.

"Lady Ariel made me promise years ago that I would not harm any creature that was brought to the retreat. I can't break my word. I also can't ask Mandra because Ariel and Jabir would be upset. If I upset them, then Pearl will get mad. I don't want to make my mate unhappy with me," Asim explained.

"I'm always making Pearl mad. It isn't all that bad," Vox grinned. "Pearl says I have a natural talent for irritating people."

Asim bit back the groan threatening to escape. Pearl was right – Vox did have a natural talent for irritating others. He had three days to set his plan in action. He just hoped none of the eggs hatched before he, Mandra and Ariel arrived at the palace.

"Pearl and I will babysit the younglings for you and Riley for a week if you'll do this," Asim finally broke down, resorting to bribery.

"A whole week? All three of them?" Vox asked, a grin slowly growing on his face at the thought of having his mate alone for a week. "What do you want me to do?"

Present Day:

"Hiding eggs? What does this have to do with the wooden creature and your mate fighting with you in battle?" Brogan asked in disgust, interrupting Asim.

"Perhaps the creatures hatched and attacked the Sarafin king and ate him. The Sarafin waged war and the creatures ate them as well," Barrack suggested.

Brogan nodded. "Possible… but what about Pearl? Where does she fit into the battle?" he asked.

"The creatures did not eat Vox. They did hatch though," Asim interjected with an exasperated sigh.

"You aren't going to go into more dirty dragon sex, are you? I have to tell you that the image of you and Pearl having hot sex together is not one I am enjoying," Barrack admitted.

"I second that," Brogan murmured.

They started to snicker but bit it back when Asim stood up and glared at them. They glanced at each other, trying to hide their amused expressions. Asim shook his head in warning.

"I'm ready to Taser your asses myself," Asim growled.

Barrack raised his hands in surrender. "We apologize, old warrior. Continue on with your grand tale of…"

"Dirty dragon sex," Brogan interjected under his breath.

"Of the great battle your mate won," Barrack continued, trying not to laugh.

Asim groaned and ran his hands down his face. He never should have shared that. Pearl would kill him and the Twin Dragons if she knew.

"She did more than win the battle, she saved my life," Asim grudgingly continued. "I will skip the details of what happened while trying to hide the eggs and continue with what happened *after* they hatched… and the trouble they brought with them."

TWELVE

One month before:

No, you've already eaten," Asim rebuked the juvenile emu with a shake of his head. "I'll need to build a higher fence if they keep growing."

Pearl chuckled. "Paul said they grow fast and he wasn't lying," she chuckled. "Oh, my, they're in the water again."

"Three and a half months old and they are already a pain in my backside," Asim growled.

"You know you love them," Pearl teased, rubbing the head of one of the emus.

"They love you. They follow you around like that damn chicken of Tina's follows her. I swear there is something wrong with the creatures on your world," Asim grumbled.

"Well, I'm not the only one they bonded with," Pearl chuckled, watching another emu tilt its head to look up at Asim.

"Can we play ball with them?" Roam called out.

"Yes, but make sure Pokey is with you," Pearl replied.

"When will their parents return?" Asim asked.

Pearl turned back and gave her mate a knowing look. "We've still found time," she teased.

"For our dragons, but what about for us?" Asim asked.

"There's nothing to say we can't enjoy a little starlight romance as well," Pearl chuckled.

The sound of giggles told Asim that Roam and Jabir were listening to them – and understanding the innuendoes lacing their grownup conversation. A pained expression crossed his face, pulling more giggles from the boys. He looked at Pearl and raised an eyebrow that spoke volumes.

"My mommy and daddy is always talkings like that," Roam whispered to Jabir.

Jabir glanced back and forth between Asim and Pearl with a frown. "My daddy makes the same faces. He looks like he has gas."

"This is what happens when you volunteer us as babysitters," Asim pointed out.

"Alright, boys, let's go play catch," Pearl laughed, turning away from her mate.

Asim shook his head and watched Pearl round up the boys and the birds. The six emus followed Pearl with almost the same devotion as the two boys. Pokey split in two so that each boy would have protection in case the birds became too rough. He turned and frowned when he felt his dragon stir and stiffen.

What is it? Asim asked, carefully surveying the landscape.

Not sure. I feel something, his dragon warily stated.

A storm, perhaps? Asim asked.

Maybe, his dragon replied.

I'd better make sure everything is secure just in case, he said.

"Hans, what do you see?"

"Credits… and a lot of them," Hans replied. "I'm glad we heard about this place. I've never seen animals like this. We should be able to get a lot for them on the black market."

"When are we going in, Zeb?" a third man asked, kneeling on one knee and staring at the structures below.

"Tonight," Zeb responded, spitting on the ground.

"That's an old warrior. He'll put up a nasty fight," Hans said, lowering the vision magnifier in his hand.

"Crag can handle him," Zeb stated with a shrug.

"It won't be easy. These dragon-shifters are a mean species. They've got that golden thing, too," Hans cautioned.

Zeb turned to look at Crag. A large man called a Drugunulite, he could turn his body to almost solid rock. The dragon might scorch him, but he couldn't turn him to ash. One strike of Crag's fist and the dragon would feel it.

"He's old. I can take him. You kill him; you kill the golden beast. I've seen it happen before," Crag said.

"What about the woman?" Hans asked, lifting the vision magnifier to his eyes again.

"We take her. She seems to know how to handle the feathered creatures and she's different. I heard she don't come from this world. We find out where she comes from and we have a whole new world to collect from," Zeb said, spitting again.

"I heard on Madaris that these warriors would pay huge credits to find a woman who could be their true mate. Even that old dragon found one! We locate the planet, take a bunch of the women, and sell them off to the highest bidder," Crag added, rising to his feet.

"They look weak," Hans commented, focusing on the white-haired female watching the two little boys play. "What about the kids?"

"Leave them. They are worthless. If they survive on their own, more power to them," Zeb replied. "I've been watching them while I was waiting for both of you to arrive. The old dragon has been coming out alone after dark to check on things. Crag, you take him out while Hans grabs the woman. I'll round up the beasts. We'll be in and out in less than an hour. No one will know we were even on the planet," Zeb instructed.

"Stupid beasts can't even figure out how to pick up a ball. This should be easy," Hans reflected, watching the feathered creatures jump and dance around the ball after one of the boys threw it.

Pearl looked up when Asim walked into the kitchen. His hair was damp from his shower and his vest was open. She glanced over at the boys playing on the floor with Pokey.

"You know you drive me crazy when you wear your vest like this," she said, walking over to run her hand over his stomach.

Asim wrapped his arm around her and pulled her against him. The smile on her lips grew when she felt his body react to her touch. Even after three years, she loved that she could still turn him on with only a touch.

"I'm not the only one who can get excited," Asim said with a sniff.

"Stop or the boys will know what is going on," Pearl warned, glancing over her shoulder.

Asim shook his head. "They are wrestling now," he chuckled.

Sure enough, the boys had shifted, Roam into his tiger cub and Jabir into his dragon form. They were wrestling with each other and with Pokey. Their parents were supposed to be back late tomorrow morning. He loved being with the boys, but he also enjoyed giving them back – for lascivious reasons, of course.

"I'm going to check on the animals. The Grombots were trying to release the emus earlier. I need to make sure they haven't discovered how to undo the new locks I installed," Asim said, grabbing her hand that was sliding up his chest and pressing her fingers to his lips. "Tonight, after they are in bed?"

"If Pokey doesn't mind babysitting duty," Pearl murmured.

"I'm hungry," Jabir suddenly said from behind them.

"Me, too!" Roam agreed, rubbing a hand across his nose. "I think I got some symbiot up my nose. Wanna see me snort it out?"

"Yew! That's gross. Can I try?" Jabir exclaimed.

"Lovely. I don't remember the girls being like this," Pearl dryly commented.

"It is a boy thing," Asim chuckled. "I will be back shortly."

"That's right, abandon me to the symbiot snorters," Pearl teased.

Asim's eyes darkened and the tiny flames she loved burned in his eyes. He still held her right hand, but she had her left one free. Leaning into him, Pearl slowly met him halfway when he bent to kiss her. She slid her free hand down between them, sliding it across his groin.

Asim pulled back to gaze down at her. Yep, the flames were much brighter now. A small, secretive smile curved her lips and she stroked him again.

"You are playing with fire, Pearl," Asim warned.

"I'll be playing with something else later," she retorted before pulling away when Jabir grumbled that he was hungry again. "I'll have dinner done by the time you get back."

"Let them play. I'm hoping it tires them out so they go to bed early tonight," Asim chuckled.

Pearl released a sigh when he pressed another hot kiss to her lips before smacking her on the ass. She glanced at the boys, but they decided they were more interested in playing with the dozens of toy trucks the symbiot created for them. She would owe Pokey something special for distracting the boys.

Warmth filled her and she could feel the symbiot's amusement. She snorted and shook her head. Just what she needed, help from a living metal sex coach – not!

"I think I can handle that part of my life on my own," she murmured under her breath.

Honestly, she felt younger than she did when she was young. She didn't know if it was because she no longer worried about Riley and Tina, the fact that dragons lived a lot longer, or just being happy, but she wasn't about to ignore the gift she had been given. Hell, if she wanted to think of herself as being sexy, and Asim thought she was too, who was she to argue? She had a few words for anyone who tried to tell her differently.

Humming under her breath, she walked into the kitchen and began preparing their evening meal. She opened the drawer, and pulled out two knives – one for cutting the vegetables and one for cutting the fresh bread. After placing them on the counter, she walked over to the refrigerator. She loved the replicator, but tonight, she wanted to prepare dinner the old-fashioned way. It helped keep her hands busy while her mind enjoyed other things – like removing Asim's clothing.

Asim shifted into his dragon, flew over the ranch, and nimbly touched down outside the barn where the emus were – or should have been. A growl of frustration escaped him when he saw the opened door of the barn. In the doorway, he could see one of the Grombots hanging by two of its arms, grinning at him.

"*Curizan spit*! Not again," he sighed. "I swear if it is the last thing I do, I'm going to design a lock that you can't undo!"

The Grombot blinked and tilted its head. Before he reached the opening, it disappeared. While the creatures normally moved so slowly that it was almost agonizing to watch, they were actually capable of moving extremely fast. As much as he hated it, he was going to need Pokey's help to round up all the beasts. Shaking his head, he pulled free the communicator that he wore at his waist.

"Let me guess, they got loose again," Pearl answered.

"Yes. I need Pokey. Both of the Grombots are loose and it looks like they released the Emus as well," he said, staring into the empty barn.

"He's on his way," Pearl chuckled. "I'll postpone dinner for a little while."

"No, go ahead and feed the boys. It shouldn't take long. I can warm up something," he said.

"If you need help, let me know. The boys would love to play tag with the emus," she offered.

"If I can't get them, I will call you," he promised.

"We're here if you need us. You know I love you. Good luck," Pearl replied with a sigh.

"I love you, too. I will contact you once I am finished," he replied, hanging up.

Asim decided he'd better try to repair the locking mechanism on the Grombots' cage first. Otherwise, it would be senseless trying to catch any of them now because they would just escape again. Grumbling under his breath, he wondered what else could go wrong tonight.

Danger!

Lost in thought, he didn't hear his dragon's warning until it was too late. When he walked into the barn, someone punched him in the jaw. The blow knocked him several meters backwards. His head snapped back and darkness descended around him. He didn't even feel it when his body hit the ground.

THIRTEEN

"That was easier than I thought," Crag grunted.

"For the dragon-shifter – now we have to capture the feathered creatures that escaped," Zeb snapped.

"What about his symbiot?" Crag asked, turning to look at Zeb.

"It won't attack us if it thinks we will kill him. Contain it in the back room; then tie the old dragon up," Zeb instructed.

"Why don't I just kill him now?" Crag demanded, looking down at Asim's inert body.

Zeb frowned and shook his head. "The creature will attack us before he dies. The only way to get away is to contain it until we are ready to leave. Once we have the woman, it won't come after us or attack us – especially if we kill the warrior."

"Whatever you say," Crag said with a shrug.

Zeb jerked his head toward the building. "Pull him into the barn," he ordered.

Crag reached down and gripped the collar of Asim's vest. He walked into the barn, dragging Asim behind him. Once he was almost to the back, he dropped Asim and turned to wait.

They didn't have long. The symbiot burst through the door. Zeb studied the enraged creature. He had seen how deadly they could be on several of the Spaceports. He pointed his blaster at Asim.

"I wouldn't," Zeb warned. "If you kill me, Crag will snap his neck before you can save him."

The symbiot took a step closer and crouched. The symbiot's body shimmered in a wide variety of colors. The display of colors reflected its feelings of aggression. Zeb gave it a nasty grin.

"Did I mention that my other friend is with the woman and the boys? You can't save them all. What is it going to be?" he demanded. He waited until the symbiot backed down. "You will go into the back room. If you try to come out, I'll have all of them killed."

Zeb knew the symbiot understood him. He could see its eyes narrow. Stepping closer to Asim, he nodded to the room in the back. "Go or they are all dead."

The symbiot hissed and rose back up. It moved with slow, deliberate movements. Zeb stiffened when it paused as it drew even with them before it snarled and continued to the back room. He followed, giving the symbiot a wide berth. Only when it was in the room did he close the distance and locked the door.

"What about this one?" Crag asked.

"Break his leg and lock him in the other barn for now. He won't be able to heal without his symbiot. We don't want him transforming into his dragon or being able to fight. We definitely don't want him and his symbiot near each other. Once we have the woman and feathered beasts, you can come back and finish the job," Zeb instructed.

"I hope we make a lot of credits off the feathered beasts. We are going to need them," Crag grumbled even as he turned and dragged Asim out of the building.

"Boys, come here," Pearl said in a sharp tone.

Jabir and Roam looked up from where they were coloring. Both sensed the authority and alarm in her voice. They scrambled to their feet and hurried into the kitchen.

"What's wrong?" Jabir asked.

Pearl's face was tight with worry. She knelt down, and whispered to the symbiot wrapped around her wrists. The thin bands of gold dissolved and divide before wrapping around each boy's arm.

"Something has happened. I don't know for sure what is going on, but Pokey is showing me images. Asim needs my help," Pearl said in a quiet, urgent voice.

"We can helps, can't we, Jabir? We are good at helping," Roam said.

Pearl reached up and touched Roam's blond hair. "I need you to hide. Can you do that for me? Can you hide where no one can find you until Pokey tells you that it is safe to come out?" she asked.

Jabir nodded. "We can goes to my favorite rock. Daddy and I made a fort in it," he said.

"Where is it?" Pearl asked, searching the little boy's face.

"It is in the meadow. It is the one with the tall rocks that sticks up," Jabir explained.

"You have to be very quiet. No one can see you," Pearl said. "Those...
They are coming. I need you to go now."

"We'll be just like Grandpa Paul – really, really quiet," Jabir promised.

"I'm always quiet. I'm a cat," Roam stated.

"Hurry and don't get caught," Pearl ordered as she stood up and
reached for the knives on the counter. "I've got some trash to take out."

"That means she's going to kick their asses," Roam whispered. "My
mommy says that when she gets mad."

"Shush! Let's go," Jabir said, shifting into his dragon.

Pearl watched both boys disappear around the corner. They were going
up the stairs to the upper balcony. Realizing that she had to trust in their
natural ability and knowing that the small symbiots attached to their arms
would help guide them, she turned her focus on the men who harmed
her mate.

Rules? Her dragon asked.

Let's start with rule number eleven, Pearl suggested with a grim smile as
her fingers curled around one of the knives she was holding.

I like that one, her dragon chuckled.

Hans silently climbed over the railing and landed on the deck. He knelt
and glanced around. Through the large section of glass windows, he
could see the woman in the food preparation area. He didn't see the
kids. He wasn't worried about them since they were too young to be a
threat.

He started forward, pausing when his view of the woman was blocked
after she activated the window shield. It wouldn't matter nor hinder his
mission to capture her. One female was no threat to a cutthroat like him.

He stood and walked across the deck. He had seen the symbiot leave a
short while ago and knew that Crag and Zeb were capable of handling it
and the old dragon warrior. He almost winced at how easy his job would
be in capturing the old woman.

He stepped up to the door and tested it. A humorless smile curved his
lips when he found it unlocked. Pulling it open, he silently stepped inside.

This is too easy, he thought as he entered before the smile died and was
replaced with a frown.

Hans stared at the woman who gazed at him with a smile on her lips.
Unease stirred inside him, but he pushed it away. His gaze ran over her
slender form. She looked cool, composed, and – he reluctantly admitted –
good in black leather for her age.

"Where I come from it is considered rude to enter someone's home
without being invited," the woman said in a cool voice.

Hans frowned. "You are coming with me," he ordered.

"I don't think so. What have you done with my mate?" the woman quietly asked.

Hans gaze narrowed on her face. He could normally tell a lot about his adversary by their eyes. A flicker of fear, a hint of desperation, and panic were normal, but hers were clear and calm. She looked as if she were ready to battle him – and felt confident that she would win. Once again, an uneasy feeling rose in his stomach. This time it was a little more difficult to push away.

"Do not give me any trouble, female. I'll snap your neck as quickly as Crag is going to snap your mate's. Then, I'll do the same to those two younglings," Hans snarled.

"Listen, asshole, I asked you a question. I'll ask one more time. What have you done with my mate?" the woman demanded.

Hans sneered at the woman's show of defiant bravado. He closed the distance between them. Stopping in front of her, he towered over her. Her face was tight with resolve and determination.

"What species are you?" Hans demanded, his gaze narrowing on her face.

"One you don't want to underestimate," she replied.

"Your mate will be dead soon. If you fight, so will you," Hans threatened. He reached out and wrapped his hand around her upper arm. "Come...."

His breath hissed out when her knee connected with his groin in a swift, hard blow. His eyes widened as pain exploded through him. Dots flashed before his eyes and his fingers loosened on her arm.

A loud groan escaped him as the pain spread. He was defenseless against her next blow. She pulled back her arm and slammed her elbow into his cheekbone. Reaching out, he grabbed at her jacket as he fell backwards, pulling her with him.

The woman's hand rose and she struggled to break free, but his larger frame and gravity were no match for her. Together they fell to the floor. Pain ripped through him and his body jerked in surprise at the source.

He froze and blinked in shock. Following the woman's gaze, he looked down at himself. It took a second for him to realize that he was dead, his mind and body just hadn't recognized it yet. The woman must have had a knife in her hand. When he pulled her down, she instinctively raised her hand to cushion her fall. Unwittingly, the knife between their bodies had pieced his heart.

"How? You are... female," Hans muttered as his body began to tremble.

"Rule number eleven: If you are going to hit someone, make sure they stay down the first time, because you might not get a second chance," she said in a quiet voice, gazing down at him with a mixture of determination and resolve.

"Rules… What rules?" Hans asked in a slightly slurred voice.

"Pearl's Rules for Living," she replied. "Where is my mate?"

"Others… Zeb has him… in… the… barn…," Hans replied before his eyes dimmed and his head fell to the side.

Take out trash, her dragon growled. *No want dead body in house.*

"Amen to that, sister," Pearl replied, stiffening her spine and pushing up off the dead man's body.

With the added boost of her dragon's strength, Pearl awkwardly dragged the man's body out of her house. Once she was done, she shifted into her dragon. She searched the darkness. She was torn between going to Asim first or making sure the boys were alright.

What gut say? Her dragon asked.

The boys – my gut says we need to find the boys, Pearl said.

Then, we find boys, her dragon replied.

Pearl felt the muscles of her dragon contract before she pushed up off the deck. Her wings swept through the air in wide, powerful strokes. She flew low to the ground, following the slight scent trail of Jabir. Her dragon's gaze swept the area, mindful of their other visitors.

Rule number twenty, her dragon whispered.

Yes, Pearl replied.

Rule number twenty was one that had protected her and the girls many times over the years. If you or your family/friends' lives are on the line, ignore all other rules except Rule Number 1. She would use her brain. She was smart, tough, and determined. She might be outnumbered and outpowered, but she had a good head on her shoulders and had enough fights under her belt to know when to fight dirty.

Whoop-ass time, her dragon growled.

Yes, it's time to open a can of whoop-ass, Pearl agreed.

FOURTEEN

Asim awoke to excruciating pain. Nausea churned in his stomach. The pain rocketed through him when he rolled to his side. It was so intense; he feared he would lose consciousness again.

Damage…, he choked out to his dragon.

Left leg broken, jaw fractured, his dragon replied, pacing inside him. *You no can shift to me.*

I know. Symbiot…, he asked, trying to breathe through the pain.

Locked away. They threaten kill mate, his dragon snarled.

Asim clenched his fists against the floor. His head was pounding, making it difficult to think. He had to get to his symbiot. He couldn't shift into his dragon with a broken leg and he couldn't fight. Breathing deeply, he forced himself to roll over. The bits of symbiots around his wrists were moving over his body. The bone in his leg would be too much for the small pieces, but they could heal his jaw.

The symbiot moved upward and slid over his jaw. Some of it slipped beneath his skin. He could feel the tingle of bone being mended. When it finished, it resurfaced through the cut on his lip and healed that as well.

"Thank you, my friend," he murmured.

The small amount of symbiot warmed under his touch. He could feel it moving down his body to his leg. Such a small amount of symbiot would take days to heal him.

"What happened?" he demanded.

Not know, his dragon replied, continuing to pace.

Asim gritted his teeth and forced himself to sit up. Sweat beaded on his forehead and he swallowed back the groan of pain. Holding his broken leg, he waited until he felt like he wasn't going to pass out before he drew in a deep breath again.

"Come to me. I need to connect with Pokey," Asim ordered in a strained voice.

The tiny strands of gold shimmered, but moved onto the palm of his hand. Asim wrapped his fingers around it and closed his eyes. Focusing, he connected with his symbiot. Within seconds, the images and conversation about what had happened while he was unconscious streamed through his mind. Panting, he released the faint connection and opened his fingers. The tiny threads of gold looked pale and listless.

"Pearl," he whispered, bowing his head.

"Where is he?" Crag asked.

"He'll be here. We need to find those damn creatures," Zeb said, glancing around the large meadow with the vision magnifier. "There! I see one of them about half way down the meadow."

"Hans should be back by now," Crag said with a frown.

Zeb lowered the vision magnifier and glared at the other man. "He said he would meet us at the barn. It may take a while if he has to carry her. The skimmer," he snapped. "We are running out of time. Let's go."

Both men slid onto a skimmer. The land transport had a long, narrow seat, a handle bar, and foot pedals that operated the speed and brakes. It was simple, but utilitarian. The bikes rose up off the ground. Leaning forward, the men shot out across the ground, cutting a path through the tall purple grass.

Behind them in the barn, two large creatures – each with four arms, two legs, and a knack for locks – climbed down from the rafters. Moving across the bare floor of the barn, the female climbed up on the shoulders of the male and inserted a piece of wire into the lock. It took several tries before the lock clicked and disengaged and the door opened. A slow smile spread over the two Grombots' faces when the enraged Werecat with wings turned to face them.

"Jabir... Roam... Are you in here?" Pearl softly called.

She climbed up onto the rocks and peered into the narrow hole in the rock. Fear gripped her when there was no answer. She turned around on top of the large boulder and searched the darkness. She froze when she saw a movement in the tall grass a short distance away.

A soft laugh escaped her when she saw the familiar eyes of an emu staring back at her. A moment later, a second and a third one joined it.

Sliding down off the rock, she listened. The smile grew when she heard Roam.

"Why's didn't we do this before?" he was saying.

"Cause we didn't know it was fun," Jabir replied.

"Boys, come here," Pearl ordered.

She blinked when the three more emus appeared near the rocks. Searching, she almost missed Jabir and Roam. Both boys peeked around the neck of an emu.

"You're riding them?" Pearl exclaimed.

"They's just like playing horsey, only better," Jabir said with a smile. "They said they would help us."

"They said...," Pearl started to repeat before she shook her head. "How?"

"They are real good at being soldiers. Jabir says they are a neutral," Roam replied.

"Not neutral – natural. They's smart, Grams," Jabir said.

Pearl turned when her dragon hissed out a warning. In the distance, she could see two skimmers heading their way. Those would be the men that the dying man had mentioned. If the men were heading in this direction, she couldn't help but wonder what they had done to Asim.

He not dead. I know if he dead, her dragon assured her.

"Boys, we need to keep them away from the barn and Asim. Jabir, can you tell the emus that I need a distraction?" Pearl asked, turning back to the little boy.

"Yes," Jabir replied.

"Whatever happens, don't let those men catch you," Pearl said.

"We won't," Roam replied with a grin. "We needs reins if we are going to goes real fast. It is hard to holds onto their necks."

The symbiots on the boys spread into a thin bridle and reins. Pearl whispered to the boys to be careful once more before she shifted back into her dragon. It was time to show these assholes who they were messing with.

Launching up off the ground, Pearl focused on her plan of attack. She needed to keep the men away from the barn long enough to find Asim and Pokey. Once they were together, there would be no stopping them.

Below her, Pearl could see the dark shapes of the emus moving through the tall grass. She was shocked at how fast they were! She estimated they had to be running at close to fifty miles per hour.

They ran in a V-shaped formation toward the men riding the skimmers. Pearl swooped down behind the men and released a long stream of dragon fire. The tall grass ignited in a flaming wall. She twisted, and rose again, rolling several times when one of the men turned on the skimmer and fired at her.

The man turned back around just in time to swerve when the emus emerged from the tall grass in front of them. The men stopped, shocked to see the birds circling them. Pearl could hear the strong, powerful legs striking the ground. Bits of grass and dirt flew up under their feet. As one, they turned back the other way.

The larger of the two men lifted a blaster and aimed for one of the young birds. In a flash, the emus scattered in all directions. The man who had fired at Pearl turned and yelled for his partner to go after the emu carrying Roam.

Pearl circled around. She couldn't release any dragon fire for fear of hitting one of the emus or the boys. Instead, she swooped down again with her claws extended.

The man – Zeb, she suspected – raised his laser rifle to shoot at Jabir. Pearl's claw snatched the rifle – and the man holding it – right off the skimmer. The added weight was too much for her dragon and she couldn't gain altitude without releasing him.

Pearl's dragon roared in pain when Zeb swung his hand up and the sharp edge of his blade sliced a deep path across her front claw. She opened her claw and released the man. Unfortunately, the move threw her off-balance. Tumbling through the air, she curled her wings protectively around her body and hit the ground on the other side of the wall of flames. Rolling several times, she finally came to a stop. Shaking her head to clear the dizziness, she shifted back into her human form.

Lying on the ground, she stared at the man on the other side. He was searching for her through the flames and smoke. Defenseless, she remained frozen.

Several long seconds passed before he turned away. Trying to push herself up, she drew in a hissing breath when her arm gave out on her. She glanced down and cursed when she saw blood dripping from under the sleeve of her jacket. This was the first time she had been hurt in her dragon form. It would seem it carried over to her human one.

"Son-of-a-bitch!" she muttered.

Standing up, she glanced through the flames before turning to look at the barn. Torn once again, she could only hope the emus were as good as Jabir said they were. She took off at a fast run for the barn.

"Where are they?" Zeb growled.

"I don't know," Crag said, glancing around. "One second they were there and the next they were gone."

"Well, find them and kill them. We'll sell them dead," Zeb ordered.

"Where are you going?" Crag asked.

"Dragon hunting," Zeb replied, checking his laser rifle.

"Tell Hans to get the ship ready," Crag grunted before he took off.

Zeb walked over to the skimmer. He released the emergency canister attached to the side and tossed it. He aimed, and fired. The canister, filled with a fire retardant, exploded in midair and created a hole in the wall of flames. Sliding his leg over the seat of the skimmer, he turned the transport around and took off through the hole. In the distance, he could see the shape of someone running. A break in the clouds cast the moonlight down on the white hair of the woman he had seen earlier.

"So, you can shift into a dragon as well," Zeb said under his breath. "Let's see how good you can fight."

FIFTEEN

Bracing himself against the wall, Asim glanced up when the door suddenly burst open. His eyes widened and a grim, pain-filled smile curved his lips but never made it to his eyes. He straightened as much as his broken leg would allow and nodded to his symbiot.

"It is good to see you, my friend," he greeted through clenched teeth. "My dragon and I need your healing powers."

His symbiot surged forward. It melted and flowed over his broken leg. Asim closed his eyes, leaned his head back, and relaxed. The warmth of healing energy flooded his body, making him whole once again. The fighting blood of his dragon ignited in his veins. When his eyes opened, the flames of an ancient dragon warrior of Valdier blazed from them.

"Our mates and the younglings are in danger," he snarled, baring his teeth.

The two Grombots that had followed his symbiot into the room turned and quickly vanished. Stepping out of his makeshift cell, Asim shifted into his dragon and took off at a run for the wide, double doors. By the time he hit the doors of the barn, his symbiot had formed armor around his body. He burst through the doors and soared up into the air. Twisting, he scanned the burning field for his mate.

His gaze narrowed on Pearl's white hair. She was running toward the barn. Behind her, a skimmer was approaching at an increasing speed.

Fury poured through him and he plunged forward. He swept over Pearl, placing himself between her and their attacker. He released a series of powerful fireballs at the skimmer. The male jerked the skimmer to the side but was unable to avoid the last fireball completely.

Asim released another burst when the man flew up into the air. The flames engulfed the skimmer. Within seconds, it exploded. The force of the explosion sent shards of the skimmer flying through the air.

Diving for the ground, Asim wrapped his body around Pearl and lowered his head to completely protect her from the flying projectiles. Molten pieces of metal rained down around them, but Pearl and his dragon were protected by the armor of his symbiot. He breathed heavily and trembled when he realized how small and fragile she felt in his claws.

He shifted back to his two-legged form and held her close to him, rubbing his nose against her cheek. The coppery smell of her blood hit him hard and he lifted his head. He didn't need to instruct his symbiot to heal Pearl – it was already moving under the sleeve of her jacket and up her arm.

"I smell blood," he groaned.

"The ass- wipe got in a lucky slice, but not before I jerked his ass off his skimmer," she said, gazing up at him. "The other man said they broke your leg."

"Yes, but my symbiot healed me," Asim said. "Where are the younglings?"

Pearl looked over his shoulder with a worried frown. "Out there on the emus," she said.

Asim glanced over his shoulder and his gaze narrowed in anger. He frantically wanted to make sure she wasn't hurt anywhere else, but he needed to take care of the threat to them first. He released her and stepped back. His body shimmered again. Once more, the gun-metal-gray, battle-scarred dragon stood in front of her. With a nod, Pearl shifted as well – her smaller, silver dragon standing proudly next to her mate. Pokey dissolved, divided into two, and created matching armor for each dragon.

With a loud roar, Pearl pushed up off the ground. Asim quickly followed. His dragon was still very protective of his mate despite her fierce nature. Together, they flew out over the field in search of the younglings.

It took nearly five fly-overs before they spied the small group emerging into the clearing near the tall rock. The emus turned in tight circles, prancing and stomping the ground. On the back of two emus, Roam and Jabir waved to Asim and Pearl.

Asim circled around and landed several meters from the birds. Pearl smoothly landed next to him. The symbiot dissolved and shook before reforming into the large Werecat with wings Jabir loved so much.

"Grams! We ran the bad man off. He rode aways on his skimmer for the mountain and didn't come back," Roam laughed, sliding off of his emu.

"That is wonderful! You were both so brave," Pearl exclaimed, bending down to pick Roam up in her arms. "Your daddy and mommy are going to be so proud of you."

"Are either of you hurt?" Asim asked, looking at Roam before he turned to look at Jabir.

"No, we's okay," Jabir said with a grin.

Asim started to take a step toward Jabir to lift the little boy down when the emu under Jabir jerked to the side and stumbled. Its legs trembled before it slowly sank down to the ground. Less than a second later, a cry escaped Jabir when he was lifted by the back of his neck off the back of the emu.

"Don't move or he dies," Zeb ordered.

Asim took a threatening step toward the man before freezing. The soft sound of Jabir's whimper of pain warned him that the man holding the boy wouldn't hesitate to kill him. His gaze narrowed in helpless rage as Zeb ruthlessly pressed his weapon against Jabir's temple.

"I should have killed you," Zeb growled.

"Release him!" Asim ordered, moving ever so slightly so that he was in front of Pearl and Roam.

"Give me the woman and I'll release the boy," Zeb demanded with a shake of his head.

"Never!" Asim snarled.

Zeb's finger tightened on the blaster in his hand. "The woman – now," he repeated in a cold voice.

"No...," Asim started to say.

"Yes," Pearl quietly interjected.

"Pearl...," Asim hissed, turning slightly in her direction.

"He'll kill Jabir. I can't let him do that," Pearl replied.

Asim watched her lower Roam to the ground and push the boy behind her. She ran her hand along her pants and smiled at him. Stepping closer, she brushed a kiss across his lips and pressed her hand against his.

"Remember rule number eleven," she whispered before stepping away and turning toward Zeb.

"Release him," she said, lifting her chin in defiance.

"Not until you take his place," Zeb countered.

Pearl stepped forward and turned to look back at Asim. A shiver ran through her when she heard Jabir release a cry and the soft thud of him hitting the ground. A second later, Zeb's cold hand gripped her neck. Pearl gave Asim a small nod, her eyes cool and calm.

Releasing a long breath, she swung her clenched fist as hard as she could down between Zeb's legs and twisted sideways at the same time as Asim released the knife she had slipped into his hand. The blade struck Zeb in the upper left shoulder. The force of it knocked him backwards several steps. Pearl followed up with a hard kick to Zeb's stomach, sending him lurching into the tall grass.

The emus followed him. The young birds went on the offensive against their attacker. They surrounded the man and began kicking him with their strong powerful legs. The group disappeared into the tall grass, following Zeb when he tried to crawl away. A shudder ran through Pearl as the sounds of the man's screams and the thuds and clucking of the emus filled the air.

"Make sure he is never a threat to us again," Asim ordered Pokey.

The symbiot shimmered and disappeared into the tall grass. Pearl scooped Jabir up into her arms and shifted into her dragon while Asim did the same with Roam. They both lifted up, carrying the boys away from the last pitiful, choked cries of their attacker.

Later that night, Pearl double checked on both of the boys. They were sprawled out on Jabir's bed, sound asleep with Pokey. It had taken a while to get both of them to calm down. She had fed them, bathed them, and finally read several books before they began yawning and their eyes drooped.

Pearl looked up when Asim opened the door, stepped in, and secured the door behind him. Her gaze softened when she saw the fatigue on his face. She walked over to him, and wrapped her arms around him.

"The boys?" Asim asked.

"Asleep. They were ready to join the hunt for the other man," Pearl chuckled, leaning back to look up at him with a questioning expression.

"I took care of Zeb and the one at our home. The other one escaped. I notified Zoran about what happened. He has dispatched several ships to find the man. I reassured Mandra, Ariel, Vox, and Riley that the boys were fine. They will be here first thing in the morning. I told them it would probably be best as I knew you were getting the boys down for the night," he said with a sigh.

"It helped being here in Mandra and Ariel's house. Jabir had his own toys and bed. Pokey is sleeping with them," she said, stepping back and guiding him to a large chair by the window. "I made you some dinner. Let me get it."

Asim tugged on her arm, pulling her onto his lap and wrapped his arms around her. He held her close, his chin against her hair and closed his eyes. Pearl could feel the heavy beat of his heart. She relaxed against him, understanding that he needed this time.

"I was afraid I was going to lose you," he murmured.

"You weren't the only one," she replied, resting her head against his shoulder and staring out at the dark. "When Hans told me what they had done to you, it pissed me off."

Asim chuckled. "You showed him!" he said, gazing down at her.

Pearl smiled. "He did it to himself, really. Neither my dragon nor I wanted a dead body in the house," she declared.

"I knew the moment that you knocked my ass in the lake that I had met a woman who was a warrior at heart. You proved it tonight," he said with a sigh and his arms tightened around her. "Tomorrow, I'm setting up a security system throughout the valley."

"No, tomorrow you are going to get up and take care of the animals like you do every day. We will not live our lives in fear because of one incident. Besides, we have an army already here! Between the Grombots and the emus, I can't imagine a safer place to live," she said sternly.

"I do believe you are right," he said, bending his head to brush a kiss across her lips.

"You bet your ass I am," Pearl retorted.

She turned and threaded her hands through his hair. Pulling his head down again, she captured his lips in a long kiss that shared the depth of her fear of losing him. Asim deepened the kiss and thanked the Goddess once more for giving him such a perfect mate.

EPILOGUE

Present Day:
"Wait a minute! What happened next?" Brogan demanded, leaning forward with his hands on his knees when Asim stopped talking.

"What do you mean 'What happened next'? We got the kids to safety," Asim said.

Brogan pushed up off the floor and grabbed the wooden sculpture. He shook it in front of Asim's face with a frown. When Asim gave him a puzzled look, Brogan released a growl of frustration and shook the wooden emu again.

"What happened to the other man? What happened to the emu that was shot?" Brogan demanded.

"Oh," Asim replied with a grin.

Barrack stood up and brushed the back of his pants. "Do you want us to hunt down the other man? We are excellent hunters," he said.

"No, no.... Crag was eventually caught for another offense and is serving time on an Antrox prison asteroid," Asim assured Barrack.

"What about the emu?" Brogan asked again.

"You know, emus are amazingly resourceful and hardy creatures. The one that was shot received only a minor wound that was healed quickly with the help of my symbiot," Asim reassured the agitated warrior.

"What about the half-blind Pactor and the Grombots and Roam and Jabir...?" Brogan added, with an intense curiosity that took Asim by surprise.

Asim chuckled and stood up. "Come, I will show you," he said.

The three men walked through the barn. Brogan and Barrack gazed around them in wonder, as if seeing the animals in it for the first time.

Grombots – more than a dozen – swung from the rafters. Large nets were strung beneath the beams to catch the little ones still learning. Brogan stumbled when a half dozen Marrats raced out in front of him. Tasiers slept or munched on thick blades of purple grass and watched them from behind the safety of the glass cubicles that separated the boys from the girls.

Asim paused in the door. Out near the corral, Pearl and Ariel laughed as they petted the newest member to their family – Hobbler and George's daughter – Isabel. Adalard and Mandra jumped to the side when half a dozen emus swept past them at a run with Jabir riding the largest one in front.

Jaguin and Sara were standing with two other men and a woman. The small group turned and smiled at Barrack, Brogan, and him. Asim heard the two men next to him draw in a startled breath when they realized the other two men were twin dragons – and they each had an arm wrapped around the small, dark-haired woman between them who was holding a toddler in her arms.

Cree and Calo murmured to Melina before walking in their direction. Asim could see the confusion and suspicion in Barrack and Brogan's eyes as the other twin dragons approached. The expressions on Cree and Calo's faces reflected their own feelings of disbelief and uncertainty.

"Asim...," Calo greeted, not looking at Asim but at Barrack and Brogan.

"What is all of this?" Barrack quietly asked, gazing at the chaotic, yet somehow normal scene before eyeing the two warriors who stopped in front of them.

"Hope. A second chance," Cree said before he clamped his lips together.

"Jaguin thought you might like to know that it is possible to find a mate – and for her to be strong enough," Calo explained, his gaze moving back to where Melina stood holding their young daughter.

Asim turned and looked at the twin warriors. "This is home – a place where family and friends come and share. It is a place where you find love and acceptance for who you are. It doesn't matter if you aren't perfect, that is what makes you special," he explained with a wave of his hand.

"In our village, everyone feared us. Our whole life we were feared and rejected for being who we were – twins," Barrack murmured, staring around him.

"We were treated the same way, but we found Melina. She loves us and fought to save our lives," Calo said, turning to look at the men. "She is our partner. She keeps us grounded."

"I understand now what Pearl and you were trying to tell us," Brogan reluctantly admitted, glancing around him as if seeing their world through different eyes.

"What is that?" Asim asked.

"That there are different rules that can help guide us this time – and help us in making the right choices," Brogan said.

"We grew up with the people of our village believing one thing – that we would never find a true mate. We were fortunate that our parents believed differently. Your mate is out there, but you will need to handle her with care, for she will not understand the ways of the dragon," Cree cautioned.

Calo nodded. "… Or the needs of twin dragons. You will need to be patient," he said.

"And follow Pearl's last rule, no matter what happens," Asim agreed.

"Which rule was that?" Barrack asked.

"Pearl's Unbreakable Rule: Family and Friends come first. Be loyal, be true… and love them like there is no tomorrow," Asim quietly shared, staring across the yard at his mate. Pearl turned to look at him, a small smile curving her lips. "Cree and Calo can explain that one to you."

Asim didn't wait to see if the twins finally understood. His gaze was locked on Pearl. She met him halfway across the yard. He could see the questioning look in her eyes fade to understanding when he gently nodded his head.

"Are they ready?" Pearl asked, lifting her hand to trace the lines near the corner of Asim's right eye.

"They will be. You were smart to ask Jaguin to have Cree, Calo, and Melina come," Asim replied, bending to brush a kiss across her lips. "Perhaps, I can talk them into taking all three Pactors home with them."

Pearl chuckled and shook her head. "You know you'd miss them as much as Ariel and Jabir would," she said.

"Fly with me," Asim suddenly said. "I know this little place in the forest not far from here…."

Pearl reached up and captured his lips. Her hand ran down between them and she brushed her hand across the front of him before pulling back with a grin. She stepped back and turned. Looking over her shoulder, she had a mischievous sparkle dancing in her eyes.

"Last one there is on the bottom," she laughed.

Asim watched his mate transform. The silver dragon flicked her tail, stroking the tip along his chest before she lifted up off the ground. Jabir, riding the emu, swept by him, laughing and waving to Pearl as she flew off.

She going to be top, his dragon snorted, impatiently pacing and wanting to pursue his mate.

I think it is time you tried the bottom, Asim said with a wicked grin.

Oh, yes! His dragon groaned when Asim sent a deliciously wicked idea to his dragon.

Asim shifted into his dragon. In a flash, the battle scarred dragon was in fast pursuit of his mate. Well, fast enough to reach her just a few seconds too late to win. Wrapping his tail around Pearl's silver tail, he locked them together and brought her gently down to the ground where the delicate silver dragon settled on top of the large male who groaned in delight.

Yes! I like, his dragon agreed.

A GRIM PET

---

by
M.K. Eidem

USA Today Best Selling Author, M.K. grew up loving to extend the stories
she'd read as a child. Now she writes her own stories and loves where
they take her.

http://www.mkeidem.com

ONE

 Lisa just smiled as Grim, for the third time, checked to make sure her cape was securely closed against the slight chill in the air before doing the same to the girls'. The capes weren't the same gray ones they had worn at the Joining Ceremony. Grim had those destroyed, never wanting to be reminded of how he nearly lost his family. Now they wore capes in the deep, purple color of his house, House Luanda.

"We are fine, Grim," Lisa told him as he went to adjust her hood again. "It's not that cold out."

"I should have considered that the sun would not have yet warmed this area when I chose it," he grumbled.

"But it will soon," she said, putting a reassuring hand over his. "I can't believe you and your Warriors were able to get all this done in such a short time."

She let her gaze travel over the newly-constructed, circular arena that now sat on the grounds in front of House Luanda. There was a raised seating area that curved around half of it, and then a gathering area for Warriors at the far end. Today was the Festival of the Goddess, but it wasn't like any festival Lisa had ever experienced back on Earth.

For Tornians, the Festival was a competition. A way for them to impress the Goddess with their strength and skill, in the hopes she would find them fit and worthy enough to bless them with a female. It was armed combat, and it wasn't uncommon for Warriors to be injured, sometimes severely.

Lisa had been horrified when Grim informed her of this and told him that there was no way she could allow the girls to witness such a thing. It would terrify them to watch Warriors, that they had come to know and love, attacking and injuring one another.

They had finally reached a compromise, and in a short time, they would discover if Grim's Warriors would accept it.

"They knew it was their Queen's wish, so it was done," Grim told her, referring to the arena as if it shouldn't surprise her.

"They are all fit and worthy males," Lisa said, smiling up at him, "but I got the best of them."

"I should never have let you out of our chambers this morning," Grim growled as he leaned down, capturing her lips in a long, deep kiss, his hands slipping under the cape he'd just taken so much time to make sure was closed. He was about to lift her up into his arms and carry her away, when he heard Alger clearing his throat, and the girls starting to giggle.

Pulling his mouth from his Lisa's, he almost ignored them all when the look in her eyes told him she wanted that too. Instead, he took a deep breath and forced himself to release her, only standing after he made sure her cape was secure again.

"Go," she encouraged softly. "We'll finish this tonight."

Giving her a stiff nod, he turned and stepped to the front of the podium to address the large crowd that had gathered. Traditionally, the Warriors that wished to compete would gather at the training fields, but Lisa had expanded the Festival into a daylong event. She had invited vendors from every corner of Luda to set up within the walls of the House and offer their food, wares, and skills for credits. When they quieted, Grim spoke.

"Warriors, today is the Festival of the Goddess." A roar of excitement went through the crowd, and Grim raised his hands to quiet them. "And we must give thanks for the many blessings she has bestowed on us." He turned and looked to Lisa, Carly, and Miki as a roar of agreement spread through the crowd.

"These blessings have changed our lives for the better," Grim continued once they quieted again. "Now, we must show the Goddess that we appreciate them." A confused silence met this statement. "As Warriors, we are used to the blood and gore that comes with battle. We must accept it. But Queen Lisa, Princesses Carly and Miki, and every other female here today do not. And I, for one, never want them to."

A low murmur of agreement answered him.

"Because of this, our battle swords and blades will not be used during the competition. Instead, only stingers shall be allowed." He gestured to the array of stingers propped up against the platform below him. "Any Warrior receiving three stings shall be deemed defeated."

Absolute silence met Grim's declaration, and Lisa let her concerned gaze travel over those before them. Had she overstepped in asking this of Grim? Rising, she went to stand beside him.

"I realize this comes as a shock to you," she said taking Grim's hand. "You believe that only by pitting your full strength and skill against your brother Warriors will you prove to the Goddess you are fit and worthy males." She let her words hang there for a moment, and saw many of the Warriors nodding their heads. "I do not believe that is truth. I do not believe that winning one competition is enough to prove you are a fit and worthy male." She saw they didn't understand.

"Was Faber not once a winner?" she asked, knowing he was. "Was he a fit and worthy Warrior?"

"No." Came the immediate reply.

"Luuken once won in his manno's House. Was he a fit and worthy warrior?" she demanded.

"No!" They shouted even louder.

"Then I say to you that while winning this competition allows others to see the strength and skills you have acquired through your dedication and sacrifice, it has absolutely nothing to do with you being a fit and worthy Warrior. It is your everyday actions that the Goddess sees, and that is what she blesses."

"If you share this belief, then from now on the victor in the Festival of Goddess competition shall receive a trophy created by Master Glassmaker Gahan, and credits equal to a Warrior's yearly compensation." A murmur of excitement went through the crowd, and Lisa raised a hand to quiet them. "Or if you do not share this belief, then you may continue the competition as it has always been with your battle swords and blades, but the Princesses and I shall not witness it. We have no desire to watch the fit and worthy males we have come to care about senselessly harming one another. The choice is yours."

Lisa stood beside Grim, silently waiting to see what the Warriors before her would decide when out of the corner of her eye she caught Alger beginning to move.

"Stay," Grim growled lowly, and Alger stilled.

Both the King's and Queen's Guard had elected not to participate in today's events. Instead, they surrounded the area where Grim and Lisa sat with the females from Earth, along with Padma, Gossamer, Gahan, Dagan, and Caitir.

Because of this, Grim was not going to let The Guard influence the others now. It would be his Warriors' decision on how they proceeded. Slowly, Warrior Tagma separated himself from the group of Warriors on the far side of the arena and moved toward his King and Queen, his battle sword strapped to his back.

Once he stood in front of them, he placed his arm across his chest and gave them a deep bow. Straightening, he released the clasp that held his sword in place and wrapped the now loose straps around the sheath-encased blade. Setting it against the wall beneath where Lisa and Grim stood, he chose the stinger that best fit his grip. Turning, he walked to the center of the arena and waited.

It didn't take long for Warrior Oya to step forward. He exchanged his weapon, took up his position across from Tagma, and saluting him with the stinger he had chosen, waited for the command.

"Begin!" Grim roared, and with a cheer from the crowd, the Festival began.

Lisa blinked back the tears that wanted to fill her eyes as she sat down. She should have had more faith in the Warriors of Luda. Should have known they would understand and be willing to change. They truly were fit and worthy males.

"My Lisa?" Grim asked quietly, concern-filled eyes looking down at her.

"I'm fine," she reassured, giving him a watery smile. "It's just hormones."

"Hormones?" He frowned at the word.

"Chemicals that are naturally in our bodies," she explained. "They increase when a female conceives. It tends to make us just a little," Lisa lifted her hand so he could see that her thumb and index finger were just barely apart, "emotional."

"I will find Hadar! He will fix this." Lisa's hand on his arm stopped him.

"No, Grim. There's nothing he can do about this. It's normal. Natural. It isn't harmful."

"Truth?"

"Truth. I was just touched that our Warriors would so readily accept this change." She had to take a deep breath to fight the new swell of tears. She knew if she didn't, Grim would be carrying her back inside Luanda.

"Mommy?" Carly's little voice had her looking down to see the eyes of her oldest locked on the two Warriors in the arena.

"Yes, baby?"

"Why is that Warrior attacking Cook?"

"Oya isn't attacking Tagma, Carly. We talked about this. Remember? They are just competing against one another."

"But it looks like he is."

"I know, but they aren't using real swords. See?" Lisa pointed to Tagma's and Oya's swords that had just clashed and the flashes of light sparked from them. "They are using stingers."

"But it still hurts," Carly argued when Tagma growled out as Oya's stinger connected with his arm.

"It does, my Carly," Grim took over the conversation, not downplaying what she was seeing. "But it is a way for a Warrior to learn and improve his skills so that when it *is* real, he won't be harmed."

"Oh." Carly was silent for a moment then her gaze went to Grim. "I still don't like it, Manno."

Grim felt his heart stutter. It had been just that morning that Carly and Miki had asked if they could call him Manno instead of Grim, and he knew it would be a long time before hearing it didn't affect him.

"That is good, my Carly. It shows the Warriors that you truly care for their well-being. Just as your mother does."

Carly's little chest puffed up at her manno's praise. It reminded Grim that it was the little things he did that truly affected those he loved. A roar from the Warriors had both Grim's and Carly's attention returning to the arena to find Tagma with three marks on his arms and Oya with only two; declaring the Captain of the Castle Guard the victor.

"Can I go make sure that Cook is okay?" Carly asked, looking back to her manno.

"Yes, Ion and Nairn will escort you." The two guards he named immediately moved to the steps.

∞ ∞ ∞ ∞ ∞

Oya grunted his thanks as he took the cloth Tagma held out, and wiped away the sweat and dirt from their battle.

"It was a good match, old friend."

"It was," Tagma agreed. "I will make sure I spend more time on the fields before we meet at the next Festival."

"It will not change the result," Oya declared. "Your time in the kitchen has dulled your skills."

"As if walking a wall has sharpened yours," Tagma fired back.

"I am not the one out of the competition," Oya told him smugly. "If you wish great rewards, you must prove you are worthy."

"Cook!" The young voice had both Warriors quickly spinning around to find Princess Carly rushing toward them, two of the Queen's Elite Guard closely following.

"Princess Carly," Tagma frowned at Ion and Nairn, even as he went down on one knee, so he was closer to her level. "This is no place for you."

"I had to make sure you were okay. Manno said you were, but..." She reached out a little hand but didn't touch the red slashes that marred his arm and chest, courtesy of Oya's stinger.

"King... your manno," Tagma corrected himself, his eyes widening slightly at how she referred to Grim, "is right. These will be gone by tomorrow."

"Truth?" Her amber gaze searched his.

"Truth, little one. You will see that for yourself when you come help me with the cookies tomorrow."

Carly was silent for a moment, and all the males surrounding them could see she was thinking.

"Alright, but I want to make sure," she said, and before anyone knew what she was about, she leaned forward and pressed a little kiss to each red slash. "Whenever I get hurt, Mommy kisses my boo-boos, and it makes them feel better. Did I make yours feel better, Cook?"

Tagma's breath caught for a moment, and he knew that even if he were in the most excruciating of pain, he would still tell her she'd made it better. "You did, little one," he told her gruffly. "Thank you."

The smile she gifted him with shone brighter than the Tornian sun. "Good. I'll see you tomorrow then." And with that, and a little wave, she was gone.

Slowly rising, Tagma looked to Oya. "I believe I just received a greater reward than you could ever receive in the arena."

"Truth," Oya agreed quietly.

∞ ∞ ∞ ∞ ∞

Lisa moved from stall to stall talking to the vendors, perusing what they had to offer. There were small bits of things she couldn't identify. Handmade jewelry. Woven baskets. And of course, there were blades and swords in every shape and size. Seeing them made her conscious of the Raptor's Claw strapped to her arm. Grim had insisted she carry it. It didn't matter that she was surrounded by her Elite Guard. She carried his offspring, and he was taking no chances.

She couldn't help but smile as she rubbed the pronounced baby bump she already sported. Grim's unborn daughter was making her presence known, making Lisa look more like she was five months pregnant, instead of the three that she was.

She knew it concerned Grim. Her rapidly growing size. He worried that conceiving his offspring would harm her, but Lisa wasn't. Yes, Tornian offspring were larger than human ones at birth, or presentation as they referred to it. And yes, the length of the pregnancy was a month shorter, but Hadar and Rebecca were constantly monitoring her, and she was feeling fine.

"Mommy, can we go see if Dagan wants to play in the garden?" Miki asked, looking up at her hopefully.

Looking a little farther down the path, Lisa saw Padma with Gossamer and Dagan at her side. They had all left the arena together during the break between rounds but had gotten separated as they wandered through the stalls.

"You don't want to watch more of the tournament?" When the girls just looked at each other, Lisa frowned. "Girls?"

"We don't like seeing them fight, Mommy," Carly whispered looking up at her with regretful eyes. "I know Manno said they aren't *really* being hurt, but they still *are* being hurt."

"I see."

"Will Manno be mad?" Miki asked.

"Mad about what?" Grim asked coming up behind them. He didn't like the way his girls jumped at his question or the guilty looks they gave him. He looked questioningly at Lisa. "My Lisa?"

"The girls were just asking if they and Dagan could go play in the garden."

Grim frowned at that, his mind going over the security issues involved. The Festival was being held on the grounds between the front entrance of House Luanda and the gate, making it easily defendable with guards stationed along the walls. The gardens his girls liked to play in were behind the House. While there were guards there, there weren't as many.

"Please, Manno?" Miki asked, and two sets of little eyes pleaded with his. Grim felt his heart melt. There was little he could deny them when his girls looked at him like that.

"You will take Ion, Nairn, and Caius with you," he finally agreed, and the guards named stepped forward.

"We will, Manno!" they squealed, jumping up and down.

"And you will *obey* them," he growled as he went down on a knee to give each of them a hug.

"We will, Manno. Truth," they promised, each kissing a cheek. With that, they went running toward Dagan, their guards running to keep up.

"It seems you were right again, my Lisa," Grim said, his gaze finally leaving the girls.

"Only because I've been a parent longer than you. One day they are going to want to watch, and that's when *you* aren't going to want them to."

"Why would I not want them to?" Grim questioned, frowning at her.

"Because that's when they are going to be watching the Warriors as a female watches a male."

"No!" Grim's denial was loud and had heads turning in their direction. "That will not happen. No male will ever be fit or worthy enough for our girls."

"I think that will be up to them to decide." Lisa hid her smile at Grim's reaction by linking her arm through his so they could walk. "But it will be a long time before you will need to worry about that."

"A *very* long time," Grim agreed.

TWO

"Come on, Dagan!" Miki shouted running passed where he had stopped on the garden path. "Carly is nearly to the rock."

Miki was the youngest and smallest of the three. Because of that, she never got anywhere first, but she tried. Now she was gaining on Carly, but when she looked back to see how close Dagan was, she found he was still at the tree but on his knees now.

Slowing, she turned then headed back to him. "Dagan? What's wrong?"

"There is something in there," he said leaning forward to peer between the full, low-hanging branches that touched the ground.

"There is?" she questioned as she dropped down beside him. "What?"

"I do not know, but I heard it."

"What are you looking at?" Carly asked, coming up behind them.

"Dagan says there's something in our tree," Miki told her sister, her gaze never leaving the tree.

"Really?" Carly dropped down beside them. "What?"

"I do not know," Dagan repeated. "But..."

Just then, a short, sharp screech came from beneath the tree causing all three of them to fall back on their butts.

"There... there *is* something under there," Miki whispered and quickly flipping over onto her hands and knees crawled closer to the tree.

"Miki, get back," Carly told her. "You don't know what it is."

"Whatever it is, it is in pain. It's afraid," Dagan said.

"How can you tell?" Carly asked looking to Dagan.

"I just can," he said, shrugging his shoulders.

"Then we need to help it," Miki said, crawling under the branches.

"Miki!" Carly tried to grab her sister's ankle, but Miki was too fast for her.

"Come on, you two, it's awesome under here."

Dagan and Carly looked at each other. Miki was always doing this. She would just take off and expect them to follow. It had gotten them all in trouble more than once.

"We cannot let her be in there alone," Dagan told her.

"I know," Carly sighed. Sometimes she hated being the older sister. "Let's go."

Together they crawled beneath the bottom limbs and were shocked at what they discovered. The low branches outside actually attached to the tree several feet up, leaving a large, open area that was like a private world meant just for them.

"Wow..." Carly whispered as she looked around.

"I told you," Miki said smugly.

"Look," Dagan said, and their gazes traveled to where he pointed at the dark form near the trunk of the tree.

Suddenly, what had appeared to be a small, non-threatening mass, rose and grew until it was nearly as tall as Miki. It spread its wings, and it let out a screech that had them covering their ears and looking at it in shock.

"It's a raptor," Carly whispered, her voice full of awe.

"He is hurt." Dagan pointed to how the tip of one of the raptor's wings hung down.

"But he can't be hurt," Miki cried out in distress. "He's the Great Raptor. Who is going to protect us now?"

The bird tipped its head to the side, its purple gaze staring at Miki as if it understood her words. Slowly, it folded its wings back into its sides.

"He can't be the Great Raptor, Miki," Carly told her. "He's not big enough. Manno said he was so big that he could block the sun."

"Truth," Miki murmured, "but then maybe he's the Great Raptor's son."

"Manno never said that in any of his stories."

"Maybe he just hasn't gotten to that story yet," Miki stuck her chin out stubbornly at her sister. "He said he had thousands of stories still to tell us."

"Truth." Carly had to agree with her sister.

"How do we help him?" Miki looked to Dagan.

"I do not know for sure," Dagan said slowly, his head leaning to the side just like the raptor's. "I have never cared for a raptor before."

"But you have cared for other animals, right?" Miki demanded. "You told us how you healed a kepie."

"Yes, but that is a much smaller bird."

"So healing a bigger one should be easier," Miki told him.

"All I did was keep it warm and make sure it had food and water. The rest it did itself."

"Oh," Miki frowned at that. "Well then, that's what we'll do for Prince."

"Prince?" Both Dagan and Carly asked.

"Well that's what he is, isn't he, if he's the Great Raptor's son? The Great Raptor protects Luda just like Manno does, and Manno is a King. So the Great Raptor is a King. And his son is a Prince, just like we are Princesses."

Dagan and Carly found themselves slowly nodding at Miki's three-year-old logic, and it seemed the raptor liked it too, as he gave a low caw and then settled back down onto the ground, its injured wing sticking out slightly. Its piercing eyes were just about to close when a call from Ion had them shooting back open.

"Princess Miki! Princess Carly!" Ion shouted, his quick steps followed by Nairn's and Caius'. "Where are you?"

"We need to go, Miki," Carly whispered, peeking between the branches once their guards had passed.

"But what about Prince?"

"He will be fine here, Miki," Dagan told her. "It is why he chose this location."

"But... he needs food and water, and look," she pointed, and they all saw a shiver go through his black body. "He's cold."

"We'll come back with those, but we have to *go*, Miki. Otherwise, Ion will tell Manno we didn't obey him, and then we *won't* be able to come see Prince."

"Oh, all right," Miki grumbled, obviously not happy but agreeing. But as they started to crawl back out, she stopped and looked at the shivering raptor. Slipping off her cape, she crawled toward the deadly creature. "Here, take this. Padma made me another one."

Carefully she draped the cape over the bird, not noticing how close she was to its sharp, deadly beak. "I'll be back as soon as I can with food and water. You just rest and try to get better." With that, she crawled out from under the tree.

"Miki," Lisa waited until the gaze of her youngest rose from the dinner plate to her. Both girls had been unusually quiet during the meal. "Ion says you lost your cape today. How?"

"I... umm..." Miki's gaze went to Carly before returning to her mother. She'd never lied to her mother before. Well, not really. She didn't count saying she'd only had two cookies when she'd actually had three. But this... "I took it off so I could explore one of the trees and forgot to put it back on."

"But it was cold out," Grim said frowning at her.

"It wasn't that bad, Manno."

"I'm disappointed in you, Miki Renee," Lisa told her. "Padma worked very hard on creating that cape for you, and you just left it?"

"I'm sorry, Mommy." Miki's little eyes filled with tears as she looked at her mother.

"Tomorrow we will go into the garden and find your cape."

"Yes, Mommy."

"Now finish eating." She looked to Carly seeing she had hardly eaten anything either. "Both of you. Then go get ready for bed."

"Yes, Mommy," they said together.

They both quickly finished their meal, then as they rose, Miki paused beside Grim. "Will you tell us another story about the Great Raptor, Manno?"

"I will, once you are in bed," Grim told her wondering why she was asking. He always told them a story, but before he could ask, they were gone.

"They're up to something," Lisa said watching the girls hurry out of the room whispering to each other.

"What could they be up to?" Grim asked frowning. "They had guards with them all day."

"Then where were they when Miki took off her cape?"

"I..." Grim realized she was right. That shouldn't have been possible. "You are right. I will find better Warriors to guard our girls."

"Grim, no, that's not what I meant. Ion and Nairn are the perfect guards for the girls." She instantly defended the two Warriors. They had more than proven themselves in her eyes with how they sacrificed themselves so she and the girls could get away when Luuken had tried to take them. "They give them the space they need to play and explore, to be little girls, while still protecting them. What I was trying to say, and apparently not doing a very good job of it, is that our girls are smart and if they wanted to keep something from us they could."

"You think that is what they are doing?"

"Yes."

"Then I will go get them to tell us what it is." Grim stood, meaning to go after his girls.

"No, Grim."

"No?" He turned to frown at her. "What do you mean? They shouldn't be keeping things from us. What if it is something that harms them?"

"Are you telling me you never kept things from your manno growing up?"

"I..." Grim's cheeks darkened. "Yes, but that is different."

"Really?" Lisa smiled as she rose and stepped into his waiting arms. "Why?"

"Because I'm male, and they are female," he told her gruffly, enfolding her in his arms.

"Really?" Lisa leaned back in his arms giving him a teasing look. "*That's the reason you're giving me? Because you're male?*"

"Females..."

"Have as much right to do what they want as any male does."

"They need to be protected," he argued.

"Truth," she agreed. "But doing one doesn't mean you can't do the other. They need to explore, Grim. Need to find their place in this world. And they can't do that if you lock them away. If you don't give them some freedom. The garden is a safe place."

"It wasn't for you," he growled, remembering Luuken.

"And that will never happen again. Not only because Wray recognized me as your Queen, but because you have tripled the guards along that portion of the wall." She reached up to gently cup his cheek. She knew it still bothered him that she was attacked in their garden. "We are safe there, Grim. Because of you."

"You mean everything to me, my Lisa. You, our girls, and the one yet to come." He reached down running a careful hand over her protruding stomach.

Lisa couldn't help but smile. Grim loved her changing shape. He was always touching and caressing her, especially her belly. He still couldn't seem to believe that *his* offspring was growing there.

"And you mean everything to us."

"Manno!" The girls' little voices called from their room. "We're ready for our story."

"And it seems the ones we currently have are impatient for their story."

"Yes, they always are." He smiled slightly at that. "So we let them keep their secret?"

"For now, yes. They won't be able to keep it to themselves for long," she told him, and together they went to their girls.

"Manno?"

"Yes, my Miki?" Grim asked, sitting down beside her on the bed she shared with her sister.

"Can you tell us a story about the Great Raptor's son?"

"His what?" Grim looked at Lisa, who was on the other side of the bed next to Carly and frowned.

"Male offspring," Lisa supplied. There were still times when Earth words slipped into their conversations that Grim didn't understand.

"Oh." He looked back to Miki. "Why would you think he had a son, Miki?"

"Well he would have to... wouldn't he? You have mommy and us. The Great Raptor must have a family too."

"I..." Grim realized that in all his existence it was something he had never considered. The Great Raptor just was. But looking at the expectation in his daughters' eyes, he knew he couldn't disappoint them.

"The Great Raptor's son helps him guard the skies of Luda...."

Lisa released a tired sigh as she rested her head on Grim's chest with a leg thrown over his, her hand resting over his heart, as her rounded stomach nestled against his flat one. Grim pulled her close, his hand gently caressing her belly.

"You did too much today," he growled gruffly.

"Not too much," she denied. "I didn't meet with Ull, as we planned, but it was a long day."

"You will see him and those with him tomorrow."

"With him?" She tilted her head up to look at him. "I thought it was just Ull I was meeting with."

"So did I, but it seems there is a Kaliszian ship traveling with him."

"Why? Because of the Ganglian ship the Kaliszians found with Earth females?"

"Yes, that is my belief."

"Then we need to get up and meet with them." Lisa started to rise, only to have Grim's arm tighten, stilling her.

"Ull has already gone back to the Searcher. He and the others will return tomorrow after you have rested."

"Oh." She laid her head back down and snuggled in closer, silently glad she didn't have to get out of bed. "You did a wonderful job coming up with that story about the Great Raptor's son."

"It was that obvious?"

"Only to me."

"They continually surprise me with their questions."

"They make you look at things differently, don't they?"

"They do," he agreed, reaching up to touch the blue and green thumbprints attached to the necklace the girls had given him just that morning, and how they requested to call him Manno.

Lisa covered his hand with hers, knowing what he was thinking. "They love you very much, Grim. So do I."

"I know," he told her gruffly, his fingers tightening on hers. "It makes me the most blessed male in all the universes, Known or Unknown. Now rest, my Lisa."

THREE

"Eat up, girls," Lisa told her daughters the next morning. "Once you're done, we are going to go find the cape you forgot in the garden yesterday."

"Yes, Mommy," they said, but Lisa caught the look they gave each other. Yes, there was definitely something going on that they didn't want Grim or her to know about. She'd have to keep a close eye on them.

"Lisa." Grim walked back into their room. He'd left a few moments ago to take a comm. "Ull and the others have transported down. They are waiting for us in my Command Room."

"Already?"

"Yes, it seems General Rayner wants to get back to Pontus as soon as possible."

"General Rayner?"

"He is the Supreme Commander of Kaliszian Defenses," Grim informed her. "The other ship traveling with the Searcher is his. He also has his True Mate with him."

"True Mate?"

"I forget you have not met a Kaliszian yet."

"No, I haven't, but Kim told me about the one that gave her a blade."

"Yes, that was General Rayner."

"It saved her life on Vesta. I would very much like to meet the male that defied Wray and gave her that blade."

Grim's lips tightened as he remembered Wray telling him exactly what had happened between him and the General. Had the General not backed down, the two Empires might now be at war, something neither wanted. They needed each other too much.

"Rayner is not a male you wish for an enemy," he told her. "That he has his True Mate with him is surprising though."

"Why? Do the Kaliszians hide away their True Mates the way you Tornians do your females?"

"No, there is no reason for them to. While Kaliszians have more than enough females, they haven't had True Mates since the Great Infection struck."

"You mean besides taking away their ability to feed their people, the Great Infection also took away the Kaliszians' ability to find true love?"

"Yes."

"That seems doubly harsh."

"Two were harmed, my Lisa," he gently reminded her, his gaze going to Carly and Miki. He had always believed he understood the horror of what Emperor Berto had done to his young females. But now, looking down at his daughters gazing up at him with so much love and trust in their little eyes, the true horror of it hit and sickened him. That type of betrayal was so unthinkable to him, so evil. If any male even *thought* about his girls that way, he would end them. Painfully.

"Grim?" Lisa asked quietly, pulling his attention from the girls. She didn't like how hard his eyes had gotten or how his skin had darkened. She'd only seen him look this way once before, and that had been after Luuken had attacked her. Looking back to her daughters, she realized what had him so upset, the thought of *their* daughters being abused that way. "It will never happen, Grim. You would never allow anyone to harm them."

"It wasn't *anyone*, Lisa," he murmured, looking at her.

"No, it wasn't. But that is something *you* would never do." Reaching for his hand, she rested it on her stomach. "To any of our offspring."

"I wouldn't, my Lisa." His hand curved protectively over her stomach. "My vow."

"I know." Stretching up on her toes, she gently kissed his lips.

"Sire." They turned to find Alger standing in the doorway. "Warrior Ull and General Rayner are waiting."

"We will be right there, Alger."

"Yes, sire," Alger bowed slightly to Lisa then left the room.

"Girls." Lisa looked to them. "Your manno and I need to go meet with some people. Ion and Nairn will stay with you."

"Can they take us out into the garden so we can find my cape?" Miki asked.

Lisa frowned. When she had informed the girls that directly after first meal they would be going to find the forgotten cape, neither had been enthusiastic.

"You want to go find your cape?"

"Yes, Mommy," Miki told her.

"Alright. Ion and Nairn can take you."

———

Looking over their shoulders to make sure Ion and Nairn weren't watching, Carly and Miki quickly scooted under the branches where the raptor rested.

"Hi, Prince. We're back," Miki said moving toward the bird that was snuggled down in the nest he had made out of her cape. "Are you feeling better?"

Unfazed that the raptor just continued to look at her, she continued. "We brought you something to eat."

That had Prince lifting his head, his purple eyes zeroing in on the strips of rashtar she was pulling from her pocket. She'd managed to slip them into her pocket at first meal while her mom and manno were talking. Sitting down in front of him, she broke off a piece and held it out to him.

"Be careful, Miki," Carly said, being the protective sister she always was.

"He won't hurt us, Carly," Miki told her with all the confidence of a three-year-old. "We're helping him."

As the girls talked, the raptor rose from his warm nest until he towered over them. Slowly, he lowered his deadly beak and carefully snatched the food from her hand.

"See," Miki said to her sister smugly. "I told you he wouldn't hurt us."

———

Lisa made no comment when Grim stepped in front of her, pausing for a moment as he opened the doors to his Command Room. She knew why he was doing it. Even though Ull and General Rayner were considered worthy males, Grim would take no chances with her and their unborn daughter's safety. After several tense moments, he moved to the side and put a protective hand on the small of her back, guiding her into the room.

Beside Alger and Agee, there were three other people in the room. One was the warrior she knew as Ull. Standing a few steps away from him was a massive male with beads in his hair, and behind him was a small, cloaked figure.

"Warrior Ull," Lisa acknowledged, her cool gaze running over him. She still wasn't sure he was the right person for this task, but she would give him the benefit of the doubt since Grim and Wray seemed to think he was.

After a moment, that dragged out long enough for Grim to start growling his displeasure, Ull bowed slightly. "Majesty."

Grim gave Ull a hard look before he led Lisa toward the other male.

"Lisa, this is General Treyvon Rayner, Supreme Commander of Kaliszian Defenses. General Rayner, my Queen, Lisa Vasteri."

"Majesty, it is a great honor to meet you." Treyvon crossed an arm over his chest and gave her a much deeper bow than Ull had. "May I present to you my True Mate, Jennifer Rayner."

The cloaked figure stepped forward, and when the cape's hood lowered, Lisa gasped. "You're from Earth!"

"I am," Jen affirmed.

"But... What? How? I just assumed you'd be Kaliszian." She turned to face Grim. "You didn't tell me she was from Earth."

"I did not know," Grim told her, frowning darkly at the General.

"It was felt that the fewer Tornians who know there were Earth females in the Kaliszian Empire, and that they could be our True Mates, the better." Treyvon ran hard eyes to the guards in the room.

"That is truth," Grim agreed, following where Rayner's gaze had gone. "Alger and Agee can be trusted. They are the Captains of my Lisa's and my Elite Guards."

"You were found on the Ganglian ship?" Lisa ignored the conversation going on between Grim and Rayner, and moved toward Jennifer.

"No, I was taken by the Ganglians over a year and a half ago."

"A year and a half..." Lisa's eyes widened. "Wait, your name is Jennifer?"

"Yes."

"As in Jennifer Teel?"

"Yes," Jen was surprised this woman made the connection so fast. "Kim is my little sister."

"Oh, my God!" Lisa was immediately hugging Jennifer before any male could move. "Does Kim know? Of course, she knows. What am I saying? She sent you here. She must be ecstatic! But wait..." Lisa pulled back slightly, frowning. "Why are you here? Why aren't you with her and Destiny? She's missed you so much and has been so worried about you."

"And I've missed and been worried about her too." Jen smiled at Lisa. She was just as Kimmy had described her. Beautiful, smart, and caring. "We spent nearly a week together before Warrior Ull arrived." Her expression cooled as she glanced at Ull. "Kimmy wanted me to stay longer, but there are more lives involved here than just ours."

"You're talking about the Ganglian ship full of Earth females the Kaliszians intercepted," Lisa said leading her to one of the couches in the room.

"Yes, Kimmy told me about what happened to you and the other females the Tornians took just like the Ganglians did us."

Grim's displeased growl had both women looking to him, and Rayner moving to step between the King and his True Mate.

"Don't growl at me, King Grim," Jen said glaring at him. "It is no different."

"She's right, Grim," Lisa told him quietly. "I know you did your best, making sure that you only took unprotected females, and that none of us were abused like Kim and Jen were, but that still doesn't make it right."

"I wasn't abused," Jen informed Lisa, "and neither were the women found on the latest Ganglian ship." She ignored Lisa's shocked look and continued. "But the Ganglians aren't as 'selective' as the Tornians. They just swept up any female they found. Young, old, married, single. It didn't matter to them."

"Oh, my God."

"That's why we need to go to Pontus first," Jen glared at Ull. "To get them and return them to Earth, along with the men that were taken with Mac and me."

"Mac?" Jen asked.

"Mackenzie Wharton. Well, Kozar now," Jen corrected. "She was the female guide that was with us when the Ganglians took us. She's now the True Mate of Treyvon's Second-in-Command, and the other reason we need to get back to Pontus."

"Those females should not be returned," Ull growled.

"That's not your decision," Jen told him, turning angry eyes on him. "They are under the protection of the Kaliszian Empire, and you have been ordered by your Emperor, my sister's husband, to return them safely. And by God, you better or you'd better hope Wray gets to you before I do!"

Grim found his lips twitching as Rayner's True Mate fearlessly challenged the first male of one of the Tornian Empire's most well-thought-of Lords.

"It seems your True Mate is as fearless when dealing with much larger males as my Lisa is," Grim murmured to Rayner.

"She is," Rayner agreed, easing his stance slightly. "She is strong and has survived more than any female should have to. And if you ever growl at her like that again, I will end you. Blood brother to the Emperor or not."

Grim's eyes narrowed for a moment, ignoring the way Alger's and Agee's hands tensed on the hilts of their swords hearing Rayner's threat. "As you should," Grim agreed, and his Captains relaxed. "Just know I feel the same about my Queen."

Looking at each other, the two dominant males realized they had more in common than they ever thought.

Later that day, Lisa found herself walking the halls of Luanda, absently running a hand over her stomach as she thought over all she had learned that day. Jennifer was truly an amazing woman. They had sat and talked while Grim, Treyvon, and Ull discussed whatever they deemed important, but what she and Jennifer had discussed was so much more.

Not only had the Kaliszians begun to find their True Mates again, some human, some not, they were also able to conceive offspring with humans. It was the other reason Jen wanted to return to Pontus. Her friend, Mackenzie, had conceived with her True Mate and while the two species were similar, the Kaliszians had no real knowledge of how to deal with a pregnant Earth female.

Lisa had immediately understood what Jen wanted. Rebecca to return to Pontus with them. She wanted Rebecca to check Mackenzie and share her knowledge of Earth females with the Kaliszian healer, Luol. Something Lisa knew Grim was going to fight her on. He would want Rebecca to remain on Luda so she could care for her until their daughter was presented. But Lisa knew that wasn't going to be possible. Oh, she wanted Rebecca here when she gave birth. But until then, there were others that needed Rebecca's skills. Jennifer had also confessed that she would like Rebecca to examine *her* because she believed she had also conceived.

Yes, it had been a busy but informative morning, and there was still more that needed to be decided. But first, she needed to check on the girls. Looking up, she saw Nairn approaching.

"You're back from the garden?"

"Yes, Majesty. Cook promised the princesses they could help him make cookies."

"Of course," Lisa smiled. Nothing kept her girls out of the kitchen when Warrior Tagma was making cookies. "Did Miki find her cape?"

"Yes, Majesty."

Lisa had gotten to know the males of Luanda well, especially those of the Elite Guard. She could tell there was something more Nairn wanted to say.

"What is it, Nairn? Did the girls disobey you?"

"No! Of course not, Majesty. The princesses are always well behaved."

"That is an untruth, Nairn," Lisa gently reprimanded. "You know they like to see if they can hide from you."

Nairn smiled slightly. "This is truth, Majesty. So we let them."

"What?!!"

The look on his Queen's face made Nairn realize she had misunderstood, and he quickly reassured her. "We know where they are, Majesty, we just let them *think* we don't."

"Oh, well that's good. Smart, too." Lisa should have realized they would never allow Carly or Miki to get away from them. "So what have they been doing, that they don't think you've noticed, that is bothering you?"

"They are spending a great deal of time beneath one of the trees."

"One of the trees?"

"Yes, it is like the one you had us move into Luanda. The one you called a 'Christmas' tree, except this one has heavy, lower branches that touch the ground."

"So they crawled under it, and you couldn't see them?"

"Yes, Majesty."

"We used to have a tree just like it in our yard back on Earth. They would play underneath it for hours."

"It seems they do here too, but..."

"But what, Nairn?"

"Miki went under it wearing her fur cape. She came back out wearing her purple one."

"She left her fur one there?"

"Yes, and they seemed to be talking, but not to each other."

Lisa frowned at that. "There wasn't anyone else there?"

"No, Majesty."

"There's nothing in the garden that can harm them is there, Nairn? No wild animals?"

"No, Majesty. We would never let them out of our sight if that were the case."

"Of course you wouldn't, Nairn. I know how much you and your brother Warriors care about the girls."

"And you, Majesty," Nairn quickly said, his cheeks darkening slightly.

"Thank you, Nairn," Lisa gave him a small smile. It still surprised her how easily flustered these big, strong Warriors could get when speaking with a female. "I will talk to Grim about this and see what he wants to do. Until you hear from either of us, allow the girls to continue to play under the tree."

"Yes, Majesty."

FOUR

"Beneath a tree?" Grim frowned as Lisa told him what she had learned, later that night after the girls were asleep.

"Yes," she said pulling her feet up under her as she cuddled into his side.

Grim reached over and dragged the afghan off the back of the couch, making sure her bare feet were covered, before responding. "There shouldn't be anything in the garden that will harm them, but I will go tomorrow and make sure."

"Thank you," she said gazing up at him.

"You do not need to thank me for seeing to our girls' protection," he told her gruffly.

"I know, but I also know there are a great many other things you need to be seeing to tomorrow. You could just have Ion or Nairn check and report back to you with what they find."

"That is truth, but this is something *I* must see to," Grim reached up touching the glass thumbprints on the necklace he wore. "After all, I am their manno."

"You are," she agreed, smiling up at him sleepily.

"And I am your male." Rising, he scooped her up into his arms. "And now I must see to you."

"Oh you must, must you?" Lisa asked as she pressed a kiss on the thick scar running down his neck.

"Yes," he told her gruffly, "You are tired. You need to rest."

"I am," she agreed, "but I'm never too tired to love my male, and I do, Grim. Love you, that is."

"And I love you, my Lisa."

"Then show me."

"I will," he vowed, and carefully lowering her into their bed, his mouth covered hers.

A fully rested and fully satisfied Lisa smiled at Grim across the table the next morning as the girls ate. Finally, knowing she needed to pull her thoughts away from what they had done in bed together the night before, she looked to their daughters. "So, girls, there is someone I would like you to meet this morning."

"Who, Mommy?" Carly asked.

"Her name is Jennifer. She is Empress Kim's older sister."

"Older sister? You mean like I am to Miki?"

"Yes, Carly."

"But, Mommy, isn't Kim part of Manno's family?" She looked to Grim. "Part of *our* family?"

"Yes, baby," Lisa told her.

"So then isn't Jennifer part of *our* family too?"

Lisa looked at Grim and realized it was something neither of them had considered, at least not the full extent of it. Yes, Jennifer was now related to them through Kim, but it was more than that. General Rayner was now family too because he was Jennifer's True Mate, and General Rayner was blood-related to Liron, the Emperor of the Kaliszian Empire. The two Empires were now forever connected.

"Yes, Carly, she is. So we need to welcome her into the family."

"But..."

"But what, Miki?" Lisa asked, frowning at her youngest.

"But... we want to go play in the garden."

"Again?" Lisa looked to Grim and saw he was frowning too. While it wasn't uncommon for the girls to play in the garden, they usually didn't play there every day.

"Yes. Pleassse, Mommy." Her amber eyes pleaded with her mother's as she drew out the please, then looked at her manno and did the same thing. "Pleassse, Manno?"

Grim was the most powerful and feared Warrior in the Tornian Empire, but looking into his Miki's eyes, he found himself as defenseless as a first-cycle trainee against an Elite Warrior.

"Why do you wish this so badly, Miki?" Grim questioned quietly.

"Well... uh... because..." Miki stuttered, her panicked gaze going to Carly beseeching her for help.

"We just really like to play out there," Carly said.

"You mean under your tree?" Lisa asked.

"How did you know?" Carly's eyes widened in amazement as she looked back to her mother.

"A little birdie told me," Lisa said teasingly, not wanting the girls to know it had been Nairn that had told her. She didn't want them to think they had no freedom.

"*Prince* told you?" Miki whispered, her little eyes going even wider. "He *talks* to you???"

"Prince?" Lisa asked giving them a confused look. "Who is Prince?"

"The Great Raptor's son," Miki told her as if it were obvious. "He hurt his wing, so we're helping him get better."

"And how are you doing that, Miki?" Grim questioned carefully, finding it took all his Warrior control to keep the alarm out of his voice. Raptors were solitary creatures that rarely attacked without cause. They killed only when it was a matter of survival. They were the symbol of House Luanda because of this. But this Raptor was injured, and even the noblest of creatures could strike out without thought when crazed by pain. The idea of his sweet, innocent daughters being exposed to such a creature made his blood run cold.

"By doing what you do for us, Manno," Miki told him. "We're making sure he's safe, keeping him warm, and bringing him food to eat. And it's working. He seemed better yesterday. Didn't he, Carly?"

"Uh-huh," Carly agreed.

"You found him the day of the Festival?" Lisa looked at her daughters. "That is why you 'forgot' your cape?"

"Prince needed it more, Mommy. He was so cold and scared."

"I don't doubt that, Miki, but you should have come and told your manno or me."

"But we couldn't, Mommy," Miki told her.

"Why, baby?"

"Because... *we* needed to help him. I promised... vowed that we would, and if we don't keep our vows," Miki's little forehead scrunched up as she searched for the word, "then we aren't worthy. Isn't that right, Manno?" She looked to Grim. "It's what you tell your Warriors, isn't it? That 'if you don't keep your vow then you aren't worthy'; and 'you must always protect those that can't protect themselves.' Well, Prince can't defend himself right now, so we have to."

"This is truth," Grim slowly admitted looking from one daughter to the other. He hadn't realized they had been listening that closely to what he told his Warriors. "A vow is a very important thing. But in giving it, you can still ask for help in keeping it, and in this, you should have asked."

"I'm sorry, Manno." Miki's little lips trembled as she looked at him. "I just wanted to be worthy... like you are."

Grim was immediately out of his chair and on his knees between where his two girls sat.

"You are, Miki, you will always be worthy, much worthier than me. You also, Carly."

"Truth, Manno?" Carly asked.

"Truth." He hugged his girls for a moment then rose. "Now, finish your meal, and then we will all go and see your Prince."

"Yes, Manno," they chorused together, and quickly returned to eating.

It was gray and overcast as the girls led Lisa and Grim to 'their' tree. Grim went down on one knee, then bent even lower still to see under the low bough he had lifted. Behind him, Lisa and the girls waited along with Nairn and Ion. He could understand why the Raptor had chosen this spot. It was well-concealed, and his Warriors wouldn't think a threat could exist in such a compact area. No Tornian male over the age of five would fit inside, but his daughters were much smaller than Tornian youth.

Reaching underneath, Grim pulled out what he found.

"Careful, Manno, Prince doesn't know you." Carly's concern was easily heard. It was something else he was still getting used to. His daughters' unconditional love and concern for him.

"There is nothing here to be concerned with, my Carly," Grim told her as he pulled out the now dirty, but empty, fur cape.

"He's gone," Miki whispered, her amber gaze going from her cape to Grim. "He didn't even say goodbye."

Suddenly, a loud screech filled the air above them, and every head looked up and found the Raptor sitting on one of the uppermost branches of the tree, staring down at them.

"My God," Lisa murmured quietly, taking in the size of the bird. She had pictured a much smaller creature in her mind, not one that seemed nearly as tall has her youngest. Its body was just as black and sleek looking as the one Gahan had created that now sat in Grim's Command Room. And while his wings rested against his body, there was no doubting he was as deadly as any Elite Warrior with his sharp, curved beak and long, lethal claws. Yet she could see the intelligence in the piercing purple of his eyes. No wonder he was the symbol for House Luanda.

Just the thought of her innocent daughters being near such a creature, let alone feeding it, sent a shiver of apprehension up Lisa's spine.

"Prince." Miki's little hands rested on her hips as she looked up and found him. There wasn't an ounce of fear in her voice. "What are you doing up there? You are supposed to be resting. We brought you first meal." Reaching into her pocket, she pulled out the piece of rashtar she'd saved from their first meal and held it up to him.

With a swiftness no one would expect from such a large, presumably injured creature, the Raptor swooped down to land directly in front of Miki.

Lisa gasped.

Ion and Nairn moved forward.

Grim drew his sword.

But the Raptor's intense, violet gaze remained fixed on Miki.

"Oh, you're better," she exclaimed happily, unaware of the tension that filled the adults around her, and apparently unconcerned that a deadly bird nearly as tall as she was had just landed in front of her. "I'm so glad. Here." She held out the rashtar to him.

Lisa held her breath as the Raptor's sharp, deadly beak lowered toward the soft, unprotected skin of her youngest's fingers. But it only bit at the rashtar, seeming to know it could harm Miki if he weren't careful.

"Prince, this is my mommy and my manno," Miki told the bird. She had watched her mommy and knew it was rude not to introduce people. "Mommy, Manno, this is Prince."

"I..." Lisa looked to Grim for a moment. She had never been introduced to a bird before, but this seemed to be important to her daughter, so she went along. "Hello, Prince," she said and bowed slightly to the bird just as she would for a real Prince. She was shocked when he returned the gesture, bowing deeper than she had, as a Prince would to a Queen. It then turned its intense gaze to Grim.

Grim was completely shocked by what was happening. While his bedtime stories about the Great Raptor had been filled with how the creature acted and responded just as an Elite Warrior would, they had been just stories handed down so a young male would know what was expected of him. No one actually thought them to be true, at least not once they grew older. But here his girls were, treating and talking to one, exactly as he had told them they should. And the Raptor was responding.

"Prince." Grim lowered his sword but didn't sheath it as he bowed his head to the creature.

The Raptor eyed the sword for a moment before it again seemed to bow to the King of Luda.

Suddenly, a deafening clap of thunder rolled across the land, and a curtain of rain began advancing toward them. With a great screech, Prince spread his wings and launched himself into the sky.

"Inside, now!" Sheathing his sword, Grim scooped Miki and Carly up, one in each arm. Then using his massive frame, he protected Lisa from the wind as he moved them toward Luanda. When tempests like this suddenly appeared, they were deadly.

Ion and Nairn held open the doors as Grim rushed his family inside, closing them just as a blinding flash of light lit up the garden. It had both girls screaming out in fright.

"Calm, little ones. You are safe."

"But Prince, Manno." Miki looked up at him, tears filling her eyes.

"He is safe," Grim reassured her. "This is what he does."

"Your vow?" she asked, her bottom lip trembling.

"My vow, my Miki."

Lisa found she was still somewhat shaken by what happened in the garden, and the rumble of the continuing storm wasn't helping to calm her nerves.

For her girls to have been so close to such a dangerous creature.

For her and Grim to not even be aware it was there.

For the tempest to appear so suddenly.

She had to fight against holding the little hands of her girls too tightly as they walked toward Grim's Command Room. She thought she'd been aware of all the dangers their new home contained, but every day she found herself learning something new. Like how a dangerous bird could be in their garden. Grim had understood that she needed to make sure her babies were okay and had gone ahead to meet the shuttle containing Ull, General Rayner, and Jennifer. Entering Grim's Command Room, she saw that everyone was there.

"I'm sorry we kept you waiting."

"It is fine, my Lisa," Grim reassured her, moving from behind his desk.

"Girls, this is Warrior Ull of House Rigel," Lisa began the introductions.

"I remember you," Carly piped in looking up at Ull. "You were at the Joining Ceremony."

Ull frowned as the taller of the young females spoke to him without permission.

"My daughter is speaking to you, Warrior Ull." Grim's deep growl expressed his displeasure at Ull's lack of response to Carly.

"I was," Ull stiltedly responded. He would never get used to these Earth females talking whenever they wished.

"You are Ynyr's brother," Carly continued, unfazed by the lack of warmth on Ull's face or in his tone.

"Yes, his older brother."

"Really? But he's already a Lord," she said giving him a confused look.

"And this is General Treyvon Rayner of the Kaliszian Empire," Lisa quickly went on, pulling Carly's gaze away from Ull. She knew from her conversations with Abby that Ull was still having trouble dealing with the fact that his *younger* brother had become a Lord before him. That, and that Abby chose Ynyr over him.

"Wow," Miki whispered, and letting go of her mother's hand, moved across the room coming to a stop in front of Treyvon. "You're almost as handsome as our manno."

"He is not!" Carly immediately defended Grim. "Manno is handsomer."

"I said *almost*," Miki spun around to argue with her sister. "Because Manno will always be much handsomer than any male in the Known Universes."

"It's more handsome," Lisa quietly corrected her daughters, while trying to keep the smile off her face. Especially when she saw the range of expressions crossing the males' faces.

Ull's was blank in shock. Treyvon's was obviously trying to hold back his amusement. But Grim's was the most expressive of all, at least to her. An unhappy frown had crossed his face at the thought that another male might rival him in Miki's eyes, but his chest had expanded with unadulterated pride at how both his daughters thought and spoke of him.

"That's enough, girls," Lisa said gently but firmly, knowing their argument would grow if she didn't stop it. "You both need to tell General Rayner you're sorry."

"Unnecessary," Treyvon began, but Lisa's piercing look silenced him.

"Yes, it is, General Rayner. Sometimes our girls forget their manners." Her gaze returned to her daughters. "Don't you, girls?"

"Yes, Mommy," they chorused together then turned to Treyvon. "Sorry."

Treyvon found himself trapped for a moment by their amber gazes before giving them a slight bow, letting them know he accepted their apology.

"And this," Lisa gestured to Jennifer, who had remained silent next to Treyvon, "is Jennifer, General Rayner's True Mate."

"Oh, you're Kim's sister!" Miki clapped her hands excitedly as she looked to Jennifer.

"I am," Jennifer agreed.

"Welcome to the family!"

"What?" Jennifer gave Lisa a confused look.

"Carly pointed out at first meal this morning that we are now family since your sister is married to Grim's brother." Lisa looked to Treyvon. "Which means you are now family too, General. Our families and Empires are now forever linked."

A sharp bolt of lightning, instantly followed by a window-rattling crack of thunder, prevented anyone from responding.

FIVE

"Manno!" the girls screamed as the room went dark for a moment after the brilliant flash of light. Grim was immediately there, wrapping them up in his protective arms.

"Calm, little ones," he murmured. "We are inside. Remember? You are safe."

"But Prince..." Miki looked up at him with wide, fear-filled eyes.

"Is with *his* manno, who is protecting him just like I am protecting you."

"You're sure?" she questioned, her little chin trembling.

"I'm sure, Miki."

"Hey, how would you like Ion and Nairn to take you to Cook?" Lisa asked as she gently rubbed each of the girls' backs. "I happen to know that he is planning on making more cookies today."

"Truth?" Carly asked, her eyes hopeful.

"Truth."

The girls looked at each other for a moment, then wiggled in Grim's arms to be released. And after each kissing one of his cheeks, they were gone.

"What kind?" The chef in Jennifer had to ask, and she found herself pinned by the powerful gazes of both the King and Queen of Luda.

It was Lisa who finally answered. "The Tornian version of shortbread cookies."

"Really? I'd love to get the recipe."

"I forgot, you were a Chef back on Earth."

"She is a Chef here also," Treyvon growled. "Her skills have enhanced the lives of our people. Her cookies and brownies are highly prized."

Lisa put a gentle hand on Grim's arm, knowing he wasn't going to like the way the General was talking to her.

"Of course she is, General," Lisa pacified and gestured to the sitting area, something that had been added to Grim's Command Room since her arrival. "I meant no offense. As I said, I had just forgotten."

As they all sat, Lisa frowned at Jennifer. "Brownies?"

"Yes." Jennifer's hand mimicked Lisa's, soothing her own mate. "One of the Zaludian ships Treyvon intercepted was carrying chocolate from Earth."

"Honestly?" Lisa's eyes widened in excitement, and for a moment she reminded Treyvon of her daughters.

"Yes, they seemed to have cleared out an entire baking aisle."

"So you have *chocolate*?"

Grim frowned at the way his Lisa stressed the unknown word. Her tone was filled with such awe and desire that he'd only ever heard before when she was in his arms.

"Yes. We have chocolate chips, chocolate chunks, chocolate bars, milk chocolate, bitter chocolate, dark chocolate, even white chocolate, and cocoa powder."

"What is this... chocolate?" Grim demanded. If it were something his Lisa desired so greatly, he would make sure she had it.

"It's something incredible from Earth," Lisa told him, her eyes still fixed on Jennifer.

"That is truth," Treyvon agreed. "My Warriors never miss last meal when my Jennifer prepares something with it. Empress Kim has even threatened your brother that she will give him no more offspring unless he has a supply of it on hand."

"What?!!" It was Grim's eyes that widened this time.

"Totally understandable," Lisa nodded, rubbing her baby bump then demanded. "What will it cost me to get some?"

"Cook?" Carly looked up from the bowl she was stirring to the old Warrior who was helping her sister.

"What is it, little one?" Tagma asked, smiling down at Miki, letting her know she was doing a fine job even though he'd have to throw that mixture out, before turning his attention to Carly.

He couldn't believe how life had changed in House Luanda since the arrival of these precious little females and their mother. He'd been a bitter, old Warrior who the Goddess hadn't seen fit to bless with a female or with the glory of dying in battle. Instead, as his skills had waned with age, he'd had to return to the kitchens and use the skills his manno had taught him before he'd begun his Warrior training.

For years now he'd begrudged his position, seeing it as a stigma of his failings instead of a chance for a different, better life. And his life was better, thanks to these little ones. They looked at what he did with such awe and wonder that it filled him with pride that being a Warrior never had. They wanted to learn from him, and it made him see his position differently, made him a different male.

"What do you know about the Great Raptor?" she asked, setting her bowl aside.

"The Great Raptor?" he asked frowning slightly.

"Uh-huh."

"Doesn't Ki..." he broke off. He knew the little ones now called King Grim, manno. The news of this had spread faster than a solar storm through the Festival. It was yet another sign of how worthy these females found Grim. "Doesn't your manno tell you about him?"

"Oh, yes. Manno tells us a new story every night."

"Really good stories," Miki added, not wanting to be left out of the conversation.

"Then why do you want *me* to tell you one?"

Carly just shrugged her little shoulders. "I just thought that maybe your manno told you different stories."

"My manno did tell me tales of the Great Raptor."

"Really?" Setting her bowl aside now, Miki plopped her elbows on the counter, her chin propped up on top of her hands, just like her sister had. "Did he tell you any about Prince?"

"Prince?" he gave her a confused look.

"Yeah, the Great Raptor's son," Carly replied as if it should be obvious.

"We met him in the garden," Miki told him. "He was hurt, and we helped him."

"What!?!" Tagma roared, startling the girls. The reflexes he thought had waned with age were never faster as he steadied them both on their stools. It also had Ion and Nairn rushing into the kitchen, swords drawn, until Tagma shook his head at them telling them that everything was fine.

"I am sorry, little ones," he continued, his voice lowering as he dropped to his knees. "I did not mean to frighten you."

"Wh... why were you upset?" Miki asked, her little voice trembling.

"I was just surprised. That is all." Tagma's mind was racing to find a way to explain his terror at the thought of these precious, little ones being so close to such a dangerous creature. "It is a very rare thing to see the Great Raptor, let alone his... son."

"Really?" Carly asked.

"Yes. My manno told me that it is a great honor for one to see... Prince."

"Really?"

"Yes. You see while the Great Raptor is out protecting the people of Luda, Prince stays behind protecting the Great Raptor's mate, his mother. Although it is said that *she* is as deadly as her mate, especially when it comes to defending those she loves."

"Like mommy is."

"Yes, little one, just like your mommy."

"They must have been so worried. Prince was in the garden for two days. Manno and Mommy would be if it were us."

"They would be," Tagma said, his throat tightening at the thought and as his gaze rose to Ion's and Nairn's. They all knew that the King and Queen of Luda wouldn't be just *worried* if their little ones were missing for two days. They would be heartsick and *enraged*! Grim would tear all of Luda apart to find them.

"So others have met Prince?" Carly asked.

"I only know of one other." Tagma thought of a story his manno had only told him once. "My manno told me that there was once a Warrior who did as the two of you have done."

"Really?"

"Yes. He found, protected, and healed an injured Raptor. Because of this, the Raptor gifted the Warrior a piece of himself."

"What did he give him?" Miki whispered.

"The Eye of the Raptor. Here." Tagma held open his hand and pointed to an unmarked spot in his palm between his thumb and forefinger where two lines met and faintly resembled a bird's head. "It allowed the Warrior to sense evil, and have the power to destroy it, protecting those under his care. As the Great Raptor does."

"Wow..." the girls both whispered, then looked at their own palms that were as unmarked as Tagma's, and were disappointed.

"Do not worry, little ones. The Eye of the Raptor has only been gifted once in all of known time, but you were still honored by meeting Prince. It has been hundreds of years since *anyone* has been given that honor. Don't you agree, Ion?" Tagma looked to the younger Warrior for help.

"Many hundreds," Ion agreed. "So long ago that I cannot even recall the last Warrior's name."

"Wow, so we are the first females to meet him?" Carly asked, her eyes going wide.

"Yes."

"That's so cool," the girls whispered looking at each other.

"You believe this 'recording' will be enough?" Ull skeptically asked after Lisa had finished speaking.

"It will be a start, at least for Trisha. I have no doubt she's been trying to figure out what happened to the girls and me. The problem is going to be you getting close enough to her to get her to listen to it, especially after the way the Ganglians took the last group of women."

"That won't be a problem."

"You think you'll be able to just 'get close' to the niece of the President of the United States? A female he considers his daughter? It would be like Grim allowing an unknown male close to any of our girls."

That had Ull snapping his mouth shut because he knew how carefully King Grim guarded his females. That *he* was even allowed to see them had surprised him.

"So you are going to have to approach when she is alone and convince her to view the recording before her guards attack. And no!" Lisa gave him a sharp look. "You can't just kill them. You are trying to build a relationship between the Tornian Empire and Earth. Your first act there can't be killing people."

Ull growled his displeasure at that.

"You also can't force the educator on her," Lisa told him in a hard voice and could see that had been his plan. "I won't subject Trisha to what the rest of us have had to go through. Trisha will either do this or not."

"And if it's not?" Ull growled.

"Then we'll have to find another way. I know I can get you enough time for Trisha to at least consider using the educator, but you and your actions will be the deciding factor." Lisa turned concerned eyes to Grim who sat beside her on the couch. "Are you and Wray sure Warrior Ull is the best male for this? Maybe I..."

Ull's roar of outrage drowned out the rest of what she was going to say as Ull surged out of his chair. Grim was instantly on his feet and in front of his Lisa, his sword drawn and pointing at Ull. General Rayner did the same, standing protectively in front of his Jennifer, but ready to assist the King if needed.

"You will not threaten *my* Queen, Warrior Ull. First male or not, I will end you if you take so much as a step toward her."

"She *dares* to question my worthiness in this!"

"When you act like this, then yes, I do." Lisa rose, and while she moved to where she could see Ull, she remained behind Grim. "This is too important, and not just for the Tornians, but also the Kaliszians and the people of Earth. Females are not possessions on Earth, Warrior Ull. They aren't going to just obey you because you are male. We are independent creatures. We make our own decisions, choose how we want to live our lives, and speak our minds. You've shown time and time again that you have trouble accepting that. Something I find difficult to believe with a mother like Isis."

"My mother..."

"Is a remarkable female." Lisa cut him off. "She stood up for what she believed in, for what she wanted, and for who she loved. That you can't appreciate that is what makes me question that you are the right male for this task. Trisha has had to survive and deal with a great deal. She's strong and independent. She isn't going to put up with your bullshit attitude toward females. She's dealt with enough assholes in her life."

"Assholes?" Ull questioned.

"Unworthy and unfit males," Lisa clarified for him. "Ones that only want to use her for their own gains."

"I am not an asshole," Ull grumbled as he sat back down.

"Maybe not to other males, but to Earth females... Jennifer?" Lisa looked to Rayner's True Mate.

"Total asshole," Jennifer agreed.

"Look, Ull," Lisa's voice softened as she moved to sit back down, and slowly Grim followed. "I know what happened at the Joining Ceremony still bothers you. That you see not being selected as a reflection of your worth, but it wasn't. It had absolutely nothing to do with *you*. You could have been the worthiest male the Known Universes have ever seen, and *still*, you wouldn't have been chosen."

"Ynyr was," the words slipped passed his lips before he could stop them.

"Truth," Lisa gave him a sympathetic look.

"Maybe I should be the one going to Earth," Lisa whispered later that night as she lay in Grim's arms, a hand absently caressing his chest as she gazed out the windows at the star-filled sky.

"No."

"But, Grim..."

"You are with offspring, Lisa."

"Truth, but that doesn't mean..."

"I would not let you go without me."

"I wouldn't want to."

"What of the girls? The other females? Do we leave them behind? Who will help and protect them if we do?"

Lisa's heart clenched at the thought of being so far away from her babies if they happened to need her. She knew someday that time would come, but that wasn't today. Then there were the other Earth females. The invited males had begun arriving, and she needed to be here to help supervise the meetings and calm fears. Releasing a deep sigh, she looked up at him. "You're right. My place, *our* place is here on Luda, but Ull is still so angry, and I don't understand why."

"He is the first male of a Lord, my Lisa. He was brought up to believe *he* would be the first, and most likely only male, in his bloodline to obtain a female."

"But why? He has three younger brothers."

"Which is unheard of. You know this, my Lisa. A female might stay with the same male long enough to give him two males, but *four*? It cast a stigma on House Rigel. No Kaliszian female would consider joining with anyone other than the future Lord."

"And then Abby chose Ynyr, a third male."

"Yes."

"But if he wants a female so badly, why didn't he put in his application to meet any of the women?"

"Pride. His younger brother is now the most powerful Lord in the Empire. He has a female, and she is already with offspring."

"Well, he'd better get over it before he gets to Earth."

"He is a Warrior. He will put his feelings aside and do what is required of him."

"He'd better," Lisa said, then forgetting Ull, stretched up so her bare breasts barely brushed his chest as she teased. "Now there is something I require of the Warrior beneath me."

"What does my Queen require of me?" Grim asked, his shaft hardening as she shifted over him, her already slick channel brushing it.

"For you to love me, my King."

"I do," Grim growled as he slowly entered her and began to thrust. "I always will. For you are my Queen. My Lisa. My everything."

With every declaration, Grim thrust harder, deeper, and the passion that never took much to rekindle between them ignited into a solar storm.

"Goddess yes, Grim!" Lisa cried out as she pressed her hands against his chest and arching her back, began to ride him. "You are mine. My King. My Grim. My everything."

"Then give me everything that is mine, my Lisa," he ordered, knowing neither of them was going to last long. Not with the way she was already tightening around him. Capturing one of the lush breasts she was so readily offering, he sucked it deep into his mouth the way he knew always pushed her over the edge, especially now that she carried his offspring.

"Grim!" she screamed as her release hit.

"Lisa!" Grim roared as he followed, and together they experienced heaven.

SIX

"Jen, I would like you to meet Rebecca Mines." Lisa introduced the two females the next morning in the sun room, after she had her guards exit, closing the door behind them. "Dr. Rebecca Mines, OB/GYN. Rebecca, this is Jennifer Rayner, General Rayner's True Mate, and Kim's sister."

"Sister?" Rebecca's eyes widened. "The one Kim was looking for when the Ganglians captured her?"

"Yes," Jen answered. "They'd taken me, and the group I was with, six months earlier."

"Wow. What are the chances of that?"

'Probably better than you think,' Jen thought but said nothing.

"Come, let's sit," Lisa gestured to the conversation area that sat in front of the wall of windows that let sunshine stream into the room.

"Wow, that's really beautiful," Jen said moving to get a closer look at the suncatcher that hung in the window. It was a myriad of colors that made you think it was just haphazardly put together, but on closer inspection, she could see the pattern repeated, like in a kaleidoscope. The shards of color it gave off in the morning light were amazing.

"Isn't it?" Lisa agreed smiling. "Dagan made it for me for the Festival of the Goddess."

"Dagan?"

"He's our clothiers, Padma's and Gossamer's, second male. He's very special."

"I'd say." Finally taking a chair, Jen waited, and Lisa turned her gaze to Rebecca.

"Rebecca, the reason I wanted you to meet us here is that there is something I need to talk to you about. And it can't go any further than this room."

"Alright..." Rebecca's gaze traveled from Lisa to Jen and back again.

"More women have been taken from Earth," Lisa told her bluntly.

"What?!!" She shot up stiffly in her chair. "Wray sent..."

"No!" Lisa cut her off. "Wray vowed to Kim that he wouldn't, and he hasn't."

"Then who?" Rebecca shot accusing eyes to Jen. "The Kaliszians?"

"Wrong again," Jen told her, her gaze hard. "The Kaliszians saved them. It was the Ganglians."

"The Ganglians..." Rebecca's words trailed off. "Oh, my God. How many survived?"

"All of them," Jen informed her. "The Ganglians didn't take them to rape. They kidnapped them so they could sell them to Tornian warriors on Vesta."

"What? No!" Rebecca denied, looking physically ill. "Callen would never..."

"Of course he wouldn't," Lisa quickly reassured her. "This was done by Reeve."

"Callen discovered this?" Rebecca asked, the color slowly returning to her face.

"No, the Kaliszians did when they intercepted a Ganglian ship in their Empire."

"I don't understand."

"Look, the Kaliszians have been intercepting Ganglian and Zaludian ships ever since Wray was shot down over Pontus," Jen told her. "They've been trying to figure out why the two are working together and they think they might have figured it out."

"And that is?"

"To disrupt the balance of power by supplying Tornian males with compatible females, and the Kaliszian people with food. If they do this, then *they* will become the two most powerful species in the Known Universes."

"But there's no way they can do that," Rebecca argued. "Neither species has a home world."

"They could because they know where Earth is, and they are the only ones, as Wray has kept its location a secret."

"But you said the Kaliszians have been intercepting their ships."

"And every time we do, they've been able to delete their navigational data. It's one of the reasons Treyvon and I wanted to speak to Wray. We want to return the women to Earth, but can't because we don't know where it is."

"And if it becomes known that there are compatible Earth females in the Kaliszian Empire..." Lisa trailed off.

"It could mean war," Rebecca whispered.

"Yes. Some of the Warriors are getting desperate, Rebecca. If they attack…"

"Treyvon and Liron would defend them. They would have no choice, not after what Aadi did."

"Alright. So what's the plan and why are you telling *me* this? I'm just a doctor."

"The plan is for Ull to go to Earth and make contact, explain what is happening, and try to negotiate a treaty that will not only protect Earth but help the Tornians and Kaliszians."

"The Tornians kidnapping us isn't going to help with that."

"We know, which is why Ull is following Jen and General Rayner to Pontus first, to pick up the women they rescued and return them to Earth."

"Along with the surviving men from the group I was taken with," Jen added.

"But not us."

"No, Rebecca, I'm sorry. I tried to get Wray to let you be returned too, but…"

"He refused."

"My new brother-in-law can be a real asshole," Jen muttered, "but in this, I have to agree with him."

"Of course you would!" Rebecca accused. "You've had it pretty cushy, haven't you? True Mate to a General. Sister to the Empress."

"Rebecca," Lisa tried to cut her off.

"Cushy?!!" Jen growled. "I've had it *cushy*? What do you know about it? Were you captured by the Ganglians? Were you forced to witness them *raping* females? Were you sold as a slave? Made to work in a mine? To live in a cave! Were you starved, Rebecca? Was your husband beaten to death right before your eyes? Did you cry every night and wish you could just *die*?"

"I…" Rebecca was cut off by the doors of the sunroom being slammed open, and a male she had never seen storming through them, despite the guards trying to stop him. He was instantly in front of Jennifer, pulling her up and into his arms.

"What is wrong, my Jennifer? Who has upset you?"

Grim stormed in bare seconds after Treyvon, his sword pulled. "Lisa?"

"It's all right, Grim. Things just got a little… heated."

"It's my fault." Rebecca slowly stood, her eyes full of regret and just a little fear of the large, Kaliszian General. His hard, glowing gaze pinned her even while he still gently held Jen. "I didn't understand her situation. I just assumed she'd been safe in the Kaliszian Empire all this time."

"While it is truth she has been in our Empire since her abduction, she has been far from safe," Treyvon growled.

"I gathered that. I'm sorry, Jen. Truly," she said when Jen looked at her over a massive bicep. "I usually don't just jump to conclusions like that, but lately..."

"Your life's been in turmoil."

"Yes."

"It's okay, Treyvon," she reached up to gently caress his cheek. "You can put me down. I overreacted too, and I have a feeling that's going to be happening a lot more for a while."

"What do you mean?" Treyvon asked, slowly putting her back on her feet. And while he released her, one hand stayed on the small of her back.

"I'll get to that, but first." She turned to face Rebecca. "I'm sorry too, Rebecca. I should have explained myself better when I said I agreed with Wray. I didn't mean that you should have to stay here, have to Join with a Tornian. What I meant was, for right now, we need to proceed as if nothing has changed. If the Ganglians or Zaludians find out what we were trying to do..."

"Lisa! You told her?" Grim frowned down at his Queen.

"She has the right to know if she's going to help," Lisa told him, not intimidated in the least at his fierce frown.

"Out!" Grim turned to face the guards. "Close the doors. No one enters."

"Yes, sire!"

"They were supposed to be doing that before," Lisa's lips twitched looking at Treyvon.

"No one keeps a Kaliszian away from his True Mate," Treyvon told her. "Especially when he knows she is in distress."

"How did you know?" Rebecca asked looking confused. "Were you walking right by? We weren't *that* loud were we?"

"It's a True Mate thing," Jen told her, not willing to go any further than that. "So are we okay? With what I said I mean? I would understand why you wouldn't be, what with not being allowed to go back too."

"Yes," Rebecca said nodding.

"Thank you, because the reason we're telling you this is that we need to ask for your help."

"*My* help?"

"Yes, as a doctor. You see there was another female with us when we were taken. Mackenzie, Mac."

"And she's not returning to Earth with the other females?"

"No, she's the True Mate to Treyvon's Second-in-Command, Nikhil... and she's pregnant."

"I see."

"It was the other reason Treyvon and I wanted to meet with Wray and get him to tell us Earth's location. We were going to go there to find my sister and bring back the information Luol, our Healer, would need to make sure Mac had a safe pregnancy. We didn't know that the new Empress was my little sister. Or that you were here."

"It must have been a shocking reunion."

"It was, especially meeting little Destiny." A smile filtered across her lips as she thought of Destiny. "Thank you by the way." Her gaze included Lisa. "Kimmy told me she couldn't have done it without the two of you."

"Kim and Rebecca did all the hard work. I was just there for support," Lisa said, downplaying her part.

"You were there for more than that. Kimmy told me how you, Rebecca, took a knife in the back to protect Destiny and that you, Lisa, distracted that psycho Risa long enough for Kim to get her out of the room."

Neither woman said anything.

"Which is why I'm hoping you'll come to Pontus with us and help Mac."

"Is this Nikhil as big as him?" Rebecca motioned to Treyvon.

"Bigger."

"Bigger?" Lisa and Rebecca said in disbelief.

"Commander Nikhil is one of the largest and most powerful Kaliszians in our Empire," Treyvon told them quietly. "He is also deeply concerned that because of this, the offspring the Goddess has blessed them with might harm his True Mate. If you were able to assist our Healer in making sure that doesn't happen, the Kaliszian Empire would be in your debt."

"As will I," Treyvon said giving Jennifer a hard look. "For I believe my True Mate is with offspring but has yet to tell me."

"I wanted Rebecca to check me first to be sure. You saw how Nikhil lost control when he just thought Mac might be."

"One of your Elite Warriors lost control?" Grim questioned moving slightly closer to Lisa.

"But for a moment. Earth females are smaller than ours. Are you saying you haven't feared for your Queen?" Treyvon looked at the difference in size between Grim and Lisa.

"I have," Grim acknowledged quietly, and the two males shared an understanding look. "Which is why if you choose to go with them, Rebecca, I must demand you be here for the presentation of our daughter." He put a protective arm around Lisa, pulling her close.

"Of course I would be," Rebecca quickly reassured Grim. "But Hadar now has enough knowledge to care for Lisa if I'm gone for a while. He did just fine when I went to check Abby."

"This is truth, Grim," Lisa looked up at him reassuringly. "And I can make sure Rebecca does a thorough scan before she leaves if that helps."

"She will," Grim growled.

"I will," Rebecca agreed.

"I really don't see why this is necessary," Rebecca said for the third time as she looked at Lisa. "The coverings I have will be fine."

"Jen said it's warm on Pontus right now, like summer back on Earth. Not winterish like it is here right now. Because of that, Padma and Caitir have been concentrating on making warmer coverings, but you're going to need something else."

"I wish the General would have let Jen come with us."

"I doubt Treyvon is going to let Jen out of his sight for a while. Not after you confirmed she's with offspring."

"Yeah, I still don't know if his reaction was cute or just damn scary."

"You mean wrapping her up in his arms, growling at everyone, and immediately carrying her back to their rooms?" Lisa asked chuckling. "Grim would have done the same to me if we hadn't been in the middle of the Assembly when he found out."

"That's true." Rebecca smiled remembering the King of Luda's reaction to Lisa announcing she carried his offspring.

"And besides, the girls wanted to see Dagan. Didn't you, girls?" She looked at Carly and Miki who were sitting across from them.

"Uh-huh," they replied. "It's been *forever* since we've gotten to play with him."

"It's only been a week," Lisa reminded them.

"Like we said," Miki told them. "*Forever.*"

"I'm also surprised Grim let *you* come alone." Rebecca gave her a questioning look. Everyone knew how protective the King of Luda was of his family, especially with warriors arriving.

"I'd hardly say I was *alone*," Lisa gave Rebecca an exasperated look. "There are three transports full of guards with us."

"Like I said, alone," Rebecca teased. Their transport coming to a stop ended the conversation.

"Come on, Mommy, let's go," Miki said reaching for the handle.

"Miki Renee, you know better," Lisa gently admonished her youngest. "We have to wait until Agee or Kirk open the door." It was a small concession for her to give if it helped Grim to not worry so much.

"Oh, yeah. I forgot. Sorry, Mommy."

"It's alright, baby. I know you were just excited, but you need to try to remember so your manno doesn't worry."

"Yes, Mommy."

Looking up as the door opened, Lisa saw Agee standing there holding out a hand.

"My Queen, the area is secure."

Taking his hand, Lisa let him help her out of the transport. It was something that was getting more and more difficult the further along she got in pregnancy.

"Thank you, Agee," she said giving him an apologetic smile, knowing he was going to have to be doing this more and more as she got heavier.

"It is not a problem, my Queen," Agee told her quietly. Then making sure Kirk was there, turned to assist Rebecca and the girls.

"Lisa," Padma called out as she walked down the path toward the transports. "What are you doing here? Why didn't you call? I would have come to you."

"I know you would have," Lisa laughed, hugging her first true friend on Luda, "but the girls wanted to play with Dagan, and honestly I wanted to get out for a while."

"Is everything okay?" Padma asked running a critical eye over her friend and Queen, as well as the number of guards that were surrounding them.

"Of course it is. Grim would never have let me out of his sight if it wasn't."

"That is truth," Padma agreed smiling slightly as she gestured toward her open door. "Come inside and we'll talk, or would you rather sit out back? It isn't that cold out today. Not with the way the sun is beating down."

"Actually, I need to speak with you about making some cooler coverings."

"For you?" Padma frowned as they waited for the guards to say her home was secure. Once that was done, they entered her home.

"No, for Rebecca," Lisa told her once the door was closed.

"I see," Padma said but didn't. "Girls, Dagan is out back."

"Can we go find him, Mommy?" Carly asked.

"Yes. Take either Agee or Kirk with you."

"Yes, Mommy," they chorused as they rushed out the back door.

SEVEN

"Look, it's the idiot."

Dagan looked up to find three young males moving toward him. He didn't like them. They were new to Luda, having recently been sent here by their mannos so the Empire's Greatest Warrior, King Grim, could train them. But when they weren't training, they liked to sneak out of House Luanda and terrorize the countryside. One day, they had discovered Dagan walking along the creek picking up pretty stones. At first, he thought they had wanted to play with him, the way Carly and Miki did, but he quickly discovered what they considered *fun* was to shove him to the ground and hit him.

The last time they'd found him, he'd gone home with his shirt torn and his body bruised. He'd lied to his mama and said he'd fallen, not only because he sometimes did, but because he knew she would be upset if he told her truth.

No one had hit him since Gahan had left the King's Glassmaker's shop, and his mama had been so happy since then. Dagan didn't want her to be sad again.

"Go away," Dagan said, backing away from them.

"Oh look, it talks," Eero, the smallest of the three, sneered. He was the one that seemed to enjoy hurting Dagan the most.

"I didn't think he could do anything but cry," Lalo, the biggest one, said.

"Let's see how long it will take this time." Dal, the leader of the three, leaned down picking up a thick stick as the other two moved to surround Dagan.

Dagan's gaze widened as he turned in a tight circle searching for a way out.

"Oh no, you unfit spawn, there's no way out this time." Dal raised the stick. "Your manno should have ended you before you drew your first breath. But since he wasn't male enough to do it, *we* will." With that, he started swinging, and with a cry, Dagan dropped to the ground protecting his head.

"Come on, Miki," Carly called out over her shoulder as she ran up the path. "I think I hear Dagan in the meadow."

The path in the woods was one the girls had been down before. It led to the small furnace that Gossamer had built for his first male, Gahan, so that he could practice his glass making skills. Dagan had shown it to them on one of their visits, confiding that he liked to go there.

Bursting into the meadow, Carly came to an abrupt halt when she saw three young males circling Dagan. She hadn't known Dagan had play dates with other friends, especially ones so close to his age.

"What game are they playing?" Miki asked, coming to stand beside her sister.

"I don't know."

"I don't like them," Miki said frowning. "They look mean."

"You know what Mommy says about judging people by how they look."

"I know but..." Just then, Dagan fell to the ground, and the three started hitting and kicking him.

"Stop that!" Carly yelled and began running directly toward the boys. When she got closer, she launched herself at the one swinging the stick. She aimed for his knees the way she'd seen one of the Warriors do at the Festival. During that match, the Warriors hadn't even been allowed stingers, and the smaller one had won the match with just such a move. Her manno had grunted his approval.

Dal didn't know what was happening. One minute he was standing there beating the idiot, the next he was on the ground, the stick flying from his grip. Kicking out, he found his attacker was gone, having rolled away with a skill *he* still hadn't mastered. Looking up, he found himself staring up into the furious amber eyes of... a *female*?

"You *will not* hurt Dagan like that!" she growled at him.

"You are bad males," Miki hissed, dropping to her knees beside Dagan. "Evil."

The other two had stopped attacking when Dal had.

"What the..." Lalo looked from the young female that had suddenly appeared next to Dagan, to the other one who was now holding the stick over Dal like it was a sword.

"You will leave. Now!" Carly ordered.

Dal's light, green-skinned face flushed emerald with embarrassment and anger that this... female would think to tell him what to do. Jumping to his feet, he took a threatening step toward her. "You *dare* speak to a warrior like that?"

"You're not a warrior," Carly told him not backing down. "Warriors are fit and worthy. They protect those smaller and weaker than them. They *don't* attack them. When I tell my manno what you've done, he's going to be angry."

"Yeah," Miki nodded in agreement, "*really* angry."

"Not if you can't tell him," Dal growled as he ripped the branch from Carly's hands and raised it. "Get her, too," he ordered the other two, gesturing with his head toward Miki.

Dagan reared up, wrapping his larger body around Miki, so he took the kicks aimed at her, and cried out "No!" But it was drowned out by an enraged screech that rent the air.

Lisa looked up, surprised when she saw Grim striding into Padma's cottage.

"Grim, what are you doing here?" she asked as she rose, moving toward him with a smile on her lips.

"I felt the need to be with you," he told her quietly as he leaned down kissing her lips gently.

"We haven't been gone that long. Not even an hour."

"Yet you were gone," he said as if that was enough of an explanation. "Where are the girls?" he asked looking around the room, his gaze taking in their absence.

"They are outside playing with Dagan. Either Agee or Kirk is with them."

"Not truth," Grim growled, his whole demeanor changing as he spun around and stormed out the door he'd just entered.

"Not truth?" Lisa asked following. "What do you mean 'not truth'?"

Grim ignored her as he roared. "Agee! Kirk! To me!"

"Sire?" The two were quickly there.

"Where are my daughters?" Grim demanded.

"The Princesses?" They looked at him in confusion. "They are in the cottage with the Queen. We escorted them inside personally."

"They went out the back door to play with Dagan," Lisa told them, reaching up to grip Grim's arm. "I told them to take one of you with them when they went to find him."

At her words, two of her most trusted Elite Guard paled. "We never saw them, Majesty. Truth."

"*Find them!*" Grim roared just as the screech of an enraged Raptor filled the air.

Dal, Eero, and Lalo looked up in horror and disbelief as a Raptor, in full attack mood, swooped down at them. Terrified, they abandoned their assault on Carly, Miki, and Dagan, and ran into the woods believing they would be safe there.

Grim raced up the path he knew his daughters had taken by the size of their small footprints. He forced away the memory of the last time he'd run on a path like this, to find his Lisa beaten and nearly abused. This time wouldn't be the same though. It couldn't be. His girls were too young, too precious.

As he rounded a bend, three bodies collided with him, each bouncing off him, flying to the side. Looking down, he saw three of his first-year trainees.

"Dal. Eero. Lalo. What are you doing here? Have you seen the Princesses?" he demanded.

"J... just exploring, King Grim," Dal stuttered, still frantically looking back the way they'd come.

"Princesses?" Lalo stammered.

"Yes, they were headed this way."

"M...meadow," Eero pointed up the path. "But they must be dead by now. There is a crazed Raptor there. It just attacked."

Grim's roar shook the trees as he raced up the path, praying to the Goddess he was in time.

"Oh, Prince," Carly walked up to the giant bird that was now standing between them and the path the trainees had taken. "Thank you for helping us."

"Yeah, Prince," Miki said getting up from the ground. "They were bad males, but Dagan isn't." She helped the dirty and bruised Dagan up. "You remember Dagan, don't you? You met him in our garden."

Prince lowered his head, cocking it to the side as he stared at Dagan, his violet gaze seeming to take in every part of him then gave the slightest of nods. When sounds of running feet were suddenly heard, he spun around, spreading out his wings protectively to conceal the three of them behind him.

Grim stormed into the meadow, his sword drawn just as the Raptor turned. Its wings were spread wide, and its deadly beak was snapping in warning. Grim took it all in, in a moment, including the fact that Carly, Miki, and Dagan were standing behind it.

Slowly sheathing his sword, Grim moved across the meadow, and Prince lowered his wings in the presence of the King, allowing him to pass. Grim dropped to his knees so he could carefully inspect each of his daughters, taking in the small scrapes and dirty coverings but finding no real harm. The same couldn't be said for Dagan.

"There it is!" Dal exclaimed. "Kill it before it attacks us again!"

"Prince didn't attack *you*," Carly exclaimed. "*You* attacked Dagan, and you would have attacked us too if Prince hadn't stopped you!"

"You lie!" Dal accused hotly.

"You dare accuse *my* daughter of telling an untruth?" Grim demanded quietly, slowly rising to face Dal.

"I..." Dal's mind raced. "She is confused. It was the idiot, the unfit one that was attacking them. We," he gestured to himself, Eero, and Lalo, "stopped him."

"Yet we found you running away."

"Only because of the Raptor," Dal claimed. "We had no way of fighting it off."

"So you chose to save yourselves instead of protecting two females?"

"I..."

Grim turned his back on the male and looked to Dagan. Going down on one knee before the unique male he'd grown fond of, he took in the darkening bruise along his jaw, the split lip, and torn shirt.

"Tell me truth, Dagan," he said gently. "What happened here?"

"I come here because I like it. It pretty," Dagan told Grim quietly. "The sun," he pointed up at the sky, "makes the ground sparkle." He pointed to where there was still some snow and Grim saw it did sparkle under Luda's sun. "It gives me ideas."

"I can see why," Grim agreed patiently. "But what happened today?"

"Like I say, I like it here, but not when they come." He peeked over Grim's shoulder at Dal, Eero, and Lalo, then quickly looked back to Grim.

"Why? What do they do?"

"They tease Dagan," he told them quietly, but everyone was able to hear. "Call me unfit, even though Dagan a good boy. They push me down. Hit me. Today they say they end me since my manno didn't." Dagan's split lip was trembling by the time he finished.

"He lies!" Dal yelled, but no one believed him.

Grim ignored Dal as he struggled to keep the rage out of his voice. He knew Dagan didn't react to it well. "You are not unfit, Dagan. You are a blessing from the Goddess, and your manno knew that from the first breath you took."

"Truth?" Dagan asked, his eyes pleading with Grim's that it was truth.

"The King of Luda doesn't speak untruths, Dagan."

And despite the split lip, Dagan's face broke out into a brilliant smile as he said, "That is truth."

Rising, Grim turned his gaze, pinning Dal and his friends as he bit out. "Kirk."

"Yes, sire," Kirk was immediately before him.

"You will take two guards and personally escort those three back to Luanda where they will be placed in containment cells until their mannos come and collect them. *If* they come to collect them." He watched all three pale.

"With pleasure, sire," Kirk replied then spinning on his heel escorted the three away.

"I'm glad they're gone, Manno." Grim looked down to find Miki looking up at him as she wrapped her arms around his leg.

"They will never harm you again, little one."

"They didn't hurt me, thanks to Dagan and Prince," she told him.

"Yeah, Prince scared them off before they could hurt us," Carly said, wrapping herself around his other leg, "but they did hurt Dagan."

"Hadar will heal him," Grim reassured her.

Grim looked at the creature that was still standing protectively between them and the remaining guards. He'd never heard tales of a real one doing such a thing. Only in the barely remembered myths that told of how the Great Raptor had once been the companion of a God. A God whose name only the stars knew now, and that this God had charged the Raptor with protecting those he deemed worthy when the God couldn't.

Those ancient myths couldn't be truth... could they?

"I thank you, Prince." Grim found himself using the name his daughters had given the bird. "For protecting those I hold precious when I wasn't able to."

The Raptor looked at the King of Luda for a moment, seeming to recognize that the King was just as deadly as it was when it came to protecting those under his care. Slowly, Prince turned his head and plucked out one of its long, jet-black feathers. When it took a step forward, Grim instinctively stiffened, even as he reached out to take the feather. But Prince dropped his head and instead offered the feather to Carly.

"For me?" Carly asked, her little voice full of wonder and when Prince nodded, she reached out to take it. "Thank you, Prince. I'll make sure to always take care of it."

Prince then looked at Miki, who gazed hopefully from Carly's feather to him. But instead of selecting a second feather, Prince gently nudged her tiny hand that was still resting on her manno's leg.

"What do you want, Prince?" Miki asked, reaching out to touch his regal head.

"Careful, Miki," Grim growled quietly, not liking the dangerous creature so close to his tiny daughter.

"But why, Manno?" Miki asked looking up at him. "Prince would never hurt me."

That's when Prince struck, embedding his razor sharp beak into the tender flesh of her tiny hand between her thumb and index finger.

Her shocked cry had Grim swinging his daughters out of harm's way, but before he could draw his sword, the Raptor was gone.

"Miki, are you alright?" Grim was once again on his knee, his hands trembling as he carefully tried to open the hand Miki had clenched to her chest, surprised to see that no blood was flowing down it.

"I... I think so," she told him. "Prince just surprised me."

"Let me see," he murmured gently.

"It doesn't hurt," she said, opening her hand so he could see it.

And there in his Miki's little hand, staring back at him, was the Eye of the Raptor.

"What does it mean, Grim?" Lisa asked later that night after the girls were asleep. They had brought Dagan back to Luanda and Hadar had healed every bruise, and every cut, while all the Earth females had come to check on him. Dagan had won every one of their hearts with his gentle way and ready smile. He had left for home happier than Lisa had ever seen the special male.

Hadar had also checked Miki's hand, but there had been nothing for him to heal. No bruise, no blood, and no puncture wound. There was only a faint violet spot in the palm of her hand. He had tried to remove it with every portable repair unit in House Luanda, but every last one of them found nothing to remove.

Now they were in their sleeping chamber, the House was quiet, and there was a roaring fire before them as Grim handed her a small glass of wine.

Grim sighed heavily as he sat down next to her on the couch. "The Raptor's feather has been given since the earliest of recorded times. Although I've never heard of a Raptor itself gifting one."

"What do you mean?"

"The finding of a Raptor's feather is a rare thing. No one knows why so finding one is an honor."

"Why?"

"Because it is believed that only true protectors are allowed to find and wear them."

"True protectors?"

"Yes, those that protect, serve, and watch over those that can't do it for themselves. The way the Great Raptor does for the people of Luda."

"But Carly is just a child."

"And yet she came to the aid of Dagan. We have both seen how protective she is of Miki... and of you. She is a worthy recipient of the Raptor's feather."

"And Miki's hand?"

"The Eye of the Raptor." Grim's voice was much more hushed this time, almost pensive.

"Why do you say it that way?" Lisa demanded, her stomach clenching.

"The Eye of the Raptor. Lisa..."

"Yes? What about it?"

"Few have ever heard of it, and even fewer know what its gift is."

"Just what did that damn bird do to my baby?!!" she demanded, setting her wine aside.

"He gave her the ability to sense the evil and darkness that is Daco."

"What?!!"

"I know of only one other that has ever been gifted the Eye. It is said that while he saved many from Daco's clutches, it came at a terrible cost."

"What cost?"

"That is not known."

"Goddess, Grim. What are we going to do?"

"Nothing."

"What do you mean *nothing*?!!"

"Calm, my Lisa," Grim told her, gently framing her face with his large hands. "First, because there is nothing we can do and second, what I've just told you is a myth. It doesn't mean it is truth."

"But..."

"No," he gently admonished her. "You said yourself that Carly was always your little Warrior, was looking out for Miki and you, even before she came here."

"This is truth," Lisa nodded calming slightly.

"As for Miki, she *never* liked Luuken."

"*No one* liked Luuken," Lisa muttered.

"Truth. So you see, it is nothing she didn't already have before. Do not place so much belief in myths that have been spoken of for thousands of years."

"I suppose you're right," she said, relaxing back into his arms, taking the glass he held out to her again.

"Of course I am. I am the King of Luda." His comment got him exactly the reaction he was hoping for. His love gave a little huff of disbelief and rolled her beautiful eyes at him, but the last bits of worry and tension left her body, and she snuggled down deeper into his embrace. "Now let us enjoy the fire and maybe... if you aren't too tired, we could light one ourselves later."

"Oh, I think that can be arranged."

EPILOGUE

Several days later…

"My Queen still doubts that you are the right male for this task, Warrior Ull," Grim said looking across his desk at the Warrior standing there.

"With all due respect to your Queen, King Grim, she knows nothing about me so is in no position to judge my abilities."

"It is not your abilities she doubts, Warrior Ull," Grim told him. "It is your attitude since the Joining Ceremony. She and Lady Abby speak regularly. As do I and Lord Ynyr."

"They feel they have the right to criticize the assistance I gave them?" Ull questioned, his rose-colored skin darkening in anger. "Assistance they requested? To you?!!"

"Neither complained of your help, Warrior Ull. In fact, Lord Ynyr repeatedly praised you, stating that without you, it would have taken him a great deal longer to get House Jamison in order. It is because of that, Wray chose you for this."

"Then what was their complaint?" It should have eased Ull's temper, hearing that his brother acknowledged and appreciated everything he had done for him. But it didn't. Instead, it made him angrier. Why would it take the word of a *third* male, Lord or not, for him a *first* male, to be given this honor? It didn't make sense, but there was a great deal that wasn't making sense to him lately.

"That you seemed... unlike yourself since the Joining Ceremony."

"They are wrong."

"I hope so because your brother warriors' futures, and perhaps that of our entire Empire, depend on the outcome of this mission." Grim let that hang for a moment then reached out to hand Ull a memory crystal. "This is the transmission Lisa recorded for her friend, Trisha. You must find her, convince her to view it, and convince her to help."

"She will," Ull growled. "My vow."

∞ ∞ ∞ ∞ ∞

"Rebecca," Grim and Ull walked to where his Lisa and a group were standing next to the shuttles. One would take Ull to the Searcher, while the other would take General Rayner, Jennifer, and Rebecca to the General's ship, the Defender. It had been decided that Rebecca would travel on the Kaliszian ship as Jennifer had become progressively sicker in the mornings. "I have informed Lord Callen that you will be on Pontus."

"What?" Rebecca asked sharper than she had intended. "Why would you do that?"

"Because Vesta is the closest Tornian planet to Pontus, and is where others will be told you are should any inquire. Its Lord needed to be informed."

"Oh, of course."

"Lord Callen is also the one that will be returning you to Luda when the time comes. Should you need him before that, for anything, contact him with this." Grim handed her a small, palm-sized object. "It is secure and will not allow others to know where you are. That is important, Rebecca. Should it become known that we have allowed a compatible female to leave our Empire..."

"Yeah, yeah, yeah. I understand. So my cover is that I'm meeting with Lord Callen."

"Cover?"

"Reason for going," she explained.

"That would be truth then."

"Rebecca!" Every head turned to see Miki running across the grounds toward them, weaving her way through the bodies that separated her from her goal. Three guards were trying to keep up.

"Miki?" Rebecca knelt down as Miki reached her. "What's wrong?"

"You can't leave!" Miki told her breathlessly. "Not without these."

Rebecca's frown turned into a smile as she opened the bag Miki had shoved into her hands. "You brought me cookies?"

"Yeah, Mommy used to always make them for us when we went on a long trip, so I thought you should have some too."

"Thank you, Miki." Rebecca hugged the little girl. "I'm sure these will make my trip much more enjoyable."

Miki smiled then backed away from Rebecca until she ran into her manno's legs. Or at least she thought they were her manno's, but when she looked up, she found herself looking into the dark eyes of Warrior Ull. Eyes that, for a moment, were darker than they should be.

"Miki," Grim lifted her up into his arms. "What have we told you about running from your guards?" That had her gaze moving to him instead of where it had remained locked on Ull's.

"But I wasn't, Manno," she told him earnestly. "Vow. I just didn't want Rebecca to leave without her cookies."

Grim released a heavy sigh realizing this was a subject he would be addressing again and again as his little one grew.

"King Grim," General Rayner's lips twitched as he nodded slightly, "and Princess Miki. It is time for us to depart."

"Safe travels, General Rayner. Remember you are carrying treasured cargo," Grim looked to Rebecca.

"No one knows that better than I do, King Grim," Treyvon told him, but his gaze went to his Jennifer.

"Bye, Uncle Treyvon. Bye, Aunt Jennifer. Bye, Rebecca." Miki waved as they walked away and Lisa didn't bother to correct her that technically she was wrong. Her girls had eagerly accepted Treyvon and Jen into the family, and if this was the way they wanted to express it, then she'd let them.

∞ ∞ ∞ ∞ ∞

Ull tipped his head to the side slightly, watching the group say their goodbyes and felt nothing. No, that wasn't truth, he felt something... something dark.

'We shouldn't be working with the Kaliszians.' The thought insidiously whispered through his mind. *'They are weak. We can take what they have, take what Earth has. That would better serve our brother warriors. It would make them see who the worthy and fit one was in his family.'*

Ull didn't know where these thoughts were coming from, but they made sense. There was no guarantee his mission to Earth would succeed. After all, what did the Emperor know? He was allowing a *female* to influence his decisions, just like the King of Luda was, as was the Supreme Commander of Kaliszian Defenses. It made them weak. Females were only ever meant for one thing. All females.

His gaze went to the little one in the King's arms and was surprised to find her staring unflinchingly back at him.

"Beware the darkness that speaks to you." Miki's words while quiet were spoken in a voice much older, wiser, and more powerful than hers could ever be. "It knows where you are most vulnerable when you are at your weakest. It then lies to you with the truth, making you believe and do things you never otherwise would. Terrible things. Beware the darkness, Warrior Ull."

"Miki," Grim growled looking down at his youngest in shock. Her hand, the one with the Raptor's Eye, gripped his neck and for a moment he felt such power radiating from it that he thought it would burn him, and her eyes seemed to glow.

"What, Manno?" she asked, her voice once again full of innocence, her touch was cool, and her eyes were the beautiful amber of her mother's.

Grim's gaze went to Ull to demand what had just happened, only to find the Warrior closing the hatch of his shuttle.

"I should have brought cookies for Warrior Ull," Miki said, watching as the shuttle flew away. "He's not very happy."

"That is truth, little one." Grim's concerned gaze remained on the shuttle.

"Maybe Trisha's cookies will make him happy. They're the best."

THE PRINCE, THE PILOT, AND THE PUPPY

("Star Puppy") A novella in the Star Series

By
Susan Grant

Bestselling, award-winning author Susan Grant is a USAF veteran who loves writing romantic, action-packed stories featuring gutsy woman and honorable men.

http://www.susangrant.com/

PROLOGUE

Bezos Station, above the Colony of Barésh
Forty-three light-years from Earth.

Puppy

    I sit on the floor with Tall Ones towering all around me. My long pink tongue dangles as I pant. I'm excited but also a little nervous about what I'm about to do. I want to please the Tall Ones I love most. To be a "good girl". A pouch containing two rings rests against my front paws. A big white bow My Trysh tied around my neck almost blocks my view of it. Rornn, my other Tall One, made me practice countless times to get ready for today. "When it comes to Earth traditions, I am woefully inexperienced," he admitted during one of those sessions. "But I want the moment to be perfect for Trysh. All right, Puppy, one more time."

    Of course, I figured it out the first try. I'm a lot smarter than he thinks, and he already thinks I'm very smart. I can see and understand much more than the Tall Ones realize. I herded My Trysh and My Rornn here, didn't I? Not that they weren't destined to be each other's Forever Mates from the beginning. They just wandered away from the scent trail for a little while. They needed me to help steer them back to it.

    Sitting as straight as I can, I try to keep my tail from wagging too hard as I listen to Colonel Duarte's booming voice. He's the pack leader of Bezos Station

—"the commander" the Tall Ones call him. Every starpilot in my Tall Ones' squadron is here in the conference room. All wear blue-and-silver formal dress uniforms, including the bride.

"Lieutenant Milton," Colonel Duarte asks her, "will you have this man to be your husband, to live together in holy marriage? Will you love him, comfort him, honor, and keep him in sickness and in health, and forsaking all others, be faithful to him as long as you both shall live?"

"I will," My Trysh says, her fingers tightly woven with My Rornn's, her voice trembling a little.

My Trysh is a lot like me. Our early lives were hard, and we never knew our fathers. Her heart was broken by that and even though the pieces knitted back together, it too easily tore along the same old scars. Our mothers were worn down by hardship but still had the strength to love us more than anything. Yet sometimes it's those who pay us no mind, who won't acknowledge us no matter how hard we try, who won't care for us or love us the way we deserve to be loved and cared for, that we seem to focus on the most. That was the case with My Trysh. She wanted nothing more than her father's attention. So much so that she almost missed seeing true love when it was right in front of her nose. She was so focused on making a mistake with My Rornn that she almost let him go.

"Lieutenant B'lenne, will you have this woman to be your wife, to live together in holy marriage? Will you love her, comfort her, honor, and keep her in sickness and in health, and forsaking all others, be faithful to her as long as you both shall live?"

My Rornn swallows, nods, then lets out a deep breath. "I will."

He takes an extra moment to answer, not because he feels hesitant or needs to think things over before deciding on his answer, but because he feels so much joy and relief that it squeezes his throat. It was the way I felt the first day I met him and he held me close. He, too, was ignored by his father. But unlike My Trysh he wanted to be. Yes, King Laren loves him, but he wants to keep My Rornn close to the den when he has the brave, confident heart of adventurer. But when it came to communicating his love for My Trysh, My Rornn was like a dog that jumps when he should sit and barks when he should listen. To My Trysh, this made his feelings seem false. But luckily, I was there to help or he might have kept tripping over his own tongue and let My Trysh get away.

It grows quiet as the bride and groom seem to forget about everyone else. That tends to happen when they look into each other's eyes. They are warriors, trained for combat, and yet they can be overpowered by a shared gaze.

Colonel Duarte clears his throat.

"Yes, Sir." Rornn crouches on one knee and beckons to me. His smile is warm. "Puppy—bring the rings."

Puppy—that's me. My Tall Ones tried a few times to give me another name, a real name they said—Cocoa, Blackie, Kaylee, Lucky—but none stuck. It's okay. My mother called me Puppy and that's who I am. I'm a yipwag, but the Tall Ones consider me a species of canine. We're more intelligent and attuned to emotions than Earth-bred dogs; we can even read minds some say. My Trysh calls me an old soul.

On cue, I snatch the important pouch in my teeth and prance down the aisle formed by the legs of standing Tall Ones. Some smile and clap their hands, others coo, "Aw," and yet still others watch me with tears rolling down their faces. That's the thing with Tall Ones. They will cry from sadness and they will cry from happiness. They'll even cry when they can't figure out why. It is a mystery to me, but every day I learn more about them, and they about me.

My Rornn lifts me high in the air—he is very tall—and holds me tucked under one arm so he can slip the special ring on My Trysh's finger. Now her eyes are wet too. I stretch up to lick My Rornn's cheek then My Trysh's chin as she leans forward to rub my ears. There is so much happiness that my heart feels ready to take flight. My tail whips fast enough to have propelled me.

How we three arrived at this moment is my favorite story. Sit, stay, and you'll see how it all began…

ONE

Trysh

"Titan Squad, this is Station Control—we have multiple bogeys out of G quadrant!"

The frantic voice filled Lieutenant Trysh Milton's headset. A distress call. It came from the station, a giant, rotating city in space. It housed thousands of people inside—military personnel like her and their families. Children. She and her squadron had just cleared the area of enemy fighters. Giddy with victory after destroying a wave of alien invaders, they were exhausted, sweaty, pumped with adrenaline. But just when they had thought it was over, it wasn't.

"Titan Squad—we've got multiple bogeys! I repeat—multiple targets. They're coming from… My God—Encke Gap!"

From an opening in Saturn's rings? How? Plowing through the rings would get you killed in an instant. Trysh gripped the joystick of her starfighter, craning her neck to see if she could get a visual on the threat. Saturn was a creamy-yellow and orange globe surrounded by an ethereal halo. Those rings were nothing like they looked when viewed from a telescope on Earth. Up close, they were snowstorms of ice particles with eddies and whorls caused by tiny embedded moons, some moons as small as hailstones. Imagine—a moon you could hold in the palm of your hand! It was breathtaking, a scene she never grew tired of admiring…until the sight of enemy alien craft pouring out from a gap in the rings pulled the last of the air from her lungs.

The Dragaar! They had but one goal—destroy the space station and then Earth. In moments, the alien fighters were upon them, firing vivid streams of plasma at the defending starfighters.

Flying at her side, the *Vash* alien exchange officer, Prince Rornn B'lenne, call sign "Charming", sounded unfazed as they joined the dogfight. "Firefly," he said, using her call sign. "Go private." The starfighter-to-starfighter channel allowed them to speak to only each other. "They must have precision-jumped through the gap."

"It's some sort of pop-up wormhole," she answered. It left her with a sick feeling. If the Dragaar had the technology to punch holes in the fabric of space at will, it was game-over. Burst after bright burst caught her eye as friendlies were destroyed. Friends...squadron-mates, killed. "We've got to do something. We're getting our asses kicked."

"We must deny them their jump gate. Close it off."

"Wormholes can't be opened and closed like that."

"Do not forget—I can make the impossible possible."

She almost laughed. He used that same dumb line the last time he tried to get her to go out with him. His propositions were hilarious, and she shot every one of them down. It was a game—their game. They were friends with no benefits. But even she couldn't deny that Rornn had a brilliant tactical mind. He was scary smart with a fresh way of looking at things that she admired. If he had figured out a way to turn this battle around, she was all ears. "Talk to me, Charming!" She strafed a crippled Dragaar fighter. It blew up, followed by the enemy knocking off two more friendlies.

"I read a research paper on the intentional disruption of small wormholes." He targeted another Dragaar. The enemy fighter exploded in brilliant fireworks. They barely escaped the debris. "It concluded that it *is* scientifically possible."

"On paper. By scientists sitting at nice safe desks stringing together a daisy chain of equations. Even if we lobbed all our R-bombs through the gate, the best we can hope for is transient instability."

"Yes. The R-bombs. See? Your mind is perfection. One relativistic bomblet salvo coming up. Cover me, Firefly." He wheeled away from her and accelerated into the invasion.

"Wait!" *Shit.* "Charming!" She used to think that "Charming" was a fitting call sign for the alien prince. Now she was convinced "lunatic" was a better fit. He was the constant instigator, the devil-may-care hotshot; she was his goal-driven, play-by-the-rules best friend who couldn't help getting swept off her feet by the riptide of his charisma. But if he had figured out a way to turn the tide of this battle, she wanted in on it.

She transmitted their intentions on the common frequency and took off after Charming, guns blazing. The HUD—heads-up display—was filled with Dragaar fighters coming straight at them. It was like driving on the wrong side of the freeway, except the oncoming cars were shooting at you.

Ahead, the wormhole whirled and wobbled in the Gap, space distorting at its edges.

"Arming R-bombs. You are still covering me, Firefly?"

"Affirmative!"

"Excellent." He rolled his starfighter and dove for the jump gate.

Suddenly her screens lit up and her pulse tripled. "I've got two bogeys locked on—No...four." Four enemies had her in their crosshairs—four evil, heartless Dragaar targeting one human. A hollow feeling in her chest followed as alarms blared and lights flashed, her starfighter's systems warning her of what she already knew. She was dead unless she shook off her pursuers.

"Coming about," Rornn said.

"Negative! Negative! I've got this. Fire your R-bombs into the Gap." It might be their only shot at saving the station, and maybe Planet Earth. But Rornn ignored her. She could picture his pale golden eyes narrowed in determination, his lips peeled back over white perfect teeth as he sped to save her. But as soon as he got within range, the Dragaar turned on him.

Rornn managed to destroy a Dragaar fighter and she got two more before his starfighter was hit by the fourth. A dramatic spray of fluids erupted from his starfighter's shattered hull, freezing instantly. She watched his ship spinning out of control. Headed for the rings.

He was going to hit.

"*Rornn!*" she screamed. Then everything went dark.

"Okey dokey. I've seen enough," said a voice in a Texas accent over her headset. "It's Taco Tuesday, and I'm starving."

Their examiner's voice shattered the moment, the horrific, wrenching moment, and yanked Trysh back to reality. She pulled off her earpieces and VR goggles, tipping her head back against the headrest in the suddenly dim and quiet simulator pod. That did not go well. Not at all. Being evaluated in simulated missions was part of keeping flying skills sharp. The virtual-reality-enhanced scenarios concocted by the instructors were notoriously difficult, designed to test you in ways you never anticipated. She had been confident she would do well today, keeping her perfect record unblemished. But that was before she let her wingman talk her into a crazy stunt turned suicide mission. Not only had she likely earned a bad grade, she'd shrieked Charming's given name like a lovesick middle-schooler.

Rornn, I'm going to kill you—I swear it—this time for real.

It was complicated enough being the daughter of General Zeke Milton —war hero, fighter-pilot extraordinaire, and friend of presidents—without raising doubts about her having won this assignment flying starfighters for the First Space Wing on Bezos Station on her own merits. Competition for the slot had been fierce, but she'd earned the right to be here fair and square. The irony was people thinking she used her father's help to get ahead when he probably couldn't pick her out of a crowd. For all the attention the Milton name got her, she'd never met the man.

When she earned her flight wings she worked up the courage to contact him, hoping her achievement would give them something in common besides their DNA. She would finally be able to tell him how she wanted to follow in his footsteps. Then he would say how proud that made him, embracing her as his own. Two attempts yielded no response. He was the Chief of Off-World Security. Her attempts to reach him may have been blocked. Or, maybe his staff didn't pass along the message. It was harder to think of the third possibility: He didn't want the unplanned byproduct of a long-forgotten affair in his life.

Her sim pod settled on hydraulic-powered truncheons to ground level. It landed with a firm thump and a hiss of machinery. Throwing open the hatch, she climbed out of her pod as a second simulator settled to the floor. She pretended to be immersed in stowing gear in her locker when Rornn walked up to her. She caught the scent of his skin, the soap he used. He was the only man she knew who smelled this good sweaty. His nutmeg-colored hair was finger combed away from his forehead, and he wore the same blue, silver-trimmed Earth System Frontier Forces (ESFF) flight suit she did. But just as the rings of Saturn looked nothing like they did viewed through a telescope from Earth, the uniform was a wholly different garment on him. There was a reason flight suits were called "bags". They weren't designed to flatter. Except if you had a body like Rornn B'lenne's. Then all bets were off.

"That sucked," she muttered, zipping her headset in its pouch. "It really, really sucked."

"It was supposed to suck. I believe the scenario was weighted against us. No matter what we tried, it would fail. Perhaps it is to keep us from getting too confident."

"If that was the goal, they succeeded." The last terrible minutes of the battle kept replaying in her mind—Rornn in a death spiral, hurtling toward the rings in his broken starfighter, and there was nothing she could do to save him. Losing him for real would devastate her. "I'm just glad you're alive, okay?" she mumbled with a sideways glance. "That's all I have to say."

His gaze sparked with surprise and delight. "That's all you *need* to say." He leaned one shoulder against the wall, arms folding, his mouth kicking up into his trademark cocky smile. *Danger, danger.* Her mind had an annoying tendency to go blank when she met his golden eyes. Yeah, a blank mind and a chest filled with butterflies. Often, he could be found in Nimbus, the station's all-ranks club, enjoying his status as the station's most-eligible bachelor. Trysh was used to seeing him surrounded by women hanging on his every word. It was one more reason he belonged in the "friend zone". That way His Royal Hotness could go through women like locusts went through cornfields back home, and it wouldn't bother her a bit.

Nope. Not at all.

If ever a person lived in a state of denial, it was her.

"Have you heard the breaking news?" Rornn announced as other starpilots climbed wearily out of their simulator pods. "Trysh Milton is glad that I am alive."

"Seal it, Charming."

"You are upset with me," he said. "I can hear it in your voice."

"The Dragaar used me to lure you away from the jump gate. You came back for me."

"I would do so again and again." He sounded unrepentant.

"We were ordered to save the station at all cost. That was our mission. You were supposed to unload the R-bombs."

"I would never leave you in danger, Trysh."

At the sudden seriousness in his voice, the use of her first name, she glanced up. Her insides contracted at the raw look in his eyes. "Never," he repeated roughly, his golden eyes defiant.

Actual lives hadn't been at stake, but their grades were. Rornn was as devoted to doing well as she was, yet he had prioritized her over passing the evaluation. That was enough of a surprise. Now his expression revealed his actions were about much more than even that. It was about protecting her—in the virtual world *and* the real one—no matter what the cost.

She almost pulled him into a kiss. Whoa. *This* after going rogue with him on the Encke Gap mission? That was her problem with Rornn B'lenne. He made it too easy to abandon her common sense. Did he possess alien powers she didn't know about? Sometimes she wished that were true. It would explain her behavior around him because nothing else made sense. Like the crush she had on him that wouldn't quit.

Crush? Talk about denial. It was more than a crush, it had been more than that for a long time. But he was off-limits for anything but friendship. The reasons were obvious, or at least she kept telling herself that. She was a commoner. He was a royal prince. She was raised by a single mom barely scraping by on tip money. His father was a king and a trillionaire. When Rornn looked at Earth women he didn't see a romantic future; he saw his next hookup. *"It seemed like a fairy tale to a girl pouring coffee for a handsome flyboy in a small-town greasy spoon, but it wasn't,"* her mother cautioned her. *"I lived in a broken-down trailer with my grandpa. Zeke was military royalty. When he said I was sweet and refreshing and not like the rest, he wasn't saying forever. It was great while it lasted, but he was never going to settle for a girl like me. That's the difference between real life and Cinderella, sweet pea."* Exactly. Cinderella got the prince and a glass slipper. Mama got a DNA test, a man's name on a birth certificate, and a few guilt checks in the mail.

Trysh turned away to unfasten the last of the VR sensors from her uniform. "I was more than capable of handling those Dragaar."

"You are more than capable, yes. But I will always protect you above all else."

"That's not the way it works," she protested.

"That's the way *I* work. When we stop caring about each other as individuals, our galaxy is doomed."

She sighed. *Touché.* Who could argue with such a profound statement? "Your ancestry is showing again." His people, the *Vash Nadah*, saved civilization from certain destruction eleven thousand years ago. If not for them, the Eight Clans, of which Rornn's family was one, humanity could have become extinct. "You can't help yourself. Chivalry is in your DNA. You're an officer and gentleman to the core."

"An officer, yes." His cheek dimpled. "But not always a perfect gentleman."

The bad-boy heat in his eyes scorched her. She deflected it with laughter. "Half the women on the station would agree with that fact. The other half you haven't taken out yet."

With that, their conversation veered back to familiar territory.

He feigned outrage. "I will not listen to your insinuations that any females other than you interest me. You are an amazing woman. Why would I want anyone else?"

"I bet you tell all the girls they're amazing. Wait—you do."

"Rumors!"

"Sure they are," she said dryly.

"If I am guilty of such an offense, which is entirely possible, I do not recall it. What I do know is that I did not mean it in the way I mean it when I say it to you."

"So, there are varying degrees of amazing."

"Indeed. You are on the farthest end of the amazing spectrum. There is no room for anyone else on the other side."

She gave him an amused sideways look as she shoved her gloves in the locker. "So, I'm your one and only."

"Finally! You have come to your senses."

"I think anytime I let you rope me into conversations like this I've actually *lost* my senses." Her body tingled, warm all over. It had nothing to do with her still pumping, post-simulator adrenaline and everything to do with their banter. She and Rornn had both been honor graduates upon completion of flight training in Texas. Since arriving on Bezos, they just as passionately jockeyed to be "top gun". But even on a purely personal level, they competed. He relentlessly tried to get her to admit she wanted him while she continuously pretended she didn't. "I don't know why you waste your breath, Charming. I'm not your target audience."

"How'd your ride go, Rornn?" A pretty maintenance attendant with mountains of strawberry-blonde hair waved as she walked by with an armful of equipment. Her eyes twinkled from under thick, perfectly curled lashes while Trysh stood there, her lip tint long gone, her plain brown hair damp from perspiration and plastered to her head.

Rornn answered with a wink and jaunty thumbs-up. The attendant touched her finger to her lips and blew him a kiss.

Exactly the kind of target I'm talking about. Trysh slammed her locker shut and started walking away. "I need tacos."

He caught up to her in a couple of long strides. "Allow me to buy you a real lunch up on the observation level. We will talk without interruption about how glad you are that I am alive."

She held up her index finger. "*Was* glad."

"We can visit that restaurant you want to try, the new one overlooking the Terra-park."

He remembered she said that? "Moon Shot? We'd need reservations, and—"

"Reservations are not needed for lunch."

"It's way too fancy and expensive for just lunch."

"Are you not worth it? To be pampered and pleasured—"

"Charming..." she warned.

He raised his hands in the air. "Friend zone. I know this. I will abide by it. Albeit sadly." Only he could make the term "friend zone" sound so endearing. Basic was the official language of the Federation. Fluency was mandatory for getting any position in the Space Forces. But on Bezos, English was used. Rornn spoke his own version, sounding a little Scottish (smooth and lyrical), a little *Vash Nadah* (oozing with privilege), with more slang words mixed in than the *Urban Dictionary*.

He pulled his flight cap out of his flightsuit leg pocket and snapped it against his open palm. Then he waited for her to exit first through the hatch into the simulated sunshine of Deck Five. At the same instant, as if they were still flying in formation, they slipped on their flight caps and sunglasses. By order of the commander, the common area was treated as if it were truly outdoors. Sometimes she could almost believe that it was. At least she knew what a real sky looked like, unlike those poor people who lived under the dome down on the surface of Barésh, the impoverished frontier mining colony that Bezos Station supervised. The people there lived and died without ever experiencing what she and the rest of the Earth personnel used to take for granted.

"If not lunch at Moon Shot, what about dinner?" Rornn asked. "Then afterward, we can go to my most favorite of spots—the observation cone." She knew he loved to sneak up there. He called it his sanctuary, his place to think. It was a restricted area, but that didn't seem to stop him—or trying to talk her into coming with him. For Rornn, rules were meant to be broken—or at least stretched severely. "We will sit and gaze out at the infinite stars," he said. "You will make your wishes, and I will grant them, one by delicious one…"

"Charming!" She couldn't help laughing. "You're such a—"

"Alien *monster*!" Shouts and chanting drew their attention to a large screen displaying news programming from home. "Earth first!" protestors shouted. "Go home! Go home!" If they could wall off Earth from the rest of the galaxy, they would. Despite everything the *Vash* Federation had given them—like cures for diseases, including cancer, which would have saved her mother's life, and the ability to travel at faster-than-light speed all over the galaxy—Earth First hated them. Hatred that ran so deep that that Earth First terrorists destroyed Glenn-Musk Station, Earth's pride and joy—their first home-built, galaxy-class space station. Hundreds of civilians and military were killed in the terror attack. When Earth First claimed responsibility for the bombing, it shocked many. Most thought the anti-alien movement was fading. But the senseless attack on the space station seemed to have emboldened the group. The Federation kindly gave Earth a replacement, an even bigger and better home in space. Bezos Station.

Bristling with weapons, a group of Interplanetary Space Marines the size of mountains carried to-go boxes out of the mess hall. Many others like them patrolled the station and down on the surface of Barésh, where there they manned a forward operating base, helping to protect both the local populace and a Doctors Without Borders group that set up shop to provide aid until permanent medical care arrived. Baréshtis were wild, unpredictable, with a moral code that defied logic, but they had welcomed Earth with open arms. They were the polar opposites of Earth First sympathizers.

"Monsters go home!" the protestors chanted. "Earth first! Earth first!"

A group of men stood watching the big screen. They wore baggy gray jumpsuits and tool belts. Cargo rats. Civilian contractors assigned to the supply squadron. "ET, don't phone home—*go* home," one of them joked, causing the rest of the group to snicker. "Frikken' bug zappers."

"Bug" was an extremely derogatory term for the *Vash*. A reference to the old belief that aliens were wide-eyed and green like bugs. Seeing Rornn walk past, one of the men elbowed a buddy. Then the entire group turned to look. Even though Rornn wore an ESFF starpilot uniform, his height, tawny skin tone, nutmeg-brown hair, and pale golden eyes marked him as a *Vash Nadah*, one of only a few serving aboard Bezos.

Trysh took Rornn by the elbow and urged him to walk faster toward the mess hall. "Let's go."

"I do not mind," he said. "They have the right to express their opinion."

Earth First, maybe. But the men who gave her pause were forty-three light-years closer and in the position to express a lot more than their opinion.

TWO

Rornn

He couldn't help smiling at the fierce way Trysh gripped his arm as they passed a group of surly cargo handlers. He could more than defend himself against such misguided souls, but if their behavior resulted in Trysh's hands on him, well, he intended to enjoy every minute.

It wasn't the first time he had experienced resistance to his presence on Bezos Station and it would not be the last, but he had learned to ignore it. Some had even disagreed with his selection to attend ESFF starpilot training in Texas too. "He's stealing an Earth officer's slot," they said. "He fucking bought his way in. He's rich enough." Several classmates jumped him one night in Texas, looking for blood. He defused the situation before anyone got hurt. He vowed that if he was to change anyone's minds about the *Vash*, it would be on the strength of his character and performance, not with his fists.

I sound more like my father every day, he thought with some dismay. The king was a staunch pacifist. It wasn't just the B'lennes who were anti-war; the entire Federation was famously averse to conflict. They went eleven thousand standard years between wars. It took Earth stepping into the picture to convince them to fight their first war in millennia, but it was a necessary war, defeating a sadistic cult leader. Inspired by the stories of bravery and battle, Rornn left home to seek a commission in the ESF Forces and become a starpilot—much to his clan's chagrin. They would prefer that he spent his days hanging out at the palace on S'aharr, their homeworld of scorching sands, attending dinners, being fitted for new outfits, making small talk with beautiful women who did not interest him, and perfecting his bajha game. He did not expect his Earth friends to have sympathy for his upbringing. But he was glad to be free of it. It was a luxurious cage, but a cage nonetheless.

"They let you go only because they think it will help get this quirky desire out of your system," his eldest brother, the crown prince, had told him. Keirr and the entire family fully expected him to return to the palace after his "little adventure".

Talk about misguided.

Luckily, as neither the heir nor the spare to the throne, he enjoyed options his two elder brothers didn't have. Becoming a starpilot was the realization of his dearest dream. Only he never anticipated he would live that dream in the company of Trysh Milton, far and away the most fascinating woman he had ever met. She was bold, bright, beautiful. She challenged and stimulated him on every conceivable level—intellectually, emotionally, physically—in the cockpit and out. It was unexpected and exhilarating. She also supported him. Of all his friends, she was the one who was always there. Their saucy banter left him feeling more alive than he ever thought possible—it was also one hell of a turn-on, as his Earth friends would say. Alas, the moment they entered the mess hall, she released him.

"You do not have to let go," he said and offered her his arm. Yanking off her cap and sunglasses, she gave him a sarcastic look and walked away, her sights set on the serving line, her ponytail swinging. His hand twitched with his urge to wind that length of hair around his fist to steer her mouth to his.

What a woman. He marveled at her as she selected a tray and eagerly accepted a plate of tacos. If only she would direct that kind of open and unfettered hunger at him. He wanted to feel her, to taste her, to hear her moan as he moved inside her. As a people, the *Vash* were not prudes. In his culture, sexuality was celebrated, often with religious zeal. But, Great Mother, with Trysh he had not come close to a simple kiss. He was used to being the best at most things he attempted, at getting any woman he wanted, but she was immune to his charms. She only had to aim her blue eyes in his direction to make him weak in the knees. But not so weak that he would let her pluck top-gun honors from his grasp again this quarter. No, not without a fight. Well, a small struggle anyway. He may have studied Earth customs with far more vigor than he did his flight manuals, but when it came to winning over a woman he really wanted he was clueless. In his culture, mates were prearranged. Luckily, as a third-born son, he was safe from having to ascend to the throne. It saved him from having to be promised to anyone, leaving him free to seek his own choices.

Trysh Milton was his choice.

But he was stuck in the dreaded "friend zone" with no way out.

"You've got that look again, my man."

Rornn turned to his good friend Declan—call sign Danger—who joined him going through the food line. Not everyone in the squadron was willing to be his friend, but what bonds of friendship he had forged were strong. Earth men like Danger were as honorable and loyal as any *Vash Nadah*. "Look?"

"I can't explain it, Charming, but you're wearing it. If you want her, go after her."

"Trysh, you mean."

Danger groaned. "Who else? Women fall at your feet, but you don't take any of them out. Not anymore. Not even for a fuck. All you do is make goo-goo eyes at Firefly."

Goo-goo eyes. Just when he thought he had all the slang words committed to memory, new ones were thrown at him. "I don't want those women. I want her."

"Then go for it. What are you waiting for? Tell her how you feel."

"I *do* tell her how I feel. Every blasted day. It does nothing."

"Then your transmissions are coming through garbled, buddy. If you want her, if you want your message to come through loud and clear, don't tell her—s*how* her how you feel. Before it's too late. She hasn't found Mr. Right yet, but she will."

Like Dr. Leonardo Treat. The man was his most recent competition for Trysh's heart. The night she went to dinner with him was one of the longest of Rornn's life. Treat—the name alone had struck fear in his gut. He was consumed with dread when she messaged him afterward to meet her in Nimbus. Rornn pretended to be sympathetic as she confessed to feeling no chemistry with the doctor. Although he was "very nice", in her words, she wouldn't go out with him again. Hurrah! It took everything he had not to openly gloat. She was still his—even though she didn't realize it.

Not yet.

"Charming. Pay attention. This is the frontier. Minutes matter, dude. When it comes to women, if you snooze, you lose."

Rornn nodded and watched her carry a tray to a table occupied by their squadron mates. Their eyes met. *Show her how you feel.* He flashed her a grin, giving her the same thumbs-up and wink he used to greet the simulator attendant, whatever her name was. Annie? Fannie? Trysh's reaction was a world apart. Her gaze turned frosty as she sat down to eat.

Rornn exhaled.

"But, more importantly, Charming, this is Taco Tuesday. Let us say thanks for the best tacos in the ESFF." Danger crossed himself then held up three fingers at the food server, indicating he wanted three tacos. The crumbled meat used for the dish had a distinct, piquant aroma. Tex-Mex, it was called. Doused in hot sauce, tacos were heaven on a plate. Nothing like them had ever been served in the palace, which made it taste even better. The more unlike home something was, the more Rornn desired it. Trysh Milton topped the list.

He turned to the server and held up four fingers.

Puppy

They took her brothers and sisters away first. "Not that one—leave it. It's the runt," the voice of a Tall One said. "Too skinny. Not good eatin'."

Another voice growled, "It's doing nothing more than taking milk. The sooner the dam is weaned, the sooner she can be bred. This is a money-making operation, not a pet store. Get rid of it."

Blissfully unaware of how her life was about to change, Puppy suckled, warmed by her mother's soft belly. For once she didn't need to compete with her stronger, bigger littermates that always pushed her away before she could eat her fill. Her world was perfect in that moment. Just warmth, milk, and her mother's gently stroking tongue. Her belly filled and drowsiness soon overtook her constant, frantic hunger...

Grabbed by the scruff of the neck, she was back in the cold, dangling high above the ground. Alarmed, she barked at the top of her lungs.

"Shut that thing up!"

"I got to fill a bucket before I can drown it."

"It's so small just stomp on it!"

"Who's gonna clean up the mess when I do—you, Yeesa?"

"Ya calling me lazy, you worthless piece of slag? Wring its neck then."

"Then bring me a bag, woman, because wringin' their necks is messy too."

"What do ya think we are—rich cogs from the compound? I ain't gonna waste no bag on a runt!"

Puppy kept crying as the Tall Ones argued. The thin skin at her nape was pinched too hard, hurting her. Then there was a thunderous sound, water hitting something hollow and hard. Puppy jolted in terror, crying louder.

Soon all the Others were barking in their cages.

"Shut that craggin' thing up, I said! It's got them all riled up. It'll turn the taste of the meat."

Puppy was dropped into icy-cold water. She managed to catch the rim of the bucket with her front paws before her head went under, her rear claws raking the slick sides. Then the bucket tipped over, spilling the water and her into the street. To the sound of the Tall Ones yelling she ran away as fast as she could.

There were Others like her in the winding alleyways, their scents unfamiliar, sharp with desperation and aggression. They chased her away from the alluring stench of trash with snarls and bared teeth. Weakening, shivering, longing for her mother, she darted from shadow to shadow. Something inside her, a voice without a sound, urged her not to lie down and give up. *Keep going. If you do, you will find your way home.* Puppy took shelter under one of the Tall Ones' boxes-that-moved. It had a low, close ceiling, and radiated heat, which comforted her. She drowsed…

A commotion jolted her from a stupor and she was no longer alone. A yipwag pup larger than she was crowded into the space next to her, a piece of meat dangling from his jaws. The aroma filled her senses. She trembled, whimpering, her hunger awakening, overwhelming. Rising on wobbly legs, her heartbeat so fast, too fast, she inched toward the visitor, her tail tucking between her hindquarters. Their eyes met. *He is like me. Lost and alone.*

With his nose, the puppy pushed a tidbit of meat toward her—

BANG BANG! Two loud booms shook the box. The pups bolted for safety.

In an instant, Puppy lost her new friend in the maze of Tall Ones' legs. She ran and ran until her little body was ready to give out. Using the last of her strength, she chose an open crate, one of many like it in a land of crates and boxes, and squeezed into the farthest corner.

But Tall Ones entered her hiding place. "This is all I could get this time. It's packed inside the med kits. After this, I don't know if I can do it anymore. Bones is getting suspicious."

"This should be enough. You kept the material separated? It's unstable if it's mixed."

"I did, I did. What do you think? I don't want the shuttle going bang."

Something heavy scraped over the floor. A sharp odor tickled Puppy's nose and she sneezed.

The Tall Ones went silent. The smell of fear and sweat was strong and distinct.

Something rammed into the space where she hid, barely missing her. A long rod. It rooted around then came slamming down. Too close. She darted away and yelped.

"It's a street dog! Jaysus. Scared the living daylights out of me. I thought the gig was up."

"Shoo! Go! Get out of here!" Puppy felt the breeze of the stick the Tall One was using to try to hit her. *Wham. Wham.* She bolted from the crate and ran, looking for another place to hide. So many crates. She dove into a large one that smelled better than the rest. Quivering, she crammed into a narrow space between round containers stored inside it.

Pain radiated from her hindquarters. Bright light burst behind her eyes with each rapid beat of her heart. She quivered, curling into a ball, almost unable to keep a whimper from escaping her throat. But the last time she made a noise, the Tall Ones tried to hit her with a stick.

The entrance to her shelter slammed shut. In the darkness, Puppy trembled as her shelter swayed and seemed to lift off the ground. There was a terrifying noise and shaking, then it subsided, replaced by a gentle swaying, a low rumbling. Her ears felt stuffy.

Then she floated off the floor.

Wonder took precedence over fear. She bobbed and bounced along the walls and ceilings of the dark, cavernous space. A delicious smell made her forget the pain in her hind leg. She pushed away from the wall to follow the scent to its source, grabbing hold of a small box with her teeth and claws lest she float away again. Glancing around for Others who would steal her prize and maim or kill her, she decided she was still alone. Frantically, she peeled off the outer covering, ripping apart the casing under that, and sank her muzzle into a warm, crumbly mess that tasted of the sweetness of her mother's milk and the savory richness of fat. It was almost too sweet, too sticky, but food meant survival. Half-choking in her frenzy to eat, awash in a swirling cloud of torn paper and crumbs, she wolfed it down.

A jerking movement knocked her loose. She dropped, hitting the floor with the remains of her meal. The den swung wildly, throwing her around. She slid across the floor and smacked into containers, hurting her ribs. Then, with a powerful boom, the crate went still. Her lungs heaved, her body hurting. She could hear the voices and footsteps of Tall Ones. Crumbs dangled from her whiskers, her nose was sticky. Bright light hurt her eyes as the entrance banged open. Faces of Tall Ones peered in. "Sarg! Sergeant Spratt! We got a hitchhiker!"

"A *what*?" Feet stomped closer.

"A stowaway. And…uh…it got into that pie you said your nurse friend was sending up."

"What! Someone got into *my* pie?" yelled the raspy voice.

"Some*thing*. It's one of those yipwags from the colony, Sarg. A street dog. A puppy."

"I want it boxed up and back out on the fourteen-hundred shuttle run! Cripes. Now it's peeing!"

More Tall Ones clustered around the opening. A faint but familiar sharp odor wafted past. Puppy wrinkled her nose and let out a double sneeze. The Tall One with the stick had smelled the same way. A bad smell. A growl began deep in her throat.

"Looks like it doesn't like us, boss."

"It ate my pie! It'll be damn lucky if *I* don't eat *it*!"

Puppy darted between their legs. The floor was slippery. She skidded as she wove between the Tall Ones' legs. Some yelled; others reached for her. She felt their fingers raking down her back as they tried to catch her; one even tried to snatch her by the tail. The thought of being thrown back in the bucket of cold, deep water gave her the speed she needed to escape her growing pack of pursuers. Ahead loomed something odd, shiny, and hard that the Tall Ones climbed and descended. Up there—she had to go. She put one paw on the step, then jerked it back in fear. But her pursuers were growing ever closer, their footsteps thundering. She leaped up to the first step, her back legs peddling. She managed to climb to the next step when hands closed around her stomach and snatched her off her feet.

Rornn

"Ask them about the sim," Danger told Trysh's good friend, Carlynn—call sign "Mooch"—as they ate lunch. "They tried to wreck the Dragaar's wormhole. Almost did."

"Seriously?" Carlynn leaned forward eagerly, her dark eyes shining. "Whose crazy-ass idea was that?"

"His," Trysh answered at the same time Rornn said, "Hers."

"That's a negative, Charming," Trysh shot back. "You went off road."

"You went with me."

"Yep. I sure did. When will I learn?" Trysh's glance left him feeling as if he had gotten seared by the hot end of a plasma launcher. He did not like to upset her, but, oh, her passion!

She snatched a bottle of hot sauce from his hand and shook some onto her tacos. "The examiner didn't even stay around to talk to us. I take that as a bad sign."

"*Au contraire*, my dear Trysh. He said he was starving for tacos." Rornn lifted a taco to his mouth and took a hearty bite. "They *are* good."

"Since when do you speak French?" Carlynn asked.

"I am a man of many talents. If you doubt me, ask Firefly."

Trysh rolled her eyes. "So much for ever having a serious conversation with you."

"I am being serious." He tried to sound contrite. "I think they programmed the scenario so that we cannot win. No one could." He spied their examiner, Major Bud Yarnell, getting up from his table, a toothpick sticking out from his mouth. "There he is now, our examiner." Rornn waved, and Trysh glared at him.

"Don't make it worse," she warned.

Yarnell walked over to the table and greeted them. He was a forthright fellow who had been a test pilot for atmospheric craft on Earth before taking the assignment to Bezos. Trysh and Rornn jumped to their feet. "At ease, everyone," he told the rest of the group at the table before eying him and Trysh as if hunting for the right words to say.

A twang of tension. Rornn could feel it in Trysh, and in him. Was it to be bad news? Perhaps Trysh was right after all, his actions in the simulator had cost them. Returning for her, abandoning the mission, he might have earned them a grade of Unsatisfactory, a U, the infamous "hook". It would sink not only his shot at top-gun honors this quarter but hers as well. True, that there could only be room for one at the top. Something they rarely talked about. He didn't want her to lose her dreams of career advancement. Nor did he wish to lose his. It was a real pickle when it came to competing for the same prize. Sometimes he wondered if they loved the competing more than the prize. But then he would see a certain intensity in her to win, a desperation, hinting that her desire to excel was more than just that.

The desire to please her father. She did not say it, but he knew it all the same.

Major Yarnell twirled his toothpick. "What the hell is wrong with you two?"

Rornn stood straighter. "I can explain, Sir. I advocated for something that was not in our orders. But Lieutenant Milton, she—"

"I did my best to provide the support he needed to complete the attack," Trysh put in. "I failed to adequately do so."

"I did not inform her I was aborting the mission," Rornn said.

"I take full responsibility," they stated at the same instant.

They exchanged glances. *No, I do*, Rornn tried to say with his eyes.

No, I do, she scowled back silently.

"The blame lies with me," Rornn insisted. "I accept the consequences of my decision. I chose to return for Trysh—Lieutenant Milton—over completing the mission."

I would do so again and again.

Twirling his toothpick with two fingers, their examiner wore a ghost of a smile on his face. "Both of you look ready to piss your pants." He shook his head. "No one lives through Encke Gap, so get the hell over that part. Colonel Amanpour never wants to discourage his flyers from thinking outside the box. Even if sometimes it isn't the right box. Keep giving this mission your all. Yes, you passed the ride. In my quarters, I have a plaque on my wall; it reads, *Never tell people how to do things. Tell them what to do and they will surprise you with their ingenuity.* Seeing that General George S. Patton was a good friend of your great-grandfather, Lieutenant Milton, I suggest you take the advice to heart. I have no further debrief. You covered it all. Now get the hell back to your lunch."

"Yes, Sir!"

They sat back down to finish their meal while enduring relentless teasing from the rest of the starpilots, who had overheard every word.

Rornn accepted it all quite happily, relieved the tension between him and Trysh had dissipated. "Now we have the perfect reason to try Moon Shot for dinner, Firefly. To celebrate that we are not being sent to the Mojave Desert to operate unmanned research drones," he joked.

"Moon Shot?" Carlynn asked, suddenly intrigued. "The two of you—alone?"

Trysh stabbed at the ice in her tea with a spoon. A flicker of discomfort in her face vanished before he could make sense of it. "Me, Rornn, and his many girlfriends."

"There are no girlfriends," Rornn argued. "One *or* many."

"There actually aren't any," Danger put in.

Trysh lifted a brow. "Tell the journalists that. The two he was charming the other night in Nimbus."

"They were guests of our station. I simply wanted them to feel at home." Rornn helplessly observed Trysh's disbelieving smirk behind her glass as she took a sip.

The entire group got up to dispose of their trays before heading back to the hangar.

Carlynn elbowed Trysh. "Heads up, Trysh. There's that new guy. The one who's interested in you."

Rornn froze. *Interested* in her? A klaxon went off inside him. This was far more of a dire situation than hooking a simulator ride. As the newcomer turned and waved, there was just enough pink coloring Trysh's cheeks and interest in her wide blue eyes to spell out an ominous warning. This rival was poised to make inroads where Rornn had so far been forbidden to enter—her heart.

———

Trysh

The new commander of the supply squadron had black hair and a wide friendly face. A nice-looking hand curved around a paper to-go cup of coffee. At this distance, she couldn't read his badge. What was his name again? Levi? Landon? Leonardo. Wait—no. Leonardo was the surgeon with the Doctors Without Borders outfit down on the surface of Barésh, her most recent attempt at finding a guy to help stamp out her unrequited, will-never-go-anywhere feelings for a *Vash* prince. When she met up with Rornn afterward to share the scant details, it hit her that two hours in the doctor's company didn't come close to only five minutes with him.

Jake, she thought. Jake Friedman. Possibly Freeling. "Hey, Jake," she called to him. "Have you settled in yet?"

"Jack," he supplied with a faint flicker of disappointment. "Jack Freeman. But, yeah, I'm good. Talk about being thrown into the fire though. It's my first squadron commander gig and first time in space. Luckily, Spratt, my sergeant, is keeping me sane."

"Box Cutter!" her eavesdropping squad mates called out. There was no such thing as privacy in a fighter squadron.

Sergeant Spratt, the cargo master, aka the cargo rat wrangler, was fast to complain to the shuttle pilots if there was damage to the cargo, as if they were the cause of it. "You hotshots are the bulls in *my* china shop," he would bellow. He was seeing a nurse attached to Doctors Without Borders. It was hard to imagine such a grump had any romantic tendencies but supposedly they were an item.

"Box cutter?" Jack asked.

"We call Spratt 'Box Cutter'. It's his unofficial call sign."

Jack's brown eyes crinkled. "Sarg tells me you're General Milton's daughter. I had no idea. I heard him give a speech once. Very inspiring. He must be pretty proud of you. A chip off the old block."

Her cheek twitched as if someone snapped her skin with a rubber band. He'd touched a chord, exposing her weak spot, a yearning to win her father's attention that never ceased. She sensed Rornn's perceptive gaze on her. He was the only person who knew the truth.

When General Milton didn't attend their graduation ceremony at the end of starpilot training, he'd demanded to know why. "When was the last time you saw him, Firefly?" He'd folded his arms, lifted a brow, and waited for her answer. She told him early in their friendship that her mother died of cancer before First Contact, before the *Vash* arrived and could have saved her. But until General Milton was a no-show at graduation, all she ever shared about her father was that they weren't close.

"When, Trysh?"

But, Zeke. Don't you want to see her? "I saw him once. When I was four years old." For the first time, she had shared the story of her father's refusal to leave his new family to see her, how he turned his back on her and Mama and walked away. "He's never seen me, outside of photos. If he ever looked at any. I wouldn't know." She shrugged.

Rornn had looked horrified. Family was so important to the *Vash Nadah* that it was part of their religion. It came before everything else in their culture. This would be incomprehensible to him, she supposed. "And you have never told me this, why?" he had asked.

"My father acts like I don't exist. That's not the kind of thing you want to tell many people."

"I am not 'many people'. Trysh." He had looked so angry. No—not angry. Hurt.

"He dated my mother while he was in Nebraska for flight training, but they broke up before I was born. She raised me alone."

"General Milton is a baby daddy."

She had almost laughed at the way "baby daddy" sounded in his accent, and to hear the slang phrase applied to legendary General Zeke Milton, Chief of Off-World Security, but Mr. Urban Dictionary looked so intense that she squelched her reaction. "He agreed to a DNA test, so I know I'm legally his."

"If I may be so bold, I have to say General Milton is not the man I thought he was." He gestured to her. "Here is this highly accomplished woman, his flesh and blood, and he cannot even take a few moments to show his pride in her."

Her heart had swelled with his compliment and his willingness to come to her defense. But he still didn't grasp the situation. "Zeke Milton is from a famous military family—a long line of heroes that go all the way back to the American Revolution. He comes from money. The best schools. A stellar reputation. My mother's family barely scraped by. She never even graduated high school. Then she gets pregnant out of wedlock at eighteen years old. Class differences, Charming. It was never going to work. Poor Mama. She really believed Zeke was going to be her happy ending. That's not his fault, is it? It's not what he signed up for. He did the right thing— he sent some money. There's no law that says he's required to be a father in anything but name only, Charming."

"Decency requires no law." His outrage had faded some, but his disappointment was still sharp.

Trysh dropped back to the present. She had been lost in thoughts of Rornn and that old conversation while Jack chatted with her. She winced, realizing she hadn't heard half of what he'd said. Charming kept sending Jack mistrusting looks as he walked next to her. Jack kept eyeing Rornn. She could sense some sort of competition thing zinging between them. Rornn had certainly never hesitated to "plow the field" on the station; why should she live a nunlike existence just because she was obsessed with her best friend?

Obsessed with, not in love with. If she kept telling herself that, it might eventually stick.

She turned back to Jack and gave him her sweetest smile. Maybe if she tried harder, Jack Freeman would grow on her over time.

A loud crying pierced the chow hall hubbub. It sounded like a crying animal.

"Hey, Captain Freeman!" one of the cargo rats bellowed. "We got ourselves a runaway stowaway!"

Rornn

"It's a puppy!" voices cried out. The crowd in the mess hall surged toward the commotion.

"Oooh. I want to see," Trysh said. "Two things I'll never turn down—a homemade brownie and the chance to hold a puppy."

These were the things Trysh desired most? An Earth confection called a brownie and a puppy?

Rornn blinked at her as she angled toward where one of the cargo rats wrestled with what looked like a puff of black-brown fur. He could not fathom how such an ear-piercing sound could come from a creature so small. It was barely larger than the size of two fists held end to end. It had a mottled dark brown coat, huge black eyes and upright ears.

It was a cute little thing.

But the noise it made… It was an unholy, ear-splitting screeching.

"Do you want to carry it down to the docks?" Jack said, hurrying after Trysh. "I'll catch it, calm it down, and you can cuddle it all you want."

Rornn narrowed his eyes. This man, Jack Freeman, was an opportunist and an interloper. The way Trysh had reacted to his clumsy probing about her father had caused Rornn's protective instincts to surge. Rornn knew that Trysh hid the pain of General Milton's rejection deep inside her. Under all her confidence, beneath all her fighter pilot swagger, it was a tight little ball of shame she concealed from everyone except Rornn. No man would ever understand her as he did. Or love her as he could.

Yes, love. He'd been a fool not to have admitted it to himself sooner. He would be even more the fool to allow her to waltz away into this other man's life without a fight. A man who would never be the mate she deserved.

Carlynn laughed. "If you could see your face."

Rornn frowned at her. "What does this Jack Freeman have that I do not?"

"A puppy?" Danger offered.

Rornn groaned. Earth people had a famous fondness for their domestic creatures. Pets—their felines and canines. Feathered beasts too. Even fish. There were no pets in residence at the palace—unless one considered the cranky, genetically engineered pink-feathered Arkeets pets, which he certainly did not. Able to pose, wings spread, on perches for hours on end, they were used for decoration. When he was a little boy, he tried petting one and it nearly bit off his finger.

Now Jack Freeman had leaped in while Rornn was "snoozing" to fulfill this unanticipated need of Trysh's. The need to hold a pet.

"She's got it bad, Charming," Carlynn said. "The feels. She keeps quiet about it, but it's right there. You can't miss it. But I guess you did."

"She has only just met him!" he protested.

"Not Jack, you goof." Carlynn laughed. "You! She's smitten. Or haven't you noticed?"

"Smitten…with me?" This was the best news imaginable. Yet, she had gone off with *him*. She made her choice. He would endeavor to unmake it.

I will win you back, Firefly. Rornn's hopes surged as the bracing promise of a new competition overtook him. He started forward.

Danger warned, "Wait, Charming, remember what I told you—"

"Minutes matter, my friend." Rornn set his jaw and strode off in the direction of the chaos.

THREE

Puppy

Yelping, Puppy struggled in the grip of a Tall One that carried the faint odor that made her sneeze in the crate she escaped earlier. The same smell as the Tall One that chased her and tried to hit her with a stick. She snarled in this one's grasp, but it only caused all the Tall Ones gathering around to laugh. Unwelcome hands from all angles stroked over her body. Instinct told her to keep fighting.

The Tall One who held her handed her to another. She used the opportunity to wrestle free. The yells of other Tall Ones boomed in her ears as she hit the ground running. Darting between their milling legs, in a strange place that smelled intoxicatingly like food, she ran, following her insistent inner voice that urged her not to stop. Not to give up.

I am not yet home.

Rornn

Jack, the cargo rat, an MP, and a hulking Space Marine chased the fleeing puppy through the mess hall. Personnel stood on tables to better watch the show. Although there was a K-9 facility on Bezos, no Earth dogs had arrived on-station yet. Studies were still being done to determine if they would be able to adapt to the variable gravity. But this was a street dog from the colony—a "yipwag" in the local dialect. And it didn't sound happy to be here in the least.

More cargo handlers from the supply squadron arrived in the mess hall, accompanied by Sergeant Spratt, whose barrel chest heaved as he joined the chase. "Doctors Without Common Sense," he complained for all to hear. "They won't listen, won't stop feeding the damn strays. Then I have to deal with an infestation in my cargo!"

A cargo handler laughed. "They eat them down in the colony, Sarg. The Baréshtis. Listening to this one screech, I can see why! Nom, nom!"

Trysh's focus veered to the man and her expression turned downright deadly. "If he touches that puppy—"

"He will not. I will see to that." Rornn recognized him as one of the members of the group cracking jokes while watching the Earth First protest. Alone, the cargo rat avoided Rornn's eyes, which did not surprise him. Cowards were usually always more cowardly alone.

Jack careened past them and lunged for the runaway. "Come to daddy." He scooped it off the floor and hugged it to his stomach. Rornn felt a strange sense of impending loss when the puppy's cries ceased in Jack's grip and Trysh's expression changed to one of rapture. He could feel her slipping away from him. But a second later, a dark stain appeared down the front of the man's gray uniform and the puppy resumed its piercing yelping, its entire body convulsing with the effort.

Jack thrust the dripping puppy to arm's length. "Great. Just great. It peed on me."

Rornn smothered a laugh. The puppy's huge panicked eyes shifted to him. Why did something in those expressive eyes hint that the act of urination had been intentional? *It seems we are on the same side.*

"Allow me." Rornn had never held a puppy in his life. As he reached for the barking little creature, he glimpsed tiny, needlelike teeth, a small pink tongue. The peculiar and foul odor of the Barésh Colony wafted from its patchy coat as he cupped his hands around its body. There was no soft, rounded belly like those of the Earth puppies he had glimpsed in Texas. Sharp bones poked out from under loose skin. He could feel every internal organ. This tiny, impossibly fragile thing was near starvation. At first, his motivation had been to impress Trysh, to compete with Jack for her affections, but all that drained away upon feeling the yipwag's terror. Gently, he held her little body against his chest, sensing she would want to feel the beating of another living thing's heart. He knew he would. "You are safe with me. I will not let anything happen to you. You are home." He knew not where that last sentiment came from, but, somehow, he felt it in his soul. The puppy trembled so hard he felt the vibrations go up his arms. Then, after a few seconds, the trembles eased.

Then there was silence.

"Holy shit," the Marine said. "Did it die?"

"That or my eardrums are permanently damaged," growled the MP.

For a terrifying instant Rornn thought he had killed it. But the puppy made a few soft grunting sounds as she rooted around with her nose. Something inside him melted as she placed one impossibly small paw over his heart. Rornn grinned at the surprised people around him, skipping over Jack to wink at Trysh, who watched him with the kind of gaze he had waited to see since the day he first met her. His grin grew even wider. "They don't call me Charming for nothing."

Trysh

Trysh spent the rest of the day taking turns with Rornn looking after the puppy in the K-9 center, leaving only when they had to be in the hangar for official duties. "You're trading away flying to make time to pet-sit?" their squadron commander, Colonel Amanpour, had asked, tugging on his earlobe as if his hearing had malfunctioned when she requested permission to swap her next shuttle run with Carlynn's. Rornn had done the same with Danger. "Isn't this the culprit that ate Box Cutter's pie?"

"I don't think she'll ever get back in his good graces, Sir, but maybe she'll help with security one day down at the docks. She won conditional acceptance into the K-9 training program. She'll need to get a little stronger before it's official. I always heard that yipwags are unbelievably smart, but you have to see it to believe it, Sir. She looks me in the eye, and it feels like there's someone home in there. A little person. It's crazy, and she's just a baby."

Amanpour had gaped at her. His bristly silver hair gleamed in an old-school, what-used-to-be Marine Corps "high and tight" style, not a clipped strand out of place. Where he would have once worn U.S. Marine Corps emblems on his uniform, Earth System Frontier Forces pins gleamed, matched by his piercing blue eyes. As the commander of the Mighty Titans Starfighter Squadron, he was her direct supervisor and the highest-ranking officer under Colonel Duarte. He was at times their boss, bully, and den mother. But in that moment, he had acted as if she were speaking in tongues. "So, you think an alien animal can be trained to do the same things Earth K-9s do."

"More things, we think. Lieutenant Frank, one of the Space Marines, adopted a stray yipwag yesterday. He says Bang-Bang's already learned a dozen commands."

"Bang-Bang..."

"Yes, Sir. That's the dog's name. We haven't named ours yet."

"'Ours'?" The colonel laughed. "Now I've heard it all. You and Charming have finally learned to share."

"We're trying, Sir."

"Don't lose your edge, Firefly," he joked.

"Never, Sir."

But that was exactly what she sensed was beginning to happen as she sat on the floor in the K-9 center that evening and watched Rornn train the puppy. After being treated, bathed, and given bowls of a nutritious mash to eat, the puppy wanted to play nonstop, dashing from Trysh to Rornn, her tummy bulging, her huge eyes full of intelligence and curiosity, her skinny little tail a blur as it wagged. From the start, she showed a clear preference for the two of them, but she also seemed to trust the MPs who managed the K-9 center. Jack, Box Cutter, and most of the folks who worked at the docks got a different reaction. It must be due to the trauma the puppy experienced on her trip from the surface to the station.

"Sit." Rornn stood in front of the puppy. The yipwag dropped her bottom to the floor. "Good girl," he praised. Sitting on one haunch, she tipped her head sideways as she awaited his next command. "Are you ready to try something new? Maybe fetch." More head tipping. "Ah, good. I am ready too. Let us shake on it." A large male hand gently clasped a tiny paw. "Did you see that, Firefly? She already knows shake!"

"Yay! Good girl!" As she clapped, she saw pure joy suffuse Rornn's face. His grin was triumphant, his golden eyes alive with excitement that he clearly wanted to share with her. He looked like a proud dad on the sidelines of a soccer field, turning to his wife after watching their kid score the winning goal. It revealed a side of him she had never expected. For the first time, she could imagine him loving a child.

Loving *her*.

Don't be ridiculous. Talk about losing her edge! This was Rornn B'lenne —sweet talker, slayer of women's hearts, jokester, hotshot, *Vash* Prince. Believing in the possibility of sharing something real with him was the same kind of thinking that got her mother in trouble. What was in those tacos at lunchtime? It had stolen her higher brain function.

But he came back for you.

As she watched Rornn carry the puppy to a dish of water then crouch next to the tiny animal as she drank, the wrenching moments in the simulator that morning filled her mind. Rornn speeding toward her starfighter to blast attacking Dragaar warcraft to smithereens. It wasn't real, it was a VR world, but the feeling that Rornn B'lenne would come back for her no matter what, no matter where, wouldn't quit. The certainty of it had been planted inside her, spreading its roots. What would it be like to go through life, knowing someone had your back like that?

"But, Zeke, don't you want to see her?" Just like that, the memory of her father turning away from her, walking out of her life, came rushing back and doused her enchantment with Rornn's actions. The memory was hazy,

almost black-and-white it was so long in the past, yet it somehow maintained its power over her. Despite all her counteracting logic, despite her longing for true love and a family of her own someday, her father's heartlessness and mother's poor choices had kept her in an emotional stranglehold. *"He was never going to settle for a girl like me. That's the difference between real life and Cinderella, sweet pea."*

Puppy leaped into Trysh's lap, a writhing, wriggling bundle of unbridled joy. In an instant, puppy kisses and a wagging tail blew away her doubts and dark thoughts. Giggling, she rubbed the puppy's warm belly as little legs kicked. A surge of love expanded in her chest. It felt as if a door inside her that she kept tightly sealed had just cracked open a little bit more.

Rornn dropped to the floor next to Trysh, one long leg sprawled out in front of him, his other bent at the knee, a shiny boot providing new excitement for the puppy as she bounded from Trysh's lap to Rornn's boot to nibble on the leather. It was chilly in the kennel area but his body blazed with heat. It was the reason she moved closer until their shoulders touched. At least that was what she told herself.

The puppy made her way to Rornn's lap, turned in a circle then curled up. Trysh folded her hand over her tiny, bony body, stroking the patchy fur. Soon, little snores told her the pup had fallen asleep. "I don't want to move," she whispered, leaning across Rornn's torso.

"Don't," Rornn whispered back. His warm breath on her cheek sent curlicues of sensation spinning down her neck and spine. "Not quite yet, at least," he said. "I like this too much."

She smirked. "I bet you do." She kept her eyes trained on the drowsing puppy, trying to pretend the rumble of his voice in his chest didn't do crazy things to her insides. She had no more luck ignoring the proximity of the rest of his body, the slivers of hot skin at his neck and forearms, his scent, and the sweet, thick heat it generated, gathering low in her belly. He was aware of her reaction to him; he had to be. He had gone very still. If she turned her head, she would find herself mouth to mouth with him. Then he would catch her staring at his lips, and his eyes would glow with knowing amusement. Because a year of experience told her he never failed to recognize his effect on her, no matter how hard she tried to hide it.

Rornn

Rornn was afraid to move, but not because he feared waking the puppy. If Trysh's hand came one micrometer closer to his hip, his efforts to hide a raging hard-on would be for naught. In that moment, he found himself praising the glory of baggy flight suits. As she petted the puppy, seemingly unaware of him or his powerful reaction to her proximity, he inhaled the fragrance of her shiny brown hair. Her pink ear with its pearl earring, so close, begged to be nibbled and kissed. The downy baby hairs at the nape of her neck were no less tempting. Great Mother, he was glad he had learned self-discipline at a young age, for it was all that kept him from wrapping her hair in his fist and crushing his mouth against hers. From jerking the zipper of her flight suit to her waist. From sliding his hand under her white T-shirt in search of the lacy bra he knew she liked to wear and thumbing the tip of one perfect breast—

Her wrist brushed against his erection, and he sucked in a quiet hiss of air.

"Hey, L-Ts," an MP said, walking into the kennel area. They jumped apart and puppy made a sleepy grunt of protest. "I'm going to close up shop and put the pup in a crate for the night. Someone will be here if she starts to cry."

Still rattled by Trysh's accidental touch, Rornn handed the limp puppy to the sergeant. His body felt like it had been left on afterburner. He was rock-hard and there was no relief in sight.

The MP carried the puppy with care to a crate with a heated, padded bottom and a water bottle. "I sure hate leaving her," Trysh said.

"As soon as we move in together, she can move in with us."

She tossed her ponytail and laughed. "Don't you wish."

"I do wish it. I want to be with you day *and* night."

Her eyes flicked to his, a brief, searching look, as if she wanted to gauge his intent. She must have decided he was joking. One corner of her mouth tucked into her cheek as she gave his arm an affectionate squeeze.

He craved more than affectionate squeezes—unless it was her thighs doing the squeezing while her legs were wrapped around his hips.

"Are you planning to stop by Nimbus after this?" she asked. "I think I'll pass. I'm beat. This has been a long day."

"I will pass as well." He offered her a hand and pulled her to her feet. She rewarded him by pausing to delightfully stretch the kinks out of her body. He admired her lithe grace, her slender neck, the curve of her lower back, the swell of her butt, her long legs. The ache in his groin tripled before he finished his impromptu inspection.

With his hands held behind his back where he hoped they would behave, he escorted her to her quarters as he had done many times over the past year, both here and in flight training on Earth. "Do you remember the nights in Texas, Firefly? When we would walk to the barracks from the club. Everything on your world was so alive—creatures singing, bats flitting." He inhaled, craving air thick with humidity, stars winking in and out of view above towering live oaks. None of which existed on S'aharr.

Or here, for that matter. "I miss it. Even the incessant buzzing of the chickadees."

She broke into a smile as they boarded the lift to Deck Four where their quarters were located. "Cicadas."

"Yes. The cicadas. I miss them. I miss Texas." He leaned in closer, and her wide eyes turned very blue. "I am just happy that once I left Earth that I did not have to miss you."

She snorted softly. "You're on a roll, Charming."

He swallowed a groan of frustration. It was like a game of bajha with a skilled opponent—he made his moves and she deftly parried each one. While he enjoyed their banter, it was time to prove that his feelings for her were no joke. He'd nearly lost her to Jack Freeman. If not for the puppy's help, he would have.

She chatted as they walked off the lift, perfectly oblivious to his building frustration. "We need to name the puppy."

"Puppy will do nicely."

"I was thinking Blackie. Or Cocoa? She's so dark."

"What if she molts? We must choose a name that transcends coat color."

She laughed. "Dogs don't molt. I don't think yipwags do either. What about Kaylee or Inara? Or Bari, since she's from Barésh?"

"Seeing her condition, I don't know if she wants to be reminded of her birthplace. I like Freeman's Folly."

"Stop it, Charming. Jack's nice."

"I'm nicer."

She laughed. "Let's stick with Puppy for now. It's easy."

"Do you not think I am nicer?" he persisted.

"Charming," she warned.

Show her how you feel. He took a steadying breath. "About us being together… How can I convince you to take me seriously?"

"When are you ever serious?"

"I am in this moment. There is no one else like you. I want to be with you and only you."

"See? This is what I'm talking about. With women, you give out compliments like candy on Halloween. It doesn't work with me, Charming."

He grimaced. "My flowery speech with females, it stems from the *Vash* culture, the way I was raised. As I have told you, it means nothing, however, you do not like it and so I will tone it down. You have my word. You are an Earth woman. I see now that I must court you differently. For this I am willing to change my ways. If you will give me the chance."

Her steps slowed. "Did you say court me?"

He could imagine what his expression looked like. Was it the "look" Danger had described? *Go after her… Minutes mattered… Show don't tell.* His friend's words echoed in his head. "I did. I do. I wish to court you, Trysh Milton."

They stopped in front of the door to her quarters. She did not reach for the entry keypad. He began to worry she would escape inside and he would lose the chance to convince her of his intentions. Maybe his last chance. Her fists landed on her waist. "What does that mean? What are you saying?"

"It means a formal declaration of my interest in you. It allows us to become more familiar with each other. Not only mentally and emotionally, but physically as well."

She made a soft choking sound. "The friend zone works for us, Charming."

"Rornn," he corrected. "For this conversation, we should use our given names."

"I don't know what kind of conversation this is."

"This is a conversation about my moving from the friend zone to the courting zone."

She seemed somewhat relieved. "Like *Vash* dating."

Courting was more of a precursor to engagement, but one step at a time. "I sense a lack of enthusiasm about the prospect, Trysh. Are you not physically attracted to me?" He braced himself for her answer.

Her laugh was not the reaction he'd expected. "Do you seriously not know? Oh, my God."

"So, you *are* attracted to me. Just as I suspected all along." Then his smugness faltered. "Is it because I am an extraterrestrial?"

"You know the answer to that too."

"Yet, I sense reluctance in you. If it is not a matter of physical attraction, and not because of my planetary origins, then what is it? What keeps us apart? I cannot talk you out of it if I don't know what it is."

"It's a long story."

"I enjoy long stories."

"You don't understand."

He flattened his hand on the wall next to her, bringing his face closer to hers. "There will come a time when I will understand everything there is to know about you."

"It's because in real life you're a prince," she blurted out, as if desperate to parry a direct blow.

"The third son. The title is meaningless."

"Not to me. We're from different social classes. It doesn't work. As friends maybe. But not as...more."

"That's it? That's the only reason?"

Groaning, she turned her back to him and unlocked the door. "Come inside." Sounding irritated, she called to the room's computer. "Lights—

medium." Illumination revealed her snug quarters that were identical to his. Their rooms on Bezos Station were smaller than most closets in the palace, but in his opinion, they offered what his previous life never could—freedom.

She gathered two glasses and filled them with water, setting them on a standard-issue round kitchen table. "We're from vastly different social classes. I'm a commoner. You're a prince. It doesn't work in real life." Her voice took on an edge he never heard before. "My father understood that. My mother didn't."

He froze. "You liken me to your father." The realization rocketed through him. She assumed he was a younger version of General Zeke Milton. Hero. Legend.

Callous bastard.

He felt both a resurgence of disgust about her sire's behavior and the instinct to protect her that followed. It made sense that her father was the root of her keeping him at arm's length. Why didn't he see it before?

She stood in the kitchen, watching him, her back to the sink, looking wary as she sipped from a glass of water. The shield had fallen over her eyes, a frequent occurrence when they first met, before they became such close friends. A shield that still came and went. He had often puzzled over it, never quite making the connection. Now he knew the reason. She feared he would treat her the way the general treated her mother. If he could prove he was nothing like her father, she would see what he had known all along—she was just the right woman for him. "I'm the third son. I've told you this. My title is meaningless."

"Not to me. You live in a palace."

"Lived. Now I live as any other ESFF officer does. And I am proud of it. You know that."

Her expression gentled. "I do," she murmured. "You're the first *Vash* Federation officer in history to graduate from ESF Forces pilot training. I'm proud to call you my friend."

He placed a hand over his heart. "I'd be honored if you called me more."

"How about I call you annoying because you're keeping me from a good night's sleep?"

"Now who can't be serious?"

She gave him a sheepish look.

He took the empty water glass from her hand and set it on the table. "Is this the only reason you have rebuffed me. Because I am a prince and you lack royal blood?"

When she nodded, he brought his hands together in a single clap. "Excellent. It narrows my plan of attack considerably."

Hot anger replaced the frostiness in her eyes. "For the short term, maybe. What if I'm not looking for a temporary hookup?"

"What if *I* am not?" Now he was growing angry. "You think that is all I want with you?"

"It's all you've ever done with the women you meet."

"Because they are not you!" he shouted. "Not...*you.*"

They stopped, their chests heaving, their gazes on fire. He almost took her right there, helped himself that kiss he craved for as long as he had known her, then everything else he had wanted, but her quiet, calm voice caught him off-guard, walked him back from the edge. "You make it seem so simple," she said. "That you can have whomever you want. Your clan rules who you'll end up with. Guaranteed it isn't going to be an Earth commoner. Yeah, I know some *Vash* royals married Earth women, but Queen Jasmine and King Rom got together while the king was still banished. Her son and daughter chose relationships that double as alliances between powerful clans. Instant *Vash* seal of approval."

"I need no seal of approval. When I joined the ESFF I left that life behind. When I marry, it will be to the woman I love."

"What about your parents? What if they don't agree with your choice?"

"They may not. Not at first. But they already know I have always forged my own path. I would want an Earth wedding. Later on, if my clan were to desire it, I would consent to formalizing things in a ceremony at the palace, but a binding legal Earth union would send the message that they cannot promise me to anyone else in my absence."

"That can happen?" Worriedly, she searched his face.

"Now that I have found you, Trysh Milton, no one will ever take me from you." He brushed the back of his hand across her cheek. The heat of her skin, her clean musk, he was hyper aware of it, of her. Everything. It filled him. Unbalanced him too. "Give me the chance. Let me prove I am nothing like your father. That I can be the mate you deserve." He pulled her closer. *Tell her how you feel.* "I love you," he said, squeezing her shoulders, and her gaze flew up to meet his. "If you need time to feel the same, it is all right. All I ask is the chance to win you over."

He brought his lips to her ear and felt her tremble, felt the tension flowing out of her. "Know this, my beloved. I will always protect you and keep you safe. You will come first with me. Now and always." They were words he borrowed from a *Vash Nadah* promise ceremony. As much as he desired to leave his old life behind, the ancient words were somehow appropriate. "For as long as I live, I will worship you. Body and soul."

She made a small whimper. He took that as an encouraging sign.

Now show her how you feel. Gently, he gently pressed the fingertips of both hands to her upturned jaw and brushed his lips across hers, a lingering, deliberate slide, then he paused to kiss one corner of her mouth. Her soft moan was the most beautiful sound he had ever heard. Her lips had parted; her breathing was shallow and fast. Her forehead gleamed with perspiration, her eyes glazed with desire as she looked up at him. That look—he had waited so long for it to be directed at him, and they had barely scraped the surface of what he longed to do with her.

"More," she said, her voice husky, as if reading his thoughts. Then she pulled him close and they kissed, deeply this time. Wrapping the loose fabric of her flightsuit in one fist, he used it to keep her pressed close to him. With his other hand he explored the curves of her body. Heat consumed him, and he ached to be inside her.

When they finally separated, she murmured against his mouth, her fingers tracing his hairline at the base of his skull. "I used to hate you for being so good at everything you do. Ground school, flying, tactics. But you're even good at this. That kiss was amazing."

He winked. "The best you ever had, yes?"

"Maybe." She took him by the collar. "I need to collect more data first." Holding his gaze, she reached for the zipper of his flight suit and slowly zipped it down to his groin.

His erection sprang free of his boxers. There was a charged pause. Her mouth tipped into a playful grin. "Boom," she said.

Laughing, he dragged her into another passionate kiss, walking her backward toward her bed. Their hands tangled as they fumbled for each other's zippers, seeing who could undress whom first. Flight suits were peeled away, boots and socks pulled off, T-shirts yanked over each other's heads. Her bra and panties, lacey confections, stood no chance against him. Then the race was on to see whose lips and hands could elicit the most groans. Now this was a competition!

Pink-tipped breasts, her slick folds, hollows and curves, every sleek muscle, her body was the most heavenly unexplored territory he had ever encountered. He made her come before he sank inside her to the hilt. She came again after only a few thrusts, her legs wrapped around his hips, her body clenching around him inside and out, his name a plea on her lips.

He was going over the edge with her. No matter how hard he tried to hold back, it was inevitable. "Trysh," he said with a note of astonishment. She was his, and he was hers. That was all he needed.

All he wanted.

Their fingers laced together, he let go in a prolonged, explosive shock-wave that grayed out his vision. He gripped her hands hard, his body convulsing. Then, finally, he lowered his head to hers as awareness crept back. Nothing compared to her. Nothing.

"Well, that's that," he said with a quiet laugh of wonder. "I can now die a happy man."

"You can't die at all," she argued. "Not allowed. You've already exceeded your quota for the day."

"At the hands of the Dragaar. Not Trysh Milton. Does that count?"

"It counts."

Grinning, he rolled them to the side, spooning her from behind, the weight of one warm breast filling his hand. "Allow me to court you," he said, his lips in her damp, tangled hair. "I will prove I can catch you."

She rotated to look at him, matching him smile for cocky smile. "Think so?"

"I know so." Chuckling, he flipped her on her back and set out to convince her of that fact as best he could.

FOUR

Puppy

Puppy soon demonstrated her mastery of "heel", matching her Tall One's steps while not tugging on the lead. Now that she was "out of the woods", as a doctor had described it, her training could begin in earnest. While her Tall Ones were busy flying, she worked with her friends at the K-9 center. She had not yet met an Earth dog, but based on reactions to her progress, yipwags far exceeded everyone's expectations.

Puppy liked being a "good girl".

"Look at that tummy! It's like a basketball." Puppy's efforts to maintain K-9 dignity evaporated the instant Her Trysh swept her up to scratch her ears and kiss her nose. Puppy licked Her Trysh everywhere that she could reach. She loved the sound of her Tall One's laugh. It was a much happier sound lately. From the start, Puppy detected something deep inside Her Trysh that she wanted to hide from others, a wound that remained raw, a secret pain. But ever since her Tall Ones began mating, Puppy sensed that the wound ached a lot less—and from what she could guess, her Tall Ones mated a lot.

They stopped at the base of a ladder, where Her Trysh placed Puppy in Her Rornn's arms for the climb up to the "observation cone". It was Her Rornn's favorite place on the station outside of Her Trysh's bed.

Restricted Area, a sign said. Unknown to the Tall Ones, Puppy could already interpret the meaning of many of the symbols posted around the station. Bang-Bang might know more verbal commands than she did, but soon Puppy would be able to read. She couldn't wait for the day the Tall ones figured it out.

She learned a lot from watching her Tall Ones. For instance, Her Trysh was more likely to balk at ignoring signs such as *Authorized Personnel Only* than Her Rornn was: "You'd better hope this doesn't get us in hot water with the squad commander, Charming."

"I dream of a good long soak in hot water. But the face I see with me is not Colonel Amanpour. It's you."

As they laughed, Puppy lifted her nose in the air, and sniffed. A smell filled the observation cone. As Tall Ones, they were not aware of it. But this scent was wrong. Bad. She wiggled to get free so she could investigate. As her Tall Ones admired each other and the sweeping view of space— countless stars and shuttle craft with blinking lights soaring between the rotating station and the planet of Barésh below—Puppy latched on to a scent trail. Yes, a very bad smell. The fur on the back of her neck stood on end.

"Now that my clan has made the official announcement of my middle brother's nuptials," Her Rornn said, "We should talk about the next steps."

"I can't wait to see your homeworld. S'aharr. But it's not for another year."

"Yes, true but…"

"But what? What's wrong?"

"Nothing is wrong. Everything is right—with you, with us. That is my worry. I would not put it past my clan to secure a promise arrangement for me now that my brother's match is complete."

"Promise arrangement—you mean like an engagement. What we talked about before."

"Yes. But with another, suitable *Vash Nadah*."

"Not a commoner," she said sourly. "Someone like you."

"Matchmaking is still alive and well on my world—my former world. But I want to cut them off at the pass, so to speak." He dropped to one knee and took her hands in his. "Will you marry me, Trysh Milton, woman at the far end of the amazing spectrum, owner of my heart?"

"When?" She sounded startled.

"Before we travel to S'aharr. But I would hope as soon as possible."

"Where?"

"Here, of course. Bezos. Colonel Duarte can perform the ceremony." He paused. "Do you not want to—?"

"Of course, I do! Yes, the answer's yes. I don't care about the details. I love you. I've never wanted anyone else but you."

Her Rornn stood and hugged her so hard that he lifted her off her feet.

Puppy reached the end of the scent trail. Behind the wall was some-thing she couldn't reach. Her hackles raised. She couldn't help growling, low and long. The bad thing was there. Something that would hurt her Tall Ones and all the others on this station. It reeked of the Tall One who chased her from the crate with the stick, and of others like him. She would find them all, but first she must protect her Tall Ones and their friends.

Barking, Puppy pawed at the wall. *Here, Tall Ones. Here!*

In an instant, Her Rornn was there. "This panel is loose." He removed it, carefully, and set it on the floor.

There it was. A small box with a bad smell.

Puppy wagged her tail harder, smiling at her Tall Ones. But Her Rornn jerked her off the floor so fast, her bark got stuck in her throat. His arm was around Trysh too, steering all three of them toward the ladder.

Trysh spoke into her comm. "Station Security, this is Lieutenant Milton." Her voice was even but urgent. "We found a device in the observation cone. A possible bomb..."

Trysh

Colonel Amanpour's office smelled like stale coffee and the slight burning odor from the copier in the admin area next door that was always malfunctioning. All the advanced technology in the galaxy at their disposal and still the office copying machine never worked right.

"Sir." Trysh reported with a salute, keeping her focus on her commander as crisp footsteps pulled up alongside her. Overhead lights glanced off Rornn's spit-shined black flight boots. She felt the breeze of his snappy salute. Puppy's paws appeared in the corner of her vision next. The yipwag waited for Rornn's gentle tug on her lead before she sat, her huge ears pricked. Her fur was glossy and thick, and she had filled out. Their little girl was growing up, the incredibly smart, joyful little yipwag that had helped dissolve the hurdles that once kept Trysh and Rornn apart. Although Puppy resided officially in the K-9 center with her canine friend Bang-Bang, she was a frequent overnight visitor at the foot of either Trysh's bed or Rornn's, depending whose quarters they settled on for the night.

Colonel Amanpour returned their salutes then leaned back in his desk chair to observe them. "At ease, Lieutenants—and you too, Puppy."

Puppy's tail gave a little swish.

Later today, she, Rornn, and Puppy would receive medals for their role in saving the station from terrorists. The team that dismantled the bomb would be honored as well. Afterward, there would be one hell of a party at Nimbus. The past few weeks had been a blur, ever since Puppy detected the improvised explosive device—an IED—hidden behind one of the wall panels in the observation cone. The yipwag had further used her talent at sniffing out explosives and the evildoers who mixed them by leading them to the members of an Earth First terror cell comprised of a couple of rogue cargo rats and a med tech who had infiltrated the Doctors Without Borders team. The suspects even had the nerve to try to blame Rornn for the bomb, knowing he often used the observation cone for personal reflection time. Earth First terrorists knew such a device would be most effective in a confined space. If it had detonated, it would have been devastating. VIPs had made the journey to the station—politicians, Off-World Security staffers, various ESF Forces brass—and General Zeke Milton.

"He's here," Colonel Amanpour said.

Even though Trysh had thought of this day for weeks, had both dreaded it and looked forward to it, the bolt of surprise upon hearing her father had arrived on Bezos Station still jarred her.

"He's with Colonel Duarte, receiving his newcomer briefing as we speak. They should be on their way down here shortly. I thought you might want a few extra moments to prepare yourself in case the prospect of seeing him is more alarming than it is pleasant."

She went still, seeing the concern in his eyes. Why, when she'd never given him any reason to worry? The secrets about her relationship with her father had always been her own...and now Rornn's too.

"Yes," Colonel Amanpour told her, confirming her worst fears. "I know the backstory."

Trysh squeezed her eyes shut for a second, then nodded. The secret was out. She was General Milton's unwanted consequence.

"Last year, after your orders were confirmed, I reviewed your personnel records—as I do with all my incoming starpilots. I saw that you were Zeke Milton's kid. I asked around after I didn't see you in his official family portrait. I found out what I needed to know." His jaw hardened but his gaze reflected sorrow, maybe even pity. It made her chest tighten, reignited the old shame. "You've never met the man," he said.

"The general's loss, Sir," Rornn broke in. His face was taut with concern and compassion, his golden eyes aglow as he shifted his gaze to her.

"*I love you*," she mouthed. She loved him for always knowing exactly what to say and do to ease her qualms. She just loved him period. Later, she would show him just how much, inch by tasty inch.

"We'll get through this together," Colonel Amanpour said, nodding. "*We* are your family, at least. The Mighty Titans Squadron will always be your home."

Trysh was not a crier. But listening to the colonel say those words made her throat ache. "Thank you, Sir," she squeezed out.

The comm chimed. "They're on the way, Sir," the colonel's assistant said.

Amanpour pushed to his feet and rubbed his hands. "Ready?"

She answered with a curt nod. Instinctively, she reached for Puppy and touched her fingertips to her soft head, a caress of thanks for bringing her and Rornn together, for giving them a reason to unite, and to love. Puppy swiveled her head and licked her palm.

Voices came closer—Colonel Duarte's and one that was familiar only because of vids she had watched. Rornn's fingertips glided down her back as, inside, she jangled with nerves, anger, and anticipation. What would happen when her father walked through that door? Would he expect a free pass back into her life? That all would be forgiven once he pinned on her medal? What about after he left? Would he then go back to ignoring her? Or would he finally play "Daddy"?

Don't get your hopes up. She made sure the hidden, vulnerable place inside her was on lock-down—at least for now. The risk of opening it up and letting him in was too great.

The two officers walked into the office. Her eyes went to Colonel Duarte first. His smile was broad. A bot-brace encased his lanky frame from his waist to his ankles. Thanks to *Vash* med tech, the brace kept him mobile while the broken back he suffered in a jet crash healed, an injury that would have otherwise left him a paraplegic for life. She had not once seen him wince in pain, even though the process was said to be extremely uncomfortable. She took some of that strength as her own, and aimed only the most pleasant of expressions in her father's direction.

Tall was her first thought. A commanding presence.

He has my blue eyes.

Her thumping heart felt ready to bounce out of her chest as he extended his hand. Her hand shook a little as she clasped his large one in hers. His grip was just right—not too hard, not too squishy. And, very slightly, damp.

He's nervous too.

It was typical of her to note such things—even in the height of battle, she was aware of the tiniest details. This was a battle too. Whether he was a friendly or a bogey, she would soon find out. No matter what, her rescuer, her chivalrous knight and their furry companion, stood at her side, ready to save her.

"Trysh," he said, letting go.

"General Milton," she replied, not ready to call him anything...more familiar. It all felt rather awkward, experiencing this moment with everyone around them, listening.

"We'll leave you two alone so you can catch up," Colonel Duarte said, his bot-brace whirring as he stepped toward the office door with Colonel Amanpour and Rornn. Puppy resisted being pulled away.

"Rornn can stay," Trysh said. "I want him to stay. And Puppy too."

General Milton beckoned to Rornn. "Of course. Trysh is right. You belong here. Let's sit. Please." Four chairs surrounded a coffee table upon which someone had set out a pitcher of water, napkins, and glasses.

Trysh kept her hands scrunched in her lap, feeling the comforting weight of Puppy's body as the yipwag leaned against her leg. Silently, the general dug in his breast pocket for a piece of paper and unfolded it, slowly, precisely. His chin reminded her of the way hers looked when she was tense. "Trysh," he said. "Your mother wrote me a letter after she was diagnosed with the cancer. I want to share part of it with you." He cleared his throat. "'I may not have been too good at finding husbands, or at school, and you may not have been a very good father to her, but it doesn't change one big fact—that she's the best thing I ever did and what you did too, Zeke, even if you never figured out how to say it.'"

Trysh was rendered mute. *I was the best thing...* So many feelings collided as she absorbed his words and her mother's. The old hunger to be noticed. To be seen. To *matter*.

He folded the note back up just as carefully as he had opened it, before slipping it back into his pocket. "Ruby was right. I didn't know how to say it, Trysh. And probably still don't. There is no excuse for how I treated you and your mother, other than that I acted selfishly, disgracefully. You *are* the best thing we did. Ruby was so proud of you. As am I." He paused. "Of course the timing of all this is probably suspect, as I am here to congratulate you on your act of valor. I deeply apologize for that and I make no attempt to justify my actions."

She lifted her eyes to his and nodded.

"On that subject, you have no doubt heard of my past sentiments toward the *Vash* Federation, particularly during the early years following First Contact. Yes, at that time I did have my doubts that joining the Federation was the best path for Earth. When the conspiracy theory emerged that the *Vash* were to blame for the attack on Glenn-Musk Station, I didn't speak out against it as I should. Earth First was responsible for the bombing. Period."

It amazed her that she could feel even more shock, but she did, hearing what her father had confessed. A lot of Earth-centrist people still refused to accept that domestic terrorism took out Glenn-Musk. They believed the *Vash* didn't want Earth to develop advanced technology that could eventually threaten the galactic pecking order, so they destroyed the station and blamed it on Earth First. On Bezos, concerns abounded that General Milton, as the Chief of Off-World Security, hadn't yet sealed holes and weak spots in security as well as he could have in the aftermath because he and others still found it difficult acceding that the terrorism originated on Earth. It left Bezos and many other critical assets vulnerable to attack. Which would have happened here—if not for Puppy's magnificent nose and Rornn's love of stargazing.

"I'm glad to hear you feel that way," she said.

Her father regarded Rornn, his eyes miraculously warming. "I am pleased to learn that you two are engaged. Trysh, I want you to know that your fiancé attempted to ask my permission to marry you. Weeks ago."

She threw a wondering wide-eyed glance at Rornn. *What? You did?*

Weirdly, Rornn didn't look smug in the way she'd expect when taking credit for something. His expression reflected a mix of conflicting emotions, his mouth skirting the edge of a frown.

"He told me he had already proposed, but that he felt the need to do things the old-fashioned way. I unfortunately left that letter unanswered as well," General Milton finished.

"I did so in hopes to have your blessing, Sir," Rornn said.

"You have it, young man." Emotion reached General Milton's eyes for the first time. "You have it," he repeated, his voice thicker. He lowered his chin and seemed to study his hands. Three stars shone on his shoulders, his many medals glittering. In contrast, sorrow etched lines on his face.

After some reflection, he glanced up. "I can't erase the years, or what I did. Today isn't the day to ask forgiveness. It must be earned, and I'm not there yet. It may take years. It may never happen. I have much to atone for, much soul searching to do. I do, however, look forward to getting to know my daughter. If she— If you…" He sighed, looking at Trysh. His voice had given out, but his beseeching gaze finished what he wanted to say.

Allowing her father into her life was a scarier prospect than anything she ever anticipated encountering in combat, a gamble that left her vulnerable to more pain. But, made stronger by Rornn's love, she was finally ready to take that chance. "Yes," she said. "I'd like that very much."

Then she exchanged a quick glance with her best friend and smiled. Her Prince Charming managed to accomplish what he'd always promised he could do. He made the impossible possible.

EPILOGUE

Puppy

It's a happy day aboard Bezos Station as I watch My Rornn slip the special ring on My Trysh's finger.

"I give you this ring to wear with love and joy," he says. "As a ring has no end, neither shall my love for you. I choose you to be my wife this day and forevermore."

Then My Trysh does the same for My Rornn, having to push a bit harder to get the band past his knuckle. "I give you this ring to wear with love and joy," she says, her eyes shining. "As a ring has no end, neither shall my love for you. I choose you to be my husband this day and forevermore."

There is much anticipation in the air as Colonel Duarte finishes the ceremony. "By the power vested in me I now pronounce you husband and wife. You may kiss the bride—and groom."

My Tall Ones' lips meet, their arms wrapping around each other. They kiss for so long that the other Tall Ones start to laugh, whoop, and whistle. Starpilots are a rowdy bunch. Colonel Duarte shouts above the cheering, "I present to you our happy couple!"

Back on the floor, I watch the party unfold, taking quick action if any crumbs drop, enjoying many scratches behind my ears, but always with my eyes, ears, and nose on alert to make sure everyone stays safe. That is, after all, my job. It reminds me that I've come a long way in a short time. I didn't do it alone. When I was small, terrified, and lost, I followed the voice inside me that said, "Never give up. Keep going. If you do, you'll find your way home." I like to think it was my mother's voice I heard. She wanted me to have the life she could not. But it took My

Rornn to convince me I would be okay. His words sing inside me now: "You are safe with me. I will not let anything happen to you. You are home."

Yes. I am home. After much searching, we all found our way home.

WIRED FOR LOVE

By

Michelle Howard

Sci-fi romance author with a love for angsty HEA's.

http://www.michellehowardwrites.com

ONE

The mewling cry cut through the night and grabbed Narelle's attention. She paused and cocked her head to the side, listening for the sound again. Silence greeted her. It was late and she hoped to stop in at The Zone for one last drink before they closed the doors for the night. Maybe squeeze in a quick chat with the striking owner and bar keep. A grin tugged at her lips. Hunter Gil definitely warranted her best effort to get there on time.

Thinking about the serious brown eyes which lightened at her approach and the slow smile Hunter always gave at her arrival was enough to hurry her steps. Another whine followed by a yip stopped her in her tracks. Tugging up the collar of her synth leather jumper against the late night chill, Narelle sighed and rolled her eyes.

"This better be worth my time."

She doubled back on the street, following the continuous whines until she reached a locked shop door. All of the lights inside the building were out, the owners probably warm and settled in their residence for the night.

Narelle huffed and tapped on the thin-framed door just in case. "Hello?"

She paused, waiting for some sign anyone remained inside.

Nothing.

"Well, I did my part." She turned, fully prepared to rush to The Zone in hopes of catching sight of Hunter.

Rapid barking brought her to an abrupt halt. Narelle cursed and turned back. This time she bypassed the front door and peered around the corner to the narrow pathway nestled between the two buildings. The tight passage reeked of rotting trash and stagnant water from the prior night's rain storm.

A dark shadow flashed against the wall on the right, heading toward her at a rapid speed. The size and shape of the threat loomed above her head. Another curse and Narelle stumbled backward but the creature kept coming, its pace picking up. Seconds from withdrawing the knife she wore at her hip, Narelle burst back onto the street and glanced over her shoulder only to come up short.

The menacing creature from the dark was…a four legged animal about knee height. A pitiful one at that. With more than a bit of trepidation, she held out her hand. "Hello there."

Distinguishing the color of the short-matted coat proved hard. A mixture of dark and light brown hair covered a shivering body beyond thin. At the sound of her voice, the animal lowered itself close to the ground and crawled toward her with hesitant steps and another whine. Narelle's heart softened as she squatted until the creature reached her.

A dog.

Not an ordinary dog, she decided, even in the dim security lights from the nearby closed shops. The eyes reflected a keen intelligence. As soon as the dog drew close enough, she ran her hands along its trembling sides, and bones met her fingers. Pointed ears flicked forward at her touch and a warm nose nudged at her chin.

"Aren't you a cute boy. Or girl." Determining the sex needed a different angle and better light.

Now the bigger question—what to do with her discovery? Pushing up to her feet, Narelle glanced longingly in the direction of the bar. She could take the dog to her temp room and hope she didn't get kicked out for violating the no living pet rule or she could continue on her path and see if Hunter had any idea on what to do.

The dog leaned into her side, bumping the back of her knee. A quick lick of its dry tongue against her fingers decided.

"Come on, boy. Or girl," she muttered and started for The Zone at a rapid pace. Her furry friend kept up, claws clacking against the wet pavers.

As she neared the popular spot for off-worlders, Narelle slowed. The door burst open and several men fell through the entrance laughing and stumbling into one another. At her side, the dog growled, drawing notice. One of the men, a regular she recognized just by his scrungy shirt and pants with a threadbare cloak thrown over his shoulder, stared.

"Wassat?" He bumped a friend and pointed behind Narelle.

She tensed, one hand dropping to the top of the dog's head. The short fur bristled beneath her fingertips.

His drunk cohorts laughed and grabbed his arm as they tugged him down the street until she no longer heard their sloppy footsteps. Breathing a sigh of relief, she stepped inside and crossed into the hum of activity representing The Zone. Due to the late hour, only a few determined customers lingered waiting for Hunter's inevitable bellow as he evicted them all exactly on closing hour.

Hoping to go undetected, Narelle took a seat in a back booth, settled the dog then watched the bustling man behind the bar. Hunter's large frame moved briskly from one end of the counter to the other, a towel slung over a broad shirt-clad shoulder. While chatting with the two customers seated on the stools, he washed and cleaned glasses. He worked with an economy of moves and Narelle allowed herself to enjoy the sight.

Smooth muscles rippled and flexed in his lower arms made bare by the rolled sleeves of the black fitted shirt. Shaggy black hair in need of a cut fell over his brow and blocked a clear view of his features. Not that Narelle minded, since she knew exactly what he looked like and could describe him with her eyes closed even after a drink or three.

At her side, the dog nudged her thigh before stretching out full length on the wine-colored bench seat.

"Are you hungry?" She rubbed a pointed ear. Deep brown eyes met her gaze, and Narelle melted. She wasn't a melt-y person, but this animal was hitting all her weak spots. "Alright. Let me see what I can do."

Taking a deep breath, she rounded the booth and pushed back her shoulders as she strode toward the bar and the one man who managed to arouse and terrify her at the same time. He looked up and their gazes connected.

Power. It radiated from him in waves and no other word perfectly described the man she approached. Sections of dark hair stood up in disarray on top where he'd no doubt run his fingers through it several times during the evening. Thick brows lowered in her direction, brown eyes narrowing.

Familiar heat from whenever they crossed paths slammed into Narelle despite her attempt at nonchalance. Everyone around them faded away. The lights, the music, none of it intruded. Her focus zeroed in on the man stripping her bare with nothing more than a look.

It was obvious Hunter didn't care if anyone saw the way he stared. A customer tried to catch his attention, but his intensity never wavered. Narelle paused to catch her breath, masking the hitch in her stride by swiveling around as if she was surveying the crowd. When she turned back around, his eyes continued to blaze in her direction.

The wiser part of her screamed run, run now and the less sane part—mainly her libido—strained to reach out and touch him. But she didn't let any of that deter her. She needed answers and not a being in this establishment doubted Hunter was the one to talk to if you had questions.

If her stomach bubbled with nerves, it was because he'd stated his interest clearly every time her travels as a smuggler brought her this way, and she'd flirt, laugh then scurry off. The last time Narelle had felt herself waiver, tempted beyond belief to give in to the sensual strings connecting them.

It always took a while to bolster her courage enough to return and face him. Even then she still denied the vivid attraction because that way lay trouble. Hunter slept his way through women and she had the terrible habit of falling in love with any man she took to her bed. Nothing good would come of her giving in to Hunter and she'd end up with a bruised heart for the endeavor.

All of this meant it was probably time to move on, time to find another stop point for her routes. At least Hunter now allowed her the illusion of pretense. Oh, he continued to eye her from across the room if he noticed her arrival and not once did he stop the wicked glances. The difference lay in the effort, deeper undertones and the knowing smiles which lacked the force and potency of earlier gestures. It was if he'd backed off and dared her to reach out for what she wanted.

And Narelle wanted. Stars and moons how she wanted!

TWO

Hunter sensed her the moment she entered his radius. Narelle Bindu. No matter how hard he worked for it, she avoided his bed as if he carried a plague. From beneath lowered lids, he watched her approach with a sensuous walk many women attempted but failed. What amused him more than anything was her complete and utter lack of awareness about her appeal.

Rapacious gazes followed her, but she neither glanced right nor left. He straightened and tossed the used towel on the bar as he folded his arms over his chest to resist the driving urge to snatch her close when she was within reach.

The last time he'd made his need obvious and propositioned the lithe green-skinned beauty, she'd not only fled The Zone but the satellite station as well, sending his worry meter off the charts until she eventually returned. Narelle wasn't ready for what he wanted to offer as evident by her disappearance, but those few days of wondering if he'd chased her away for good still scared Hunter. She'd driven him to new heights with her avoidance tactics, causing a reaction no other woman before her ever had.

Time. He needed time to draw her in to satisfy their mutual desire for one another. Eyeing the rounded curve of her breasts from the low cut of her top, his lower half sprung to life. No denying he wanted her, but he wouldn't push as hard again.

The problem resided in his growing worry that he didn't have much time left. Narelle in the last couple of visits exuded an unseen before restless vibe Hunter couldn't pin down. It was almost as if she planned to disappear permanently.

His heart clenched. He wouldn't allow her to vanish without getting one taste. The vow grounded Hunter and loosened the knot in his gut. He ignored thinking about why it mattered so much.

In her black leather synth suit, she appeared a woman well versed in the seductive arts. Long legs, body sleek and a fluid swing of those curvy hips. One only had to look into her gray eyes to reinforce the impression. Daring and full of allure.

Except for now. Now she looked worried. Tense lines creased her forehead. Pearly white teeth nibbled on the full bottom lip, turning the green flesh a darker shade of emerald.

Hunter growled, his lips curling up at the sexy gesture. She was pretty. Beyond damn pretty and he liked everything about her including the small scar on the upper right side of her lip. He had dreams about that scar. About her lips. About kissing her until neither of them resisted the undeniable pull drawing them close.

Pale green skin hinted at her heritage as a Nordo, the short black horns on her temple no longer than his thumb confirmed it. Nordos coming and going at his rough and ready bar wasn't unusual but his visceral reaction to Narelle was.

Hunter leaned forward and braced his forearms on the counter separating them as she stopped at the bar. Deep and stormy, her eyes flared in appreciation, and Hunter luxuriated in a moment of pride for maintaining his former military physique. "What can I get you tonight, Narelle?"

"My usual." A sassy wink accompanied her order.

His cock surged in response as he turned to mix the fruity beverage with a surprising strong hit of alcohol. The first time she'd requested the drink, Hunter had eyed her luscious form from head to toe wondering if he'd be scooping her off the floor later. All hair and ass not an extra pound to be found yet she'd handled the heavy dose of alcohol like a pro.

Today she wore the red mass in a tight bun but curls slivered free. Sometimes at night, he dreamed about pulling on those strands while she was on her knees, mouth to his hardening length.

"I'll have what she's having, Hunter," an irritating customer yelled out from across the bar. One dark look from Hunter had the man paling and ducking his head back to the full glass of clear liquid already in front of him.

Over his shoulder, Hunter winked at Narelle, catching her smirk before she wiped the expression clear. The gods forbid he should ever think she found anything about him appealing. With the mixer humming away as he prepared her drink, Hunter wondered what her story was. Like most of his patrons, she kept her lips sealed about her private life, but he'd made no secret of his interest in exploring the heated attraction which ignited whenever their paths crossed.

Drink finished, he walked back toward her and held it slightly out of reach. Her brows pinched and an exasperated huff escaped her lips. "Get it over with, Hunter."

He grinned. She knew him well. "Stay after closing and talk to me."

"Fine."

The full glass almost hit the floor with a crash. Hunter caught it before the blue bubbling liquid spilled and handed it over. "What did you say?"

Her eyes rolled. "You heard me."

"Allow me time to replay the moment in my head."

He almost had it. A glitter in her gaze, a slight curve of her lips and a twitch of that damn scar. Then she banked the spurt of humor. Hunter vowed he'd see her laugh one of these days.

Narelle bit her inner cheek as she leaned her hip to the side. Amusement faded and doubt clouded her features. "I was hoping we could talk in private for a minute."

All intentions to get a pretty smile from her before he headed to his lonely bed vanished. "What's wrong?"

She shifted nervously, head jerking to the side. Hunter tried to see over her shoulder but she leaned closer, blocking his view of the bar, and her citrus fresh scent washed over him. He swallowed back a groan and gave her his full attention.

"I found something outside before getting here. I wanted to see if you could help me."

Narelle never asked for help. At least he didn't think she was the type to ask for help. All cocky confidence and sheer bravado with a veneer of vulnerability that made Hunter want to wrap his arms around her and never let go. Except she refused his every attempt to move what they shared from light banter to something hot and physical.

"You know I'll help you, Narelle. All you have to do is ask."

Her shoulders dropped and her eyes brightened as she shot him a half grin. She pointed over her shoulder without turning. "When you close come see me at the back table."

Annoyance nipped at his patience, but Hunter gave in with a firm nod. "I'll only be a little while."

Putting words to action, he signaled the closing of the bar by hitting the overhead lights twice. Long use to the abrupt nature when he declared it time to go, customers began settling their tab and rising to their feet.

"Out now!"

Chairs scooted back and patrons leaped to their feet faster. Humor twitched the sides of his lips. He may have been forceful a time or two escorting wayward customers out the door.

Quiet settled after the place emptied, and he tallied the night's earnings with half a mind to the task, the other half firmly on Narelle, who never moved from her spot in the back. Blonde highlights gleamed in the loose sections of hair, which fell about her face from the knot atop her head.

She'd positioned herself well, and he only caught glimpses of her profile as she nibbled her lips and alternately looked down at her lap.

Hunter couldn't imagine what could have driven her to him but wasn't going to complain. More than anything, he'd love to have the challenging woman indebted to him. He shut out every light except the smaller ones running over the main bar and the corner stage where he sometimes paid to have performers come in.

Keeping his steps light, despite the beginning twinges in his right knee, Hunter approached her table. Unobserved he took note of the way her hands continually clenched on the table. The invisible barrier she normally kept around him was lowered. Hunter sensed changes he had yet to pinpoint, and his cock stretched in pleasure.

"Narelle?"

She jumped to her feet but relaxed instantly. "Sorry. Thanks, Hunter."

Her nerves pissed him off, but he shrugged off her gratitude and crossed his arms. "You wanna tell me what's going on?"

"It's best I show you." She moved to the side, revealing the shadowy form of an animal resting on the bench seat.

The animal lifted his head, a fine shiver running through its painfully thin body. Pointed ears with black tips twitched. Black fur formed a mask around the eye and muzzle area. Hunter's gaze grew greedy in its scan as he looked the animal over. Brown hair, darker in spots, long tail but a body which hinted at its former muscled strength.

Uncontrollable emotions hit Hunter all at once. Memories he didn't want to revisit ran through his mind, their dark intensity killing his desire. Light hearted play vanished and his prior years in the service returned in a flash. Pain lined by grief and anger at the injustice of his past slapped him in the face.

Straightening, he glared from the animal to Narelle. "What game are you playing at Narelle, and where'd you get that?"

Narelle didn't like the look Hunter aimed her way. Instantly put on the defense, she reached back and planted a hand on the dog's head. "Not a game. I found him…or her on the streets before coming here."

"Him. And you need to contact the military government to come and pick him up. Right away."

The way Hunter's gaze never strayed from the animal unnerved Narelle. Every muscle in his body locked and coiled in preparation to attack. She shifted her stance in an effort to protect the bedraggled mutt from this side of the man she'd never seen before.

Opting for a simpler question, she asked, "How do you know it's a he?"

His brow arched, and he shot her a disapproving look. "Because only males were bred and created as war mongrels."

War mongrels? She vaguely recalled the term. "The dog is from a military program?"

How had it ended up on this out of the way satellite station? Only criminals, runaways and those looking to stay under the radar ever came here. Government personnel rarely ventured this far off their designated track to police anything.

"Yes."

Narelle had the unnerving feeling she'd stepped over some invisible line without trying. The dog or war mongrel as he referred whimpered and slid closer to her hip. Warm brown eyes peered up at her and Narelle softened.

She tried again. "You were in the military, right? He's hungry, Hunter. At least we can feed him before contacting the authorities to find out where he belongs."

"Damn it, Narelle!" He exploded and took two steps away as he drove his hands through his midnight hair. His broad back stretched beneath the shirt. A harsh exhale followed. "You don't know what you're getting into."

She surged to her feet equally roused. "Explain it then. It's a dog, Hunter. A lost and hungry animal. I can't believe you'd refuse a simple request to feed it."

He spun around and pointed a finger at her. "It's not a dog! It's a war mongrel, trained to search, attack and kill enemy forces with his partner."

She trembled in the face of the fury he made no attempts to hide. "Partner? How do you know all of this by looking at him? Maybe he's someone's pet."

His doubtful look cast in her direction left her flushing. "Someone's harmless pet wouldn't have a jack output located in his left ear."

The dog pushed up to its haunches and cocked his large triangular head to the side. Intelligence gleamed in the round eyes and despite his weakened state, Narelle could believe Hunter's assertions.

"Is there a way to contact his partner?"

Hunter glanced at her sharply. Fear and another stab of pain darted through his eyes. "You have no idea what you're asking me, Narelle."

Those strong hints of emotion hit Narelle hard and struck a like chord within. Unable to resist, she moved toward him, her hand landing on his bare forearm. "I'm sorry, Hunter. Maybe I should go. I just thought you'd—"

"Fuck!" Another strong blast of emotion before he used her hand to jerk her forward. Off balance in her heeled boots, Narelle fell in his direction. Firm, warm arms wrapped around her waist and clenched her tightly against the hard length of his body. "How do you do this to me?"

The better question was how he managed to take her off guard. Struggling, she pushed at his chest. "Hunter!"

Hard lips pressed to her parted mouth. Shocked and tempted, Narelle stilled. Hunter ran his hands up to the middle of her back, keeping her steady as his tongue plundered the depths of her mouth. Passion and restrained desire from their past flirtations burst through. Narelle moaned from the heat of the lips devouring hers.

Blunt fingers kneaded her spine, and like liquid, Narelle melted into his hold. Every touch, every stroke fanned the flames. A broken moan slipped past her iron control. Mentally cursing, she wanted to hold back. Anything to keep Hunter from realizing how much she craved what he offered each and every time she showed at The Zone.

It wasn't a short kiss. Nor a long one either. The length carried enough time for him to completely disarm and disorient Narelle. With obvious reluctance, she eased away. It only worked because Hunter allowed it. Her lids fluttered open to witness the wetness of his bottom lip, which he licked as if savoring her taste.

She touched a finger to her own tender mouth. Breasts full and heavy, she stared, trying to figure out how this changed things because Narelle knew it had. Something very important shifted between them with the kiss.

Hunter released her, moving back slightly. "Get rid of the animal, Narelle."

"I can't." What didn't he understand? She waved an arm behind her. "Look at him. He's obviously starved and hasn't eaten in a while. His coat is matted in places and I'm not sure how long he's been loose on the streets."

The dog didn't make a sound, head tilted to the side as if he knew they discussed his fate. No whine or begging eyes as she assumed most dogs did. Acceptance stared back and for some reason the look hit Narelle hard.

She faced Hunter again. "Please."

His sigh drew her gaze to his full lips. Lips she'd kissed a moment ago. Pain flashed across his face before his expression blanked. "You're asking for a lot."

"You were a soldier at one point. Maybe you could contact someone to find out how he ended up here." Narelle remembered mention of Hunter's past in the military. Rumors claimed he'd been a Jutak warrior, but he never confirmed or denied. He did acknowledge being in the Vargos war though.

"I don't have to contact anyone to get that information. I can use his output jack if he'll let me and get at least information about his partner."

Relief rolled over her, and Narelle grinned. "Good."

She ran a hand over the dog's head. Or maybe she should refer to it by its proper name of war mongrel. A bony shoulder pushed harder at her side.

"If it works," Hunter warned, lips pursed and glare in full force. "He might not let me."

And part of Hunter hoped the war mongrel wouldn't. He didn't want to do this. He didn't want to connect back with a past best left behind him. But Narelle's grey eyes softened to a cloudy blue, pulling at something in his chest he couldn't resist.

"At least we can try."

He wanted to ignore her plea. It was best for all of them to ignore it. Yet Hunter knew he wouldn't. Right now with her gaze shining with hope, Hunter found Narelle hard to resist. It was always that way when she was around. The woman could ask for anything from him with that look in her eyes and Hunter would work to get it for her.

"Alright."

THREE

"Alright."

Narelle hoped she hid her relief when Hunter gave in.

"Get him out of the booth. I'll need space to work."

She shifted about the table and the war mongrel moved, leaping to the floor before she could call him. "He's pretty smart."

Hunter snorted, going down to one knee beside the animal. "They usually were. Only the best for the government."

Unable to take her eyes off of Hunter, Narelle rested her butt on the edge of the table. From this angle, she stood above him. Waves of black hair taunted and she wanted to grip the strands, test if they were as soft as they looked. Black synth fabric spread over broad shoulders. The sleeves rolled to his elbows revealed a fine dusting of black hair on his forearms.

Throat tight as desire began a slow curl in her belly, she asked, "How does the jack thing work?"

Hunter tipped his head up and grinned. Narelle's insides clenched. His face might be scarred and weather beaten from a life built on hardship, but his grin was worth every credit she had in her offshore account and then some. The uptick at the corner of his mouth, the fuller bottom lip and his even teeth melted a portion of the wall she tried to keep up around him.

Jealousy flared. Despite not giving in to his flirting, she wondered how many women took him up on the offer to spend time in the bed of the apartment he lived in above the bar. Hunter was too potent for his own good and every female who crossed the door of The Zone agreed with her. The attraction wasn't in his looks. No, it was in the aura he emanated with seeming easy.

"Jack output." He held up his right wrist to reveal smooth, tanned skin she wanted to lick. "You are aware I had to undergo surgical enhance-ments when I transferred?"

"You were in the Vargos war. All of the frontline soldiers received adjustments." Adjustments was the nicest term Narelle could think of for what a lot of those men and women went through. An average humanoid wouldn't have survived in the war going against the aliens intent on taking over this sector, so the government added cyber enhancements. Legs, arms and other body parts deemed in need of strengthening.

"I was a Jutak warrior first."

Elite soldiers based on the planet Enotia. They worked for their govern-ment and fought injustice wherever needed.

"What does that have to do with this?" Narelle was honestly curious. This was the most personal information he'd shared. Granted, most of the blame lay at her feet since she ran when Hunter pushed.

His stare hardened. "Not all Jutaks are Enotian. Some of us joined because of being half-breeds or not being accepted on our own worlds. My reason was a little different."

Not knowing what to say, Narelle remained quiet. Hunter looked away as he continued to speak. "Have you ever heard of Lomus?"

"Yes. The planet was the first to be destroyed by the Vargos. Scientist believe it will never be habitable again and all of the Lomanis died in their fight to stop the Vargos. They failed."

"Not all of them died." His low muttered whisper left her stunned.

"Hunter?" Narelle shoved her hips off the table and approached, but the dark look in his eyes when he glanced up stopped her.

"Very few of us lived. We escaped to other planets and hid who we were. No one wanted to hear about the Vargos back then."

No, they hadn't. The Lomanis had appealed for help within months of the Vargos attacking their home world, but it was viewed as a difference between two races and not requiring official involvement from the govern-ment. Only the Vargos hadn't been satisfied with annihilating their adopted planet and the native Lomanis who gave them sanctuary.

They waited years, building their tech and their armies then launched an all out war against every planet in the vicinity. Once the government got involved, the battles escalated and it took ten years to defeat them and end the war.

"How old were you when you left Lomus, Hunter?"

"Young. My mother and father wasted no time in getting us to a shuttle and leaving when they saw what was inevitable. I became a Jutak warrior as soon as I was old enough, because I knew they wouldn't question my origins or reveal the secret to anyone."

The Jutaks lived by their own brand of justice working within the lines of the law. Barely.

Hunter returned his attention to the dog and his wrist. "I only told you, so you don't panic when you watch what I'm about to do."

Narelle had no time to digest the warning before Hunter rubbed at his wrist with his thumb and his skin parted to reveal a small square compartment which snapped open. Her eyes widened at the intricate array of wires and blipping lights inside. She'd never actually seen the evidence of the modifications on those soldiers.

Hunter's actions drew the attention of the war mongrel who perked up and pawed at Hunter's thigh.

"Haltzo. Sitzen." The sharp commands flew from Hunter's mouth.

Narelle didn't understand the foreign words, but the war mongrel sat at attention, haunches quivering. His gaze never left Hunter's face.

"Lomanis apparently have a natural affinity for machine and tech. I discovered this after the fact." Hunter kept his voice low but didn't turn in her direction. Narelle focused knowing this was important.

"Ofen."

The dog's left ear folded back to reveal a panel which Hunter opened further. Narelle pressed a hand to her stomach. A section along the side of the animal's head slid away filled with electronics and a small probe extended.

"Um…Hunter. What are you doing?" Though she had a vague idea.

For the first time since agreeing, she sensed a hesitation in his actions. "I'm going to see if I can get an idea of his partner although I'm fairly sure the soldier is dead."

Worry set in and she jerked upright from her slumped pose. Despite wanting to help the stray, concern rose. She didn't want to do anything at the expense of Hunter. "Maybe you shouldn't do this."

The war mongrel's upper lip peeled back on a snarl, sharp teeth flashing as it lunged.

"Haltzo!" Another snapped order from Hunter to the war mongrel. "Sit down, Narelle and no sudden moves."

Exhaling sharply, she resumed her half-sit, half-lean on the table behind her. Her heart thumped on pace with her increased breathing. "Be careful, Hunter."

"Always, baby."

She rolled her eyes at the cocky tone, crossed her legs at the ankle and waited. Hunter connected the probe to a port in his wrist and flinched. Observing in silence as requested, Narelle gripped the edge of the table behind her.

When Hunter tipped his head to the side, the whites of his eyes darkened until the entire orbs turned black. Narelle sucked in a gasp. She didn't know much about Lomanis. Was this normal? The war mongrel whined and a red flush stained Hunter's cheeks. Should she interfere?

But no, he'd been explicit in his instructions, and she didn't want to do anything to interrupt what was happening.

Information downloaded at a rapid pace into the section of Hunter's brain designed for this process. He gritted his teeth against the accompanying twinges of pain from linking with a war mongrel he wasn't supposed to connect with. The familiar rush brought its own brand of hurt.

Images and memories occurred in flashes but enough for Hunter to piece together the details. The surface file ended abruptly. Releasing an unsteady breath, Hunter detached, closed the flap on his wrist and locked the war mongrel's jack output. Once everything was secure, he braced one hand on the floor and closed his eyes. The burn assured his eyes had changed during the process. What did Narelle think? Would she be freaked? Appalled at how *other* he really was?

No time to think of her reaction. He'd been correct in his initial assumption. "The soldier or his handler died on a mission. Not sure how Bogan survived and why it didn't return to the nearest base or command site as it's trained to do."

"Bogan," Narelle murmured and the dog's ears flickered, looking toward her for the first time since gaining Hunter's attention.

"Also known as K9-15." Hunter rose to his feet, battling an over-whelming wave of grief that came with the brief moment of connection. A connection he hadn't felt in years. For good reason. A man only survived the sort of pain he'd gone through one time in his life if he was lucky. More than that and a person was left devastated to the point of no return.

For Hunter, it had almost come to that. "The war mongrel needs to eat. I'll see what I can pull together in the kitchen. Again, no guarantee it will accept the food."

Truth be told he wasn't sure how K9-15 survived. The lack of a handler and government assistance should have consigned the war mongrel to death. Of course, it looked like the animal was close enough to that state already.

"It's a he not an it." Narelle's interjection pulled Hunter's gaze back to her.

This was the soft side he'd sensed beneath her tough exterior. She needed to understand. "War mongrels were created to be weapons. Disposable. You had to treat it as such. Attachments were strictly forbidden."

For all the good it did. One thing the government failed to take into consideration was the bond which grew between man and animal. Intense training, cyber-connections and depending on one another in life and death situations tended to create a level of trust and intimacy which could never be avoided. Bonds formed on less.

Narelle's eyes softened as she stared at Bogan, who stood next to his thigh. "Too late for the warning. I think this guy is attached."

Hunter hoped she was wrong. Very wrong. He'd already been down that road and had the scars to prove it.

FOUR

"We need to return him."

Narelle didn't want to address Hunter's comment and changed the subject. "Did you find out what you needed?"

Hunter tossed her a knowing smirk. "K9-15 was the last in his batch created as a war mongrel. Excelled at his training. Almost didn't make the WIRED program though. War mongrels who didn't pass the program were put down as failures."

"Why?" Narelle couldn't imagine putting down this beautiful animal.

"They couldn't find a handler to sync with him."

Narelle's brows lowered. "That doesn't make sense. That's the purpose of the project."

Hunter shrugged and clicked his teeth. "Komm."

Bogan obediently followed him into the back kitchen. Hunter pulled out a dish and filled it with a broken protein bar. After studying the grainy bits, the food disappeared in a gulp. Brown eyes shot to Hunter, and Narelle held her breath as Hunter added several more pieces.

"Every K9 is different. Most bonded easily, but from what I've seen in his memory banks, Bogan only made it because of Joseph Donner. That's the soldier who died on their last assignment together."

Staring at the dog as he daintily nibbled on the food left Narelle at a loss. "But you can help him, right?"

"A lot doesn't add up." Hunter shook his head, then went back to filling a bowl with water and setting it next to Bogan.

"What do you mean?" Narelle pressed.

Hunter spared her a glance and grasped the back of his neck with another of those telling sighs. "Even injured and without his handler, K9-

15 shouldn't have come near you or let you near him. It's not in the training."

"Maybe he went against his training."

Remorse and a heavy dose of anger formed Hunter's frown. "It's best for all if you contact the government and return him, Narelle."

He kept pushing for what she knew was the right step but something Narelle couldn't put her finger on held her back. Why did she feel this strong affinity for the dog? She'd never had a pet or a desire to own one. "I can't, Hunter. Don't ask me to do that yet."

Broad fingers jammed through the waves of his hair as he pursed his lips. "You do realize the possibility of it...*him* surviving is slim? Look at him, Narelle. There's the very real danger to anyone if he decides to attack. He's a highly-trained asset. War mongrels weren't meant to last without their handlers. I should know."

The last statement was telling as was the brief glimpse of grief twisting his features. "What does that mean?"

"It means unless he can sync to another handler, he's going to die anyway."

Brutal, hard, honest truth. She expected no less from this man who teased and enticed with a single glance. "What if you sync with him?"

No hiding his obvious distaste. "No."

Narelle occupied her hands by shuffling the container of packaged protein bars on the counter. Anything to keep from touching Hunter to ease his pain as she wanted. "But you have experience. You seem to know about this handler stuff. With your adjustments, couldn't you do it?"

"I'm not in the military any more for a reason."

Hunter's rough growl rasped against her senses. Hiding her renewed desire, Narelle studied his expression. There was more he wasn't telling. Secrets. Hunter Gils was a man of many secrets. But then so was she. Anyone who came to this off the track location came because they needed a place to hide. A place where no one questioned.

Letting the matter drop was the right thing to do. Contacting the government to get their property was the appropriate step to take. Yet, Narelle hesitated. Hunter knew a lot more than he was letting on. Following instinct, she asked, "You were in the WIRED program, weren't you?"

His head snapped up. "Whether I was or not is secured classified information. My role in the military during the Vargos war is top secret."

"That a yes?" It seemed natural to push. "Sounds like a yes."

His brows pinched deeper, and a snarl rattled. "Don't go there, Narelle."

She ignored the warning even as her breasts swelled in the face of his demand. "I'm only asking because you can help him. I know it."

As if a switch flipped, Hunter's demeanor changed. Anger dissipated and something else took its place. The lines of his shoulders eased. He shifted the weight of his hips, the cocky stance drawing her gaze down to note his prominent arousal against the cloth of the black cargo pants.

When she found the energy to bring her eyes back up, wicked glee and pure seduction stared back at her. "I'll try. For a price."

"A price? What price?" She stiffened and backed up a step. She knew exactly what he wanted.

Hunter took a step forward, negating the attempt at distance. "One night."

Narelle's heart pounded. Licking her lips, she repeated his words "One night? For what?"

Pinning her to the wall with his body, his rough palm cupped her cheek. "It ends now. No more games. You know what I want in exchange."

Shivers worked their way through her body. Tendrils of desire awakened and coiled around her lower half. She tried to speak and had to clear her throat twice. "Are you really so desperate you'd bargain for a night to get me in bed?"

"Yes." Simple and ruthless. No remorse in the blunt tone he used. "You have no idea how desperate I am to crawl between your thighs and see if you're as hot on the inside as you are on the outside."

"Pathetic, Hunter. You're pathetic." But her voice thickened. "What makes you think I want to sleep with you?"

His lips twitched. "Oh, we wouldn't be sleeping."

Need burned a path of arousal straight from her nipples to the place between her thighs. Narelle jerked her face away from his tender touch. She wanted him but if she slept with Hunter how would she resist him in the future? Without a doubt sex with him would be like no other. He possessed the ability to shred her heart if given the chance.

She swallowed and forced the answer past dry lips. "No. I'm not sleeping with you."

His hand dropped and Narelle immediately missed the contact. He shrugged broad shoulders and moved away, freeing her from the press of his hard body. "Fine. I'll contact the authorities and make arrangements for them to pick up K9-15."

"Bastard," she spat, out of control and stepped to the side. Far enough away to control the urge to strike out physically. To hurt him for forcing her into this position.

All traces of humor washed from his face. "Bastard? No, not a bastard, but I am a man tired of the chase. Give me what I want, Narelle, and I'll give you what you want."

"You don't know what I want."

His head tipped to the side. "I know exactly what you want because it mirrors my own dreams. I want to drown in the scent of you. I want your soft skin beneath my hands no matter how rough they are. I want to stroke deep into the heart of you as you clench around me with the hunger we both have for one another. Deny it if you must but I know, Narelle. I see it in your eyes every time you refuse me."

"I'm not falling for you baiting me."

Hunter leaned close, but Narelle refused to give ground again. Amusement twinkled in his eyes. "Coward."

The whisper wafted across her cheek, and her insides clenched. Damn him. Damn him for knowing exactly what he did to her.

"I'm not a coward."

His lips quirked. "Then ask for what you want, and I promise to give it to you."

Demand and pleasure all wrapped into one sensuous statement. She could have him, touch him. Narelle balled her fists and stood tall. "You'll help the war mongrel, Bogan?"

An abrupt nod as he folded his arms across his chest.

She'd like to knock the smug grin from his face. "Agreed."

His brown gaze smoldered. "Tell me. I need to hear what you're agreeing to."

"One night, Hunter. You and I. In exchange, you'll try to sync with Bogan."

Too easy. Hunter couldn't believe he'd gotten her to give in. Fine trembles ran through him. Finally. At last he had a means of finally getting what he wanted from Narelle. He'd have her in his bed and all it entailed.

Bogan shifted about, reminding him of his presence. Hunter didn't want to do this. No, he *really* didn't want to do this. Helping Narelle and the war mongrel would open wounds long ago healed. It also meant revealing more of himself than he wanted to. None of that would stop him from this course of action though.

"But you sync with Bogan first. If it doesn't work, I owe you nothing."

He grunted. Always planning a way out. "Agreed. If the war mongrel rejects me, I won't hold you to our bargain."

There was a very real chance of that anyway. Tension eased from her shoulders and Hunter suffered a moment of regret for his methods but quickly squashed it. They both wanted this. He'd merely provided Narelle a way of accepting which allowed her to still deny she wanted him every bit as much as he wanted her. If this didn't work, he'd find another means of getting her in his bed.

Hunter turned toward the war mongrel, who lay stretched out on the floor, head planted on his front paws. Hunter crouched and made sure to establish eye contact. He signaled with his hand and used the verbal commands all soldiers in the special unit had been taught. "Komm."

Bogan perked to attention, trotted over to Hunter and sat. Hunter took a deep breath. "Ofen."

The slot by his ear opened again with a snick. Hunter rubbed at his inner wrist activating the pad. A press of his thumb, and the probe slid out. If this worked he'd once more be connected to a war mongrel. Something Hunter had avoided after the loss of his partner during the last mission he'd undertaken with his team.

Against his will, memories blasted forward. As lead, Hunter and his war mongrel Riktor entered the structure first to scout. The animal saved Hunter by ignoring a direct command for the first time ever and pushed Hunter far enough away to protect him from most of the blast. The rest of Hunter's team hadn't been so fortunate. They'd all died, leaving Hunter to walk away with massive scarring, a bad knee and malfunctioning adjustments. The list of injuries he'd sustained would have been enough to shake any soldier. Knowing everyone in his unit died created a wound that would never heal. Losing K9-03 ripped him to pieces and ruined any thought of going back to the lines.

As the sole survivor, Hunter's superiors reviewed the incident over and over before clearing him of any wrongdoing. He received his discharge at the same time the Vargos were defeated thanks to that last battle. Sure, he, Riktor and the team were listed as responsible for turning the tide during the war, but the cost had been high. Too high.

"Hunter, is everything okay?"

Narelle's softly voiced question dispelled the memories of the past. Hunter shook his head to clear it. "Fine."

She winced, and he wished he could take back the rough bite in his tone. Instead he focused on Bogan. There'd be time later to woo her with sweet words. He inserted the probe, and the initial jolt after such a long time shocked his system. The biotronics from his adjustments were powerful. Unlike earlier when he accessed the surface memories, Hunter needed to allow Bogan to connect with him on an intimate level to create the reciprocal feedback necessary for a successful sync.

With the war mongrel's history of unsuccessful matches this would be difficult. On his side, Hunter was counting on his heritage as Lomanis to aid him. Closing his eyes, he relaxed his guard and opened himself.

It didn't take long. He sensed the moment the biotronics in Bogan made contact with his. Another jolt followed by resistance on the war mongrel's part and a low whine.

"Gott, biet rel," Hunter soothed as he opened his eyes. *Good war mongrel.* "Gemfach." *Easy.*

Hunter needed to get through the animal's natural barrier to accepting another. As he expected, his own reluctance to bond again in this manner worked against him as well. Another whine from Bogan as if craving the contact but afraid.

"Gemfach," Hunter repeated running a hand over the bristling hair on his back. The short strands needed a good washing and a brushing. Something the sync would automatically take care of. "Gemfach."

His tone came through, and Bogan held still, every muscle quivering. Part of the block keeping the sync from taking place cracked. The well of emotions from the animal bombarded Hunter until he gritted his teeth against the onslaught. Grief, fear, anger and confusion. The loss of Donner had hit Bogan hard. During the mental surge, Hunter caught the handler's death in a series of slide images from the war mongrel's perspective.

Whatever assignment the two had been on ended with Donner's death and Bogan returning to the pick-up zone as trained. But not before he'd dragged the young's man body for hours attempting to bring him back. Hunter's throat locked. Riktor would have done the same for him in a similar situation. What the military failed to grasp was that syncing between a war mongrel and the soldier handler was more than computer programming and training.

Trust, love and an unshakeable bond grew. One would think the extensive testing would have revealed this. Or maybe it had and the government didn't care because the Vargos war meant more than worrying about a small elected group.

At some point Bogan realized the futility of his efforts and reluctantly left his partner behind. No one arrived to retrieve him. Days passed until hunger and fear drove Bogan in search of contact with another. How he ended up here was unclear. Static and breaks in Bogan's recording mechanism prevented Hunter from seeing those details. Probably due to the war mongrel's waning condition.

The next footage showed Narelle crouching beside the animal and then their trek to The Zone. Hunter swallowed, hesitating about the next step. If it worked, it would be irreversible. He'd be permanently linked again to a partner and all the potential pain which came along with it.

Hunter firmed his voice. "Trijl, Bogan." *Sync.*

Despite what he expected, the connection slammed into Hunter with the force of a fighter jet. Stomach dropping, he staggered to one knee. Narelle gasped behind him. Bogan rose to his haunches and snapped in her direction.

"Zut, Bogan. Haltzo." Hunter tightened his free hand on the war mongrel's ruff, keeping him from lunging for the woman behind him.

Bogan strained against Hunter's hold. His brown eyes rolled, gaze darting around. If Bogan hurt Narelle, even accidentally in his panicked state, Hunter wouldn't hesitate to shut him down with a pulse from the probe joining them.

After a warning growl, he settled and Hunter heaved a sigh of relief. He cut his gaze to Narelle. "Don't fucking move again!"

She glared.

"I mean it, Narelle. You asked for this."

"Forgive me for being concerned."

Due to his own anger her sharp voiced words almost passed him by. Then it hit him what she'd revealed. A slow smile curled his lips. "Forgiven, sweetheart."

She huffed and tipped her chin up. Hunter chuckled, but his laughter was interrupted by a wet tongue licking his hand. Right. He straightened, eyeing the wrist with the open panel and the probe inserted into the jack output on the side of Bogan's head.

"Let's try this again." After a warning glance at Narelle, Hunter turned Bogan's muzzle in his direction and used the same order from earlier. "Las. Trijl."

Bogan tried. Hunter sensed the effort on the war mongrel's behalf, but they hadn't been paired together, likely weren't a good match in any way. Eyes narrowed, Hunter relied on what he'd learned from his time with Riktor and pushed harder for the sync. His Lomanis genetics responded.

Burning at his temple signaled his eyes going black. In place of the walls and floor of his kitchen, code displayed over his vision. His brain translated the information at a pace no one could consciously track yet Hunter had instant understanding. The data download allowed him to see what he needed to accomplish the sync.

With meticulous care, Hunter layered his biotronics over the ones left behind from John Donner. A quiver ran down the spine of the war mongrel. He continued to rub his left hand over Bogan's fur. Then the shift occurred. Bogan's body filled out beneath his fingertips, bulk forming in place of his scrawny frame. Adjustments accounted for the change now that Hunter had jumpstarted them.

Hunter frowned, his concentration increasing. One more thing. Bogan started to shake, excitement overruling Hunter's orders. Almost there. Another burst of energy on Hunter's part.

Sync.

Perfect fucking sync.

Basic commands scrolled across Hunter's left eye adjustment. Commands he already knew by heart from being in the WIRED program. He and Bogan were in sync. Hunter stood up, a wave of dizziness rolling through him. Movement from the corner of his eye had him holding up a warning hand to Narelle. Her lips firmed and an odd spurt of humor prodded. She didn't listen for shit.

"Did it work?" she asked.

"Yes." He cleared his throat to relieve the dryness. As the disorientation from bonding with the war mongrel wore off, Hunter drew a deep breath. He faced Narelle, unconcerned about how he looked. This was what he'd waited for. He didn't care he'd had to play dirty to get it. "Now I've met my end of the bargain, where were we?"

FIVE

Narelle wanted to curse as she followed Hunter into his apartment above The Zone. Bogan trotted behind them, the change in his appearance and demeanor still amazing to her. His tail wagged from side to side, his shoulder brushing Hunter's leg with each step. Gone was the gaunt body and malnourished look. Instead, a robust large dog stood in its place, tan hair smoothed down as if he'd been bathed and brushed.

As Hunter opened the door, Bogan shot ahead through the crack. Nose to the floor, he went from one corner to another.

"Gemfach. Komm." Hunter tapped his upper thigh and Bogan returned to his side, tongue lolling in an obvious sign of happiness. Hunter scratched the pointed ears. "Gott, biet rel."

Curiosity got the best of her despite the nerves of being in Hunter's private space. "What language is that? The translator keeps giving the foreign words."

"There wouldn't be a translation. Most of the genetic coding to create the war mongrels came from security trained dogs on a planet called Earth. Doctors and scientists thought it wise to customize the commands using a mix of several languages from the same planet. Only soldiers in the program and the war mongrels would understand them."

"Huh." Narelle pushed the tips of her fingers into the front slit pockets of her jumpsuit. She didn't want Hunter to note her need to fidget. "Why'd he run around your place?"

"Checking for any danger. Instinct, training and a bit of science thrown in." Hunter pointed to a small alcove. "Gehe." *Go.*

After circling Hunter's legs twice, Bogan went to the corner and stretched out prone.

"Las." *Stay.*

Hunter directed his attention to Narelle. Her heart rate picked up, and her nipples betrayed her by stabbing against the front of her synth suit. As if he knew, his eyes crinkled at the corners and her stomach wobbled in response.

Narelle wanted to follow the line of questions but Hunter's gaze held a knowing glint. "Are you thinking of backing out?"

The taunt hit the mark, and Narelle stiffened. Yeah, he knew what he did to her. She couldn't hide it. Even now her body readied for him. Swollen breasts, elevated respiration, and an undeniable ache at her core. All of it affirmed her growing arousal.

"I gave my word, Hunter."

Hunter's mouth quirked, the corner tipping up in a devastating half-smile. "Then get over here."

Damn him. He stood in the center of the room, his living space as simple as the man himself. Overstuffed chairs, functional table and light source and hard floors battered and streaked with age. Her gaze shot up toward where he probably slept. Narelle squeezed her thighs together and tipped her head toward the set of metal grated stairs and loft area. "Bedroom I assume."

"Mmm."

Gathering her courage Narelle met his stare with a smirk of her own and added an extra swivel to her hips as she walked toward him.

Not that Hunter waited for her to reach him. Two steps brought him up against her and his arms whipped about her waist, causing Narelle to gasp. His mouth slanted over hers before she could protest. His tongue slid between her parted lips as he bent her backward over his arms.

Narelle should have floundered in his hold. Panicked at least. But Hunter braced his weight and nibbled at her mouth as he murmured, "I won't drop you after waiting this long."

A snort of laughter bubbled from her lips. Narelle placed her hands tentatively in the overlong strands of his hair. "That would be a waste."

Hunter lifted his head. Desire. Unlike her, he didn't try to hide it. Cheeks flushed and lids at half-mast, his desire for her was clear to see. Electric currents charged the air between them. Narelle caught her breath, blinking at the savage expression that crossed his face.

"I think I'm going to need every bit of tonight to sate my desire for you."

She swallowed. "One night is all we agreed to, Hunter."

"One night, Narelle. I remember the terms." He gripped her hair in one fist and yanked. Her neck arched back, and she soaked her panties from the dominant move. His other hand pressed the small of her back until her chest smacked into his. Her hands flew to his shoulders for balance, but there was no balance for being with Hunter.

His every action kept her off rhythm. And deep down inside, a part of her thrilled to his rough handling. Violent scarring marred one side of his face, the criss-cross hatches going down to his neck but none of it took away from his undeniable attractiveness. He focused on her with single minded determination, sparks flaring from his brown eyes. Tiny lines fanned from the corners stress or laughter she couldn't tell, but she liked them as well.

There wasn't much about Hunter she didn't like. Narelle started to say something else, maybe resume the teasing that came naturally to the both of them, when he swooped down and lifted her in his arms. She squealed, stunned to silence, and his mouth was on her again. This kiss was as powerful as the one before it but more. So much more, and she had no words to explain it.

It didn't deter Hunter who stumbled his way to the stairs. Their lips mashed together, heads twisting, tongues tangling. Narelle drowned in the sensations, searching for relief as her lower region pulsed and throbbed. Hunter broke away on a raw groan. Showing no signs her weight bothered him, he climbed the steps to the loft two at a time. When they reached the top, Narelle glanced around and realized it was nothing more than a platform space with the large bed taking up a good bit of the floor. Moonlight gleamed through a small window.

In smooth easy glides, Hunter lowered her to her feet, his hands taking every opportunity to touch and stroke. By the time she stood on her own, Narelle was a goner. No need to protest or deny the inevitable.

Not that it would mean anything. Both of them were going into this with their eyes open and Narelle hoped she didn't let Hunter deep enough to hurt her.

His rough thumb rubbed at the crease between her brows. "Such heavy thoughts and all I want to do is make you feel good, baby."

Hunter worried Narelle might change her mind. If she did…he didn't want to complete the thought. He lusted, he wanted, he craved. His cock throbbed against the front of his pants and the thought of her leaving before he got to explore to his heart's content hit him in the gut. She couldn't walk out at this point. He'd fall to the floor on his knees and whine like a baby with his favorite treat snatched away.

Her head tipped to the side as she toyed with his hair. "You think it's that easy?"

Hunter battled the pain of his growing erection and kept his groan muffled. He tugged her other hand and led the way to his bed. He was glad he'd brought the massive frame and thick air mattress. Not only did it fit his large form, but it enabled him a lot of room to play. And Hunter had every intention of playing with his sassy menace.

"Ask me after." He flicked a finger over her pouting lips, then ran his thumb over the delectable scar on her lip.

Narelle bit the tip. Hard. "You're cocky."

He cupped his hard length then slid the fastening of his pants open. Her waiting expression dared him to say it. Not going there. However, he wanted something else. "Take off your clothes, Narelle, unless you want me to rip them off."

Like a bloom in its first blush, pops of red seared her cheeks. The urge to swat him was also there. It took everything in Hunter not to laugh in her face. She wanted to hit him alright but was trapped by the bargain.

Nimble fingers flew over the front closure, and the top of the sexy suit parted giving Hunter his first up and close view of the tantalizing green skin beneath. Large mounds, plump and ripe just waiting for his mouth popped out. Forgetting about his own clothes, Hunter choked as she slid the tight material down her torso, over her hips and then down her legs.

Short red hairs formed a neat triangle at the apex of her thighs. His mouth watered from the sight. She had to bend over to undue her boots and Hunter almost stopped breathing. He ripped his shirt over his head not sure where it landed, toed off his boots and shoved his pants down then gripped his dick and pumped twice. "Fuck, Narelle. I need you now. I'm not sure how long I'll last the first time."

Naked at last, she strolled toward him, mouth curved in a teasing smile. "What about those plans to make me feel good?"

Words didn't describe what she did to him. Of all the women to cross his path, only Narelle brought out this savage side to him. His craving for her bordered on obsession and although he realized this, nothing would steer him away from every bit of the pleasure he planned to drain from her tonight.

As soon as she drew close, he pulled her in tight, smoothed his hands down the slope of her back and cupped her round ass with a firm squeeze. Narelle's breath quickened and the tiny sound sent another surge of arousal through him. Hunter sported an erection hard enough to pound her through the mattress.

A little nudge in the right direction and they fell onto his bed, though he was careful to keep his weight off of her. Narelle grasped at him and Hunter grinned. "I'm right here, woman. No need to claw at me."

This time she did slap at his shoulder but Hunter knew the perfect way to soothe her ire. He nibbled at the slim column of her throat. "Mmm, you taste better than I could imagine."

He nipped her ear and she jerked then melted in his arms. Her moan was a symphony to his senses. "That's right, baby. Give into it."

He continued to murmur nonsensical things as he licked at her skin and lapped at her collarbone until he stopped to stare at the breasts pointed in his direction. The gift before him deserved the right amount of attention so he used his hands to tease at the budded tips first, enjoying her hum of gratification. When Narelle undulated beneath him, he lowered his head to take one succulent morsel in his mouth and sucked.

"Yes! Hunter, don't stop." Desperate hands dug at his hair and Narelle's hips began to pump and twist about.

The plea contained notes of want, need and demand. Hunter let her nipple go with a plop then placed a gentle kiss on the crinkled flesh before switching to her other breast. The minute his mouth made contact, Narelle arched up on a whimper. He firmed his hold at her waist, keeping her still for his torture, though his body wanted to explode.

"I knew you'd be this hot. All those nights of dreaming about you, wanting you."

Hunter made his way down the luscious body splayed out on his bed, inhaling deeply the slight musky scent of her arousal. When he reached her feminine juncture, he parted the folds with two fingers and brushed his thumb over the swollen button, which darkened from green to a deep jeweled tone.

The muscles in Narelle's upper thighs quivered as he rubbed the nub back and forth, wetness gathering on his fingers. Smiling, Hunter lowered his head and feasted.

Soon Narelle's husky moans filled his bedroom, the bed creaked from her rocking hips and Hunter sensed her on the verge of coming.

"Hunter! You bastard if you stop now, I'll kill you."

The threat gave him pause, and Hunter laughed. He didn't believe she had a shot in space of taking him, but the thought amused him. "Why the rush, baby?"

He blew on her sensitized flesh and her hands slammed down on his head as her thighs locked about his ears. This time he dropped a kiss on her inner thigh and laughed long and loud. Only with Narelle did he always battle the need to let down his guard. She brought out the playful side of him. Hunter didn't have a lot of cause to be playful in his life and valued these moments more than she'd ever know.

"You made promises." She tipped her head up to meet his gaze down the slope of her belly.

Propping his weight on his elbows and breaking the stranglehold she had on his neck, he made a decision. He hadn't intended to drag it out, but now he needed to watch her find her release again and again. "You're right."

Hunter's smile was wolfish and Narelle felt a brief flash of fear. But no, he wouldn't hurt her. More and more, Narelle wondered if she was the one who'd end up hurting him. His eyes gleamed and warned of wicked plans.

Two fingers slid between her wet mound and stroked. Narelle clenched then forced herself to relax at the delicious sensations he wrought. When she imagined this, the one thing she hadn't expected was Hunter's determination to see to her pleasure as well as his own. She rocked her hips in time to his touch.

Another explosive burst drew close as Hunter built up the steady rise in flames licking through her insides.

"Up," he pulled his hands away and guided Narelle to her knees.

"Hunter, what are you doing?"

When he spun her around, she started to question him but Hunter's hand glided down her torso and dove back between her spread thighs.

Her head fell back against his shoulder. What he was doing felt amazing. Her thighs quivered and she couldn't fight the rhythmic clenching as she worked against his hand. She looped her arms behind her about his neck, fingers thrusting into the wild strands of hair. "Oh, yes."

"Come for me," he coaxed. "Come for me and let me see you in all your glory."

Wet slicked between her thighs. Short, hard pumps. Fast, smooth glides. Narelle gasped head thrashing on his shoulder as she fought to hold out longer. More. She wanted more before it ended.

"Hunter."

"Let it go, baby."

Narelle tried to fight the power of his pull on her but his fingers pierced her knuckle deep, stroking a place so deep inside, she didn't know it existed. She almost bucked off of him as her body betrayed her.

Trembling, Narelle barely noticed Hunter turn her back and ease her down to the bed.

"With me," he growled. "I want you with me this time."

Smooth and easy, he glided into her ready channel with little difficulty. Inside she pulsed and stretched from his width but accepted the intrusion. Another shudder rolled over Narelle and she arched up chest to chest, hands clinging to the broad shoulders spread above her, while she tried to catch her breath.

Her heart pattered off beat. The seamless ease with which he wrung an orgasm from her was frightening.

Intense brown eyes filled with arrogance and victory, pinned her to the bed. Frozen, bound by more than the physical, Narelle struggled. No, no. This wasn't how it was supposed to be. She shook her head but Hunter lowered his face to her throat, his muffled groan hard to miss. "I've waited for this."

Gentle swipes from his tongue, the press of firm lips at the pulse pounding out of sync then he braced up on his forearms, moved—and tore apart any illusions Narelle had of this staying simple. Using nothing but the sheer grace of his body, Hunter changed this from two people just having sex. It became deeper, ties seeking to bind her in a way she wouldn't want to escape.

Instinctively, Narelle knew it was deliberate on his part and a spurt of anger tugged at her senses. Feelings she refused to look at were ruthlessly shoved down in order to focus on the anger.

How dare he? How dare he force her to feel more than she this...this bet warranted?

Hair fell across Hunter's brow as he grunted with each punch of his hips. "Tonight, we don't hide," he muttered. "You're mine. All mine. Every bit of you."

Waves of pleasure dragged at her without mercy. Sweat glinted on his jaw as he kept his head down driving into her body.

"Why?" The helpless cry broke free. She pounded a fist on his shoulder.

Slowly, he eased out until only the thick crown of him remained. He licked his lips but never took his gaze from her face. "Because you want to shut me out and if all I get is tonight, you're going to let me in this once."

When he slammed forward giving her every inch of him, Narelle fell into the intimate circle he created where only the two of them existed. Her knees clamped about his sides, toes curled into the sheets.

With every stroke, he rocked her body back and forth on the linen. Narelle whimpered as his thrust grew erratic, hitting her in the same spot repeatedly. Her vision darkened as her breath grew ragged. Back bowed, she clenched her fingers on his shoulders as the world around her erupted in a haze of colors.

"Yes! Fuck, yes!"

Breath hot against her shoulder he collapsed right after. Sweat cooled on their bodies, moisture clinging to the crease between her breasts. Narelle panted, unable to stop running her hands up Hunter's damp back. Damn him! Sex had never been this explosive before and with a man she knew good and well wasn't right for her. Or maybe he was perfect for her.

Narelle expelled her breath on a sigh, her quivering thighs loosening their fierce grip on Hunter. Her heart continued to thunder in her chest as his softening length slid free. A whisper soft kiss landed on her cheek as he shifted his weight and slid to the side of her on the bed, his arms clasped tight about her waist. Narelle flowed with the movement, ending on her side facing him. It required more energy than she could spare to resist.

The tender look in his eyes did strange things to her and Narelle wanted to run and hide. Hunter must have sensed or read her mind because his hands held firm and his brows lowered, the relaxed look on his face fading. "Don't."

Narelle considered a sniping response, but one look at the eager light in his gaze dared her. With a sniff, she rolled her eyes and flipped over, giving him her back.

His muted chuckle as he cuddled close caused a reluctant smile to tilt her lips. Another kiss landed on the curve of her shoulder, the wet dip of his tongue teasing in its wake.

"All trouble and worth it," he murmured huskily.

SIX

Narelle woke in slow increments. The first thing she noticed was the heavy weight over her waist. A muscled forearm clamped possessively over her. At her back, warm heat created a cozy nest among the twisted blankets. More cozy than she should feel with this man. She wanted to doze back off and snuggle into the warm weight behind her.

That would only make leaving harder.

Easing away slightly, Narelle had one thought at the forefront of her mind. Get up and get out. All before Hunter woke and decided to talk about…their night. Or whatever this was. Every touch tonight, every smile in her direction sliced through her heart.

Another slide and Hunter's arm fell to the covers, granting her freedom. As she rose and stood beside the massive bed, Narelle's gaze was drawn back to the man sprawled over most of it. A beautiful network of scars on the far right of his back marred the muscles. Her fingers had traced the lines of some, but the way he tensed at the touch warned her away from probing.

Similar meshwork marks from knee to mid-calf ruined his right leg. With his leg bent it was hard to miss. It didn't matter though. Hunter's body appealed to her scars and all. Now that she knew what he looked like beneath the dark clothes he favored, it would be difficult to resist him in the future.

Temptation called, and Narelle moved the sheet slightly, stopping after baring his lower half to her view.

Military fit as she once heard a friend say about a former lover. Hunter retained a muscled, sleek frame. Toned and tight, she'd reaped the benefit of his powerful thrusts, the slap of those hard thighs. And his chest.

Narelle knew her gaze had grown dreamy as she reminisced about stroking every inch over a chest he'd pressed against her like a leaden weight, keeping her immobile as he rutted into her sex.

Round butt cheeks as hard as they appeared twitched as if he sensed her stare. No denying he had a great body. Nibbling her bottom lip, she stepped away. If she didn't force herself to move, she'd never leave. Her gaze searched for where they'd thrown her clothes.

Across the room, curled in a ball, but head up Bogan snuffled and his tail gave one wag. He must have snuck up after they'd fallen asleep. Vigorous bouts of sex tended to tire anyone out. She glanced back at Hunter's sleeping form.

Emotions held her locked in place. She inhaled sharply, mad at herself for her inability to compartmentalize this. Unfortunately, the breath she took only filled her lungs with the smell of the man himself. Dark, masculine and the hint of some woodsy scent. She took another whiff against her better judgment and reevaluated. If danger had a smell that lingered in the air as well.

Walk away her inner voice warned. Before her heart engaged further. Narelle gathered her clothes and dressed, her gaze constantly going to Hunter as if drawn by a magnetic force. Curses fell silently off her tongue as she ripped her eyes away from the impressive sight of his body there for the taking if she wanted a second round.

A mirthless grin curled her lips. More like the fifth round. She stuffed her feet into her boots, feeling the twinges in her sensitive parts attesting to a night well spent with a man who knew his way around a woman's body. She'd have some light bruising and tender parts tomorrow.

And just like that her mind delved back into flashes of having sex with Hunter. The way he'd pressed into her welcoming body, the powerful thrust of his hips as he'd leaned over her, his breath warm on her face. Then he'd lined up his face next to hers and whispered every dirty thought he'd ever had about her in her ear.

Putting into words the things he'd thought about stirred Narelle in ways she hadn't imagined. His seductive voice lent another layer to the passion igniting between them and she'd had one explosive climax after another.

Hunter woke when an elbow jabbed his rib followed by a knee which grazed his dick. He bit off a curse and managed not to move as Narelle shifted. He held his breath awaiting what she'd do next. Only a brief pause and the sheets fell about his hips to his upper thighs. Hunter's erection sprung to life in anticipation of a robust repeat session of earlier.

The covers slipped more baring him completely. He grinned. Maybe

Narelle planned to wake him in an unexpected way. He listened. Able to discern the rustle of clothing, he stiffened. Wait! Would she really try to sneak out without saying *anything* to him?

Hunter stayed still until he definitely heard the sounds of her now shod feet. Light scuffles as she made her way to the stairs leading to the lower level were the last straw. He rolled to the side and opened his eyes, interrupting her stealthy escape. "Narelle."

Hands on the railing, she spun with a gasp. "I thought you were asleep."

Obviously. "I woke as you tried to slip out."

She dropped her hand, planted both on her hips and notched up her determined chin. He wished he didn't find the pose enchanting. "I was leaving. My end of the bargain was met."

Insulted, Hunter sat up, tossing the sheets to the side and out of his way. This had been far from a casual fuck. "Without saying goodbye?"

What happened between them was more than a bargain. Naked, Hunter met her glare for glare. He smirked when her gaze dipped to his straining erection. Hunger flashed across her features. Now that he'd had a taste, he wanted more as well.

Narelle's gaze shifted lower as she took in the uneven map of twisted red lines from his right knee to lower calf. It took everything not to hide them. The scars came as a result of emergency repair surgery on his adjustments. They worked well enough, but if he strained the biotronics past their endurance the circuitry misfired thus part of the reason for his discharge from the service. His last mission may have helped end the war against the Vargos but the price had been high.

When Narelle finally lifted her defiant gaze, Hunter realized she wouldn't change her mind about leaving. She stomped down their stairs in clear dismissal.

At her refusal to give in, his jaw tightened and frustration flickered. Hunter chased after her. "What are you playing at, Narelle?"

"I'm not playing," she returned without stopping.

Control slipped and Hunter fisted his hands as they both drew to a halt in his living area. "You know this isn't over between us."

She spun on her heels glaring. "On the contrary, Hunter. This was never meant to be more than an interlude."

She wanted to play it this way? Pretend the heat which exploded between them every time they crossed paths didn't exist? "What do you think is going to happen next, Narelle? That you'll walk out the door and I just forget about you?"

For a minute the bravado weakened. The tough girl façade faded. Then she shored up her defenses. "Hunter, let this go. I'm not the one for you."

Hunter restrained the urge to punch a hole in the wall. She was exactly the one for him. Trouble was, Hunter didn't know how to convince her of the fact. He bit back a snarl of fury as she crossed toward the door and hesitated hand on the knob. Something like regret flashed over her features. "I hope everything works out with the war mongrel."

Narelle slipped through the opening of the door and closed it behind her before Hunter could respond. Defeat lashed at his senses and the bitter taste of loss filled his mouth. He muttered all the way back to his bedroom, kicking at his clothes on the floor and ignoring the lingering scent of their lovemaking from the tumbled sheets.

Bogan trotted over and nosed at Hunter's leg. With a sigh, Hunter gave up for now and decided there was no need in chasing her. She'd be back in his bar again. He had to believe that and the next time, he planned to be prepared. Narelle was his and now that he'd had a taste, he wasn't letting her go.

In the meantime, Hunter took a quick shower unable to focus with the scent of her on every inch of his skin. Afterwards, he settled at the cramped desk shoved in the corner. The click clack of Bogan's nails followed. He booted up the old computer with its top of the line interior workings. To any who sought to rob him, the would be criminals would overlook this out of date tech, never knowing what he had housed on it.

Hunter keyed in his password and paused briefly as he thought about what he was about to do. One more step, one more door to his past opened. This could only bring back bad memories. Bogan groaned and nudged against Hunter in order to rest his muzzle on his thigh. Hunter scratched the animal behind the ear.

"All in or nothing." With that announcement, he keyed in a site he had avoided over the last few years having no need to maintain contact with the information or the people. But niggling concern played at the back of his mind and Hunter refused to let the puzzle sit unanswered. He glanced at the tan and black war mongrel. "I need to find out how you ended up here and how to get you back."

Mysteries never sat well with him.

SEVEN

Narelle hated the desire urging her to return to Hunter as she strode down the silent street. His determined glance as she'd basically run away affected her more than she wanted to admit. But Narelle couldn't lower her guard and let him in. She knew her weaknesses. Without much effort he'd have her love whether he wanted it or not.

If she wasn't careful there was more than physical pain at stake. It was her heart. A heart in need of avoiding the experience if Hunter didn't feel the same way.

Truth to be told, Hunter was a distraction she didn't need. As she hurried from the entrance of The Zone her thighs twinged. Zaps of discomfort reminding Narelle of the passion which had flared during the night with Hunter. She'd imagined sex with him on numerous occasions, but reality far exceeded anything she'd dreamed.

At least she'd gotten him to agree to take on the dog. Or what had he called it? Her brows creased in deep thought. War mongrel. That's right. One of the many things which tied to his secretive military past. Though not so secretive since he'd shared quite a bit with her today.

Narelle walked a good way beyond The Zone, debating if she wanted to take her shuttle and leave immediately or return to the temp housing unit. Might be better to leave in the morning when she wasn't half sex drunk from the orgasms Hunter gave her. Her body clenched in remembrance and she missed a step.

To her left a voice called out, "Did you just leave The Zone?"

Stiffening, Narelle's pace slowed as a solitary figure separated himself from the shadows. "Who cares?"

The dark-haired man dressed in common leathers from head to toe tipped his head to the side and smiled. "Asking for a friend."

While the smile increased his face from attractive to downright handsome, the blank look in his eyes said something all too different. There was death in the icy blue stare setting off all sorts of warnings.

Narelle fingered the knife strapped to her thigh and moved forward. "Can't help you."

Much to her dismay, he skip-jogged to catch up with her. "Well at least tell me if you know Hunter Gils. I'm hoping to catch up with him. We knew each other in the past."

Narelle shot him a look from the side of her eyes he couldn't mistake and withdrew her knife. Still striding down the street at a pace which required him to keep up or get lost, she said, "Can't help you with that either."

If she wasn't mistaken, the next sound he made was a low, dark growl. Before Narelle could react, he grabbed her by the elbow, yanked her to a stop and spun her around to face him fully. She flowed with the abrupt motion, sliding the grip of the knife in her palm and slashing out at his mid-section.

He called her an unsavory name as his hand fell away and Narelle chuckled as she crouched and they circled one another. "Not the first time someone's said that about me."

Not responding to her jibe, he launched a flurry of kicks and punches in her direction. Narelle blocked each and backed up, victory singing in her blood as she cut his forearm and blood spattered to the ground. Another curse. Much more intense than the last.

"You're exactly the type Hunter would go for." It almost sounded like approval in his voice. "He has an eye for strong women. Females with a little fight in them."

Narelle didn't like hearing herself compared to Hunter's *type*. She ducked, avoiding a fist to the face, but he struck again and the hit landed on her side, sending the breath out of her on a groan.

Crap, he had fists of steel. She couldn't take too many direct blows like that one or he'd have her laid out in no time.

Stepping away with her weapon up and ready, Narelle couldn't resist a taunt of her own. "You could always go to The Zone and look for Hunter yourself."

In ordinary circumstances, she would never give someone up like this but Narelle had every bit of faith in Hunter handling himself just fine against this man. He had former soldier written all over him. The way he held himself, the fighting stance and the way his gaze never left hers told its own story. But his presence contained none of the deadly energy found circling the man she'd just left.

"No need. You're exactly the break I've been waiting for. He hasn't let another close to him in years. Not one friend or lover."

Before Narelle could ponder that statement, he stopped playing with her. Lightning fast moves Narelle couldn't hope to counter came at her. The crack of a fist to the jaw sent blood spurting from her abused tongue, another strike to her soft belly left a fiery trail of pain, followed by a sweeping kick, which landed her on the ground.

The knife flew from her grip as Narelle crashed into the ground and cried out. Her head rocked twice, pain exploded and stars raced across her vision. Body tensing, she prepared to meet her death bravely. The only measure of relief came from knowing Hunter would be pissed and this stranger, whoever he was, had no idea what he'd started.

She might fight the attraction between her and the owner of The Zone but Narelle wasn't foolish enough to believe Hunter wouldn't take her death personally. For some reason, he wanted her beyond one night of passion.

Despite the pain, her lips curled in a grin at the thought. Her attacker crouched beside her, his leather pants rippling. He braced a palm on the ground and leaned close to hover above her face. "You find something funny?"

She choked out a laugh. "Only that I wish I could be there when you get fucked up by Hunter."

He snarled and gripped her hair, pulling her head back and putting a strain on her neck as he next spoke. "We'll see about that. It's long past time for Hunter Gils to pay his dues."

Not understanding amidst the pain and confusion, Narelle blinked. Nausea swirled and she spat another wad of blood out. "Maybe you should talk to him yourself. Hunter and I aren't exactly friends."

Truth. They'd had sex. No plans for more.

A grim smile crossed his handsome face. He dragged a finger down her cheek, across her jaw and stopped at the pounding pulse in her throat. The move threatened in its simplicity. Justified fear surged as he pressed down with his whole palm surrounding her lifeline. The throbbing beat jumped in response, causing him to release a ruthless chuckle.

Every bit of her body ached, but Narelle considered a vicious head-butt to escape. Blue shards dared her to make the move. She remained still, knowing he was one wrong word away from snapping her neck no matter his issue with Hunter.

As if he had all the time in the world, her attacker loosened his grip, and continued his forefinger's prior journey. The blunt digit tapped further down before landing on her collarbone. Narelle couldn't control her shiver. He traced an odd pattern on the tender skin, then yanked hard enough on her hair with his other hand to pull the roots. Narelle screamed against her will.

"Hunter always did like marking his women," he whispered. "Possessive and stupid at the same time. For future reference, if you want to deny
belonging to a man, make sure he doesn't leave his love bruises all over
your throat."

Barking in the distance dispelled the eerie quiet of the night. He stood
suddenly, the flap of his leather coat swishing. *Bogan.* Without a doubt in
her mind, Narelle knew it had to be the war mongrel. She rolled to her
side, gasping but determined. Sharp pain pierced her side.

Groaning, she pressed against the injury and pushed up to her knees.
The world spun in a sickening circle and she crashed back to her stomach.

Damn it, Narelle knew she should have left the sexy bartender alone.
Anger renewed at Hunter pushing the matter between them but her eyes
closed against her will. She hoped to the dark beyond she didn't pass out.
If she did, Hunter would probably freak when he found her.

Thinking of him brought a small measure of calm. Her pulse slowed its
erratic pace and Narelle could no longer hold off the inevitable as she fell
forward and surrendered to the encroaching darkness.

Hunter finished the file he'd downloaded and was no closer to figuring
out how the government lost such a valuable commodity like the war
mongrel. They were notorious for keeping track of every person or
machine they spent money on. Only problem was, if Hunter probed
further, he was bound to draw attention he didn't want or need.

As he shut down the system, Bogan sat up with a whine, gaze locked
on Hunter's face. Pushing away from his make shift desk, Hunter turned
completely toward the corner where the war mongrel shook with nervous
energy. Ignoring his naked state, Hunter attempted to soothe the animal.
"Gemfach, Bogan. Komm."

Instead of coming toward him as he'd commanded, Bogan alerted, tail
straight out and body angled at the window. Hunter stood and crossed the
space to place a hand on the war mongrel's head. He and the others
soldiers had learned the small physical contact would sometimes comfort
the animals when they appeared on edge.

Bogan didn't relax.

Hunter crouched beside him, hoping to connect, but Bogan avoided his
gaze. Deliberately. Frustration mixed with empathy bubbled up for the
animal who no longer had a handler. He didn't need this.

Thanks to Narelle, Hunter was left in a position he detested. Still the
war mongrel wasn't completely to blame for his behavior. Their training
prohibited ignoring a nearby threat of any sort, which meant something
was wrong. The idea alone brought out Hunter's own protective nature.
"What is it?"

He didn't expect an answer but the animal's entire body quivered with the need to move. Brows drawn close, it took a moment for Hunter's senses to attune using their newly formed sync. Whatever it was had the war mongrel really disturbed.

Trying to puzzle it out wouldn't get Hunter anywhere and the more he stood waiting, the more agitated Bogan grew, letting out another low whine.

All at once the obvious answer came to Hunter. Only one thing, one person could have caused the war mongrel's strong reaction.

Narelle.

Despite the trijl he now shared with Bogan, the animal for some reason had also endeared himself to Narelle. If Bogan's body language was anything to go by then she was in danger.

"Gehe! Suche." *Go! Search!* The command snapped out, Hunter's own urgency lending it a resounding bite.

Bogan launched from his spot and headed for the bedroom window. His lean body streamed through the space easily, back paws clipping the frame as he cleared the opening. Hunter leaned out to catch a glimpse of him going down the rickety outdoor stairs and off into the night, his muscled brown body low to the ground in stealth mode.

"Shit!" Hunter delayed for a bare moment. Then he backed away from the window to drag on his pants. Foregoing a shirt, he grabbed his hand-held laser and two knives which he tucked into his boots after slamming them on his feet. A back-up pistol stashed in the waist of his pants and he was ready.

Hunching his large body over, Hunter climbed through the window following the path Bogan had taken. As he barreled down the now deserted streets, more curses slipped past Hunter's lips. He worked harder than ever to reopen the sync with Bogan as he passed by familiar buildings.

'Bogan, bericht! Bericht!'

No response, only a blank space where he should have keyed into the war mongrel. Fear, a forgotten foe, paid an unwanted visit but Hunter shoved it far away into the recess of his mind. No time to dwell on what was happening to send Bogan darting off into the night.

Ice cold calm descended over Hunter, his training and years in the military coming back with all too familiar ease.

Track. Corner. Destroy.

Three simple mandates he'd lived by as a soldier during the Vargos War. Hunter didn't want to be that man again, but he would be if he had to. For Narelle.

System access. Online. Activate protocol.

The command given was subconscious but one Hunter didn't regret. His head only stung a little from the blip of pain as he allowed his

Lomanis heritage to fully merge with the government adjustments. He'd only told Narelle part of the truth. Lomanis were far better at integrating with electronics then he'd implied. It was why he'd been selected to lead raid after raid during the war. The scientists couldn't figure it out and Hunter never explained.

He took to all the messing around in his brain with more ease than the other soldiers. Out of the twenty-five recruits in the WIRED program, he'd synced with his war mongrel Riktor on the first day they were introduced, suffering the least amount of discomfiture.

Now Hunter would use his legacy to force the connection with Bogan if he had to. Blaming the animal for the small tugs of resistance and defiance was pointless. Hunter wasn't his original handler after all. But Narelle's safety was at stake and it meant all bets were off.

With that thought in mind, Hunter forced the sync with the war mongrel at the same time he reissued the command. *'Bericht!'* Report.

Rapid fire code scrolled across Hunter's optic screen and a blinking square representing Bogan appeared, moving faster than the average animal. But then Bogan wasn't an average animal. He was government engineered property bred to assist during a war that no longer existed.

The animal's speed reminded Hunter of another war mongrel with the same instinctive drive to rescue. Riktor. Hunter's stomach knotted. Losing the war mongrel he'd been synced with had caused Hunter unspeakable pain which took months to recover from. After that last mission, he'd made a promise to never put himself through the same striking torment again. Ever.

Yet here he was, racing through the streets after a war mongrel and a woman who had the potential to destroy Hunter's whole world.

"Bogan, haltzo." Despite the distance, his shout should reach Bogan's enhanced auditory adjustments. To increase the odds, he sent the order via the sync as well.

Narelle's scream ripped through the night and the hair on Hunter's arms stood on end.

No mercy, he thought as he rushed forward, forcing himself to breath in and out. Whoever thought to mess with Narelle would soon learn she had a man willing to kill for her. Death would be too kind for them.

The red square hovering on his optic screen slowed briefly then took off like a shot. Panic flared and Hunter increased his speed. The blown adjustments in his right knee protested the demand he placed on them but responded. As he hurdled toward Narelle, Hunter knew his image would appear blurred to any observers.

"Hang on, beauty," he murmured, not giving in to the fear gnawing at his insides. She would be fine.

No other outcome was acceptable.

EIGHT

The area Hunter traced Bogan to was a less than desirable section of town. He couldn't imagine why or what would have drawn Narelle this way unless she was using the credit by the hour rentals.

Short, successive barks ahead signaled Bogan's position. Hunter slowed to a half-jog and withdrew his laser as he neared. Then he spotted the crumpled figure on the ground and his heart stopped in his chest.

"Narelle!" Hunter rushed to her side, sliding to his knees.

The blow to his chest caught him off guard and Hunter flew backward, his body slamming onto the ground feet away. Instinct had him rolling to his front, the laser still clutch in his grip.

Coming toward him from the darkened alley, a cloak figure chuckled. "I knew she'd be the means to bring you out. Always on guard, always close to the pathetic bar you run."

Footsteps clacked, drawing closer with each muttered word. Hunter rose, never taking his gaze off the man. Flashes of blond hair winked in the flickers of light cast from a nearby street source.

"Who are you?" Not that the answer mattered. Hunter planned to kill him for daring to touch Narelle.

"Don't you recognize the man you ruined?"

Voice harsh and grating, but not familiar. Hunter strained to place the features as the man came to a stop beside Narelle's prone figure. Bogan approached from the opposite direction, stiff legged and snarling.

"Haltzo. Las."

For once, the war mongrel obeyed his order instantly and froze in his tracks. Fur ruffled in ridges along his back in a clear indication of the animal's agitation. His upper lips peeled back revealing deadly teeth capable of crushing bones if caught between his powerful jaws.

The stranger glanced down at Bogan and sneered. "Another K9? You always managed to end up winning in the end while the rest of us suffered for your actions."

Blue eyes met his and knowledge broke through Hunter's confusion as his muscles locked in place. The last mission—Hunter's greatest success and failure. It wasn't possible though. There were no survivors from his team. The government had been adamant as they disclosed the devastating news to Hunter upon waking from his surgery. "How?"

Even as Hunter asked the question, his mind snatched him back to the fateful day which had changed the tide of the Vargos war. With his war mongrel, Riktor, by his side and his team of five, they'd gone into the communication center fast and hard. Intel hinted this location housed several of the masterminds directing the efforts of the Vargos ships and their commanders.

If Hunter's team could take them out, it would shift the tide of battle. Strike a much needed blow against an enemy which seemed to haunt and follow Hunter his entire life.

Trailing behind Riktor, Hunter led his squad to what would be their doom.

"Clear."

"Clear."

Each room they checked was empty. Disappointment cast a pall. They'd been so sure. So certain this was it. Hunter exchanged a glance with each of his men dressed from head to toe in battle gear and received a chin lift in return. They would keep going. Search the grounds next if necessary before giving up.

The washed-out bunker hummed with abandoned computronics. But no sign of Vargos soldiers. In the last room at the back of the place, Hunter lowered his weapon and cursed. Jestin entered behind him, pushing up his protective goggles and pursed his lips, vivid green gaze glowing with frustration.

"How'd we get it wrong?" Noah questioned in a rough voice, his usually laughing blue eyes narrowed.

"Wait." Lukain, Hunter's right hand, paused next to a blinking screen on one of the tables shoved against a wall and leaned forward. "This is it. It's running code. Sending direction to their troops."

The resounding cheer left Hunter with a relieved grin. "Blow that shit."

Before the last word left his mouth, five lasers blasted away. And then Hunter heard it. A sound that curled his last meal in his belly and threatened to send it back up in a rush. He should have known this was too easy.

Low tones beeped from above. Everyone's gaze jerked toward the ceiling and the digital timer counting down on a wall mounted plate.

35

34

33

No time to find the source of the bomb. No time to get Riktor to seek and deactivate.

"Go! Go! Go!" Hunter yelled, waving them back through the door they'd entered.

The distance from the narrow hallway to the only exit seemed miles away. Sweat trickled beneath Hunter's blast helmet and soaked his collar. Boots pounded around him as his friends, men he'd fought with raced to beat time.

Riktor used his trijl to send a mirror timer over Hunter's optic adjustment, adding the clock over his vision.

"Riktor! Komme!"

Ignoring his order for the first time, the stubborn war mongrel stayed in the back.

30

29

28

"Fuck!" Hunter roared as the initial blast ricocheted behind them. Too soon. A secondary incendiary device blew from the left, rocking the structure and sending plumes of dirt and dust down on their heads. Air whistled through his lips and with his heart in his throat, Hunter wondered if this was the end.

In front of him, Lukain stumbled going to one knee. Jestin snagged him under one arm and yanked him back to his feet. Too close for Hunter's piece of mind, but they were close. Almost out.

"Step lively ladies!" They were all WIRED and his command pinged on everyone's auditory adjustments.

Laughter broke out though gazes remained steely and determined. Four Vargos appeared in front of them and rushed forward, their yellow skin visible easily in the simple loincloths they wore. Weapons fired around them. Hunter aimed for head shots. The aliens dropped one by one, clearing the way.

Nearing the exit, the wall of the arched doorway shook. Hunter thrust a shoulder against it for support, ignoring the immediate pain that shot down his right side.

A few feet and all of his men would be free of the building.

13

12

11

Riktor soared past the soldiers and leaped on Hunter's chest, knocking him back and all the way out. Before he could reprimand his partner, the war mongrel turned and raced back into the crumbling building.

"Haltzo! Las!"

Riktor picked up speed as he crossed the threshold. Fire burst through the windows as a series of mini explosions detonated.

3

2

1

Hunter's last sight was of Riktor at the rear, trying to herd his men through faster with nips at their heels then the biggest explosion of all.

The past faded and the present wrenched Hunter violently forward in time to this moment. A moment in which every member of his team was dead and K9-3, Riktor had sacrificed his life in an attempt to save those very same men.

Except.

"How did you survive, Lukain?" Mixed emotions tore at Hunter's psyche. He wanted to be thrilled at the knowledge one of his men had made it out after all.

Narelle groaned, pulling his attention.

Yet nothing about an injured Narelle and a very angry soldier lent itself to Hunter feeling the slightest bit of joy. He fought the urge to go to her. To check on how bad she'd been hurt.

Lukain stepped forward, setting off a fresh round of rumbles from Bogan. "Would you believe Riktor? During the final explosion, everything was smoke and burned flesh around me. I knew the others were gone and yet your war mongrel had more loyalty than you, Hunter. He dragged me to a section where the wall had been decimated. His biotronics failed once he managed to get me out."

Pain winged its way through Hunter's heart. He owed his life to Riktor as well. The bravery his partner exhibited in the face of death could never be matched. Knowing the war mongrel had continued to complete the mission and gave his life to save another meant a lot to Hunter though he wasn't sure the revelation had been intended to uplift Hunter in any way.

Lukain shook his head. His mouth twisted in a wry grin. "Crazy animal always did have an intense rescue drive. Fur burned clear away and skin shredded, he locked on my leg and didn't stop tugging until I was clear of the debris."

The back of Hunter's eyes burned. He swallowed past the thickness in his throat.

"Reminded me of that time you were pinned and he set up a frenzy of barking that led us right to you before that squad of Vargos discovered our presence at the Enteg battle."

Because Riktor had been more than any scientist could have imagined. Strength, intelligence and loyalty bred in his lean muscled body.

"Why stay hidden? It's been years." Hunter couldn't fathom a reason that would have sent his friend and fellow soldier on this reckless path. If it came down to it, Hunter would take him out.

Anger wiped away whatever pleasantness had been on Lukain's face. Blues eyes lit with limitless rage. "I got to a medic center off world but was ruined. My adjustments were all blown and irreparable. Useless, Hunter! I was useless and all because of you."

"You blame me when it was my war mongrel who got you out?! You're alive because of Riktor. Both of us are."

"This isn't living, Hunter." Lukain whipped back the side of his long leather and ripped upward the shirt he wore.

Bile rose in Hunter's throat. From the shoulders down, metal panels intermixed with twisted scarred flesh. The jagged pattern continued down to the band of his pants leading Hunter to believe the damage was extensive. This went beyond seamless military adjustments and synth skin. "What did you do?"

A sneer crossed Lukain's face. "Not pretty, right? My adjustments were shot. Blown and no good. The medics had to remove them or risk poisoning my blood from the leaks and fried wiring. I couldn't get better because I'd been declared dead and even if I wasn't, the military no longer had a need for me. The war was over. We'd taken out the Vargos fucking communications hub and their troops fell apart."

Lukain let his shirt drop and the coat closed part way to hide his mutilated body. "Only thing left was to use scrap parts. Fucking scrap parts on *me*, a decorated soldier who helped win the shitty war!"

Lukain's hoarse screaming set off Bogan and the war mongrel launched passed Hunter, snarling on the defensive. Lukain screamed as ninety pounds of genetically engineered K9 powered into him. Jaws snapped and bit until Bogan clamped a secure hold on Lukain's upper arm, claws digging for purchase on the man's chest. Hunter couldn't risk firing without hitting the animal.

"Give it up, Lukain."

His former friend and team mate punched at Bogan's snout over and over until the war mongrel released on a yelp. Hunter raised his laser but hesitated. Memories of shared laughter rang in his ears.

Lukain used the opportunity to take off, black leather swirling about him as he vanished into the night. Bogan's hind legs scrabbled as he spun around to give chase.

"Haltzo, Bogan!" Hunter didn't want the animal after Lukain and the unknown.

With Lukain gone, Hunter did what he'd wanted to do from the moment of arrival and hurried toward Narelle. He brushed a hand over her red waves, clearing his view to her face. She groaned but didn't wake. Hunter tucked his weapon at the waist of his pants, hands going over her body to check for injuries but an aggressive shoulder shove from Bogan knocked him backward.

Oblivious to Hunter's glare, Bogan nosed at Narelle's face causing a flinch. Stunned at the war mongrel's behavior, Hunter took a minute to give the order. "Bewachen."

Ignoring the order, Bogan snarled, upper lip peeled back as he positioned himself over Narelle's limp form. From his protective stance, Hunter sensed the animal wouldn't give easily. To make matters worst, he'd also somehow shut down the sync from his side preventing Hunter from accessing him that way. If the scientist had ever hinted at such a thing even being possible, he didn't recollect yet Bogan had done it twice.

"Bogan, sitzen."

Another low growl, flashing teeth which could tear through an enemy. Hunter had witnessed such during the war and it wasn't pretty. Getting to Narelle was priority but not if it put her at risk. Any abrupt movement would trigger Bogan to attack and Hunter didn't want Narelle caught in the middle.

Commands rolled through his mind as he sought the best option to regain control of the situation. Hunter needed Bogan to stand down without traumatizing the animal further. He may have synced with him but there was no bond in place. No opportunity for a rapport to develop. That came from months of working together and Hunter didn't have months.

Keeping his gaze on the war mongrel, Hunter straightened from the kneeling position to emphasize his height. "Gott, biet rel. Gemfach."

Brown eyes flickered and Bogan's pointed ears twitched at Hunter's soothing tone. He continued to croon, keeping his voice low which took minutes Narelle didn't have.

"Gemfach," he whispered and extended his hand palm up.

Bogan darted a look at Hunter's hand, gaze confused. The growls shifted to a low whimper.

"Bewachen."

Though his body tensed, Bogan refused to move. Hunter glared, trying to force calm. It was clear Bogan had been without a handler for a while, but he wouldn't be able to ignore training and protocol for long. A directive was meant to be followed thanks to months of training and a firm reward system.

Hunter repeated the command to guard, adding another layer of authority to his voice. "Bewachen."

At last Bogan backed off on a low growl with stiff legged motions and shifted his focus to their surroundings.

Blowing out a breath, Hunter knew nothing would slip past the war mongrel in guard mode. Returning to Narelle's side, he cupped her face in his hands, taking in the injuries with a quick visual assessment. Injuries which seemed limited to a green bruise darker then her own jade skin tones under her left eye and a split lip.

Anger swirled at the thought of Lukain hitting her in the face but Hunter pushed the emotion back. Now wasn't the time or place. Leaning forward as his heart rate settled, Hunter tapped her cheeks. She'd been still the entire time, worrying him. "Come on, beauty. Open those pretty eyes."

Another groan and then Narelle's lashes fluttered. Relief sent Hunter's breath escaping in a rush. He didn't care what it said about him. They'd only shared one night but already she had him hooked. Hooked to the point he wasn't going to let her get away easy.

If Narelle thought to escape what was between them, Hunter would show her different.

Gray eyes met his, dazed confusion tipping her mouth down in the corners. "W-w-what happened?"

Hoarse and weak, the question held none of her usual fiery tones. Narelle blinked and creased lines formed on her brow. She lifted a shaky hand to her temple, glancing over her short horns. With a wince, she dropped her arm to her side.

Hunter scooted closer. "Narelle, baby, I need you to sit up. I'm going to lift you in my arms."

As soon as he touched her, Narelle whimpered, shattering Hunter's calm. He cursed and slid his hands under her hip and back, flinching when she moaned.

"Hunter."

Relief crashed into him even as his lips flattened. "It's alright, baby. I have you."

Hunter stood cradling her close, arcs of fire lancing down his knee from the added weight. Didn't matter. He'd withstand any hurt or pain for her. Hunter scanned the area. In the dark he couldn't see much. Bogan whined. Hunter switched his optics to night vision but still saw no signs of Lukain returning.

This time, Bogan brushed against his leg.

"Gott, biet rel."

With Bogan at his side, Hunter hustled back to The Zone, never stopping his scan of the area.

NINE

Not as bad as she expected. Narelle stared into the mirror mounted on the wall in Hunter's bathroom. Sure her lip was busted. She poked at her puffy eyelid. A black eye in her future too. Overall not more than she could handle.

Sighing, Narelle stepped back with only a breath-stealing twinge in her side. It could have been worse. Obviously, Lukain hadn't wanted to do permanent damage. Only enough to get Hunter's attention. She flipped the light off and with a deep breath returned to where Hunter waited with the war mongrel pacing in front of him.

In the lower living area, Hunter leaned against the wall and studied her calmly. Beneath his gaze, Narelle felt like a bug under his attention. So far, he'd followed her every step only stopping once she entered the bathroom to clean her scrapes.

"Na-relle."

She loved and hated the way he said her name. The tender look accompanied by a slight drawl as he curled the l's on the end softened her ire. Dropping onto the lounger, her aching muscles sighed in relief. Hunter growled in annoyance but Narelle added a raised palm to her warning. "Don't, Hunter."

Since returning, he'd at least taken the opportunity to put on a shirt doing Narelle the favor of covering his upper body from her lustful glances. She might have been slightly battered but apparently her libido was up and working fine.

His brow quirked, and his lips drew into a thin line. "Don't what, Narelle? Throw you over my lap for being stupid?"

Hunter straightened from his slouch and his gaze darkened. He shoved his hands into his front pockets, pulling the pants taut against his thick thighs. The relaxed pose did nothing to ease the sense of danger emanating from his vibrant potency. "Or don't care that you were almost killed shortly after leaving my bed."

He said the last in a low even tone, making it all the more deadly for the whispered volume.

"I wasn't almost killed." Beneath his stare, Narelle fought hard not to squirm. "You're being ridiculous. This is a rogue satellite station. The criminal element will always come and go. I'm fully aware of this and take the necessary precautions whenever I'm here."

Her rational explanation had little effect on him. If anything, Hunter seemed to grow angrier and Narelle's heart rate increased with a tiny frisson of fear. This wasn't the bar owner who intimidated patrons enough they never caused trouble in his place. This was the former soldier who refused to waiver.

Both were completely unlike the man who'd touched her with reverence and passion earlier tonight. Another shiver. She'd need to tread carefully.

"And did those precautions do you any good tonight?" he snarled.

She'd had enough of his derision and upped her glare to match his. "They would have except this guy had a hard-on for you."

"Exactly!"

Narelle mentally banged her head on an invisible wall. She hadn't meant to acknowledge the threat. No need to make this bigger than it needed to be since she planned to leave sooner rather than later. Hunter could deal with his own drama.

He dropped his hands from his pockets and prowled closer. "Do you know what it did to me to see you hurt like that?"

Why did he have to utter the question in such a soft voice? The look in Hunter's gaze spoke volumes and as Narelle was quickly learning, he had no problem exposing his emotions for her.

Having nothing to counter with, Narelle held her silence. Hunter turned away, freeing her from the volatile moment. "I'm making a few calls to see if I can figure this out. In the meantime, you stay here."

He didn't even give her the courtesy of facing her when he made the decree. Instead, he jammed a finger in Bogan's direction. The war mongrel sat in a corner, ears pricked at attention. "Bewachen."

Not sure what instructions he'd given the war mongrel, Narelle jumped to her feet intending to give Hunter a definitive piece of her mind. Much to her surprise, Bogan hip checked her and she stumbled back. When she tried to go around him to follow Hunter as he dashed upstairs, Bogan yipped and blocked her path.

"You've got to be kidding!"

Hunter's laughter trailed behind him as he left her alone with the war mongrel, who suddenly looked like it would take a bite out of her if she so much as blinked wrong. Gone was the injured animal she'd found in the alley. In its place was a creature bred to follow a soldier's command.

He did it well too, brown gaze staring at Narelle waiting for her next move. She dropped back down on the lounger. Great. Now she had two stubborn males to deal with.

Bracing his palms on the desk, Hunter waited for the screen in front of him to load and connect. There was only one person he trusted to speak with about Narelle's attack and Lukain's sudden reappearance from the dead. It was a long shot using this long-forgotten link. One he'd had during the war but no longer needed. Until today. Until Narelle.

"Code 76Z-8"

Hunter waited. Minutes he couldn't spare if he wanted to get to the bottom of this. Please let someone else also still be monitoring the old frequency.

"Acknowledged. Go."

Familiar. Not a strange soldier on the other end he'd have to rely on. "Ezra?"

"Here, Hunter."

He and Ezra had been on the same last mission but on different teams. Ezra's team had walked away, Hunter's hadn't.

"I need your special help."

A pause. Hunter held his breath.

"Whatever you need man. How soon?"

"Emergency. As soon as possible." His friend wouldn't question the urgency.

"Acknowledged. Send the data."

Relief left him shuddering. Now there was another who'd be able to help get to the bottom of what was going on. Hunter needed to understand why there was a war mongrel unaccounted for and how Lukain managed to stay off the radar.

Hunter gathered what little he had and sent the file he'd compiled to the other soldier via the secured connection.

Ezra made no attempt to hide his amazement. "*You* completed another trijl with a war mongrel?"

Ezra alone knew Hunter's reasoning for wanting to avoid that state. Unwilling to explain until they could get together in person, Hunter settled for a simple one word answer. "Yes."

Another stretch of silence and then Ezra answered, "Expect me in two or three days at the most."

Hunter exhaled. The feeling of having help to address the situation overwhelmed. "Thank you, man."

A derisive grunt gave Ezra's thoughts on the matter. "I owe you, Gils. We all do."

Skin crawling and wanting to avoid any conversation shift about the war, Hunter ended the transmission. He headed back to the lower level and braced himself for Narelle's ire. Using Bogan to keep her from leaving or disappearing to find more trouble was wrong but Hunter didn't regret it. Whatever it took to protect Narelle.

Even from herself.

When he returned down stairs, Narelle sat stiffly shooting glares in his direction. Holding back a chuckle, Hunter bit his inner cheek. She might have thought she looked tough but the dark expression on her face only served to show how attractive she was with a pout.

Bogan turned to watch Hunter approach and he signaled the war mongrel to stay with a hand gesture. Instantly, the animal dropped down beside Narelle's feet, the tip of his nose planted on the toes of her boots.

Narelle slid from the sofa to the floor to sit beside Bogan. "Don't turn him on me again."

Hunter accepted her grumble but didn't respond. He'd do whatever necessary to keep Narelle safe. Taking the seat across from her and Bogan, Hunter stretched his legs out. "Tell me everything from the beginning. Start with the moment you left here."

Silky red hair slipped over her shoulder as she faced him. Wearing one of his long sleeve buttoned down white shirts since her synth suit was ruined, she appeared innocent and sweet. Hunter knew better. She had a sharp tongue and a sharper bite.

Her green skin was a lighter tone than its usual deep emerald. His gaze traveled over the short blunt horns at her temple. Next time he had her under him, Hunter planned to test their sensitivity by licking them. The bruise under her eye brought back his own rage but he quelled it under the need for more information. At least her lip looked better.

After a moment of staring at her, which he didn't back down from she huffed. "Fine."

Hunter listened to every detail as Narelle spoke. His knee throbbed from the strain of earlier and he absently rubbed at the ache. His leg would never be the same again. Hunter accepted the reality like he accepted the ruined adjustments which enhanced the limb were beyond repair as well. He was lucky though. He was alive. Not many could say the same and none in his unit.

Although he now had Lukain to consider and his admitted vendetta. Hunter shook away the turmoil of the past and gazed at a now silent Narelle as she knelt beside Bogan. Her hands rested on the war mongrel's nape, fingers lightly scratching. It continued to amaze him how easy the animal accepted her.

Bogan waffled and stretched flat out, legs sprawled as Narelle bent over him and shifted the scratching to a vigorous full body rub along his side.

"He likes you." The deep belly groan from the animal had Hunter smiling.

Narelle's head dipped but she didn't glance Hunter's way. "I like him too."

Which meant when the time came to contact the government and return Bogan she would more than likely flip. Hunter sighed and straightened from his relaxed pose. He wasn't looking forward to that moment.

Narelle rose at the same time as he but Hunter managed to speak first. "I have a friend who will help figure this out."

"And Bogan?" her stubborn chin tipped up.

"And Bogan," Hunter agreed, closing the distance between them.

"Well, that takes care of that. I can go now and leave you to it."

To her credit, Narelle didn't flinch from his glare. She remained in her spot until his chest bumped her front.

He was close. Lips, breath. Things she shouldn't find erotic but the soft nature of the light brushes of contact were. Raised around rough men, Narelle was hard to intimidate but Hunter had a way about him. He made her knees weak and it had nothing to do with lingering pain from the attack.

She pressed her hands up to his chest to create space between them. Solid heat emanated from beneath her palms and muscles contracted under the shirt he wore.

"Stay, Narelle. Let me protect you until we can stop my old teammate."

If only she could. Staying meant fighting the temptation of being in his presence. It meant resisting the urge to lick the small scars marring his face. Scars which spoke of a battle well won. "I don't want you hurt in place of me, Hunter."

Incredulity crossed his face. His gaze darkened, a frown twisting his lips as his hands gripped her hips and pulled her snug against him. "But it's okay if someone with a grievance against me hurts you."

The low growl vibrating under her fingers warned Narelle to consider her answer carefully. "I just think it would be better if I left."

Hunter snorted. "You've been identified as a way to hurt me. A way to make me lose my mind if something were to happen. Trust me when I say Lukain will follow where you go in his attempts to strike at me. Give me the time I need to stop him before it gets too far."

Narelle's mind stuck on the first statements. Knowing she meant that much to this sexy soldier was still hard to believe but there was no denying it. She risked a glance at his 'I don't give a fuck face' and her heart rate sped up.

She hoped he didn't see her ears heating and decided to tease. "You're that confident in your skills?"

Hunter's lids lowered over his eyes, the look one of sensuous promise. He skimmed his lips over her cheek. Warm breath feathered her face. "Baby, I'm confident of my skills in everything."

And he should be. It didn't take a genius to figure out what else he meant and Narelle now had firsthand experience with his boast. Their position allowed her to feel the hard bulge of his erection at her mid-section, but she decided to ignore the obvious. They'd have to face this... thing between them later.

"Alright. I'll stay til you find out what's going on. That's all, so don't think this is permission to roll over me."

TEN

Three days later found Hunter's eyes narrowed on Narelle as she descended from his upstairs apartment. She was proving more difficult to seduce into staying than he'd initially expected. If he came out and announced his desire to pursue something permanent with her, she'd flee.

As it was, Narelle purposely avoided the counter where he worked, strolling around the crowded tables making her way to the well-lit area and the small space some customers used as the dance floor at The Zone. Avid gazes turned in her direction.

Male gazes.

As usual, heavy pounding beats blasted from the micro speakers. Narelle put one hand beneath the fall of red hair shoving it back from her face as her curvy hips began to sway from side to side. Hunter fisted the wet rag in his hand. It was an erotic sight and he wasn't immune. Since the night of the attack, she stayed with him, sleeping in his bed while he tossed on the sofa much to his frustration.

She spun around, matching the beat of the pulsing music as it increased. Hunter slammed his hands down on the counter and turned away to wait on a customer. He refused to stare and lust after her as if they hadn't shared mind numbing passion.

Tonight, tonight he'd get her back where she belonged.

"Is that her?"

Hunter jerked, then a wide smile split his face at the man standing across the bar from him. Dressed head to toe in leather and body armor, the dark-haired former soldier kept his gaze on the dance floor.

"Ezra, you made good time."

"I left as soon as you contacted me." At last Ezra turned from Narelle to face Hunter. His grim expression eased a little, and the corner of his lips quirked upward beneath the shadow of his beard. "Never thought you'd reach out about a woman."

Hunter grunted and tipped his head to his side. "Not just her."

Ezra leaned forward to see beyond the counter where Hunter stood, his ankle length coat parting to reveal several weapons at his hip and across his shoulder.

"Fuck, you weren't lying!" Losing his legendary composure, Ezra ran a hand through his hair and shook his head as he settled back. "I'm almost tempted not to ask."

"Don't have an answer either way."

At the sight of a stranger peering at him, Bogan sat up from his prone position and tilted his head to the side. Curiosity gleamed from the brown orbs fastened to Ezra but the war mongrel remained quiet waiting for his cue from Hunter.

Folding his arms over his chest, Ezra shot Hunter a wry look. "Nothing easy with you, Hunter."

Since he agreed, Hunter didn't take offense to the statement. He waved at one of his employees to take over the bar then pointed at one of the corner tables. "Lets talk over there. Less ears to hear what I want to discuss."

Ezra nodded abruptly and strode away. Hunter assured himself of Narelle's position before moving. Lost to the music, she danced in the same spot, leaving him free to step away and speak with his old friend. Bogan trotted at his heels, attuned to any command from him.

It amazed and unnerved Hunter to have another war mongrel looking to him as a handler. He didn't want the responsibility or the feelings which came with being synced with an animal. Sadness and pain lay that way. Especially since Hunter knew no matter how this ended, Bogan belonged to the government and wasn't his to keep.

The moment the military received notification of Bogan's survival, they'd be all over The Zone demanding the return of their property and Hunter would be in no position to refuse. Once again he'd suffer the pain of separation but of a different sort.

Against his will, his gaze sought Narelle. Her green skin appeared dull beneath the flashing lights, but Hunter knew better. He'd kissed the emerald flesh, stroked all over her soft, giving body. There was nothing dull about the pearlescent beauty. Her red hair swished along her back almost as if following the beat of the music. A group of male customers gathered their courage and danced closer.

She winked and flirted but at least kept a decent bit of distance from them. Unclenching his balled fists, Hunter strode toward a smirking Ezra.

"Is she the one?"

The one. During missions, soldiers often talked about the one, a woman in their current lives or hoped to have in their life. Someone who would care if they came back safely. It was a way to keep despair at bay. As if actually planning for a future meant they had a future. Was Narelle his one? Hunter hated to admit she probably was. Now he'd have to convince her of the same.

To Ezra, he said, "Maybe."

The amused grunt made it plain Ezra saw through him. His friend propped his elbows on the table, all humor falling away. "Tell me what you have going on."

Hunter recounted the attack on Narelle ending with his surprise about Lukain's appearance. "Not one whisper about his survival."

"How did he manage that trick?"

Hunter merely arched a brow at the question. Shit if he knew.

"Right." Ezra rapped his knuckles on the table and slouched back. "So Lukain's back from the dead and you have a lost war mongrel."

Hunter agreed Bogan's presence skewed matters. "What are the odds of a war mongrel running loose? One which ends up at The Zone where I work and run things."

"Slim and why I didn't hesitate when you reached out. There are no coincidences when the government is involved."

Hunter nodded, pleased they were of the same mind. "Were you able to find anything?"

A look flashed across Ezra's brutal features, his eyes darkening from brilliant blue to a fathomless navy. "Officially there are no unaccounted for war mongrels. While not in active duties since the war ended, they are being used for research and study. Anything more, I couldn't find out unless I wanted to trigger the obvious flags they have set."

Lie. Ezra was good at tech. Better than Hunter and his Lomanis heritage. If Ezra wanted he could root through every file available and not give a hint of his cyber presence. Of course that detail wasn't one he shared with many, so Hunter didn't call him on it. He had his own secrets he didn't want to share.

"What's the *unofficial* verdict?"

Another grunt but more annoyed. "The bastards are running tests to reactivate that segment of the WIRED program."

Hunter stiffened, but Ezra lowered his voice and continued. "Instead of active combat missions they are looking to use the animals and their handlers to infiltrate perceived threats."

Anger rose fast and furious in Hunter. Essentially turning them into high risk spies. Utilizing the skills they'd trained for in those type of situations after all they'd been through was unimaginable.

"How long?" Hunter snarled, gripping the edge of the table to control his rage. "How long have they been doing this?"

"Less than a year." Ezra ran a palm over his face. "Look, if you can stay low—"

Every muscle went tight. "What do you mean?"

Ezra met Hunter's gaze evenly. "A few participants may have been involuntarily recruited."

Blood boiling, Hunter instinctively moved forward bumping the table. He narrowed his focus to read the truth of what Ezra just revealed. Involuntarily recruited. Drawn against their will into a game of subterfuge. The thought of the men he knew being forced into what many viewed as a living nightmare curled his stomach.

After the Vargos war, soldiers were reassigned, most to less intense situations. Occasionally base assignments with non-travel stipulations. Unlike Hunter, not everyone who'd attained permanent injuries were let go with recompense. He'd stumbled on minor success owning The Zone, while others sold their talents and skills as mercenaries to earn enough to survive.

Lips parted to speak, Hunter broke off at the low whine from his side. Bogan was up on his haunches and pressing into Hunter's lower leg and hip. He ran a hand over the brown ruff in a soothing stroke while never moving his gaze from Ezra. "Do you think Bogan is a part of this new venture?"

Ezra shrugged. "More than likely it seems possible. Any word or hint about his original handler?"

"He's dead."

Ezra flinched. He'd been WIRED too but not in the K9 division. Still Ezra had witnessed what happened when one or the other died and the trijl was violently ripped asunder. "Before or after being recruited for this program?"

There was no way for Hunter to tell. Sections of Bogan's memory pertaining to his handler's death were skipped or just plain missing. Those huge glaring holes now held a more ominous meaning. What if they'd been deliberately deleted instead of damaged as he'd assumed? Better yet, why not clear it all out? Had Bogan truly escaped or had he been purposely left behind?

Too many questions to ponder. "Not sure. It still leaves me in the wind on the why."

"To draw you in?"

Ezra's question was valid but didn't ring true for Hunter. The ruined adjustments in his leg didn't make him a likely candidate for whatever was being devised. In addition, Bogan already had a track record of being difficult to partner. There was no guarantee putting the war mongrel with Hunter would have netted the result they wanted.

He shook his head. "It's not clicking. Lukain made it clear he wants revenge. Can't see him working with the government considering his anger that night."

Leaving him with two separate issues. In which case Hunter could consider himself fucked.

"I'll see what else I can discover." Ezra pulled up the collar of his leather and stood. "I'm gonna hang about a bit. I'll be around and you can reach me on the old frequency like before."

On his way out, a few dared stare at the tall stranger covered in leather but hastened to turn away as he drew closer to their tables to leave. Hunter blew out a breath and signaled Bogan. "Komm."

After a slight hesitation, Hunter chose the direction which took him closest to the dance area and Narelle. At the same moment, she glanced his way. Her steps stumbled but she recovered smoothly, turning her back on him deliberately.

Yeah, tonight he'd end their stand off and enjoy every minute of it.

ELEVEN

After dancing until her feet hurt, Narelle headed upstairs before Hunter. The Zone wouldn't close for a few hours but she needed the time to wrap her head around the look he'd shot her way. Tonight he'd push for more and she wasn't sure she wouldn't give in. Even if it was a bad idea.

The attack a few days ago served as a vivid reminder of why she needed to get on her ship and leave. Not come back. Not think about the man who caused her to have such wicked, wicked thoughts about the two of them sweating and rolling around in his big bed.

Her nipples peaked at the idea. Breath growing short, she reached the door to his apartment above The Zone. At her side, Bogan's head bumped her thighs. Another Hunter dictate. Narelle scooted aside and waited until Bogan searched the place before locking the door.

Ever since the attack, Hunter had given a command which kept the animal by her if she wasn't with him in the bar. Narelle ran her hands over the black tipped ears, at least he was good company. Bogan licked her fingers and Narelle chuckled. "It's just you and me, buddy."

A quick shower later found Narelle wearing another one of the shirts Hunter offered since he refused to let her go to her ship and grab her own personal things. She refused to sleep in her patched synth suit.

Hunter continued to believe she was a target, though Narelle felt the threat was over. She made her way to his bed where the sheets smelled of him, the pillows scented with his masculine essence and sighed.

Bogan padded over and nudged her arm closest to the edge of the bed. "Right. You're going to watch the place until he gets back."

After three days of the same, the routine was familiar. Narelle snuggled deep into the covers, smothering her yawn. Tomorrow. Tomorrow she'd leave with or without Hunter's agreement.

As she dozed off, Bogan settled with a groan somewhere on the floor and she fell into a deep sleep with the sounds of canine snores in her ear.

What felt like moments later, her eyes blinked open in the dark. The bed shifted beside her and the warm weight of a male presence squeeze in beside her. Narelle considered protesting but lacked the spirit. Her lids lowered on the cusp of dozing off when lips pressed to the curve of her shoulder where the shirt dipped.

"Hunter?"

The weight of his arm curled about her waist and tugged her against his nude body. Narelle stiffened and her eyes flickered open.

"Shh. Let me hold you. We'll fight tomorrow and have make-up sex after. It will give me time to have a nap before opening The Zone."

Narelle crammed a fist in her mouth to muffle her laugh. When she had her mirth under control she spoke into the darkness. "What makes you think I'm having sex with you again?"

Hunter nuzzled the back of her neck and Narelle's body did the melt-y thing once more. "Because I plan to make you mad in the morning."

Shameless. Hunter Gils was shameless, but Narelle admitted to looking forward to how he'd execute the fight and the make-up sex. Exhaustion pulled at her and instead of saying anything else, Narelle found herself falling to sleep while being held by the man she should be running from.

Hunter felt the moment Narelle dropped off. He buried his nose in her hair, the scent one he recognized because she'd used his cleansing solution. Didn't matter. Beneath it all she smelled like his. She belonged to him. Now he only had to convince her to stay.

Holding Narelle tight and shifting his hand to palm her belly beneath his shirt, Hunter settled down to rest. Moments later, his senses screamed to life. Bogan leaped to his feet with a flurry of barks. Glass shattered as his bedroom window blew inward and Hunter rolled with Narelle to the floor at the farthest side.

Terror flashed over her upturned face. "Hunt—"

"Stay down!" Hunter pushed her beneath the bed frame, and jerked open a hidden compartment in the flooring. He whipped out two lasers and thrust one into Narelle's hand. Hunter met her gaze pleased to see her hanging on to control despite her heaving breaths. "It has to be Lukain."

Hunter knew it to his soul and the other man would pay for this.

"Face me if you want her to live, Hunter." The shouted dare was followed by Bogan's snarls and growls.

Hunter kissed Narelle, tongue and lips tangling briefly then lunged up, weapon in hand. Beside the window, Bogan stood, fur bristling. As soon as the war mongrel caught sight of Hunter, he cocked his head to the side.

"Gehe! Suche, Bogan."

Like a shot, Bogan took off through the window. Hunter grabbed his pants, vaguely aware of Narelle handing him a shirt which he jammed his arms in and pulled over his head.

"Go after him. I'll be right behind you."

Hunter toed on his boots and spared a second to point at the green skinned beauty who'd carved a space in his heart without trying. "Don't let Lukain see you when you follow."

Then he raced out the window, worried he'd be forced to watch another partner die. The tan and black coat became a distant blur. Damn animal was barely giving him a chance to catch up.

He shouldn't have synced with another war mongrel. If possible, Lukain would take out Bogan to lash out at him. Hunter tried to swallow past the knot in his throat.

Using every bit of his strength, he pushed to keep sight of Bogan knowing the war mongrel was his only chance to track Lukain. Ahead Bogan slowed almost to the exact spot of Narelle's earlier attack and the tall form of his former team mate stepped forward.

"You think sending your friend would scare me, Hunter? You forget I'm already a dead man."

Ezra. He must mean Ezra since he was the only one Hunter had discussed the matter with.

Lukain shook his head. "I have nothing to live for except vengeance. You'll pay for how I suffered."

For the man he once was, the friendship they'd once shared, Hunter attempted to reason. "Lukain, what happened to you was terrible. The war effected all of us. I have scars, I lost friends. But it's time to walk away. Live a life with some measure of happiness."

Lukain's gaze narrowed as he withdrew his laser. "Easy for you to say. With another K9 by your side and a woman who cares for you."

Hunter tried again. "You could meet the one, your special person."

"Drop your weapon, Hunter." Lukain snorted. "Maybe I'll believe you're sincere."

If he did, Hunter wouldn't stand a chance. "Your vow, Lukain. Don't harm the war mongrel."

It was risky but with the moment upon him, Hunter didn't want to have to kill the last living member of his team.

Surprise glittered in Lukain's blue eyes and his arm lowered slightly. "You'd take my word?"

"Yes." They'd been soldiers. Men of honor following orders.

"Fine. Drop your weapon and I won't kill the K9."

Hunter let his laser clatter to the ground. He signaled Bogan to back off, almost shuddering when the animal complied.

Lukain laughed, the chilling sound lacking any vestige of humor. "Fool. I won't rest until you're dead or I take away what you don't deserve."

Too late Hunter realized Lukain had the laser aimed to the far right of Hunter. Toward Bogan. Then beyond. Panic flared. No. Not possible. Heart thundering in his ears, Hunter turned slowly and saw her.

Narelle stood behind him, the laser he lent her in an ironclad grip, her eyes on Lukain. Hunter knew how it would all play out. Lukain was going to kill the woman he loved.

Love.

It was easy to acknowledge now because no other emotion could explain why his heart clenched at the thought of losing her. Hunter faced the gleeful ex-soldier. He'd never get his weapon from the ground in time. "Lukain, for all the gods sake, don't."

The answer was written on Lukain's face.

"Don't," Hunter whispered the ragged plea then Lukain fired.

TWELVE

Hunter moved faster than he thought possible, forcing his adjustments to give him the speed needed. Narelle's scream tore through him. Already in motion to cover her with his own body, lasers blasted around him. One from Narelle as she dove to the side, and Hunter wanted to kiss her for having the sense to get out of the way while wanting to strangle her.

Lukain's shot went wide, chipping the building behind. Another laser blasted from somewhere overhead. Bogan barked in a frenzy, the sound nothing like he'd heard the war mongrel make before.

"Hunter." Narelle choked out his name.

Hunter's hands wrapped around her and squeezed. He whispered words of thanks, shaking at how close he'd come to losing her. On the thought, he pushed back. "I told you not to let him see you."

She patted Hunter's black tee shirt, the glazed look in her eyes ripping him to shreds. He brushed his thumbs over her cheeks. "I'm fine. You?"

"You need to call off the war mongrel."

Narelle had her arm up and the laser aimed in the direction of the new voice. Warmth spread through Hunter as he turned, keeping a hand at her lower back. "Do I have you to thank?"

Ezra's expression pinched tight. "I wish, but your K9 ruined my shot. Jumped on Lukain and went for his throat."

A painful yelp had Narelle jerking away from him. Hunter flinched at the sight that met his gaze. Lukain was dead. Of that Hunter was certain.

Bogan lay on his side twitching, sparks flaring from the optic center. Narelle raced over and dropped to her knees. "Hunter, quick. Bogan's hurt."

More than hurt. Lukain lay sprawled on the ground, blood and gore representing how brutal Bogan had been. At the cost of his own life. Killing a soldier went against protocol, and it was easy to discern he'd fried the primary biotronics in his brain. But he'd done it. The war mongrel had risked his life to save him and Narelle.

Swallowing past the thickness in his throat, Hunter squatted next to them. "Gott, biet rel."

He smoothed a hand over Bogan's heaving side and despite everything he'd done to avoid this, he was going to lose another animal he was synced to.

"Why, Bogan?" But Hunter knew the answer. Brown eyes glazed with pain stared at him and a wet tongue licked the back of Hunter's hand.

Shit. Fucking rescue drive. Science couldn't breed it out of an animal or train it into submission no matter how hard they tried.

Hunter blinked away moisture. "I'm going to lift him, Narelle."

He wouldn't leave Bogan behind. Narelle scooted back, then got to her feet. Hunter picked up Bogan and eased his weight over his shoulders until his four legs draped Hunter's chest, front legs on the right and hind legs on the left.

Ezra stepped up to them, his icy blue stare toned down. "I'm sorry, man. I tried to stay close to The Zone in case Lukain returned."

Hunter nodded and pushed down the pain. "Let's go."

Hunter's bar bustled with activity. This wouldn't be an uncommon occurrence, except it was after hours and the bodies filling the space were government drones not paying customers out for a drink.

It had been simple enough to reach his old government contacts at the WIRED program and they'd sent a team to retrieve their possession immediately. That was how they referred to Bogan. A possession. Data transmissions had been shoved in Hunter's face as proof of ownership and leaving him nothing to fight back with.

The sooner they left the sooner he could console Narelle, who failed miserably at appearing stoic. Shock was setting in, and her skin had lost its jeweled tones. He stroked a hand up her back, attempting to soothe. She wouldn't go upstairs or lay down so Hunter kept her close wanting the officials to hurry up and leave. Unfortunately, the ass in charge wouldn't stop talking.

"K9-15 was slated to be put down. Considering all the issues getting a handler to work with him, the scientist weren't interested in a repeat after Donner's death but the stupid animal didn't return for decommission like he was trained to do."

Decommission. In other words, killed. Bogan had returned but for whatever reason contact hadn't been made. Maybe he was smart enough to know what they planned and avoided it.

"Bogan worked well enough taking down Lukain. That made him an asset." Hunter felt it worth mentioning but Godav, head man in charge and all around ass, smirked.

"The only reason you had success doing the trijl with number 15 is because he and K9-3 were bred from the same genetic combination."

Hunter jerked, the words hitting him harder than any blow. Bogan and Riktor came from the same stock. No wonder both animals displayed the same undying spirit and loyalty.

Godav watched Bogan as the animal was placed on a hover board, quivering but still alive for the moment. "Anyway, you've shown us that he does have some use after all and we plan to see if we can duplicate it in future war mongrels."

For their stupid spy program.

"You're taking him back?" Hunter asked the obvious, though inside he tempered the urge to punch Godav in the face.

"The damage is severe, and I doubt he can be salvaged but it won't hurt to try. His memory bank might be good for future study."

Narelle gasped behind Hunter and locked her hands on the back of his shirt. Godav waved the drones in white lab coats forward and they left. With Bogan

Hunter pressed his lips tight, then nodded. "Right. Thanks for filling in the pieces."

Jerk that he was, Godav smiled at Narelle before departing. It wasn't easy but Hunter stayed until the ship carrying the best partner a soldier could have faded in the skyline.

Narelle pushed at his shoulder. Nothing masked the misery on her face. "Why Hunter? Why did you let them take Bogan?"

Hardening his heart, Hunter gave her the only answer he could. "I told you in the beginning, Narelle. He belongs to the government."

EPILOGUE

Gasping, Hunter fell atop Narelle, her legs limply dropping away from the tight clench about his waist. Using the last of his energy, he rolled to the side and tugged her close. "Stay."

She moaned, entwining her arms about his neck. "Is that what this was about? I already agreed to stay, Hunter."

The last few weeks, Narelle needed the comfort of sex and the reassuring familiarity of hanging at The Zone. Hunter for his part didn't pressure her. Initially. After a week of watching and waiting, while sleeping on his couch, he'd finally cornered her and demanded she give them a chance.

"A chance at what?" She pretended confusion in order to watch him spear his fingers through his hair.

"Relationship, Narelle. A relationship with me. I love you, damn it."

Her next teasing words stalled. "You love me?"

She'd thought it. Almost sensed it without him saying anything. He'd coddled her after the loss of Bogan then let her run a ridiculous tab in his bar which left her passed out at a table. No one had bothered her and she'd awakened to Hunter carrying her to his bed where he tucked her in. Alone.

Hunter propped up on one forearm and traced a pattern on her shoulder then trailed his finger down to her elbow. "I'm making sure you don't change your mind."

Worry glinted from his dark gaze. Narelle was the cause of it. She hadn't returned the words he'd said, but he hadn't pushed. Instead it must have brewed in the back of his mind leaving him wondering if she really meant it when she'd agreed not to take her shuttle and leave.

Which she'd thought about in a moment of panic. She'd squashed the notion and it was time to let Hunter in on her own secret. Of sorts. Gliding a hand over his sweat dampened hair, Narelle said, "I love you too, Hunter."

His mouth parted, but no words came out. Narelle waited until it went beyond normal.

"Hunter?" She pushed up on her hip.

"You love me?"

Did he have to appear stunned? Narelle groaned. "You scared me. Yes, I love you."

For a moment he'd actually had her wondering if she should have kept the words to herself. The world flipped around and Narelle found herself on her back a looming Hunter braced above her. "You're moving in, you're never leaving. I'll track you down if you try."

Filled with joy at his possessive tone, Narelle laughed and brushed her hands over his shoulders. "It won't hurt if you keep having sex with me like this to convince me to stay."

"Done."

He responded so fast she chuckled again. About to tease him more, she was interrupted by a ding from the old fashioned computer on his desk. Hunter was up and out of the bed before she could blink.

"Yes. Yes. When? Now?" Hunter glanced at her. "How bad is it?"

Narelle stood and snatched up her black leather pants and a deep leather corset in purple. Hunter had allowed her to retrieve her belongings and only fussed a little about her wardrobe. According to him, the leather drew more stares than he appreciated.

Hunter ended the call and bent to pull on his own pants. "We need to go downstairs. Ezra's here."

Narelle hadn't gotten to really know Hunter's shadowy friend. One glimpse from those frigid blue eyes and she'd wanted to avoid further contact. Downstairs in The Zone, Hunter activated sensors to turn the main overhead lights on only.

Leaning against the bar, her hand on the knife at her hip, Narelle waited while Hunter opened the door and let Ezra in. Behind him a hover-board floated with a familiar tan and black animal.

"Bogan!" Narelle crossed the room, her hands rubbing the short furred coat, blinded by tears of happiness.

To her dawning horror, Bogan remained reclined on the hoverboard and didn't react to her presence by so much as a twitch. Hunter came over to exchange a glance with Ezra. "What happened?"

"Your pal Godav had K9-15 upgraded. New adjustments because he'd blown the ones in his brain. Unfortunate for them considering how much credits went in to saving him for future use, Bogan hasn't responded. Won't sync which was a problem before hand. Won't follow commands.

Shit according to Godav he won't move at all and all their tests show he's fully restored."

Narelle gasped. "They sent him here?"

She found it hard to imagine. The government certainly weren't doing it out of the kindness of their hearts.

"Godav said he was to be decommissioned but remembered you seem to have a soft spot for the war mongrel." Ezra flicked a glance in Narelle's direction. "He also mentioned your girlfriend might want to say goodbye."

"Bastard," Hunter snarled, coming closer. "Is he going to show up with a pack of white coats and take Bogan back?"

Ezra raised his hands. "Said he's yours free and clear if you want him. Sent a data chip confirming ownership."

Ezra tossed the silver disc at Hunter who caught it, gaze never leaving Bogan's prone form. "Thank you, Ezra. I owe you."

"I'll hold you to that." The man's eyes darkened in a way Narelle couldn't define. Then he turned and left, the door closing behind him.

Narelle licked her lips and continued to glide her hands over Bogan. "Do you think...do you think you can help him?"

She hated to ask. Hunter had been as devastated as her at the loss of Bogan. Perhaps he thought he hid the hurt but she'd caught the pain in his eyes when he thought she wasn't looking.

"I can try. I'm not sure what they did or what they changed."

"It doesn't matter. Do it for Bogan. He saved our lives, Hunter."

He gave a succinct nod and released the jack output. Hunter palmed the war mongrel's head and lowered his own but not before Narelle caught a glimpse of his eyes going completely black.

Hunter refused to disappoint Narelle. He saw the tripwire designed to notify the government the moment Bogan came online. Fucking Godav. It was nothing to deactivate it along with the standard failsafe regarding attacks on soldiers. Hunter didn't want to risk losing the war mongrel again if placed in a similar circumstance. Bogan would be free to defend against anyone who posed a threat, soldier or not.

As to the reason Bogan remained catatonic, Hunter identified the problem and corrected it. A simple thought and Bogan's biotronics clicked over, operating at optimum efficiency. He dropped his hand to his side and Bogan lurched up. He licked Hunter's face, whining as his tail wagged then shifted as he tried to crawl into Narelle's arms. She staggered back on a laugh and Hunter caught her from behind. "Whoa."

He helped lower Bogan to the floor and went to one knee. The new wireless additions negated a live probe for the next step. "Trijl, Bogan."

The connection snapped into place with ease. Joy burst through Hunter's chest. "Gott biet rel."

Narelle placed a hand on his shoulder. "Looks like you have your partner back."

He did. He did indeed.

Perfect fucking sync.

RESCUED BY THE CYBORG

(A Cy-Ops Sci-fi Romance)

By
Cara Bristol

USA Today bestselling author Cara Bristol writes science fiction romance
with heart, heat and humor.

http://carabristol.com/

ONE

Hissing and growling, the *Ka-Tê* emerged from the jungle.

Solia hid her face under her good wing, feigning unconsciousness. *Will it be me? Please, not me.* Tears trickled from her eyes. If her life was spared, another's would be taken.

Her hair registered disturbance in the air as the *Ka-Tê* approached. Through a tiny gap in the vanes of her wing, Solia caught sight of dirty, razor-like claws. Two sets of feet stopped beside the electro-cage.

No. no. no.

A hiss. "Save this one for last." A long tail snapped.

Her hair prickled as they moved on; her heart pounded as she listened for an indication they'd stopped at the adjacent cage containing the human girl. She heard no buzz of the force field shutting off or cry from the captive.

It would be the other one, then—the sentient who rolled silently in her cage. Without legs, she moved on a *rotae*, a natural wheel. Solia had never seen such a creature and wouldn't have guessed she was female except the *Ka-Tê* somehow knew. They'd killed the males first, reserving the females for a special torture.

The force field hummed.

"Get out." The microimplant behind Solia's ear translated the snarl into *Faria*. "Now."

The hiss was followed by a cry of pain from the sentient. *Make it quick.*

Make it quick. Nothing could save the creature, but Solia prayed she wouldn't suffer for long.

"Run. Run for your life." The *Ka-Tê* laughed.

Branches snapped as the sentient fled. She wouldn't get far. None of them did. Solia bit her lip until it bled and squeezed her eyes shut.

Laughter. Grunts. Screams. Then growling, chomping, and slurping. Bile rose in Solia's throat, and tears seeped past her shuttered eyelids. Finally, the jungle rustled as the predators moved on. Silence fell. The rusty scent of blood drifted on humid air.

"She never had a chance," the human girl whispered.

Holding her broken left wing tight to her body, Solia sat up. "No." Traffickers had delivered to the *Ka-Tê* eighteen hostages: six males and twelve females. All the men, one of them the human girl's husband, had been slaughtered at the start then, each day thereafter, the *Ka-Tê* came for a female.

Now, only two remained.

"Which—which one of us do you think they'll take next?" the human asked. Rachel, her name was.

"I don't know," Solia said. The human woman had never stopped hoping for a rescue. It wasn't going to happen. No one knew they were here, and no one would risk a landing if they did. The Association of Planets had charted Katnia as a forbidden zone.

Rachel choked and pressed a knuckle to her mouth. "If I hadn't complained so much…John was working long hours. I hardly got to see him. So he booked a cruise to surprise me."

Solia had heard the story several times. "It's not your fault. You couldn't have guessed slavers would attack." Thinking the pirates coveted the ship, the overwhelmed, outgunned crew had directed the passengers to the escape pods. The slavers had swooped in and scooped up Solia's pod, taken everyone aboard prisoner, and handed them over to the *Ka-Tê*. Each day, another female was raped and murdered, the victims' screams and creatures' laughter and grunts breaking the silence of the jungle. Dwindling numbers marked the passage of time.

"How's your wing?" Rachel asked. "Does it still hurt?"

"It's all right, unless I move it." With a swipe of his powerful claws, one of the *Ka-Tê* had almost torn her wing from her body to prevent her flying out of reach.

"If we could talk to them, reason with them—but they can't speak. They hiss and growl," Rachel said. "How can you communicate with animals?"

"They're not animals, exactly," Solia said. The *Ka-Tê* were humanoid felines, vicious, indiscriminate predators who had decimated their ecosystem by hunting nearly to extinction most large animals on their planet. Birds, which could sometimes escape, and rodents too small to catch, had survived. "They have a language." An ugly, guttural one.

"All I hear is growling."

"I can understand some of their vocalizations. I'm a linguist." She'd worked day and night, charting the ancient languages for the Farian ambassador's presentation to the AOP. After completing the project, she'd treated herself to a star cruise. And ended up here.

"So you can talk to them! Tell them we can be ransomed."

Solia touched her throat, shaking her head. "I don't have the anatomical structures allowing me to make those sounds. My aural implant helps me translate languages, but I can't speak Katnian. They're not interested in money. They want the kill."

"I never knew such creatures existed," Rachel said.

"I knew because of my work with languages and my connections to the Association of Planets." The AOP had barred Katnia from the alliance and issued a galaxy-wide travel advisory, except pirates and slavers didn't obey advisories.

Rachel hugged herself. "I won't let them rape and torture me. I'd rather kill myself."

A swift death was the best they could hope for. Solia had thought long and hard how to provoke the creatures to anger so they would kill her quickly, but doubted she would be successful.

"But there's nothing here!" The human girl struck the invisible force field with her fist, crying out as electricity jolted through her with a sizzle. While causing considerable pain, the voltage wasn't high enough to kill. Rachel flung herself onto the ground, dug her fingers into the dirt, and threw a handful at the force field. Sparks, earth, and rocks sprayed. Her sobs of despair were the most heartbreaking sounds Solia had ever heard, and she realized the human girl finally had lost hope.

TWO

"Did you like my present, Uncle Guy?" Jessamine grinned. With the loss of another tooth, her smile appeared even more mischievous.

Guy winced. He'd forgotten about it! "I'm sorry, sweetie. Uncle Guy had to launch the ship, so he didn't get the chance to open it yet." He loved his seven-year-old niece like crazy; however, her antics put a cyborg's patience to the test. R&R on Terra with his sister and her family had gone well, but he'd be lying if he said returning to work wasn't a bit of a relief. His sister had her hands full with that little moppet.

"You…open…away." Jessamine's image and audio flickered as a solar storm broke up the transmission.

"What was that?"

"You…open it right away."

"I will. Promise."

His sister, Jill, appeared on the view screen. "I'm sorry, Guy. If I'd… inkling…what Jessamine had—"

"Don't tell him!" Jessamine cried. "He hasn't…yet. You'll spoil…surprise."

"Oh, he's going…surprised." Although the image pixilated, the censuring glare Jill shot at her daughter still came through. Their mother had employed that look when they were kids. It never had failed to have the desired effect on him and Jill, but it didn't work so well on Jessamine.

His niece's insistence he open the gift immediately and his sister's apology had him a bit worried. What could Jessamine have given him? His bags had been collected and loaded onto the shuttle by a Cyber Operations robo when he'd kissed his family goodbye. Jessamine had hugged his neck with candy-sticky fingers. "I'm going to miss you, Uncle Guy. I got you a special present. Be sure you open it right away."

"Will do. Thank you," he'd said. "I'll miss you, too, munchkin."

He'd boarded the shuttle, but an unexpected solar storm had interfered with the electronics, necessitating his full attention—and he'd forgotten about the gift.

Guy eyed his sister and niece. "Maybe you'd better tell me what it is—"

Their images wavered then the transmission went black.

So much for that. Once clear of the solar storm, he would run back to his cabin. Many pilots might have switched to computer control during a solar incident, but, like most cyborgs, Guy preferred hands-on when situations got a little dicey. Sometimes decisions had to be made in a flash, and Guy preferred to be the one making them.

Solar wind rocked the ship, but Guy's hands remained steady on the stick as he boosted power to the engines. The added thrust would burn more fuel, but he'd clear the storm quicker.

Once the ship was free, he set a course for Alpha Nine Seven, a space station in the Herlian sector where he would meet up with his mission partner, Brock Mann. Cy-Ops had gotten word the terrorist nation planet Lamis-Odg had set up another outpost, and he and Brock had been ordered to investigate. Guy switched piloting to the computer and left the cockpit. Now, the gift.

What could Jessamine have given him?

Ping! An encrypted communiqué from Cy-Ops Director Carter Aymes shot into his cyberbrain. He opened a frequency, but continued to shoulder his way through the narrow corridor.

Where are you? Carter asked.

Just left Terra. Had to bypass a solar wind storm, so I went a little out of my way, but I'll be on Alpha Nine Seven as scheduled.

Change in plans. I'm sending Kai Andros to A-9-7. I need you for recon in the Katnian sector.

Katnia? What's going on?

Intel has picked up signs of activity.

What kind of activity?

A ship reportedly landed.

Every captain and navigator steered clear of Katnia. Even the AOP, which had waited far too long to take action against the terrorist nation planet Lamis-Odg, recognized the threat posed by the *Ka-Tê*. If those creatures ever left their planet, they would go on a killing spree the likes of which the galaxy had never seen. The only thing keeping them in check was a lack of technology enabling them to leave. *Who would be stupid enough to land there?*

Pirates. They attacked a star cruiser a few weeks ago. An escape pod with eighteen people vanished.

Guy stopped dead outside his stateroom. *You're not suggesting they took the hostages to Katnia?*

I would prefer to imagine anything else, but this particular pirate group, calling itself Quasar, has been known to hide out on Katnia in the past. No one, not even intergalactic authorities will follow them there. I have a bad feeling they've been providing the Ka-Tê hostages as prey in exchange for a safe haven from prosecution. Viciousness was inbred in the *Ka-Tê*. Their nature was what it was—but for a sentient species to *give* them victims... Sometimes Cyber Operations fought a losing battle in its mission to keep the galaxy safe from terror. *So you want me to search for survivors?*

Negative. It's too dangerous. Do a recon from orbit. See if you can pick up any tracers from ships that might have been in the area. To be on the safe side, run a scan for nonnative life forms. If you detect any anomalies, we'll send a team in full armor. Don't do anything stupid. Even a cyborg is no match for the Ka-Tê. They hunt in packs.

Roger. He didn't have a problem with *not* risking his life. Guy cocked his head as his cochlear implant detected a faint noise not part of the shuttle.

How did everything go on Terra? Carter paused. *Are you okay?*

I'm fine. Shit happens. He shrugged. *I needed to go home anyway. My family missed me, and my niece is growing up. She's a little pistol.*

Well, I'm sorry.

Guy's gut tightened. He appreciated Carter's concern about his broken engagement, but he didn't care to discuss it. He wanted to move on. *I'm over it. Her loss. Anything else?*

No. Keep me informed.

The noise was growing louder and seemed to originate from inside his cabin. *Will do.*

Aymes out, Carter said.

Roarke out.

Guy pushed into his cabin. Next to his bags was the gift—a box tied with a big red bow. The carton was moving. And mewing. "Oh, Jessamine, what did you do?"

The box bumped into his foot. Atop the lid his niece had written: *LIVE ANAMUL. OPEN ~~IMED~~ IMID SOON!*

He ripped off the bow and peeled back the top. Inside, an angry, frightened kitten hissed. Jessamine's cat had birthed a litter, and he recognized this baby by its gray coat, four white feet, and a blotch shaped like a star on its button nose.

Sighing, he reached into the carton.

The kitten growled and swiped its claws across his skin.

"Ow!" Guy yanked his hand back. The kitten leaped out and dove under the berth.

Great. Just great. How could his niece have done such a thing? She shouldn't have boxed up a live animal—even if she did punch air holes in the carton. If she hadn't contacted him and insisted he open the present, the kitten might have remained inside for quite a while.

In the corner of the container, he spotted a slip of paper, partially shredded. He unfolded it.

Dear Uncle Guy,

I know you are sad, and I want you to be happy. I am giving you one of Fluffy's kittens so you won't be lonely. I named her Mittzi becuz she has four wite white mittens. Pleez come home again, soon.

Jessamine

XOXO

His sister worried about him, but Carter, too, and now Jessamine? He hadn't hidden his feelings well enough if his seven-year-old niece could pick up on them.

His fiancée's defection had devastated him.

He'd met Mariah in a cocktail lounge at the Darius 4 Pleasure Resort. Later, they'd laughed at the cliché of their meeting, how their eyes had locked across the crowded room. He'd wended his way among the floating tables, introduced himself, and offered to buy her a drink. For him, it had been love at first sight. Mariah had claimed the same, but after what had happened, he wondered.

She'd been swept away by the romance of dating a cyber operative. A cyborg. An elite breed of computer-enhanced men. Rough. Tough. Sexy as hell. Her description—not his. Her admiration embarrassed him. He hadn't chosen to become a cyborg; tragic circumstances had forced it upon him. He was proud of his service to the galaxy, but he didn't consider himself special in any way.

Still, she'd made him feel like the luckiest man in the galaxy—for sure, one of the luckiest cyborgs. Guy could count on one hand the number of cyber operatives who had steady, healthy relationships: Brock Mann and Penelope Aaron, Kai and Mariska Andros, Dale Homme and Illumina, March Fellows and Empress Julietta, and Sonny Masters and Amanda Mansfield. Five fingers—five couples out of hundreds of agents.

After their vacation, they'd continued to see each other and, after a year of intergalactic dating, Guy had popped the question. Mariah had accepted and begun planning the wedding of the millennium. He'd put in for a month's R&R so they could get married and go on a honeymoon. Undercover for months at a time, he'd been unable to be there when she wanted his opinion on the wedding arrangements. His inability to participate hadn't thrilled her, but he'd assumed she understood.

Turned out he wasn't one of the lucky ones.

Mariah had fallen for the fantasy of being the wife of a secret cyber operations agent more than she appreciated the reality. Two months before the wedding date, she sent him a Dear John letter.

Yeah, their breakup was as clichéd as their meeting.

Dear Guy,

I'm so sorry. I can't marry you. I haven't been able to find the words to tell you, but I met someone else. Someday you'll find the right woman who will be everything you need her to be.

Mariah.

Sent from her PerComm, it had popped into his cyberbrain during a meeting with Cy-Ops HQ.

Nice. But his reaction to being jilted had proved her point. Cyborgs *were* a different breed. While his human side wanted to punch the wall, his computer-controlled cyborg brain carried on with the strategy session like nothing had happened. Two months later, he went home, using scheduled R&R for a family visit instead of a wedding. Curious and precocious, Jessamine kept him on his toes and amused him, even if she did wear him out after a while.

He couldn't keep a kitten.

Guy dropped to all fours and peered under the berth. "Here, kitty kitty."

The kitten arched in the corner, the fur on her back standing straight up.

"It's okay, Mittzi. It's okay."

She hissed.

"Nobody's going to hurt you," he said in a soothing voice and reached for her.

Mittzi took another swipe, but he latched onto her and hauled her out. Guy got to his feet again, and, holding the growling kitten against his chest, stroked her fur. She was a fierce little thing. A fighter. What was Jessamine thinking to put her in a box?

A pretty little cat with huge green eyes and long white whiskers, Mittzi's fluffy kitten fur would turn sleek and shiny when she matured. Guy estimated her age at two months. Old enough to be away from mama kitty, but barely. She did indeed sport mittens—four white paws, the front right a little higher than the other three, making it look like the other three had slipped down her legs.

Guy sat on the bunk and held her, speaking in a low voice, all the while petting her. Gradually her racing heart slowed and her body relaxed. Mittzi began to purr. She *was* adorable. To humor his niece, he'd peeked at the frolicking kittens and said, "Yeah, they're cute," but truly hadn't paid much attention.

"Which one is your favorite, Uncle Guy?" she had asked.

"The one with the white socks." He'd randomly pointed to this one, not realizing the significance of the question.

Guy held up Mittzi. "We're going to have to find you a permanent home. I'm not around enough to own a pet."

The kitten highlighted his unsuitability for long-term relationships. If he couldn't keep a cat—why had he thought he could handle marriage? Perhaps Mariah had a legitimate gripe. He'd missed every single wedding-planning session—even the vid-con ones. He'd been undercover and incommunicado, unable to tell her he couldn't attend. No wonder she'd gotten fed up and left him.

Still, the way she had done it...

Keeping Mittzi was out of the question.

"As soon as I finish this assignment, we'll head to the Alpha Nine Seven," he told the kitten. "You're so cute, somebody on the space station will take you. In the meantime, I'll rustle up some rations. Hope you like reconstituted fish. I hope the 3-D replicator can come up with a litter box."

THREE

Mittzi padded into the cockpit and made herself comfortable on Guy's lap. Once she'd recovered from the trauma of being boxed, her affectionate, playful nature had revealed itself. Though he'd fixed her a bed, she'd insisted on sleeping next to him in his berth last night. Unfortunately, he was starting to get attached, a situation he did not need. He'd suffered enough heartbreak without having to give up a pet he cared for.

"Computer, put Katnia on the screen and magnify four hundred times." He'd switched to voice command. The silence of space travel, of being alone, had never bothered him before, but this trip, he'd needed to hear a voice, even a digital, terse one.

"Done," replied the computer.

A lush jungle appeared. Covered with dense forests and plant life found nowhere else in the galaxy, Katnia was a botanist's dream. It could have been a zoologist's fantasy until the *Ka-Tê* had killed off most of its wildlife. Only a few remained, and their numbers had dwindled to near extinction. Only insects, tiny rodents, and small birds still flourished.

The first indication of the *Ka-Tê's* viciousness had occurred a century ago when a scientific exploration team landed on the planet. Half of the landing party had died at the hands of the creatures. The survivors named the planet Katnia and the resident species *Ka-Tê* because they resembled hairless panthers. The misnaming had spawned a belief the predators were related to cats. DNA analysis had disproven genetic similarity, but the myth had persisted.

"Scan the surface for life-forms alien to Katnia," Guy ordered. "Report any anomalies."

"Scanning," said the computer.

For several minutes the only sound in the cockpit was Mittzi purring, and then the computer spoke. "The exospheric molecular analysis has been completed."

"Report."

"Plasma diffusion with a molecular array consistent with a class B attack cruiser has been detected."

Guy accessed his databanks in the microprocessor embedded between the hemispheres of his brain and pulled up a list of individuals and organizations known to run class B attack cruisers. It was a short list.

Quasar.

"Identical plasmic trace elements were detected in the troposphere and at ground level," the ship's AI said.

"You're saying a craft landed on the planet's surface?"

"The probability is 99.87 percent."

"How long ago?"

"Adjusting for weather and atmospheric conditions, the range would be between two and three weeks. The surface scan for alien life has been completed."

"What did you find?" He held his breath. *Report nothing. Please, report nothing.*

"One alien life-form has been identified."

He clenched a fist. "What?"

"One alien life-form has been identified."

Fuck. "What is it?

"A Farian female."

"There's a Faria on the planet?"

"Affirmative."

"Alive?"

"Affirmative, but life signs appear weakened. There is an 88.32 percent probability of expiration within twenty-four hours."

"Transmit coordinates to my microprocessor."

Numbers buzzed into his brain.

"Are there any other sentient life-forms besides *Ka-Tê* on the planet?" he asked.

"Negative," the computer said.

"Any deceased?"

"Affirmative. Scan detected remains of seventeen sentient beings including two humans, one Arcanian, one Rotaenian, two Xenians…" The computer reeled off a list matching those reported as missing after the pirate attack.

Guy set Mittzi in the vacant Nav seat and opened a hailing frequency to HQ.

What did you find out? the director asked.

The Ka-Tê have a Faria. Quasar landed on the planet.

Fuck! Only the one individual? No others?

Seventeen are dead.

I'll dispatch an extraction team for the Faria. ETA in twenty-six hours.

That will be too late. She won't last that long. I'm going in.

Negative. It's too dangerous for one person. I can't risk losing a cyborg.

Cy-Ops agents risked their lives all the time, undertaking missions against the odds, but one weighed the danger against the possible outcome. Carter was right. One lone cyborg against a pack of *Ka-Tê*? He and the Faria both would die. But all Guy could focus on was a survivor needed help. *I can't let her die,* he shot back.

Roarke, this is not a suggestion: I'm ordering you to remain on the ship.

No can do. Critical minutes were draining away while he argued with his superior. The predators wouldn't allow the Faria to expire from her injuries; they would torture her to death. It was what they did, what they lived for.

Dammit Guy—

Roarke, out. Guy closed the channel. There'd be hell to pay later, but Carter could put it on his tab.

He locked the ship in orbit, scooped up Mittzi, and hurried from the cockpit. He deposited the kitten in his cabin where she'd be safe during his absence. In the armory, he stripped and pulled on a protective mesh vest. It wasn't totally impervious to penetration, but it would provide a temporary barrier to the claws of a *Ka-Tê*. Blood-borne nanocytes could heal many injuries but wouldn't help if he was gutted. Over the mesh, he donned a mottled-green uniform to help him blend with the flora. The *Ka-Tê* had sharp eyesight; fortunately, a cyborg's was sharper.

He grabbed a couple of photon blasters, pressed his thumb to the DNA scanner, and programmed the weapon to respond only to his touch. If he were to be jumped, at least the *Ka-Tê* couldn't shoot him with his own weapon—although that was least likely of all the possible scenarios. *Ka-Tê* preferred to bite and slash; no one had ever known them to use weapons. Biologists had speculated the *Ka-Tê* didn't have the manual dexterity, but Guy intended to take no chances.

Well, other than landing on the planet.

Suited up and packing, he squeezed into the two-seater landing module that would shoot him to the planet's surface.

FOUR

The pod set down in the jungle three kilometers from the Faria's coordinates. Cloaking had to be deactivated for landing, and getting closer might have alerted the *Ka-Tê* to his presence. Fortunately, dense foliage most likely blocked the view of the pod dropping from the sky.

He climbed out of the tiny craft, reactivated its cloaking device, and the module disappeared from sight. If any *Ka-Tê* wandered by, they *might* notice a faint shimmer, but, from a distance, the pod was undetectable. Guy plotted its location in his cyberbrain so he could find it.

Following the coordinates, he set off into the jungle. Fronds, ferns, and other spore-producing plants slapped at his legs as he picked his way over thick roots and vines sprawling across the floor. Trees spired up to the sky to fan out in a dense canopy of variegated green.

Lush. Beautiful. Eerie.

A hush of death thickened the air.

On his missions, Guy had tromped through many jungles on many planets. In each one except on Katnia, the screech, crash, chatter, and howl of forest animals blended into a cacophony of endless noise. Jungles were never quiet.

This one was.

His acute cybervision and hearing detected insect activity and a twitter of tiny birds, but only faint traces of larger animals. Mammals, reptiles, amphibians, larger birds—most of them of any size had been killed.

Although the dense vegetation helped to muffle sound, with the absence of animal chatter, unusual noises would stand out. Guy trod carefully. *Don't want the Ka-Tê to hear me before I hear them.*

While the creatures had decimated the fauna, they'd done little to touch the flora. He'd never seen a jungle so thick, so undisturbed, almost primordial. Layers of dead and decaying plant matter padded the spongy ground.

Snap! Grrrr. Snap! Grrrr.

Hackles rose on his nape. Cocking his head, he listened to the growls. Two frequencies—two creatures. He ducked behind a thick, half-rotted tree.

Moments later they appeared, padding on all fours. They did sort of resemble hairless panthers, their long, muscular bodies moving with a feline sway, but they weren't cats of any kind. Their heads were too bulbous, their jaws oversized with a jutting under bite. Random tufts of bristly hair protruded from leathery skin. Despite the intelligence sparking in their yellow-green eyes, they were the ugliest creatures he'd ever seen. Slime crawlers were more attractive.

One of them paused, raised its head, and sniffed.

Guy gripped his blaster, ready to shoot.

The creature roared, revealing a mouthful of sharp, yellowed teeth. Red stained its muzzle, and Guy's stomach churned as he realized it was blood from a recent kill. On a planet with few animals, that could mean—

What if I'm too late? What if they already killed her?

The *Ka-Tê* glanced at each other, hissed, and moved on.

When he could no longer hear them, he raced through the jungle. Closer to his destination, he encountered two more creatures and had to duck behind another tree, making sure to remain upwind. He had no idea how sharp their sense of smell was. After they passed, he hit the jungle again. He neared the coordinates, human and cyber senses on high alert. Parting the fronds, he peered into a clearing.

A Faria lay motionless on the ground, her silvery wings torn and bloodied, one bent at an unnatural angle. Her clothing hung in shreds on her battered body. Deep wounds crisscrossed her arms, legs, and abdomen. She looked broken.

Don't be dead.

Guy had rescued many people—but had lost even more. Some he hadn't been able to get to in time; others were alive, but later succumbed. Though intellectually he knew saving everyone was outside his control, each death scarred him. For the ones lost, he fought harder to save the ones he could. He sensed losing this little Faria would be the greatest loss of all.

He cocked an ear for the *Ka-Tê* then, hearing nothing, sprinted into the clearing. A shimmer revealed an electro-cage surrounded the Faria, the force field beamed from a half-buried unit. To his knowledge, the *Ka-Tê* didn't have the technology to create a containment field—but Quasar did. Pressing his lips together, Guy fired his blaster at a molehill-sized mound. The energy field collapsed with a crackle.

Silvery, luminous skin had dulled to gray. Gaping wounds had bled into the dirt, darkening the soil around the Faria. There was no telling how much blood she'd lost. He cursed himself for not bringing an emergency medi-kit. Pressing his fingers to her throat, he sought a pulse. Too faint, but there.

He tucked his blaster into the holster so he could ease an arm under her shoulders. She moaned in pain.

"I know, sweetheart. I'm going to get you out of here," he murmured. He hoped he wasn't too late. When he started to lift her, her eyes flew open. She cried out and jerked, her good wing spasming. "Hey, hey, it's okay," he murmured. "My name is Guy. I'm here to help. What's your name, sweetheart?"

The fear in her eyes muted. "So-Solia," she answered. Silvery tears welled. "R-Rachel never gave up hope we'd be rescued until the end. B-but then she did…"

"There's someone else here?" Had the computer missed one? Unusual, but possible, considering the density of the vegetation. He'd take Solia to the ship and then come back for the other survivor.

She shook her head. "No, they're all dead. The *Ka-Tê* killed them, except for Rachel. She took her own life."

"I'm sorry," he said, recognizing her need to process the horrors she'd witnessed. "I wish we had time to talk, but we don't. I'm going to carry you so we can move fast and get out of here. Okay?"

She nodded.

As he moved to scoop her up, the hair on his nape prickled. He whipped around. A *Ka-Tê* sprang at him out of nowhere like it had been catapulted. Guy threw himself over Solia and struck out with his arm. As he flung the creature away, its claws sliced through his sleeve and dug into his biceps.

Solia screamed.

The *Ka-Tê's* barbed tail switched. Yellow eyes gleamed with intelligent malice. It snarled and leaped. If he'd been alone, cyber reflexes would have enabled him to dodge it, but he served as the sole barricade between the creature and Solia. It landed on him, raking with its claws. His uniform shredded, but the mesh protected his chest. Mostly. One razor-sharp claw pierced through to his skin. The *Ka-Tê* roared and lunged for his throat, but Guy grabbed its neck with one hand, thrust the muzzle of the blaster to its temple, and shot it in the head. Blood and brains sprayed him in the face.

He shoved the limp body into the dirt as two more creatures galloped from the jungle. He shot them both then whirled around as a couple more leaped from the thicket. *Fuck, how many are there?* He dispatched them as well.

Five down. His heart hammered for long seconds as he waited for others to appear.

Hic-hic-hic. Solia gasped for air, her body shaking.

He wished he could comfort her, but the snarls, her scream, and the scent of blood would draw more *Ka-Tê*. "I'm sorry, sweetheart, we gotta go."

Gently, he hoisted her over his shoulder. Not the most comfortable position for her, but it allowed him one hand free to shoot. Banding his arm across her thighs, he sprinted into the thicket. He tried to tread quietly, but speed mattered more than silence. He and Solia were bleeding. Any *Ka-Tê* in the vicinity might track the blood scent. Hiding wasn't an option.

His cyberbrain homed in on the pod's coordinates as he ran, knocking away branches, fronds, and giant ferns with his blaster hand. He plowed through a stream rather than leaping over it, to minimize the impact on Solia. She was limp and silent except for her muffled whimpers when he jolted her.

"How are you doing, sweetheart?" he asked.

"A-a-all right."

"We're almost there." It disturbed him the *Ka-Tê* had sneaked up on him. His cyberhearing could detect sounds even dogs couldn't hear. Only a cyborg's instinct had saved them. His injured arm throbbed, but nanocytes had already rushed the site to initiate healing. By the time they reached the ship, the wound would be a memory. A bad one. How could he not have heard the thing approach?

Rawr! Rawr! RAWR! Snarls split the air as if creatures closed in, but that couldn't be possible. He had a head start, and he was fast. *Rawr!* "They're farther away than they sound," he reassured her.

"They have us in their sights." Her voice quavered. "They know you're armed, so they're hanging back, calling for reinforcements before they attack."

"It might sound that way—"

"No, you don't understand. I'm telling you what they *said*."

The certainty in her voice got his attention. "What?"

"I'm a linguist with an aptitude for languages enhanced by an implant. Their vocalizations might sound like animal growls, but it's a language."

"You speak Katnian?"

"No, but I understand it. Four of them are following us. They're calling others to intercept us, ambush us up ahead."

Oh. Fuck. "Hang on." He tightened his grip. Nanos pushed power to his legs, and he burned through the jungle. Foliage blurred as he ran.

RAWR! Fuck, if that one didn't sound close. Scientists had hypothesized a *Ka-Tê's* speed rivaled a Terran cheetah. A cyborg with prosthetic legs and a nano infusion, he was faster than a cheetah—but no one had *clocked* a *Ka-Tê*. What if they were much faster?

Solia cried out as he vaulted over obstacles and came down hard. He knew she felt every jolt in her battered, torn body, but he didn't dare slow.

His cyberbrain led him to the pod. Activating his wireless, he transmitted a signal and switched off the cloaking device. The ship shimmered into view, and the hatch opened. He dove in, holstered his weapon, and swiped his hand across the reader to seal the door. He expelled a breath.

Well, that got the pulse pounding. He buckled Solia into the Nav seat. Her complexion was grayer, duller. Her head lolled.

"Solia!" He patted her face. "Stay with me, sweetheart!"

She opened her eyes. "I'm here."

Thud!

Solia screamed.

A monstrous *Ka-Tê* leaped onto the nose, clawing at the window, trying to get at them. Its maw opened wide in a muffled roar. The pod's construction provided a sound barrier, but the sight of the sharp, yellowed fangs and teeth was bad enough.

Solia emitted terrified huffing noises.

The pod rocked as the creatures threw themselves at the tiny ship.

"You're safe. They can't penetrate the craft," he said and flung himself into the pilot's seat. "But we're not sticking around, either." His fingers flew over the launch screen.

Thrusters ignited. He hoped the *Ka-Tê* on the ground got fried.

The pod lifted off. The creature on the window hung on.

"It will fall off. Don't look at it," he said.

She already had her eyes squeezed shut. Her knuckles whitened on the seat's armrest.

If Solia hadn't been injured, he would have shot the pod to the sky and done a loop the loop and dumped the *Ka-Tê's* hairless ass back down to Katnia. But he couldn't subject an injured woman to the g-forces. However, he had a few other tricks up his sleeve.

The pod rose into the sky with the *Ka-Tê* clinging to it. He was a stubborn fucker. Clear of the canopy, Guy opened the throttle and lifted the nose. The *Ka-Tê* slid and hit the view window. The tiny pod arced into the sky. Guy kept his eye on the altimeter. When he achieved enough clearance from the ground, he leveled out and then lowered the nose. The *Ka-Tê's* eyes widened with alarm. He clawed at the pod, fighting gravity. He lost the battle, fell from the craft, and disappeared.

Guy raised the nose. The pod scaled the sky and zoomed out of the atmosphere.

FIVE

Report! The pod had no sooner docked on the shuttle than Carter's hail came through. Guy braced himself for a reaming, although, in truth, Carter was one of the good guys. The director could be a pain in the ass, sometimes, but every single cyborg in Cy-Ops owed him his life. Including him.

I got her, he answered. Carrying an unconscious Solia, he climbed out of the pod and hurried down the passage.

Her?

Solia. The Faria. The Ka-Tê had her. She's alive, but barely.

Shit. No others, right?

No. I intend to take Solia to the Cybermed station in sector seven. She needs more help than conventional medicine can give her. Her wing is in bad shape. Guy waited for the denial. Classified top secret and extremely specialized, Cybermed facilities weren't public hospitals. Rarely did they treat people who weren't undergoing cybernetic surgical modification. But Cybermed was the only medical facility with a chance of saving Solia's damaged wing. The left one had been nearly severed from her body; it hung by a tendon. It was amazing she'd survived. If it wasn't fixed properly, she would never fly again.

I'll let them know to expect you. Carter didn't question or hesitate.

Moments like these were why every single Cy-Ops agent would kill for the man. *Thank you.*

What else did you find out? the director asked.

Ka-Tê are fast, strong, and vicious. Maybe no one but a cyborg would stand a chance, and I'm not even sure of that. I was barely able to outrun them. He might not have beaten them to the pod, if Solia hadn't warned him. *Also, they have a language.*

You're kidding. They don't just snarl and growl?

Solia is a linguist. She understands the sounds.

The pirates who delivered the captives managed to communicate. Maybe we can, too? We can find out what motivates them.

Now you sound like the AOP, Guy said.

Don't be nasty.

Though Cy-Ops and the Association of Planets each wanted safety for the galaxy, they disagreed on strategy. The AOP's policy acceptance of diversity, of live and let live, put them at a disadvantage with terrorists bent on achieving their aims at any cost. The alliance's naiveté sometimes resulted in tragedy—leaving Cy-Ops to clean up the mess.

Guy entered the compact med bay and positioned the unconscious Solia on the berth. Faria glowed with a natural luminosity; her skin had dulled to ash. Waist-length silver hair had grayed and lay lank and lifeless. She looked dead. Only the faint rise and fall of her chest revealed she was still alive.

He palmed a screen and accessed the bridge. Keying in a code, he set a course for Cybermed and then swept a bio scanner over Solia. Vitals barely registered. He read the diagnostic. Major blood loss. Organs failing. Shock. She was sinking fast. No MEDs exploded in the background, no soldiers moaned, but the past slammed into him. Truman was dead; he couldn't lose this little Faria, too. She'd saved their lives, *his* life, by warning him the *Ka-Tê* were closing in. She couldn't die now!

He yanked open a cabinet, grabbed an infuser loaded with *nano-temp.* Pressing it against her neck, he injected the generic microrobotic cells into her bloodstream to jump-start healing. Would it work on a Faria? He wasn't sure, but, in any case, the effects would be temporary at best because her body would break down and flush out the nano-temp. But, with a little luck, it would stabilize her until arrival at Cybermed. Next, he injected her with a dose of *hemogen* to speed the production and maturation of blood cells. "Hang on, sweetheart," he murmured.

He ran another scan and released his breath in a relieved whoosh when he saw an improvement in her vitals.

Guy stripped off his shredded shirt and the netting. His nanos, permanent ones programmed to his genetics and chemistry, had sealed the punctures to his torso. All he had to show for the attack was pinker skin. In a few hours, his skin would darken, and only memories of the experience would remain.

Those would never disappear.

He realized he still had Carter on an open channel. *I don't entirely disagree with the AOP's containment strategy,* Guy told the director. *The Ka-Tê have killed most of their animal life. Unless they start eating insects, pretty soon they'll starve to death.* If it was his decision, he'd charge in with a full unit and wipe every single *Ka-Tê* off the face of Katnia for what they'd done to Solia… which was why they didn't put cyber operatives in charge of interplanetary relations. *The AOP is correct in its assumption. If we leave them alone, karma and nature will take care of them. However, with mercenaries and pirates feeding them, that's not going to happen. So far, the pirates have had the sense not to give the Ka-Tê passage off the planet. But if that changes, or the Ka-Tê acquire the technology to leave on their own, they'll make Lamis-Odg look like Vestian altar boys.*

What do you suggest?

In the short term, heightened surveillance of the sector. We have to prevent offworlders from contacting the Ka-Tê. If another trafficking incident occurs, we should consider extermination.

Ironically, the "Kumbaya"-singing AOP would fight Cy-Ops tooth and nail. Where the organization had failed to move decisively against threats to the galaxy, addressing a problem in such a direct manner *would* spur the alliance into military action—against Cy-Ops. The AOP would lose, of course.

I'll increase drone surveillance. The other will require more consideration.

Of course. Exterminating an entire species was a grave last resort.

Now about your insubordination. You disobeyed a direct order. Consider yourself on two-week paid leave, effective upon delivery of the Faria to Cybermed. I'm assigning someone else to your mission with Brock.

Fine. He shrugged. Carter had to maintain order, but if Guy had it to do over again, he wouldn't change his decision. Administrative leave amounted to a slap on the wrist—Carter could have thrown him in the brig. Instead, his pay wasn't even being docked. Forced time off suited his intentions anyway. He couldn't dump Solia at Cybermed and leave. He had to ensure she recovered and got back to her people and—boy, he was a dumb fucker. *Thanks,* he said.

Good call on your part. If I threw every agent who went rogue into the brig, I wouldn't have a Cyber Operations team.

Cyborgs didn't take orders well. Shit happened. For all their muscle power, brain power counted more. You had to be able to think on your feet in the field. What they did exceptionally well was guard each other's backs. That included Carter's. Guy and his fellow agents liked to yank Carter's chain because he ran the organization—had founded it—but he belonged to the brotherhood, too.

I'll keep you posted, he promised, although Carter would know what happened before Guy did.

Good luck.

The link disconnected, and Guy focused on Solia. Her lashes formed dark crescents on her pale-gray cheeks. All the Faria he'd met had glowed and sparkled like they were illuminated from within. Solia's light had been nearly extinguished. Unconscious, she looked so small and defenseless. She *was* small and defenseless. Nano-temp would help, but she wasn't out of the woods yet.

The med-bay door slid open to admit Mittzi. "Meow?" It almost sounded like, "Where have you been?"

He'd left the kitten in his quarters—but had forgotten to lock the access/exit. Guy sighed and picked her up. "What mischief did you get into while I was gone?" he asked and petted her.

Between her shoulder blades, he could feel the small lump of a microchip ID tracker. A good thing to have, considering how much she moved about. If she disappeared and got herself wedged into a duct, he could locate her from the ping.

Mittzi blinked, her green eyes wide and innocent appearing. White feet contrasted with dark-gray fluffy fur. Some people were dog lovers; others preferred reptiles; some the limbless, but empathetic, *ikantani*, but who couldn't respond to a kitten this cute? He'd keep her if his work permitted it. Maybe somebody on the Cybermed station would want her. He'd ask around.

In the meantime, he would leave her with Solia. Piloting actions from the med bay were limited. On the bridge, he could override the presets and boost power to get them to Cybermed faster. He could keep an eye on Solia via the monitor. In her condition, she probably wouldn't rouse. If she did, Mittzi would keep her company. Petting an animal was supposed to be calming, wasn't it?

Guy deposited the kitten on the berth with an admonition to behave, reprogrammed the entry/exit so the kitten couldn't get out, and headed for the bridge.

SIX

What *was* that?

Something kept poking her. Solia rose to consciousness but buried her face in her wing and squeezed her eyelids even tighter. She didn't want to see what existed in the light. Monsters were real, and they didn't just creep in the night. *Don't look. Stay here.* Here, wherever that was, with her eyes closed, was warm, pain-free, safe.

Safe from what? What was she forgetting?

Pat. Pat. Something pawed at her feathers. Then a *rumble*. Pat. Pat. Poke. Something sharp, like a claw scraped across her face.

Claw.

Ka-Tê.

Jungle.

Cage. Death. Her lids sprang open. Two green *Ka-Tê* eyes stared into hers. The creature yawned, revealing a mouthful of small, sharp teeth, and then struck out with its paw.

Solia shrieked. The creature somersaulted and disappeared. Dragging her broken, torn wing, Solia stumbled for the door and plowed into a massive chest.

"What's happened? What's wrong?" A man gripped her shoulders. Though he barricaded the way, his presence exuded safety, calmed her panic. More memories flashed. Racing through the jungle. This man carrying her to a pod. Bodies hitting the window, scratching, clawing, trying to crack it open. The man—Guy— had rescued her from Katnia. The floor hummed beneath her feet. She was on a ship now.

But one of the creatures—"K-K-*Ka-Tê*. Here."

"What? Where?" Disbelief knit his brows.

Solia gulped air and pointed. "Under the berth. It's little, but I woke up, and it was on me, scratching my face. It had green eyes. Claws." She patted her cheeks. There didn't seem to be any injury.

"Mittzi." Guy shook his head. He got down on all fours to peer under the bunk.

"Be careful."

He reached under the berth and pulled out a ball of gray fur with white feet. Maybe *Ka-Tê* were born furry but lost their hair as they matured? The creature spoke, emitting an odd little *meow* noise. Neither language training nor the implant provided a translation. It clung to Guy, showing no sign of savagery, but maybe viciousness developed with time, too.

"It's not a *Ka-Tê*, it's a *kitten*, a baby *cat*," Guy said, his tone gentle. "Don't you have *felines* on Faria?"

"That's a cat?" She eyed the long tail, the fluffy fur, the round, whiskered face. This was one of the animal species humans adopted as pets? "No, I've heard about them, but we don't have any kind of feline on Faria."

"Her name is Mittzi. She's not a threat. Do you want to pet her?" He held out the animal. Cupped in his hands, the kitten appeared tiny, but looks could be deceiving. Guy was the largest man she'd ever met, and he had big hands to match. Next to him, anything would seem little. Even a Ka—kitten.

"No!" She shrank back. Now that she was awake, and the animal wasn't sitting on her chest a hair's distance from her face, it looked harmless, but she couldn't bring herself to touch it.

"I'm sorry," he said. "I left Mittzi with you for company. I had no idea she would frighten you."

"It was touching my face—staring at me with those…eyes." She realized how ridiculous she sounded. With a better glimpse—from a safe distance—she could see the vast dissimilarity between this animal and the *Ka-Tê*. Still… "Aren't cats predators?" She recalled the little bit she knew of the animals native to Earth.

"Most domesticated cats will hunt if they're allowed to roam, but unless you're a mouse or a small bird, you don't have to worry. Cats are also prey animals. Coyotes, even large dogs, will kill cats."

At the top of the Katnian food chain, *Ka-Tê* had no predators. Unless you counted this man. He'd faced them and survived. Not only that, he'd taken out several.

"I'll stow Mittzi in my cabin," he said. "I'll be right back."

Solia pressed against the wall. She hated feeling so afraid, so out of control. "Wait!" she called before he disappeared.

He glanced at her. Solia crept forward. Though everything in her cried out against it, she reached out a trembling hand. Guy smiled encouragingly. She touched the kitten.

"Meow?"

She yanked her hand away and fled for the corner.

"Back in a few," Guy said.

The door closed behind him. Her heart thudded in her ears. *I did it. I touched it.* The small feat represented a major victory. Solia wrapped her good wing around her body. The broken one drooped, and she couldn't move it, but at least it didn't hurt anymore. She eyed the healing slashes across her body. The gaping cuts had knit together? Already? *How long have I been here?* She rubbed her forehead.

Guy reentered. "I'm sorry. Cats bear a faint resemblance to *Ka-Tê*—the hairless ones more so—but it never occurred to me Mittzi would scare you."

"It's okay. It...Mittzi...surprised me. How long have I been here? We're on a larger ship, right?"'

He nodded. "We're on my shuttle. You've been here about two hours."

"That's all?" She studied her arms and legs, which the *Ka-Tê* had slashed. From the healing state of her injuries, she would have guessed days.

"I injected you with nanos."

"Nanos?"

"Nano-temp," he amended. "Short-acting nanocytes. Your body will flush them out, but before that happens, they'll boost healing. You lost a lot of blood, so I gave you a shot of hemogen. I'm happy to see your natural color returning."

"Are you a physician?"

"Medic, MMU. Former Terran United military. I served on a mobile med unit in the field."

"And now you..."

"Do other things," he said. "You should get back into bed. If you're moving around, you could do additional damage to your wing before we get to Cybermed."

"Cybermed!" She pressed a hand to her throat. "I don't want to become a cyborg!" Too late, she realized *he* was one. Nothing else could explain his fast reflexes when the *Ka-Tê* jumped him, how he'd managed to outrun them, why he was so large and *muscled*.

He twisted his mouth. "Few do. Becoming a cyborg is a last resort. Cybermed won't transform you. That would require neuro surgery to implant a microprocessor and a complete infusion of permanent self-regenerating nanos programmed to your specific DNA.

"I'm taking you to Cybermed because if anyone can reattach your wing, they can. Any other medical facility would amputate it. If you want to fly again, this is your option."

Amputate? Faria couldn't live without wings. Losing one resulted in a severe handicap; two resulted in death. "I-I want to save my wing, but I thought it was improving. I can't move it, but it doesn't hurt."

"That's due to the pain-dampening effects of the nano-temp. My plan is to get you to Cybermed before it wears off."

"Can't you give me another injection?"

"Not a good idea. Nano-temp won't change your biochemistry, but it does speed healing and regeneration. Your wing could heal broken. Cybermed could fix that—but it would be better if they didn't have to. As it is, you're going to need some rehab." He gestured to the berth.

Her legs had begun to wobble after standing so long, anyway. Faria flew more than they walked, so their limbs weren't strong. She got into bed and shifted to avoid putting pressure on her wing. Lying down made Guy seem more massive. The Farian people didn't grow very tall. Solia was five feet. The tallest Faria barely topped five and a half, and Guy was way over the mark. Six and a half at least.

Carrying her, he'd run through the hot, humid jungle without breaking a sweat. Muscles bulged in his arms, his chest, his thighs, and she'd bet they rippled across his abdomen, too. Would his body feel as hard as it looked? Her hair tingled. *I shouldn't be thinking of him like that.*

But that was like unringing a bell—it couldn't be done. She felt herself silver.

"Your color continues to improve. Good!" he said. He pushed his sleeves up, drawing attention to his change in clothing—and that his wounds had vanished. The *Ka-Tê* had slashed him.

"Your injuries...they're better?"

"Yes, I heal very fast."

"Because you're a cyborg?"

He nodded.

"How did you become a cyborg?"

"Can I get you anything to eat? Are you hungry?"

Solia pressed a hand to her stomach. "Yes." The *Ka-Tê* had thrown some fruit into the cage a few times. Apparently, they didn't want their captives to starve to death before they could kill them—or be too weak to run—not that any of them had gotten far. The last time they'd bothered to feed her had been three days ago.

"I'll get you something to eat. Is there anyone you'd like me to contact? I've already notified the Farian authorities, but is there anyone specific you'd like to talk to? Parents?" He paused. "Husband?"

"No." *He's being kind. He's not asking because he's interested.*

Nor would it do if he was. Romantic attention from an offworlder would have to be discouraged. She couldn't marry a non-Faria. Special abilities could be lost if they bred outside their race. Besides, Faria mated for life with no chance of dissolution for a bad choice. So one had to be very, very sure.

Who said anything about marriage? whispered a saucy little voice.

Exactly, she flung back. *He's not interested in me. He's doing his duty.*

Didn't they say insanity wasn't talking to yourself, but answering?

"I'll get your food," he said.

He left, and she fanned herself. Her face revealed her emotions in a heartbeat. All Faria were expressive; they silvered and glowed when excited or aroused. Guy had ignored her question about how he'd become a cyborg—but she never should have asked. It had probably been a painful experience. A man of his confidence and capabilities would never be interested in a rude little Faria linguist who screamed when confronted with a harmless baby animal.

See, you are interested!

No, I'm not!

Not to mention a crazy Faria who talked to herself.

SEVEN

After Guy programmed the ship's food replicator to produce Farian cuisine, the dispenser produced some fruit-scented biscuits, a thick purple drink, and some hard squares of something he couldn't begin to guess at. The replicator could provide a little bit of most cuisines but offered limited variety within any one food group.

On impulse, he had the machine dispense a sandwich for himself—vegetarian, so he wouldn't gross her out. Would she want to eat with him? She needed to rest. Her body required recovery time, and she had a long, hard rehab ahead of her.

Can't believe I put the cat in the room with her. Bad call. How could he have been so stupid? Solia wasn't the first person to believe the misconception the *Ka-Tê* were felines. However, their genetics were no closer to a cat's than a guinea pig was to an Arcanian. Worlds apart. Mittzi's tiny teeth and claws couldn't begin to compare to a *Ka-Tê's*.

Talk about your close calls. They'd barely made it off the planet.

He wished he knew who to contact on Solia's behalf. When he'd informed the Farian authorities about her rescue and condition, they'd reported she had no next of kin. Just because she didn't have a spouse didn't mean she didn't have a boyfriend or somebody who cared about her.

Guy knocked on the door before entering. Solia sat in bed, the light cover pulled up to her waist. "I did the best I could to get you Farian food," he said.

"Anything you brought will be fine. I could eat a horse." She grinned. "Isn't that a Terran saying?"

He smiled. "Yes. Have you seen a horse?"

She shook her head.

Guy chuckled. "You'll prefer what I brought you, then." He rolled a bed tray to the berth and placed her meal on it. "I got myself a sandwich. Maybe we could eat together?"

"I would like that."

He pulled up a chair. The nano-temp and hemogen had done wonders. While her skin hadn't regained its normal glow, it was more silver than gray, and her hair seemed more alive. The biggest problem was her broken wing. Would Cybermed be able to reattach it so that it functioned? He hoped so. The alternative would be to replace her natural wings with prosthetics. Cybermed had done that once—with excellent results—but still only once. He didn't want to upset her, so he kept his concerns to himself.

"Please, eat!" He motioned and bit into his sandwich.

Solia ate with delicate nibbles. "I need to apologize," she said. "I overreacted to the kitten."

"You don't need to apologize," he said. "It was my fault. I never should have left her with you."

"I scared her as much as she scared me. Is she okay?"

"Mittzi is fine. No harm done."

"On Faria, people sometimes adopt *moochins*. They are round furry animals with long tails and large eyes. Children love them. I imagine having a pet aboard your spacecraft provides company on long flights."

Guy made a face. "I didn't plan to adopt Mittzi, and, in fact, I need to find a permanent home for her. Jessamine, my niece, thought I needed a pet, so she surprised me with a kitten. I didn't find her until I was underway."

Solia's laughter tinkled like chimes in the wind. "Oh." She nibbled at the fruit biscuit then patted her mouth with a napkin and asked, "Do you have a lot of family on Terra?"

"A sister, brother-in-law, and niece."

"You're not mated, then?"

"No," he said tersely.

"I'm sorry. My question is painful for you."

"It's all right. I was engaged to be married, but my fiancée met someone else."

It surprised him he hadn't felt greater pain over his broken engagement —and that Solia had noticed what he did feel. He hadn't thought he'd reacted to her question. He wasn't sure he liked that someone could read him. Being a cyborg, he could switch off emotional displays. In the field, hiding emotion was a prerequisite for staying alive. "What about you? Don't you have family? A mate?" Turnabout was fair play.

For a moment, her hair seemed to dull before it regained its sheen. "My parents were killed when I was a small child. I grew up in an orphanage. Faria mate for life. Dissolution of the mating bond is not possible. Only in rare, extreme instances are unions annulled. I haven't met the man I want to spend my life with. My job doesn't leave me a lot of time to meet people, so no boyfriend."

Her single status pleased him, though it shouldn't. It was none of his business. "You said you're a linguist?"

She nodded. "All Faria have special gifts. I have a natural ear for language and vocal nuance." The corner of her mouth curved slightly. "When you mentioned your broken relationship, there was the slightest catch in your voice. Most people would never notice."

He'd have to be more careful in the future. He cocked his head. "That's how you were able to communicate with the *Ka-Tê*."

"I could understand them." She rubbed her throat. "Vocal anatomy won't allow me to replicate their sounds, so I can't speak to them. I don't think it would have made a difference." She swallowed. "Understanding made it worse. They spoke freely around us, laughed. I knew what would happen."

Guy sucked air through his teeth. "I'm sorry."

"They considered me the prize. They like 'flying things,' even though they tore my wing so I couldn't escape. They were saving me for last. Rather than kill me outright like they did so many others, they intended to keep me alive and play with me for a while. Torture me just short of death. A human woman named Rachel was in the cage next to me. They would have killed her next, but she slit her own throat with a rock and thwarted their plans. They took their anger out on me. Slashed me with their claws."

Having faced his own traumas, he understood pain and terror, hopelessness. Truman's death had scarred him but also had motivated his enlistment in Cyber Operations. Carter had saved his life. Now he needed to pay it forward by saving others.

"I enlisted in the Terran military as a medic, intending to put in my time then allow the government to pay for medical school. They sent me to the front lines, patching up soldiers on the battlefield," he explained. "One day, they brought an unconscious guy into the mobile medical unit. He'd been tortured by Lamis-Odg—and booby-trapped with a microexplosive device. I didn't know that. In tending to his injuries, I triggered the MED.

"It killed him, and I woke up in the hospital as a torso with a head, my arms and legs blown off." Guy touched his left ear. He'd lost that, too—not to mention hearing on that side. "It's true what they say about phantom limbs. I could still feel my arms and legs, but they were gone, along with my military career, my hopes of becoming a physician. Then a man I'd never met visited me and offered me the chance of lifetime." He paused, the memories washing over him like it was yesterday. He took a breath. "You asked how I became a cyborg. That's how."

Solia's eyes rounded with sympathy. "Thank you for sharing your story."

Why had he? He'd never told Mariah—but then, she hadn't asked. It hadn't struck him as odd until now. How could she have professed to love him and not wondered about his past?

Carter had given him a new lease on life. There were no strings attached, but when the Cy-Ops director recruited him for Cyber Operations, of course Guy had agreed. How could he do anything else? The entire cyber operative force was built of men and women Carter had pulled from the wreckage of some disaster or other. Field agents gave the director a hard time, but, like Guy, none of them forgot how much they owed him. They'd march into hell for him.

Hell assumed many deceptive forms. It sprawled over the Lamis-Ogd desert where *iwani* sand demons lived beneath the dunes, it rose high into the sky like the deadly forests of DeltaNu 9084. And it was an eerie, silent jungle where vicious predators preyed on anyone foolish enough to land.

If Carter hadn't sent him to Katnia, Solia would have perished along with the others.

Mariah had claimed he cared more for others than he did for her. "Sometimes I think I need to become a victim to get your attention," she'd thrown at him after he'd missed yet another wedding-planning session. They'd patched it up, he'd thought. Mariah had had his love. When he was home, he'd focused on her.

But he wasn't available enough to suit his socialite fiancée who loved good times and lots of attention. Her gaiety and frivolity had attracted him when they met. With her, he could forget reality, the death, danger, and darkness of his missions. He had loved her, welcoming her lightness to distract him from the ugliness. She had adored the romance of dating a cyborg, a field agent—until he'd had to fulfill his commitment.

He could see now that marriage had been a pie-in-the-sky dream, and he'd face the same situation with any other woman. What wife would accept "being abandoned" six, eight, ten months of the year?

Mariah hadn't been the first woman unable to accept his duty—she'd only been the first to promise it wouldn't be an issue.

But it had been.

In Solia's eyes, he saw sympathy, and, if he wasn't mistaken, the beginnings of hero worship. To her, he was a knight who'd ridden in on a white charger. He had no charger, only two prosthetic legs with arms to match. He was a half man, half machine who did a job few others would even attempt. His assignments were gritty, dirty, bloody—and those were the easy ones.

Exit now. "I'd better get back to the bridge." He grabbed his half-eaten sandwich and pushed to his feet. Solia had finished all of her meal. "Do you care for anything else to eat or drink?" He averted his gaze, focused on the exit.

"No, that was more than enough, thank you."

"There's a comm system." He pointed to a screen. "If you need anything, call me."

She did not respond, so he risked a glance. Her little chin came up, and her shoulders squared. "I'll be fine."

He was acting like an asshole, but it would be better in the long run if she didn't get ideas.

Better for whom?

"We'll arrive at the Cybermed station tomorrow." He'd see her settled, contact Carter, and request he be put back on duty. He'd completed his job here. Time to move on.

"Guy, wait!" Her voice stopped him midflight.

Don't ask me to stay. He'd hate to hurt her feelings by rejecting her.

His heart thudded. He had to leave. "Yes?"

"Would you...would you bring Mittzi to me?"

She wants the kitten, not me.

"Of course." He nodded and fled.

EIGHT

"Are you sure you'll be all right?" Guy asked. As she'd requested, he'd delivered Mittzi. Now that she could see it clearly, the kitten was no bigger than a baby moochin and just as cute. But still terrifying.

I will defeat my fear. The kitten can't hurt me. I will defeat my fear. "I'll be fine."

"Use the comm link if you need me to retrieve her." He set the kitten on the floor and fled again.

Language was Solia's primary gift, but the mother she'd never known had been an empath, and she'd inherited a fair amount of perception. Though Guy appeared calm on the surface, emotions tugged him in opposite directions. She'd sensed his disquiet and found herself asking questions she shouldn't have voiced.

When will I learn? Men liked her at first—until the relationship progressed, and they realized she could read them. Between a language ability enabling her to detect nuances in vocalization and a moderate amount of empathy, *true* feelings were revealed to her. She recognized dishonesty even when masked. People themselves weren't aware how many little lies they told.

"I'm fine."

"I'm sorry. I didn't mean to hurt you."

"I don't know what happened."

Or the lies they kept to themselves. The silent hurts, the resentments, the jealousies.

Even she lied. She had told Guy an untruth. Yes, she was busy with her job and was cognizant of the commitment a lifetime mating represented, and therefore cautious, but the real truth was nobody wanted *her*. When men discovered she could read them, they fled. Nobody wanted their emotional defenses breached.

"It's like you're crawling around inside my head," an ex-lover had said.

She read emotions, not minds, but that was a difference significant only to her.

Guy had been harder to get a handle on than most until, midway through dinner, his discomfort had washed over her like a wave.

She admired how he devoted his new lease on life to help others. He was the sole reason she was still alive. He was a good man, a caring man. A hero.

But even he had lied by omission—he hadn't been entirely honest about what would happen at Cybermed. He'd presented it as a solution, but it concerned him—and that worried her. So many emotions swirled around, the truth had gotten murky. One emotion remained clear: fear. Hers.

The kitten padded toward her and jumped onto the bed. Solia employed every iota of self-control not to shriek and leap off the berth. *Touch it. Pick it up.*

She couldn't—not yet. Unlike the *Ka-Tê*, which had radiated evil, the kitten projected no malice, only curiosity. Solia's heart pounded, but since she wasn't fleeing down the corridor, progress had occurred. She exhaled her tension and wiggled her toes.

The kitten pounced, wrapping her front legs around Solia's ankles and biting her feet through the bed covering. *Get it off. Get it off.* Solia kicked, her heart fluttering. The more she thrashed, the more determined the kitten became.

Slowly reality filtered through the panic. No pain. No injury. The kitten meant no harm; it was playing.

Her racing pulse slowed.

Do it. You have to do it. Solia reached out and picked it up. When it made no move to attack, she gained confidence. A ball of fluff, Mittzi weighed nearly nothing, and her fur was softer than a moochin's. Solia brought her closer for a better inspection. *I'm holding it!*

Round green eyes stared out of a gray furry face. Long white whiskers stuck out below a tiny button nose. White mittened feet dangled. Not a fang or claw in sight. "Meow?"

"You're not so scary."

Moochins liked to be held and petted. Maybe kittens liked the same? She set Mittzi on her lap and stroked her side. A rumbling noise, like a little motor, vibrated from the kitten. Pleasure. Happiness. The kitten liked the attention.

Don't we all?

She scratched behind its ears. The kitten purred louder and rubbed against her hand. *Guy must have thought I was crazy to panic the way I did.* "I scared you, too, didn't I?" The kitten had run beneath the berth to hide. That should have been a clue she presented no threat, except panic had blinded her.

Solia released the last of her fear in a long sigh and fluttered her good wing. Mittzi's gaze zeroed in. "Oh, you like that, do you?" Solia fluttered it again and tried to move the broken one, but it hung limp.

"What am I going to do, Mittzi? What if I can't fly again?" Cybermed offered no guarantees; she understood that. Her people pitied *groundlings* as damaged goods. Her attunement to language subtleties and empathy already counted as two strikes against finding a mate. Becoming a groundling would end her chances for good. No Faria would accept a mate unable to fly.

She and Guy had experienced similar horrors, and she'd sensed a rapport, but he'd fled like he couldn't get away fast enough. They'd been conversing, and then…a wave of discomfort had washed over him. Had she probed too deeply with her questions? She reacted to nuances, to what people didn't say, which unnerved them. Had she done that with Guy? Her senses were so developed, the habit so ingrained, she acted on what she knew to be true before considering the consequences.

Maybe she assumed too much. His departure might not have anything to do with her. He had duties, responsibilities—like getting her to Cybermed. He couldn't be expected to play nursemaid.

"Why did he run, Mittzi?"

The kitten didn't answer—didn't understand. She didn't have the language ability if she did comprehend. But that didn't mean she didn't communicate. Her throat rumbled with a kind of purring, communicating relaxation and pleasure.

Solia drew her hand from head to her tail in a light caress. "You don't care that I'm odd, do you? We can be friends. What do you think?"

Mittzi purred. The little creature reacted to touch and tone in manner, not unlike the nuances Solia picked up on. She sensed emotion and intent and reacted to it. "We're not different, you and I, are we?"

NINE

Guy relinquished piloting to the computer. The space station doors yawned open, and the ship glided in and docked. Panels slid shut, the bay repressurized, and the temperature warmed.

"The shuttle bay has returned to life support mode. You may disembark," the computer announced. An orderly with a hover gurney headed for the ship.

Guy met him as he guided the litter onboard. "She's in the med bay. Follow me."

Dressed like a crewman, Solia perched on the berth's edge with Mittzi on her lap. The *Ka-Tê* had shredded her clothing, so he'd rustled up a uniform, slitting the back to accommodate her wings. The smallest uniform he could find still swamped her slight frame.

"We're ready?' she asked.

Guy nodded at the orderly. "He'll check you in."

"May I bring Mittzi?"

"The cat?" The medical attendant shook his head. "No. Animals aren't allowed."

"I understand." Solia placed the kitten on the berth and eased to her feet. "I'm ready, then." She looked at Guy. "You're coming, aren't you?"

She'd survived a terrifying experience on Katnia. While surgery couldn't compare to what she'd already been through, it was scary enough to face without family or friends to visit, without anyone to hold her hand through the long, painful rehabilitation. Her vulnerability tugged at him to stay—and made him uncomfortable. What if she came to depend on him? Worse, what if he came to depend on her? To need her sweet smiles, to hear her tinkling voice? He'd changed his mind a half dozen times whether to stay or go.

Carter had given him the time off, but that was when Solia had been part of his mission objective. He'd worried about her all night but had kept his distance, because in the long run, avoidance served them both for the best. Mariah had been right; he couldn't be a woman's forever man.

"I'll see you settled, but then I need to report to duty," he lied. "Are you sure there isn't somebody you want me to call?"

She shook her head. "I shouldn't have asked. You don't need to come with me. I'll be fine." She smiled, but her silvery sparkle dulled.

The hover gurney lowered, and the orderly helped her onto it. Electro-restraints snapped around her legs and torso.

"No! No, no!" She thrashed, fighting the bands. "Take it off! Take it off!"

"Stop, you'll hurt yourself," the attendant said. "Restraints are to prevent you from falling."

She pulled at the bands. "No! No!" She gasped for air, and her face grayed.

"Remove the restraints," Guy ordered, knowing Solia flashed back to her captivity on Katnia. What good was physical protection if it harmed her psychologically?

"I have to follow procedures."

Guy opened a link to Carter. *We're at Cybermed, and I'm two seconds from punching someone.*

Why?

An orderly strapped Solia to a gurney. She's having a panic attack. I don't care about rules. Get admin to undo the restraints — or I'll do it.

Solia was crying, tugging at bonds she couldn't break.

"Time to roll," the orderly said.

His head would roll. Guy couldn't wait for Carter. He stepped forward—

The orderly clapped a hand to his ear and tilted his head. "I under-stand," he spoke as a message came through his earpiece. He lowered his hand and scowled at Guy. "Admin ordered the restraints removed."

"You'd better do it, then."

With a press of a button, the bands fell away. Solia gulped air. Silver tears leaked from her eyes and slid into her hair. Guy touched her shoulder. This clinched it. He would stay. What if something else happened? She needed him to run interference, hell, to hold her hand. Cybermed performed miracles of science—with cold precision. Solia wouldn't get the due of a cyborg candidate or potential Cy-Ops recruit. She was an injured woman who'd been through hell and now found herself a long way from home in a frightening place about to undergo a scary procedure.

"I'm coming with you," he informed her. He recalled the devastating loss, the depression, the incredible aloneness upon waking up at Cybermed. And he'd been a big, tough military man.

She sniffed. "Thank you. W-what about Mittzi?"

"She'll have food and water. She'll be okay by herself." At least until he could sneak her into the Cybermed installation.

White. White. Everywhere. Walls, ceiling, and the lights. The white blinded her. Guiding the gurney through the maze of corridors, the orderly marched on her left, the snap of his heels conveying his irritation. Was he mad at being overruled or because the man responsible gripped her hand on the right?

Guy's strong, reassuring touch calmed her. When the orderly had strapped her to the stretcher, she'd flashed to her captivity in the electro-cage and had lost it. She would have torn off her other wing to free herself from the gurney. Somehow, Guy had gotten the attendant to release her. He squeezed her hand now, and she smiled up at him gratefully.

"You don't need to stay with me," she said. *Don't leave. Please, don't leave.* She felt so weak for needing him, but her upcoming surgery in this strange, white place scared her to death.

"I want to be here. Nobody should go through this alone," he said.

Did he mean it, or was he being nice after her meltdown? She attempted to get a read on his emotions, but hers were in such a jumble, she couldn't fight through the muddle to make sense of anything. Or maybe he'd managed to block her.

"Thank you." She swallowed. "What happens now?"

"Surgery," the orderly said.

"Testing and examination first, I imagine," Guy contradicted.

"That's not what's on the schedule," he replied. The gurney stopped outside a door marked Surgical Unit 10. "We're here."

"This is fast," Guy echoed her thoughts. "What's going on?"

The orderly shrugged. "I do what I'm told. You seem to be in the know. Talk to the doc." He guided the gurney into a room whiter and brighter than the corridors then left.

A dark-haired woman in a surgical uniform entered through a door at the rear of the room. "You must be Solia. I'm Dr. Aileen Beckman. I'll be examining you, and hopefully, operating on your wing today."

"About that." Guy frowned. "I thought there would be testing then surgery later…"

"You are?"

"Guy Roarke."

"The medic. You forwarded the images of her wing and administered the nano-temp."

"And hemogen." He nodded.

"I've reviewed the medical records and images, and based on those, my professional opinion is time is critical. We require some nerve and muscles tests, which can be quite painful, so we'll do them under anesthesia and perform whichever surgery is indicated."

"You mean, reattach my wing," Solia said.

"That's what I'm *hoping* for," Dr. Beckman said. "You need to be prepared for removal."

"Amputate? I'd be a groundling." She shook her head. Tears welled and spilled over. This was almost as bad as being sold to the *Ka-Tê*.

"We'll do everything we can to prevent that. Unfortunately, the administration of nano-temp, necessary to save your life, initiated a premature healing of your wing and surrounding nerves and muscles. The partial healing has created complications."

Guy sucked in a breath. "I compromised the reattachment?"

"You did the right thing under the circumstances. Without nano-temp, she wouldn't have survived. I'm not saying her wing can't be reattached, only that I won't know until I get in there. I wanted to prepare you."

How did one prepare to become a groundling? What would she do if she had to spend the rest of her life walking?

"Solia. I-I—" Guy's voice sounded as broken as her wing. "I'm so sorry…"

She didn't blame him. How could she? If not for him, she'd be a pile of bones on Katnia. She grabbed his hand. "You didn't cause this. The *Ka-Tê* did."

"I should have tried something else."

"There was nothing else you could have done," Dr. Beckman said. "I reviewed the scans. She would have died if you hadn't administered nano-temp. But we don't have time to waste. Do either of you have any more questions?"

Will I ever fly again? That was her question, but the doctor had already said she didn't know.

"No," she said.

Guy looked grim. "No."

TEN

Guy paced outside SU-10. Beckman hadn't offered an estimate of time required for the procedure, but surgery seemed to be dragging on. Maybe that was positive? Maybe reattachment required a long time? Or had something gone wrong? What if Beckman had had to amputate? If she was a cyborg, he could have pinged her for an update.

Spinning on his heel, he stalked down the hall in the opposite direction.

I did this. If I hadn't given Solia the nano-temp, the odds would have been better. Neither the doctor nor Solia blamed him, but that didn't erase his responsibility. *Another life destroyed.* He hadn't considered anything but nano-temp. Guy punched the air. If she lost her wing, he'd never forgive himself.

What the hell was taking so long?

Any news? A message from Carter shot into his brain.

No. Not yet.

How long has she been in surgery?

More than five hours. Five hours, thirteen minutes, and twelve seconds. He didn't need to check the time. His cyborg brain kept track.

Yours lasted twelve.

But I became a cyborg. They're attaching a wing. A robo-tech is doing the actual procedure. Robos had the precision required to reconnect delicate blood vessels and nerves.

Who's the overseeing physician?

Beckman. Aileen Beckman.

She's good. One of the best.

Guy spun on his heel again.

You're not responsible for this, Carter said.

Why would you say that?

You take things to heart.

I am responsible. He should have considered alternatives.

Nano-temp saved her life.

How did you—never mind. Of course Carter had gotten a full report. He kept tabs on everything and had connections everywhere. Cy-Ops and the auxiliary Cybermed were under his control.

We do the best we can within the limits of our abilities. We give people chances, not guarantees.

Exactly. He was supposed to have given Solia a chance—not hinder the chance she had. He'd known the healing boost could be problematic, so he'd only given her one injection. Why hadn't he tried something other than nano-temp first?

You need to stop beating yourself up about Truman.

This isn't about him. But thank you for reminding me how I fucked that up, too.

We all have demons. Some days they make us stronger, some days they do a number on us. Solia's situation isn't your fault—nor is Truman's death.

I gave her the nano-temp. I triggered the fucking MED.

The infantryman who'd been blown up hadn't been any old soldier. Truman Haynes had been his best friend since childhood. They'd enlisted in the Terran military together, his buddy going the infantry route while Guy had become a medic. Truman's unit had been ambushed. Guy had been on duty in the mobile medical unit when his friend was brought in. His injuries were serious but not imminently life-threatening. Other soldiers were in far worse condition. Truman would have survived—until Guy examined him and triggered the microexplosive device planted by the enemy.

Guy lost all four limbs and his right ear. Cybernetic surgery had saved his life and given him new arms and legs and sharper hearing. There hadn't been enough left of Truman to piece anything together.

"Mr. Roarke?" Dr. Beckman poked her head into the hall.

The doc is here. Gotta go.

Let me know. Carter signed off.

"How is she? Did you save her wing?" Guy scanned Beckman's face. Her expression was schooled; he couldn't read it.

"We reattached it—" She held up her hand, silencing the *whoop* he would have made. "It's too soon to tell if it will take or how much function she'll have if it does. Solia is sedated in a stasis tank to minimize movement and to speed neural, muscular, and osteo regeneration. She received an infusion of nano-temp."

The same robotic cells that had caused the problem.

"What are the odds of a full recovery?"

"I wouldn't begin to—"

"Tell me."

"Twenty percent."

Fuck. Guy opened and closed his fists, staring at his lifelike prosthetics. "I lost all my limbs and became a cyborg! How is it Cybermed can give me two fake arms and legs, but reattaching a natural wing is a 20 percenter?"

"It's touch-and-go for cyborg transformations, too. Half of them fail. The difference is the prosthetic limbs you received were functional at the start. Her wing was damaged, blood supply cut off. Nerves were severed. Tendons were shredded."

"Can I see her?"

Beckman nodded. "For a *brief* moment. Do you know how to get to the stasis unit?"

"I can find it." A schematic in his cyberbrain gave him an unerring sense of direction.

"Five minutes," Beckman said. "I'll have the unit programmed to admit you. If you overstay your time, you *will* be escorted out."

"Got it."

The entry scanner read his DNA and let him in. In a tank large enough to accommodate the span of her wings, Solia was submerged in ice-blue gel. Her natural silver pallor had grayed again, and her hair lay dull, wet, and flat against her scalp. Her wings were spread almost to full extension, surprising Guy with their length. In the air, she would appear like a graceful silver butterfly.

He gripped the edge of the tank. *You have to be okay. You have to.*

Life or wing. Logically, there had been one choice. If she had died, saving the wing would not have been an issue, but flying meant everything to a Faria. If the reattachment didn't work, Solia would be devastated. *He* would be devastated. Guy leaned over and stroked her wet, lank hair. "I'm right here with you, sweetheart," he whispered. "You can do this. You'll fly again."

You have to.

Three days later

"Solia, can you hear me? Wake up, sweetheart."

Her body levitated at a forty-five degree angle in suspended animation, the force field holding her aloft to avoid pressure on her healing wings. Immobilizers positioned both limbs at half extension now and prevented her from moving them while healing and regeneration progressed. After twenty-four hours in the post-surgical stasis recovery tank, she'd been moved to this unit, where she'd been for two days, still under sedation until this morning.

She looked so fragile, so delicate. In sleep, her face relaxed, and her lashes curved into feathery crescents on her silver cheeks. Her natural color was almost normal. Her hair had regained its body and life and seemed to crackle.

They'd stopped sedating her, so she should be waking up. Why wasn't she?

Guy palmed the medscreen and hacked into her records, scanning the notes. She'd received several more doses of nano-temp. Neural, muscular, and osteo regeneration was progressing, according to Beckman, who had upgraded her prognosis from 20 to 30 percent. Guy had triumphed over far worse odds on missions, and her numbers were trending in the right direction, but they were still too low for his comfort.

He erased his access signature and closed out her records. Cybermed administration could still find out he'd peeked—if they knew what to look for.

Perhaps he shouldn't wake her, but he needed to speak to her more than anything. "Solia! It's Guy."

Her eyelids fluttered, and her nose wrinkled.

"Wake up, sweetheart. Talk to me."

Her eyes opened. Confusion clouded her gaze. She shifted her head from side to side. Panic flared in her eyes when she tried to move her wing but couldn't.

"You're in Cybermed. You're okay. You're safe."

The panic and fog cleared, and she blinked. "Guy?"

He smiled. "It's me."

"I had the operation?"

"You did. Three days ago," he said.

Her eyes widened. "Three days? Did it work—my wings—can I fly?"

Her muscles strained as she again attempted to flutter her injured wing.

"Don't do that," he said. "You need to remain still. You're in suspension until your wing heals enough for you to use it." He wished he could hold her hand to comfort her, but the force field didn't allow him to touch her.

"How long will that be?"

"Another day or two, the doctor said." Beckman hadn't said; he'd read it in the records. Like most physicians, she probably considered herself too busy to deliver regular updates. "You'll begin with some strengthening exercises before they'll let you fly."

Her lower lip trembled. "Thank you. If you hadn't brought me here, I'd never fly again."

He couldn't bring himself to tell her it wasn't a sure thing. *Thirty percent will have to suffice. She's beaten the odds before. She survived on Katnia when all the others were killed.*

"You stayed the whole three days?"

He nodded. "I'll be here until you're ready to leave."

"Until I fly out of here." A smile lit up her face. Her hair sparkled. This was the healthiest he'd seen her. She was healing, even if the state of her wings was uncertain.

"Until you fly out of here," he repeated. Dammit, she *would*. She *would*.

"Then what happens?"

"Then I'll take you home to Faria." An ache settled in the pit of his stomach.

Her smile waned a bit before widening, "How is Mittzi?"

"Good. Getting into everything. She disappeared once. I found her in an air duct. I have no idea how she squeezed in there." The ping of the kitten's ID tracking chip had allowed him to locate her. Otherwise, she'd probably still be MIA.

Solia giggled. "You're staying on the shuttle?"

He nodded and grinned. "I have to keep an eye on Mittzi." He wouldn't have left Solia's side at all, excerpt Cybermed personnel wouldn't let him stay overnight. They'd limited his visits to three short intervals per day.

Her cheeks dimpled, and then she sobered. "You don't need to stay with me. I'm so grateful for all you've done. You have important work. I don't want to keep you from your duties."

"Your recovery is the most important thing. You can't run me off that easily."

A yellow light flashed overhead, and a loud beeping started.

Solia jerked. "What's happening? Is something wrong?"

"Nothing wrong," he said. "It's my signal I have to leave. They only allow short visits."

Even Carter hadn't been able to bend the rules on that one. The ward supervisor who oversaw visiting hours had been adamant. He'd over-stayed the warning once, and she'd threatened to deny him access privi-leges if it happened again. She could *try*. He was a cyborg. He could hack his way in—but that would cause an incident, and Carter frowned on inci-dents. So, Guy would play by the rules. Until he needed to do otherwise.

"It's late evening now," he said. "I'll come see you in the morning, okay?"

"I'd like that."

"Get some rest. I'll be back soon."

Guy adjusted his jacket and then swiped the access screen to the suspension recovery room, but instead of the door opening with a beep and green light, a red *ACCESS DENIED* message flashed.

Had something happened to Solia? His pulse spiked. Activating his wireless, he hacked into the system and forced his way in.

The unit was vacant. Had Solia taken a turn for the worse? Could she have hemorrhaged? Had she been brought back into surgery? She couldn't have…died? Every horrible possibility rushed into his brain. Fingers flying over the medscreen, he hacked in.

Susp ph term. Pt trpt to rhbt. Cybermed shorthand for: Suspension phase terminated. Patient transported to rehabilitation.

Relief whooshed out in a huge sigh. Solia had transitioned to the next treatment phase. He perused the rest of the updates. No more favorable advancement in prognosis had been noted, but Beckman hadn't downgraded her condition, either. After erasing his presence, he hightailed it across the Cybermed campus to Solia's new location.

Wings unfettered but folded at her sides, Solia sat in bed.

"Guy!" she exclaimed with a beaming smile. "I moved my wing today!"

"You did? That's wonderful!"

"I just finished my first rehab session. They wouldn't let me fly, but they had me extend and curl my wing. I did a bunch of flutters. Watch—" She unfolded her previously broken wing then brought it close to her body.

"I'm so happy for you, but should you be doing that?" he chided gently. He had a hunch she wasn't supposed to be exercising without therapeutic oversight.

Her glowing face sparkled with flashes of silver. "Well, no. I didn't think it would hurt to bend the rules a little."

He might be a rule breaker, but *she* needed to follow directions exactly to maximize her chance of recovery. Still, he didn't want to douse her excitement or optimism. A positive, can-do attitude often determined success or failure.

"Speaking of bending the rules…" Guy peered into the corridor. The ward supervisor was engaged in a conversation at the far end. Good. He closed the door then approached the bed. "You have a special visitor."

Solia knitted her brows. "Visitor? When? Who? Who would come to see me?"

Guy unfastened his jacket. Before he got it all the way undone, Mittzi poked her head out. "Meow?"

"Mittzi!" Solia cried.

Guy placed the kitten into her outstretched palms.

She hugged the purring fur ball. "You sneaked her in?"

He grinned and nodded.

"Is it...safe? I mean, I just had surgery."

He'd considered the possibility of microbiotic contagion, especially since the staff had kept Solia in a sterile environment. "Yes," he said. "I ran her through the decontamination unit on the shuttle." He chuckled. "She didn't like it much." Mittzi had emerged from the unit, hissing and spitting and had treated him to the cold shoulder for hours. "If anyone comes, give her back so I can hide her."

"Okay." She grinned. "Thank you for bringing her."

Guy pulled a chair closer to the bed and sat. Solia glowed from the inside out. Her hair gleamed as if each individual strand were a tiny thread of light. He'd met a few Faria; they were considered to be the most attractive creatures in the galaxy, but Solia's beauty was in a class of its own. As she healed and returned to her normal state, she *shone*, the contrast to her grayness when he'd first found her, revealing the degree of her injury. She'd been closer to death than he'd realized.

His heart thudded. He lost a lot of people in his line of work. Like Carter had said, Cy-Ops didn't offer guarantees, only chances, and sometimes the latter were slim. Losing Solia would hit harder than the other losses. She deserved to live and to glow and to fly.

Barring an unforeseen complication, she would survive. Beckman had notated a 99.24 percent probability of survival. Flying? Still an iffy 30 percent. Anything short of a full recovery would break Solia's heart.

"I brought something else for you," he said.

Solia looked up, and Guy withdrew a pendant from his jacket. A crystal reflecting rainbows of light dangled on a gossamer chain.

"For me?" She shook her head. "I can't accept something so beautiful."

He held up his hand. "Hear me out. The crystal hides a microtransmitter and tracking device. If you ever get into trouble, all you have to do is hold the crystal for three seconds like this, and it will shoot a signal to my brain, and I can find you." He handed it to her. "Try it on."

Solia fastened the necklace around her neck—and it disappeared.

"It's gone!" She patted the bed. "Did I drop it?"

"You're still wearing it," he said. "Special properties render it invisible when it touches the body."

She fingered her skin below her throat. "I feel it!" She peered down at her chest. "But I can't see it." She lifted it away by the chain, and the crystal materialized. "It's like magic. Now you see it, now you don't."

"If no one can see it, they won't take it from you."

"Well, thank you."

The kitten swatted at it.

"No, Mittzi!" she chided with a smile, and dropped the crystal. It vanished. Mittzi stared. "I'll be leaving one way or another in about two weeks, they told me." Her glow dimmed. "What will I do if I can't fly?"

He wanted to promise her everything would be okay, but he couldn't mislead her. He wouldn't stand for someone lying to him, and he wouldn't do it to her. "Stay positive," he said. "Your overall recovery is much better than expected. You had a good therapy session. Just stay focused."

"That's sound advice. I need to do that."

"What will you do when you leave here?" Guy asked.

"I'll continue my work on the Farian language project."

A pang shot through him at the idea of never seeing her again. Maybe another time, another place, they could meet up and talk about old times. By then, she probably would be mated. He delivered a burst of nanos to calm his emotional reaction so she wouldn't pick up on it. He couldn't offer a future, so why should he resent someone who could?

He admired her courage during her abduction, her tenacity to proceed with life. He would make a poor lifetime mate for a courageous but delicate Faria. A jaded cyborg, he had nothing to offer except long absences, a lack of communication, and constant worry. That kind of life could smother the strongest love. Mariah had realized that, which was why he couldn't blame her for jilting him. He didn't approve of how she'd done it, but the basic decision had been understandable.

He couldn't leave Cy-Ops. He owed too many people: his buddy who'd been blown up, Carter who'd given him a second chance, and the victims he hadn't been able to save. For each one he lost, Guy vowed to save two more. Pay it forward.

He had nothing to offer Solia, except the necklace as a token of his continued protection. He couldn't be her mate, but he could be her protector. *Wherever you are, whenever you need help, I'll be there.*

"What will you do next?" she asked.

Think about you. "Catch up with my next mission."

"If you need to leave..."

"Hey, you can't get rid of me that easy." He flashed a smile. "I want to see you well." Wanted to spend every last minute with her. There. He'd admitted it. For all the good it did. They had no future. His issues could keep a psychiatrist in business for years. His life operated on adrenalin and danger; she needed to be protected from that. He offered darkness and menace; she was lightness and hope.

"Your job must be very dangerous."

"Sometimes, but I'm prepared." She didn't need to know how many times he'd barely gotten out alive.

Beneath the covers, Solia scratched a finger against the fabric. Mittzi danced sideways on the bed and then pounced. Although the kitten had scared her at first, the two had become fast friends. Maybe... "You like Mittzi a lot, don't you?"

"She's adorable. Very affectionate and playful."

"How would you feel about taking her?"

"You mean..."

"Adopting her. I have to find her a home, and you two get along so well..."

"I'd love to!" Solia's face lit up.

He cleared his throat. "Good." One problem solved.

Footsteps outside drew close. "Somebody's coming," he whispered.

Solia handed Mittzi to him, and he tucked her inside his jacket and fastened it.

"Meow?"

"Shh!" he and Solia warned as the panel slid open.

The ward supervisor had a nondescript unlined face, her features symmetrical, unremarkable. Her age was indeterminate; she could have been fifty—or thirty. She scanned the room, the jerk of her eye movements so slight it would be virtually undetectable—except to a cyborg whose programming noted minute variations. "Why is the entry panel closed?" she demanded. "What is going on in here?" Her voice conveyed suspicion, but her blank expression didn't change.

"We were talking," Solia said.

"You do not need to close the door to talk."

"You do if you want privacy," she said.

"Rules are rules. The door must remain open."

Mittzi batted her paw against the inside of his jacket.

"What is wrong with your uniform?"

"I have a symbiont." He fabricated a story. "It keeps my heart beating."

Solia choked to cover a laugh. He didn't dare glance at her, or he would crack up, too. He crossed his fingers that his "symbiont" wouldn't meow.

"You should get a cybernetic cardiac unit," the ward supervisor advised. "They are far superior to human organs or symbionts."

"I'll take it under advisement."

"Remember, rules require doors remain open at all times in the event of an emergency."

"Won't monitors alert the medical staff of an emergency?" Solia asked.

"The rules require—"

"We understand," Guy said. "We'll leave the door open."

The ward supervisor executed a sharp pivot and left the room.

"Android," he and Solia said in unison.

Guy unfastened his jacket a little to let Mittzi stick her head out but kept her tucked inside, his back to the open door.

"How did you know?" Solia asked.

"She has a cookie-cutter face," he explained. "Her eyes, her nostrils are exactly the same size. Her nose and mouth are centered perfectly. Her hair follicles are spaced the same distance. How did you figure it out?"

"Her voice sounded close to organic, but I detected a slight digital signature. I wonder if an android could be programmed to speak to the *Ka-Tē?*"

"The ward supervisor had the right personality," he said.

"Guy!" She gaped at him, but humor twinkled in her eyes, and her lips twitched.

"I apologize," he said. "I insulted androids everywhere." He tucked Mittzi's head inside his jacket. "I'd better put her on the ship before they send an organic life-form who won't be fooled into believing a kitten is a symbiont."

They laughed again, the intimacy of shared humor warming his chest. Then came regret. *This is what I'll never have.* "I'll keep Mittzi until you're ready to leave."

"Will you bring her back for a visit?"

He nodded. "Of course." He touched her shoulder. "I'll see you again tomorrow."

ELEVEN

"Anytime you're ready." The therapist stepped out of the way.

Moment of truth. Solia had bristled at ten days of therapy restriction, limiting her to repetitive strengthening and flexibility exercises. She'd wanted to spread her wings and fly! Now that she had the go-ahead, fear slithered through her. What if her wings didn't work? What if she couldn't lift off? What if she couldn't stay aloft?

Arms folded, Guy leaned against the wall, a picture of relaxation and confidence. As he had every day after her first therapy session, he'd come to watch her progress and offer encouragement. He buoyed her when the arduous, sometimes painful therapy caused her spirits to flag. Not having a guarantee was hell, but the therapist pushed her harder and longer with each session, and she'd grown a lot stronger.

Now she would find out if the pain and hard work had been worth it.

Guy pushed away from the wall and flashed a thumbs-up.

Solia inhaled a deep breath. *I can do this.*

Crouching, she unfolded her wings and leaped. Contracting her dorsal muscles, she brought her wings downward in a strong stroke, forcing a draft over the top, which increased the pressure underneath. She lifted off the ground.

I'm doing it! I'm doing it! Another downward stroke, and another, and she became airborne. The flowing breeze caressed her face like a familiar lover's kiss. Oh, how she'd missed this! Flapping, she glided around the therapy gym. Who needed air? She could soar on euphoria alone. She climbed to the dome ceiling then swooped low on a rush of air and emotion.

"I'm flying! I'm flying!" She laughed as tears coursed down her cheeks.

"You are, sweetheart, you are!" Guy applauded.

Round and round the gym she went. Muscles in her back contracted and released. Wings moved up and down. Giggling, she buzzed her therapist, who ducked then she flew high and circled.

Euphoric, she flew a lazy figure eight then glided to ground level, settled on her feet then leaped into the air again because she could.

She flew for fifteen minutes before her therapist waved at her to end her flight session. Her first time airborne since the capture and attack, she considered ignoring him, but fatigue had begun to set in, so she landed and folded her wings like a good little patient. She skipped to Guy. "I did it! I did it!"

"You sure did!" He caught her as she bounded into his arms, and he swung her around. Laughing, they twirled together in a dance of shared joy. His hands gripped her waist, holding her against his solid, muscular rock-hard body. Warm, masculine musk filled her senses and created an unexpected pang. Their gazes locked. His eyes beamed with happiness for her, but as they stared at one another, the emotion turned heated. Abruptly, he set her on her feet and stepped away.

His gentle smile lessened the sting. "You flew like an angel," he said. "I'm so very, very happy for you, sweetheart."

An odd awkwardness hovered on the air, but it couldn't dampen her relief and joy. She could fly again!

"You did very well," said her therapist.

She jumped; she hadn't heard him approach. Solia whirled around. "What's next? When can I do it again?"

"Tomorrow morning," he replied. "If it goes as well, you can fly in the afternoon, too. Then, the next day, we'll increase the flight duration. By the end of the week, you'll be ready to leave."

"That's wonderful!" A measure of her excitement dimmed with her mixed fortune. She was thrilled and looked forward to resuming her life, but, once she left the facility, Guy would vanish from her life. She would only have memories and Mittzi to remember him by.

The therapist stepped to the computer to update the medical records.

"Come on," Guy said. "I'll walk you to your room." He cocked his head. "Or, if you don't want to go back yet, Cybermed has a garden."

"Yes, let's go there." Now that their friendship had an end date, she didn't want to miss a second of his company.

"Tell me if you get tired."

"I'll be fine," she said. Forced to walk during her convalescence, her legs had grown stronger.

They didn't have to foot it the entire way; they caught a horizontal transporter that zipped them to the other side of the space station. "Many people undergoing cybernetic transformation and receiving prosthetic limbs can't walk far in the beginning, so there's assistance," Guy explained.

She gasped in delight when they entered a garden filled with trees, bushes, grasses, and flowers from across the galaxy. Squat purple and pink trees from Xenia added dramatic color, roses and peonies from Terra perfumed the air, leafy Arcanian bushes with pop-up eyes watched over everything. A bubbling fountain harmonized to the melody of birdsong.

"It's beautiful!" She tilted her head to watch a cawing bird with brilliant plumage circling against a realistic but faux-blue sky. A winged rodent leaped from one tree and glided to the next. Buzzing insects zipped from flower to flower.

"Shall we take a stroll?"

"Let's!" she said.

They set off down a stone pathway, and she sensed the gaze of an Arcanian shrub following them. She giggled.

"What's so funny?"

"The bush! It's watching us."

"Yeah, it's a little creepy, isn't it?" he said. "Have you ever been to Arcania?"

She shook her head.

"Many creatures on the planet have multiple eyes—by multiple, I mean more than two, including the Arcanians themselves. They have six of them, which they can move independently."

"You've seen a lot of wondrous things," she said.

"I have." His eyes blazed.

He means me! Solia silvered under his appreciative scrutiny, but she sensed strong ambivalence. Longing warred with regret, but regret would win. *He wants me, but he won't act on it.*

Guy had sought out her company, conversed with her, laughed with her. Often touched her in small ways he wasn't aware of. His attraction radiated clearly—but so did his turmoil over it, and their predictable parting left her feeling rejected.

"Look!" He touched her elbow and pointed to two fuzzy balls with tails rolling in lavender grass. "Aren't those from Faria?" His touch lingered on her arm longer than necessary to get her attention.

"Yes. Those are moochins."

He leaned in and whispered, "We could sneak Mittzi in here. She would love it." His breath sent shivers up her spine, as did his use of the plural. We. Like they were a couple sharing a life, an intimate moment.

"We could," she agreed. *Kiss me.*

He wouldn't, though—and shyness prevented her from making the first move. *Don't be such a fraidy moochin.* She'd survived capture by Quasar, an attack by the *Ka-Tê*—not to mention surgery and a painful rehab. What was so daunting about telling a man she liked him?

She wet her lips. "We would have to do it soon. I-I leave next week."

"After your next flight, I'll grab Mittzi and meet you back here." His conspiratorial smile set her heart to pounding.

Do it. Say something. "When I leave, I'll miss"—*you*—"Cybermed." Coward!

"You will? I didn't miss it. Cybermed saved my life, but the surgery and rehabilitation were long and painful. I was glad to be discharged."

"I meant...the garden." She winced. *Just say it. Tell him how you feel.*

"I hear Faria has lovely gardens."

"You've never been to Faria?" she asked.

"No. I would like to visit someday."

Someday. "You should. I could be your guide. Show you around."

"I'll look you up," he said. His tone said he'd never visit.

She was a job to him. He might be attracted to her, but that didn't count for anything. The euphoria of flying should have been enough to buoy her good mood, but the magic of the day dulled, leaving her dispirited. "I'm getting a bit tired. We should go back."

"I'm sorry. Of course." He gripped her elbow to assist her, and she seesawed between wrenching away to protect her heart and leaning into him to soak in his presence. In the end, she did neither—she walked beside him, her heart aching.

Alone in the conference room, Solia knotted her hands in her lap. Why had she been called? Who would want to speak to her? She'd been resting in her room when a man with military bearing summoned her to a vid conference.

"Who is it?" she'd asked.

"I am not at liberty to say," he'd said. "Come with me. You do not wish to keep him waiting."

"Keep who waiting?"

"You'll find out soon enough."

Then he'd deposited her in the vid room and left. Where she waited. Keeping *her* waiting was okay, apparently.

The screen flickered, and then a man's image appeared. Perhaps it was an illusion created by the vid, but he appeared to be one of the biggest men she'd ever seen—except for Guy and the other men who were undergoing transformation to cyborg. She'd run into some of them as she entered and left the therapy gym. Was the man on the screen a cyborg, too?

"Hello, Solia," he said. "I'm Carter Aymes. You're wondering what this is all about." His smile was friendly, but there was no mistaking the authority in his posture or his direct gaze.

She straightened. "Yes, I am."

"I'm with an organization called Cyber Operations. You've already met my colleague, Guy Roarke."

So Guy worked for Cyber Operations. He'd said little about his "work," and any time she had brought it up, he'd changed the subject. What exactly did Cyber Operations do? And how were cyborgs involved? It was a short leap to connect Cybermed with Cyber Operations.

"I've been following your progress."

He had? That sounded...ominous. Or maybe he was checking on his "investment"? Cyber Operations must have footed the bill for her surgery and rehab. She'd be forever grateful, but would Cy-Ops expect a return on its investment?

"I can't imagine what you want to talk to me about, Mr. Aymes."

"Carter, please." He smiled. "I'll get to specifics in a moment, I promise. I believe you intend to resume mapping ancient languages?"

"Yes." What else could she do? If Guy had shown an inclination to pursue a relationship, she might have considered other options, but that hadn't worked out.

"I have a proposition. An offer."

Was this where Cy-Ops demanded payback? We fixed you so you could fly; now you owe us? She did owe them, but how high would the price be? Did Cy-Ops own her now?

"Guy has informed me of your special language abilities, that you understand the *Ka-Tê*."

"I understand their language, but I don't have the anatomical vocal structures to speak it."

"How much do you know about cyborgs?"

She lifted a shoulder. "As much as the average person, I guess. Cyborgs are like remanufactured or reengineered humans."

"Close." Carter smiled. "What turns humans or any intelligent lifeform into a cybernetic organism is a microprocessor in the brain and nanocytes, robotic cells programmed to their specific DNA. The microprocessor interfaces with their organic brain. To cut to the chase, with the appropriate programming, cyborgs have the ability to communicate in every language—except one."

"Let me guess—Katnian?"

"That's the one. Your abduction and rescue have heightened the need for us to learn Katnian."

"I don't think anyone other than the *Ka-Tê* can speak the language."

"Not naturally, perhaps, but electronically? We've begun a research and development project for an AI Katnian vocal simulator. Until we learned of your ability to communicate with the *Ka-Tê*, we didn't realize it was possible to communicate with them. We intend to write code translating the Katnian language and then mimicking the sound using a voice implant—"

Alarm shot through her, and she jumped to her feet. "I'm no guinea pig —" She put a hand to her throat.

"No, no," Carter said. "You wouldn't be a test subject. We need you as a translator, to help us decipher the language, convert it into code, and then determine if what is being transmitted electronically is accurate. We would test the device on androids first, and if it works, it could be incorporated into cybernetic microprocessors."

"Oh." Her face tingled, signaling she was silvering with embarrassment. She dropped into her seat. Being contacted out of the blue by the clandestine Cy-Ops had caused her to jump to conclusions. She already had one implant—her language assist one. She had nothing against cyborgs—how could she, she was half in love with Guy already—but she didn't desire to become one. "That makes sense," she said in a small voice.

"I would like to offer you a position with Cyber Operations on the KVS Project, the Katnian Vocal Simulator. The job comes with a lucrative compensation and benefits package, and the satisfaction of potentially saving lives. Our goal is to stop the trafficking that provides the *Ka-Tê* with prey, but, until that happens, a vocal simulator will give our agents an edge of protection in the field to enable them to rescue more people."

She and Guy had barely escaped alive. He had managed to outrun them, but only because she'd been able to warn him. Otherwise, he would have run *into* them and couldn't have fought off an entire pack.

"I see where comprehension would be helpful, but what will talking to the *Ka-Tê* gain?" They were vicious, merciless creatures.

"Honestly? I'm not sure. We haven't tried to communicate with them because we haven't been able to. However, Quasar has engaged in commerce—albeit of the horrific kind—and avoided being slaughtered themselves, which suggests communication may be possible. I have a hunch the *Ka-Tê* understand other languages, although they can't speak them. Or maybe they can. Those are some of the questions we might get answered if we can communicate. In any case, the KVS project will make Cy-Ops agents safer if they land on the planet."

No agent should have to risk his life the way Guy had done. Solia shuddered. If she could help...Guy and Cy-Ops had saved her life and restored her ability to fly. Maybe, in some small way, she could repay what she owed and protect someone else. She would do it for Rachel and the others who'd died on Katnia. "Where would I work?"

"At the research facility at Cy-Ops HQ. I can't divulge where it is, and you'd be transported under blackout. Project details are classified. You won't be able to discuss or share your work with anyone."

"When would I start?"

"Immediately. Upon discharge from Cybermed, a ship will transport you to HQ."

"What about my job? What will I tell the Farian ambassador? This will leave him in a lurch."

"Not a problem," Carter said. "I have connections with the Association of Planets, and I can be quite convincing."

No kidding. She was actually considering this!

"Besides, due to your hospitalization and rehab, you've already been absent longer than anticipated. They've hired substitutes to fill in."

Did she have the guts to do this? Con: she'd have to leave her home planet. She wouldn't be able to tell people what she did or have visitors. Pro: she could save lives, repay her debt to Cyber Operations, put her language abilities to the test, and maybe, just maybe, see Guy again. He had to report to HQ sometimes, didn't he?

"I'll do it."

"Welcome to Cyber Operations, Solia." Carter beamed.

TWELVE

The breeze of Solia's wings kissed Guy's face as he escorted her to the launch bay. His heart dropped like a lead weight into the pit of his stomach. *You're going to do this? Let her fly out of your life? Just because other relationships didn't pan out doesn't mean this one wouldn't.*

We don't have a relationship. We have a friendship.

Whose fault is that?

He'd have to be blind to miss her longing glances, her crestfallen expression. If he gave her an inkling he returned her feelings, a more lasting relationship might develop.

Maybe—until he disappeared for months on end. He couldn't expect her to put up with his absences. Mariah had proven it wouldn't work. His job didn't allow for a wife, a pet, or a permanent residence with a picket fence—whatever the hell a picket fence was. If he couldn't adopt a kitten, how would he keep a woman happy?

He stroked Mittzi as he carried her. He would miss the little fur ball and her amusing antics.

They entered the bustling launch bay, and he spotted Carter's ship, the serial number revealing it was a Cyber-4, a cruiser used for nonoperational purposes, typically personnel transport. Cyber-1 and 2 were fighter craft. Cyber-3 carried cargo. "Well," he said. "This is it."

Solia settled to the ground. "I can carry Mittzi now."

He handed her over with a sense of loss. Besides his affection for her, the kitten symbolized what he couldn't have.

Everything you won't allow yourself to have? "You're wearing the amulet, right?"

"Right here." She pulled it away from her throat, and the crystal sparkled under the artificial lights. Mittzi swatted at it. "D-Do you ever get to Cy-Ops HQ?" she asked.

When he'd mentioned Solia's Katnian language ability to Carter, he hadn't expected the sneaky bastard to recruit her! On the positive side, there wasn't a single place in the entire galaxy safer than Cyber Operations headquarters. He wouldn't need to worry. Not about her safety, anyway. Cy-Ops agents and civilian employees came and went out of HQ, and Solia would turn heads. Perhaps others wouldn't have his hands-off policy.

Solia wouldn't take a tumble with just anybody. Faria mated for life. When she chose to get involved, the relationship would be permanent. His stomach knotted at the thought of her marrying. A growl erupted in his throat, and he coughed to cover it.

Solia's alarmed gaze shot to his face. "What's wrong? Why are you angry?"

"I'm not. Well, maybe a little, but only at myself," he said.

"Why?"

He shook his head. "Not important." He exhaled. "You—be careful. You'll be safe at Cy-Ops. Carter will watch over you. You have the amulet. If you're on furlough or anywhere and you need help, I'll be there."

She bowed her head then raised it and wet her lips. "What if I need...a *friend*?" Her tone filled in the details words omitted. What if she needed a lover? A mate? That's what she meant.

His heart ached. He wished he could be her lover. For her, and for himself. But history had proven otherwise. In the long run, leaving her with false hope would be crueler than outright rejection, but he strove for the kindest way to let her down. "We'll always be friends," he said as if he'd misunderstood. He paused, hating himself as he prepared to deliver the *coup de grâce*. "You're feeling grateful, but you don't need to. I was doing my job." *I am such an asshole.*

Her face grayed. "Then there's nothing else to say, except goodbye."

"Goodbye, Solia." Guy kissed her cheek, his lips lingering for a fraction of a moment while he inhaled her scent.

Holding Mittzi to her chest, she flew to the waiting craft and boarded.

———

"Hello, I'm Solia," she said.

"What is that?" Ridges across the *Surelian's* face and neck bulged as he eyed Mittzi.

"It's a baby cat. My pet. I was told it would be okay to bring her. She's harmless." The kitten contradicted the assertion by hissing and growling.

"Mittzi!" she chided. "I'm sorry. I don't know why she's acting this way." Even without the hissing, the kitten's emotions would have been easy to read. She radiated dislike.

Solia had expected the Cy-Ops crew to be Terran like Guy and Carter. Foolish. She herself was Faria, an alien to the Earth people. Why wouldn't Cy-Ops employ sentients from other planets?

"Follow me. I'll show you to your cabin." An edgy impatience rolled off him. "Once you're settled, we'll get underway."

"I'm sorry. I didn't mean to keep you waiting." She hadn't realized she'd been holding up the launch.

He didn't acknowledge her apology but spun on his heel and marched down the narrow passage. She followed, doubt and sadness weighing heavy on her. First impressions often provided a good indication of what one could expect later on. Would her new job be like this? All business, no warmth? No civility? The man hadn't even introduced himself.

Am I doing the right thing? There was still time to back out. She could march off the spacecraft and go home to Faria.

Except her doubts had more to do with Guy than the Surelian's attitude. She'd put her heart on the line and told him how she felt—and he'd rejected her. He'd understood what she meant by "friend" but pretended otherwise. Grateful? Of course! How could she not be? But it was insulting for him to believe that's why she'd begun to care for him. Solia swiped at her eyes. He'd communicated his feelings enough; he wasn't interested in her *in that way.*

Rebuff them before they rebuff you. How much of her pickiness in choosing a mate had originated from fear of rejection? She'd thought she needed a Farian mate—until she met Guy. Then her standards had seemed more like impediments to finding love.

Before, she had hoped to run into him at HQ. Now, she prayed she wouldn't. Still, she didn't regret taking the job—if she could assist in preventing torture and murder by the *Ka-Tê*, then she had to do it.

Nor should she judge Cy-Ops based on the actions of one surly Surelian. She kept a firm grip on Mittzi who had stopped hissing but continued to growl. Like all members of his race, the Surelian was bald, and his skin had a greenish cast. Ridges crawled up the back of his neck, along with a tattoo. His somewhat disheveled uniform covered most of the tat, except for a point. Something about the marking looked familiar. She frowned.

A rumble vibrated through the ship as it prepared for launch. *This is it! No backing out now.* She fell against the wall as the craft took off. They hadn't wasted any time in leaving.

"In here." The Surelian gestured to a cabin.

A very sturdy, almost-reinforced metal door slid open. None of the shuttles she'd ever flown on had such stout doors. Maybe reinforcements were normal on a Cyber Operations ship. She tried to remember the other cabins they'd passed. She hadn't paid attention to the doors.

"You will stay here…until we arrive," he said.

Solia fingered her amulet. Like an eddy picking up leaves, nervousness swirled in her stomach. Something seemed off. "H-how long is the trip?"

The Surelian's gaze snapped to her necklace. "What is that?"

"W-what?" She dropped the pendant.

"Your necklace—it disappeared." The Surelian's hand shot out, grabbing for her throat.

Mittzi hissed, and Solia fell back into the tiny cabin. The Surelian's nails scraped her skin as he latched onto the amulet and yanked. The chain cut into her neck before it broke. "The captain will be very interested in this." He stepped back, and the door slid shut with a thud.

Solia clutched her bleeding throat, gaping at the door. Mittzi growled.

"It's okay, Mittzi. It's okay." But it wasn't. Cy-Ops procedure and protocols might be unfamiliar to her, but this was plain wrong. The crew member had stolen her amulet! She surveyed the tiny cabin, which contained a hard, narrow bunk without any bed covering and an exposed commode.

Not a cabin, a *cell*.

She rushed at the door, but it remained solidly shut. Clutching Mittzi, she ran her free hand over the door and wall for a release. There was no access screen. She banged on the panel. "Let me out! Help! Let me out!"

Nobody responded. Could they hear her through the solidness and the engine noise? *Did I get on the wrong ship? This can't be a Cyber Operations vessel.* Except, Guy would have known if it wasn't right. He'd pointed out the ship! Fear curdled in her stomach. Solia sank onto the bunk, hugged Mittzi. *What am I going to do now?*

THIRTEEN

Guy watched from the observation area as the Cy-Ops cruiser took Solia away. His whole body ached, but cyborgs didn't cry.

Friends. We'll always be friends. Grateful. Had he really uttered those words to her? From the moment he'd laid eyes on her slight, broken body in the Katnian jungle, their futures had been fused. There would never be another woman for him.

He waited until Cyber-4 disappeared before he stalked to his own ship. The sooner he could focus on work, the sooner he could begin to forget. *Right. As if that would ever happen.* He rushed through the preflight check and got the okay to leave. He'd cleared Cybermed airspace when Carter pinged.

Where's Solia? the director asked.

On Cyber-4. The ship just left. Guy answered.

Fuck!

What? What's wrong?

Quasar attacked and boarded Cyber-4 en route to Cybermed. They airlocked the crew. No. No. Guy had seen Cyber-4. Read the serial number. It had docked at Cybermed… Solia had boarded. *What are you saying?*

Quasar has Solia. I've dispatched a fleet to intercept the vessel. They have orders not to fire on the ship, but we can't predict what Quasar will do.

Guy balled his fist, jerked back at the last second before he slammed it into his shuttle's console. *No cyber operative would give up the ship.*

The crew members were civilian employees, not cyber operatives. Guy, it wasn't a random hijacking. Cy-Ops intercepted a partial communiqué between Quasar cells. They wanted Solia, not the ship.

Why?

Because of her language ability. They had an informant on Faria and learned of her implant. Quasar's sacrificial offerings have opened up an alliance with Katnia, but I suspect they want a more direct means of communication.

What does Quasar get out of it? How could this have happened?

A planet free of interference. No one will go near Katnia. Traffickers have a perfect place to hide hostages, and, if they rebel, they feed them to the Ka-Tê.

Bastards.

We'll get Solia back.

I'll get her back. How many crew members were lost?

Four. I have to notify next of kin.

Guy gritted his teeth. Ejected into space, the air-locked crew members had suffered a painful death. Quasar had no mercy. It was critical he get to Solia and get to her fast. He switched to manual, opened the throttle to full power.

Cy-Ops should have been a haven. Instead, Carter hadn't even been able to get her there! However, he didn't blame the director, but himself. Why hadn't he boarded the ship, checked it out? Met the crew? He would have recognized something didn't add up. Instead, he'd been focused on sending her away because he was the asshole who couldn't admit to loving her.

Shoot me Cyber-4's tracking signature, Guy communicated to Carter.

Wish I could. Quasar uploaded software to alter the trace.

So, we don't know where they're headed?

No.

Carter signed off, and Guy accessed his cyberbrain, hoping for a ping from the amulet. Nothing. *Dammit. Come on, sweetheart. Activate the beacon.* How long would it take before Solia realized something had gone wrong? Without a tracker, the ship could disappear into the vastness of space. Would the hijackers go to Katnia? Or hide out until the heat cooled? What would they do with Solia? *I'm coming, sweetheart. I'm coming. Just tell me where you are.*

A flashing message signaled a hail from Earth. Guy opened the line and kept his hands steady on the stick.

"Uncle Guy?" Jessamine appeared on the screen.

He loved his niece, but this was not a good time for a chat. "Hi, sweetie," he said. "I'd love to talk to you, but I'm kind of in the middle of something really important."

"Mommy said you might be busy, but I was wondering about Mittzi. You like her, don't you?"

Mittzi was on the hijacked ship, too, but she was the least of his worries. "I like her. Right now she's with a lady friend." A sharp pang shot through him. *Friend.* If the unspeakable happened, that would be her last memory of him—he'd wanted to be her *friend.* "Is Mommy there?" he asked. "Let me speak to her."

"I'm here." His sister Jill appeared.

"I'm involved in a situation," he said. "I don't mean to be rude, but I can't talk to Jess right now."

"I'm sorry. I made the mistake of warning her you might not keep the kitten, and she got concerned. Take care, and we'll talk later."

"Thanks." He closed the channel.

Jessamine had some timing. The cat. He shook his head.

The cat! He almost vaulted out of his seat. Guy accessed his cyberbrain. *Yes! There it is. Right there.*

FOURTEEN

Mittzi chased her tail, but the situation was too alarming for Solia to be amused. She'd been kidnapped by Quasar. Again. She'd remembered where she'd seen the tattoo—on her captors who'd delivered her to Katnia.

Were they taking her back there? Solia wrapped her wings around herself. *I'll die there.* She would have the last time if Guy hadn't rescued her. That kind of luck wouldn't happen again. Guy assumed she was en route to Cy-Ops headquarters, and Quasar had taken the pendant she could have signaled him with.

Mittzi did a backflip and then raced around the tiny cell. "Mittzi, come here." Solia scooped her up. "Settle down. I can't think when you're bouncing around." The kitten had disliked the Surelian right from the start. *I should have paid attention.* Heartsick over Guy, she'd ignored the clues: Mittzi's reaction, the Surelian's rudeness, his disheveled attire. He wore a crewman's uniform, but it was wrinkled and ill-fitting. She'd allowed him to push her into a cabin clearly not a passenger stateroom. The director of Cy-Ops would not have assigned her a cabin with a bare metal bunk! She was locked in the brig. Nearly all ships had them in case passengers overcome by space sickness went a little crazy and needed to be contained.

She'd fiddled with the necklace at the worst possible time. If not for that, the Surelian never would have noticed it. She hugged the kitten. "What are we going to do, Mittzi?" She scanned the cell. Everything was welded or bolted down. "Everything" encompassed two items: the cold, hard bunk upon which she sat—and the commode.

The berth came in one solid piece, the edge rolled into a lip around the perimeter to hold a mattress—which was not provided, leaving the bunk

with all the comfort of a laboratory table. Solia shifted Mittzi off her lap
and went to inspect the commode. The toilet came in two pieces: a single
base unit and a metal seat. Did the latter come off? She lifted the seat, and
it wiggled.

Dropping to her knees, she peered at the underside. Two bolts attached
the seat to the unit. She wiggled the seat. If she could loosen the fasteners
more... A toilet seat wasn't the best weapon in the galaxy, but she had
nothing else.

Mittzi jumped off the berth to check things out. "If this works, we need
to be ready to run," she told her. "And, most of all, you need to be
very quiet."

"Meow?" the kitten said.

"That's what I'm talking about. None of that." She pressed a finger to
her lips. "Shh."

Wiggling the toilet seat back and forth, she managed to loosen the nuts
enough to unscrew them from the bolts then pull off the metal seat. It was
quite heavy, but residual nano-temp bestowed her with strength she
wouldn't ordinarily have. She practiced her swing. She would aim for the
head and keep hitting until the Surelian—or whoever opened the door—
went down. Hopefully, only one person would come for her.

She'd never beaten anyone before—never so much as hit somebody—
but she would not go back to Katnia. *I'm fighting for my life. And Mittzi's. If
they kill me, they'll kill poor little Mittzi, too.*

Once they escaped the cell, they would hide. She and Mittzi would
squeeze into a duct and hunker down. When she didn't arrive at HQ,
Carter would guess something had gone wrong, and Cy-Ops would search
for the ship. He would contact Guy who would rescue them. "Guy will
find us, Mittzi. Don't worry." He might want to be her *friend*, but he'd
promised to protect her.

Clutching her makeshift weapon, Solia waited for someone to open
the door.

Curled into a ball, Mittzi napped. Solia lost track of the number of times
she'd thought she heard a noise and leaped up to position herself beside
the door. Vigilance was hard to maintain when minutes bled into hours,
but she couldn't afford to let down her guard. Her life was at stake. At
some point, she imagined a change in the engine's growl, and she tensed,
but nothing happened.

Finally, the door hummed. Heart in her throat, she sprang off the bunk.
A shadow spilled inside the cell, and, with all her might, she swung the
toilet seat.

FIFTEEN

Guy jerked his arm in time to avoid being brained by a commode. Pain ricocheted as a heavy metal seat—wielded by the woman he was trying to save—smashed into his forearm.

"Guy!" Solia gasped. "How did you get here? Are you all right? I'm so sorry! I'm sorry!"

"I'm fine. No harm done." His prosthetic limb had absorbed the blow without serious injury. The same wouldn't have been true of his head. Fortunately, cyber-reflexes had thrown up the hand not gripping the photon blaster, or the weapon might have discharged. Solia had a heck of a swing. "Come on! Let's get out before they notice the ship has been disabled." He pulled the seat from her hands. It clattered as it hit the floor.

She touched her throat. "They took my necklace. How did you find me?"

"Mittzi." He grabbed the kitten. "She has a subdermal ID tracking chip. The signal was weak, but I was able to pick it up. With my wireless implant, I hacked into Cyber-4's computer, slowed the ship, opened the emergency bay doors, and docked a shuttle pod."

"You got in without their noticing? Aren't there warning indicators?"

"I disabled those as well and reprogrammed the computer to display a normal gauge reading. But I couldn't disguise the sound of the engine slowing."

"I noticed that! I thought it was my imagination."

"That's why we need to hustle. If one of them catches on, they'll investigate." He passed her the kitten. "Hang onto Mittzi." He gripped the blaster in his right hand, cupped her elbow with his left, and ushered her out of the brig.

"Stay close behind me," he advised. "If we get involved in a firefight, drop to the ground and stay low. If anything happens to me, run for the escape pod launch bay. It's portside aft. I programmed the pod to respond to your voice commands. It will take you to my shuttle."

He wished he'd brought a weapon for her in case something happened to him. His scan of Cyber-4 had identified six men on board. One, possibly two, would be on the bridge—the others could be anywhere.

With Solia following, he scooted down the passage.

Guy checked the corridor. "It's clear. You first," he whispered and motioned for her to go around him. The emergency pod launch was located at the terminus of the portside corridor, which contained several staterooms and the galley. Someone could be inside any of those cabins. He wanted his body between them and Solia.

She squeezed by. Mittzi meowed.

Whoosh.

A door behind him opened.

Guy whipped around, raising his weapon. An armed man emerged, spotted him, and slapped his comm link. "Intruders!" he shouted as he aimed. Guy fired at the same time the man discharged his weapon, the blast singeing Guy's ear before it hit the wall, showering the passage with sparks. The man fell over dead with a smoking hole in his chest.

"Go! Go! Go!" Guy sprinted around the corner. "They're coming!" The man's communication to his co-conspirators had gone through—cyber-hearing detected several men approaching. He herded Solia toward the bay. Activating his wireless, he accessed Cyber-4's computer.

He sealed the entry and then jammed the bridge's controls to prevent the traffickers from opening the large external panel and sucking them into the space or locking them inside the launch bay. Solia scrambled into the pod with Mittzi, and Guy followed. While she buckled in, he transmitted an electronic signal. As the panels to space opened, he fired up the pod. Thrusters ignited, and they shot into the black.

Solia's eyes were wide. "We made it!"

"We made it!" He squeezed her hand.

She peered through the viewing window. "I don't see your shuttle."

"It's cloaked," he said. Cyber-4 had been cloaked, too, until he'd hacked in and lowered the shields.

"What will happen to Quasar?"

"A Cyber Operations fighter is on the way. Quasar will be given an opportunity to surrender or Cy-Ops will destroy the ship." Though the Cyber-4 was low-level in terms of technology, the equipment and tech it did have couldn't be allowed to fall into enemy hands. Via wireless, he messaged the arriving fighter Solia was off the ship.

The computer guided the pod to his shuttle and docked it. After the bay sealed and pressurized, Guy helped Solia out and led her to the bridge.

"What happens now?" she asked.

"Now, we scram." If Cy-Ops blew up Cyber-4, they needed to be out of range.

"Would it be okay if I cleaned up?" Solia asked.

"That's a good idea," he said. "I mean, not that you need to, but—" He was botching this. Hair mussed, feathers ruffled, clothing wrinkled, she'd never looked more appealing to him. He had her back safe and sound.

"I understand." She smiled and laid a hand on his arm. Her simple touch ricocheted through his body. How could he have considered walking away from her? How badly had he screwed things up? They needed to talk, but first things first.

"You can use the captain's stateroom," he said. "It's starboard, midship. I'll come find you when I'm done here?"

She nodded and left the bridge.

Guy opened up the throttle. When he'd put enough distance between them and the action, he set a course for Cy-Ops headquarters, reduced to cruise speed, and switched to computer-pilot.

He pinged Carter. *We're headed to HQ.*

She still wants to work for Cy-Ops, then?

Haven't asked her yet, but we're headed that way. They could always change course if she wanted to return to Faria.

I received notification the hijackers have surrendered. They'll be interrogated. We might get some good intel. With Solia's assistance, we stand to make some headway toward resolving the Katnia problem. However, after what happened, she may decide she doesn't want to work for Cy-Ops.

She might. I'm not going to push her. It has to be her decision. Roarke out.

Guy spun around in his chair and rubbed his forearm where Solia had struck him with the toilet seat. He grinned. His little Faria had a lot of fight in her.

But she wasn't his. Not yet. He'd rejected her; would she give him another chance?

He pushed off from his chair.

Outside the captain's stateroom—his cabin—Guy halted, stomach in knots. *Please let me make it right.* He knocked.

The door opened, and Solia stood there. She'd bathed and smoothed her hair and feathers, and had donned his robe—backward, to accommodate her wings. The garment was so large on her, it puddled on the floor. His mouth dried. He cleared his throat. "Can I come in?"

She stepped aside.

"Where's Mittzi?" he asked.

"I dropped her off in the galley. Found some reconstituted fish and gave her water."

"Oh, good. Are you hungry?"

"No." She tightened the belt. "I, uh, hope you don't mind my borrowing a robe."

"It's fine." He liked seeing her in his robe. Even worn backward. Especially backward.

She took a breath, and her breasts swelled. "Thank you for saving me—again."

"I'll always be there to save you, Solia."

"It doesn't need to be a habit." A small smile curved her lips, but then she moved away. "Are we headed to Cy-Ops HQ?"

He nodded. "Unless you've changed your mind about signing on. We can change course." He wanted to change course, turn back the clock to the moment on the Cybermed dock, and change his answer. Give her the right one, this time. "If you want to go home, I'll take you there."

"No. I want to help more than ever now."

Guy swallowed. Tension thickened the air. "About what I said before... about being friends..."

She waved her hands. "It's all right. I understand. I shouldn't have said anything."

"I don't want to be your friend," he growled.

She flinched, and her eyes clouded with silver tears.

Could he mess this up any more? "No, that's not what I meant. I do want to be your friend—but also your lover, if you'll have me, if you'll give me another chance—not that I deserve one."

Her jaw dropped.

"I'm not good at relationships. I have...issues. I screw up, a lot. I don't know if I'll ever fix all my mistakes. And I'm gone for months at a time—"

Solia leaped, and he caught her waist. Her legs wrapped around his hips, and her wings enveloped them both. "You really aren't good at this," she said with a giggle, and kissed him.

Her lips mated with his. Her touch and scent filled his head and imprinted on his heart. He was a wanderer who couldn't settle, but, in Solia, he'd found a home. He explored her mouth, the textures and taste, stirring urges to know all of her. Against her tummy, he hardened, and when she squeezed her legs to tighten the embrace, he groaned at the hot pleasure coursing through his veins.

Soft breasts pressed against his chest. They kissed: long slow ones, frantic fast ones, teasing and light, hard and deep, all manner of kissing. He'd swear the room tilted.

Breathless, they broke apart. Holding her with one hand, he stroked her silvery, gleaming hair with the other. She gasped and arched her neck. He planted kisses against her throat while threading his fingers through the lustrous, silken strands. She moaned and grabbed his hand, stilling it.

She panted. "You're going to end this before we start if you keep doing that."

His jaw dropped. "Are you saying your hair…"

"Is sensitive…*sexually* sensitive."

He couldn't prevent a grin from creasing his face.

Solia silvered.

He wound a strand of hair around an index finger. Desire sparked in her eyes. She wiggled out of his embrace and let the robe fall to the floor.

Perfection revealed.

"Are you just going to stare at me?" She motioned to his uniform.

"I-uh figured we should, uh—I don't know. Talk. Work things out." He tried to be strong, to say what he needed to say.

"Knowing you want me is enough for now."

"I wanted you the moment I saw you."

Her entire body glowed. She motioned again for him to disrobe.

How could he deny her? He unfastened and shrugged out of his clothing. She flew into his arms. "Do, uh, Faria do it in flight?" He held her tight against him. The head of his manhood nudged her entrance.

She giggled. "Sometimes. We can do it the Terran way, if that's your pleasure."

He collapsed onto the berth. They caressed and kissed each other to the peak of desire, teasing and tempting. She kneaded and stroked his nano-infused muscles. He was fascinated by her hair and the smoothness of her curves and skin. When they joined, ecstasy quickly claimed them both.

She pillowed her head on his shoulder, and her wings covered them, keeping them warm. He touched her hair. She sighed with a contentment echoing through him. She was better than he deserved, and he'd spend every day of his life, proving himself worthy of her.

The cabin door whooshed open. They sprang up in bed.

"Meow?" Mittzi sauntered in.

Guy laughed. "We need to put a bell on that cat." Or seal the door.

"Good idea," she agreed. "Later." She kissed him. Desire swirled.

Later. Definitely later.

STAR CRUISE: SONGBIRD

By

Veronica Scott

Scifi romance author Veronica Scott grew up in a house with a library as its heart. Dad loved science fiction, Mom loved ancient history and Veronica thought there needed to be more romance in everything.

https://veronicascott.wordpress.com/

To my daughters, Valerie and Elizabeth; my brother, David and my best friend, Daniel,
for all their encouragement and support!

ONE

"Do you need more pain meds?" Dr. Emily Shane asked the question while she was making her notes about the exam she'd just concluded.

Grant Barton, newly arrived member of the *Nebula Zephyr's* security team shook his head immediately. "Never touch them."

"I'm not sure the aversion is in your best interests." Eyebrows raised, the doctor assessed him. "The scan shows extensive nerve damage from an old wound. Why didn't the military specialists run you through the rejuve resonator and repair everything?"

Grant pulled on his shirt and slid off the examining table. "You know the rules, doc, a guy can't go through the procedure more than three times and I'd already had my trifecta. Are we done? I'm due on duty." He respected the doctor, given all her own military experience, but he wasn't about to start down the pain meds route. He'd tough it out like he always did.

Without waiting for her to do more than nod, he was out the door and exiting the sickbay, into the crowded corridors of Level A.

The ship's AI spoke in his ear. "All Security Officers, I have a situation in the casino observatory level."

Grant hastened his pace. "I'm right there, responding now. What's up?"

"There's an unruly crowd gathering. Passenger Karissa Dawnstar was doing an autograph signing and apparently word has spread."

"There's no such event on the calendar for today." Jake Dilon, head of the ship's security detail spoke up on the private com.

He sure sounds pissed. Grant paused at the entrance to the casino. The crowd was huge and growing, jostling for position in the line to reach the observatory. The queue snaked between the gaming tables.

"Our passenger and her entourage are alarmed," the AI said.

"Listen, there must be a couple hundred people here," Grant said. "I'm going in the back way and extract the lady. Then the rest of you can do crowd control and disperse these fans. It'll be easier to persuade them to leave when Karissa isn't here anymore."

"Go for it," Jake said.

Grant backed out of the casino and ran to the nearest crew-only gravlift. Once inside the system he transferred to the small tube giving access to the observatory. Emerging from the concealed door at the far end, he found himself behind the singer and her entourage, who were backed against the bulkhead by a clamoring crowd, only a small table separating them from the fans. The singer herself was easy to identify, clad in a sparkling, short blue and green dress, lavender boots to the knees and her towering pink hair ornamented with silver braids. He shouldered his way through the crowd and touched her arm. Startled, she turned to him, her blue eyes wide with fear.

"Ship's security, Miss Dawnstar, here to get you out." Grant took her elbow in a firm grip and towed her sideways, away from her entourage.

A cry went up from the front row of fans. A stocky individual Grant recognized from the briefing earlier in the day as Karissa's manager, glared at him. "What the seven hells do you think you're doing, pal?"

"Removing this lady from a bad situation before anyone gets hurt," Grant said. "You'll be hearing from my boss later about this unauthorized event."

"It's fine, Ted," Karissa said, keeping pace with Grant. "This is out of control, we've got kids here and someone might get trampled. I'll catch up with you later."

Surprised but relieved she was so sensible; Grant got them both into the gravlift and sealed the portal in the other man's face.

"Do you mind letting go?" Karissa raised her eyebrows and glanced at his hand on her arm. "Unless I'm under arrest?"

"Sorry." He released her and allowed himself to drift a little away from her in the silvery antigrav stream. "Someone's going to be in trouble for this stunt, but not you, unless it was your idea." He keyed his com to report in. "I've got Karissa and we're on the move."

"Good work. We're clearing the casino now," Jake answered. "A Level is congested, can you take her to my office on level 13 until the situation clears? Then you can escort her to her suite."

"Will do." Raising his voice from the nearly inaudible tones the AI utilized for private communications, he addressed his companion. "We'll have to hang out in my boss's office for a bit."

"So I'm in detention?" Tilting her head, she smiled.

"No, of course not, Miss Dawnstar." *Very important passenger, keep the tone congenial.* He might not relish this job but it was his employment for now and he couldn't afford to blow it off over annoyance with a pop star. "This was for your safety and the safety of the other passengers."

"Just Karissa," she said. Hands on her hips as she floated in the gravlift, she raised her eyebrows. "And you are?"

"Sorry, Officer Grant Barton." He reached out to shake the hand she offered and tried not to stare at her wildly decorated fingernails and the jewel-encrusted ring big as his palm. "Should have introduced myself earlier but I was concentrating on the extraction."

Everything he said seemed to amuse her, as she chuckled now. "Like a dentist?"

"What? No, sorry, military terminology for removing personnel when it's considered imperative they be immediately relocated out of a hostile environment and taken to a secure area."

"My fans certainly aren't hostile." Her frown was epic, her arched eyebrows punctuating her displeasure. "Over-enthusiastic sometimes maybe."

"There were way too many of them crammed into that small space and a lack of proper exits. The AI tells me we never use the Observatory for events."

She shrugged. "I was glad to see you, I'll admit. Ted— my manager— said the pop up signing was approved so take it up with him."

"Arranging events is above my pay grade, thankfully. I'm sure my boss will be talking to the guy. We get off here." He extended a hand to stop their progress and then opened the portal to the admin deck. Checking to see other than a few crew members, the corridor was empty, he allowed her to precede him. "We go left and the office is just a few doors down."

One of the women in the corridor drew the other out of the way with a giggle. "Karissa! I can't believe I ran into you here, in crew territory."

The singer gave a little wave as she strutted along the corridor in the amazing boots. "Grant here is giving me a tour. A private tour." She winked and he could feel his face getting red.

"Will you sign an autograph for me?" asked the other woman.

"Of course." Karissa pulled an autograph chit from her pocket and scrawled her name with one elegant fingertip. The chip beeped and emitted the first few notes of her signature song, as a tiny holo of the singer floated above the surface. "Special for you."

The crew member hugged it to her chest, eyes wide.

"We should be going." Grant touched Karissa's elbow. He gave the staffer a stern look. "Don't broadcast our guest's whereabouts."

"No, sir. Of course not."

He breathed a sigh of relief once he'd gotten Karissa into the Security Office. Hastily he cleared some equipment off a chair and she sat.

"Nice place you got here."

Was she being sarcastic? He racked his brain for what to say next. "Would you care for something to drink? We have real Terran coffee."

"Fruit juice would be good, bluecranmikka if you have that."

The AI spoke. "I'll have a bottle delivered in two minutes, Passenger Dawnstar."

Karissa fluffed her hair and settled into the chair. "Thanks."

Grant felt awkward. Sitting behind the boss's desk didn't strike him as appropriate; neither did leaning on the wall as if he was guarding the singer. He glanced at the shiptime readout on the wall. He was going to be late. He keyed the staff only com. "How's it going up there, boss?"

"A few hundred passengers where they shouldn't be. Unhappy at missing their chance to see the singer. Going to take us a while to sort it all out. I've got the cruise director up here too, since I'm sure the CLC Line expects us to be tactful and she's better at it than I am." Jake Dilon was as unflappable as ever but Grant could read between the lines. The impromptu, unauthorized autograph session had really messed up the traffic flow in the casino and the gambling revenue was a priority to their employer. "Can you keep our passenger on ice a while longer? I know you were off duty— "

"No problem, sir. I'm on it." He closed the com loop. "I bet the casino manager is going to go supernova."

One of the AI's robos glided into the room and presented Karissa with a chilled bottle of her requested fruit drink and left just as smoothly.

"Problem?" Karissa opened the container and took a healthy swallow.

He realized he'd spoken out loud. "Your manager's stunt is taking more time to undo than we'd expected. I'm sorry but you and I'll have to stay here out of the way a bit longer."

Still holding her drink, she rose and made a slow tour of the office, examining the few knickknacks and holos Jake had on display. Over her shoulder, she said, "You're not a fan, I gather?"

"Fan?"

"Of my music." She laughed. "I must sound conceited but most people would be thrilled to have a one on one session with me. You haven't even asked for an autograph."

"I'm sure your music is wonderful. I've been downrange for the last few years so I'm not up on popular culture." He checked the time again and looked up to see her frowning at him.

"Downrange? More military slang?"

"Means I've been outside the Sectors, in places I can't talk about."

She nodded. "Am I making you nervous? Or am I keeping you from something, a date maybe?" Karissa pointed at the shiptime indicator on the wall. "You keep checking."

Reluctantly he said, "Not a date. I have a—a pet, who requires exercise."

"A pet on board the ship? What an unexpected answer! So Fido needs a walk, does he? Let's go—I could use some exercise."

"It's not that simple," he said.

"Is the pet exercising area open to passengers?"

"Not the one I use." He admitted. "But—"

"This office is boring," she said. "Now I'm not a Socialite who'd probably *die* of boredom if you kept me here, but you can't dangle a chance to take a pet for its walk in front of me and then yank it away. Too cruel, Officer Barton. Be mean to me and I might have to write you into a song."

Before he could decide if she was kidding, Karissa laughed and went to toss her now empty drink container into the refuse reclaimer. "I insist and I *am* the headliner on this tour your cruise line is running. I could pull rank." Hands on her hips, head tilted she stared at him. "Hey, I'm *kidding*. Lighten up, Officer. Now, where do we go to collect the pet?"

With the uneasy feeling he'd been overtaken by a whirlwind, he escorted Karissa from the office and down the gravlift to the crew quarters decks. "We're uh on the move, Jake, but still in non- passenger country."

"Why? What happened?"

"Our passenger was bored. It's my time slot to give Valkyr his exercise and she wants to tag along." Grant felt uncomfortable with the nature of the entire situation.

"All right, I can't say I'm excited about the idea but it'll keep her out of my hair and out of view. We should be clear to get her back to her own cabin by the time you're done." Jake hesitated. "Keep it professional."

"Of course, sir." He shot the singer a sidewise glance. "I never heard of her before this cruise."

"You've heard of her now." Jake signed off.

"We have to pick up Valkyr in my quarters," he said to his companion. "It'll only be a moment."

"I'm sure the crew quarters are quite memorable." She laughed and followed him. "I'm getting the fifty credit tour today."

The corridor to his cabin was empty, much to Grant's relief. He felt there was enough of a circus going on without more witnesses. The portal slid aside and he allowed her to precede him into the room.

Karissa stopped in her tracks once she was across the threshold. "You didn't tell me you had a bird!" Before he could stop her, she went forward to where Valkyr sat on his special perch. "You're gorgeous, big boy." She extended her hand to stroke the glossy iridescent black wing.

Grant had no conscious memory of moving but he had her in an iron grip, with his back to the bird and her safely to the side.

"What the seven hells—" She yanked away from him.

"Valkyr is a Qaazamir hunting eagle—he could bite off one of your fingers without any problem and his talons can inflict enough damage to kill a human. *Never* approach a wild, feral animal as if it's a house pet."

She looked chastened. "He's beautiful. And he doesn't act upset. Or threatening."

"You're in his space and he's doesn't know you." Grant pivoted on his heel to check the eagle's reaction. Valkyr sat on his perch calmly, blinking at them, as if he hadn't a care in the world. He preened, fluffing out his feathers, raising his elegant crest of white and doing a bit of grooming, then spread his wings wide for a moment in an imposing display, before settling on the perch.

"Give me a moment to get my gear and we'll go," Grant said. "Promise me you won't get close to him."

Karissa nodded but didn't take her eyes off the bird, apparently still fascinated. Grant was uneasy as he headed toward his bedroom.

Won't hurt the pretty one. She admires me.

Amused, Grant admitted to himself Karissa worked her celebrity magic on animals as well as most humans. He acknowledged Valkyr's comment with a quick thought and hastened back wearing his special handler's glove and shirt with the padded shoulder. Going to the perch, he held out his left hand and Valkyr sidled off the perch onto his fist, clutching him with the huge talons capable of causing devastating damage.

"Wow," said Karissa, coming closer. "His claws are like knives. How can you hold him without getting hurt?"

"The glove and the shoulder of my shirt are made from woven cartefl fibers, strongest material in the Sectors," Grant said. "In the old days, a handler had to wear bulky leather gloves and thick padding but modern tech makes things much easier. Shall we go?"

Karissa moved toward the door but gave him a dubious frown. "You just carry him through the ship? What if he gets spooked and flies away?"

"Valkyr is a highly trained military asset," he said, entering the corridor behind her. "And a registered sentient. He knows how to behave in a noncombat situation. This way."

"So the two of you were in the war?"

He really didn't want to talk about his past or explain himself to this pop star. "Yes. We were in the Special Forces Z Unit until recently. Z for zoological."

"I watched part of a documentary on them once," Karissa said as she entered the gravlift.

Valkyr liked antigrav and flared his wings to the full 8' span, posing dramatically as they drifted downward toward the hangar deck.

Don't show off for her too much. Grant chuckled a bit as Karissa gasped at the display his companion was making.

"How can you keep him on a spaceship?" Karissa asked, her voice full of reproach. "How can that possibly be good for him?"

They stepped off at the hangar deck, Valkyr folding his wings obligingly so Grant could get through the portal. "This a temporary job for me. I needed a place to land after the military, while I figured out our next steps."

The hangar deck was the single largest space on the *Nebula Zephyr*, as big as the two cargo decks combined, and ran the entire length and breadth of the ship. Currently the three shuttles, the captain's flitter and two small exterior maintenance vehicles were parked neatly in their assigned spaces, with plenty of room left over for incoming shuttles when the liner was in orbit above a planet.

A crewman greeted them, staring at Karissa so hard Grant was amazed the man managed any coherent words. "Deck's clear, as ordered. You have an hour."

"Thanks." Grant watched the man leave as Karissa gave him a wave and threw him a kiss. The crew member stumbled and all but fell into the gravlift.

"What now?" she asked.

"Now he flies." Grant lifted his arm in a rapid motion and Valkyr launched himself into the air, flying low across the deck at first and then beating his wings to gain height. He was soon lost to view in the far end of the deck. "Ready when you are, Maeve."

"Who's Maeve?"

"The ship's controlling AI. She helps me with these sessions."

Two small drones flew from somewhere in the vast recesses of the deck, circling Grant and Karissa. "Chef Stephanie provided the usual select morsels," Maeve said, her voice echoing a bit in the space.

"Good, Valkyr's definitely hungry. Let's get him hunting." He turned to Karissa. "The eagle prefers live prey but we simulate the experience as best we can. Maeve's gotten adroit at dueling with him in the air, gives him a good workout."

For the next few minutes, the ship's AI flew her drones across the deck, high above their heads, and then abruptly the two separated like startled birds, going in opposite directions. Valkyr pursued one, zigging and zagging on its tail, before he flew above it and pounced, catching the drone in his claws. With a triumphant shriek, the eagle took the drone high into the superstructure, landing on a convenient strut. Grant could hear the crunch from where he stood, as Valkyr compressed the soft metal to get at the raw meat inside. The broken drone fell to the deck. The bird took off after the other drone and an elegant aerial combat ensued, with Maeve unexpectedly adding a third drone to the chase.

Grant was frustrated he couldn't link with Valkyr as he usually did when the eagle flew, but he felt he had to maintain situational awareness since he was responsible for Karissa's safety.

"Your bird's amazing in the air," she said as Valkyr 'killed' the second drone and soared above them. "But surely even this exercise can't be enough for him?"

Surprised at her insight, Grant shook his head. "No, but better than nothing. This is how we did training while we were on board military vessels, going to or from a mission. But Valkyr prefers to fly on a real world, using the thermals."

"Why don't you two just go home then?" She gestured at the ship around them. "Why live on a ship?"

"There's nothing for us on Qaazamir." Grant was blunt. "His species has gone extinct, due to chemicals the colonists put into the environment."

"How sad." Karissa turned her gaze to him. "And you? No family?"

Grant was silent. He did not have to explain himself to amuse this woman. Baring his deepest sorrows to her wasn't part of his job. The sour bitterness of his past welled up and he swallowed hard. *Just a few minutes left,* he warned Valkyr on their private mental channel.

"You can escort Miss Dawnstar to her cabin now," Jake said in his ear. "We've cleared the crowd."

"With pleasure." He turned to her. "My boss says we can get you to your cabin. Let me land Valkyr and we'll drop him off in my quarters on the way to yours."

"Don't cut him short on his treat for me. I can wait." She strolled away to sit on a convenient pile of tech crates. "Got nothing important to do."

Her dismissive attitude intrigued him. "Don't you have to get ready for the performance tomorrow?"

"I've sung all those songs so many times, I can do it in my sleep. And my dancers and I aren't doing any new routines on the ship. Just the tried and true hits, the best of Karissa." Her smile was forced and didn't warm her eyes. "Rehearsals tomorrow, for your information."

Valkyr swooped in, landing on his shoulder and drawing his beak across Grant's cheek in a careful caress. *The hunting was good today, did you see?*

You've lost none of your skills. Grant indicated the gravlift portal. "I only get the hangar deck for an hour at a time, so we should be going. Passengers are definitely not allowed down here, other than for embarking or departing."

"Well, I'm not doing either one today." She laughed and joined him on the step into the gravlift. "I enjoyed watching the session, thank you, both of you."

Valkyr preened again and dropped one glossy black feather. Grant caught it and offered it to Karissa. "Valkyr must really like you—he doesn't give his feathers to just anyone."

She blushed a little as she accepted the gift, running the soft vanes through her fingers and admiring the play of iridescent colors—dark green and blue. "I'm honored."

TWO

Grant figured his brush with celebrity was now ended and he was relieved. Getting Karissa back to her cabin had been fairly easy, encountering only a few passengers along the way, who were too surprised by the chance encounter to ask for autographs or personal trideos with the star, especially as Grant kept her moving with a firm hand on her elbow. He ushered her into her suite, where the stocky manager and his own boss waited, along with the cruise director. Grant saluted and was dismissed.

Therefore he was surprised at the morning security staff briefing next day when Jake said, "You're off your normal assignments for then next week or so."

"What am I going to be doing? Am I in violation of some rule or code?"

"Quite the contrary. Seems you were a hit with Karissa yesterday. She's requested you as her security liaison for the rest of the trip." Jake grinned. "Soft duty."

"I'm no bodyguard."

Unsmiling, Jake raised his eyebrows. "Hey, we were all trained to do personal protection, once upon a time in the Special Forces. Besides the lady has her own bodyguards, although where the seven hells they were yesterday in the mob scene at the Observatory I don't know. You just need to watch out for her in connection to the *Zephyr*, keep things smooth. And safe. No more unauthorized setups like her manager pulled yesterday."

Red, the second in command in Security, punched him playfully in the shoulder. "Most guys would give their right arm to spend a week with Karissa. As a married man, I exclude myself but you're a bachelor, enjoy the opportunity."

Grant felt as if the bulkheads were closing in on him. "I'm not most guys. She was very pleasant but I don't want to be that visible."

"The lady asked for you, end of story," Jake said. "Suck it up for a week and then you can go back to general shipboard patrol duties. The CLC Line has a lot riding on this rock-and-roll tour going well. We all have to do our part. Report to the theater after this meeting—she'll be rehearsing most of the day as I understand the schedule."

So Grant slipped into the closed theater complex on Level B and stopped for a moment to watch the band currently on stage, lesser lights who'd had a hit or two a long time ago. Even he vaguely remembered the song the musicians were running through now. It had been big when he went into the service. Shaking his head at the way a single event like a fluke hit song could shape a person's entire life, he asked a stagehand where Karissa was and headed backstage.

Maeve could transform parts of certain decks into different configurations and for this tour she'd added capacity to the already large theater and expanded the dressing room areas. He heard raised voices, even over the music from the stage out front, as he went in the direction of the headliners' area.

"I'm not going to insert your latest protégée into the 'Inner Sector Girls' routine, much less have her sing my lyrics," Karissa said. "It's not my job to help you launch another singer or get into her pants."

"Darling, you wound me. Where would you be if I hadn't pushed your career in the early days?" The manager gestured dramatically. "Why won't you do me this tiny favor, costing you nothing?"

"My fans paid to see me, not some wannabe. My integrity's at stake." Karissa wasn't giving an inch. "You've pulled this too often, Ted."

Grant cleared his throat and the pair turned to him, both scowling, although Karissa broke into a pleased smile a moment later. He nodded at the people surrounding her and her obstreperous manager. "May I suggest taking this discussion somewhere more private?"

She glanced at the crowd of dancers, stage techs and others, who were trying to avoid catching her eye. "They've heard it all before, trust me. But the discussion, as you called it, is over." She walked away from her manager, presumably heading for her dressing room. "We should probably talk about my schedule today, right, Officer Barton?"

Taking her cue, he followed, brushing past the obviously disgruntled manager.

Karissa barely waited for the portal to her private room to open before flinging herself inside and going to the feelgood dispenser. "Lords of Space, he makes me so angry. I can't wait for this tour to be over."

Grant shut the door and lingered there, at a loss for what to say.

She turned to him with two bottles of a high end juice mix. "Want one? Or something stronger?"

"It's kind of early, isn't it? And I'm on duty."

"Oh, right." She set one down and opened the other, taking a long drink. "You'll find we rock stars don't care what time of day it is. Our inner chronos are all messed up. For your information, Mr. Judgmental, I've been to rehab twice, so I completely avoid the hard stuff myself. Just trying to be polite, in case you wanted a feelgood." She sauntered to the couch and flopped down, legs akimbo.

"I was in rehab once myself," he said, stung by her assessment of his character. "I don't judge."

She paused in the act of raising the bottle to her lips and stared at him, eyes narrowed. "You?"

"Pain meds. I have a lingering injury that conventional treatments can't resolve. So the docs dosed me up with the best stuff. Thought they were doing me a favor." He closed his eyes for a moment, remembering that grim time on the hospital ship. "I was out of my head, either high or craving the next fix. The only thing that helped pull me out of the hell was my link with Valkyr. He and I fought the addiction together because that was no way to live and if I died he'd be alone. I don't touch anything now, not even headclear. I prefer the pain."

"One day at a time," she said with a nod.

"Exactly."

"Does Valkyr have another flying session today?"

He shook his head in answer to her question, glad they'd left the topic of addiction. "It's a big deal for the captain to have the hangar deck cleared so we only do it once a week. That's why yesterday's time was so important not to miss. So what's on the schedule for today?"

"You're all business, all the time, aren't you?" She surveyed him for a moment. "Actually, I like that about you. It's refreshing. Sit down, why don't you?"

He took a chair and dragged it closer to the couch. "Schedule?"

She sighed. "Rehearsal and sound check this morning. Meet and greet this afternoon. Concert tonight. After party with cruise high rollers and then I'm free."

"Where can I find the head of your private security detail? I should co-ordinate with him or her."

She pointed a finger at him. "You're it, end of story."

"Miss Dawnstar, I'm assigned to co-ordinate with the ship for you, not be your personal bodyguard."

"Ted fired them all before the cruise started. Said they were doing a lousy job and he'd hire new guys when we reached Calillia Three. I guess he figured I'd be safe enough on the ship." She gestured at the bulkheads around them. "Stalkers can't get me here, right?"

He was appalled. "Do you have stalkers?"

"Maybe. I get some creepy fan mail but I never see it—it all goes through a service. Anything too whack in tone gets reported to the authorities. There've been a few incidents over the years, but that's part of the job." She shrugged. "You want your fans to relate to your music, sometimes they get a little confused and think you're relating to them personally, you know?"

She was so nonchalant he was almost fooled but he detected an air of stress below the casual words. This woman was worried about something but refusing to admit it. "And you agreed to travel without protection?"

"My contract states Ted's in charge of all security." She rose and threw the bottle into the recycler, picking up the spare she'd gotten for him. "The fucking contract I can't wait to end. Ten years he's had me wrapped up in fine print and unfavorable clauses. Well not any more and he knows it. Calillia is the end of the line. I'm not re-signing, not with him anyway. I'm not a green kid to be taken advantage of anymore."

Feeling he'd stepped into a whirlwind, he had more questions but there was a ping from the door com. "You're needed on stage, Miss Dawnstar."

Setting the half-finished juice down, she straightened her shoulders and flashed a brilliant, totally phony smile. "Show time. Excuse me while I do the magic."

He opened the portal for her and she swept past him, plunging into the crowd waiting in the hall. Multiple voices called for her to render decisions on costumes, makeup, revisions to dance steps and more as she made her way to the stage. Everyone wanted a piece of her time. He shook his head, amazed at the babble. Who knew there was so much involved in simply singing for people?

As she conferred with her band and dancers on stage, he prowled the backstage and then the audience area, taking note of possible problems. He'd never been in this part of the ship before. He and Maeve conferred over what surveillance she conducted in this area, which was less than he expected and he asked her to extend a few more ganglions into the hull. He'd just completed that discussion when a blast of music from the stage drew his attention and he allowed himself a few moments to watch Karissa in action.

Even though he could tell she wasn't putting much energy into the rehearsal, her voice was amazing in its range and purity. She only sang snippets, stopping frequently while sound levels were adjusted or the dancers tried different steps. It was nearly impossible to watch anything else when she was in the spotlight and he took himself severely to task. He had to ignore her and focus on potential dangers. That was his job here. He made a mental note to ask Jake to assign extra officers to any public events, now he knew she had no private security at all. 'One is none' was an axiom in the Special Forces Teams and he knew he required backup for bigger events than this rehearsal.

Eventually the session ended and he escorted Karissa to her suite, where she ate a light lunch. He was invited to help himself to the ample buffet Chef Stephanie had sent up, and made a sandwich, which he ate in a corner of the main room while Karissa nibbled at her own food and dealt with an endless series of people wanting her time. Ted was there, with a young woman Grant assumed was the new protégée in question, but he left the singer alone and concentrated on a messy public display of affection with his companion.

Eventually Karissa retired to her private rooms with her dresser, and hair and makeup artists, returning an hour later in full regalia, hair piled on her head, turquoise and lavender today, her short skirt a kaleidoscope of colors, and her top bespangled. She wore fanciful tights and a pair of ruby red shoes with heels so high he wondered how she walked. But rather than exhibiting any unsteadiness, Karissa prowled through the room, secure in her public persona. Her face was beautiful, seeming bare of makeup, which Grant suspected was the height of artifice and cosmetic skills. She pointed at him and he noticed her nails were elaborately painted, with gilded tips. He had to tear his gaze away from her enhanced eyelashes, coated with glitter and feathery extensions reminding him of Valkyr's crest.

"Ready to go, Officer Barton? Time for me to meet my public, who paid your employer for the privilege. I hope I won't disappoint."

She swept out of the room into the corridor, surrounded by her people, and guided by the *Zephyr's* cruise director. Grant stayed close. "Is the room ready? We're on our way," he told his boss over the security link.

"All clear. I've posted extra crowd control, as you requested. Must be several hundred."

Jake's comment was an understatement, he saw as they approached. The line to get into the session was long and the cheers and outcry as Karissa approached was loud and enthusiastic. She was animated, waving and thanking people for coming to see her. He scanned the crowd as he walked by on the way into the venue, but didn't see anyone whose demeanor set off alarm bells. There were two monks from an order based on Calillia, which surprised him. But they stood silently in the queue, serene in their subdued red and black robes.

I guess even monks can have their favorites. Maybe the pair were just traveling back to their home world and curious about the fuss. Calillia was known as the self-designated Musical Center of the Galaxy after all and the monks were in charge of several of the thousand year songs.

The room was set up much more efficiently than the makeshift tables in the Observatory had been, and he was pleased to see two of his fellow officers ready to assist in moving people safely in and out after their moment with Karissa was over, as well as a number of the cruise director's staff.

Trideos of Karissa's top hits played to help keep the waiting crowd occupied.

Things went smoothly. Grant took his position behind the singer, scanning the room and the people in line but detecting no threats. Karissa was a natural at working the crowd, sweet with the many young girls, gently teasing with the adults, commenting to each person on something. He was amazed as the afternoon wore on. How could she sound so fresh and genuinely pleased as basically the same remarks were made to her over and over? She posed for personal trideos and signed all manner of items.

The monks arrived at the table in due time and were deferential, praising her legendary vocal range. "We're happy you're coming to our planet," one said as the other nodded. "We'd love to show you our temple. I have an invitation for you from our high priest as there's a special section of the 'Thousand Year Song to the Heavens' coming up during your stay. A rare opportunity." He reached inside his robes and Grant tensed, but the man brought out a rolled parchment, tied with a golden thread, which he held out to Karissa.

"I'll have to see how my schedule goes but the offer's very kind." She took the scroll but was already shifting her attention to the next person, having signed the monks' *Nebula Zephyr* commemorative program with a flourish.

The duo lingered. "There are ancient artifacts we're sure you'd find of interest. We have instruments going back hundreds of years. We'd be happy to allow you to play any of them. Your gift is unprecedented."

"She already said she'd see what she can do to carve out time," Grant said. "Miss Dawnstar has many commitments already."

The monk glared at him, which surprised Grant. Weren't monks supposed to be serene and accepting of fate? Maybe not on Calillia.

"As she is from our world originally, we're sure she'll want to pay proper tribute to the influences of her childhood."

He sensed Karissa's stress in the rigid set of her shoulders and the way she was remaining silent. "The scroll was a nice touch but why don't you send a proposal in care of the ship?" he said. "We need to keep the line moving here."

"Yes, please do send me the invitation," Karissa chimed in.

One of Jake's men came up in response to Grant's subvocal request, interposing himself between the monks and the next person in line. "Sorry, gentlemen, each passenger only gets two minutes with Karissa. There's still quite a crowd." Efficiently the other officer encouraged them to step away from the table and toward the exit. Few people had the resolve to stand up to an ex-Special Forces operator encouraging them to move along in no uncertain terms.

Karissa reached for her water and he noticed her hand shaking. He leaned over her shoulder, creating a moment of semi privacy for her. "Do you want to take a break?"

Closing her eyes, she sighed. "I want to get out of this room and off this ship and fly far far away."

The bitterness of her tone surprised him. Before he could reply, she popped her eyelids open dramatically and gave him the big phony smile as if practicing the crowd pleasing artifice. "But I can't disappoint my fans." She turned to the next person in line, a small child and held out her hand. "You waited a long time to see me, didn't you? That was so nice of you! What's your favorite song?"

As the overawed child stammered and the excited parent rushed to fill the conversational gap in great detail, Grant moved back, feeling a wave of pity for her. But this success was what she'd worked so hard to attain, right? So she had to take the good with the bad, but it all seemed like harder work than he'd realized.

A man ten feet away in the queue caught his attention. He was sweating despite Maeve's careful control of the room temperature for maximum comfort, and he clutched a bouquet of flowers as if his life depended on it. "Possible trouble," he said under his breath on the security comlink. He had his hand on his stunner as the man reached the table.

Handing Karissa the somewhat crumpled flowers, the fan grabbed her hand and dropped to his knees, pulling her off balance over the table. "Marry me," he said, planting a slobbery kiss on her cheek. He was aiming for her lips but Karissa averted her face with a gasp. "We're fated to be together. You know it and I know it. I've heard you singing your love to me—"

Grant broke the man's grip on her hand and pulled her away from the table, shielding her with his body as the security team closed in to take the stalker out with minimum fuss. Only the guy didn't want to go, fighting the guards, yelling obscenities at them and appealing to Karissa to rescue him. It was over in the space of a few moments, the cruise director moving in to reassure those still in line.

Karissa seemed reluctant to leave his embrace and Grant found he was equally unwilling to let her go. He settled for drawing her aside, toward the rear of the room and making himself a barrier for the curious glances. "We'll shut this down now," he said as he forced himself to release her, his senses beguiled by her perfume. "You've had enough today."

"No, I have to finish the signing," she said in a low voice. "Thank you for getting him off me."

"Of course." Grant took one of her scarves from her belt and wiped her face carefully where the man's lips had rested. "He won't be allowed anywhere near you the rest of the cruise, I promise. The captain'll confine him to his cabin and Maeve will monitor."

Eyes wide, she stared at him. "Do I look all right?"

"Perfect," he said.

She squared her shoulders. "Then we'd better get on with it. I imagine some of the kids in line were scared. Well, seven hells, I was scared too."

He was dubious about the wisdom of her continuing to interact with her public today but Karissa was already walking to the table, so he shoved the scarf into his pocket and followed. She made cheerful conversation with the next few fans, giving them extra time and glossing over any remarks about the disturbing moments with the obsessed fan.

As the afternoon wore on with no further incidents, Grant checked his chrono. Leaning over, he said in her ear, "We're already an hour past the posted ending time."

"How many more?"

"I've had the guys cut off the line outside the room, no more people adding themselves. About ten. You've done enough—you still have to perform tonight."

She sighed. "Ten I can do."

He could tell she was forcing herself to be 'on', her smile more brilliant than ever and her voice extra cheery. It grated on his ears and he was ruthless about sweeping her from her chair and escorting her from the room as the last fan walked away dazed from a brush with the celebrity. Making an executive decision, he took her as far as he could in the relative peace and quiet of the crew-only passages.

"Has anyone told you about the schedule for tomorrow?" she asked as they walked.

"I apologize but I haven't had time to come up to speed on all the details since I was just assigned today."

"Don't worry about it. In the morning I'll be sleeping in, after the performance and the party tonight. But in the afternoon I'm filming a music trideo on the beach level." She gave him a wry glance. "It's basically a commercial for the CLC Line but my manager saw fit to agree so I'm stuck. I was wondering if Valkyr could be in the trideo?"

"He's not a performing pet," Grant said with heat, insulted. "He's a trained war bird."

"I know, of course he doesn't do tricks or stunts. I truly thought he might like it. You might like it. I'm guessing the captain doesn't shut the beach level down for you two. Or not often. But it'll be a closed set for me, for two or three hours. I was hoping he might think it was a treat."

Now Grant was embarrassed, as she explained the thinking behind her request. "I'll see if I can get permission. Valkyr has to stay in my cabin except for authorized excursions. Line liability and all."

"If I ask, they'll say yes." She was supremely confident.

"Probably so, but I also need to ask Valkyr."

"Oh." Plainly she hadn't considered the eagle's opinion. "Well, he gave me a feather yesterday so perhaps he'll be willing to do a cameo fly by in exchange for a few hours at the beach."

She retired to her room as soon as they reached her suite, Grant escorting her through the throng of people.

"How long do you need?" he asked, low voiced, as he stopped at her bedroom doorway.

"I can only take an hour," she said. "Then my team and I have a lot of work to do to create Karissa for the concert stage."

He eyed her up and down in disbelief. "You could step on stage right now."

"Flatterer." She patted his cheek. "You're sweet, Officer Barton, but my costumes are much more involved than this get up. Not to mention the makeup. People expect the full show, even on board a ship." Her glance went past him and she sighed. "Here comes Ted. What can he possibly want now?"

"He can wait." Grant ruthlessly pushed her across the threshold and keyed the portal shut, taking up a guard stance in front of the door.

Ted stutter stepped to avoid running right into him and glared. "I need to talk to her. Get out of my way."

"Come back in an hour." Grant gave him what he knew was a blank stare. He'd used it to good effect on annoying senior officers many a time in the military.

"Listen you, your authority or whatever you think you have here doesn't extend to deciding who she can see and when, nor does it apply to me. I'm her manager."

"I'm aware of your position, sir. My orders come from the captain via my superior officer and I'm to honor Miss Dawnstar's requests as far as I can within ship safety parameters. She said she needs an hour and she's going to get it." Grant stood a foot taller than the blustering manager and he wasn't going to give an inch unless Jake or the captain came and gave him a direct order, neither of which was likely. Karissa had been on her last legs when she returned to the suite and needed the rest before performing.

Ted suddenly seemed to realize everyone in the suite was watching them. He spun on his heel and stalked off to the always present buffet and drinks table, pouring himself a large feelgood and making conversation with several cute young staffers whose function on the tour eluded Grant. The women had the right access badges though, so he made no objection.

The hour went by at lightspeed and Karissa emerged from the bedroom. "Thanks," she said, as there was a surge of people in her direction. "All right, we've got a show to do, let's get cracking."

She made her way to the theater area, moving with a group through the corridors of the *Zephyr* and attracting a lot of attention.

Grant wasn't invited into the large room where she and her team worked their costume, hair and makeup magic, although Ted went in, giving him a triumphant glare. Grant didn't feel it was within his mission parameters to block Karissa's own people from her, absent a direct request from her. Unfortunately. He waited with feigned patience to escort her to the backstage area.

When the singer emerged from the room where she'd been getting ready, he was astounded. She looked as if she'd stepped straight from a trideo, her sexy costume elaborate and glittering in the lights, her multicolored hair caught up in coils by all manner of elaborate, bejeweled accessories. Even he could tell her shoes were works of art, with heels designed to resemble stacked planets, standing six inches high. Obviously enjoying his reaction, she pirouetted on the absurd heels; hand on her hip, coquettish and grinning over her shoulder. "Well?"

Seeing him apparently as a total loss for words, she laughed and held out her hand. "Escort me," she said like a queen.

He did so, surrounded by her team, including the backup singers and the six dancers, all of whom joined Karissa when she reached the backstage area. Gently she let go of Grant's arm and stepped away, gathering her team for a pep talk. He stayed alert, watching everyone else in the area, ready to challenge anyone acting suspicious.

The show was already going on at full volume. Karissa's was the final set of the evening and when she ran onstage, her dancers bouncing and doing acrobatics around her, the roar was astounding. Grant stood in the wings, as close to the stage as he could, and watched the performance. Karissa strutted, she danced, she teased, she brought a child on stage for a brief chat, she sang full throated. The crowd loved it all. He had a hard time keeping his eye on the audience, watching for problems, because she was so riveting.

"First time at a show?" asked an older woman standing next to him. "This is nothing compared to what she'll do at the big concert on Calillia next week. There'll be multiple costume changes and aerial components. And maybe some new songs, although she's been quiet about her songwriting lately. She doesn't want Ted getting the rights to any more of her stuff if she can help it. Things are unfixably sour between them now." She laughed self-consciously and held out her hand. "I'm Desdusan, by the way, her chief makeup artist. Chief busybody too. I try to look out for her as much as I can. Been with Karissa for nine years, ever since she hit the bigtime with 'Twisted Comets'. She'll probably sing that for the encore."

"I hate to admit it but I've never heard her music before—it's all new to me," he said as they shook.

The woman did a double take. "You're kidding, right? You're probably the only person in the Sectors who hasn't heard at least one Karissa song."

"I have now," he pointed out, annoyed to feel so defensive

As expected, Karissa left the stage briefly at the end of her set and re-entered skipping and beaming at the crowd as the applause rose to deafening levels. She sang the encore with as much energy and enthusiasm as she'd opened the concert . Then she waved to the crowd and danced off. Grant followed her as Desdusan gave her a bottle of water and the two women headed for the dressing room. "Did you like it?" Karissa asked him over her shoulder.

"Full of energy and feeling," he said. "Clearly I missed a lot while I was on active duty."

His answer appeared to please her. "Give me a few minutes to freshen my makeup and then we'll be off to the official afterparty."

The gala was held in one of the *Zephyr*'s big ballrooms and attendance was restricted to high rollers who could afford the steep ticket price for mingling with the members of the various bands. Karissa's group was in the far corner, with an extra cordon of security staff in dress uniforms, who verified the eager passengers had paid the extra rider to spend time in her orbit. Grant's job was to stay close to her but unobtrusively, which he did. He was surprised to see the two monks again, seated at a table inside Karissa's space. The Calillians made no attempt to talk to her and seemed content to merely watch the festivities.

"The monks are somewhat unsettling," she said to Grant in a low voice at one point. "Some of the sects on Calillia are pretty radical in their beliefs. I'd rather not have rabid fans from their ranks."

"Do you want me to ask them to leave?"

She shook her head. "They must have paid the fee like everyone else and they're keeping their distance. I don't know for a fact their order is one of the loony fringe. I found it spooky how they wouldn't take no for an answer earlier though."

"I'll keep an eye on them," he said as Ted ushered the next pair of influential people he wanted her to meet towards where he and Karissa had taken a moment to be private.

She patted his arm. "I'm counting on that, Officer Barton."

"Grant," he said before he could stop himself. Annoyed at his own unprofessional lapse, he swore under his breath. He wasn't here to get on first name basis with the most famous singer in the Sectors.

Eyes wide as she smiled, Karissa whispered, "Grant," in a teasing tone and turned away to greet Ted's special guests.

Grant retreated to the far bulkhead, where he could see the entire room and take himself to task for getting too caught up in the casual atmosphere surrounding Karissa. He was here to guard her, not get to know her.

The evening couldn't end soon enough for him. He was disturbed to watch the singer switch from her fruit juices to harder feelgoods late in the evening after what she'd said about her trips to rehab, but it wasn't his place to intervene. Ted was urging her on and plying her with exotic drinks. The party got wilder, the music got louder and he grew restive. Somewhere around two AM, ship's time, the event officially ended and he escorted her to her cabin, surrounded by a group of fans and hangers-on. Surprisingly Ted stayed behind in the lounge at the ballroom, deep in conversation with two nubile dancers from one of the other bands' performance staff.

At the entry to Karissa's suite, Grant was prepared to bar the others from entering, but she waved them inside with a tipsy gesture. She kicked off her sky high shoes and settled onto a couch, immediately flanked by several of her dancers. "Join us," she said in Grant's direction, as someone brought her another drink.

"I'm off duty." He made his decision and his boss could ream his ass over it later. Everyone present had a badge as part of her staff, she was safely in her own cabin and he'd been on duty almost twenty four hours straight.

"See you at the beach then. Bring the bird." She gave her attention to the male dancer on her left, who was rubbing her arm and attempting to whisper in her ear.

Grant left without a backward glance. He understood adrenaline must run high after a show, especially with the kind of adulation and applause she'd gotten. He knew how necessary it was to let off steam and come down from the high, although in his case, it was usually the aftereffects of a deadly mission, where he'd had to kill people. He found he didn't want to watch Karissa and her people in their private party. *It's not my world.*

THREE

After showering, he spent time with Valkyr, summarizing the day's events and then went to bed, but he couldn't sleep. He tossed and turned but his senses were on high alert, as if there was some danger lurking. Finally he gave up, rising and throwing on sweatpants and a T shirt, deciding to do a bit of research for his current assignment.

Which wasn't to say Karissa had gotten under his skin but he had to admit to himself he was curious about her story.

Seated at the desk, he watched trideo news reports from the early days of her career, when she was hardly the Sectors-wide sensation she'd become. Faintly he heard a ping from his door com.

"Who in the seven hells would be disturbing me at this hour?" He shut off the trideo feed and strode to the door, flicking it open, ready to verbally blast anyone of less rank than the captain.

There was a woman huddled on the deck, leaning on the bulkhead next to his cabin door. Grant needed only a glance to realize it was Karissa, face bare of makeup, her hair a shoulder length curtain of shiny jet black. She was barefoot and wearing a gauzy nightgown under an unbelted satin robe. She held out one trembling hand to him. "Help me?"

Blessing the Lords of Space the corridor was empty, he scooped her up and carried her into his cabin, straight through to the bedroom as there was nowhere to lay her down in his main room, Valkyr's perch taking up most of the space.

She struggled for breath, wheezing a bit. "Maeve let me into the crew gravlift."

"What's wrong?" He was no medic but he checked her pulse, which was thready and he was alarmed by how pale she was.

"Did you see me drinking?" she asked.

"You consumed quite a bit." He tried to keep his tone neutral.

"Bastard Ted spiked my juice with something, tryin' to get me hooked again. One sip and I was a goner. He's always got a stash of high end stuff, likes to party with his girls and get fully engulfed in the joy." She opened her eyes and fisted her hand in his T shirt, dragging him closer. "I swear to you after the second time in rehab, I said no more. Clean and sober. But he thinks if he gets me addicted again I'll be under his thumb, re-sign the contract and make him more millions of credits." Eyes wide, she sat up, one hand going to her abdomen. "I'm gonna throw up."

He got her to the bathroom and held her hair aside as she emptied her stomach. "Feel better?"

"Can't breathe too well." She was visibly struggling, her chest rising and falling as she wheezed. "After you left, I was disappointed we didn't get to talk I tried to figure out what was the matter with you—you left like a comet blasting out of orbit—realized then how high I was, not just post-show jacked up but really high." She rolled her head against his arm. "Threw everyone out. Took four headclear but the injects aren't working."

"You need the doctor," he said.

Despite her physical distress, Karissa grabbed his arm in a desperate hold. "Gotta keep this quiet. No press."

"Dr. Shane is discreet."

She leaned against the pillows and closed her eyes. "I trust you. Grant. S'why I'm here." Her lips curved in a tiny smile but even as he noticed her expression, the blue tinge in her skin alarmed him and he opened the senior officer comlink.

"Dilon here." Jake's voice was calm. Nothing ever fazed him.

"I've got a situation in my cabin and I need Dr. Shane right away." Grant glanced at Karissa. "I think it's an emergency. Possibly a drug over- dose. And we need to keep this completely quiet, sir."

"Bring the person to the sickbay and I'll meet you there," Emily Shane said on the link.

"I can't, doc, not unless there's no other way."

"We'll be right down," Jake said, obviously getting the picture Grant must be talking about Karissa. "But Emily makes the final call as to whether the patient gets transferred to sickbay."

"Yes, sir."

Rumpled, yawning, dressed in casual clothes, Dr. Shane and her husband arrived at Grant's cabin in no time and he was banished to the main room with Jake, while Emily examined Karissa in the privacy of his bedroom.

"I see why you said this needed to be kept quiet," Jake said as the two men waited. "We do have entertainment media on board for the cruise. If word got out Karissa overdosed—"

"She said her manager spiked her drink, got her unintentionally high."
Jake regarded him steadily, unsmiling. "Did you see him do it?"

"I observed him giving her drinks, but as far as putting something into
them, no." Reluctantly he shook his head.

"Unless she's going to press charges, which I somehow doubt, we've
got no play here, other than taking care of a passenger who became
extremely unwell in the middle of the night. And we don't discuss medical
information." Jake grinned for a second. "Emily's beaten the privacy
concerns into my head for sure. She usually won't tell me anything unless
I make it a formal production, safety of the ship level need-to-know. Or
Captain Fleming asks her." The security chief snagged a chair and sat
down. "How did Karissa end up here?"

"She thought I could help and keep things quiet. I think she may have
panicked a bit also, not being able to breathe right." Grant stood at modi-
fied parade rest, giving a report to his senior officer, making the situation
less personal. "That's all. Maeve let her use the crew passageways and
access this deck. You'd have to ask the AI why she allowed it."

"So Karissa wasn't here when she got sick?"

"No. And Maeve's records will bear me out."

"I'll be straight with you, this situation has all kinds of 'doesn't look
good' written all over it. The potential for bad publicity for the Line is
immense. Are you involved with her?" Jake held up one hand before
Grant could speak. "I wouldn't be in your personal business but you're
assigned to guard her, which makes it Ship business."

Grant stood straight. "In no way am I personally involved with Karissa
Dawnstar." *But under other circumstances I'd sure like to be.* Finding her on
his doorstep, in need of help, had aroused all his protective instincts,
which added fuel to the attraction he was already fighting. "I'd never jeopardize the life of a protectee by embarking on a personal relationship."

"Keep it that way. You don't want to be explaining yourself to Captain
Fleming on the bridge, trust me. Only a few more days until we reach
Calillia and she becomes someone else's assignment. Then you can do
whatever you want."

Then I'll never see her again—our orbits are too far apart.

Interrupting his lecture to himself, Emily emerged from the bedroom
and Grant let his anxiety out as he asked, "How is she?"

"I gave her something to counteract the overdose of headclear and
whatever she'd been consuming in her drinks all night. She's breathing
better, no need to go to sickbay at this time." The doctor walked over to
Jake and he put his arm around her waist. She smiled at him, ruffling his
hair a bit with one hand. "Middle of the night house calls are no fun.
Hazards of being married to a doctor."

"He called me first, if you remember," Jake said.

"I was still blissfully asleep at that point." She turned to Grant. "This may be awkward for you but she needs to be watched tonight, to be sure the respiratory distress doesn't manifest again. I suspect she may have an underlying, previously undiagnosed condition aggravated by whatever she took. Probably mild until the overdose stressed her system. But I can't discuss it further with you two. I did give her a recommendation to seek out her own doctor when she reaches Calillia. So can you watch her, Grant? Here?"

"Is that what she wants? Rather than us getting her back to her own cabin?" Jake asked.

We'll watch.

Grant was startled by the firm comment in his head from Valkyr.

"Yes. She feels safe with your choice of bodyguard," Emily said to her husband, Grant's boss. "But if you're not willing to do this, Grant, I totally understand and we'll come up with another way to monitor her outside sickbay for a few hours."

"She came to me for help so I feel I need to see it through."

Emily gave him a few notes on complications to watch out for and then the couple left. Grant could tell Jake wasn't happy about the situation but he was relieved his boss hadn't overridden Karissa's request. He went back to the bedroom, quietly peeking in. Slender hand pillowing her cheek, the singer was peacefully asleep. He could hear her soft breathing and was reassured at how regular it was. The color in her cheeks was better as well. Quietly he drew a chair to the bedside and took up watch, allowing himself to sink into the semi sleep of a warrior, resting but alert.

For the most part she slept soundly but at one point he realized she was weeping in her sleep, so he leaned over and whispered in her ear. "Hey, it's okay, I'm here and Valkyr's here and we won't let anything bother you, my word on it. No bad dreams allowed." She seemed to relax at the sound of his voice, turning toward him without waking up but to his relief the tears stopped. Grant took her hand and leaned back in his chair.

Around eight in the morning, ship's time, Jake pinged him. "How's the patient?"

"Still sleeping, no problems."

"I want you to skip the morning briefing, stay with her. Emily's going to stop by and check on her and bring some of her own clothes for Karissa to change into. We'll have to try to create the impression she went out early, somewhere on the ship, and is going back to her cabin, no big deal. But I'm afraid she'll still get press. Use the crew passageways as much as you can. I'm surprised her entourage hasn't reported her missing."

"After the party last night her staff probably thinks she's sleeping in."

"Will she still be doing the trideo shoot this afternoon, on the beach deck? We moved mountains to get it closed off for four hours, just for her." Jake sounded annoyed.

"Knowing her, she'll insist on it," Grant replied. "As soon as I get a reading on the situation, I'll report back."

"Keep me posted." Jake signed off.

Karissa stretched and yawned, opening her eyes. "So it wasn't a dream? I did come to you?"

"Yes, thank goodness. Do you remember the doctor coming to see you?"

"She was nice." Sitting up, Karissa scooted to the center of the bed and started rearranging the pillows to support her back. "She thinks I have mild asthma but I haven't noticed trouble breathing before." She gave him a shy smile. "Thank you for coping with me."

He was at a loss for what to say. "I'm glad you didn't wait too long. Listen, I only have limited capability to cook in my quarters but I can make you some coffee? Or I could rustle up some toast maybe."

She put a hand on her stomach and made a face. "Coffee, yes, I need the energy. Then maybe I'll try the toast."

"Dr. Shane will be stopping by soon with some of her clothes for you. I think the idea is for us to get you back to your suite with the least amount of notice and comment," he said over his shoulder as he left the room.

She followed him. "Do I embarrass you?"

"Of course not. I'm glad you came to me. But you yourself said the press was on board and hungry for any hint of gossip. You in a nightgown and robe, casually strolling through the corridors will create talk."

"True." She paused at Valkyr's perch and held out her hand to the bird.

"He's not a dog, he doesn't sniff you to make friends," Grant said with amusement. "He already gave you a feather."

The bird shifted on his perch and eyed her for a moment before lifting his crest and making a soft noise deep in his throat. Karissa slowly extended her fingertips to brush the shiny feathers. "So soft. Did you ask him if he was willing to be in the trideo today?"

"Indeed I did and he was pleased. He relished the idea of access to the beach, although I told him there won't be fish."

"Does he eat fish?"

"Valkyr is a top predator – he eats whatever he chooses. If you want to offer him a treat, I have special cakes in a box on the desk."

When he re-entered the room with two cups of steaming coffee, she was holding one of the bird snacks crumbled in her palm and Valkyr was delicately picking up parts with his beak. Brushing her hands off as the bird completed his meal, she joined Grant and accepted her coffee. They sat on his small couch.

"Are you going to press charges?"

"Against Ted?" She seemed surprised. "No, there'd be no proof, my word against his and I'm the one who's been to rehab twice. The rock star. Who'd believe me?"

"I do."

She rewarded him with a genuine smile. "And I appreciate your trust. No, I just have to get through this coming week, the concert series on Calillia, and then he and I are through. I'll be free. That's all I want—my freedom after ten years." She leaned forward. "Do you know what it's worth to be my manager? To handle all my affairs?"

"Millions of credits, I imagine."

She nodded. "And power in the industry. Standing. Respect. The ability to make magic happen for other people too, or so they hope. He's been trading on my efforts for too long. I don't mean to sound ungrateful because I wouldn't have gotten where I wanted to be without him, but after the first few years I realized I was his indentured servant and the contract I'd signed was all in his favor. I'm quite poor actually, comparatively speaking. He owns the whole Karissa image, the music, the clever souvenirs, all of it."

"Sounds like you need a lawyer."

"Oh I have one, a damn good one, which Ted has no idea about. As soon as the contract is done there's going to be a forensic audit the likes of which the Sectors has never seen. It'll be a cold day in all seven hells before I sign another contract with anyone to manage me, because I can manage myself." Rising, she paced the length of the room. "Besides, I'm fucking tired. You have no idea how stressful it is to have hundreds of people dependent on me, on my voice. To perform whether I'm sick or sad or I've broken my leg in a stupid accident and have to hobble." She paused, her expression so distressed he set his cup down and instinctively went to her, catching her in his arms and making soothing noises as he stroked her hair.

"I'm sure it must be a huge responsibility," he said.

"I just wanted to make music, to write songs and share them," she murmured as she put her arms around his waist, resting her head on his chest. "And somewhere along the way it became this giant circus. You'll see, when I do the shows on Calillia."

"Am I invited?" he said. "I've gotten quite fond of your songs after the show yesterday."

"Special backstage access for you," she said with a smile.

There was a ping at the door and regretfully Grant walked away from her. "That'll be Dr. Shane, no doubt."

Emily swept in, organized and crisp. She'd brought a backpack full of clothes and she and Karissa retired to the bedroom so the singer could change. After satisfying herself Karissa was healthy enough to be on her own this morning, Dr. Shane left and Grant got dressed in his CLC Line uniform.

"See you this afternoon, Valkyr," Karissa said to the bird with a final stroke down the beautiful feathers on his back.

There were a few people in the corridor, which Grant regretted but there was nothing he could do about it. He just had to hope his shipmates wouldn't jump to conclusions or gossip. Karissa immediately began chatting about the mechanics of the trideo and what part Valkyr could play. They took the crew passageways and emerged into the corridor to her cabin, to find a small crowd of her people waiting outside her door.

"Oh, didn't I tell you I was going for a tour of the engine room this morning?" she said brightly. "Sorry."

Ted pushed his way to the front of the group and stood with his fisted hands on his hips. "Why would you want to see the engines?" he asked, his gaze flickering over Grant suspiciously.

"Why not?" she asked dreamily. "I might write a song about them." She turned to Grant with a smile. "Thanks for escorting me but for the next few hours I'll be safe in my suite, getting ready for the trideo. You can meet us on the beach deck at one in the afternoon." Karissa swaggered toward the door. "I'm starved, someone order up the breakfast buffet."

Grant was livid with the manager for trying to get Karissa hooked on pernicious drugs and possibly causing her an overdose, but he choked back the hot words rising in his throat. She hadn't asked him to intervene and she seemed to have a plan for handling Ted for the critical next few days. As he walked away, he had to remind himself he'd just met these people and they had complex relationships going back a decade. He was merely the security officer assigned to her on this ship. Sure, he felt like there was a connection between the singer and himself but when would he ever be able to act upon it? Karissa Dawnstar wasn't an ordinary woman you could just ask out on a date.

Or could you?

When he and Valkyr reported to the beach deck a few minutes early, and made it past the security cordon, he was astounded at how much activity and how many people were required to make a simple music trideo. Two *Zephyr* lifeguards stood by and a small group of passengers who'd won a lottery to be extras were corralled by an assistant director at one end of the beach.

He launched Valkyr into the air. *If she's serious about doing a scene with you, I'll let you know but in the meantime, enjoy the afternoon.*

He heard gasps as the eagle spread his magnificent wings and arrowed out to 'sea', eager to explore his newfound playground. Grant had no trouble finding Karissa herself, in the center of all the activity. She beckoned him over and pirouetted, hand on her hip. "What do you think? Best outfit yet?"

"I'd think you were fishing for compliments, if I didn't know you better," he said, giving the tight, old fashioned bathing suit a cursory glance and studying her face, trying to see how healthy she was under all the makeup and glitz.

Laughing, she leaned closer to speak privately. "I'm fine, don't look so worried. I'm tough. We film these trideos in bits and pieces so there won't be any sustained dances or songs to perform. Besides, the music is already recorded. After today I have a couple of days off, until the rehearsal down on Calillia."

He took a deep breath. "About those days off—"

An officious director pushed past him. "Miss Dawnstar, we need you at the water's edge now, with the children. The kids can only be on set for so long and we still have to set up the dream sequence."

"Hold that thought," she told Grant. "Pick a good spot to do your security surveillance thing and enjoy the chaos. We'll have a chance to chat later. I'm not needed in every shot."

"Valkyr is here," he called after her. "If you still need him."

She waved to signify she'd heard and kept going as the director chattered in her ear.

Grant never realized the making of a trideo was so complicated and painstaking. Maybe it wasn't unless a major star like Karissa was involved as the centerpiece. Mostly he tried to stay out of the way, while keeping an eye on the extras for anyone who might be a threat. The lifeguards had to rescue a child extra who slipped, fell in the gentle waves and panicked. At one point he had to ask Valkyr to fly over a different part of the beach, as he was distracting the crew.

True to her word, Karissa managed to extricate herself after about two hours and came to meet him. "The assistant director's doing a sequence with the dancers now and I'm not involved. Sit with me while I have a snack?"

"Of course."

He grabbed an assortment of tempting food from the catering table for them both and she snagged two bottles of her favorite juice. "Sealed tight," she said with a wry tone in her voice, holding the containers high. "I'm not taking any more chances of imbibing extra ingredients."

He followed her to a ring of chairs off to the side, all of which were empty. As she sat in the one with her name inscribed on the back in glittery pink lettering he saw her shiver. Maeve maintained balmy breezes on this deck to heighten the authenticity, but concerned Karissa might be getting a chill, he tracked down Desdusan and obtained a robe for the star.

"Is this going well so far?" he asked as she bit into her sandwich after he draped the robe over her shoulders. "You said it was going to be chaos and I believe you now."

"Organized chaos though." She grinned. "I think all parties involved will be satisfied when the end product is released." She studied him as she took a long drink of the juice. "Didn't you have something you wanted to say to me about my days off?"

"Are you actually from Calillia? Or was that a publicity thing?"

"Ooh, been studying up on my dossier, have you?" Her tone was teasing. "Yeah, as it happens, Ted was on Calillia for a big gig, heard the choir from my orphanage perform and me perform a solo, and offered me a contract. I was about to age out of the government care system and terrified what I'd do, where I'd go, so I was only too happy to sign on with him. The press loves the fact I'm such a big name in music now and I come from the planet known grandiosely as the Musical Center of the Galaxy. Ted probably would have invented my origin story if it wasn't true."

"You're my current assignment," he said with dignity. "So of course I had to do the proper in-depth research."

"You make me feel like a mission objective," she said teasingly. "Maybe I'd like that. You're probably quite single minded and intense."

He took a deep breath at her comment but stuck with his subject, tempting though it might be to flirt more openly. Flirting wasn't one of his skills. "And you've never been back until now?"

She shook her head. "No good reason to visit. I was a foundling left on the proverbial doorstep in a basket, so no close ties here. I probably would have auditioned for one of the Thousand Year Choirs but there was no guarantee I'd be accepted into a good one and a girl like me wasn't likely to ever rise to soloist. I have no patience for singing the solemn notes. I like to write my own stuff."

"I was wondering if you'd like to go down to Calillia tomorrow for the day with me and Valkyr, just the three of us, like anonymous tourists? "

Mouth open in surprise, she stared at him. "Are you serious?"

"Why not? You said yourself you don't have any rehearsals or commitments."

"Valkyr is hardly anonymous."

"Yeah, I'll admit he'll attract attention but if you don't wear all the Karissa stuff—"

Laughing as if she might fall from the chair, she gasped out, "The 'Karissa stuff'? My costume designer and the makeup artists will be highly offended. I'll have you know this effect is extremely challenging to create. And expensive."

"I'll take your word for it. And I've seen how effective it is on stage. But I've also seen the real Karissa underneath. I like her," he said simply. "And I'd like to take that girl for a day exploring the city, have some good local food for lunch, see the sights, let my eagle have some flight time in the nature preserve at the edge of the city. Spacers with exotic pets are a commonplace sight in a port city. No one'll look twice—well they won't look more than twice—at Valkyr. If anyone recognizes you, we can say you're her stand-in or stunt double or something. Don't sing and we can pull it off. I promise."

Eyes narrowed, Karissa stared at him for a long moment. He hoped he hadn't seriously overstepped his bounds. "You honestly think we can manage a day of privacy?"

"My word as a soldier," he said. "I wouldn't ask otherwise. I'm not taking you into any kind of dangerous situation. But you can't tell anyone ahead of time either."

"All right, I'll do it. I can't even remember the last time I got to do something as delightfully mundane as being a simple tourist. Pick me up right after breakfast."

"I'll be there."

Ted and the director came up to them. "We should finish the mermaid sequence now."

"Coming. Thank you, Officer Barton," she said with formality, handing him her plate and giving him a saucy wink at the same time.

The final scene of the day was just Karissa, standing on the beach facing the ocean. Maeve had been requested to change the lighting of the holographic 'sky' to a pearlescent sunset. As Karissa sang lyrics about dreams and hopes, Valkyr swept in over the water, making a tremendous display of his wings, and landed on her outstretched fist, sheathed by Grant's special glove. He was amazed she could bear the eagle's weight without staggering but Valkyr assured him he'd made the landing as lightly as possible. As soon as the director yelled "Cut," Grant stepped in to take his warbird and remove him from a crowd of people who wanted to pet and admire him, heedless of the beak and talons. He had to leave the deck to take Valkyr back to his cabin, so Red covered for him with Karissa. By the time Grant re-entered the beach deck, the shoot was over, trideo techs were packing the gear and the singer had gone to her cabin, Red accompanying her.

"We're done for the day," Red said over the comlink. "Our guest is in her suite and says she doesn't need anything else. So I'm off duty and you can stand down as well."

Feeling disappointed, Grant acknowledged the transmission and returned to his cabin. Already it was hard to believe she'd actually been in his space the night before. The scarf he'd taken from his pocket and laid on the desk caught his attention and he twirled the fabric into a circle with his index finger. A whiff of her signature perfume drifted from the silk and he took a deep breath. *I should give this back to her.* But it might be his only remembrance of his unlikely brush with Karissa.

Were they really going to go sightseeing tomorrow on Calillia? She'd said yes, but she might have changed her mind by tomorrow, or had it changed for her by Ted.

As he reheated his basic meal, Grant said a small prayer to the Lords of Space that he'd be given the day he hoped for in her company. It had been a long time since he'd wanted anything so badly and the realization took him by surprise.

FOUR

He made his way to her cabin in the morning, dressed in civilian clothes and feeling slightly uneasy. She let him into the suite and he was relieved to find her with unadorned face and hair, dressed in the clothes Dr. Shane had let her borrow two nights before. As usual she pirouetted for his approval, laughing. "Not my usual style—I hope you're not disappointed."

"I could never be disappointed by you," he said. "Shall we go?"

As she grabbed a little embroidered purse, she said, "I thought we were taking Valkyr with us, for a free flight session?"

He led her along the corridor as rapidly as he dared. The few people they passed didn't spare them a second glance. "We are but we have to stop by my cabin to pick him up. If I'd brought him up here, we'd be attracting a whole lot more attention." He opened the entry to the crew passageway and breathed a sigh of relief once his highly recognizable companion was safely inside and out of public view.

"You hate the skulking and hiding, don't you?" she asked as they took the gravlift down to the crew quarters.

"I understand the need," he said. "I just wish it didn't have to be that way."

She looped her arm through his and squeezed. "Well, we'll just be two people in the crowd on Calillia today, with a giant bird of course."

Valkyr submitted without protest to having a lightweight leash placed on his ankle before the bird took his position on the reinforced shoulder pad of Grant's shirt. "A Customs requirement, even though Valkyr has all his papers in order."

Karissa laughed. "The leash wouldn't stop him for a moment if he wanted to get away, right?"

"Right, but what the bureaucrats don't know, we won't tell them."

He led her to the hangar deck and as they stepped inside she exclaimed. "Much busier than when we were here before."

Since the *Zephyr* was now in orbit around Calillia, shuttles were coming and going.

Karissa hung back a bit, chewing the tip of her fingernail. "I'm not sure my disguise is good enough to stand up in a shuttle full of people. I'm counting on this day so much and I don't want to ruin it. If I'm spotted, we'll have the press on us as soon as we land and we might as well come back. Or I can hop the shuttle back alone anyway, so at least Valkyr gets his chance to fly."

Grant took her hand. "Don't worry so much. I've planned much more complicated missions in the Special Forces. Right this way to your special transport, courtesy of Captain Fleming." He led her along the bulkhead, working his way down the landing bay until they reached the captain's personal vehicle, a trim smaller shuttle.

A pilot stood waiting for them. Grant made quick introductions and then they entered the shuttle.

"I don't know how you pulled this off," the pilot said. "And I don't care—it's an honor to fly you anywhere, Miss Dawnstar." He gave her a salute and headed for the cockpit.

Karissa sank into one of the seats. "You aren't going to be in trouble are you? We aren't stealing this or anything?"

"I did have to explain to my boss why I needed to talk to the captain and then approached the captain, but they both saw the wisdom of your commuting to the surface in a private shuttle. I can actually fly it—I'm rated for all kinds of small vehicles, up to certain classes of fighters, but the captain drew the line at that idea."

"I'm glad, means we can spend more time talking." She patted the seat beside her. "Come, sit."

Grant got Valkyr established on a portable perch clamped into an all-purpose receptacle on the shuttle's bulkhead, and then was only too happy to join her. "We didn't get to talk too much about what you'd like to do today."

She held up her hand and enumerated her choices. "First we have to take Valkyr for his flying time. Then I've been craving a proper Calillian *estuvanza* lunch—it's a meal made up of special dishes with fresh sea food and spices only found on this planet, but we'd have to go off the tourist track to eat the genuine article, prepared the old style."

"Absolutely. This day is for you. Any sights you want to take in?"

Rubbing her forehead, Karissa hesitated. "I might want to go by the orphanage where I grew up, but I'm not sure. Let's see how I feel after lunch, all right?"

Once the shuttle landed, Grant led her to the CLC Line office at the spaceport, near their assigned landing pad, where he picked up the initiator for a groundcar. After loading Valkyr into the backseat, where the bird sat perched on the edge of the cushions, broadcasting unhappy thoughts, Grant gave the car's AI instructions and it smoothly drive them out of the spaceport and through the outskirts of the city.

Karissa checked on Valkyr. "Your usually debonair eagle is grumpy today. Even I can tell, the way his feathers are ruffled."

"He loathes riding in a groundcar when he could be flying." Grant executed a turn, merging onto the expressway.

"We're going to Mountain Vista park?" she said.

"Yes, I researched what was available and this was the best place to fly Valkyr, in proximity to the port."

"Good choice, Probably won't be too busy on a weekday either. You did do your research." She ran her hand through her hair, fluffing it out and smiled.

"How does it feel to be back?"

"I'll let you know later but thanks for arranging all this. It's nicer to kind of sneak home, rather than arrive in a blaze of press and the lord mayor giving me the key and all the fuss. Which will happen the day after tomorrow, by the way. You'll find it endlessly amusing no doubt."

His heart fell. "I'm only assigned to guard you as long as you're on board our ship. I'm not included after you debark. Has Ted talked to you about what security preparations he's made?" If people were relying on him, they needed to think again because she was only the *Nebula Zephyr's* charge while she remained a passenger. There was no way Captain Fleming and Jake were going to send him planetside to do security. Nor would it be appropriate, not in any official capacity.

"He was babbling something about hiring local off duty cops," she said.

"Totally inadequate for a person of your stature. Not to be disrespectful to Calillia law enforcement but I doubt they have the proper experience with keeping high value targets safe." The mere idea made him livid and nervous for her.

"Ted doesn't want to spend a penny on me if he can help it, now he sees I'm adamant about ending the contract." Karissa turned in her seat to face him. "Could you come along unofficially?"

"Take personal leave, like today?" Which was exactly what he was contemplating.

She nodded. "I know it's asking a lot. I could reimburse—"

He held up his hand. "Don't even think about offering to pay me."

He drove in silence for a mile or so.

"I'm sorry, I didn't mean to insult you," she said. "I just didn't want to presume on our friendship. Can you at least come to the first day of rehearsal? And the shows of course. I'll get you an all access badge." She touched his hand. "As my friend? I've gotten used to having you there to depend on. Being back on Calillia, at the same time the contract is ending, is overwhelming. Scary."

"Of course I'll be there, let Ted try to keep me away. My boss will be willing to give me the time off." He curled his fingers around hers and squeezed gently. "I vote we stop talking about this and concentrate on being tourists today."

The road became a gentle but inexorable incline, and then began curving though impressive foothills, with deep valleys off to the side. Chirping, Valkyr shifted restlessly in the back.

"If we had more time, I'd take him into the mountains themselves," Grant said as he directed the groundcar into an isolated turnout at the highest point. "At home on Qaazamir, that's where his kind lived, in the peaks."

He got the eagle out, riding his fist, and the three of them hiked a short trail leading from the parking area to the edge of a vast valley, stretching as far as the eye could see, ringed by the higher mountains marching into the distance. Grant gave Valkyr the signal and he catapulted himself into the void, rising on the updraft until Grant could no longer see him.

"How do you know he'll come back?" Karissa asked.

"If he chose to stay here, believing he could be happy, I wouldn't try to dissuade him," Grant said. "But he won't." He held out his hand. "I have a snack in the car, courtesy of Chef Stephanie. Valkyr will be quite a while, especially if he finds good hunting, so shall we go sit in the shade and munch?"

Holding hands they made their way back to the parking lot, retrieved his backpack and adjourned to the eating area, shaded by old growth trees. Karissa helped him lay out the delicacies the ship's chef had prepared for her—scrumptious pastries and tiny sandwiches with breakfast style meats, plus bottles of her favorite juice concoction.

"I'd get fat if I lived on your ship," she said later, helping herself to the fourth pastry. "Luckily I work off immense amounts of energy doing the shows." She studied Grant for a moment. "Why are you so sure Valkyr won't want to stay here? I mean, mountains, right?" She waved her hand in the direction of the ravine.

"Not our mountains though. It's not home." Leaning back, Grant finished his juice and said, "Qaazamir eagles bond at birth with their handler, establishing the mental link. Actually, Valkyr bonded with my great grandfather."

Mouth open in shock, she asked, "How old is he?"

"Two hundred or so. It was common for the birds to be passed down in the same family line. As long as the DNA of the descendants contained certain dominant markers, the bird treated each the same as his original partner. He only bonds to one human at a time, so the new handler must be present at the death of the previous owner, or immediately thereafter. Of course sometimes birds were stolen by upstarts the elders hadn't selected. Clan wars were fought over good nesting areas. An egg was the most desired dowry." Grant drew idle patterns in the dirt beside the grassy patch he was sitting on. Realizing with chagrin he was sketching clan insignia, he brushed his hand over the drawing to obliterate the symbols. "There was an entire indigenous culture on Qaazamir, rich traditions."

"What happened?"

"The Sectors happened. Qaazamir was colonized early on, before many of the laws and protections were developed. If the planet was discovered for the first time now, there'd be no colonization because the planet had inhabitants and the birds would still exist. My people would still exist." He stared at the horizon. These were matters of which he normally never spoke. "But the colonists pushed the rightful owners of the planet aside, mined the rich ores, polluted the water and the ground… it's a toxic hellhole now. In fact, what happened on Qaazamir was the primary reason the Sectors established safeguards. But by then it was too late for us. We had a dying planet. My ancestors refused to accept reality for a long time. The elders thought having won their case at the Sectors Supreme Court meant everything would be fine. But the corporate colonists left and the poisons remained. The high court's judgment had no requirement on the defendants for restoring the ecological damage already done."

"You—you were the upstart who took the bird? Took Valkyr?"

He nodded. "I could see the way the extinction trend was going. Valkyr had passed to my great aunt and then my father. I was already in the Special Forces when he was dying of amphbagan fever, a wasting disease caused by the poisons leaching from the ground, but I got compassionate leave and made it home in time. I took Valkyr with my father's blessing, if not the permission of the elders. I tried to find a female so he could mate, but by then there were no more females. The last few clutches of eggs were deformed and failed to hatch. I was banished in absentia for stealing Valkyr from my cousin."

He turned his gaze on Karissa, who was leaning forward, chin resting on her hand, apparently mesmerized by his story. "My father and I felt as long as one Qaazamir eagle flew free somewhere in the galaxy, our people, our traditions would not have perished. There are no birds and hardly any people left on Qaazamir. It's a wasteland. The military was happy to accept Valkyr and me into the Z Command, to carry out unique missions behind enemy lines."

"What happened? Why are you here?"

He shrugged with a nonchalance he didn't feel. "Ten years is a long time, a guy gets busted up too many times and he can't be put back together completely any more. Becomes a burden to his teammates, a dangerous weakness. So we retired."

She stared at him. "But then how did you end up on the *Zephyr*?"

"I was on a classified task force once with Red—you met him yesterday—and when he heard I was mustering out, he suggested I take a berth on the *Zephyr* to buy myself time to figure out a future. The CLC Line is owned by veterans and they take care of their own, which is why I have the latitude to keep Valkyr on board." He straightened feeling oddly exhausted by all the talking about himself.

"This assignment is beneath you, isn't it? Guarding me?"

"What?" He was startled, trying to think what he could have said to give her a mistaken impression. "Of course not, your safety and security are highly important. And today," he said with clenched jaw, "Is not an 'assignment', not to me. It was a day to spend with a girl I really like."

She left the table and came to him, hugging him. "I didn't mean it that way, which you'd know if you took a moment to not be offended and to think. I just meant you've done such important work, such dangerous things and now you're watching over one silly singer who happens to be famous. Keeping her overeager fans at bay. You should be doing grander things, more life and death things."

"There's nothing I'd rather be doing right now," he said with perfect truth.

She raised her face to him. "You really like me, Officer Barton?" Her smile was mischievous and inviting and her eyes twinkled.

"Grant." It was the most natural thing in the world to kiss her, his lips against her soft ones, his tongue tracing the seam, asking for permission to explore. Karissa sighed and opened herself to him, her tongue twining with his. He pulled her closer to him, her soft curves fitting his hard frame as she went on tiptoe to deepen the caress. With one hand he brushed the side of her breast and she sighed with pleasure at his touch.

He broke the kiss off before she was ready and her small protest reassured him. "I've earned the right to do what I want," he said softly, looping her silky hair behind her ear. "And what I want more than anything is time with you."

Startling them, Valkyr came shrieking dramatically overhead, before he veered off to catch another updraft and commence aerial acrobatics.

"He's jealous, a bit," Grant said. "He wants your attention today too."

"Is he done flying already?"

He checked his mental link with the bird. "No, he's found good hunting and spectacular cliffs with generous updrafts. He just came back to check on us."

"The signs say there's a trail, over there," Karissa said, pointing to the west. "Feel like a hike?" She held out her hand.

"Why not?"

Eventually the path ended in a meadow full of flowers, overlooking another sheer drop, with a small waterfall. Karissa said she wanted to work on some songs, so he boosted her to the top of a nice flat rock and watched her get out her special AI and headphones, before he settled into a watchful position at the base of the formation, and opened his link with Valkyr wider, to share the incredible sensations of soaring.

The return drive into town was peaceful, Valkyr drowsing in the backseat after all his exertions. Grant parked at the edge of one of the squares and they set off hand in hand to find the special lunch she'd been craving.

Head up, Karissa stopped dead in the middle of the street, sniffing the air. "That's it! Whoever is cooking what I'm smelling right now knows what he or she is doing."

Laughing, Grant pivoted her to face the family style restaurant they were standing in front of. "Well, finding a place was easy. Let's see if the manager will accommodate an exotic war bird."

The receptionist's eyes widened at Valkyr on Grant's shoulder but she led them to a table in the garden out back, shielded from the street, featuring a small fountain, and left them with the menus.

"I can't read this," he said. "My hypno implants are for spoken languages only. We really are off the beaten track if the menu doesn't have Basic."

"Trust me to order for you?" Karissa's eyes were gleaming as she issued the playful challenge.

"Sure." He folded the menu and set it aside, but his attention was caught by people staring at them from the open restaurant door. Gut tightening, he wasn't at all surprised when the receptionist retraced her path to their table, trailed by an older couple and a child.

"I recognize you!" the woman said with excitement. "I just saw you on the entertainment news this morning!"

With shock he realized she was talking to *him*.

"I'm sorry, but that's impossible," he said. "I'm no one famous."

"Yes, yes, see, they say you're the blessed singer Karissa's new boyfriend." The girl pulled an AI from her pocket and retrieved the particular trideo broadcast, playing it for him on the tablecloth.

The entertainment reporter had caught him putting the robe over Karissa's shoulders at the trideo shoot on the ship's beach yesterday. She was gazing up at him with an unmistakably fond smile and he hardly recognized the expression of tenderness on his.

"Seven hells." He jumped up from his chair hard enough to knock it over, sending Valkyr into startled flight that made the restaurant staff shriek and cower.

Karissa stood up. "Calm down, everyone." She pointed at Valkyr. "You too. Land it now, mister."

Shockingly to Grant, the bird obeyed her admonition, resuming his perch on the back of a sturdy chair.

The locals apparently hadn't realized who she was until just now. Eyes wide, the group stared at her. "Karissa! Here, in our little restaurant?"

"Yes, I wanted to show my friend the true joys of Calillia food, not the stuff they serve tourists at the spaceport," she said, addressing the oldest woman, who had the unmistakable air of being in charge. "Your food smelled so wonderful, it drew me in. I'd like to buy out the entire restaurant for two hours, so we can eat in privacy, how much?"

The old woman named a price and Karissa doubled it.

"Done. And after we're done eating, I'll sign autographs for you—all of you." Karissa raised her voice and pointed to the crowd of cooks and servers jammed into the doorway. "You can all have pictures with me," she said. "But you have to keep my secret until he and I, and the bird, have left. Can you do that?"

"Of course. It's an honor to cook for you," said the proprietress.

And no hardship to accept a payment probably equal to an entire week's worth of dinners. Angry thoughts in his head, Grant was still reeling from seeing himself on the Sectors news feed.

"We wanted to do some exploring in town later," Karissa added, "So if you can keep my secret until I've gone back to my ship tonight, I'll send tickets to my concert, enough for all of you and your family members to be my special guests. I just wanted to be reacquainted with my home in peace today, you know? Before the hoopla?"

The old woman straightened and glared at her employees and family. "We will keep the lady's secret until tonight, understand?"

Her staff and family members nodded with impressive solemnity. Obviously her word was law to them.

"Well, what are you hanging around her for? You, go put up the closed sign, draw the curtains and lock the doors. The rest of you, back to the kitchen. The food won't cook itself."

"May we have a pitcher of spiced virtunna juice over ice? I haven't tasted any in years—it's my favorite," Karissa said.

Bowing and retreating, the staff left the garden. The elderly woman lingered. "I'm sorry my granddaughter upset your friend."

"Actually she did us a favor, letting us know the news was out there. We had no idea. Please don't worry about it. The juice?"

"Coming at once."

As the lady left the garden in dignified manner, Karissa laughed a little. "That's never happened to me before, having my companion recognized first. I think my disguise was fooling them, just as we'd hoped."

He paced to the fountain and stood watching the fish dart here and there, without really seeing them.

She followed, resting her hand on his arm. "Hey. I'm sorry. I should have thought about the fact the entertainment reporter might still be lingering on the set yesterday. I'm so used to the constant media coverage."

He laid his hand over hers. "I guess I should have been more discreet too. The *Zephyr* seems like such a closed world, but of course it isn't. I can't believe I let my situational awareness slip so badly." He smiled at her. "You have a terrible effect on my control, lady."

"Good. I'm glad to hear it." She studied him, head tilted. "There's more to it though, isn't there?"

"In the Special Forces we don't allow anyone to take facial shots that could be used to identify us. I'm not happy about this, even though the media apparently don't have my name. Just some snide remarks about the 'security guard' with a crush on you." He tried to keep his tone light.

"Which you and I both know is not the truth. Besides, you're out of the service now." She put her hands on her hips. "I can't deny the fact—the glare of publicity is part and parcel of being with me. No matter how careful we are, privacy is next to impossible. I regard myself as lucky to have had so much of a day to myself, thanks to you. Would you rather forget this" —she waved her hand at the garden—"And just go back to the ship?"

He knew he was behaving like an asshole over something that couldn't be fixed now. His face and his name no doubt, were out there in the Sectors media. He might as well suck it up, rather than ruin the special day he was trying to give her.

His special day with a girl he was drawn to like a moth to a flame. Liked too much.

You wish her to lay your eggs.

Valkyr's comment made him laugh. *Not exactly, pal.*

"Why are you laughing?"

Feeling the heat in his cheeks, he chuckled self-consciously. No way was he explaining the bird's comment. Lucky she couldn't speak to the eagle. "Valkyr made a remark."

Karissa shot the bird a suspicious glance. "Which I'm guessing wasn't too flattering?"

Grant caught her in his arms. "Oh no, it was very flattering but expressed in avian terms. Some things don't translate well." He gave her a kiss. "Let's forget this and have the amazing lunch you promised me."

Just then the owner and her waiters brought out the first of a seemingly never ending series of dishes, beginning with mildly spiced and ending with selections so hot Grant's mouth was on fire.

Then the servers brought the traditional dessert, a creamy confection with cake that melted on his tongue and made the entire menu he'd been served come together perfectly. He leaned back in his chair. "I'm too stuffed to move."

"Maybe we should just nap in the sun like Valkyr for the rest of the day," Karissa said with a laugh.

"No, I promised you a tour of the marketplace before we went back, so we'd better not linger here." He glanced at his chrono. "We have plenty of time before the captain's shuttle has to return to the *Zephyr*."

He sat and watched while Karissa paid the bill, posed for numerous photos with everyone and reconfirmed tickets would be sent for the concert if no word leaked out until midnight about her having been at the restaurant.

"I'll tell people my ovens were broken and so we had to close," the owner said. She had one of her daughters escort them through a private alleyway into the edge of the bustling market square.

"I need to walk off that fantastic meal," Grant said as they meandered arm in arm down the sidewalk. "I'm not going to eat any dinner, for sure."

"It was perfect, just what I've been craving for years. Thank you."

"My pleasure." Grant heard music and paused to listen. "Is that a thousand year song? Where's it coming from?"

Shading her eyes with her hand, she surveyed the buildings, finally pointing at one with an elaborate façade of gilded carvings. "Probably that temple. We can go listen if you like."

"What's the deal with these songs? Do generations of people really sing the same tune night and day for a thousand years?"

She nodded. "Sometimes it's the same song but more often there will be new verses being written daily or weekly, and given to the choirs and soloists. The musical variety depends on the funding and the purpose for the song. But the music never stops, not for anything. There's a story once of a huge fire and the choir moved outside and continued singing while the building fell. Anyone can commission a thousand year song although as you can imagine it takes massive resources, so typically only the most elite families or temples will do so. I have heard of villages putting all their resources into it, but the village was long gone and forgotten by the time the song concluded."

"A thousand years? People actually sign up to sing the same song for their entire lives, and never hear the final notes?" He scratched his head, pondering the mystery. "Their children won't even hear the final notes. Why do it?"

"Why do human beings do anything? Why did the people from Terra venture out in their generation ships before the hyperspeed drives were invented? The songs are a part of the Calillia religion. Legend says the music brings the blessings of the gods upon the planet and the people. In fact, it was gods who started the first songs, millennia ago. If you believe in myths." She gave him a shrewd glance. "Nowadays much of the planet's economy is based on the songs and supporting the needs of the singers so the tourists come."

Pulling him with her, Karissa ducked into the back of a large song temple, where the choir he'd heard was faithfully singing the chorus and refrain of their life's work.

"See this?" Karissa pointed at an elaborate, slow moving device beside the door. "This was the style of chronograph when the song started. It's measuring how long the chorus has been singing, and how much time is left."

"How long?"

She eyed the device. "Eight hundred years, give or take a decade or two."

"Two hundred years to go." He surveyed the choir, some fifty strong, standing on tiered steps at the front of the large, airy open space, putting a great deal of energy into the harmony. Shaking his head, he towed her outside again. "And you would have been in one of those choirs all this time?"

"Most likely."

"I can't imagine you doing that—you'd go crazy."

She laughed. "Probably. Or start singing my own lyrics and be punished. Ted, for all his faults and our legal problems now, did me a huge favor when he plucked me from the orphanage."

"Do the songs ever end in actual fact?"

"Oh yes, two ended during my life here and there was a huge celebration each time. Usually a special set of verses is written for the last year of the performance and the director might even add extra singers. The honor of singing the final notes is given to the best singer in the chorus and he or she then retires to a life of luxury and ease, because they were so honored. None are scheduled to end this year though, sorry."

"Life must feel flat, being in a chorus after finishing the song, with nothing to do. Anticlimactic."

"Oh the singers get hired into other choirs fairly quickly. The singing goes on night and day." She quickened her pace. "I want to get some souvenirs for Desdusan, maybe something nice for Dr. Shane for lending me her clothes—you'll have to advise me."

Laughing, he caught up to her at a stall featuring scarves painted with musical motifs. "I know less than nothing about Dr. Shane's preferences and her husband—my boss incidentally—wouldn't like it if I did."

She made her selections and paid with credits in hand, before they wandered further, examining knickknacks, laughing and teasing and having the fun day he'd hoped for when he issued the invitation. He kept his peripheral awareness high, in case anyone else recognized him from the damn trideo, but the market was busy and they were just another tourist couple window shopping.

He realized she'd stopped walking and had his arm in an iron grip. "Oh no," she said.

On high alert, ready for any challenge, he scanned the environment for a threat and perceived none.

"That's too cruel." Karissa left his side and darted across the street to a booth he realized was lined with cages, huge enclosures housing dozens of birds. She started throwing open the doors to the cages and encouraging the birds to take wing, in some cases scooping up the brightly colored creatures and throwing them into the air. Yelling curses, the merchant came out of the office to the rear of the stall. Grant drew him aside and assured him they'd pay double for the merchandise he was losing.

Karissa acted like a woman obsessed, going from cage to cage on her mission.

Her actions attracted a crowd as the flocks of gorgeous birds took wing, singing and warbling their joy.

Grant joined her at the last cage, in the back of the stall. Valkyr, who'd been an impassive observer of the frenzy, for which Grant was grateful, sat straighter and flexed his wings. "We owe this guy a huge stock of credits now."

"I don't care, it was worth it." Grant realized she was crying. "Caged songbirds, they were caged songbirds. Condemned to a life no one should live."

He gathered her close, wondering how much of her own situation and return to Calillia today had influenced her overwhelming reaction to the plight of the birds.

"There's one left in there, at the back," she said. "I think she's hurt but I can't get her to come out."

Valkyr launched off his shoulder with a sharp whistle and forced his way into the cage in question, which fortunately had a wide oblong door.

What the seven hells are you doing? Grant couldn't imagine the eagle was trying to attack one lone songbird after ignoring entire flocks of them, but Valkyr's odd behavior was alarming.

Mine.

The eagle was in a mantling position, shoulders arched, wings spread protectively over the last bird. Grant caught a glimpse of white feathers and a gleaming green eye at Valkyr's feet, and heard cooing.

All right, let me look. Examining the simple wire cage, Grant found a way to lift off the entire top, which he did, and then reached in to take the bird Valkyr was so jealously protecting, his eagle moving aside an inch at a time. Valkyr hopped out of the cage and flapped the short distance to Grant's shoulder, craning his head to stare at the rescued bird, lying in the human's hands.

Her heart was beating so fast, Grant was afraid she'd die. One wing was bent at an awkward angle, painfully broken.

"Poor thing," said Karissa, drawing a fingertip along the bird's head. "Such beautiful white feathers."

Mine, mine, mine. Mine to protect. Make her well.

"Easy, boy, we'll do what we can," he said out loud. Over his shoulder he told Karissa, "Valkyr seems to have fallen into love at first sight here."

"How sweet." She turned from the credit transaction she was concluding with the now smiling vendor. Grant guessed he'd probably realized he was dealing with the famous Karissa and therefore he had a critically short window of opportunity to get her out of the marketplace before a mob scene occurred that would make the crush at the Observatory Deck a few days ago minor by comparison. "But he—but they—can't mate, can they?" she asked in confusion.

"Take her for a moment." Grant poured the bird into Karissa's hand, moved Valkyr to a temporary perch, stripped off his shirt and then his undershirt, wrapping the bird carefully, not to disturb the broken wing. He shrugged back into his overshirt with the reinforced pad for Valkyr and grabbed Karissa by the elbow. "We have to run, before this guy tells all his friends who you are."

They sprinted for the car. He heard shouts behind him and redoubled his pace. Valkyr launched from his shoulder and flew a few threatening swoops above the heads of the first wave of people coming to see Karissa as the couple reached the groundcar and threw themselves inside. Revving the motor to the red line, Grant hit the street, going toward the spaceport at a high rate of speed.

"What about Valkyr?" Karissa glanced back anxiously.

"He knows our destination. He'll catch up. Are you okay?"

"Fine. Never a dull moment."

"Not with you." He grinned. "How's our new lady friend?"

"Calmer since you wrapped her up. Valkyr does realize he can't actually be her mate, doesn't he? She's a Calillia songbird, not a Qaazamir eagle."

"He won't hurt her. The female Qaazamir eagles had beautiful white plumage so I think her feathers attracted him to some extent but who can say ultimately? Two beings come together and their souls…connect."

"Coming from you, Officer Barton, that's almost poetic." She gave him a teasing smile. "Can we take her to Dr. Shane?"

"We could, although Emily does veterinary work grudgingly. Only because she wasn't trained on it," he hastened to add as Karissa frowned. "But I have someone else in mind to ask for help. I've sent the shuttle pilot a message to be ready to leave as soon as we arrive and Valkyr joins us. You got the bird's papers from the merchant, right?"

"Yes, although the certificates are probably forged. I'm sorry about this."

"About what?" Perplexed, he gave her a quick sidewise glance.

"Ruining our afternoon. I know you wanted to have dinner on Calillia later and watch the moons rise. I just—I couldn't stand seeing all those beautiful rare birds crammed into the cages, destined for a life as pets. Most of them would have died soon from crowding and improper care."

He reached over to squeeze her hand. "I get it. No problem. I think we were running out of time on our anonymity anyway. I saw more than a few second and third glances from people, even before the bird incident."

He signed the CLC Line car in and waited for Valkyr to arrive, which he did fairly soon. Grant led the way to the *Zephyr's* shuttle, but he didn't breathe freely until the pilot lifted off and he was sure there'd be no repeat of the crowd scene. Valkyr sat on the seat opposite Karissa, staring fixedly at the wounded bird, crooning and occasionally ducking his head to rub his huge beak along the other bird's head. She welcomed the avian caress, arching into him and cooing her own small noises.

"What are you going to name her?" Grant asked.

"Lully." Cheeks flushed, Karissa seemed a bit embarrassed. "One of the nurses at the orphanage gave me a stuffed animal I named Lully and for years I couldn't sleep without her. Eventually she got 'lost' during laundering and the attendants said I was too big for stuffed toys. Do you think that's an acceptable name?"

Beautiful, like my mate.

"Valkyr approves."

Can he talk to her? Tell her everything's going to be ok?"

Grant realized he hadn't considered the interspecies communication aspect. *Can you?*

Not yet. Impressions only. Calming thoughts. There will be time.

"I'll buy her from you," he said. "If Valkyr is so attached to her, I hate to separate them."

"I'll give her to you, as long as I get full visitation rights."

When they reached the *Nebula Zephyr* and had thanked the pilot, Grant didn't even try to take Valkyr to the cabin where he belonged. Instead he took Karissa and both birds deep into the ship, to the hydroponics deck. He'd already asked Maeve to contact the person he was seeking.

Karissa gawked as she moved through the long trays of greenery. "I really will have seen the whole ship by the time I leave, won't I? What are we doing here?"

There was an open air office at the rear of the deck, surrounded by gorgeous rosebushes in full flower, and the woman working there paused as they approached. Wiping her hands, she came forward to greet them.

"Karissa Dawnstar, meet Tyrelle Embersson, our Special Hydroponics Officer. She's from Tulavarra." Grant hoped he wasn't going to have to give explanations about Tyrelle. Her story was complicated and not relevant to today. Much. Only her special powers.

"I attended your concert last week with my husband," Tyrelle said as the two women shook hands. "You have a lovely voice. Somewhat obscured by all the other elements of the show, but definitely one of a kind. Incredible range for a human."

"Tyrelle sings too," Grant said.

"Among other things." The woman with a nod and a sweet smile, as if she had a secret she wasn't sharing. "May I see the bird?"

Karissa unwrapped the shirt. The white bird was noticeably calmer now.

Valkyr gave a triumphant chirp and Grant had to push him back.

"Yes, your mate will be fine," Tyrelle said to the eagle. She took the songbird in her own hands, closed her eyes and hummed. Lully sat still for a moment and then flared out the no-longer-broken wing as if stretching after a long nap, spreading the wing on the other side a moment later. She stood and launched herself from Tyrelle's hands, flying in a circle around the hydroponics deck, before landing on Valkyr's broad back, where she settled with much ruffling of feathers and began to groom herself, and him.

"So now you have two birds," Tyrelle said to Grant. "Captain Fleming won't tolerate a flock, you know. And how are you doing?"

He was embarrassed to have her ask in front of Karissa. "Also better, thank you."

Tyrelle placed her hands on his temples. A cool wave spread through him as she worked her healing magic and he felt the chronic pain from the last of his war injuries dim and recede. Tyrelle's treatments with her special powers had done more good for him than any combination of conventional medicine and painkillers. Detecting a subtle trembling in her fingers, he pulled back. "Don't overdo it," he said, catching her jade green hand and squeezing gently. "Your husband will be mad at me and he's not exactly a small man."

"Yes, I had been busy today even before I got your com message. We'll do more another day. You won't need too many more treatments before the deep seated nerve problem is cured. No more pain." Tyrelle smiled.

"There are quite a few com calls for Miss Dawnstar piling up in the queue," Maeve said unexpectedly out of the thin air. "Your manager is threatening to complain to the captain about Grant and Jake is holding him off."

"I took a personal day and it's none of the bastard's business." Anger made Grant's voice unusually brusque.

"The media is probably going crazy after our day on Calillia and wanting more information," Karissa said with a grimace. "Good publicity but still…it'll scare Ted. He hates not being in control of everything I do and who I do it with. I'd better go back to my cabin and deal with the uproar."

Karissa said goodbye to Tyrelle and Grant escorted her out of the hydroponics deck.

"I have to take these two to my own cabin first," Grant said. "Come with me?"

She hesitated. "I think I'd better deal with Ted on my own. And then he'll want to go over the plans for our move to the hotel on Calillia tomorrow, and the set up for rehearsal the day after." She went on tiptoe to kiss his cheek. "Thank you for the wonderful day today."

Valkyr on his shoulder put him off balance and Lully in his hands made things even more awkward and he couldn't reach out to hug her as he longed to do. "When can I see you again?" His heart pounded at the thought she might not feel as strongly as he did about spending more time together. *Don't let this have been a shipboard flirtation.*

"Not tired yet of all the glitz of being seen with a rock star?"

"Fuck that. I'll never be tired of being with you, getting to know you better. Today was special for me. Minimum of glitz." He hated being in the corridor, even though only a few crew members were coming and going. He'd been anticipating their dinner and a chance to talk more.

"If you can get time off, come to the arena the day after tomorrow and watch the rehearsal for a while. You can bring Valkyr of course. I'll make sure an all access pass is at the box office in your name." She gave him a shy smile. "We could do dinner afterward, just us."

"It's a date," he said, leaning forward to kiss her on the lips, not caring who was watching.

As she walked away toward the passenger access portal, he added, "Promise you'll call me if you need anything before then."

Karissa waved and was gone.

FIVE

Next day he was back to his regular duties, patrolling the corridors and decks of the *Nebula Zephyr*, dealing with minor passenger problems and one issue of shoplifting in the jewelry store on Level A. He couldn't wait for his shift to end so he could rush to his cabin and view the special feed of news Maeve had collected for him from the broadcasts emanating from Calillia. Everything to do with Karissa was what he'd asked the AI for and she obliged.

He ate his reheated dinner while the trideo clips played, many of them the same shots of Karissa being welcomed home by the President of the planet, given the key to the city as she predicted. A high priest recited a lengthy blessing and a choir from her old orphanage sang. Grant saw her wiping away a tear before she hugged all the children, thanking them and inviting them to her concert.

Frustration chafed him, not to be there at her side.

He thought he recognized Leclaire, the stalkerish fan from the *Nebula Zephyr* signing, in one of the crowd scenes but even though he asked Maeve to focus in on the segment, he couldn't be sure. He did see the same two monks again, this time flanking the high priest. *I hope they're not pressing her to tour their temple again.*

To his eyes, she was doing the "Karissa act," smiling brilliantly and being self-protective. In one clip he caught a flicker of a disagreement between Karissa and Ted but as soon as the manager realized there were trideo cameras trained on him, he'd pulled her out of view, behind a group of other people.

You miss her. Head tilted, Valkyr paused in his munching on dinner and chirped, startling Lully off her perch next to his.

We'll see her tomorrow.

He'd called the arena to verify the fact rehearsals started in the early afternoon, so he arranged to be on Callilia before then, taking the regular
shuttle from the *Zephyr* to the planet, renting a groundcar and parking at
the sprawling venue. There was an all access pass waiting for him as
promised and he and Valkyr entered the arena through the staff entrance.
A giant stage had been constructed in the center of the area, and Karissa's
band was doing sound checks as he walked through.

The man you wish to keep away from your lady. In that group to the left.

Startled, Grant checked out a group sitting in the bleachers, being
addressed by some sort of a guide. She was giving instructions for their
meet and greet with Karissa, to occur shortly. And sure enough, as Valkyr
had said, there was Mr. Leclaire, sitting at the back of the group, pale and
sweating. Grant kept himself from displaying any outward signs of
unease, but he searched for a security person or member of the police to no
avail. Proceeding backstage, he cornered Desdusan. "Where's the head of
security?"

Shaking her head, she said, "There isn't one. The city detailed a couple
of cops though, for crowd control. I think you'll find them walking the
perimeter."

"Thanks. Can you tell Karissa I'm here but I have something to take
care of?"

She looked puzzled but agreed, going off with her armful of costumes.

Grant sent Valkyr aloft to keep an eye on Mr. Leclaire while he finally
located one of the Calillia police. Fortunately the woman and her partner
took him seriously after he showed them his CLC security credentials. The
senior cop promised to go speak to the fan and evaluate the risk.

"I thought Karissa's manager was going to get a restraining order on
the guy," Grant said.

The cop shook her head. "I checked the file before we came over here,
figured she must have some stalker issues, as big a star as she is. Nothing.
But if this guy is trouble, we'll get him flustered enough to be deemed a
suspicious character and eject him."

"Thanks." Grant walked backstage again, distressed by the thought he
might have kept Mr. Leclaire from being in the same room with Karissa
this afternoon but the stalker could still attend the concerts.

He went straight to the star's dressing room. When he knocked at her
door and was told to come in, he expected her to be surrounded by the
usual annoying throngs of people but there was only Desdusan and a
couple he didn't know.

Karissa was in the middle of a costume fitting, with Desdusan assisting
the designer, who was unknown to Grant. He stopped in his tracks as he

realized the fourth person in the room was a D'nvannae Brother. On closer examination, the man wore the black leather garb and had the stance and attitude of the assassin order, but not the facial tattoo. Still, he made a note to himself about the fact Karissa numbered dangerous people among her acquaintances.

She cried out with pleasure at seeing him, breaking into a wide grin. "I'm so glad you're here!" Ignoring the efforts of the two women working on her elaborate dress, she rushed to him for a hug and a kiss. Having her back in his arms was a relief, abruptly shattered by Valkyr's laconic thought.

Police taking that man away now.

Keeping her hold on him, Karissa drew back a bit. "What's wrong?"

He glanced from her to the other people in the room, unsure how much to say.

"Oh, you can speak freely. These are my friends, Twilka Zabour the designer and her husband Khevan. Twilka's the one who helped me find my own high powered attorney on the sly, so I can safely exit this onerous contract with Ted when it ends, and set up my own company to handle my rights. And Desdusan is loyal. She won't betray me to Ted."

The wardrobe mistress nodded, her lips set in a thin line. "He's treated her so badly all these years."

Grant shook hands with Twilka and her husband. "Are you aware Ted's hired no security for this event? Not for today, not for the concerts—he's relying on the local police and the arena staff. Insufficient protection for a star of your magnitude, in my opinion."

Khevan nodded. "Indeed the security is sadly lacking, I agree."

"Valkyr spotted Mr. Leclaire in your meet and greet group for this afternoon and I was able to persuade the cops to escort him out, but there's no restraining order on him. He can come right back. I'm not trying to scare you," he said hastily as she went pale under the elaborate makeup. "And I noticed the monks were at your welcoming ceremony yesterday and here in the arena again today. They worry me—I can't quite put my finger on it, but something's not right there."

"I can certainly look out for Karissa when my wife and I are here," Khevan offered. "But we're only able to stay for the first concert."

"I have commitments in the next Sector," Twilka said. "We could stay—"

"No, I know how important that gig is to you. I'll be fine. I have Grant. I do have you, don't I?"

"Of course." He kissed her cheek.

"I could arrange to have some of our affiliates take on the personal security," Khevan said, handing Grant a business card.

Karissa shook her head. "No, Ted has the total control of arrangements for three more days. Remember the lawyer said I can't risk breaching any contract terms or I might trigger the automatic extension?"

Twilka said what Grant was thinking. "Darling girl, Ted can't hold you like a slave. Even if the contract extension did get triggered, your lawyer will fight it for you. I can get you away to one of my father's estates in the Inner Sectors to wait out the lawsuit."

Karissa shook her head. "I know that and I appreciate the offer, but meanwhile Ted would have all the rights to all my music. He'd have the rights to the embodiment of me. He could even put his latest floozy on stage lip synching to my songs and I couldn't stop him. And we all know how long lawsuits drag out. Ted will fight like a wild raging beast to hang onto to his rights, if I let the contract tip over into an extension, if I give him any slightest opening."

Grant checked with Twilka for confirmation and she nodded slowly. "My father's lawyer said the interlocking subparagraphs and trigger clauses were the most pernicious he'd ever seen."

"Well then, we have to keep you safe and happy for a few more days," Grant said, giving her a small shake.

"I'm so glad I met you," she answered.

Twilka pulled at her arm gently. "I hate to interrupt this lovely moment but I have to finish the fitting so I can go away and get this gown ready for the stage. The multiple changes you want to pull off during the performance make this tricky. But I do love a challenge."

There was a knock on the door. "We'll be ready for you onstage in five, Miss Dawnstar," said a disembodied voice.

"I'll go wait out there," Grant said as the three women gasped and rushed behind a screen set up to shield the other end of the room from view. "Check things out."

He wandered the backstage area, nodding to the few people he knew or recognized from the small crew that had been with Karissa on the *Zephyr*. He saw a pile of antigrav units heaped on the table and headed over to inspect them, being familiar with the tech from his days in the service. Two performers were standing there, sorting through the units and complaining.

"Yeah, mine kept shorting out on me this morning," said one. "Gave me a heart attack."

"They haven't been maintained in oh forever, cheapass management," said the other, rejecting three of the units and grimacing at a fourth.

"May I?" Grant reached past them for one to examine. He was dismayed at how worn the height sensors were and the condition of the antigrav repulsors. "Is one of these for Karissa?"

"No, she has her own, lucky her," said the first performer. "See you up there," he said to his friend and sauntered off.

"We used to have a guy who did nothing but maintain these," the remaining performer said to Grant. "Ted fired him about a year ago. He'd probably fire half of us too, to keep costs down, except the crowds expect Karissa to have a full troupe. I'll be glad when this tour is over. I'm out of here. Got a better offer from someone else." He slung his chosen unit over his shoulder and stalked off.

Hearing the music start, Grant hastily grabbed the best remaining unit and affixed it to his own belt, just in case.

"Tell your bird to stay out of the way," the stage manager said to him as he stood in the wings.

I heard. Valkyr sounded grumpy.

Keep your eyes on her for me when she's in the air, old friend.

Karissa went past with a little wave, deep in conversation with three people.

The rehearsal was like the one on the *Zephyr*, only on a grander scale. The crew did more sound checks, various bits of choreography were tinkered with, Karissa sang fragments of songs, sometimes repeatedly. Then it was time to practice the aerial acrobatic portion of the show.

Karissa was singing and then she lifted into the air, rising high above the stage, surrounded by her aerial acrobats, all moving in precisely choreographed routines designed to frame and complement her activity. She began to drift on a leisurely tour of the arena, so all the ticket holders at a concert could say they'd seen her up close and in person, Grant guessed. She waved at the small group waiting for their meet and greet as she flew above them and blew kisses. The acrobats stayed in a concentration above the stage.

Something isn't right. She falters.

Valkyr's urgent thought was followed by two screams, one from the bird himself and one from Karissa as the antigrav unit sputtered and cut out. Grant was in the air, arrowing towards her as she spiraled down, using every bit of his military training to wring extra speed and lift from the commercial unit he'd had the foresight to wear.

Valkyr had his talons hooked into straps and belts on Karissa's costume and was exerting maximum effort to slow her fall. Slender as she was, she was too heavy for him to lift but the eagle strained to keep her from plummeting directly onto the hard floor and suffering life threatening injuries. Wings wide, he was buying time for Grant.

Praying to the Lords of Space for mercy, Grant managed to get within six feet of the pair, rising under them. *Drop her to me, before you injure yourself too badly.*

Valkyr retracted his talons and a screaming Karissa fell directly into Grant's arms. He kept his balance by the narrowest of margins and got them safely landed on the floor, where she clung to him, weeping. Still carrying her, he went to a small vehicle used by the arena staff, set her on the seat and got in the driver's side, taking her to the backstage area where a crowd waited.

"Don't move," he told her, jumping out and coming to pick her up. "Make way," he ordered the crowd. "Get a doctor—she should be checked out."

Someone ran to do his bidding. Desdusan paced with him, stroking Karissa's hair. "I was so scared."

"You and me both," the singer mumbled, clinging tighter to Grant.

Ted stood in Grant's path.

"Listen you son of a bitch, I want to see all new, top of the line antigrav units here tonight, with a certified tech to maintain them, by six o'clock. No one, and I mean no one, least of all Karissa herself is going aloft until you get the new units," Grant said to Ted. "Am I making myself clear?"

"Who the seven hells do you think you are, giving me orders?" Ted tried bluster.

"I'm the guy who just saved your singer's life. I'm the guy who'll have this show shut down for safety violations faster than you can blink if you don't get out of my way and follow my orders." Grant shouldered past the red faced manager and got them to Karissa's dressing room, shutting the door even on Desdusan.

He carried the singer to the couch and sat, with her on his lap.

She was trembling violently. "I could have died, if you and Valkyr weren't here. Thank you."

"Hey," he tilted her chin up so he could see her.

"I must be a mess," she wailed. "Don't look at me."

"All I want to do is look at you and be happy you're here, warm and safe. No more rehearsal today."

"But—"

"No buts. You need to recuperate from the shock of a near miss and I'm guessing you'll have a few pulled muscles at the least. Tomorrow, I'll be here to test the new units and the first time you go aloft, Valkyr and I'll be in the air with you, until you and I are both satisfied everything's ok." He left her for a moment to fetch an afghan on a nearby chair and draped the fabric over her as she shivered.

"From the girls at the orphanage where I grew up," she said with a watery smile, pulling the soft woven fabric more tightly around herself. "I need to do something really nice for them."

"Worry about it later. Or maybe after you're done with Ted and his bullshit." He got one of her scarves and wiped her face as clean of the smeared makeup as he could get it.

Desdusan's voice came from the door com. "The doctor's here."

"Raincheck on dinner?" he said, rising to open the portal for them.

"Tomorrow? But can't you go back to the hotel with me?"

"Of course, but only to make sure you're ok. You need to rest."

"Is Valkyr all right?"

I'm fine, wings in one piece, the eagle said when Grant asked. *My shoulder joints ache as if I'd tried to carry off a mountain gazelle.*

We'll check with Tyrelle as soon as we get back to the ship.

He waited while the doctor examined Karissa and prescribed a mild muscle relaxant, which she refused to take. "I've been to rehab twice, you must be aware of my past if you work at the arena. No drugs. I don't care how mild the meds are. I'll take a long soak in a hot bath, with special salts, do some stretches and be fine."

Grant and Valkyr followed the limousine to the hotel in his rented ground car, and then made their way to her suite, over the initial objections of the hotel staff, who weren't too sure about the giant eagle. By the time he got to her rooms, Karissa was already in the tub, modestly shielded by towering bubbles.

She opened her eyes as he came in, feeling awkward to be in her presence while she was naked, and blew a few of the bubbles at him. "Like a scene in a madcap trideo romance, isn't it?"

"I've got to get going back to the ship, but I wanted to make sure you're doing ok."

"I wish you could stay." She swirled her hand through the waters, dislodging some of the bubbles. The pillowy tops of her breasts were visible and as the bubbles drifted he got momentary glimpses of the rest of her shapely form and he could feel himself responding, all the blood rushing to his groin.

He drew a deep breath. "There's nothing I'd like more, but I don't think it's a good idea."

She pouted for a moment before grinning. "We could just talk."

"Uh huh. Or you could get your rest and be ready for tomorrow's rehearsal and the string of concerts to come," he said.

She flipped a handful of the bubbles at him. "You're no fun, Officer Barton. But I will admit I'm aching all over. Lords bless Valkyr for breaking my fall and you catching me, but even then, it wasn't a picnic."

He came to sit on the edge of the tub and took her hand, resolutely keeping his gaze focused on her face rather than the enticing expanse of skin the bubbles failed to hide. "I promise I'll be here tomorrow, we'll have dinner and then I'll stay the night, if you still want me to."

"I'll want you to, very much," she said, staring into his eyes. "It's a date."

He brought his own military grade antigrav unit to rehearsal the next day, intending to give it to Karissa if he wasn't satisfied with the new equipment, but Ted had followed orders grudgingly, and there was a stack of shiny, top of the line antigrav pads on the table backstage, zealously guarded by a tech. Several of the acrobats pulled Grant aside on his way to Karissa's dressing room to thank him for saving her, and for intervening to get them new equipment.

She was alone with Desdusan, who greeted him and left the room, closing the portal behind her.

"How are you doing today?" he asked, taking her into his arms for a kiss.

"Sore," she admitted. "I'll be taking it easy through rehearsal. You're going to fly with me, right?"

He nodded and went to inspect her new antigrav unit, lying on the couch. "I asked Maeve to do some research for me and I think I found the perfect place for dinner. A five star restaurant serving Calillia cuisine cooked in the normal way and also nouvelle style, done with ingredients from other worlds. Has great reviews."

"I should have known you'd do your research." She laughed. "I'm flattered. But will the food there be better than what we had at the family restaurant whose name escapes me?"

"Probably not. It might cost less though, considering you had to buy out her restaurant to bribe her into silence. Did you get her and her people their tickets?"

"Of course. I had Desdusan do it, rather than trust the task to Ted or his minions. Did you see the coverage of yesterday's incident?"

"Yes." He tried to keep his tone casual, not to appear upset by receiving even more unwanted publicity. "Too bad the meet and greet group was here and some of them recorded it."

"I'm told ticket sales have tripled. Ted wanted me to add a show and I said no, since the date would fall outside the contract term. People want to see if I fall again." She shivered a little.

"You won't and once a person hears you sing, they'll forget all about the macabre possibility."

He and Valkyr flanked her as she rose into the air later, and flew alongside her as she made the circle of the arena several times to get the feel of the new antigrav, and did part of her routine. When Karissa landed, she was beaming and the watching crowd of musicians, dancers and crew applauded. "So much more powerful than the old one. I feel much safer, thank you."

"There's an emergency backup so if the power on the main unit did fail, you'd drift to the ground," he said. "For once Ted did the right thing and got you top of the line equipment. After this concert tour is done, you and I should do some training. Your technique is a bit rough. Beautiful," he added hastily, "But rough."

Biting her lip, she had a strange expression on her face, brow furrowed. "After? But when does the *Nebula Zephyr* sail for her next port?"

He cleared his throat. He'd forgotten about the ship and the fact

Karissa wasn't traveling with them to the next Sector Hub. "Two days after the final concert."

"We have to talk," she said, frowning.

"At dinner." He could wait. Tonight they'd have all the time in the world to talk...and do other things. "I think you have a rehearsal to get through?"

She stuck her tongue out at him and ostentatiously pivoted to listen to the stage director. Grant took his customary place in the wings and watched, making a few mental notes of things he wanted to mention to her, not about the show or her singing of course, but mechanics of the production.

The session was about done when he heard a rising murmur of excitement and turned to see Ted strutting into the area with a large entourage, accompanied by a man even Grant recognized.

"Patric Bowdene," Desdusan said the name as if she was praying. "*The* most famous singer in the entire Sectors. And the most reclusive. How did Ted pull this off?"

"I thought he retired," Grant said.

"Well apparently Ted found a way to lever him out of his privacy."

Karissa came off stage and Ted waved her over. She was absorbed into the crowd surrounding Patric, with Ted making enthusiastic introductions before Grant could say anything, and the entire group moved off toward her dressing room.

"I'd better go," Desdusan said. "She'll need help getting out of the costume and into her dress for dinner with you."

"Which I'll bet is going to be delayed," Grant said, unable to keep a certain annoyance out of his voice. "Chances for a fellow singer to meet Patric come once in a lifetime, if ever. Tell her I understand and I'll wait outside with Valkyr, let him get some fresh air flying. When she's ready to leave she can send someone to let me know."

"Will do." The older woman moved off.

Valkyr appreciated the opportunity to do more freewheeling acrobatics than the confines of the arena allowed for, and the time passed. Grant kept an eye on the arena but from where he was standing he couldn't see the VIP parking, so he had no way to know when Patric and his massive entourage might be leaving. Finally, as the sun was setting, he called Valkyr to him and walked back inside, startled to find the place pretty much empty and the lights off. Uneasy, he hurried toward the backstage area, only to be met by Desdusan.

"They've gone," she said.

"Good. Then Karissa and I can go have our dinner."

She shook her head. "She went with them. Ted insisted. I'm sorry—she asked me to let you know."

"She stood me up?" Anger and puzzlement warred inside his head. Sensing his mood, Valkyr shifted on his shoulder, spreading his wings as if about to take flight.

Eyes downcast, Desdusan looked miserable as she nodded. "I overheard Ted saying he's gotten Patric to agree to sing a duet with Karissa tomorrow as a special guest and they needed to discuss the arrangements. I think Ted's up to something sneaky, as usual."

"She could have said no because she had a prior commitment tonight. Or invited me to join them. She and Patric could have talked in the morning. Despite that fucking contract I keep hearing about, he doesn't own her." He knew he shouldn't be venting his feelings to Desdusan but the words poured out. He took a breath to regain control of his emotions.

"I'm sure she'll call you later," the costumer said. "She knows how to reach you on the ship."

He caught her sleeve as she stepped away. "If you see her, tell her I was disappointed of course but I understood. Even if I don't, between you and me. But there'd better be a raincheck."

Nodding, Desdusan murmured agreement and walked away into the shadows.

There was no call from Karissa that evening. Grant was on duty the next day but eagerly anticipating seeing her at the concert in the evening. Surely they could catch a few private moments between the show and the after party, and make new plans.

Midmorning he was summoned to Jake's office, which was unprecedented.

"What's up, boss?"

"Take a seat." Jake nodded at the chair by the desk. "Sorry to pull you in like this but I'm afraid I've got bad news."

"Something's happened to Karissa?" Icy dread formed a ball in the pit of his stomach. Some other hazard he should have anticipated, like the faulty antigrav? He started planning how he could get to her side in the quickest fashion.

"No, she's fine as far as I know but it does concern her." Jake's face was unusually grim. "Her manager filed a restraining order against you this morning. You're not to be allowed within a hundred yards of her, no contact, and you're explicitly barred from attending any event of any size at which she is expected to be present, including her concerts."

He was sure he hadn't heard right. He was so stunned that he got a worried mental inquiry from Valkyr, roused from his nap by Grant's distress. *I'm fine, tell you later* he reassured the eagle. "You—you've got to be kidding."

Jake held out a paper. "Printed this copy off for you. Came through to the captain this morning. It's official all right."

"The captain?"

Jake nodded. "All he wants to know is there's nothing which will reflect badly on the line or the ship but we stand behind our people."

Grant let out a short, bitter laugh. "That bastard Ted couldn't even be bothered to take out an order against Mr. Leclaire after he stalked Karissa here on the *Zephyr* and showed up at her rehearsal to do another meet and greet. I saved her life and he gets one against me?"

"I was surprised. I thought things were going well between you and her," Jake said.

"I thought so too. Maybe Ted thinks I'm a threat to his control. He brought in Patric to sing with her yesterday."

"*The* Patric? As in the King of Celestial Notes?" Jake sounded a bit awed.

Grant glanced at the printout in his hand and grimaced. "She signed this."

"I saw. Man, I am so sorry."

Shoving all his emotions into a black hole in his heart, Grant straightened. "Tell the captain there's nothing for him to worry about. I acknowledge receipt of this order. Was there anything else, sir?"

"No, you can resume your regular duties."

Grant went back to the deck he'd been patrolling, barely paying attention to the passengers and crew he met along the way. The rest of the morning passed in a haze.

He spent the evening in his cabin constructing an elaborate birdbath for Lully, and trying not to think about what he'd expected to be doing. He kept hoping for a message from Karissa herself, or failing that, some word from Desdusan. The only thing to come through from Calillia was a notification from the arena his all access pass had been cancelled.

The next day was even worse, as he tried not to think about the concert, which he was legally forbidden to attend. He declined a well meant invitation from Red and his wife to join them for dinner and another from Jake and Dr. Shane to join them for drinks and a movie. He appreciated having good friends on board who were trying to keep him distracted, although he was embarrassed anyone knew so much about his private affairs.

He took Valkyr and Lully for a scheduled flight session on the hangar deck when he got off duty and while the birds cavorted and chased Maeve's drones, he sat with his back against a shuttle and tried to wrench his mind into the discipline required to meditate and cleanse the soul of adverse emotions. The ritual was an ancient one, from his planet and he'd had some success with it when he was recovering from his final career-ending set of war-related injuries but tonight the desired calm mental state refused to arrive. Moby, the ship's cat, sat beside him for a while and he found it more restful to pet her soft fur and listen to the purr.

Lully is afraid of the cat. I have assured her Moby is a friend but still she fears.

Regretfully, Grant urged Moby to go somewhere else, to her indignation, and then stood to receive Valkyr on his shoulder. Lully settled in on the eagle's back, as was her custom.

As the hangar crew filtered back onto the deck, Grant headed for his cabin, seriously contemplating getting drunk, which he never did. And certainly not over a woman. *But Karissa isn't just any woman.* Not to him.

She's a queen of the flock.

Valkyr's thought was complimentary, his next equally so. *As a warrior of Qaazamir, you deserve to fly with her.*

I may never get the chance again. But I appreciate your support. Grant unlocked his cabin and stepped inside.

The more fool she then. There are few to match what you bring to the flight.

He was surprised, as the eagle rarely made personal comments but Valkyr was already absorbed in a mutual preening session with Lully. He checked his message queue but there was nothing.

Maeve spoke on the private channel. "I've been monitoring the planetary broadcasts. Would you like me to project a realtime trideo of the concert for you?"

He wondered if the CLC Line had the remotest understanding of how much Maeve remained a military AI at heart, with civilian rules existing to be broken in favor of loyalty to her crew. He was sure Captain Fleming got it. Grant didn't answer her right away, going to the kitchen and fishing a readymade meal from the stasis cabinet, then putting it away again, not hungry. Did he want to see Karissa perform all out? Dance and sing and duet with Patric no doubt, who oozed the sexual magnetism underlying his title as king of celestial music?

Jealous much? "All right. Thank you, Maeve." Maybe viewing the concert in this way would be closure and he could mourn the relationship that never had the proper chance to become more than an unlikely friendship and move on. He quashed the tiny hope he might still hear from her, the idea their connection hadn't been so easily set aside.

The AI placed a crystal clear trideo inside the cabin, taking up every inch of space not occupied by the birds. He stumbled to the couch. "Whatever feed you're pirating here is top notch."

"The sound is enhanced as well," Maeve said.

He'd seen much of the concert in bits and pieces over the last few days but watching how the entire thing came together was something else. Karissa took his breath away when she came onstage for the first song, an actual pain in his chest at seeing her. The first half hour went by in a whirl of her older songs, loud, with a driving beat and much action from the dancers. Karissa's costumes were her usual mix of bright colors and quirky accessories, matched by her technicolor swirled hair and elaborately painted nails, each a work of art. And the shoes, with their incredibly high heels. Eventually she disappeared offstage at the end of a long set, 'disappearing' in a cloud of glittery pink smoke while the dancers and band member took center stage to fill in the time as she changed costumes. Holographic cartoon characters also danced and flew above the stage and cavorted at intervals around the arena to entertain the crowd.

Then she was back, asking the audience if they'd missed her and getting the expected roar in response. She was wearing one of the dresses Twilka had been working so hard on, metallic and shiny, sexy. She sang newer songs, engaged in banter with her crew, invited a little girl onstage…Grant was impressed at what a consummate show woman she was. He didn't care for the way the spotlight made her a perfect target if there was anyone in the arena who wished her ill. He hoped Ted had done something about banning the dangerously infatuated Mr. Leclaire.

Karissa soared into the air for the song where aerial acrobatics were required and when she finished he realized his hands were fisted and he was on the edge of the couch, as if he'd been prepared to launch himself into the air to catch her again.

She flies well. Valkyr was approving.

"You never said that to me," Grant said, half humorously.

You fly as a warrior, to do battle. She flies as a queen, all grace and elegance. She mastered her fear from the other day well.

Surprising him no end, Lully warbled along with Karissa on one slower song, a beautiful descant accenting the singer's voice. He was happy to see the bird standing tall, wings tucked and tail flared, singing her heart out. He wished Karissa could have seen how happy the rescued bird was now.

The concert ended and the crowd pleaded for an encore. When Karissa re-emerged onstage, she had Patric by the hand and the stadium went wild. Karissa invited them to give her special guest a warm welcome, Patric kissed her hand and then hauled her close for a more intimate caress. The couple launched into one of the king's classic hits, singing to each other.

"I've seen enough," Grant said.

The trideo winked out.

SIX

It required all his hardwon discipline as a soldier to fall asleep later that evening and he tossed and turned for a long time first.

Somewhere around two AM ship time, he thought he heard a voice telling him to wake up and realized it was Maeve. Sitting up, rubbing his face, he said, "What is it? Do we have an emergency?"

The AI was silent but there was a ping from his cabin portal com.

Hoping against hope he was right about who might be visiting him in the middle of the night, he hurried to the door and opened it. "You came," he said, his heart pounding in his chest.

"You—you aren't mad at me?"

He drew Karissa into his cabin, closing the portal and taking her in his arms. "How could I be?" Lowering his head, he captured her lips in a kiss he made deep and involved, the singer responding to him with passion. Her body molded to his as he held her close. When the kiss ended, he buried his face in her shiny black hair, breathing in the perfume that was hers alone. "Are you all right?" he said.

"Not how did I get here, or why did I sign the fucking order or—" Eyes wide, she stared at him, a tremulous smile on her well kissed lips.

"I missed you," he said simply, sweeping her into his arms again. "How long do we have?"

"A couple of hours. Ted thinks I'm visiting Twilka and Khevan on their space yacht but I have to be back on Calillia by noon. He's afraid to tangle with them—she's rich and influential, and he's an ex D'nvannae Brother—so when they invited me, he couldn't say no. Then Twilka had her shuttle pilot bring me over. Maeve let me aboard and gave me access to the crew decks."

"And here you are," he said, scarcely able to believe his own eyes.

She took his hand and led him toward the bedroom, stopping for a moment at the birds' perches and petting a drowsy Lully gently. "She looks so much better—her feathers are glowing."

"Valkyr is a devoted mate." Grant tugged her to continue walking. "Eagles and songbirds do fit together sometimes." Next moment he was horrified to see tears tracking down her cheeks. "Sweetheart, what is it? Am I assuming too much here?"

Karissa shook her head, wiping away the tears with her fingers. "I thought you'd be so angry and hurt. I was afraid you'd never speak to me again."

"Ted's probably fucking terrified of me and he should be," Grant said. "I hoped it was something to do with the damn contract he holds over you. I was going to be on your doorstep the moment that thing expired after the last concert and find out if you were coerced into signing the restraining order. But if you told me to my face there was nothing between us, I would walk away, you know that, don't you? If me out of your life was what you wanted."

She cried harder. "Never. I can't bear the thought of losing you."

"Shh, you won't." He picked her up and carried her into the bedroom, placing her softly on the narrow bed. He went into the bathroom and got her a handful of tissues. Sitting on the end of the bed while she leaned on the pillows, he said, "So what did happen?"

"Years ago, after the second time I went into rehab, Ted had his lawyer insert a new clause in the contract, giving him control over who I had in my personal life. To keep out the undesirables, he said, to help me stay clean and sober." She shrugged. "I agreed then because I didn't care. I never expected to meet someone like you, not in my world." She put her hand on his cheek. "You're pretty special, Officer Barton."

"The name is *Grant*." He laughed, happy to be sitting here with her, teasing each other. "I watched a trideo of the concert. Undoubtedly a terrific evening you gave your fans. Valkyr said you flew well."

Eyes widening, she mimicked shock. "I know a high compliment when I hear one. Tell him I'm honored." She went to throw the tissues away. "I wanted you to be there for the concert so badly. I'm glad you got to see it at least."

"What's the deal with Patric?"

Her face clouded over. "Ted wants me to do a tour with him. Of course I'd have to renew the contract."

"Do you want to do a tour with him?" He studied her face.

"It's every artist's dream to work with the king of the celestial notes. It could elevate a career in all kinds of ways. But no." She shook her head. "What I really want to do with my life going forward is to be able to write my own songs again, and sing them. Different songs. Songs that feed the soul. I've moved on from my 'Inner Sectors Girls' phase, fun though that was. I'm sure I'll sing the oldies again but not as much. No more huge concert tours, no more giving away pieces of myself to fans and the media."

He pulled her onto his lap. "This is the conversation we were going to have at the dinner we missed."

"Yes. I'm never going to let anyone run my life again. I'll be in control of my music and my creative choices. But I-I want a partner. Someone to be there for me. Until I met you I didn't even think such a thing was possible for me. I envied Twilka and her husband so much for what they have together."

"I don't know them, but I'll tell you what I was going to say at dinner. I know nothing about the music business but I know how to manage and organize and get things done efficiently. I wasn't always a solo operator in the service. I led teams and missions, some quite complex."

"So dinner was going to be a job interview?" Her smile was warm. "I kind of expected something else."

"Not exactly." Grant kissed her hard. "I was trying to figure out what place I could have in your world, beyond keeping you safe and making sure you were properly respected and cherished." He took a deep breath. "Beyond loving you with all my heart. A man like me has to have a purpose in life. Lack of goals, lack of personal challenge was why I've been drifting since I retired. With Qaazamir a dead planet essentially, what could I do?"

"You love me?"

"With all my heart," he repeated.

"But?"

He shook his head. "No buts. I want to stand by your side for the rest of our lives. No qualification or hesitation. But I'm not cut out to be the glorified bodyguard, not even for you. I'd have figured something out, but after I watched your two rehearsals, I knew what need I could fill."

"I want to do so many things," she said. "It'll be fun to plan together. I don't need Ted for show business management any more—he's been coasting on my success and contacts for the past five years or so, once I hit big. No one refuses my calls nowadays. And Twilka's lawyer will handle any contracts I do sign. None of which are going to touch my personal life. That's for me and you." She ran her hand up under his T-shirt. "I do have other needs, you know." Shifting on his lap, she deliberately rolled over his aching erection with her well-toned dancer's derriere.

"Oh now we're having a different conversation, are we?" He unfastened her buttons and she shrugged out of her top.

"I kinda hoped we were done with conversation all together," she said as he laid her back on the bed.

"I am if you are." Grant worked to get her pants off, throwing the garment on the floor. He took a moment to admire her lacy underwear, stroking one hand over the pink satin cups of her bra, holding her full breasts barely restrained. Running one hand down her taut abdomen and under the filmy lace of her panties, he inserted his finger into her warm channel, penetrating her folds, and massaged the sensitive bud. Leaning over to kiss her, he murmured, "So ready for me—that makes me hot."

"I've been ready for you practically since we met." Her tongue traced the seam of his lips and he parted to give her entry, even as he continued to work his fingers in and out, making her squirm under him and moan in pleasure. Karissa broke off the kiss, throwing her head back to gasp as she climaxed, going rigid under him for a moment. "Oh so that's what it's like to be a mission objective," she said with a satisfied smile.

"That was the first reconnaissance only," he said, unfastening the bra to give himself access to her breasts. Watching her face to see what pleased her, he rolled the budded nipples in his fingers and lowered his head to kiss and tease with his tongue.

"You have too many clothes on," she said after he'd played for a few moments, tugging at his shirt. "I demand equal access."

Obligingly he sat up so she could remove his shirt and then Karissa unfastened the string holding his sweatpants and slid them down his legs and off. Free of the fabric restraint, his cock jutted, ready for her attention. She licked the head as if it were a delicacy and then took him into her mouth, swirling her tongue over and along the shaft, and exerting suction so skillfully she had him bucking his hips, unable to resist the sensuous torture. He laid back, fisted his hands in the scrollwork of the headboard and let her take her pleasure as she wished. She stroked the hard length of him and then paid attention to his aching balls, rolling them in one hand for a moment, before moving on to massage the incredibly sensitive area behind them.

Eventually, she sat up, keeping one hand on his cock and running the other over his abdomen, up to his flat nipples, circling them lazily while he forced himself to keep his hands off her.

"I like having you at my mercy," she said, "But I think the game's gone on long enough." She maneuvered herself to where she could straddle him, lowering herself slowly onto his rigid shaft, inch by inch. Karissa could do things to him internally with her incredible muscles, honed by her dancing, he'd never felt before and she used those skills to drive him crazy with need as she took him into her soft warmth.

His aching cock firmly seated inside his lover, Grant's control snapped and he let go of the bed, taking her in his arms and rolling them over, still connected, so he could thrust with all his strength. Karissa laughed and put her arms around him, her lips seeking his for another penetrating kiss as their bodies moved in unison, joined in pleasure and emotion.

His climax was long and hard, and he felt her go into her own orgasm with him. He thought if he died right this instant, he'd die happy.

Karissa was a woman in a billion and she was his.

———

Eventually they came up for air, after a more leisurely lovemaking session and took a shower together in his tiny bathroom, to the accompaniment of much laughter from them both. Swathed in towels, Grant and Karissa sat jammed together on the couch and Maeve replayed the trideo of the concert for them, while they munched on special treats she'd delivered via robo server.

"Where did the food come from?" Grant asked. "We don't get service on crew decks."

"I diverted it from First Class. If anyone notices, I'll state the controller malfunctioned." Maeve was calm and cool.

"I promised to write a song just for her," Karissa said as the robo server departed. "It's going to be entitled 'Lady of the Stars', a love song." She hummed a fragment of a tune. "I've already got the melody."

Lully woke up and warbled along with the portion of the concert she'd like before, and a delighted Karissa chimed in, so Grant had her dueting in his cabin not only with the bird, but with herself.

The encore segment began.

"I didn't watch this," Grant said.

"I'd just as soon not," Karissa agreed. "Turn it off, Maeve? Patric has a beautiful voice but he's full of himself and sure he's the Lords of Space's gift to women."

"I couldn't handle seeing you in another man's arms," he admitted.

She kissed him. "Pure acting on my part. We got offstage and I gave him hell for grabbing me and groping me. He's not to do pull the same stunt again at the next concert or I'll slap him and walk off the stage." She stretched. "I'm afraid I have to be getting back."

"Will you be able to rest before the show? I shouldn't have kept you here so long but I hated to lose a single moment," he said. "You won't be able to come back."

"No," she agreed. "Twilka delayed her departure as long as she could, to let me come to you once. But she has a deadline to meet. It's going to be a long two days before I'm in your arms again."

"But then we won't have to be apart for any reason—no one and nothing is coming between us," he said. "Better for you not to take risks before then." He followed her into the bedroom to admire the view as she got dressed and put on his own clothes. "I'll escort you to the hangar bay."

"I did tell you I have my personal lawyer working on getting the restraining order lifted at midnight two days from now? Right after the contract ends? I can't do it any sooner or I would."

"Don't worry. It'll be fine. Have there been any incidents while I was out of the picture? Mr. Leclaire show up again?"

"No," she said as they walked down the crew corridor. "The monks have been ever present pests though. Ted and the high priest have been very cozy."

"What do they want?"

She shrugged. "Well the high priest wanted me to sing a special, private concert for their leadership and high ranking patrons and I said no. Maybe Ted thinks he can still change my mind. Or maybe he likes them. I have no idea and I don't care. Let him send his new little protégée to enhance their evening."

Grant let the subject drop but he made a private resolve to do what research he could on the sect. He escorted her to the private shuttle on the hangar dock and waited until she was securely inside before he left the area. No more sleep for him. He had a lot to do, beginning with a long chat with his boss, but he was happier than he'd been in years, he realized, and at peace.

Grant lay hidden in his chosen position, taken up much earlier in the day and he'd not moved since. He was as close to the artists' exit of the arena as he could get. He'd wanted to infiltrate the arena itself but Karissa had begged him not to risk anything that might give Ted an edge to extend the contract. Reluctantly he agreed, although as a former Special Forces operator, penetrating a music venue was like a simple training exercise for him. He also thought she was worrying needlessly about how much power a contract clause could possibly give the man but wasn't going to heighten her anxiety. As soon as midnight struck, the plan was she'd come out to him, or send Desdusan if the restraining order had been lifted. Then they'd be off to make their own new start, free of Ted.

He had Valkyr flying surveillance over the arena grounds, just in case, and he was listening to a vidcom of the concert in his ear piece. All had gone smoothly, no hitches in the show, no incidents, but he had that insidious little tingle in the back of his head warning him not to let his guard down.

Large group of monks leaving the building, carrying someone. Cargo entrance. They have a woman prisoner.

Valkyr's urgent thought came as the announcer's voice in his ear registered shock Karissa hadn't come out for the encore with Patric. Ted's new singer, Valma, was singing her part in the duet.

"Seven hells!" He was up and running for the cargo dock in a heart-beat, his personal blaster in hand. *Track them.*

They've loaded her into the back of a small cargo hauler.

He redoubled his speed, making a mad sprint in the open. If the monks got Karissa away from the arena he'd have a hard time finding her, although she'd agreed to wear a tracker for him, hidden in her hair ornaments. Grant threw himself into a parked maintenance vehicle, hotwiring the initiator and tearing off at breakneck speed, heading for the only exit close to the cargo bay. *Status?*

I see you. The truck moves slowly. You still have time to catch it.

Firing his blaster at the driver of the truck, who slumped in the seat as the windshield vaporized, Grant drove straight at the medium sized cargo hauler. The man riding shotgun with the driver apparently took control of the vehicle and straightened its path, again heading for the gate. Grant shot out the antigrav units closest to him, sending the truck into an uncontrollable skid, tipped on its side, and ramming the fence before coming to a halt.

He drove his own tiny vehicle to the rear of the truck. Blaster in hand, he wrenched open the door. "Hand her over."

Hands raised, braced against the tilt of the vehicle, a monk grinned at him. "Gladly."

A gagged and bound Desdusan was shoved into his arms as the monks fled in all directions.

Swearing, he lowered the woman to the grass and ripped off the gag.

"A group of other monks took Karissa," she said, breathing in harsh gasps. "I saw her get into a groundcar. Older model, black, with red trim. They headed for the main audience member exit."

Find her, he sent to Valkyr, even as he was checking the readout for the tracker, which showed a stationary target.

"Someone will come," he said to Desdusan apologetically as he rose.

"I'm fine, go on, save Karissa."

As sirens blared, he wasn't too surprised to find Karissa's elaborate wig and crown of ornaments lying on the cargo dock. Grant faded into cover and made his way to where he'd left his own vehicle, parked on the periphery of the vast lot. The police activity was concentrated on the abandoned truck at the cargo gate as he opened the back of his groundcar and extracted an individual speedcycle, built to go fast and dangerous. Buying the bike earlier in the day had used up a substantial portion of his credits, but he'd wanted to be prepared for any contingency.

The speeder was an air and ground model so he ascended straight up and took off toward the mountains. True to his word, he'd researched the particular sect paying so much attention to Karissa both on the *Zephyr* and here on the planet. The order guarded their information closely but hadn't expected to be hacked by someone with the refined skills of a military operator so he'd learned where their primary temple was located, on a mountain peak outside the city, and the information they'd been running a Thousand Year Song rumored to be close to completion. Maybe the sect snatched Karissa to sing the final verses. But why go to so much effort and risk? True, her vocal range was rare, if not almost unheard of, but couldn't any competent singer handle the song? And what did they expect to do with her after the song was complete?

He'd found the salacious tales of how in centuries long past, the ultimate singer became a human sacrifice to please the gods with his or her voice in the afterlife, but surely no one was mad enough to believe in that stuff nowadays?

While he pondered, he flew at a high rate of speed and received updates from Valkyr.

Following the car described, the bird reported. *They go to the destination you identified but the road winds. There is no other habitation in the immediate area.*

I'm going the direct route. I'll be there before they are. Recon the site, then check back on the car.

He sent an anonymous report to the Calillia authorities but without much hope of help arriving in time. If they came at all. The planetary government was pretty hands off about anything to do with the Thousand Year Song business. And who knew what Ted might be saying right now. Desdusan would give her version so obviously something nefarious was happening but would her testimony be enough to spark official action?

One is none, as his branch of the service always said, and here he was, the one person who had a chance of reaching Karissa. But he had Valkyr and no one on this planet could possibly imagine what the eagle was capable of doing. The human races had a deep seated fear of attack by a wild animal and Valkyr in full battle mode was terrifying.

Over the location now. The bird sent a visual, as he'd been trained to do, and Grant put the speedster on auto, so he could concentrate on the layout.

Can you tell where the singers are?

Grant felt Valkyr's movements as the eagle drifted over the temple, riding the thermals and searching. *Here.*

The choir was singing in an outdoor amphitheater, next to a stage surrounded on three sides by ornate pillars, with the fourth side being the sheer mountain wall, as the peak towered far above the plateau where the complex had been built. There was no roof over the stage.

Got it.

He was over the site now, drifting silently in the night sky on antigrav alone, having cut the power. *Check on Karissa.*

The car has arrived in the outer courtyard. She walks with a group of men in the direction of the singers.

He left the speedster on auto, locked into a circular staging flight, high above the temple, and flew himself to the temple using his personal anti-grav pads. As he drifted closer to the ground, he heard the choir. There was no audience and the attention of the earnest singers was locked on their director. Cloaked in his personal disruption shield, Grant landed on the far side of the stage and moved to hide behind the pillar closest to the raised dais where he believed the monks intended Karissa to stand and sing. Blaster at the ready, he waited.

They are nearly there. She walks freely.

Grant took a deep breath and consciously slowed his heart rate as Karissa came into view on the path skirting the building, leading to the stage. She and a man in elaborately decorated vestments walked ahead of the others. Two of the monks were the men he'd encountered before. She didn't seem to be under any coercion.

"Now you understand your part must begin eight beats before the choir completes the last verse?" the high priest was saying.

She nodded. "I got that. Let me sit and study the score so I'm ready."

The high priest led her onto the stage, indicating the dais with one hand. "You'll stand here, facing the mountain."

"Not the audience?" She shrugged. "Have it your way. You do understand I'm going to be pressing charges against you and your sect when this is over? I'm here under duress and if it was anything but the end of a Thousand Year Song, I wouldn't give you so much as a single note."

Don't threaten them, sweetheart. He admired her spirit but this whole setup was ominous and weird.

The priest bowed. "Again, I apologize but when our singer was killed in an accident six months ago and you repeatedly refused to help us for payment, or out of charity, we were left with no choice. The song must end properly. "

"Go away and let me warm up my voice. I just sang an entire concert, in case that's escaped your attention."

Tense, Grant waited while the official stepped a few paces away to answer a question from one of his subordinates. Seizing the moment, Grant crossed the few feet of stage between him and Karissa, placing himself between her and the monks, and decloaked. Blaster in hand, he said, "This farce has gone on long enough. Say goodnight to the lovely lady because she's leaving with me. Now."

Karissa gasped and surged to her feet. "You came!"

"And we are leaving. Stay behind me." He sent the autopilot on the speedster a subvocal command, to land in a clear space close to the stage.

"I can't," she said. "Not until I've sung for them."

The high priest's face was a study in oily triumph as he bowed his head to her.

"These people kidnapped you, and Desdusan, who got banged up but is okay by the way, and you want to stay and do them a favor?" He could hardly get the words out.

She laid a hand on his arm but stayed behind him. "It's a thousand years, coming down to tonight, to this moment in time. How can I walk away and break the song?"

"We admit our methods were wrong, but once she's sung the concluding verses, you will both be free to go, with our undying gratitude," the priest said.

Grant didn't trust his manner, which exuded superiority, or the odd glee in the man's eyes. *This guy knows something we don't.*

"You have the blaster," the priest said. "Guard your lady while she sings and then depart unmolested."

He backed up, Karissa moving with him, until they stood on the other side of the stage. He kept his focus on the priest but said in a whisper, "I don't trust this whole setup."

"I have to sing. I'm too much of a Calillian to refuse. I'm sorry—"

He shook his head. "Don't apologize for being yourself. I don't like it one bit but I'll back you. Just be ready to jump when I say so as soon as the song is done."

"Agreed." She gave him a squeeze around the waist and kissed his ear. "I need to loosen up my voice. The night air and the altitude are causing me problems."

He escorted her to the stage and stood as close as he could while she ran through scales. The choir continued to sing their part unabated, which he found unsettling. None of all this byplay, not even his waving a blaster at their high priest, had produced so much as one wrong note. The performers certainly did take their song seriously.

Karissa took a deep breath, stood straight and began to sing, softly at first as her melody cut across the one the choir was belting out, but then their harmony began to fade as the men and women performed their final notes, and her voice dominated, ringing out in the still night air, echoing off the mountain.

The high priest and six monks came to stand in a semi-circle at the edge of the stage, watching Karissa almost hungrily, Grant thought. He indicated the need for them to keep their distance with a menacing gesture of his blaster. The choir director left his podium and came to attempt to direct Karissa but she was in full flood on the music and ignored him. The choir filed out of the amphitheater, which again had Grant's hackles up as he found it unbelievable the celebrants wouldn't remain to hear the end of the Thousand Year Song.

Get ready, he warned Valkyr. *Things may get hairy.*

A mist had begun to creep across the lawn, moving onto the stage. Grant realized the hair was standing up on the back of his neck and his arms, and his nerves were tingling. His blaster felt as if it weighed a ton and he had to struggle to hold the weapon level. There were odd sounds behind him, in the direction of the mountain, and flashes of orange and electric blue light hit his peripheral vision. The monks, who were facing the cliff, as was Karissa, gesticulated and whispered eagerly among themselves.

He wished he knew how much of the song remained.

"Eons ago," the high priest said conversationally, "A race of powerful aliens used gates to visit other worlds. The Mnuc'osan technology was sound-based, harnessing harmonics and waves far beyond any understanding humankind has yet reached. Something happened on their home world—no one knows what —and many exploring parties found themselves stranded as the central power source flickered and died. On one planet, the primitive local inhabitants revered music, as it happened. A smart Mnuc'osan figured out that by sustaining and building upon a certain set of sounds for a thousand of the planet's years, enough power could be accumulated for the gate to be coaxed to open and the travelers could go home."

"Are you telling me this whole Thousand Year Song thing was started by a bunch of stranded alien scientists?" Grant asked.

The priest nodded. "Many of our party have gone home in exactly this way now, although we don't know what awaits them. Now it's my turn, with the last of my companions. But the final notes must hit certain key frequencies to activate the gate, which is why we needed Karissa so desperately when our lead singer died in an accident."

"So you were the ancient 'gods' the Calillians sang to appease?"

Grant observed the priest had lost a bit of his human form, the face elongating, the body growing taller and thinner. He blinked hard to keep his focus against the forces in play and the assault from the song Karissa was valiantly singing.

"Apparently the superstitious natives thought it was a religious pursuit. We of course had to hide our true purpose. And our identities. As the planet became more civilized, it was essential to maintain a society structured to revere and continue the singing, even when there was no longer any belief in the gods."

He and four of the other monks were definitely transforming into wraithlike beings as Grant watched. The remainder of the group stayed human, barely paying any attention to the conversation between Grant and the high priest. He heard one man murmur, "Heaven" as he pointed at the mountain wall.

The wraiths began to drift past Grant, toward the mountain. He moved closer to Karissa, stepping onto the stage with her, and checked the mountain with one rapid glance. A portion of the solid stone had transformed into an oddly shaped, gaping maelstrom of mist and colors.

"What happens to us when you've gone?" asked one of the human monks plaintively.

"I neither know nor care," said the wraith.

Karissa grabbed Grant by the arm, fingers digging into him and sang a few more notes, ending on a high crescendo, holding the final bell-like tone for an impossible time. She rocked on her heels as she finished, and Grant caught her as she stumbled.

The wraiths flowed into the gate she'd opened for them as if sucked into a vacuum, attenuating as they streamed past the stage, partially obscured by the mist.

The wraith who'd been the high priest in his previous form paused, swirling around them in a dizzying wave of colors, accompanied by an oddly putrid scent. "Your manager expected us to kill you. This was our bargain with him. Ted said he was the beneficiary of your life insurance and your will when it came to your intellectual property. Petty human concerns." The wraith laughed and the sound was discordant in such an eerie way that Grant had to fight not to blast it with his weapon, fearing to do so would have no effect and might trigger some kind of deadly vengeance by the uncanny alien. "But you served the Mnuc'osan interests well this night, and as I am the last to leave this benighted planet, there's no need for further secrecy. You may live. The knowledge is yours, if you survive what comes."

With a shriek of high speed wind, the wraith spun away from them, plunging into the heart of the gate as if it had no further power to resist the summons from its home.

One of the monks screamed and ran after the being, entering the eerie mists in the heart of the mountain.

"You promised us heaven," cried another as he too ran stumbling after his fellow. He fell into the still swirling colors and vanished from view with an anguished shriek.

Now the rest of the monks crowded forward. Grant grabbed a dazed Karissa and sprinted for the speedster.

There was a small explosion of sound, colors streaming all around them in such density Grant was blinded for a moment, although he kept moving forward, carrying Karissa. He heard screams and groans as he literally ran into the speedster with such force he knew he'd be bruised later. Vision clearing a bit, he helped her take a seat in front of him and then he was lifting off into the air, even as a group of men ran toward them, cursing and begging her to sing more.

"We need the gate to heaven," one yelled. "It must reopen. We were promised forgiveness for our sins and a life in paradise."

"Take it up with your masters," Grant yelled. "The Thousand Year Song is done."

He took the speedster aloft in a wide swoop over the plateau and risked a glance at the place where the gate had been. Part of a man lay at the base of the mountain slab, as if he'd been cut in half trying to escape when the gate closed. Karissa averted her eyes.

Valkyr swooped down to fly next to them. *The mountain rumbles. My winged brothers have abandoned the heights and flee.*

Sure enough, a broad swath of the sky was obscured by huge flocks of birds, all streaming away from the mountain, just as he, Karissa and Valkyr were fleeing. Grant heard a loud rumble behind him, growing louder until it filled his ears and drowned all other sounds, leaving him temporarily deaf. He banked the speedster and watched as the entire face of the mountain detached and slid away in the blink of an eye, taking the temple and the road and everything else with it. The dust cloud boiled toward them and Grant flew as high as he dared pushing the engine to give him all the power it had as he set a course to escape the disaster zone.

Eventually he landed in a clear spot, on a swath of green pasture, and lifted Karissa off the speedster to hold her tight.

"I was there and I can't believe it," she said. "No one else will either."

"I guess they opened their gate once too often," he said.

"I wonder what the Mnuc'osan found when they got home, if they got home?"

"We'll never know." He gave her a hug and a kiss. "But we are going to file all the criminal charges we can think of against Ted for plotting attempted murder while concocting this scheme with the monks. I recommend we don't explain the alien connection."

"Not at all?" She frowned. "Not even to the Sectors authorities?"

"I have certain contacts from my Special Forces days—I'll give them a heads up, but it seems the active threat is over. And Calillia can go on with its tradition of the Thousand Year Songs as a tourist attraction, no harm, no foul, right?"

"Right." She sighed. "Nowadays no one actually believes the songs bring good luck or favors from the gods."

"So can I be seen publicly with you, my songbird?"?" Grant grinned.

"My lawyer sent me a message right before the last set of the concert. We're all clear, the contract expired and the restraining order is cancelled too. You do realize we'll never be free of the media scrutiny, the fan interest?"

"I accept the challenge," he said. "It's the price for being with you and loving you. And once I'm in charge of security and other arrangements, the situation will be a lot more controlled. Less chaos. More privacy."

Valkyr landed on the speedster and chirped.

Karissa reached out to stroke his head. "Thank you," she said. "Thank you both."

"Where to now?" Grant asked. "Your hotel?"

"Can we go home? To the *Zephyr*? I know we can't stay there long term but it feels safe to me, cozy."

"You're the rock star who can afford to buy an entire hotel and you want to sleep in my tiny bachelor officer's cabin?" He laughed.

She wagged her finger. "Not a bachelor any more, Officer Barton."

Lully will be worried. We should go.

"The name is Grant," he whispered, pulling her close, right before he kissed her.

Karissa's final concert on Callillia was a sellout. Hastily arranged as a charity event, to raise funds for the orphanage where she'd grown up, as well as to benefit the surviving victims of the mountain landslide, which wiped out several villages, the performance was as smooth as Grant could make it. Twilka connected them with an experienced producer and many of the other performers donated their time and expertise.

Ted had left the planet, right ahead of the Sectors-wide warrants being issued for his arrest.

Grant stood in his usual spot backstage and watched as his beloved sang her heart out on one of her classic hits. Then she changed pace, telling the audience, "I've been writing new songs, inspired by being home on Calillia again, and other life events." She glanced at him and blew him a kiss as the band went into the first notes of what people in the know felt was going to be her next mega hit.

Alone in the spotlight, her black hair flowing and her dress a marvel of layers of iridescent silk in many colors, sprinkled with glowing points of light like distant stars, she sang about an eagle and a songbird brought together by destiny, kept apart by forces beyond their control, yet fighting to be together, united in their unshakable love.

She wears my feathers in her hair. Does she know the Qaazamiri meaning when a woman wears such a token from a warrior and his eagle?

Valkyr's voice in his head sounded amused.

"She does," Grant said.

Good.

Karissa rose slowly into the air, her antigrav the best military grade unit available. Her dress swirled gracefully around her. The spotlight caught Valkyr and Lully as the birds flew with her, the three of them twining in an intricate aerial ballet that complemented her lyrics perfectly. Lully sang full throated, her notes accenting Karissa's in an impossibly perfect harmony.

As she sang the final note, the light went out and Karissa descended to the stage amid the thunderous applause and cheers of the crowd. Grant was on the darkened stage to catch her in his arms and they were kissing when the lights came up again.

The songbird and the eagle, together for the world to see.

TIME TRAP

A Project Enterprise Story

By

Pauline Baird Jones

Pauline doesn't love reality, so she writes perilously fun books mixed with romance and humor.

http://paulinebjones.com

ONE

Master Sergeant Briggs—yes, he had a first name, but only his mother had ever used it—stared somewhat balefully at the crate delivered to him by the lowliest Airman currently stationed on the so-secret-they-weren't-even-supposed-to-think-about-it Garradian outpost. No one had wanted to be the one to bring it to him. Rumor was, there was a no-fly zone over his "recuperation sector." What a bunch of wimps. So he was kinda grouchy about being side-lined for his *health*. And turning a year older.

Who wouldn't be? Jeez, he'd been banished to a freaking hut. So he'd gotten shot. It was a graze. That maybe got an alien infection, but he'd kicked that to the curb. And what do they do? They park him on a bay overlooking a freaking ocean. It was hot, but it wasn't the heat bugging him. It was all this freaking fresh air. Like he was some kind of beach bum or suffering a mid-life crisis, instead of a guy who lived and died for planes and spaceships and the motors that made them move. His lungs needed engine fumes, not tropical breezes. He needed work, not a birthday present.

He glared at the crate. It didn't flee. Just sat there. Only two people he knew would be brassy enough to send him a birthday present, especially right now.

Sara Donovan and Doc Clementyne.

He could hear them laughing all the way from the Milky Way. They wouldn't be laughing when they turned forty five. Five years to fifty. How the hotel did that happen? He wasn't supposed to get older if he took a trip to a galaxy far, far away. He was pretty sure someone had promised him he'd get younger if he signed on the dotted line. Or if not younger, then that he wouldn't get older. Some kind of paradox or something.

About to stomp away from the crate, he hesitated. Donovan and the Doc did know him pretty well. Were they busting his chops? Or sending him a lifeline?

If they didn't want to drop and give him twenty when he got back to Earth, there'd better be something interesting in there. He pulled out his army knife—one on steroids—and selected a chunky blade. He applied this—with force—to the nails holding the lid down. Yanked the lid back and tossed it aside. There was a note on top of the straw. At least they'd been smart enough not to send him an actual birthday card.

We found this in the Area 51 garage sale and immediately thought of you.
Cha-cha-cha,
Donovan and Doc (and their significant others)
P.S. According to the files, this was collected on 2789645. Ring any bells?

Area 51 garage sale. He chuckled. He should have known. Those two did know the way to make his engineer's heart happy. He dug through the straw, tossing it aside. The late afternoon wind would clear it away. The wind was like the tide. It came. It went. Every freaking day. Weren't even any damn birds chirping on this blasted place. What kind of island didn't have birds?

His hand struck metal, he felt around for the edges, and lifted it clear. Heavy little sucker. It pulled at his wound, but he ignored that and carried it over to the rough table he'd built on his second day of exile, using some of the driftwood washed in by foxtrot tide. The base doc could tell him to take it easy, but she couldn't make him do it. If he'd had the parts, he'd have given the table an engine. And driven it back to the base.

He set the big disc down on top of the table and stepped back to study it. Not exactly promising. Looked like a manhole cover. Maybe those two were jerking his chain. Only his knowledge of Donovan and the Doc kept him from heaving it into the surf.

And the fact that Area 51 did not save manhole covers, not even for garage sales.

2789645? Actually that did ring a few bells.

He pulled up the stool he'd also made, and considered the item, rubbing his chin thoughtfully. If memory served—which it might not now that he was so foxtrot old—that was the first planet they'd dropped a team on back in the early days of Project Enterprise, when they weren't sure any of it was going to work.

The planet had had a barely habitable atmosphere, some algae that only excited the botanists and this. The geeks had studied it for a while, but had lost interest when it didn't do anything. No one had asked him to look at it then, and he'd had other priorities, so he didn't care.

Now? He might care a little.

He'd gotten that desperate.

Why had they sent him this thing? Something about it must have interested them. He leaned back wondering how they got their hands on it, and then how they got it to him for his birthday—all without getting him or themselves flagged and hauled in to explain. Until he remembered who they were. Alone, those two were dangerous. Together? Lethal. He liked that about them. And they could dance. He'd always hoped to find a permanent dance partner—but he didn't hang out in the right places for that kind of woman.

He sighed. Reached out a finger and flicked the edge of the metal. He wasn't worried about touching it. If there'd been any danger in touching it, someone would already be dead. Or turned into an alien.

It was thicker than a manhole cover. No sign of a seam on the sides. He ran his hands across the top. It was rough, mostly from mild corrosion, he decided. His fingers found indentations that could be an alien version of screws or bolts. He lifted it up and studied the rim, rolling it left, then right. Lines were cut in the rim, not unlike a coin, but then his fingers found two depressions, side by side. He pushed them both. They gave, but nothing happened. Not a surprise. The geeks had probably done that much. He pulled out his cheaters—one of those gifts that keep on giving for crossing into over-forty range—and studied the rim. Was there a seam?

He turned it over. The bottom was dotted with multiple ovals that formed a circular grid across the surface. He touched one of the holes. It indented about an inch. He felt around. Was that wiring he felt in there?

"What do you do?" he muttered. The wind and the tide didn't know.

Time to see if he could open this bad boy up. Be nice to put one over on the geeks of Area 51.

TWO

They dropped through the time tunnel in a dark rush, the landing a jolt that shook Madison all the way from her toes to the top of her head. Good thing she knew how to stick a landing. She didn't move and thought she wasn't breathing until her nostrils filled with the pungent scent of cleaning supplies and the dust their arrival had stirred up. With her knees still bent from the landing, she wiggled her nose, trying to head off an errant sneeze.

The fear of getting shot helped. This was their most vulnerable moment. It took a few seconds for all the molecules to settle, during which they were an easy target.

When no one shot them, she eased her weapon free and flicked it to stun. She wasn't supposed to kill people for fear of messing up the timeline. But they could kill her. So not fair.

After another moment of assessing silence, she pulled out her handy little scans-for-almost-everything device with her other hand, and flicked it on. The scanner had a fancier name but even its initials were too long to remember. With her weapon extended, she lifted the scanner up next to it and studied the faintly glowing screen, looking for something she might have to shoot, well, stun. No other life signs, at least in the immediate vicinity. She adjusted the settings with her thumb, scanning wider. No one but them so far.

Of course, the opposition could be wearing a fancy heat-blocking suit, too. But for now the intel that had sent them here looked to be decent. She didn't let herself get optimistic. There was still a lot that could go wrong.

Sir Rupert's claws dug into her shoulder, as he poked his beak up out of his specially designed-for-him backpack. He wasn't good at whispering, so he used his claws to ask for an update. She felt the soft brush of feathers against her neck and lifted her index finger, her signal for "just a minute." She changed the settings again, this time scanning for threats inside this room. Found nothing, which would be one of the reasons she'd chosen to arrive here. Even the tightest security types didn't think about teching up the janitor's closet. Not that they really needed to double down in this room when this outpost was thick with beyond-the-latest in protection and detection technology—if their intel was right.

There should be—yup, there they were. The master security feed wires ran into, and out of, a box in the corner of this room. This would be the other reason she'd chosen to arrive here. One really didn't want to land in a motion-sensor-rich zone to take out, say, the motion sensors.

She navigated around a bucket, then a mop. Man, you'd think people would come up with a better way to clean in the future.

She scanned the junction box for alarms, then felt along the sides with her fingers—she liked to use high and low tech—and when she was satisfied there were no trip wires, she shone her light on what looked like a keyhole. She looked closer. Amazing. It was a keyhole. She shook her head, pulled out a lock pick, and popped it open. The guts were high tech again, so she used her handy dandy line-tapping thingy, and soon she was looking at the station's video feeds on a small screen. She shifted between the various views, looking for signs of trouble. This station was, according to the intel, a kind of safe house and time travel research center.

As she studied the feeds, she also noted the arrangement of hallways, sleeping areas, offices, a couple of labs, the arrival and departures room, and the inevitable time command center. It pretty much matched the map she'd been given prior to her briefing, and according to her time chronometer, she had nailed her time landing.

She gave herself a mental thumbs-up because her hands were full.

Once she was sure of her route, she fired up the recording program, just in case anyone was monitoring this particular time. While that was doing its thing, she went into the guts of the programming, studying their scanning and blocking tech. She wasn't a geek, but thanks to good briefings, she played one during time ops. She frowned. It wasn't at the level she'd been told to expect. A niggle of unease created a nagging, unreachable itch between her shoulder blades. If she could have, she'd have flashed out right then, but how did she explain the niggle to the very tough new guy, who probably had something to prove since he'd just been promoted?

Still uneasy, she turned off anything she couldn't false feed, then started her recordings looping. It was kind of old school, but Madison was really old school. And she liked to throw in curveballs so the opposition couldn't get a good file on her. Being predictable was the kiss of death in the time travel biz.

She went super high tech on the motion sensors. Motion sensors were evil. And sneaky. The motion sensors were easier to mess over than she'd expected, too. Her niggle went up a notch.

Sir Rupert must have felt her stiffen. He emerged from his pack and perched on her shoulder so he could ruffle his wings. "Well?"

"Too easy," she told him. Of course, there was no way to know if anything she'd done had worked until they opened that door. At that point they'd either get shot or not. Their geeks could jump forward in time and get the latest devices, but so could the Time Service. It was a quiet battle of wits fought across the whole canvas of time, though neither side culled much tech from early in time. Wasn't much call for catapults in a time outpost, or anywhere else she'd been. Though she remained hopeful. In her opinion there was something kinda majestic about hurling large objects long distances.

"One or two niggles?" Sir Rupert asked.

They might have done a few too many ops together. "I'm up to two."

"Tell me when you hit three," he said.

"Roger that."

For a parrot, he had some big, brass ones. And like her, he knew that so much access to so much tech meant these outposts were getting harder and harder to crack, even with good intel from their spies in the Service. They both knew that the quality of the intel had been declining. Hard to pinpoint exactly when with time travel in the mix. All that bouncing around in time, sometimes she forgot what she knew and when. It was the new guy, a former security chief on a space station, who had figured out they had a mole. Which could mean their spies had been erased or reprogrammed.

She closed the panel and turned toward the door but wasn't quite ready to cross the space between. She reminded herself this intel was supposed to be solid as a rock—one traveling through space and time. Which meant it was solid until it wasn't.

She still had doubts about a mole, or so Madison had heard, but *She* must have approved the mission. Madison also knew that the details had been tightly controlled. Only Madison, Sir Issac, the new guy, and *She* knew about it. Even the geek who'd talked her through the tech didn't know when or where they were headed.

And Madison was the only one who had picked the exact time and place. Knowing that didn't help the niggle, in fact, it made it worse, but not quite to a level three yet. Had Madison somehow given them away? She trusted everyone but *She*, but not because Madison thought *She* was a mole. It was *She's* utter ruthlessness that made Madison uneasy around her. It was probably a good quality for a Rebellion leader, but it did make a lowly minion uneasy. Madison could admit that this prejudice could also have something to do with when she'd been born, at a time when heroes beat the bad guys by being heroic instead of ruthless.

She hesitated, trying to pinpoint where her uneasy originated from. Madison had been told it was almost impossible to jump back in time and change the outcome of an op—there was even an equation for it. But "almost" wasn't for sure, and that didn't mean the opposition hadn't learned how—or that *She* would tell her minions if the opposition had closed that loophole. Frankly, the way both sides had agents bouncing around in time, it was miracle they didn't collide in transit.

So Madison had two rules. She never believed everything she was told, and she always expected the worst—without going full on pessimist about it. More in the vein of "it was what it was," with a little of "what will be will be" thrown in there.

She'd escaped the Time Service agents more than once because of her rules.

And because she believed the niggles in the middle of her back.

According to their intel source, the mole had been, or was here on this outpost right now, only in another time. Dwelling on him being here, but not *here*, made her head hurt. She worked better without a headache. The science said that because all of time was aligned somehow—blah, blah, complicated equation—there were echoes, that these echoes could bleed through both time and space. There were certain species that could perceive these echoes. Wasn't it a nice coincidence that Sir Rupert was one of those species?

All they had to do was get in, let him look around, and leave without getting captured or wiped out of existence by the Time Service.

Easy peasy.

In other words, just another day—or millennium—in the Rebellion.

She realized Sir Rupert had left her shoulder. He was standing in front of a large disc that had been propped up against the wall, partly concealed by some cleaning paraphernalia.

"I haven't seen one of these for, well, for a very long time."

Madison directed her pinpoint beam at it. "What is it?"

"It's a transport pad. This is the precursor to the time travel launch pads."

"Seriously?" She shouldn't take the time, but they were in what the geeks would call a minor time flux. Which meant they had lots of time until they didn't. She joined the bird, running her light over what looked like a manhole cover. "You've gotta be kidding. Who had the nerve to use that thing?"

Sir Rupert regarded her with some amusement in his dark eyes. "I did."

"Oh. Well." She grinned. "No one ever said you lacked nerve."

He ruffled his wings, like he might be pleased.

"Let's get going," he said. He fluttered back up onto her shoulder, and worked his way back into the pack, his moment of nostalgia for the good old days over.

"You're the boss," she said, then added. "Keep your beak down." Maybe if he dug his claws into her niggle, it would go away. Or at least give it a nice scratch. She activated the door and when it slid back, she peered out. The silence—and lack of shots fired at them—were somewhat reassuring. She stepped out and turned left, padding silently down the hall toward the command center.

THREE

Briggs fitted the outside cover back in place. It had been an interesting exercise getting it open. A mix of WD-40 and a magnet did the trick. Sometimes you had to go low tech on high tech crap. The interior had been interesting. Not as interesting as an interstellar engine, but better than an inanimate table.

He was pretty sure he'd found the break in the wiring—some duct tape fixed that—and then he'd traced said wiring back to what had to be the on/off switch on the outer rim. The power source had been the most interesting thing about the disc. Even almost depleted, it looked like it packed a lot in a small space. He'd almost taken it out—that would interest the geeks more than anything about the disc—but he wanted to see if he could turn the sucker on first. If he could get one over on the geeks at Area 51, well, that would be his second birthday present.

He tightened everything down, then turned it over so the dots were facing up. He had his cellphone—he couldn't phone home, but they'd launched a small satellite because the geeks missed being able to text—set up to record some video. Geeks always wanted proof. He adjusted it using the selfie stick he'd gotten as a joke gift at the Doc's bachelor party. This he'd rigged into a crude tripod. Now he carefully zoomed it in on the disc and turned on recording. He circled back to the device, careful not to block the video. He looked at the camera, he should probably say something, but he was better with tools than words. Didn't they say pictures were worth more anyway? He depressed the switch on the side and stepped back.

This time something happened.

There was a low hum that slowly built to just shy of annoying. He heard the moveable parts inside start to move. First one of the dots turned faintly red, then red flowed across the top of the disc. More humming and moving parts sounds, and the circles turned from red to green all at the same time, sending beams of green light toward the sky at least six feet in the air.

Interesting. Still not sure what it did.

He was tempted to stick a finger into one of the beams, but he knew better. Funny how knowing didn't stop the wanting.

Oh, the human condition.

He looked around, found a stick, and carried it back to the beams. He poked it into one of the green lights. The stick glowed green, but nothing happened for a count of three, maybe four, then the end of the stick vanished.

Okay. Birthday present number three. Got to keep all his fingers. And he now knew this thing did something. Wasn't sure what, but something. He went and shut off the video, then turned back to do the same to the disc, but right then the hum increased in intensity and the green lights began to pulse.

FOUR

Thanks to a sudden increase in her niggle—and a minor change in airflow —Madison ducked before the first shot sizzled past where she'd been standing. Crouched behind a control panel, she fired back and was already changing position before that shot reached the other side of the room. She might have heard a muffled thump, as if someone had dropped to the floor. Hopefully it was not of their own free will. Fire was returned where she'd been, then tracked to each side.

That would be why she kept moving.

Sir Rupert, who had poked his beak out of the pack so he could use his super power, now ducked back down, so far it felt like his claws were digging into her rear. The pack had some deflective qualities, which she hoped they wouldn't need.

Memo to self: if it niggled like a trap, it was probably a trap. It could be a fluke, she reminded herself. Maybe someone dropped in and found everything off. Bad luck happened, too. It wasn't always a trap. Only time would tell which it was, an irony she wished she had time to appreciate.

She got a dig in the back, which meant Sir Rupert thought it was time to go.

Good idea, might be hard to make happen. She didn't have time to check, but she had a feeling all the station's stuff was back on. Supposedly this suit would mask their location and could do an emergency flashout even with blocking tech deployed, but a failed flash out would mark her position for them like a big arrow in the sky. Not even she could tumble and dance herself out of the kind of fire that would attract. And—there was that thing about not believing everything she was told. A stench was growing around this op that was making her question everything. But Sir

Rupert would have told her immediately if the mole was in the op information chain.

They might still be able to jump out from the closet, if they could get there. Unless that gap had been left open on purpose, a gap in coverage designed to lure them in. All roads led to this being a trap, but that should have been impossible. As if she hadn't learned that the impossible was only impossible until it wasn't.

She kept her body between Sir Rupert and the incoming—he was more important than she was—as she began to retreat along the shortest route back to the closet. And—this is why she got picked for these missions—as a former gymnast, she knew how to move in ways even highly trained Time Service agents didn't expect. She initiated an intricate and random series of tumbles, leaps, and rolls—careful to keep her pack from coming close to touching the ground, or any other objects, or being exposed to enemy fire. Music in her head helped, though she missed hearing the real thing.

As opportunities presented, she fired back and even went high at one point. No one ever expected that. She fired down on them from some kind of file cabinet, and then dropped down, using it for cover while she got her bearings.

Lots of shots incoming. And they were blue, which meant they were trying to stun her. For now. But the color of the shots told her something else.

This was a Time Service Interdiction Squad. Their best and brightest. Could it be Boris out there—she shut that thought off at the root. *Don't go there.*

If they caught sight of Sir Rupert, they wouldn't settle for knocking her out. They would not risk him getting off this outpost with what could be in his head. Would their scanning be able to separate his profile from hers? The pack was supposed to prevent that, too. But...oddly enough, sometimes the super tech got too sophisticated for its own good and missed the small stuff. Like a parrot. She would have liked to figure out what gave them away—apparently still hoping this wasn't a trap—but she was too busy dealing with what was.

She had a slight edge, or so she hoped. Unlike many of the other rebels, she'd never been a Time Service agent, so their intel on her should be limited to those scans taken during past ops, which varied based on the sophistication of the tech used at the time. With time travel in the mix, she never said never. But at least they'd never had a chance to dig around inside her head. People could try to be unpredictable, but they tended to be unpredictable in ways that sophisticated tech could predict. Yeah, another equation.

She reached the hallway opening and flattened against the wall in a low crouch, angled so that Sir Rupert was protected as much as possible.

She felt the vibration as more station systems came online. Didn't have time to see if they'd found her video loops. She was pretty sure they'd be able to track her soon, if they weren't already.

Just in case they weren't, she dug in her pocket for one of the pebbles she invariably kept there for moments like this, and tossed it well away from where she wanted to go. It clinked against the metal floor and a flurry of shots crisscrossed the spot. Still blue.

The volume of shots confirmed her suspicion she was up against a squad. Kind of flattering. In a not wonderful way.

None of the shots had come from the door she wanted to go through. Apparently she was supposed to just dive through. Because the best and brightest the Time Service could muster would leave one door unguarded.

She did a crouching roll across the opening—she did have a bird on her back—and fired multiple rounds through the opening, laying down a wide spread to clear her path ahead, then she was up, following her fire down the hall. It was a nice narrow hallway with no alcoves to hide in. Hopefully the hostiles on her heels would be just far enough behind to give her time to get to the closet.

The doors lining the hall were all metal, so any that were partly open she lit up as she ran past. Amazing how hot a metal door got from even one energy blast. Her weapon wasn't set to stun. Not anymore.

She heard cursing, and at least one body hitting the ground. Shots came from behind now, tracking after her like angry bees. She was still doing her gymnast thing, but the hallway was narrow. She needed to get out of it and fast. She returned fire from a low position, her flip taking her into the shallow protection of the closet door. Her shoulder was out just far enough to catch a blast that almost spun her away from the door. That wasn't a stun. But not a kill shot either. She staggered from the hit and pain, but managed to stick it. Sir Rupert gave a soft squawk.

"You hit?" She pressed in closer, angling to protect him, fired off some shots and hit the control to open the door, ignoring the pain spreading out from her shoulder and trying to cloud her thinking.

"No."

She fired another spread, then the door opened at her back, and they were inside the closet. The door closed and she fired on it, aiming at the handle and hinges until they glowed bright red. Only then did she reach up and try to flash out.

Not a huge shock when they didn't.

Might be damage from the hit, but most likely the opposition closed the hole they used to get in. Also meant their intel on the suit was wrong. Or they'd upgraded for it already, but—

"Blocked?" Sir Rupert asked, making his way back to her shoulder.

"Yeah." She should have tried to jump sooner—

"They locked this place down before they started firing," Sir Rupert said, as if he knew what she was thinking. Which he probably did. He was that smart. He didn't waste time bemoaning the failure of the suit to perform as advertised.

Multiple shots made the metal door rattle in its frame. They had maybe thirty seconds. Probably less.

"The transport pad," Sir Rupert said.

"Why did I know you were going to say that?" Had she had the same thought? Was that why she'd retreated here? Sometimes if felt like even she didn't know what she was thinking. She crossed to it and started to lower it.

"Not that side."

"Heavy bugger." She flipped it over, wincing as pain flared brighter in her shoulder. She blinked spots away, kicked the bucket and mop to the side so there'd be room for it to lay flat. She glanced back. Red spots were appearing on the metal door. Spots that glowed and expanded as the metal began to melt.

"Turn it on here." Sir Isaac's beak touched the spot, then he hopped on the device.

She depressed the spot. There was a hum, but it felt like a long time before the circles turned red.

She glanced back again, maybe ten seconds, and they'd be through. She pointed her weapon at the door, preparing to take a stand if she had to. Sir Rupert was the one who had to escape. She took a quick look back, but he was gone. Just a pattern of green beams shooting up from the disc and piercing the ceiling.

"Man, I hope you know where we're going."

A pinhole opened in the door, growing rapidly as they concentrated fire on that spot. The shots were red now. One red beam skimmed by her other shoulder as she scrambled onto the device. The door burst open, weapons firing at, and sparking off, the green beams—then the room vanished in a tunnel that was both familiar and not familiar. Just a transport pad, she reminded herself, but the ride felt like more than that. It was beyond rough. She tumbled and bounced around in the tunnel. Saw the white light coming and tried to slow down. Couldn't. Tried to aim for the center. Didn't think she'd nailed it.

She might be about to find out about catapults, though....

The transit sped up. Wasn't going to stick this landing. Be lucky she didn't break something. With a spin she flew head first through the center of the circle of light....

FIVE

Something catapulted out of the green beams of light like it had been hurled, something that squawked loudly as it tumbled beak over claws, just missing Briggs' head. The spinning tumble continued unchecked toward a stand of palm-like trees. Somehow it recovered, made a narrow pass between two tree trunks, then circled back to a landing on the peak of the cottage. It ruffled its feathers as if annoyed, then began to preen itself.

A parrot? He blinked. The green body, with a band of red just above the beak looked parrot-like.

"That's not something you see every day." Particularly in this birdless place. Too bad he'd already turned off the video. No one would believe he really saw a parrot shooting out of that thing.

The bird looked up and Briggs had the odd feeling it had understood him. He'd heard parrots were pretty smart. He glanced back at the disc. At least now he was pretty sure it was some kind of a transport pad. Definitely needed to get the power supply out—

He heard the hum build again and turned fully around, just in time to catch what flew out next. Instinctively his arms wrapped around the very humanoid—very female—form it ejected. He staggered a few steps and then went down. The sand was harder than he'd have thought. His breath rushed out as they slid toward the water, his arms still wrapped around the woman.

When they hit wet sand, they slowed, and finally stopped. He felt water soaking into his shirt and heard the waves hitting close to his head. Took him a couple of tries before he could grab some shallow breaths. Each one was filled with the smell of salt, woman, and singed something.

He could feel the female struggling to catch her breath, too. Yeah, she was definitely female. Almost every inch of her was pressed against a lot of him, creating a different problem in catching his breath.

In the sudden silence, the bird squawked once.

Over on the table, the disc's beams flickered, there was a popping sound from inside, and it went dark, smoke puffing out the holes on the top. Great. Now he didn't even have a depleted power supply to show the geeks.

"Ow."

Her voice was pained, but, well, nice. She took a couple of deep breaths that increased Briggs' male holding a female problem. He wasn't as old as he'd thought. He would have shifted her off, didn't want it to get embarrassing, and he would like to catch his breath, but the thing digging into his ribs felt a lot like some kind of gun. If she twitched wrong...

She muttered something that could have been a cuss word.

"...that hurt."

It was something of a relief she spoke very American sounding English, but also a worry. What was she doing on this top-secret outpost? He'd bet real money this was not what Donovan and Doc had had in mind when they sent him the disc to play with.

The weapon retreated as she rolled off him and onto the sand. She didn't get up, just lay there staring at the sky, her chest rising and falling quickly.

He yanked his gaze off her chest and sat up. Only, the changed angle made her harder to see. Was that some kind of high-tech camo? If it was, it was damaged. One second she was part of the horizon, next he could see her very nicely put together figure encased in a black suit.

She muttered again but all he heard was, "...buggers shoot better than I thought they could..."

She lifted the hand holding the weapon, then looked at it as if surprised to find it in her hand. It was impressive she'd kept hold of it during that landing. She stared at it then looked at him. She seemed about to say something, but instead she rolled over and got up, the movement of her body smooth and graceful.

Oh yeah, she was a girl. If he'd had any doubts after the close proximity check. Almost idly, he thought, bet she could dance a great cha-cha. And he wished he could get a better look at that weapon. It wasn't like anything he'd ever seen, even around this outpost.

"You're flickering."

That sounded like it came from the peak of the hut. Briggs got up, not nearly as smoothly as the woman. Because he was a guy, and he had his pride, he kept the wincing to a minimum. His wound had not liked the slam against woman or ground, though other parts of him hadn't minded the woman-slamming part. He thought he saw her touch something near her shoulder, and the camo faded, leaving just the black suit. Now he could see it had lines of silver running through the tight fitting black. He gave a half tug at the neck of his tee shirt. Very, very tight fitting. He'd have spent more time matching brief memory with reality, but, as if she just realized he might be dangerous, she lifted the gun and pointed it at him.

His gaze narrowed. He was not in the mood to get shot again. He made a half move toward her.

"Don't." She flicked something on the weapon.

He assessed his chances. He could take it from her. Did he want to? She looked like kind of cute standing there and the look in her eyes said she really didn't want to shoot him. There was definitely a glint of humor in her chocolate-brown eyes.

Her lips twitched. "Stun hurts almost as bad as getting shot." She rotated one shoulder. "And getting shot is the pits."

He couldn't argue with that, his hand lifting to cover his own protesting injury. He should have just taken it from her while they were on the ground. His gut said she was dangerous, but something else told him she wasn't dangerous to him—at least—he backed away from finishing that thought. Took a tug at his tee shirt neck again. Damn the heat in this place.

"You okay?"

He started to answer, but realized she wasn't talking to him.

"I am fine." The bird squawked once, then flew down, making a neat landing on her shoulder.

All she needed was an eyepatch to look like a pirate, standing there with her shoulders back, her chin up, and her feet planted. Her grin was sassy.

"Thanks for breaking my, um, fall," she said.

More heat bloomed where it shouldn't. He opened his mouth to answer, but she holstered the weapon like a pirate. Then she reached up toward a now visible line of buttons situated just below her shoulder blade and pressed one of them.

There was a distinct pop and smoke jetted out of her suit from the back.

The bird glanced back. "Well, that's embarrassing."

SIX

Embarrassing didn't quite cover it. At least the big guy, the very nice looking big guy—she flicked her gaze up and down—seemed pretty unfazed by their abrupt arrival—and failure to depart. He might even be kind of amused.

Madison might be impressed.

And, by the way, she'd totally lost her fascination with catapults. She was lucky he'd been there to catch her. Of course, he was big enough to catch two of her. She studied him. He had looked annoyed when she first pointed her ray gun at him, but now? Hard to say. Was that a twinkle buried deep in his eyes? She liked the eyes, with or without a twinkle. Even drawn in a line, his mouth was—she ran a fingertip along hers and sighed. Made her gaze move on. Military haircut and bearing. The tee shirt was stretched across a chest she had good reason to know was well-muscled and unyielding. And yet, the landing had managed to be pleasant for all that.

His denim shorts exposed tree-trunk legs planted in a way that should have made her nervous. Okay, he did make her a little nervous. He could probably take her down with his pinkie finger. She felt a little color steal into her cheeks as she recalled how it felt to be held against him. All of him. The iron bars of his arms around her. His afternoon beard had been nicely rough against her cheek, his mouth temptingly close.

Did he date older women? Who pointed ray guns at him?

Sir Rupert's wings brushed the side of her head, as he lifted off, circling the clearing, then landing on a rough-hewn table parked in front of a rustic cottage. Had she landed in *Robinson Crusoe* land? The guy sure looked the part.

Sir Rupert gave a small squawk, his version of a snort, perhaps, his claws lifting briefly. So what if the big guy was the only non-time traveling male she'd met in, well, she didn't know how long. It wasn't that relationships were discouraged in the Rebellion. The new guy had a wife. But it was tough to get involved with someone who could be years younger than you, or crazy ancient, when you finally had that date. At least it was easy to shake off the bad ones. Don't call me, I'll call you took on a whole new meaning in time travel.

As if he sensed her random and inappropriate thought processes, Sir Rupert ruffled his fathers and walked around the manhole cover. Still troubled by the rustic setting, she considered the big guy, then decided he could have already taken her down if he were so inclined. She let her hand drop away from her weapon—oh yeah, that hurt—and walked over next to the boss.

"Won't that just take us back," she stopped, slanting a glance at the guy, "where we came from?"

The big guy appeared to hesitate, too, then walked to the other side of the table from her. "If I was asked, I'd say you depleted the power source and that thing won't take you anywhere."

He was a pretty cool customer. Despite the, um, rustic surroundings, he'd clearly had contact with tech. Fixing tech was not her skill set. Breaking it? Yeah, she had that down pat.

"No," Sir Rupert said, continuing to circle the disc as if that would somehow make it work again. He angled his head to look at her. "They knew right where to shoot."

Now that he'd mentioned it, she felt air from what must be a hole in the shoulder of her suit. And possibly some sluggish bleeding. And just like that the pain rose in a wave. This made the horizon waver for several seconds and her stomach gave a nauseous bump. She firmly pushed it all to the back of her brain. Because the niggle was back between her shoulder blades.

The squad couldn't use the manhole cover to follow them here, so that might be a relief, but could they track them some other way? She looked around again. Where was here? She turned back to the big guy, tried out a smile. It felt like it hit a deflector shield and fell into the sand at her feet with a painful plop. He crossed his arms over his chest—man, that was a great chest if his tee shirt wasn't lying—and she knew it wasn't.

"We don't care for Time Service agents around here."

Madison looked quickly at Sir Rupert. He was the boss.

"Neither do we," he said.

The big guys brows arched skeptically. If he'd had dealings with the Service, which he clearly had, she did not blame him.

"You're not Time Service...agents..." The sardonic tone faltered a bit as his gaze fell on Sir Rupert.

Okay, so he'd run into agents, but not Sir Rupert's *Militarian* species. That was interesting. What would he think when he found out the bird was in charge of the op? Sir Rupert gave her a tiny nod, though his glance also advised caution. Like she didn't know that.

"We're, well, I guess you'd call us the opposition." Tip-toeing through minefields was her thing, assuming it was an actual minefield. But emotional mine fields? Not so much. Her ears were starting to buzz as the pain indicated it did not like being ignored. "Do you mind if I sit down? I don't feel that great."

She got a hard stare from the big guy and a very brief nod. She gripped the table as she sank onto the stool. She leaned an elbow on the table and tried to slow her breathing. Cause each breath hurt like a son of a gun. Been a while since she'd taken a hit this bad. If it had hit her somewhere else—but Sir Rupert was right, whoever fired it had known right where to point and shoot.

Must be frustrating when he or she saw Madison vanish via the manhole cover. She would have chuckled, but that would hurt, too. Through a growing haze she met the big guy's hard, distrustful gaze. So why did she sense something else from him? Why wasn't she that worried?

"I'd let you point my ray gun at me, but it only works for me." She lifted it clear of the holster and set it on the table top, then shoved it toward the big guy. Sir Rupert let out a muted squawk that she took to be a protest. Or agreement. Sometimes it was hard for her to tell.

"DNA or handprint?" The big guy asked, managing to keep one eye on them, as he snagged her ray gun and studied it with what she'd call professional interest.

"DNA," she told him, her voice oddly distant from the rest of her.

He quirked a brow. "Ray gun?"

"It has a fancy name that I can't ever remember," she admitted. And that's what they'd called them in the books and movies from her time, a time where a girl like her wouldn't have got to look at one, let alone get to point and shoot one at bad guys.

She could tell by the way he handled it, he was comfortable with weapons. If her head would clear, she'd figure out what that meant for them. Beads of sweat began to track down the sides of her face and the wavering horizon began to blur. She needed to stay awake, to stay focused. There was her niggle…

Sir Rupert fluttered over to the edge of the table with a worried squawk. "You are injured. I should have realized…"

His words kind of faded so she missed the end. The horizon steadied for a second, long enough for her to see two moons, dim in the late afternoon sky, but definitely two moons hanging there over the big guy's shoulder.

She rubbed her mouth, her hand coming away damp with cold sweat. "This isn't Earth."

The big guy lowered her weapon, his gaze sharpening.

Sir Rupert looked up, his feathers ruffling.

"What year is this?" She tried to look around, but that was a very bad idea. Spikes of pain shot up from her shoulder, stabbing into her brain and everything spun fast enough to ramp up the nausea. From a long way away she heard her voice say, "Usually I can make a good guess, but this place doesn't give much away." She tried to grin, but it felt like it wavered more than the horizon. She was talking too much, but couldn't stop herself.

"Who are you?" He had his Sphinx on, though he did glance at the bird this time.

"I am Sir Rupert." He ruffled his feathers importantly.

It might actually be his real name. Birds didn't have the same risks with sharing their real names. It was hard to track down a flock and pick out the one bird who could erase you from existence. Time was not only fluid, but apparently had a sense of humor. Let's make sure, it said, probably snickering somewhere out there, that you remember people you can never see again, because they didn't exist anymore. And then let's put you in position to fix all kinds of time paradoxes. But not that one.

Never that one, thank you so much, Boris.

The big guy was looking at her now, she realized, though it seemed his expression had softened. Or her gaze was getting blurrier. Probably that one. He wanted a name, she realized fuzzily.

"Scarlet Doe." It embarrassed her to say it out loud. Even about to pass out from pain, she blushed. She met his ironic gaze. "I told them it was the worst fake—"

"Code name," Sir Rupert interposed.

"*Code* name, worst code name ever." The big guy's brows rose and his look said, give me something better than that if you want my help. She couldn't give him her real name, so she gave him the one she'd used in her head for so long it felt like her real name. "Madison. You can call me Madison."

Her insides tensed, despite the pain that caused, as the name dropped into the gentle sea breeze and rose through the air toward the warm, high sun. The horizon didn't tremble or reverberate, at least not in a time-ish way. That's how she would have known that somewhere that name had registered with someone. Real names in time travel were dangerous, existence threatening, but so was time travel. Besides, all they could do now was kill her. For her, well, she didn't exist, though it had been a near thing, a fluke in time. But even she needed something to anchor her to her past, even if it was gone. It was so easy to lose yourself in time. And for someone who had been doing it as long as she had? That anchor was as critical to her survival as staying hidden.

They all knew it, so they were careful about using those anchors outside their own minds. Until now, not even Sir Rupert had heard the name Madison. Which begged the question, why had she told the big guy? And the answer came back in two parts.

He would know a lie if he heard it.

And for some reason she was too foggy to figure out, it was important he believed her. She wanted him to trust her.

"And you are?" she asked, then was sorry because he probably only had a real name.

"Briggs."

It felt like her chin sank deeper into the palm she rested it on. "Briggs." She smiled at him, felt the cloudiness of her gaze, even as she worried at how much their arrival would put him at risk. "Nice to meet you, Briggs."

He frowned and stepped closer. "You are hurt."

"Yes." She felt the clouds going dark, felt herself listing to the side—felt those strong arms lock around her for the second time. "Thanks again," she murmured, her head dropping to rest against his truly wonderful chest as her lights went out.

SEVEN

Briggs carried Madison inside the hut and settled her on his bed. Her waist was ringed with a belt loaded with neatly slotted equipment. The only one missing was her ray gun. He removed the gear, then the belt, and tossed it aside. Only then did he lower her—feeling something stirring inside himself, a something not appropriate to the situation, as he did so. But doing it felt oddly familiar, as if they'd done this before. Which was not possible. So—maybe it just felt right, the kind of right that he hadn't felt for a long time. It hadn't been so long that he hadn't recognized the look in her eyes, an interest she hadn't tried to hide. Was it a tactical move? Hadn't felt like it, and the interest had stayed in there as the fog closed in, and took her down.

Before he could stop himself, he smoothed the hair back from her face, noticing how her lashes fanned across the upper curve of her cheeks. Her skin was pale beneath her tan, revealing a sprinkling of freckles across a nose that tipped up on the end. His gaze lingered on parted pink lips, noted the rapid rise and fall of her chest. He pulled his hand back, though his fingers wanted to linger on the soft skin and trace the lines and curves of her face. And then move lower…

She'd never make it onto a magazine cover. She was short, her body more compact than thin. Very fit, with signs of strength in her limbs and body. That was okay. He'd never been interested in half-starved waifs with big, sad eyes. What he'd seen of her eyes, they for sure they hadn't been sad. Serious, sassy, amused, and interested, but not sad.

She did interest him. He faced it because he needed to take care. If this was some kind of move on the base here, well, he had to make sure that didn't happen.

Madison. Even as he considered how this might be a play, his hands moved down her arms, then flexed her legs, trying to assess her injuries. He checked her ribs, but was defeated by the suit. She seemed to have been sealed inside it.

"Put your fingers here," the bird said, tapping its beak between her breasts.

He gave the bird a wary look.

"To open the seal on her uniform," it added.

Briggs decided he didn't want to know what the bird was thinking when he hesitated. He touched the suit, careful to keep his fingers in the center. But his knuckles brushed curves as he tried to find a seam. Felt like a creepy guy, even when his thumb finally found something. He pushed and a gap appeared. He pushed a little harder and his fingers brushed against soft, firm skin. He didn't yank back. That would be obvious, even to a bird. She didn't stir. Breathing a bit easier—okay, nothing was easy about this, but he doggedly worked to open it wider.

The vulnerability of her situation called to his sense of honor, the reason he'd joined the Air Force. To serve. To protect. But then there was that other call. It wasn't just a guy and a gal call, though it had started that way when she slammed into him.

There was something about her that had made a stealthy pass through his defenses, not just the base's. She was wrong for him in every way— including too young. He could be her father. Maybe if he repeated that enough, if would finally sink in. But that wasn't going to happen while he was sitting here opening her suit while the warm, clean scent of her filled his nostrils. Here he'd thought it would be better to smell anything but fresh, sea breezes. It was a reminder to be careful what you thought you wanted because the universe was listening and happy to show you where you were wrong.

He tried taking a deep breath, but that just made it worse, so he held his breath and finished exposing her from waist to neck. Underneath she wore a light weight tank top that hugged her skin and revealed the fact that the suit had seriously compressed her...chest.

Briggs massaged his temple, but stopped when he caught the bird looking at him in a way that was kinda unnerving. Like it knew exactly he was thinking. The skin he could see was smooth and also lightly tanned. No sign of tan lines—not that he was looking. Much.

He averted his gaze from the danger zones and eased the suit off her shoulders—sweat beading on his skin and hers—dang tropics—until the suit was folded down around her waist. Normally he'd have been interested in that suit. Of course, he'd left normal when the parrot bounced out of the disc. His gaze accidentally tracked across her tee shirt and he found one reason to be glad it wasn't cold. Just the one, though. Because the heat outside was not helping him at all with the heat stirring inside.

"Where did she get hit?" His voice came out husky, but maybe the bird didn't notice.

"Back left shoulder."

He shifted her onto her uninjured side and all heat fled in the face of a cold rage that wasn't any more appropriate than the—his mind rejected lust. Oh, he wanted her, he admitted reluctantly, but well, he needed to move on. She needed his help. He studied her injury.

It was an ugly, sluggishly bleeding gash high on her back, partly inside, and partly above the rounded edge of her tee shirt. The force of something had driven bits of wires, small pieces of metal, and cloth into her skin, but —he studied it carefully—he didn't think it was deep, despite the debris. He could probably patch it up, but—his thoughts strayed to the alien infection that had put him in the infirmary for several days....

"She should see a doc." And what would that involve? Their presence was a security breach that was going to be hard to explain. He glanced at the bird, who was perched on the bed examining her injury with a bird-like, but oddly professional, interest.

"It could have been worse," the bird said, relieved. "Can you apply first aid?"

The bird said. Had he just thought that? It wasn't a shock that a parrot, or parrot-looking bird, could talk. It even had the croaking overtones of a parrot. But this was *talking*, not just talking. He shouldn't be surprised. They'd been looking for non-human, sentient alien life from the first flight of Project Enterprise. It was even possible this wasn't the first contact with a non-humanoid, since there were other ships out there nosing around. It was his first, however. Until now their people had had contact with only humanoid aliens.

Briggs nodded, dug his first aid kit out of his duffle. and opened it. He found the supplies he needed and started cleaning and disinfecting the wound. He didn't hesitate, even when she stirred and muttered in pain. He'd tended battle wounds before. And this was a battle wound, no question. He might have cussed under his breath, but he kept going. It had to be done. When he was sure it was cleaned, he studied the injury carefully. There were signs of scorching around the edges. His lips tightened. Someone had used an energy—a ray gun—on her. And she'd fired back, he reminded himself. Still pissed him off someone had hurt her.

He doused the area with antiseptic, waited for it to dry, then carefully applied Super Glue to close the torn skin. He sprayed on some pain killer, then covered it with a light bandage and eased her onto her back again. Only then did he look at the bird, trying to decide what to ask.

The bird hopped up on the headboard and looked around. "Are you marooned in this place?"

Briggs sat back, shifting to ease his wound, which was complaining about the workout, now that he wasn't busy focusing on Madison's injury.

Madison. That probably wasn't her real name either, but it meant something to her. He'd felt it, felt truth in it somewhere. "I'm recuperating." His annoyance with this broke into his tone. "The base..."

He stopped that sentence unfinished. For all he knew, these two were attempting to infiltrate the base. Just because they looked like time travelers and she'd asked what year it was, and they'd appeared out of a disc, didn't mean they'd traveled through time. It could be a simple transport pad. A decoy? Donovan's handwriting had looked genuine, but it wasn't like he could give her a call and ask. And it might have been an unintended consequence. He had been the one to fix it and turn it on—something no one at the base or Area 51 would have approved. In his boredom, he'd been careless. He could face the uncomfortable truth now that he was forty-five and probably more mature.

"You are wise to take care. The people hunting us are ruthless and highly trained. If they find you useful, they will take you, and reprogram you to serve their needs." The bird moved one way along the headboard, then moved back.

"And if they don't find me useful?" Briggs asked, his gut tightening at the thought of the "useful" people at the base, including Doc Clementyne's brother, Robert. Robert, who had finally found happiness and purpose in his life.

"They will erase you from time. It will be as if you never lived."

He frowned. "But wouldn't that..."

"Do you think they care about fallout to others?"

"The time service—"

"...has changed," the bird said. "Absolute power corrupts absolutely. They began trying to fix and repair time breaches, but at some point their focus changed. And now it ripples back through all time in an unchecked rotten flow."

"But—" he started to protest, but how would he know that big events hadn't changed? Or if this bird spoke the truth. They were the 'opposition,' but that didn't make them allies. Even if he had a built-in prejudice against the time service thanks to Doc. The bird could be talking to earn his sympathy and turn him into a weapon against its enemy.

"The only place they take care is around large events, because these anchor time and time will push back."

If the bird could have smiled grimly, Briggs sensed it would have.

"They learned that lesson the hard way, but they did not learn enough."

Briggs studied the bird, but it was not like he had experience reading a bird's face for truth or lies. Odd that his gut felt it spoke the truth—the truth as the bird knew it, he decided.

"Why are they after you two?"

"We are hunting a traitor and they seek to stop us before we can return to our base with that information." The bird ruffled its wings and stepped lightly along the headboard again. "They did not factor in the transport pad or they would not have left it for us to find."

Was the bird sure about that? That thing didn't seem like the kind of thing you left lying around in an unsecured area.

"We found it in a storage closet, shoved into a corner," the bird said, as if it heard Briggs' thought.

Had it had the same thought?

"I can not be sure it was not part of the trap," the bird conceded. It looked around. "I do not think it meant us to come here, however."

Yeah, a trap that depended on him turning that thing on at the right time wasn't a very good trap. More like a lucky chance if these people were as bad as the bird thought they were.

The bird looked around now. "I did not expect to arrive here."

Briggs let himself grin. "Where did you think you were going?"

The bird regarded him solemnly. "Anywhere that wasn't where we were." It paused, then added, "But more useful than here."

Briggs' grin widened. He was kind of starting to like the bird. He grinned. "Yeah, I'm not thrilled to be here either," he admitted.

The bird regarded him in a way that might be thoughtful. "You should leave."

Briggs' gaze narrowed. There'd been a warning in there. Did it expect trouble to follow them here? He looked at the bird. "How do I know your trouble won't follow me?"

"It is our job to contain it," the bird said.

Briggs didn't try to hide his skepticism. Then his brows lowered in a scowl.

"They can't get here on that," Briggs pointed out, already sure that wasn't how trouble was gonna arrive.

"No," the bird's head bobbed as if it was aware of the irony, "but nevertheless, they will come."

EIGHT

"I'm afraid I have to agree with Sir Rupert." Madison's voice was husky, but calm.

Briggs twisted around to look at her. The fog was clearing from her eyes, revealing worry. He saw something else in there though, something he recognized because he'd seen it many times during his years in the USAF.

The look of a warrior preparing to meet the enemy.

"And thank you for the third time." She shifted her shoulders. "It feels much better."

Better wasn't fighting fit, but he also knew when someone couldn't be talked out of a fight. Not someone with that stubborn jaw line.

"You're welcome." He kept his tone even with an effort. He wanted to argue with her. He wanted to grab her and change her mind the old-fashioned way. Not that he wanted to get caught with his pants down when the enemy arrived. If they arrived. And when had her enemies become his? A smile tugged at the edges of her mouth, and regret filtered into her expression. She could be his daughter, he reminded himself. It didn't help as much as he'd hoped it would because she didn't look at him like he was her dad. Was it because he wanted her to be older that it seemed like she was older than she looked?

"You never said what year this is?" she prompted softly.

He hesitated, but couldn't think of a good reason not to tell her. "2017."

Her eyes widened. "Really?" She glanced up at the bird. It ruffled its wings, which could be its version of surprised. "But I thought—" She stopped, then asked, "Where…"

"That's classified." His non-disclosure agreement didn't say he couldn't mention the base to time travelers, but there were all kinds of clauses about not talking to anyone—including yourself—and getting shot if you did. So it added up to not disclosing to time travelers in his opinion. And the kind of shooting in the agreement? It wasn't the kind that required recuperating in a hut or anywhere else.

"I need to get up." She reached out and he did, too, maybe to stop her, but her fingers slid between his, her palm brushing against his and he forgot about stopping her. Might have made him think about pushing her back down. Warmth surged from where their hands touched and it felt like they'd always held hands and always would. There was the heat of desire in the mix, but also the warmth of a wood fire, the kind that invited you to settle in, to stay, and make something that lasted—

His fingers tightened involuntarily on hers. There was no fool like an old fool...

For several seconds, it felt like she returned his grip, probably just so she could swing her legs over the edge of the bed and rest them on the floor. Side by side, her head barely reached the top of his shoulder. He waited for her to free her hand, but she didn't. If anything her grip tightened. Her breath came in quick bursts for several seconds and she bit her lower lip. He had to stop himself from reaching for her as she lost color, but after a moment or two, her breathing slowed and some of her color came back. Her lips formed into a thin, stubborn line.

She looked at him, her smile wavering a bit, and finally there was some sad in her eyes. He didn't mind because there were other things in there, too. If he died right now...well, he wouldn't be happy, but it would be better than seeing her walk away...

The bird flew over to the top of the rustic dresser, breaking into whatever was happening between them. It walked one way along the top, then back, almost as if it were pacing.

She hesitated, her shoulders stiffening as resolve pushed out every other emotion in her eyes.

"How big is our possible risk zone?" she asked.

It stopped, a wing came up, as if rubbing the lower part of its beak. "They'll come in on a tight beam because they won't know what they're jumping into."

"They won't like that," she said with a grin. "Couple of hundred yards? More? Less?"

The bird appeared to nod. "Less, I think."

Madison shifted a bit, so that she half faced Briggs, their hands still linked.

"Is that enough to keep your people safe?"

"If it wasn't, could you do anything about it?" he asked, though without heat. He figured she was trying to find out what she needed to know, without actually finding it out. He appreciated the effort, even if he wasn't sure it would work. She had no idea what this island contained.

She nodded. "There are some things we could do." She glanced around. "Defensively, this isn't the best location. Or the worst."

"The structure will give them something to focus on," the bird pointed out, his tone in the range of 'it was what it was."

Wary and trust contended for the upper hand inside his head. Last time he'd felt like this, he'd been trying to decide if he could trust Doc Clementyne—but he hadn't felt like this around Doc. Then he had needed to only believe his head, not his heart. Could he trust either when all he wanted to do was sit here and hold her hand? Okay, not all he wanted to do. His lips twisted wryly.

"That should be enough," he admitted. If he'd put Robert Clementyne at risk, there was nowhere in time or space he could hide from Doc Clementyne.

She squeezed his hand one last time and then released it so she could stand up. This time she didn't face him when she said, "You need to go."

She didn't know he couldn't, even if he wanted to, which he didn't. He'd never walked away from an important fight in his life. But there was more to it than this girl and his uneasy feelings for her. More that was both complicated and simple. It was his fault the base and its people were at risk. He'd opened the door these two came through. And he had to close it. He couldn't die trying. He had to live and do it. That was the simple part. The complicated part? He stared at her profile. He sure as hotel wasn't leaving her—these two to face the incoming alone. That wasn't in his DNA—though it was the first time he'd felt the need to protect a bird.

"No," he said, his tone mild, but firm.

She spun to face him, her head tipped to one side as, he guessed, she assessed his resolve. Finally she glanced at the bird. It almost seemed like it shrugged.

"We could use the help."

"The risk—" she said, but her protest lacked force.

"I'm guessing we don't have a lot of time to argue. Is the ray gun your only weapon?"

Her posture changed. Kind of reminded him of Donovan when she was preparing to toss someone on their ass. He rose, towering over her with his brows arched. Not that Donovan had ever managed to toss him. After a pause, she nodded.

"How many hostiles incoming?"

She wasn't the one who answered him.

"At least six. Highly trained and outfitted with dangerous and deadly technology they've stolen from the future."

Briggs mouth straightened into a line, and he shot a look at Madison. She seemed startled, but not annoyed. Was she surprised by what the bird had told him? Who was in charge? Who got to decide what? He could take orders, but—as if she sensed the question, she spoke.

"Sir Rupert is my," she hesitated, "...boss. I'm his bodyguard. It's my job to get him safely back to our base." He knew his gaze narrowed sharply because she added, "But it is always in my brief to protect innocents from hostile actions of the Time Service squads. You do not have to believe me, but I am as committed to protecting your people as you are."

"We are committed to that," the bird amended. "It is why we do what we do. To protect all living things from the damage done by the Time Service."

Because he couldn't do it to the bird, he directed a drilling gaze on Madison, using all the technique he'd learned during his years in the military. She didn't flinch or look away. Her lips might have twitched once.

"So," he said, finally, "six hostiles incoming?" That didn't seem too bad, even with fancy dancy technology.

"There might have been more than six who attacked us," she cautioned with a frown. "There was a lot of incoming fire, but they could have upgraded their weapons from our last, um, encounter." She rubbed her forehead. "I didn't get a look at any of them. Just heard one or two go down."

"So what's your highest estimate?" Briggs pressed.

Her lips twisted wryly. "They might wait to reconstitute their squad before they come after us. Or they might call in backup. Twelve is the most I've ever seen them risk on a single op." She frowned. "It depends on what they think they'll jump into."

"If they believe you are alone, injured, and cut off from assistance," the bird said, "they will not wait for backup."

"But..." she started to protest, then stopped. "They would have brought a full force if they thought we jumped back to our base. But they know the manhole cover wouldn't take us there." She looked more hopeful.

Briggs grinned at the "manhole cover."

"But..." she murmured, the look she exchanged with the bird was interesting.

"What?" he asked, adding impatiently, "I need to know."

"He is correct. He does need to know."

Madison shifted her shoulder as if it pained her, but she met his gaze with sober determination. "If they saw Sir Rupert during the op, they will come in at full strength and loaded to kill. They can not afford to let him return to our base alive."

Did he need to know why?

"I told you we were seeking to identify a traitor, a mole in our organization," the bird said.

He frowned as a thought occurred to him. "How will they track you?" From where he sat, the disc looked dead out there on the table.

Once more it seemed that Madison looked at the bird for permission.

"He needs to know," the bird said again.

"I do," Briggs said grimly.

Madison patted her waist, then looked around, found the things from her belt he'd tossed onto the bed, and went over to them. She sorted through the small pile until she found the one she wanted. She activated it and directed it at the suit, watching a small screen. She finally made a face, speaking to the parrot, not him.

"Yeah, it's got an active tracking beacon."

"What...the suit?"

She nodded.

"Can you turn it off?"

In normal circumstances no one could find this outpost, since it had cloaking technology, but these two had made it in, so that probably wouldn't keep out their incoming squad. He could summon help, lots of it, but he had a feeling that conventional defenses wouldn't work in this situation.

"Maybe," she said, but once again she looked at the bird. "They might already have a fix on it."

"You want to use it to draw them in," he said, because it was what he would have done.

"We could try to leave, but if they already have this location..." She shrugged and did it very well.

He'd meant he had to be a grownup and not look—more than once. Apparently he was not as mature as he'd hoped. He glanced up, found her watching, humor and something else in her eyes. If she weren't younger than him....

She met his gaze steadily. "It's the best way for us and for your...for anyone here. They don't know the terrain, won't know what they are jumping into, but if they follow the beam in, they'll be less likely to look around, at least until they've got what they want."

He frowned. "A couple of hundred yards isn't that narrow." Had she seriously thought she could cover that much ground?

"I assess they will come in at considerably less than one hundred yards," the parrot said. "Their scanning will see the trees as obstacles to avoid, so the clear space on the beach is where they will most likely land."

Madison nodded. "And they'll know, if I'm conscious, they won't have that much time. I will have sensed them incoming."

Briggs blinked, not sure what to say. She could sense that?

"She's a very good time jumper," the bird said. It began to pace once more. "I do not believe they saw me. I transported before the door was breached. They'll know you were injured and that your suit was damaged and that the pad was the only way out."

"You think they'll be overconfident," Briggs suggested.

"Not a good reason for us to be overconfident," Madison said. "Their tech will be formidable, even if they think I'm down or almost down."

Her worried gaze met his. He should care they were up against some scary dudes with scary stuff, but words lost their power when she looked at him like that. He was treading in deep water, no question, but if it came down to a choice, he had to choose the base, its people over her.

She gave a slight nod, as if she knew it and agreed. "So we fight."

"Was there ever any doubt?" the bird asked.

"How long do you think we have?" Briggs asked now, his brain kicking into strategy mode.

Madison frowned. "That thing wasn't supposed to send us through time, just space."

Briggs blinked.

"What happened before your transit?" the bird asked.

"There might have been some shooting," she admitted. "More shooting, I mean," she added, with a sidelong glance at Briggs. "While I was in the beams."

"The concentrated weapons fire must have boosted the power and the signal, enabling that pad to connect to this one," the bird said. It fluttered over to the back of the chair, and moved back and forth on this now. "It is only thing that explains it."

"I'm not going to ask what would have happened if there'd been no pad to connect to," Madison said.

Since she hadn't asked, the bird didn't appear inclined to answer.

It was nice to know he'd been right about what the disc did. He might be forty-five but he still had it. "The other pad must have had a better power source," he mused, then gave himself a shake. It didn't matter now. "How long do we have to plan?" It was need-to-know.

Madison hesitated. "Oddly enough, the trip through time will give us more time. We might get three hours, but safe number is more like one hour."

One hour? Briggs tensed. "Then I need to make a call."

"I need to walk around, get a feel for the location," Madison said. She started to turn.

"Wait." She stopped, one brown eyebrow lifted. "This is my turf. I know the terrain," Boy, did he know it. "I'm in charge."

She hesitated, glanced at the bird and nodded. "But Sir Rupert leaves the area. He can't be seen."

"During your call, could you get me access to a computer," the bird asked. "I could endeavor to send out an SOS."

"You think help will come in time?" Briggs asked, not thrilled at more time travelers arriving.

The bird moved its beak from side to side. "There is not enough time, I know, ironic, but these are the limitations we live—or die—with."

"He could get the word out about our traitor," Madison said.

"I don't like it," Briggs said.

"Then I will go find some birds to, um, hang with."

Briggs blinked, not sure whether to laugh or grind his teeth. "There aren't any birds on this...in this place."

"No birds?" Madison looked shocked, then shook her head. "We're running out of time."

Briggs hesitated, then went with his gut and prayed it wasn't letting him down. "I'll arrange a safe place and a way to send your message." But he'd also make sure Robert was warned.

"Your plan," the bird said, "you must disable, not kill them."

"That's not—"

"Not all of them are willing," Madison said, clear reluctance in her voice. "And we don't know what impact their deaths would have on the timeline."

"You're in one batcrap crazy business," he said. "Okay, I know how to disable."

"Thank you," the bird said.

He shook his head. "I'll go make my call."

He stalked out the door toward the water. His chest heaved twice, then he lifted his radio.

Madison stared at Briggs' back for several seconds, then turned back to Sir Rupert, but she didn't know what to say or even ask.

"Trust him," the bird said.

"I do." She glanced out the door again. "He doesn't trust me, us."

"No." His wings fluttered and he lifted off, coming to where he could look out the door, too. "You should collect your things and get out of that suit."

"If they don't see a heat signature connected to the suit—" she protested.

"Trust him to work something out."

She looked down at the bird, but he wasn't looking at her. He hadn't done this once already, had he? Not that he'd tell her if he had. He would try to steer them away from where it went wrong—she rubbed her temple. It always ached when she tried to think her way through the paradoxes of time travel. She was tired of it, she realized. Tired of doing the same operations, tired of looking for Boris—the one who had changed her life for all time. She chose to be happy, as happy as possible, because why give up more of her life to a faceless nosebleed waste of space. But she felt out of juice.

This place, that man, had made her realize how very fast she'd been running, trying to stay ahead of how alone she was. And how very much she wanted to not be alone anymore.

I don't know how many more fights I have in me. Even thinking the words made her realize she did know. She had one left, because she couldn't let that man down. She couldn't let him die because she'd made a mistake. She hadn't trusted her niggle.

That couldn't, it wouldn't ever happen again.

NINE

Briggs had told Robert not to get out of the chopper, but he was too much like his sister. The impossible not only didn't scare him, he thought it could be beat. He grinned at Briggs, his curious gaze tracking past him to Madison and the bird. His eyes widened in delight and he passed Briggs, his hand held out.

"Robert," he flicked a glance back at Briggs, "and I'm not supposed to ask your name."

"Madison," she said. "And this is Sir Rupert."

Her smile was so natural for Robert, Briggs felt a stab of something that couldn't be what it felt like because Robert had a wife. But then he processed the fact she'd told him their names. Trust. She trusted them.

"How do you do?" the bird said, waving a claw in greeting, Briggs supposed.

Briggs lips compressed when Madison shot him a questioning look. He trusted her, he realized, but Doc—this was the brother that had been lost to her. Nothing could happen to Robert.

"We were wondering if you could take Sir Rupert with you. He kind of needs to send up an SOS to our base."

If anything Robert looked even more curious. "How do you do that?"

"Facebook," the bird said.

Both he and Robert did a double take.

"Facebook?" Robert slanted a look at Briggs.

"We all have an emergency account," Madison explained. "We use Facebook memes all the time to send messages. And those quizzes. Sometimes we use the quizzes."

"I don't," Briggs admitted, a bit dazed, "have an account. But—"

"It won't be instantaneous," Robert said, "but we should be able to get you connected. Emily loves Facebook."

Madison half opened her mouth, then closed it.

"His wife," Briggs said. She needed to know what was at stake here. And to know he trusted her.

She met his gaze, gratitude in the worried depths.

Robert half turned toward the chopper. "Let's get your stuff unloaded." He hesitated. "Sure you won't need more help?"

"We'll be fine. Just help," Briggs had to swallow, "the bird with his meme thing."

Robert laughed as the bird flew a small circle then landed on his shoulder. "I always wanted to be a pirate," he said, stroking the bird.

Briggs could be wrong, but he thought the bird rolled its eyes.

Briggs stared out over water reflecting light from the waning sun. Night was incoming, probably at the same time as the bad guys—the guys he hoped were bad guys. It had been a busy almost hour, one far too short, since Robert had left with the bird.

Madison had traded her suit for some camo, though not without a protest.

"If you're in there, we won't have enough fire power." She was not going to be bait on any op with him.

So they'd filled the suit with bags of hot water and arranged it on the bed. He'd hesitated, then looked at her. "We may not have a choice. If we can't stop them—"

She nodded.

She wanted to kill them, he realized. There was more than getting shot in the shoulder that drove her, but he didn't have time to find out. He snorted silently. Time. What a mess time travel made of things that should be simple, straightforward. "Can you do this?"

He kept his tone neutral, but with a layer of hard he used when he sensed an Airman on the point of wavering.

She looked at him then. "I can do what has to be done."

She might as well have said, *I can do what must be done one more time.* She was at her limit. Maxed out. But she'd do it. He wanted to—but they both needed to get under cover.

"Will you do one thing for me?" she asked, her voice so quiet, he almost missed her words.

"If I can."

Her lips trembled into a small smile. "I promise it won't hurt."

She turned until she fully faced him and reached out with one hand, settling it lightly on his chest close to his heart. Her chin lifted. "There's not much time…."

She lifted onto her toes, her lips parted, but she was too short. His lips quirked, Briggs bent his head, and met her halfway. She didn't seem to know what she was doing, but it didn't matter. He hadn't forgotten how to kiss a girl. His arms found their way around to her back and he pulled her close and maybe off her feet entirely. Desire tried to surge out of control, but he didn't turn it loose.

There was no time. No time….

He felt her stiffen and lifted his head.

"They're coming."

For half a second, he couldn't let go. Then his arms slackened. She stepped back. He couldn't, not until she created the distance. His hand shook slightly as he touched her hair one last time. He dropped his arm to his side, his fingers clenched.

"Right," he said. "Let's do this."

———————

Briggs had helped Madison slide into the sniper's blind they'd built, one on either side of the target zone, then he piled foliage across the opening. She dug deeper into the dead leaves and other debris as she heard his crunching footsteps taking him to his position. Plants gave off a heat signature, too, so the dense foliage should muddy hers, particularly when they had a nice clean one inside the cottage to focus on.

Their positions would also provide a good crossfire situation. She had two weapons—a tranquilizer rifle and one with real bullets, already positioned for sniping. She only had to shift her hand to grab a stun grenade.

She considered her instructions again, making sure they were clear in her mind before things went hot.

The plan was good. He knew strategy, was just the kind of person the Time Service liked to acquire. She had to make sure that didn't happen.

As the clock ticked down to zero, she felt calm settle over her mind, her body alert, but not tense. If this was her last performance, she intended to make it a good one.

They wore headset radios, tuned to a frequency his people were unlikely to stumble across, but they were only useful until the shooting started. Her headset crackled.

"Romeo Tango Golf," she heard Briggs say.

Ready to go.

"Mike Tango," she answered. *Me too.* She felt the change as the time bubble formed. "Hotel India," she said. *Hostiles incoming.* She lifted the tranquilizer rifle, tucked it into her shoulder, and prepared for her first target.

The horizon shimmered a bit, and then Briggs saw six dark figures appear along the beach line. Almost immediately they were gone. They'd activated their camo, he realized but they'd be moving in toward the hut. In the moonlight falling across the beach, he saw footsteps appear in the sand and grinned. No one had come up with a way to hide footprints.

They reached the table and stopped, probably looking at the dead transport disc. He activated the drone. It rose slowly, until it was about chest height, hovering in the shadowy doorway of the hut.

"What's that sound?" one of them asked. The footprints turned, first one, then all of them angled toward the hut. They began to track forward.

Keep coming, he thought, *just a little further.* When they were close enough, he sent the drone out of the doorway and activated the EMP device the drone carried. There was a flash of bright light. *Hello, electromagnetic pulse.*

The drone went dead.

But so did their fancy tech.

They went from blending into the horizon to dark shadows backlit by the rising moons.

Madison fired her first shot, then a second. Nice. Two shadows down. The other turned toward the shots, giving Briggs a chance to lob a stun grenade into the middle of them. Another bright, blinding flash. Followed by the sound of muffled thumps into soft sand.

Don't move, he wanted to tell Madison. But their radios had been taken out by the EMP, too.

He waited for his night vision to return. There were dark lumps around the hut's doorway. But were they all down? He lowered his night sight and their heat signatures popped them out. No sign of movement. With his weapon ready, he kicked out of his blind and approached them.

Madison appeared out of the dark on the other side. He lifted a hand to stop her before she stepped into the light.

"Cover me," he ordered. He pulled out the plastic zip ties and secured the first guy, feet and hands, then moved to the second. One figure shifted a bit and a shot hissed out, hitting its target. The moving stopped. Even as Briggs secured each one, his mind was repeating over and over, "Too easy…"

A sharp cry, cut off before it was complete came from Madison's position. Briggs dropped down between two of the prone figures as something blue sizzled past, close enough for him to feel the heat. A bright cage of lights dropped over him and the figures. He heard the crackle of it, felt its heat maybe two inches above his head. And from Madison's direction, he saw another one appear, trapping her inside.

Madison felt the niggle too late to escape the energy trap. The heat of it traveled along her weapon, forcing her to drop it. Then two figures emerged from either side of the hut, both with their camo already down. One circled the cage that held Briggs trapped.

"Sometimes it pays to be late to the party," the one closest to her said. His voice was icy cold, crisply devoid of anything that might give away his origins. He stopped and looked at his downed team. "We need to know what happened."

Briggs wasn't down in the sense this agent meant, but he was not moving. She did not see how it would help, but she clung to the faint hope as the man's attention shifted to her. She was the only one who appeared to be standing. He walked over until they stood a few feet apart. His gaze traveled up, down, and then back up to her face. His gaze narrowed. His hand lifted and it took all her resolve not to flinch, but it was just a light. With her night vision lost, she couldn't see his reaction, but she heard his sharp intake of breath.

"Not possible," he said. "You're...not possible."

Her vision clearing, she studied him now.

"Boris," she said. "You're Boris. You're the one who erased my family." It was the only way he could have recognized her. Because of him, they didn't exist. She didn't exist.

"Boris?" The man seemed puzzled, though it was hard to be sure in the moonlight.

"Boris Karloff. The always bad guy."

Now he chuckled. "That depends on your perspective, I suppose. I did what had to be done."

"You erased my family, my brother, and the people he was meant to save died. You had no right to do any of it."

He shrugged. "Apparently I missed my target."

"I was away," preparing for the Olympics that had never happened for her, she thought painfully, "they came for me first. But they were not in time to save...." She couldn't continue. Didn't need to. He knew what he'd done.

His quiet laugh chilled her to the bone as he came closer. Stopping only when he was just shy of the shimmering cage that held her back from killing him with her bare hands. She'd tried not to think about meeting him, because it would have eaten her up inside, but now that he was there? She wanted him dead.

"You really believe that? You believe they were too late?" He laughed again.

Madison felt cold go deeper into her bones as she stared into his cold blue eyes. Funny how fear changed the cold. Cold should just be cold.

He shook his head, his gaze mocking. "You were young, but surely in time you must have realized you were the one they wanted. It was never about your family. It was always about you."

The one true thing she'd learned during her time with the rebellion was how to hide her feelings. It served her well now. She stared at him from blank eyes, while her brain raced, trying to feel her way to truth. His words would hurt later, if she lived, if she found out he was right. This moment, the talking, it wouldn't last. He couldn't erase someone who didn't exist, but he could kill her. She was human.

And if she died, so did Briggs. And when he died, they'd search this place and find his people. She didn't know what was here, but she could tell Briggs believed there were people here the Time Service would want. Somehow she had to keep him talking. Time, almost she laughed, they needed time.

"And why was a thirteen-year-old gymnast such a threat to the Time Service?" She was impressed with the bored scorn that infused the question. Girl gymnasts weren't that big of a deal when she was training. But she'd lost that dream, too. And why had she mattered to the Rebellion? No, now was not the time for those questions. If she wanted answers, she had to live.

"You don't know, do you?" His laugh held surprise. "You are one of the most gifted time sensitives in, well, history."

She didn't even blink. "And you didn't want that?" She didn't try to hide her disbelief. *Never trust a Time Service agent.* It was the first rule in the Rebellion.

"Oh, we would have, but your other gift was a deal breaker. They didn't tell you that you have a complete, built-in resistance to the mind wipe, did they? I'm sure it was just an oversight. There you have it. You couldn't be turned. No use to us, but very useful to the Rebellion. We couldn't risk you or any future heirs being out there, so you had to be erased." He paused. "How every clever *She* was to hide you from us. We never even had a whiff of you in all this time."

"Are you so sure you weren't mind wiped?" Madison asked, as hope faded. She could see death in his eyes. He was going to kill her. She couldn't think her way out of this cage. If Sir Rupert had called in help—it was possible they'd get here in time to clean up the scene. But she wouldn't make it. Briggs would die—or worse, be taken to use.

He shrugged. "I never needed to be persuaded to join. I like my job." He walked around her cage, looking her over like an animal being assessed for slaughter.

He was drawing out the moment so she'd suffer, she realized. He did like his job. "It's a pity," he said.

"What's a pity?" she asked, knowing he wasn't capable of feeling pity.

"That you won't live long enough to ask her if I've lied to you." He lifted his gun, letting her see as he flicked it to the kill setting. His other hand held the cage control.

He'd have to drop it to shoot her.

She might be able to move fast enough.

He stepped so that the tip of his ray gun almost touched the cage and was pointed at her heart.

Her breaking heart.

I'm so sorry, Briggs.

TEN

Briggs froze, keeping his head down, his body slack. As he went down, he'd felt something hard pressing into his thigh. If it was the drone…inch by careful inch, he eased his hand down. His fingers brushed against it, then curled around it. He traced it. Yeah, that was the drone, the EMP device still attached. He'd left the trigger back in the blind, but that would be dead anyway. There was a chance, a slight chance, that the device had enough charge left. He'd not set it to full charge, just in case. Didn't want to cause any problems on the base.

His guard moved closer and Briggs lowered his lashes, feeling the dull thud of his heart as Boris spoke to Madison. It was clear he meant to kill her.

Don't think about it. Deal with it later if we make it. His fingers traced the shape, found the device. He was running out of time. There. His finger found the manual trigger.

"It's a pity you won't live long enough to ask her if I've lied to you."

Briggs pressed the button, praying at the same time. The flash was smaller this time, but the cage disappeared. His guard was close and slow to react. Briggs took him down and out and was already headed toward the two figures silhouetted against the rising moons. They disappeared into the shadows of the trees. He could hear the scuffle, the panting breaths of a desperate struggle. A grunt of pain and then silence.

Afraid to hope, Briggs darted toward where he'd last seen them—

Madison stepped out of the shadows, her face white, her eyes haunted.

He grabbed her and pulled her close, his hands running down her back, then up, as if to assure himself it was her, that she was alive.

"Is he dead?" He spoke matter-of-factly into her ear. A contrast to the frantic beat of his heart and hers.

She shook her head. "I...no." She inhaled shakily. "I wanted to but..." She stopped. His grip tightened.

"Wait here. Don't move." He headed into the shadows, found the guy she'd called Boris, and dragged him out into the moonlight. He had a nasty swelling bruise on his chin and was bleeding sluggishly from a wound in his side. Briggs used more zip ties on him and his sidekick. He angled his head and studied Boris's partner. She did look a bit like a Natasha...

Once he was sure they were all well secured, he went back to Madison.

She hadn't moved though now her body shuddered with shock. Now the words she'd exchanged with Boris came back with echoing force. He didn't know what to say or do, other than to hold her again. He wanted to tell her it would be all right, but the words stuck in his throat.

How could anything be all right for her? She'd lost so much. Questions formed and were discarded before they were uttered. Nothing sounded right.

"I'm sorry," he finally said. "I'm sorry."

She looked up at him then. "I am, too."

Madison shuddered with the adrenalin that had carried her through the fight with Boris. He was a good fighter, but a lousy gymnast. The super power he hadn't seen coming. And the knife strapped to her leg.

She was still surprised she hadn't killed him. He'd been worse than she'd imagined. A cold, killing machine.

Maybe that was why she couldn't do it. It took her too close to the edge of becoming like him, becoming him.

"You," she was close enough to feel Briggs swallow, "could stay here, you know. We're a motley crew, so you'd fit right in."

She was surprised to hear, to feel herself chuckle. Knew she'd find him grinning, felt her own lips stretching into something like a grin. It was a relief to feel the drama ratchet down. She'd never wanted to be one of the drama girls, not with the team or without. It was even a relief to feel the pain in her shoulder and the slow creep of blood from the wound she'd reopened—

She started to answer him, but stiffened instead, spinning to face the rippling horizon once more. As *She* and the new guy's cells settled into this time, she stepped protectively in front of Briggs. *She* noted the movement and her lips twisted wryly. The new guy moved forward to examine their catch.

"Nice work," he said, his wary gaze moving between Madison and their boss.

"That's Boris," she said, adding, "the one who erased my family."

"He's dead?" *She* asked.

"No." Madison lifted her shoulders in a sigh. "I'm not like him. I'm not a killer."

The new guy straightened, eyeing Madison carefully. "What do you want me to do with him?"

"I want you to keep him away from me," she said. Briggs stepped up next to her, his hand on her shoulder.

"You had help, I see," *She* said. Her gaze returned to Madison. "You can't trust them, you know, him least of all."

"Even a Time Service agent will tell the truth when he knows it will cause more damage than a lie," Madison said evenly.

She's gaze flicked toward Briggs. "We can talk about this later—"

Madison felt Briggs grip on her shoulder tighten, then loosen, as if he'd forced himself to do it. She shook her head.

"I'm not going back. I can't do it anymore."

"You could still be a target—"

"I don't exist, remember?" Her lips twisted wryly. "And according to him, you can't rearrange my brain. So you're going to have to trust me. And leave me alone to get on with my life."

She didn't like it, but the new guy was watching.

"We're supposed to be the good guys, remember?" Madison said.

She thinned her lips, but she gave a half nod. "Sir Rupert…"

There was a raucous caw-caw from the trees, then he sailed into view, landing lightly on Madison's shoulder.

"I think this island needs birds," he said. "Not to mention someone who can make sure you don't interfere with…anyone's future."

Madison reached up and stroked under his chin. "Thank you," she said softly.

The slightest slump in *She's* shoulders was the only sign he'd tipped the balance. Her blank gaze tracked between Madison and Briggs. "I don't suppose you're going to introduce us."

"Not a chance." Madison met and held her gaze. "I've done more than enough time. You know that's true."

The new guy spoke again. "We are the good guys, are we not, ma'am?"

"Of course." *She* gave a shrug that was not quite casual. "You did good work. We'll all miss you."

"You'd better," she let iron filter into her tone, "miss me, I mean."

She glanced at the new guy and finally did sigh. "You have my word." She nudged one of the men with a toe. "You have no idea how good she is…was," she said. "You will miss her."

The new guy grinned. "At least we got our mole."

Madison's smile was real this time. She glanced at Sir Rupert. "Good job."

Now that it was decided, *She* turned brisk. "Tag them for transport," she ordered. With a half salute for them, she vanished in a shimmer of horizon.

"I'll keep an eye on her," the new guy promised, before he and the catch of the day vanished.

Madison tensed, reaching out with her senses, but there was nothing but the night breeze and the light from the two moons. And a man and a bird. She gave a small chuckle, then laughed with sudden joy. It had been a long time...she sobered thinking about how long.

She faced the man. "I hope you meant it, because I can't go anywhere now."

Sir Rupert, as if he realized he was a bit in the way, lifted off, circling the clearing before landing on the table. Madison would have liked more space than that, but it was what it was.

The man rested his hands on her waist and she saw joy in his eyes, too, manly joy of course. But also hesitation.

"What's wrong?" she asked, lifting her hand so it rested against a cheek roughened by the beard he hadn't had time to shave.

"Today was my birthday," he admitted, with a rueful scowl. "That thing was a present sent by a couple of friends."

"Happy...birthday?" She couldn't remember the last time she'd been in real time to celebrate a birthday, or been with anyone who would have cared.

"I'm forty-five," he muttered.

Madison looked at him, trying to understand his problem.

"I'm a lot older than you," he muttered, even lower than before.

Her eyes widened and she couldn't help the half chuckle, half snort. "Sorry, but," she bit her lip. "You said this was 2017, right?" He nodded warily. "Briggs," was this the first time she'd said his name out loud? "I was born in, um, 1946."

She could see him doing the math.

"1946?"

She nodded. His hands slid further around her, moving up her back, then down her shoulders while heat built swiftly inside her. Heat and longing and an aching restlessness. His mouth turned up slowly, the smile sexy with lots of hot in his eyes.

"You're in really good shape."

"I try to work out and...and...eat right," she said, breathlessly, her lips aching for his. Had she only known this man a few hours?

"Do you know what my friend, do you know what Robert said, before he took the bird away?"

Madison almost lost her breath at this sign of trust and at the way his hand trembled as he smoothed the hair back off her face.

"What...did Robert say?" she asked.

"He said, you should keep her."

"Did...he?"

He bent his head toward her mouth. She pushed up on her toes, but his mouth was just a bit out of reach.

"Can I keep you, Madison?"

"Please," she said and finally his mouth covered hers. His arms banded around her, so that all of her was pressed against a lot of him. He was a big guy. But now there was time to get to know all of him. Lots and lots of lovely time.

COURTING DISASTER: STARDOG 2

Laurie A. Green

By

Laurie A. Green

Laurie A. Green is a three-time RWA Golden Heart® finalist, an award-winning author, and a science fiction romance enthusiast who founded the SFR Brigade community of writers.

http://www.laurieagreen.com/

ONE

Three Calendars After Operation Reset
  Carduwan Fifth Fleet Headquarters
  Talstar Station

Captain Navene Jagger smiled as he gazed out the viewport of the immense space station. Talstar. Home of the Universal Flight Academy, orbiting the lush blue world of Veros. Good memories here. Heady times with his fellow cadets during the three calendars it had required to earn his wings. He'd left the program with salutatorian honors.

But without Drea.

His smile slipped. Not every recollection of Talstar was a good one. The broken engagement. The devastation in Drea's eyes. Watching her walk away for the last time. It had been his greatest defeat—Hades, his *only* defeat. And he'd no one to blame but himself.

He'd left Talstar the day after graduation, abandoned his plans to test her father's Mennelsohn prototypes, and promptly joined the Carduwan military.

That had been ten calendars ago. Ten very long calendars. He'd spent the first seven trying to apologize to Drea for the unforgiveable, trying to prove to her he'd changed, trying desperately to win her back.

Until...*Sair* happened. Drea had fallen in love with an escaped slave. A nobody. Or so he'd thought.

That was when he'd finally grasped the scale of the wedge he'd driven between them by a few acts of foolish, ego-driven folly. *He'd* done this. *He'd* destroyed their relationship. Not Drea. And, Gods knew, not even Sair.

That realization had sparked his transformation. He'd reinvented himself, stopped being a ladies' man, stopped being *anything* other than a dedicated officer married to his career. He didn't have love...but at least he had pride. And purpose.

Jagger compartmentalized his lingering heartache and studied the mirror in the officers' lounge, doing one final inspection of his uniform. Every detail in perfect order. High and tight. Square and shiny. Dark hair cut to military precision. Brown eyes keen and confident. The very picture of a capable officer. He needed to make a big impression on what could turn out to be a monumental day.

Jagger left the lounge for the Fifth Fleet command offices to see Admiral Kareek. He'd been expecting this summons by his superior since he'd received orders to bring his mid-range battleship, *Imperative*, to berth at Talstar and report in. A new destroyer was about to be commissioned into the Carduwan fleet, and rumor in the ranks was that *Meritorious* was earmarked for his command. A successful tour with the fleet's newest and most advanced warship would surely herald a promotion to Senior Captain. It was what he lived for now.

Jagger picked up his step in anticipation. He'd paid his dues, many-fold. Three calendars had passed since he'd been loaned as a young buck captain to the covert Network fleet. He'd served as a kingpin in bringing down the mighty Ithian Alliance—heady days of flying a one-man Stiletto fighter. After Operation Reset, he'd been rewarded with the skipperdom of an aging heavy battlecruiser, *Jaden*, before the big kick upstairs to *Imperative*, a Dominion class destroyer with a crew complement of five hundred.

He was primed and ready for this next big challenge, a task that would surely deem him worthy, eventually, to carry the mantle of Fleet Admiral. To step into the very shoes of the man he'd been summoned to meet with today.

He presented himself to the ID scanner outside the admiral's offices. "Captain Navene Jagger. Appointment with Admiral Kareek." Several beams plotted his face, matching it to a simultaneous retinal scan, and the security locks clicked open. An automated voice announced his arrival and appointment time to the admiral's flag lieutenant working at his station in the anteroom.

The lieutenant saluted him. "Good morning, Captain Jagger. Admiral Kareek just received an important comm. He'll be with you in a moment."

Jagger returned the salute, nodded his understanding and milled about the room, examining the admiral's various citations and diplomas. He didn't want to risk wrinkling his flawless uniform by taking a seat. Better to stand tight and keep the shine on.

Five tempas later, the admiral himself opened his office seal and hailed in his booming voice, "Captain Jagger. Good to see you. Come in."

"Good morning, Admiral."

"Sorry about the stutter in the schedule. Had to drop everything to speak to a VIP." The man moved behind his desk and gave Jagger a shrewd grin. "Congressmen, you know."

"I understand, sir."

"Have a seat."

Jagger settled into one of the plush chairs before the admiral's desk, back straight, feet planted in front of him—his "seated at attention" mode.

"You were expecting to have a chat about the *Meritorius*."

Isn't that why I'm here? "It had crossed my mind, sir."

"I'm sure you've heard the scuttlebutt. Your peers are saying the ship is already yours."

"I never put much stock in rumors, sir. But I'd be more than honored to accept the command."

"Good answer." The admiral settled back in his chair, studying him. "You have a spotless record, Captain. You served the Network well. Admiral Ry Mennelsohn speaks of you in glowing terms."

Jagger shifted at the mention of Drea's brother. "Thank you, Sir."

"Your commands have been highlighted by the defeat and capture of two undocumented Alliance ships, all without loss of life on either side of the skirmish. Remarkable feats. Your superiors are quite impressed with you."

"I'm proud of my record, sir."

"There's just one hitch." Kareek leaned forward, planting his elbows on the desk. "Your pride, son."

"Sir?"

"You have an ego the size of the Bradley Rift, my boy. And sooner or later, it's going to trip you up. Those rogue ships you went after? You broke several rules of engagement in the pursuit. Since the outcome was for the greater glory of the Carduwan Fifth Fleet, you were given kudos instead of a reprimand, but you and I both know how much you risked in the attempt."

Jagger frowned. Kareek was questioning his suitability? "Admiral, I—"

"Hold your thoughts, Captain. I know you were a first-rate starfighter jock. And I know the academy tends to encourage a bold abandon in its young pilots. But you moved up to battleship command some time ago, and that brash bravado of yours hasn't mellowed one wit. That could be a dangerous wild card when you're responsible for a thousand lives. One day that pride is going to become a liability, and the brass doesn't want to see it jeopardize our latest and greatest battleship. If you want to evolve into the most elite of the elite—and I *know* you do—you need to acquire a healthy dose of humble."

It felt like the deck had given way beneath his feet. Kareek was *denying* him his due? "Are you saying you don't think I'm ready for the *Meritorious*?"

"I'm saying I can't offer you that command today."

What? Jagger raised his head and threw back his shoulders, firing all guns. "Sir, I'm the most senior of your promotable captains, and my service record is unmatched. No one is better prepared to skipper the *Meritorious*."

"Ah." The admiral wagged a finger at him. "You see. There's that infamous Jagger pride talking when it ought to be your conscience listening."

"I was merely—"

"I know what you were doing," the admiral rumbled, cutting him off with a firm wave of his hand. Kareek picked up his comm and checked the screen. "Truth is, the *Meritorious* command hasn't been decided. In the coming weeks, she'll be put through a series of space trials. Her commanding officer will be named upon completion of those tests." The admiral laid his comm back on the desk. "In the meantime, I have another assignment for you."

Jagger cocked his head. *What in Hades...* "Another, sir?"

"Yes. This morning I received a personal request from an old friend. Ambassador Gant. I believe you know him."

Jagger's mouth twisted in a half grin. Hell, the man had nearly been his uncle until he'd destroyed his chances with Drea. "Jaeo *Mennelsohn*. Yes, sir. I know him quite well."

"Probably why he requested you for this assignment, then." The admiral's black gaze settled on him. "It's sensitive. Your mission would be to fly a transport through the Bradley Rift. There are dangerous rogues cruising the sector—*Refugees*, they call themselves. Alliance holdouts who aren't happy with Gant's appointment as ambassador to Rathskia. Something to do with that whole business of him serving as commodore of the Network Fleet. At any rate, the ambassador has requested you be the one to provide safe escort to the embassy for his daughter and a companion."

"His daughter?" Jagger straightened. Jaeo's daughter—Drea's cousin—had gone missing four calendars ago—along with Jaeo's original ship, *Phantom*. "Daea Mennelsohn's been found?"

The admiral again consulted his comm screen. "No, no reference to a Daea. The girl's name is Ketsia. His recently adopted ward, as I understand it."

Ketsia? Had he heard that name before?

"She was part of the package when Jaeo recently married a Rathskian woman," the admiral explained.

"Yes, sir. I was invited to their wedding, but wasn't able to attend due to ship inspections." Jagger didn't add that he'd been grateful for the obligation. It was better to steer clear of Mennelsohn family doings than have to face the reality of Drea's happy bond with Sair.

"At any rate, this Ketsia is now his responsibility, and it seems her private transport came under fire by a renegade while en route to the ambassador from Purmia. Her pilot managed to shake the bastards loose and hightail it to the nearest safe spaceport—Talstar Station—meaning she has now fallen under the protection of the Carduwan Fleet."

"And I'm to escort her to Rathskia onboard the *Imperative*?"

The admiral shook his head. "No, Captain. *Imperative* will remain at dock. You'll have a new ship for this mission. The *Sheeban*."

"Never heard of her, sir."

"No one has." The admiral stood, gathering up the com in one beefy hand. "This is a covert mission we don't want linked to the Carduwan fleet. The politics are…delicate, so you won't be in standard uniform."

"I don't understand, sir."

"Certain sympathizers in the House of Planets just instituted a compact decreeing Bradley Rift a safe zone for these so-called Refugees, so it's off-limits to military vessels, and commercial transports steer clear due to navigational risks. The renegades believe that in order for Jaeo's daughter to reach him, a second ship will attempt to skirt the Rift. Intelligence tells us they're lying in wait for a potential target—a second private luxury transport or military vessel circumnavigating the area. We're going to fool them. You're going to take a worthless cargo and a civilian craft straight through the heart of the beast and blend in with the countless other space-freighter jocks who risk shortcuts through the territory. They won't expect it."

"Why wouldn't the Mennelsohn family just send *Specter* to retrieve her? The ship's DEDspace drive capability would make any threat a non-issue."

"Yes, but there's a catch. The Refugees have convinced their sympathizers that the Network is still a threat to them. They've pressured the House of Planets to restrict DEDspace engagement anywhere within a parsec of the Rift. If it's violated without due cause, well…trust me, son, it would become a political fireball."

And political fireballs tended to incinerate military careers. Jagger never backed off from a challenge, but this plan seemed hastily drawn and full of question marks. "What if these Refugees seize my cargo and find Jaeo's daughter onboard?"

"Highly unlikely. Even if you're approached, they'll first scan your cargo for valuables, and you won't be carrying anything of interest. They'll be looking for a bigger score. But regardless, we'll supply you both with a complete set of alternate identities and data histories as a precaution."

Jagger locked eyes with the admiral. "You're going to send me into the

Rift in a cargo ship with the ambassador's daughter onboard...and no defenses?"

"*Sheeban* has defenses, Captain. Paracannons, for one. And...other options." The admiral got to his feet. "There's a very short window on this, so you need to get underway before the rogues figure out what we're up to."

"Without a full briefing, sir?"

"No time. You'll receive your detailed mission instructions via a data-cell once you've left dock. Report to the Quartermasters in the next ten tempas to be outfitted for your civvy uniform. They'll provide you with new credentials, the transport's drive card, and any further info you'll need. The ambassador's daughter and her companion are being escorted to your transport, but you'll have time to undergo craft orientation."

"And the rest of the crew? When will they report?"

The admiral gave him a somber look and steepled his fingers together before him. "You *are* the crew, son."

TWO

Jagger stood at the docking bay entrance, trying to find any positives in this gigadam boondoggle. He'd be flying solo, he reminded himself, just like the glory days of slicing through space in his Rimcraft Stiletto. It might not be all bad. That thought tumbled and burned the moment he caught sight of the shipwreck at the end of the boarding passage.

He checked the bay number again. Yes. Right bay. He just couldn't believe what was berthed there.

The *Sheeban*'s battered two-deck carcass could've been a clunky, mid-ranged compost hauler that had seen its best days millennia ago. They wanted him to transport an ambassador's daughter on this wreck? What was the story here?

And his newly requisitioned uniform? Not a uniform at all. A worn set of coveralls, untailored, drab gray, and lacking any insignias. People were going to take him for a second-rate mechanic in these faded greaseskins instead of a top-flight Carduwan officer.

But that wasn't the worst of it. The garb came complete with a battered helmet and face shield. What was he supposed to be—a pilot or a test-flight dummy?

Judging by the look of his vessel, it was the latter.

The admiral couldn't be serious about this. Was this Kareek's idea of a joke? Or an elaborate hazing meant to take him down a peg or two before he was presented with command of the *Meritorious*?

He glanced at the small packet the quartermaster had pressed into his hand. "There's a purser's safe under the pilot's console," the non-com had told him. "Use these lock codes to open it once you've cleared station and are on course for the Rift. It contains your classified directive from Command."

This "directive" had better shed a lot more light on the situation. Like why was he being issued spacejunk to transport a diplomat's ward safely through a very treacherous region of space.

It was always an option to refuse a mission, but—Jagger heaved a weighty sigh—that had Career Ending Catastrophe stamped all over it.

Though maybe he'd luck out and this Ketsia wouldn't be the sort to settle for an antiquated monstrosity to ferry her to the ambassador. Maybe she'd refuse to step foot on the derelict, and the mission would be cancelled before it began, with no black mark on his record.

Jagger strode up to the entry and punched in the access code he'd been given. The hatch popped, allowing him into the airlock. He pulled and activated the electropad containing the ship's orientation, doing a quick walk-through of the main deck of the *Sheeban*.

The inside of the ship looked nothing like the outside, thank the Gods —clean, pristine and polished to a shine, though clearly vintage. Someone had either meticulously maintained her interior, or she'd had a first-rate restorer lend his talents to her innards. It seemed a strange inequity, but at least the part of the ship he'd have to live in for the two-week flight was passable.

He did a sweep inspection of the galley, forward lounge, and three small cabins on the main deck, placated that everything appeared tidy and spiffed. After taking the lift up to the Flight Deck, he inspected the pilot's console. His electropad provided flight instructions and instrumentation layout. All very straightforward.

He'd just returned to main deck when he caught sight of three figures approaching the boarding passage on the exterior monitors.

His passengers had arrived.

He returned to the airlock and opened the seal to greet them.

The young girl had paused with her entourage midway up the boarding passage, appraising *Sheeban* not with a look of utter disdain but pure reverence. Her mouth parted to form a silent word his lip-reading skills couldn't decipher. The two uniform-clad-but-not-up-to-military-standard males escorting her were most likely flight officers from her private transport.

Jagger popped off the ridiculous helmet and gave Jaeo's dependent a quick once-over, puzzling at the expression of rapture that still lingered on her face. How could a wreck like *Sheeban* get this reaction from anyone?

Jagger made his way down the boarding passage to greet the party, which was when he realized that Ketsia wasn't the mid-teen girl he'd been expecting. Petite, yes, but a beauty of at least twenty calendars, with flaw-less deep bronze skin, a generous smile, shimmering black hair, and the most luminous ebony eyes he'd seen in his thirty calendars.

Ketsia Mennelsohn wasn't just a surprise, she was an EMP exploding through his systems.

She turned as he approached, her poise transforming a simple black suit into a garment of stately elegance. With a graceful bend to her knees, she lowered her case to the ramp beside her feet.

Jagger came to a stop a respectful three strides out from her and her escorts. "Captain Jagger with the Carduwan Fifth Fleet."

One of the men stepped forward to make proper introductions—possibly her pilot, judging by the fringed shoulder boards and elaborate gold chevrons marching down the sleeves of the uniform. "I'm Captain Farrol of the Trigate transport yacht." He emphasized the last two words, his gaze making a critical sweep over the battered hull of the *Sheeban*. "This is Roham, my co-pilot. And may I introduce Ms. Ketsia Tayah, ward of Ambassador Gant."

"Captain." Jagger shook the man's hand mechanically. "Co." His attention settled on the young woman. "Ms. Tayah. It will be a pleasure serving you on behalf of the Carduwan Fleet."

"Thank you, Captain Jagger." She accepted his offered hand and slanted her head in an affirming nod. The unabridged definition of charming. She wasn't Rathskian, as he'd expected. Based on her features, he guessed she was Tectolian, a subspecies rumored to have originated on a scattering of sun-blessed islands in some forgotten sea.

Jagger addressed her chaperones. "Which of you will be accompanying Ms. Tayah to Rathskia?"

"Neither, I'm afraid," Farrol said regretfully. "We've been ordered to remain with the yacht to oversee repairs. She took quite a strafing from the renegades."

"I see." No question the lightly-armed luxury craft had gotten the worst of a skirmish with a rogue guerilla gunship. His gaze returned to Ketsia. "I was told you'd have a companion."

She gracefully bent and hefted the case beside her feet in one hand. "I do."

Jagger scowled at her luggage, noting the hard sides and narrow slots. Not a bag then—a crate. "You're bringing an animal aboard?" Jagger regretted his gruff tone as soon as it slipped out. Intolerance wasn't one of his more admirable qualities.

"Not just an animal." She gave him a wary—and utterly heart-stopping—smile. "My StarDog."

"A pet?" He tried, and failed, not to sound cynical.

"A *friend*," Ketsia clarified.

"I wasn't aware I'd be transporting live cargo."

"Luna's not cargo, Captain. She's well-trained, and she was reared on starships, so she won't be any trouble."

Her yacht jock spoke up. "You can rest assured the animal won't sully your…" Captain Farrol squinted at the *Sheeban* with obvious distaste. "…fine ship."

Bringing a scowl to bear on the man, Jagger squared his shoulders and pointedly let the helmet drop from his hand to bounce by the chin strap. Junkheap or not, no one insulted any ship *he* captained. "My conveyance may not be much to look at, but I assure you she'll finish the job you started."

Farrol's eyes narrowed, and he turned to Ketsia. "Are you *quite* comfortable with your transport, Ms. Tayah? It's an unusual situation, to be sure. If you're not completely satisfied…"

The woman's gaze settled once again on the ancient ship before flitting to Jagger. "I have every confidence in the plans. And this ship." She gave the men a smile full of conviction. "Thank you, gentlemen. You can be on your way."

"Very well. We'll return to the repair docks then. But if you should change your mind—"

"You're good to go, Captain," Ketsia said then lifted her radiant eyes back to Jagger's. "I've been assured I'll be in the best of hands."

Wait. Was that a hint of snark in her tone? How much did this woman know about him? It wouldn't be like Jaeo to fill his daughter in on his history with the Mennelsohns. Would it?

The men muttered their farewells and ambled off with several dubious glances back at *Sheeban*.

"Right," Jagger said, reaching for the crate. "We need to get underway. I can stow the animal while you get settled in your quarters."

Now her black eyes snapped with alarm. "You won't be stowing her anywhere. She stays with me. And her name is Luna."

No Sundog—or whatever she'd called the creature—was going to have free run of his ship. "I'm sorry, ma'am, but we have strict protocols regarding live cargo."

"With all due respect, Captain, it seems your military protocols have been thoroughly dispensed with for this mission. Luna stays with me."

So this beautiful face had a bite to it? He didn't like making exceptions, but he owed a lot to Jaeo, and by extension, his family. Jagger backed off a step, dropping his voice a full octave to rumble, "Noted. I can allow it a trial, but if it causes any mischief, I'll insist it be confined."

"*She* won't be any trouble." Ketsia lowered her head to soothe the creature in a voice soft with affection. "Will you, baby?" That gentle lilt caressed Jagger's awareness like a whisper, making his imagination fire and his traitorous pulse rate spike.

Lock it down! He gave his face a mental slap. *Even if women were still on your menu, this one is totally off-limits.*

Ketsia lifted her chin, and her black gaze returned to his face. "So, as I understand it, we're supposed to be married?"

Jagger managed not to choke on his tongue. "Pardon?"

"I was told in case of trouble, our story is that we're Dallan and Adey Tion, a bonded pair of independent freighters, transporting seeds to the new colony on Arst."

"Now there's a brilliant cover." Jagger huffed out a breath and donned his helmet, snapping the chin strap into place. Not bad enough that they'd given him a shoddy relic to fly, but they'd married him off, as well?

Ketsia lowered her head, but her eyes remained fixed on his faceplate. "They didn't tell you this?"

"Only the essentials for now, due to the short window." Jagger subconsciously ran a hand over the code card in the thigh pocket of his coveralls. As soon as they disembarked, he'd pull the datacube and get up to speed.

"Captain Jagger, am I to understand you don't fully comprehend your mission?"

She was questioning his fitness? "Ms. Mennelsohn, if you have any doubts about my qualifications or my suitability—"

"It's Ms. Tayah."

"—then it's your prerogative to request a different escort. But the truth is I'm woefully *overqualified* to carry out my orders."

She lifted an eyebrow and crossed her arms. "I'm aware of your sterling qualifications, Captain."

He returned her glare, satisfied the faceplate concealed the ire heating his face. She wouldn't hear it in his words. "Further, Ambassador Mennelsohn specifically requested me for this duty."

"Ambassador Gant. He hasn't gone by Mennelsohn for many calendars." She peered up at him dubiously.

He met her skepticism with a deep frown. "I'm aware of that."

"Could you please take that off?" she asked quietly. "Because I feel like I'm talking to a machine."

A machine, was he? With one quick swipe at the catch under his chin, Jagger clamped his hands on the sides of the helmet and lifted it free of his head, stowing it under one arm.

"I imagine—"

He savored the satisfaction of seeing her eyes widen and her mouth part slightly, truncating her thought.

His subspecies tended to sport sharp, pinched features and a pronounced beak for a nose. Jagger's face was atypical for his kind. Most women found him attractive, and downright alpha when his eyes went stormy. Miss Rathskian Ambassador's Daughter appeared to be no exception.

"What did you imagine?" he challenged in a deep, rolling bass.

The StarDog answered with a low growl from inside the case.

"Luna, no," Ketsia whispered, placing her hand over the wire mesh door.

"I don't think your animal likes me."

"That's one thing we can both agree on." Her eyes flashed with exasperation.

Sweet Hades. Even when she was angry, she was...captivating.

And that set all the sirens blaring in the early warning system in his heart. The same awareness detector that hadn't sounded in three long calendars.

Jagger composed himself before announcing, "Unless you wish to request other arrangements, we'll deploy in five tempas."

"The arrangements..." She met his lock-jawed challenge before her eyes cut back to the *Sheeban*'s sorry carcass. "...suit me fine."

"Noted," Jagger said flatly. "Let me show you to your cabin before we get underway."

THREE

Once he'd piloted *Sheeban* clear of her berth, Jagger input the course into the nav-system and pulled the packet with the code card from the thigh pocket of his coveralls. He opened it and dumped the contents into his palm. Along with the safe's lock code, a square of paper slipped out. Jagger unfolded it to discover a handwritten note from Admiral Kareek himself.

Captain Jagger:

The fact that you're reading this letter means you didn't file a protest of your assignment at first sight of this junk dealer reject. If so, you will have pleasantly surprised me. It proves you've got more mettle than I gave you credit for.

But then, if you have half the intelligence your IQ tests avow, you might have realized that neither the Carduwan government nor Ambassador Gant would allow his ward to be transported through a dangerous sector of space in a second-rate shit-hauler.

There's a reason he chose you...and a reason he had this ship delivered to Talstar for your assignment.

Once you're set to leave dock, insert the enclosed datacube into the side port of your helmet for your full briefing of mission parameters and this craft's capabilities. Let me assure you that, despite appearances, piloting this vessel will afford you a very unique opportunity.

Once you leave the Talstar Traffic Perimeter, you'll make no further contact with Command to maintain your cover. We can't risk a rogue ship picking up any official communications from the Sheeban. *You are to dispose of this message and the instructional datacell in the ship's waste incinerator before you enter the Bradley Rift.*

Be safe out there, Captain Jagger. Take good care of your passenger. Much is riding on your success.

Jagger lowered the note to his thigh. The admiral's last words carried the punch he was sure the man had intended.

So Jaeo himself had arranged for the delivery of the *Sheeban* especially for this assignment? Then there had to be a lot more to the old girl than just a scuffed carcass and faded paint.

That much was heartening. He looked forward to *this* briefing.

He plugged the code into the purser safe and opened it to extract the datacell.

After reaching up to locate the helmet input port with his fingers, he plugged in the device containing his full brief.

The inside of his faceplate exploded to life in a vivid, 3D display.

Ketsia checked the fit of the scruffy gray coveralls in the imager on the wall of her quarters. Hardly flattering, but at least the material was comfortable.

She glanced at the helmet resting sideways on her bed—*rack*, she mentally corrected. Luna had made a den of it, and only the StarDog's bushy tail was visible, jutting out the opening.

"Don't get too comfortable. I'm going to need that."

Luna chittered back at her softly.

"Ha," Ketsia huffed. "No, it isn't. You'll just have to find something else to cuddle up in."

She moved to the bed and lifted the helmet, rousing Luna by spilling her out onto the covers. The StarDog flicked her pointed ears, clicked her teeth, and deftly jumped to the arm of her coveralls, climbing up to perch on her shoulder in a blurr of white and black. Ketsia eased the headgear on, fixing the strap and initializing the feed. The 3D displays glowed to life on the inner surface of the faceplate.

Ketsia scanned the read-outs and smiled.

Luna squeaked.

"Well, yes, he does seem a little arrogant—"

Luna interrupted with a sharp trill.

Ket winced and clamped her hands over the helmet's ear vents. "All right, incredibly arrogant. But Jaeo believes Captain Jagger can get us through the Rift safely. We'll be with him for two weeks, so we should try to be allies."

The little StarDog sneezed.

"We should still try."

Ketsia left her quarters with Luna balanced on her right shoulder, and scouted the main deck for the captain. Not finding him, she headed up the lift to the upper deck. He didn't need to be at his console to fly the ship, but she supposed he'd gravitated there out of habit.

Sure enough, she found him slouched in a flight couch, his visor pointed out the port toward the stars.

"Captain Jagger," Ketsia greeted.

He lowered the leg he'd braced against the console and straightened in his seat. "Ms. Mennelsohn."

"Ms. Tayah. But please call me Ketsia to dispense with formalities."

"Fair enough." He gave a subtle nod. "Call me Jagger, if you prefer."

From the angle of his head, halfway between her and the port, she couldn't tell if he was looking at her or out into space.

She gave him a tight smile. "Mind if I man the co console?"

"I see you dressed for the occasion," he quipped, not acknowledging the unusual enhancement of a StarDog parked on her shoulder.

"Yes." She settled in the co-pilot's couch and ran her fingers over the worn sleeve of the coveralls. "Best to look the part, even if the plan is not to be spotted."

"A sensible precaution," he agreed.

"Do you think we'll fool the rogues?" she asked.

"Probably." His visor turned fully in her direction. "But there's more to worry about in the Rift than renegades. Slavers, human traffickers, drug-runners, and fugitives tend to populate it, too. Still, none are likely to take note of us. Crop seeds don't present a desirable bounty to spaceborne criminals."

Ketsia focused on the proximity scan readouts on the left side of her visor. No blips on the screen out to the scan range of a million milos.

"So I assume you've now had your full briefing? Did it come as a surprise?"

The Carduwan captain's mouth eased into a guarded smile. "Quite. Recovered two calendars ago from a boneyard on Dartis and with just her interior restored to date, she only looks the part of rat-hulled spacejunk." He reached out to pat the monitor, as if in apology to the craft. "But our lowly *Sheeban* is none other than the legend herself—*Banshee*. Zaviar Mennelsohn's celebrated original prototype."

Luna added a happy trill to his glowing valuation.

"And yet you took this assignment thinking you were flying into the Rift in a battered hulk of a ship. Why would you do it?"

"I've never been one to question duty." He straightened his legs, pushing himself back into the flight couch.

"I seriously doubt that," Ketsia muttered.

"Regardless," Jagger replied in a clipped tone. "I did it for Jaeo. We go back a long way."

Ketsia nodded. "Back to your Flight Academy days."

Jagger's face shield quickly angled her way, but he simply responded,

"That's correct," and looked away again, with no apparent curiosity about how deep her knowledge of his history ran.

In truth, it was pretty shallow. A few mentions by Jaeo...and her personal knowledge of Captain Jagger from her ordeal on the Network command ship, *Spirit*. But it was obvious he didn't remember that frightened, disoriented seventeen-year-old girl who'd clung to Sair like he was her only lifeline to sanity.

"Do you mind if I fly her for a while?" Ketsia asked.

The captain braced his feet against the deck and straightened his spine, his body language registering clear surprise. "You know how to fly *Banshee*?"

"Yes. Jaeo used to take me along when he checked her out of the museum on *Spirit* for maintenance runs." Ketsia skimmed her fingertips along the armrest of her flight couch. "He taught me."

"You have a functional unit?" Jagger asked, tipping his helmet toward the one she wore.

"Of course. Fully functional." She laughed softly. "I'm not just wearing it for looks."

Captain Jagger glanced at his monitor, reached over to flip a couple of switches, and went still, apparently scanning the readouts hidden on the inside of his visor—the same data Ketsia was receiving on hers—for their status. He could relax. They were in the clear, still days away from entering the Bradley Rift.

"Be my guest," he finally agreed.

Ketsia raised her head and her voice along with it, "*Sheeban*. Co-pilot assuming command."

The ship pinged an acknowledgement, and the helm was transferred from Jagger's drive helmet to hers, flashing a line of blue letters: Pilot transfer: Dallan Tion to Adey Tion.

"The ship was programmed with our cover names," Ketsia remarked.

"Fleet wouldn't overlook obvious details."

He drummed his fingers on the arm rest and his body went rock-still. Was he scanning every detail of his readouts for trouble? He may have allowed her to take the con out of curiosity, but he clearly wasn't comfortable with her piloting capabilities.

"Relax, Captain," she reassured him. "I've flown her dozens of times without the slightest mishap."

"Duly noted," he said, after attempting to casually clear his throat.

Luna became active on her shoulder, moving from side-to-side and softly chittering her brand of encouragement. Ketsia laughed at her antics and reached up to scratch her little buddy's neck.

She caught the slow swivel of Jagger's helmet from the vu-port to Luna's bouncing shoulder dance.

"Where do StarDogs hail from?" he asked. "Never encountered one before."

Despite his face being half-hidden by the visor, he seemed genuinely interested. "They hail from a talented bio-engineer." Ketsia pressed her knuckles to the base of her helmet and eased it back to a more comfortable position. "They're recombinant canine, weasel, mongoose, and feline DNA, created to serve as starship mascots and vermin exterminators." Giving him a sly smile, the one expression visible to him below her faceshield, she added, "And as Network spies on Alliance ships, if the rumors are true."

"Huh." He shifted in his seat. "And how does an ambassador's daughter come by such an animal?"

She affectionately stroked Luna's soft fur. "She was a gift."

"From a man friend?"

Ketsia sniffed. What, did he think men regularly showered her with exotic gifts? "From two friends, actually. Taro and Adini Shall. A couple who crewed for Jaeo on *Wisdom* when he was flying for the Network. The same vessel that had to be destroyed in spaceport during a covert Network mission."

"I remember *Wisdom*," Jagger said in a low voice. "She was a good ship."

Did he also remember that it was Captain Drea Mennelsohn who'd destroyed her uncle's ship to keep it out of enemy hands? The same Drea Mennelsohn he'd probably flown with during Operation Reset, and who was now bondmate to her good friend Sair.

He'd certainly gotten quiet.

"Jaeo returned later to retrieve his crew. I met Taro and Adini on his new vessel, *Acumen*."

"And how did Jaeo's crew come by a StarDog?" Jagger eventually inquired.

"Adini told me Luna was the sole survivor of an Ithian raid on the bio-engineer's StarDog lab on Carduwa. It happened about six moons before Operation Reset, when Luna was just a tiny StarPup."

"And the animal somehow ended up in their hands?"

"It wasn't random. Adini was the bio-engineer's daughter," Ketsia said, glancing his way. "She smuggled Luna off Carduwa on a ship that Taro crewed as navigator at the time. It was just after they met. In fact, another StarDog was the reason they met at all. Adini ended up having to barter the other StarDog to Taro's captain to pay for transport. Luna is the last of her genetic copies. She meant a lot to them."

"And yet they gave her to you?"

"It's more like a permanent loan." Ketsia lifted the StarDog off her shoulder and into her lap, sliding her fingers through the animal's silky black and white coat. "While I was aboard *Acumen*, Luna and I formed a special bond. We can...understand each other. When it came time for me to leave the ship, Adini said she didn't see how they could separate us, so she told me to keep Luna with me. It was really hard for Adini and Taro to say goodbye to her."

"That seems extraordinarily kind of them."

"They're extraordinarily kind people. Taro is Tectolian, like me. He reminds me so much of my brother. A brother I haven't seen...since I was a child."

"Why is that?"

Ketsia drew a deep breath. It still hurt to remember this part of her life. "Because I was taken from my family on Tectol as part of a tribute." She paused, trying to gain control of her emotions before finishing. "I was sent to Ithis as slave stock...until Captain Drea Mennelsohn saved us, just before Operation Reset."

Jagger's body stiffened, and he faced forward in his seat. "You were one of the escapees Drea brought to *Spirit*?"

"Yes." Ketsia's gaze cut to Jagger's visor. "One of two hundred."

She was one of Sair's!

Jagger fought to quell his reaction. Sair—*Drea's* Sair and now *Congressman* Sair—a former breeding slave on Ithis. A man with a harem of two hundred females....which had apparently included Ketsia. He clamped his jaw so tight that his molars ached.

He'd been on *Spirit* when Drea brought the women to refuge, still stinging from Drea's rejection. Still reeling from the choice she'd made.

Sair.

And now to discover this woman had been one of the man's females on Ithis? Gigadam!

Jagger bolted to his feet and turned for the lift.

Her puzzled voice chased after him. "Jagger? Is something wrong?"

"Just getting some lunch." He doubted his terse reply would fool her, but he needed to sort out his head without her present to see how much this new wrinkle had thrown him.

She was one of Sair's. Haley's Crest!

He stepped on to the lift and escaped to the main deck then stormed into the galley. Rifling through the refrigeration unit, he chose two meals from the well-stocked provisions. He ripped open the packages and thrust the containers into the fren-oven to heat while he stood glaring at the galley wall.

Sair had done what Jagger couldn't. He'd made Drea happy. Together, the two of them had saved the universe. Operation Reset would most likely have failed catastrophically if it hadn't been for the sacrifices they'd both made.

And now they were bondmates.

Happily bonded...with a young daughter.

He still cursed himself for the impetuous, ego-fueled deeds that had cost him the love of his life. He'd often questioned why Drea would choose a man like Sair—a breeding stud with two hundred women—when his own transgressions amounted to no more than a handful of hurried, no-strings-attached encounters during flight academy.

Was it to teach him a lesson? To repay him with the same pain he'd caused her?

Jagger leaned against the galley wall and rocked his head back, thumping his helmet against the bulkhead.

No. Drea's actions hadn't been vindictive, as much as he'd wanted to believe it was all about him. She loved Sair. With every atom of her being. And Sair loved her back, with a fierce loyalty no one could deny. Not after what had happened to her in the battle over Ithis. Not after Sair had stood by her side when the rest of the universe—including Drea's own brother—had written her off.

"I remember you."

Jagger raised his head from the wall. Ketsia stood before him, her hands clasped, the visor in place over her eyes. "You should be at your console," he growled.

"I used to watch you walking the *Spirit* corridors. You always looked... so lost. Haunted. And that's what I was feeling, too."

Jagger straightened. "I wasn't lost. I was a Network officer with a job to do. And we were facing impossible odds."

"But you seemed so...broken. I always wondered—"

Jagger ignored the flare of pain in his gut, and cut her off with the snap of his upraised palm—the universal hand signal for 'halt.' "*Sheeban*. Pilot, assuming command." An audible beep and acknowledgment flashed inside his visor.

Ketsia's hands lowered to her sides, weighted by her clenched fists. "Why did you do that?"

Jagger pushed off the wall with his shoulders and loomed over her. "You're distracted by inconsequential nonsense, and your attention isn't on the controls, where it should be."

Ketsia's mouth dropped open. Her little StarDog wrapped itself protectively around her shoulders, chittering at him angrily.

"That thing had better not bite."

Luna stopped scolding, and her beady black eyes locked on him. It was almost like she could—

"This *thing* can understand every word you say," Ketsia said quietly. Her lower lip trembled, but whether from hurt or rage, he couldn't tell with her eyes hidden. "If you'll excuse us, we'll return to our cabin." She stalked out of the galley without her lunch, but with Luna facing backward on her shoulder, glaring at him.

Jagger turned to brace a shoulder against the wall, teeth set on edge. He hadn't handled this well at all, but he damned sure didn't need her rubbing his nose in the past, whether she'd meant to or not.

When he'd accepted this mission, he'd had no idea who Ketsia was or that she'd been present onboard *Spirit* during the darkest chapter of his life.

Did she know? Had Drea told her the story? Or Sair? Or Jaeo?

Yes. He'd made thoughtless, unprincipled mistakes as a young cadet—and he'd paid for those follies with his future. But he wasn't that man anymore. Losing everything that truly mattered to him had turned him to stone inside. He couldn't even remember when he'd last been with a woman.

Yet somehow Fate had seen fit to throw him together with this Tectolian beauty—of all people, one of Sair's harem.

Get your head back in the game!

Yes, dammit, he had a mission to perform. Get Ketsia Tayah home safely to Ambassador Gant, by way of a treacherous dark nebula where bloodthirsty criminals lurked. Fighting this reckless attraction for a black-eyed seraph who seemed set on opening old wounds was definitely not in his game plan.

FOUR

Admiral Kareek's voice echoed in Jagger's head. *"You have an ego the size of the Bradley Rift, my boy. And sooner or later, it's going to trip you up."*

It had tripped him up.

His pride had been calling the shots since he'd walked out of the admiral's office—first with his frustration at not being granted command of *Meritorious*, and then his disgust at being saddled with an aging ship he'd believed below his station.

And finally...with the way he'd treated Ketsia. She'd done nothing to deserve his admonishment. Maybe he really was the prideful bastard his superiors believed him to be.

Ketsia had avoided him by staying in her cabin for the last two days, apparently only venturing into the galley for a meal when she knew he was busy in other parts of the ship. At least he could hear her talking to her StarDog from time to time, so he knew she was still alive and breathing.

His fault, he admitted to himself. Totally his doing.

It didn't matter that she seemed to trip all his toggles on so many emotional levels—especially when he refused to acknowledge he still *had* emotions. It wasn't her fault that their shared history was anchored in territory he never wanted to navigate again. He was a Carduwan officer, for Crest's sake, and she was his responsibility. He owed her adopted father—and by extension, *her*—every courtesy. He'd been entirely unprofessional.

And it stopped now. Starting with a very humble apology.

Yes, he could do humble. It was within his range.

He clicked on the ship's intercom, summoning a semblance of calm he wasn't feeling. "Could you come to the Flight Deck? There's something I'd like to show you."

He winced. That sounded like some unimaginative pickup line. And he should know. He'd used it more than once in the long ago and best forgotten.

Worse yet, he hadn't even said 'please.' Lords, when was the last time *that* word had been part of his vocabulary?

A long pause preceded her equally composed response. "I'm on my way."

He kept his eyes on the display monitor when she walked onto the Flight Deck a few moments later.

Ketsia took in the trim lines of the man's uniform. Captain Navene Jagger cut quite the dashing figure in those threadbare coveralls. He looked every inch the outstanding officer she believed him to be. But she didn't understand how she'd triggered such a negative reaction in the man that he'd stalked off the Flight Deck to escape her company.

Was it somehow connected to her assuming the controls of *Banshee*? He'd certainly been quick to wrest control back into his no doubt capable hands.

Or was it the fact she'd followed him? Or her childish admission that she remembered him from *Spirit*?

Hades, she'd *obsessed* over him. Watched him, and watched for him. Like some sad little orphan puppy pining for a glimpse of her hero.

Now the man seemed to resent who and what she was—or who she'd been—on some very deep level…but why?

And why summon her to the Flight Deck now? Unless he was looking for another fight.

"Have you ever seen the Rift?" he asked, without turning her way.

She pulled up short. "The Bradley Rift? You can see it?"

"At this distance, yes. It's quite impressive. You might want to take a look." He gestured to the monitor in front of the co-pilot console. "You won't have this view once we've entered the region."

She approached him with care in her step and in her tone. "Why is that?"

"The dust and gas clouds are only visible from a distance through *Banshee*'s filters. Once we're inside the nebula, the particles will be too thinly disbursed to detect on the monitor even though they'll obscure our scanners."

Ketsia lifted off her helmet and peered at the screen before her, mesmerized by the images emerging from the swirling blue-green-red-violet chaos. "I see monsters."

He managed an off-kilter smile. "Most people do."

The man should smile more often. It was a nice look for him. Much nicer than the hard frown and harsh words she'd spent two days avoiding.

Ketsia traced a circle around one section of the screen. "Here there be dragons," she said quietly. "Two of them. Intertwined. Both breathing fire."

"That's called pareidolia. Your brain trying to recognize familiar patterns where none exist, trying to make sense out of nonsense in the chaos."

Yeah, her brain had been attempting to do just that ever since the baffling nonsense in the galley.

"Look." Ketsia reached out to hit the magnification on one section of the image. "There's Luna."

Jagger studied the area she pointed to. "It does indeed look like your little StarDog."

Oh Hades. That smile! Ketsia forced her attention back to the monitor. "What formed the Rift?"

He gestured to the center of the monitor. "Long ago, a star went supernova in this sector and blasted everything around it to oblivion with hot gases. When the supernova eventually burned out billions of calendars later, the Bradley Rift was left behind. An atypical dark nebula filled with charged particles that make navigation difficult and scanning impossible except at close range. That's why outlaws have used it as a hideout for centuries."

"What do you mean by 'atypical'?"

"Something prevented new stars from forming in the region after the event. It's left scientists quite baffled."

"So she's a mystery girl."

Jagger gave a soft laugh. "I guess you could say that."

She liked this Captain Jagger—the more soft-spoken, genteel version of the Asshole Space Jock she'd recently sparred with. Even if she might be partly to blame for bringing out the ASJ side of him.

"I want to apologize to you," he offered, stopping her thoughts cold, "for my behavior the other day. You're under my protection, and I didn't treat you with the courtesy you deserve. It won't happen again."

Ketsia traced a random image on the monitor with the tip of her finger. "Was it something I said?"

Jagger adjusted the controls. "Yes. And no. You mentioned the *Spirit*. I have some bad memories connected to that."

She tilted her head quizzically. "To *Spirit*?"

"To that time on *Spirit*."

She gave a slow bob of her head. "It wasn't exactly a happy time for me either."

Still perched on her shoulder, the StarDog raised up on its little feet and extended its nose with pointed ears pricked. Chittering quietly, it fixed its soft brown eyes intently on his visor. Then, without warning, the beast leaped, landing on his shoulder. Jagger stiffened, fighting the impulse to throw the animal to the deck. "What's it doing?"

"Trying to make friends," Ketsia answered.

"Seems more like an aggressive takeover."

She laughed. "She's not aggressive. In fact, I think she's starting to like you."

"I'm not sure the feeling is mutual."

Ketsia gave him a pensive grin. "Just give her a chance. She'll be your best friend once you get to know her."

Jagger reached up slowly to run his palm over the little beastie, bracing for a nip or a sharp bite. Instead, the little StarDog...purred? It actually purred like a domestic feline as Jagger stroked its soft, thick fur. And like a feline, it arched its back and rubbed against the side of his helmet then licked his hand like a canine.

"What are StarDogs made of again?" Jagger asked.

"Recombinant weasel, mongoose, canine, and feline DNA. All the best properties of each to create a lethal vermin hunter and loyal companion perfectly suited to a starship environment."

"Luna?" Jagger asked, rubbing his thumb over the animal's tilted head. "Is that your name? Maybe short for Lunatic?"

"No." Ketsia snickered. "Taro and Adini's other StarDog was named Katrina, after a legendary queen. So Taro named this copy 'Luna,' in honor of that same high queen's shieldcrest—the moons of LaGuardia."

"I've never heard that legend."

"You're not LaGuardian."

"Neither are you."

"No. But Adini is. Half LaGuardian and half Purmian."

"Now there's a lethal combination." Jagger grinned, remembering Drea's petite and fiery Purmian first mate and close friend, Commander Zjel Shenna. At least, that was what everyone had called Zjel back in the Network days. Except for him. He'd always called her Spitfire.

Of course, now everyone called her Duchess.

Luna nuzzled Jagger's ear, making a quiet gurgling sound followed by a few soft barks.

"What's she doing now?"

"Communicating." Ketsia laughed. "She's saying, 'Pay more attention to me. You're getting distracted.'"

"Sorry, girl." Jagger rubbed the StarDog's ears.

"It's good to see you make friends."

Jagger gave a sly smile. "I wouldn't go that far."

"How far would you go?" Ketsia blushed, an appealing shade of pink over her lovely bronze skin. "Wait. I didn't mean…"

Jagger just languished behind his faceshield and watched Ketsia squirm. He couldn't help himself. She was an adorable squirmer. A stunning, tongue-tied, ebony-haired, pink-lipped seductress who had no clue what she could do to a man just by saying the wrong thing at the right time.

But she was also ten calendars his junior…and his duty and responsibility.

He needed to keep his head in the game and his cock out of it.

"It's all right," Jagger reassured her. "I didn't take that in the usual context."

Now it was Ket who stared. Sans faceshield. Until she dropped her eyes in utter discomposure.

Right. So there seemed to be a spark on both sides of this fuse.

And here they were, alone together on a vessel navigating a dark nebula.

This might turn out to be more dangerous for the two of them than all the bad guys roaming the Rift combined.

FIVE

They were four days into the Rift, and so far, no danger had materialized —in either sense of the word.

While Jagger was awake, it was easier. He could shift his thoughts from forbidden territory to an underperforming circuit or a scheduled course adjustment to keep his mind on the straight and true.

But after he turned the controls over to auto-pilot—or Ketsia—and went to tumble into his rack for a few haras rest, his imagination took over and ran amok. No way to whip his growing preoccupation back into submission when his subconscious was the officer on deck. Somehow, he had to find a way—honorably—to get through seven more days with his sanity and lust both thoroughly in check.

Gigadam. This wasn't a scenario he'd even remotely imagined he'd be facing.

He'd tried reverse psychology. At first, the mere thought of Ketsia with Sair was enough to snuff out any rising flames. But lately, even those tormenting images had flip-flopped into edgy yearning.

It didn't help that her cabin was right next to his, just one wall separating them. And it was certainly no easy thing to catch her subtle side-eye or the tiny hitch in her stride whenever he was near, and know she was waging some inner battle with herself, as well.

But was she fighting an urge to run *to* him or *away* from him? Strike that. Maybe it was better if he didn't know.

Her little StarDog seemed to be warming up to him and accepting him into her pack—or clowder, or boogle, or whatever term was used for a StarDog family. Little Luna was now just as likely to jump onto his shoulder as Ketsia brushed by him in the corridor as she was to stay with her mistress.

And Ketsia didn't seem to mind.

Sometimes, the pint-sized creature would stay with him for haras, chittering, cooing, and purring softly beside his ear. *Not helping, little one.*

He had no idea what she was going on about. If only he could speak StarDog, he might be privy to her mistress's deepest secrets.

No, cancel that. He didn't want to go there. He didn't want to know what the beauty really thought of him.

Luna suddenly jumped from his shoulder and skittered across the deck and up the wall to a duct outlet—her method of moving quickly between decks—and disappeared.

Flight Deck seemed suddenly quiet and secluded without the little beast for company.

And without Ketsia.

Jagger kicked back in his flight couch, folded his arms, scanned his readouts, and stared out into the emptiness of the Bradley Rift.

Captain Navene Jagger was quite possibly the most fascinating man Ketsia had ever met. It had taken days of living and interacting together, alone aboard the *Banshee*, before she finally began to see through the layers of staid Carduwan officer to the man at the core.

Luna had seen through him much sooner.

As soon as the little StarDog started warming up to him, Ket knew there had to be a prince in there somewhere. Luna was never wrong about people. Ever.

Yes, Jagger put up quite a solid front—often arrogant and aloof. Sometimes rude. Occasionally scornful. But she'd had a few rare glimpses at another side of him. Like those brief moments when they'd shared their visions of creatures swirling in the depth of the Rift. He'd even laughed once, and she'd been completely enchanted. It was a genuine laugh, unhindered by layers of protocol and decorum.

She wanted to hear that laugh again.

She hoped it would be soon.

Once in the galley, she opened the chiller and selected a meal then paused and selected a second. Jagger had been parked at the pilot console for most of the morning. He'd probably appreciate some lunch.

A short time later, she carried their meals up the lift to the Flight Deck.

Stepping off the unit, she noted the slight angling of Jagger's helmet to the left, a subtle pointer that he was aware of her presence. There was no way that tiny gesture should've unleashed such a large flock of butterflies in her midsection, but it did.

"I brought you some lunch," she said, extending the steaming bowl of marro-broth and rice as she approached.

"You didn't need to do that," he told her.

She shrugged. "You've been sequestered on Flight Deck for hours. I thought you might be hungry."

He accepted the bowl from her with a nod. "Thank you."

She settled into the co-pilot console and cupped her bowl in her hands. "Anything on the scopes?"

"Nothing. But that can be deceptive. Here in the Rift, the sensors wouldn't pick up another ship unless it's right on top of us."

Ketsia did a quick scan of the sensors on her faceplate. "That's unnerving."

"Good with the bad," Jagger answered. "It means other ships can't detect us either. Not in the usual way."

"Can they detect us in an *unusual* way?"

Jagger didn't look her way, but his mouth quirked in a soft smile before he answered. "Yes. Via visuals. Line of sight."

"So that's why you've parked yourself up here on Flight Deck? So you can watch for anything that might be coming?"

"Partly." He flicked a couple of switches on his monitor and swiveled in his flight couch, tilting the visor up to take in his surroundings. "But partly because it's a chance to fly the legend."

Ketsia smiled "I didn't know *Banshee* was considered a legend."

"Oh, yes. Zaviar Mennelsohn's grand experiment." Jagger ran a hand over the console. "His original B-class vessel."

"Zaviar," Ket repeated quietly. "Jaeo's brother."

"His genius older brother." *And Drea's father.* "May he rest in peace." Jagger did a quick check of the blip that had entered scan range. No heat signature. Just a rock. "The siblings had a bitter falling out. Part of the reason Jaeo changed his name to Gant, as I understand it."

"What happened?"

"Not sure. Except…" Jagger paused to tug at the collar of his flight suit, "it had something to do with a woman, and it happened over ten calendars ago." The Mennelsohn brothers' feud had erupted just after he and Drea had parted company, so he didn't have firsthand knowledge of the events. "Anyway, this ship was Zaviar's champion. The first ship to prove his theories that DEDspace existed. The first vessel to cross the flashpoint barrier. That was some thirty calendars ago, right here in the Rift." If his memory served, Drea's father had had some crazy notion that the charged particles in the Bradley Rift interacted with Dark Energy Dimension space. But it was a crazy idea that had proven to be right.

"I don't know much about DEDspace…except that it hurts," Ket remarked.

Jagger turned his head back to the stars. "The price we pay for slipping the bonds of 3D."

"To gain, we know pain," Ket quipped.

"A classic Jaeo-ism." Jagger gave her a grin. She wished she could see the expressive brown eyes that accompanied it.

Ketsia gestured to the monitor. "Would you mind if I take the controls for a bit?"

After the last episode, she didn't know how Jagger would react to her request, but he just shrugged with a bob of his helmet. "The con is yours."

"Practice makes practiced," Ket replied with a smile. "*Sheeban*. Co-pilot Adey Tion, assuming command."

The ship pinged as it traded the control to her drive helmet. She gave the instrumentation a quick scan, noting nothing untoward in the status of the various systems and controls. Then performed a visual sweep of the surrounding Rift.

All quiet in outer space.

Though her inner space was quite another matter altogether.

Jagger observed Ket from the relative obscurity of his helmet. Bringing him lunch. Keeping him company. Now assuming control of the ship and loitering on the Flight Deck for a time. It was almost like she enjoyed the camaraderie. "Practice makes practiced," he repeated. "You picked that up from Jaeo, too."

"Actually..." He noted the long pause and the tension in her voice. "Jaeo picked it up from his bondmate Lonna, and Lonna picked it up from my sister. They were close friends."

"You have a sister?"

"Had."

Jagger looked her way. It was obviously a topic better not pursued, but he couldn't contain his curiosity. "She wasn't rescued from Ithis with you and the others?"

"No." Ketsia seemed to fold into herself. "She died about a year before Operation Reset."

"I'm sorry." Jagger squinted at some of the readouts. Poor kid. Must've been tough on her to lose her sibling.

"Her death is the reason Sair escaped."

Jagger's mind went instantly to torpedo lock. Ketsia's *sister* was the reason Sair ran? Why? How? He struggled not to show any reaction to her statement. "Was he somehow responsible?"

"No. But he blamed himself for not protecting her..." Ketsia fell silent, and though Jagger couldn't see her eyes, he could read her grief in the slump of her shoulders and fall of her head. There was a lot more she wasn't disclosing, but he didn't want to press her. Not now. His curiosity about Sair's previous entanglements could wait for another time and a different avenue.

Yet it seemed Ketsia's sister had been the catalyst for everything—for Sair's escape and the fated meeting with Drea. Like the fabled butterfly that flapped its wings on Parol and caused a tidal swell on Veros, a series of actions and reactions had made ripples in the universe, and the sum of that force had robbed him of his future with Drea.

Like Hades. There was no force. There was only you being a heartless idiot.

Right. He needed to put a lid on this. Find a way to douse the burn of past mistakes to stop them from flaring back to life, again and again.

But then Ketsia drew in a deep breath and added her quiet but cool addendum, "Sair was my sister's bondmate."

"He…" Their convo had just jumped to flashpoint in a hurry, and he was struggling to give chase. Sair had bonded with her sister while a slave? "How is that even possible?"

"The usual way. They exchanged vows."

"I meant how was he allowed to bond?"

"You know who he was? What the Network discovered about him?"

"Yes." Jagger expelled a slow breath. "I was there for the briefing on *Spirit.*"

"Well, the Ithians knew, too. The premier gave him…certain allowances…*exemptions* that he would never have afforded to the other slaves. He allowed Sair and Saybin to bond."

Jagger jerked, twisting his head away. "Your sister's name was Saybin?"

"Yes."

The name Sair and Drea had given their infant daughter. Resentment flared in his gut. Drea had been so accepting of Sair's sexual past that she'd allowed her daughter to be named for his former mate…

Yet she couldn't forgive me?

The affront made his words come bitter and grating when they shouldn't have been spoken at all. "It must've been difficult for him to be with you after she died."

Now Ketsia went quiet. She gazed out at the silent stars, her visor panning a slow arc from horizon to horizon. Then her voice came, cold as space. "For the record, Sair never touched me. Not in a sexual way. He was never anything but kind to me."

Wait. What? Jagger leveled his attention on her from behind the smokescreen of his visor. "He had the choice *not* to touch you?"

Her chin lifted in defiance when she turned her head his way. "I was barely fifteen calendars old when I was added to the breeding stock. Not too young in the eyes of the Ithians, but Sair wouldn't have it."

"So..." he muttered. "You're a virgin then?" He mentally gave himself a punch for being so tactless.

"I never said that."

Mental images of Ketsia in the arms of another man filled his head and twisted into a knotted cord of jealousy deep in his gut. "So what are you saying?" God, he had no right to question her. But—

"I was with someone...once," she confessed in a broken voice.

"And it wasn't Sair?"

Her head snapped his way, her mouth set in a deep frown. "I told you it wasn't."

"Yes. Right." Jagger huffed.

Ketsia cocked her head. Her voice carried an edge when she asked, "Why is that so difficult for a man like you to understand?"

Jagger's shoulders went rigid. "A man like me?"

Her throat worked against the chin strap of her helmet and her mouth pressed into a thin line, but she didn't respond.

Did she know about his fall from grace? Maybe even from Drea herself? How did he expect her to see him then? As a cheater? A two-timer? A disloyal bastard?

"What kind of man is that, Ketsia?"

For a moment, she didn't speak. Then, reaching up, she removed her helmet, slanting her head as she turned to face him. "A man who's distant. Insulated. Isolated. Unreachable. Untrusting, even of himself."

Jagger clenched his teeth, baring them. "You're dead wrong if you think that's me."

It was a lie. She'd nailed it. She'd seen right through his defenses, swept aside the layers, and exposed the vulnerability he'd hidden away. He felt like he'd been stripped naked before her eyes.

And not in a pleasant, desirable way.

She continued to stare at him. And just when her scrutiny couldn't have gotten any more agonizing, she said, "What happened, Jagger?"

Jagger closed his hand like a claw on the armrest. "Don't do this. Don't bring Drea into this."

Ketsia's mouth fell open. Shock and realization sparked in her eyes. "Drea? Drea *Mennelsohn*?"

Gods! She hadn't known. Here he thought she'd been taunting him, but she'd obviously had no idea of the history he and Drea shared.

Until he'd just spilled it out on the deck at her feet.

But Ketsia didn't know the reasons Drea had left him. What an unfaithful wretch he'd been. What an undeserving bastard. And he couldn't admit to that part. He didn't want to see the loathing fill her eyes.

"I need some water." Jagger bolted out of his console and stalked to the lift, punching the controls to take him the hell away from her. While the unit descended, he stood rigid with his hands closed into fists at his sides.

It had all been a game, just a stupid competition. A way for the students to thumb their noses at overbearing instructors at flight academy. Cockpit sex with his female peers. *It didn't mean anything*, he'd justified to himself again and again. There were no emotions involved; it was just a stunt with a willing partner. An expected tradition.

Five times he'd gotten away with it. Five times he'd accepted the quaint handmade trophies, the lewd congratulations and thumps on the back from his friends and peers. And each time his conscience took him to task, his inner asshole told him it was all okay. No one was getting hurt. She'd never know.

And besides, for the sake of staying focused on training, he and Drea had agreed to hold off on intimacy until after graduation, so…well, he couldn't cheat on his fiancée when he wasn't even sleeping with her. Right?

Wrong.

So, so wrong.

Nothing could ever ease the memory of the shattered look on Drea's face or the pain of betrayal in her eyes when she'd discovered the truth.

She'd walked away. After first setting on him with a vengeance in the final academy dogfight exercises and stripping him of valedictorian honors, she'd walked away.

He couldn't believe he'd lost her. For seven calendars, he'd refused to believe. He'd tried again and again to tell her, and show her, how much he still loved her. That he'd do anything to win her back.

He barraged her—with messages, audios, invitations, gifts—for all of those seven long calendars. She'd denied them all. Rejected his gestures just as completely as she'd rejected him. Until they both started flying for the Network, allies in a common cause. And then she'd had no choice but to talk to him. With communications re-established, he was sure they'd reconcile. He convinced himself that when enough time had passed to soothe her pain and cool her anger, she'd come back to him.

Until the night she'd made her feelings clear to him at the officers' dinner on *Spirit*. The same night she'd introduced him to an escaped slave named Sair.

The lift door opened, and Jagger strode for the galley, drew a tall tumbler of water from the tap, and swallowed it down in several long gulps. He thrust it back under the tap for another fill, barely registering the gentle ping in his helmet or the blue letters flashing an alert that he had the helm.

"Jagger." All the muscles in his shoulders went tight at the sound of Ket's voice in the corridor. "I'm sorry. I didn't know this was about Drea. I just—"

He turned on his heel and marched up to her, stopping well inside her personal space. She watched him silently, with no helmet to obstruct that beautiful face or startled expression. He clawed at his own chin strap to release it, jacking the helmet off to drop it to the deck. Intending to tell her to stay the hell out of his head and keep the fuck out of his past.

But she stood her ground, peering up at him with those lovely widened eyes, with those perfect, beckoning lips.

So he kissed her.

Hard.

Without thinking. Without restraint.

She didn't back away. Didn't flee. Didn't slap him hard across the face, like she had every right to do.

She froze. Clearly not enjoying his attentions…but accepting them.

Haley's Crest! What was he doing?

She was his mission. His *responsibility*.

He broke off abruptly, blinking himself back into the here and now. "Gods, Ketsia, I didn't… I don't… Crest, you have my apologies."

"It's all right."

"No, it's completely wrong. I could be court-martialed for doing something so asinine."

She raised her soft hands to frame his cheeks and her black eyes met his. "This was between us. I promise you, no one is ever going to know."

"Why did you follow me?" he asked, his voice hoarse and choked. "Why come after me?"

"Because you needed a friend."

"You think so? We've spent a few days together, and you think you know all about me? What makes me tick?" Jagger fought to control the resentment churning inside him—the frustration, the fascination…and the fury. "Do you know what I did to Drea to make her leave me? Did she tell you the whole ugly story?"

His question hung suspended in time, until Ketsia slowly shook her head. "Drea never spoke about you."

Drea never…

Her words sliced through him like a dagger. He couldn't stand seeing the compassion in Ketsia's eyes when she revealed how completely Drea had gotten over him.

She never mentioned me?

His heart turned to granite. "Let me fill you in. I *cheated* on her. Many times. Had sex with other women while we were engaged." He saw how she took the blow of his words—the shock of the initial blast, the slow recoil, the measured recovery. "Now tell me, am I still the kind of man you want to comfort? The sort you want to pity?"

Her dark eyes glinted. "I'd never pity you."

"Then why did you *follow* me?" He closed his hands around her slender waist and lifted her, parking her on the galley table. He moved in close, so close he could feel the heat of her breath on his face. "What do you *want* from me, Ket?"

Her lips parted, but she made no sound. A sudden electric tingle coursed through his body, followed by the sharp buzz of the ship's warning system.

A buzz that grew insistently louder.

Jagger's attention dropped to his discarded helmet, and he uttered a curse. Abandoning Ketsia, he swept it up off the deck to park it on his head.

"Proximity alarm," he snapped. "We're being scanned."

SIX

Jagger bolted out of the lift and sprinted for the pilot's couch.

Outside the port, an unmarked Parolian frigate floated off *Sheeban*'s starboard bow, hot-firing its retros to bring its ungainly hulk to a full stop. Her crew must've been as surprised to have come upon *Sheeban* as Jagger was to be come upon.

Jagger sliced sideways into his command console and opened a channel. "*Sheeban*, hailing hauler. State your business."

"Acknowledged, *Sheeban*. *Keltoose* here, corporate spacefreighter. It wasn't our intention to enter your space at velocity."

Jagger took a deep breath. "Cords and bounds, *Keltoose*?" Freighter lingo for 'Where are you headed?'

"Veros." The trajectory was right, but it didn't mean the ship wasn't ferrying pirates. The captain didn't offer anything further except a question. "And you, *Sheeban*?"

"Set for Arst, bearing crop seed." He'd just offered more than was usual protocol, but he hoped the frigate was just a frigate who'd take him at his word, and not a privateer who might decide he was hiding something important.

Which he was.

Ketsia slipped into the co-console beside him, her helmet back in place. Luna followed, slinking into her lap to curl into a ball and softly chitter. Jagger gave her an acknowledging nod.

Though he'd have felt more comfortable if both she and her pet stayed below decks, the *Keltoose* had scanned them, so they knew he had a second aboard. Her instincts were dead on. It looked far less suspicious if she parked herself on the Flight Deck for the encounter, like any other co worth her carbon would do.

"Apologies for the unintentional intercept, *Sheeban*. We wish you every luck in making safe port." Jagger thought he heard subtle laughter behind the captain's voice. His crew seemed to be enjoying a joke among themselves that a battered hulk like *Sheeban* would even survive the journey. "We'll reset course, and be on our way."

"Acknowledged, *Keltoose*. Closing channel." Let them laugh. If they as much as twitched in the wrong direction, they'd be saying hello to a hefty duo of paracannons secreted beneath *Banshee*'s deceptive exterior. Or damn the Compact, Jagger could smoke them with a quick blast of short-range Mennelsohn DEDdrive, leaving them floundering in a whirlpool of twisted time-space dimensions. His ego would delight in either of those solutions.

But his better sense told him the right course was to let them leave in peace, still laughing and clueless about both the ship's capabilities *and* what she carried. His ego was just going to have to take this one for the team.

The *Keltoose* fired several bursts of its navigational thrusters and pushed itself out of *Sheeban*'s personal space, skirting her and continuing in the general direction of planet Veros. Jagger kept a steady eye on his visor readings for any hint of deviation—a common ploy for blacklane bandits—but the departing ship stayed true to course.

Once the freighter had slipped out of scan range, he relaxed. All was well. Just a chance encounter in the murk of the Rift. Hopefully, the last until they reached their destination in seven days.

The tension in his muscles began to ease to parade rest then did an about-face when Ketsia slid off her helmet and locked her black diamond eyes on his faceplate. "We need to talk."

Jagger cocked his head. "About the freighter?"

Ket leveled him with a searching look. "About what the freighter interrupted."

Jagger bowed his head and crossed his arms. "The freighter interrupted nothing, if you're good for your word."

"I am."

"Then I think we're done here." He rose from his console to check a component that was registering hot on his helmet display.

Ketsia stayed put in her flight couch. "Are you in the habit of shuttling aside anything you don't know how to deal with, Captain?"

That question was a two-barreled lase-pistol.

"I'm in the habit of being the best officer I can be. On occasion, I might falter. But I try never to make the same mistake twice."

Her voice went low. "So what happened in the galley was a mistake?"

"I believe," Jagger answered matter-of-factly, "I've already conceded that."

He was painfully aware of the tight set of her mouth and sharp line of her shoulders when she turned her face away to peer out into the stars.

He rose to locate and pull the overheating capacitor from its slot in the instrumentation behind his flight couch. "I need to run a diagnostic. I'll be in the maintenance bay."

Jagger moved toward the lift, feeling like he couldn't retreat fast enough for his own good.

Ket was so done with Captain Navene Jagger. She didn't think she could suffer another moment with the man on this small ship.

Him and his overblown, infuriating, insolent pride.

Luna might've sniffed out a prince somewhere inside, but there was definitely a black-hearted ogre guarding the door.

Fine. He could stay glued to his Flight Deck, and she'd stay here in her quarters with Luna—conveniently out of his sight and out of his way—for the balance of the voyage. They'd managed just fine without his company for an entire day already. Once he'd delivered them to Jaeo six days hence, he could fly on to Hades for all she cared.

Luna crawled into her lap and whimpered, ever sensitive to her sullen mood. How in the Gods' known universe could she have ever believed she was falling for such a conceited, narcissistic jerk? After what she'd been through, he was the last man—

A gentle rap on her cabin door was followed by Jagger's soft query. "Ketsia?"

Jagger waited outside Ketsia's quarters. She didn't respond. After a long silence, he was reaching out to knock again when the soft click of her cabin seal sounded.

Ketsia appeared, her face obscured by her helmet except for the quivering downward spike of her mouth. Luna balanced on one shoulder, cooing, her long, furry tail wrapped protectively around the front of Ketsia's neck.

"I know I've been an asshole, Ket." He lowered his head, at the same time raising his eyes to give her a soulful look. "Truth is, I can't seem to help myself where you're concerned."

"Is that supposed to pass for an apology?"

Jagger braced a hand against the corridor wall and shifted his weight. "No. This is. I'm very sorry for how I treated you."

"Apology accepted. Is there anything else?"

"Yeah." Jagger lowered his head and hooked his thumbs in the pockets of his coveralls. "I think you called it earlier. We do need to talk."

She stared at him through her visor. Her answer came on a shaky exhale. "I really think it's better we don't. We're only six days out now…"

"I know." His gaze dropped to his deck boots, and his face took on a pained expression. "But it could be a very long six days, so if you change your mind…"

She gave a stoic nod and quietly shut the seal to her quarters.

He turned back to the lift before realizing the thin wail of the proximity alarm was rising from the helmet he carried in his hand. Jagger scrambled for the Flight Deck.

SEVEN

"*Sheeban*, prepare to be boarded."

Jagger clamped his hand over the armrest of his flight couch. The *Keltoose* was back. She'd probably never actually left the vicinity after her captain's clever duck and feint to keep up appearances.

And he'd been an absolute fool to accept the deception at face value.

Now, with the freighter on top of him, bristling with unsheathed cannons and missile mounts, his options for escape were nil. He couldn't take action without drawing their fire and endangering Ketsia. He had no choice but to let the pirates board and discern for themselves that he carried no cargo of interest or value.

Except for Ketsia herself.

Another ship came into range on his readouts. Hades, a monster ship a good ten times the size of the freighter. Jagger held in a blistering curse. They'd come back—with reinforcements—for a reason. Crop seeds were nothing but ballast, but a young, attractive female like Ket would be solid gold for human traffickers.

He'd really screwed up. Let himself get distracted when his mind should've been on his duty. He'd failed her...and he'd failed Jaeo, too.

Jagger made a fist. He'd be damned if he'd let these bastards take her, even if it meant going down in the blazing hellfire of a close-quarters fire-fight to protect her.

"Adey, report to the Flight Deck, double time!"

"Right here," Ketsia answered from his side. She slid into her station, helmet in place but Luna nowhere to be seen. "I heard them, Dallan."

He muted his mic and said, off channel, "I need you to stay at your con. Let me do the talking. Don't let them hear your voice unless it's life or death."

She faced forward, the knuckles of her left hand going white where she had a death grip on the side of her flight couch.

A trio of hollow thuds reverberated through *Sheeban*'s interior—the sound of the mothership's cargo arm making contact with the outer hull and pulling their vessel into her massive shuttle bay.

"Open your outer hatch, *Sheeban*, or by all that's unholy, we'll breach you," a deep voice demanded.

Jagger pulled in a breath between clenched teeth and exchanged looks with Ketsia. "Aye, ya bleakers. We're opening." He flicked a toggle and pushed off the flight couch, giving Ketsia a hand signal to sit tight. "And I'll be collectin' intentions at the a-lock." Freighters slang for 'What the hades do you think you're doing boarding my ship?'

He cut off the open channel and bent down close to Ket. "You know how to raise and fire the paracannons or take her to flashpoint?"

She gave a tense nod. "Yes. But I've only done it a couple of times."

"That'll work." Jagger licked his lips. "My code words are 'trigger' for the cannons and 'flash' if you need to make a run. If I say either, it's an emergency. Don't hesitate, k?"

Ket never took her eyes off the monitor. "K."

"It's going to be fine." It was a hollow reassurance after just telling her two drastic options they might have to employ.

Jagger eased his hand onto her shoulder in a comforting grip before pounding to the lift, hitting the control for main deck with the flat of his palm. Before the lift closed, he caught a brief glimpse of Ketsia's blacked-out faceplate peering over her shoulder at him from her co-couch.

Jagger was tall by Carduwan standards, but felt a runt in the presence of the four towering Ithians—*rogues!*—who stood hunched in *Banshee*'s corridor, weapons drawn and beaded on him. If these were rogues, this behemoth mothership that had swallowed them had to be a Hammerhead Destroyer—no doubt one of the two that had gone missing when their government was nullified by Operation Reset.

This was escalating to worst case scenario in a hurry. He was glad the helmet concealed his initial expression as he skidded to a stop and conjured up a degree of outrage before wrenching off his headgear.

"Hope the quad of ye have a gigadam good cause for an uninvited layover," he growled between clenched teeth.

One of the Ithians stepped forward, his voice calm and a tinge amused as he spoke in universal. "I think it will be in your best interest to stand down, Captain...?"

"Tion." Jagger's upper lip twitched in a bared-teeth sneer. "And who would I have the distinct displeasure of addressing?"

"Call me Rinn."

"Captain, is it?"

The Ithian lowered his head with his voice. "Just Rinn will do."

"What's your calling here?"

The men exchanged looks, and Rinn leveled a steely glare on Jagger. "We'll be asking the questions, Tion. Where's the rest of your crew?"

"My co is on the Flight Deck. We *be* the crew."

"Call her down."

Her. The Ithians knew Ket was female. A clammy chill swamped his blood. He couldn't let them take her, so best play the card as it lay. *"Her* would be my bondmate, and ya best not have any dark designs on her status."

"We have no interest in the whore trade, Tion. But for your own safety and hers…call her down."

If Jagger gave Ketsia either code, they'd have a fair shot at escape, but they'd still have to contend with the four angry, armed giants onboard *Banshee.* Best not take that chance for now. Ket's safety was his ultimate concern, and he didn't want her injured—or worse—in an on-deck laze-pistol blitz. As long as one of them was wearing a drive helmet, their options remained open, and Jagger was sure Ket had the good sense to know that.

Never taking his eyes off the four men, Jagger raised the helmet and spoke into it. "Adey, these four Ithians want a chat as one." He was giving her fair warning what she'd be walking into. Facing members of the subspecies that had enslaved her and forced her to breed was not going to be easy.

"And what if I have no hanker to chat them back?" came her clipped response.

Jagger almost smiled. She'd pulled off one damned fine freighter impersonation there, shot through with attitude.

"Best appease the asking, m'love. They're claiming you're not their mark, so I'm beholdin' them to that promise." Jagger kept a soft edge on his words, so the men would see Dallan Tion had full respect and deep affection for his partner, Adey. A strong pair-bond made them appear less vulnerable.

"'ight. I'm down." Perfect air of disgruntled disdain she'd put on that reply. He'd never suspected Ketsia had such fine-tuned talents as an actress. Another tiny slant in their favor.

She joined them in moments, covering the deck in a bold stride that didn't waver even upon sighting the four titans hunkered down in the corridor.

She stopped eight paces away. "I'd like ta say I'm happy ta make your acquaintance, but it'd be a gigadam lie. Why'd you board us, then?"

"Please remove your helmet, Ms. Tion," Rinn asked in a quiet voice.

She stood her ground and crossed her arms defiantly. "Think I'll be keepin' my face to myself and my mate, ya hedgers."

"I understand your reluctance. But it's tantamount we establish your identity."

"Aren't ya the fine talker, though? Bet you were amongst those high n' mighty once."

"Are you asking if I'm a holdout from the Old Alliance, Ms. Tion?"

"Don't much care. All I know is I'm lookin' at a pack of roughs now."

Rinn exchanged a grin with his comrades. "While I admire your pluck, Ms. Tion, I recommend you cooperate so we aren't forced to deal with your obstinance. Remove your headgear."

"Fine." The scorn she'd put in that extended F was brilliant. As long as she was amusing the head Ithian and not angering him, Jagger wouldn't intercede in their little tête–à–tête.

Ketsia tilted her head to the side and toppled off her helmet, letting her tangled hair fall over her face to partially obscure her features.

"Ah. Tectolian, are you?" Rinn rumbled as one of his men ran a scanner beam over her face.

"Born'n raised," Adey Tion replied.

Jagger tried to hide the tightening of his muscles with a lazy loll of his head to one side and a disgruntled exhale. He was confident the Carduwan military had deleted their real histories and inserted their cover data into all the major ID databases…but what system would rogue Ithians access? "This time we're burnin' is costin' us percents," Jagger complained. "Maybe let's get to the pork and tell us whatchu want?"

Rinn turned to Jagger with a less than pleasant expression. "Your profits—or lack of them—are of no concern to us. Your intentions and your cargo is what we've yet to ascertain."

Sounded like their aliases had passed muster. "Ya care for a spy of my product, do ya?"

"We've already determined the nature of your cargo."

"Then why—"

"What we're questioning is the third lifesign on your ship. A small one. Is there an animal stowed away somewhere on this vessel?"

"*Hadeees*, yes," Jagger answered emphatically, attempting to draw the Ithians' attention to him and away from Ketsia's visible fist-clench. "It's a cat-thing we picked up on Veros to keep the vermin down. Would be bad for the bottom line t'show up on Arst with a cargo that's been et. The creatures mostly feral so you're not likely to glance her."

"It's a cat, you say?"

"Cat. Ish. Look at the lifesign. Feline-size, right?"

"Call the beast," Rinn instructed.

"I tol' ya, she's feral. Beastie don't answer when yelled for."

"Call her."

Jagger scratched his cheek and rolled his eyes. "What's the name again?" he asked Ketsia.

"Berra," she said flatly.

The LaGuardian word for "hide." Clever.

Jagger sauntered over to a vent opening. "Berrrrrra, here, kitkit," he called. "Ya hungry, ya beastie?" He made a show of patting his pocket with his hand before turning to ask Rinn. "Ya wouldn't happen to have any food on ya?"

"No," Rinn snapped. "As a rule, I don't carry feline food on my person."

"Might help, is all." Jagger shrugged. "Berra! Berra!"

"Secure them," Rinn commanded.

The Ithians seized both him and Ketsia, making quick work of wrestling their arms behind them and locking restraints on their wrists in spite of their shouts of protest.

Jagger managed to put himself between the Ithians and Ket, alarmed by their sudden aggression. "What in Hades are ya doin'?" he cried, with a quick glance at their discarded drive helmets that had been kicked to the side of the corridor.

"Responding to your trickery," Rinn replied coldly. "You're pretending to call the animal while in truth commanding it to hide. In the LaGuardian tongue. Quite suspicious." He leaned lower to get in Jagger's face. "Since neither of you look LaGuardian and we're on the hunt for a LaGuardian bio-product called a StarDog."

"Berra's the name the cat-thing came with. What's this..." Jagger locked down any reaction and put on his best clueless face. "WhatDog?"

"*Star*Dog," Rinn answered.

"Look all ya want, ya bozers," Jagger said through clenched teeth. "Ya'll only find the cat-thing. But take the gigadam 'straints off us, now!"

"Of course. Pram, you can remove their restraints..."

One of his underlings scowled darkly.

"...once they're locked in a detention cell on our vessel."

"What? You're not takin' us off our ship, ya bleakers!" Jagger yelled, maneuvering to wrap his fingers around Ketsia's wrist. This had disaster written all over it, and he wouldn't allow these thugs to separate them.

Rinn loomed over him, sour-faced and hard-eyed. "You'd be best advised to cooperate fully." His eyes cut to Ket for a quick, appreciative assessment. "For both of your sakes. Do you get my meaning?"

Jagger froze, understanding his threat only too well. "I get ya."

"Good. I'm glad we've reached this understanding." Rinn turned to stride away with a quick jerk of his thumb. "Take them."

Their cell was cramped and spartan, with just a bare mattress on the floor and a head with a wash basin and no privacy, save for a waist-high partition. This wasn't going to be easy on Ketsia. Pretending to be married as a cover and having to act out the role before observers were two very different things.

Jagger turned to her and gathered her into his arms. She momentarily went rigid then eased against him when he whispered close to her ear, "You okay?"

"Terrific," she answered with a cynical huff. Hearing her utter one of Jaeo Gant's pet phrases almost made him smile. Almost.

Jagger tilted his head, pretending to nuzzle her hair. "You did great."

His reaction to the brush of her lips against his cheek was all kinds of disturbing in their present predicament. As was his brief musing on just how far they'd have to take this marital farce.

"Thanks for that," she answered.

He leaned her back so he could look into her eyes, before pulling her near to bury his mouth in the silky cascade of her hair. "Why do they want Luna?"

Ketsia slid her hand around his waist and up his back as she pressed closer. *Damn!* That move must've looked very convincing on their captor's surv-cam. At least, his body seemed to think so, even when his head knew differently.

"She's a courier," Ketsia breathed.

Wait! Luna was some sort of messenger, and no one had thought to bring him up to speed on this before *now?*

Including Ketsia?

Jagger skimmed his lips along her cheek until he reached her mouth. Then he pressed forward, exacting a subtle revenge for her nondisclosure. Ketsia sucked in a silent, trembling breath when he took her lower lip gently between this teeth. "For who?"

"Jaeo."

Luna was carrying a communiqué for Ambassador Gant? And using him to deliver it? Without his knowledge? This mission was sinking to a whole new level of sucker punch.

Haley's Crest. What kind of a friend was Gant?

"Nice surprise." Jagger exhaled, easing back until she could see the fury arcing behind his eyes.

"Sorry," she mouthed.

He nodded, very slightly. Not an acceptance of the apology, only an acknowledgement of her duplicity.

He released her, slowly turning away to park his hands on his hips and study the details of their cell. It was a clear message to Ketsia that he wasn't pleased, but it carried another purpose. His captors would expect this inspection. He meant to play his role well.

Solid bars held them, not a detainment beam. That might be a good thing. Bars could be breached, force beams not so much. They were in an end cell in a bank of four with an open viewing area surrounding the quad. And they were the only prisoners. Also useful.

He spied the lens reflection of the overhead surv-cam parked in the ceiling above their cell, no doubt rigged for sound. There appeared to be just the one and not multiple devices, probably because their cell had served as a brig for wayward crewmen rather than actual prisoners. Fortunately, a single spy-eye was easier to deal with.

Across from their cell, a ventilation screen set into the lower wall of the open space looked like a promising option at first glance, but not for him. Ket might be able to squeeze through that space if she were athletic enough.

Jagger's gaze cut her way, and he swallowed hard around that thought. He'd bet she was athletic as Hades with that trim, supple body. When their eyes connected, Jagger quickly looked away.

If the Ithians held them long, they'd soon be sharing that tiny bed to keep up appearances. If this was the live or die situation it was shaping up to be, they might be forced to act the part of a mated pair.

Certainly not the hardest thing he'd ever done for the sake of duty, but he was only half of the equation.

How would Ket feel about her role?

Cross that abyss when you reach it.

Right now, there were about forty million other details he needed to be focusing on.

Their cell—all of six footspans by eight footspans—had barely enough room to move around each other without becoming dance partners, and not nearly enough to hold a grudge. Especially when Ket kept watching him with those long-lashed dusky eyes of hers.

Eyes that conveyed she was clearly both worried and sorry for the nondisclosure regarding Luna.

And it certainly worked. After just one of her long, poignant looks, he was over being angry.

Jagger spent the next few haras pondering what information the StarDog could be carrying that was so gigadam important that the Ithians had learned of it and wanted to intercept it. Maybe he didn't *want* to know. Maybe the less informed, the better. Especially if the Ithians got desperate enough to resort to some of their more inventive tortures.

Hades.

He could take it. He had the training and techniques to overcome all but the worst of what these rogues could dish out. But he couldn't let them zero in on Ketsia. Or use her body as a means to make him talk.

That was where the dread lay for him. Because there was no denying it: sometime in the last few days, Ketsia had become more than just his mission. And he wasn't keen on exploring how *much* more she meant to him if the Ithians unleashed their diabolical imaginations on her.

He'd do everything in his power to prevent that. For starters, he didn't intend to let Ketsia out of his sight, even for a moment.

His wandering gaze strayed to the narrow bed again, where she'd stretched out to rest. The worn gray jumpsuit followed every delectable hollow and rise of her lissome body like a cozy second skin. His hands twitched, and he curled his fingers tight until his fingernails dug into his palms.

He'd have thought being imprisoned by rogue Ithians who suspected him of harboring a bio-engineered spy would be enough to keep his mind centered on escape and survival. But one glance at his comely cellmate, and his concentration seemed to vanish like the dawn mists on Veros.

Some brands of torture were self-inflicted.

After losing the battle to keep his attention averted elsewhere, Jagger's legs went on auto-pilot, moving him to stand over Ketsia before lowering him to sit on the edge of the mattress at her side. His gaze settled softly on her face.

"Tired?" he asked. Really? In the history of the universe, had anyone ever asked a more stupid question?

"Yeah," she replied. "You?"

He skirted a potential invitation to join her. So not appropriate. "Not yet." He reached out to graze his thumb lightly across her cheek. *Just playing the part,* he told himself, to which himself answered, *You're an asshole.*

Guilty as charged.

But he'd thought he'd cured himself of that brand of assholedom when he'd evolved into a military space monk. He'd successfully weaned himself of the need for women entirely. Relegated such inconsequential urges squarely to the realm of his past.

And then along came Ketsia...

And now this tiny little cell to share with her.

So much for self-discipline.

"What are you thinking?" she asked.

"Trying to figure our options," he lied.

"Any luck?"

"Not so far."

"Then why don't you rest." She scooted to the far side of the mattress, making as much room for him as possible. Even with the added inch or so, it meant they'd end up locked in a horizontal embrace. In bed.

Not happening.

Jagger lurched to his feet. "You rest," he croaked. "I'm going to keep working ideas." Which were exactly nil—but the thought of sleeping beside Ketsia was more than his short-circuiting self-discipline could handle right now.

Pride goeth before a fall?

Shut up, Jagger.

EIGHT

The sharp clank of metal on metal brought Jagger to full alert.

A giant stood just outside their cell—the one who went by the name of Pram—holding a square tray in each hand.

"Lovers' spat?" the Ithian asked, his gaze moving from the spot where Jagger had propped himself against the cold cell bars to linger on Ketsia where she lay curled up on the bed.

"No, ya bleeker." Jagger pushed off the floor and went to Ketsia's side, extending his hand to help her up. "The rack's so small, we need to take turns durin' the night."

The man ogled Ketsia as she brushed the wrinkles from her flightsuit. "Who wouldn't want a turn?"

Ketsia's head snapped up.

"Want to lose your tongue?" Jagger spat, his rage far from staged...and unfortunately, his accent far from freighter-esque.

The Ithian didn't notice. "Mind yourself, Spacerat. You're already living on borrowed time."

"What's your meaning?"

"We find that SpaceDog on your ship, and you won't be leaving this plane alive, you cocky little Cardi," the Ithian barked.

So they hadn't found Luna yet. Thank Hades.

"But then again, we don't find a SpaceDog, and you still may not be leaving alive. You nor your mate, though I'm guessing she'd outlive you..." His lips parted in a grotesque smile. "...by a couple of days, at least."

Jagger made a threatening move toward the man. "You can park those eyes elsewhere, ya palie...or risk having them join your tongue."

The Ithian *tsk*ed. "Better not push your luck with idle threats, little Studman."

"We ain't the ones doin' the pushin', now are we?" Jagger fired back. He didn't like the leer the man laid on Ketsia. There was no question what the Ithian had on his mind.

"I brought food. If you want to eat, step to the back of your cell."

They did as instructed, Ketsia reaching out to snag and clutch Jagger's hand in her own. She was shaking—though whether from anger or fear, he wasn't sure.

The Ithian flipped up the access at the bottom of the bars and slid the trays across the floor into their cell. "It's nothing fancy." His gaze lingered on Ketsia again. "I can imagine much tastier fare."

She gave Pram a defiant glower. "Don't care much for your manners. Wonderin' if a short chat with your superior would cure that?"

The man physically recoiled as if Ket had sunk a poisoned dart in his heel.

At least the Ithian leader, Rinn, had an air of respectability, and it seemed this Pram feared him. That could work to their advantage later.

If they had a later.

"I'll be back," Pram said in a gravelly voice that sounded more threatening than informative. "Mind yourselves." He left the containment area. Jagger sensed the tension leave Ket's body as soon as the bastard had stepped out of sight and closed the seal behind him.

They settled side-by-side on the mattress with legs crossed and the trays in their laps. Jagger ate the few mouthfuls of tasteless gruel that had been slopped onto the trays. *Nothing fancy* had been a gross understatement. If they were detained for any length of time, they were likely to starve to death.

Once they'd finished, Jagger gathered up the empties and tried to push them back out the access, but it only opened one way—inward. No way Ket would be wriggling through there if an opportunity for escape arose. He angled the trays through the cell bars and let them drop to the floor outside with a clatter.

Ketsia took one of his hands in both of hers. "Lie with me, Dallan."

His head and his thoughts swiveled back to her. "What?"

"You need rest. Trying to sleep with a row of bars at your back isn't going to keep you sharp."

He gave her a slow, half-hearted smile. "Lying with you isn't likely to do that either."

She ducked her head then met his eyes again. "Was that a compliment?"

Jagger went still, wiping all expression from his face. "Maybe a warning."

Her dark eyes shone with a quiet, black fire, and she answered in her

Adey voice, "You don't scare me, Spacer." She leaned closer so the Ithians couldn't eavesdrop on her addendum, speaking low and slow directly into his ear. "We need to talk." She motioned toward the bed.

Jagger stiffly acquiesced, easing onto the stale mattress and wrapping his arms around Ketsia when she cozied up to him. She made it look convincing for the Ithians—trailing her fingertips over his parted lips, drawing her hand down his chest, brushing the tip of her nose against his cheek. Maybe a bit too convincing. "I need to explain."

"Listening." Hades, it wasn't just the Ithians who were being persuaded. His heart kicked hard in his chest, and his blood made a frantic detour south. When she pressed her lips to his, he pressed back.

She responded, moving into him, accepting the demands of his mouth. He lost himself in the heat of the moment. Couldn't break free of the spell, couldn't stop himself from angling his head and taking the warmth and sweetness she offered him.

Desire flared, breaking free of containment, peppering his blood with primal want and hot-blooded need. He ensnared her in his arms, drawing her tight to his chest, moving his hands to mold and possess her. Wanting to own every part of her.

Gigadam, this wasn't the time or place to consider breaking his vow of celibacy. Not here. Not now. And certainly not with *her*. What the *Hades* was he thinking? He eased away from her on the mattress, disentangling his arms.

She closed her fist on his flightsuit collar, drawing him back. She leaned forward to press her mouth into the space between his cheek and the mattress and whispered, "What Luna's carrying…"

He closed his eyes, forcing himself to focus on her words, not her actions. "Yeah?"

She kissed his cheek. "Intercepted comms." Her lips brushed his right eyelid. "…the rogues…" She shifted to his left lid. "…are organizing."

Jagger ran his hand languidly down her side, held her gaze, and nodded. If her cryptic words meant what he thought they did, Luna was smuggling information that could indict these Alliance holdouts as dangerous cells. It would give Carduwa and a host of House of Planets allies the legal grounds to enter the Rift to pursue and capture these Ithian rogues so they could be brought to trial for their plotting.

And if Rinn and his crew had gotten intel that a StarDog would be their undoing…

That explained why the Ithians had doubled back. They must've detected Luna's presence during their first encounter, begged off as an innocent cargo ship, then returned with their mothership to seize the *Sheeban* and determine if she was, in fact, carrying the StarDog they were looking for.

And if they found Luna aboard…

There could be only one outcome for the two of them. For the *three* of them. Execution.

The assault on Ketsia's hired yacht wasn't at all what he'd been led to believe. It wasn't Ketsia who'd drawn their fire. It was the information Luna carried. This was clearly a politically-backed operation, and Jaeo was no doubt in it up to his elbows. But how could the man have put Ketsia in harm's way?

He was trusting you to make sure that didn't happen.

Ketsia met his eyes, her mouth forming a question when a loud clank sounded in the quiet.

They both jumped and scrambled to their feet when the seal opened, and Pram stepped through into the observation area.

"Shower time for the prisoners," he announced, his face breaking into a hideous sneer. "Choice is yours. Take them together…" He ogled Ketsia. "Or separately."

Before Jagger found the wits to respond, Ketsia stepped forward. "Together," she answered boldly. "I'm not lettin' him out of my sight for a secta with you miscreants about."

She interwove her fingers with his and gave him a cocky tip of her head.

The girl had brass.

Beautiful, entrancing…and *gutsier* than he'd given her credit for. Definitely his kind of girl.

And that was when Jagger realized just how lost he truly was.

Because, Hades help him, he might just be falling for her.

NINE

Jagger moved his hands to the neck of Ketsia's jumpsuit and undid the catches, peeling the fabric down to expose her bare shoulders and the deep V of cleavage between her breasts. There he stopped. He couldn't finish. He'd be damned if he'd strip her naked in front of this salivating bastard, Pram.

Elsewhere on the ship, his superior apparently had the same thought. A harsh command crackled over Pram's comm device, and the man put on a sour face and begrudgingly sauntered out of the shower bays, leaving them to their privacy.

"I thought he'd never leave," Ket quipped in a perfect deadpan.

Gods, she was something special. Too special for him. Too special to be in *this situation* with him.

This shower ploy didn't fool him. The Ithians weren't concerned with their hygiene. They were up to something, he just hadn't worked out what it was.

Ketsia snapped her fingers in front of his eyes. "Hey. Still with me? Going to finish what you started, Spacer...or am I?"

Jagger went for a teasing spousal reply, "Be my guest."

And damned if she didn't.

When she'd kicked off the last thread of her clothing, Jagger had to remind himself to breathe. Then she placed her hands on the top catch of his coveralls, and he forgot how again.

"No need to be shy," she whispered, "since we've done this together at least a thousand times." She tweaked open the fifth and sixth catches of his flight suit, and knelt to remove his deck boots.

"Don't I wish."

Ketsia set his boots aside and rose. He fought to hold eye contact and not let his gaze wander. "Fortunately…" Her mouth quirked, and she pushed the uniform off his shoulders. "I'm not the modest sort."

"So I see."

"Probably lucky for both of us."

"Speak for yourself."

She crouched, tugging his uniform down to his ankles and off over his feet.

Well, they certainly had no secrets between them now.

She took his hand and led him into the bays, flicking one of the hydro controls to start the stream. He stepped to the next showerhead and activated it.

Here, also, surv-cams were set into the ceiling. Jagger did a quick flick of his gaze to the lens to alert Ketsia, and she nodded her understanding. She seemed undaunted, Gods love her. Probably due to her former experience as a slave.

Side-by-side, they soaped, lathered, and rinsed. Jagger summoned every last shred of willpower to look the part of a spouse comfortable with showering with his mate, and not some horny fool with his tongue lolling out of his mouth. But in the quick glances he stole…Gods, she was beautiful. Her bronze skin glowed in the dim light of the bay as she lifted her face to the stream and let the water cascade over her skin.

When Ketsia turned to rinse her hair, Jagger stepped closer. "Let me help."

She handled his intrusion into her personal space like a trooper, leaning back as he ran his fingers through the dense curtain of her dark hair, swaying with each pass of his hands. After he'd gently wrung the moisture from her tresses, she circled to face him, pinning him to the bay wall with a very unexpected and very sweet kiss.

"Ketsia," he whispered, folding her into his arms. This was crazy, but nothing felt more natural or more perfect than holding her right then, her body warm and shedding rivulets of water in the steam. "I'll get you out of this."

"You mean you'll get *us* out," she retorted. "We leave together. Or not at all."

She was wrong about that. If an opportunity came for escape, with or without him, he'd send her off without a second thought.

But how he'd make that happen, he didn't know.

Jagger reached out to shut off the water then plucked a towel from the hook and wrapped it around Ketsia before taking the second one for himself.

"Time's up," Pram's gravelly voice sounded from near the seal. Jagger hadn't heard him enter. How long had the man been standing there, watching them?

Jagger's eyes flicked over the bare floor where they'd discarded their clothes. "Our outfits seem to be on the miss," he said in an accusing tone.

"Being laundered," Pram rumbled with a sneer. "You'll get them back by morning."

Ah. That was what the Ithians were after. They were checking every stitch of the garments for concealed information, leaving them *without* those stitches. At least Ketsia had her towel, though it only wrapped her from shoulder to thigh, just covering the bare essentials.

"We'll die from chill in that cell," Jagger protested.

"My superior ordered a blanket provided." He put a hand on the coarse fold of material slung over his shoulder. "Kind man that he is."

"Why not let her have it now? Ya can see she's a-shiverin'. She ain't faring well on your blasted iceboat."

Pram eyed her with relish. "You'll get it when you're back in your cell."

"Cock that!" Jagger removed the towel twisted around his hips and wrapped it around her waist, giving her more coverage. She looked up at him, her brows arched in surprise. He didn't have much issue with strutting around naked if it would keep her warmer and give this pervert less of her to drool over.

"Have you no pride, man?" Pram growled, sounding quite unhappy with Ketsia's wardrobe addition.

He and Ketsia exchanged looks, and Jagger snorted.

"Back to your cell," their guard ordered.

Jagger placed an arm around her back, a pointedly possessive gesture, as they walked together down the corridors. He turned a spiteful eye on Pram. "When are ya going to let us back to our ship?"

"When we've found what we're looking for."

"And when ya don't?"

Pram slammed the bars shut behind them, scowling. "We will. We know you're hiding something."

Jagger held his arms out and glanced down at his body. "Doesn't seem so, does it?"

The man's face reddened. "On your *ship*, Spacerat. Wherever that SpaceDog is hiding, we'll find it. And then the two of you will have Hades to pay, won't you?" A slow grin bowed his mouth, and his attention shifted to Ketsia. "Looking forward to that."

After taking a moment to gloat, the Ithian thrust the blanket through the bars and stalked out of the observation area.

Ket plucked the blanket from the deck and turned to draw it around Jagger's bare body. "You seem to have gotten pretty comfortable in your own skin."

"I admit it felt a bit…awkward at first." He swept a lock of her dark hair off her shoulder. "Until it didn't."

She gave him a tiny smile.

"I know this hasn't been easy for ya…Adey. But I'm very proud of ya."

She eased into his arms and tucked her face into the hollow of his neck. "It hasn't been all bad…Dallan," she answered, matching his lazy freighter drawl.

He cocked his head. "No?"

She shifted back to meet his eyes. "I'm with the one I care about."

He had no answer for that, only a dull ache that settled in his heart. Was it Ketsia talking? Or Adey?

"There's something I need to tell you…" Her lower lip quivered, and she caught it tight between her teeth.

"What is it?" He closed his hands over her shoulders, and slanted his head to speak in a low voice. "Tell me."

"Could we…" Without a telltale movement of her head, she flicked her eyes to the overhead surveillance. "…lie down? Under the blanket."

Jagger glanced down at the swatch of scratchy material she'd draped around him. He swallowed around the destroyer-sized lump that rose in his throat. This was a bad idea. Yes, he was attracted to her. Yes, she seemed to be attracted to him. But the situation had surely only confused her feelings. What they used to call Stockholm Syndrome, though nobody knew where the tag had originated. Except that it wasn't her captors she'd become enamored with, it was her fellow prisoner.

"You know they're watching."

"It's what they're expecting." She touched his arm, her fingertips trailing lightly on his skin. "And our time may be short."

Jagger couldn't deny that cruel reality. He nodded cautiously.

As they eased down on the mattress together, she moved close, tugging the blanket up over their heads to block the surv-cam. Jagger's heart hammered in his chest.

He knew where this could lead, where his body clearly wanted to take it, but hadn't he already had his fall from honor for one lifetime? It would be so easy to take advantage of the situation…but Gods-damn, he didn't want to be that man.

"That one experience I told you about…my only time?" she said.

Gods, this wasn't starting well. Jagger gave a slow blink. "Yeah."

"I was raped," she said. "By an Ithian. When I was a slave."

The breath left his lungs, and for a moment, his heart went still. "Gods. Ket."

"It was my owner's son."

"I'm…so sorry." He started to ease away. "Being held is probably the last thing you want."

She caught his upper arms. "No, I'm trying to tell you it's exactly what I need." She drew him back to her. "Right now."

His body sagged under the weight of her words. His Ket—his beautiful Ket—had been violated in the worst possible way, and now faced death without ever knowing the gentle hand of a considerate lover. It was completely unfair, but yet, he couldn't be that man. It was wrong, ethically, morally, professionally—

"It's true that there were times I didn't like you much. I'd never met a man so owned by his pride before. But then you came to my cabin...to apologize...and you were so humble. So caring." She drew him closer, molding her succulent, towel-wrapped curves against his chest. "That's when I saw who you really are." She tenderly brushed the stray lock of hair from his eyes. "So if we only live for a few more hours..."

Gods, the temptation. But even if she thought she wanted this, she'd only regret it later. "Ket—"

She placed the pad of her finger to his lips, silencing him. "Sair once told me that someday I'd find a man—the right man—who I'd want with all my heart." She peered at him, her eyes large and luminous in the faint light. "Now I know that man is you."

Jagger went still. "The last guy in this galaxy who deserves you?"

She exhaled a quiet *oh.* "You see? That's the Jagger I fell in love with."

"You didn't..." His denial died on the vine when it met her soft, coaxing lips. A siren and temptress who meant to have him, and Gods knew he wasn't strong enough to dissuade her, or man enough to reject what she was offering.

With a groan of defeat, he surrendered. Let her bathe his face and throat in kisses. Let her roam his body and break down all his barriers.

Beneath the blanket, she swept the towel away to discard it on the floor beside their bed. His gaze fixed on the twin swell of her breasts before he skimmed a hand up to caress and fondle her. Then he bent to take a tight peak between his lips to taste her, tease her, explore her.

He drew his tongue in a languid path over her lush curves, pleasuring her with lips and teeth, lingering and loitering until she was gasping aloud. "Dallan!"

So beautiful. Everything about her, beautiful. The silk of her skin, the salt of her flesh. The way she closed her eyes and arched her back.

She sought him out, tightened her hand around his erection, tentatively stroking the length of him in a feathery caress before gripping him more boldly. She worked him. Gods, no, it was more than that. She *owned* him.

"Adey!" Jagger cried, sucking in air as his need flared hot and spiraled into tight knots of tension. He dropped a hand to clutch the mattress, already pushed to the brink of containment. Three calendars—three long calendars of self-denial surged within him, demanding release.

But he refused to go there without taking her with him.

"Dallan," Ket whispered. "Touch me."

He slipped one hand into the valley between her thighs to stroke the center of her heat. She moved with him, closing her eyes. Her body rocking with his rhythm.

"Please. Please, now." Beneath her entreaty, she added in a breathy postscript for him alone, "Jagger."

He positioned himself and was careful, tender, in taking her. Though he was sure any injury to her body was long healed, it didn't mean the wounds to her spirit had closed.

Yet she didn't stiffen beneath him, didn't press her hands to his shoulders to push him away. There was no hesitation, no rejection, no change of heart, only the welcoming embrace of her body accepting him home, and the soft cries of her encouragement.

Thrusting his hips, looking into her eyes, he touched and stroked her, allowed the hot thermals of need to build...and crest...and carry them both to a sudden and violent climax.

They soared as one and imploded as one then lay pressed together, clutching and huffing until the tingling eased. When their gasps for air mellowed to mere pants, Jagger slipped his arms around her back and rolled beneath the blanket, bringing her atop him to melt against his still-heaving chest.

"I love you," Ketsia whispered, and he knew it wasn't Adey who'd made the heartfelt declaration.

"Ket," Jagger mouthed, closing his eyes and splaying his fingers wide on her back. "There truly is no way in sweet Hades I deserve you."

TEN

Tucked into Jagger's arms, it was the first time in years that Ketsia could remember sleeping so soundly. The universe finally felt right to her heart, though she knew in her head it couldn't be more wrong. That they were a long way from any shot at a happy ending.

Against her, Jagger exhaled softly, his beautiful chest rising and falling with each quiet breath. Last night, he'd sworn to her that he was the last man in the universe she should ever want, and then—with a little urging —he'd proven he was the only one in creation she'd ever need.

If only it hadn't taken a calamity to help them discover each other.

A click echoed through the empty cell block, and tension stiffened her muscles. Pram was back. And judging from the low-level lighting, it wasn't even shift cycle yet. This couldn't be good. Under the blanket, she rewrapped the towel tightly around her body and looked toward the seal.

The click sounded again.

But not from the seal.

From the ventilation duct in the lower wall.

Ketsia did a slow roll away from Jagger to face the opening. A barely perceptible coo sounded in the twilight.

Luna?

She couldn't speak to her StarDog. The Ithians might hear or see. So she tugged a portion of the blanket up to block her hands from the over-head surveillance and signed toward the opening. *Luna? Be very quiet.*

Another quiet click sounded, and this time Ketsia saw it was caused by a vent screen fastener falling to the floor. It joined two others that already rested there. Luna was attempting to remove the screen.

Jagger's forearm tightened around her body, his corded muscles going taut. "What's that sound?"

"It's nothing," Ket replied. "Just the ductwork cooling." She gave him a subtle wink and a tiny head gesture toward the air vent.

Jagger rubbed his eyes and blinked then fixed his attention on the screen.

No wonder the Ithians hadn't located her little buddy on *Banshee*. She'd found her way onto the Ithian destroyer and had probably been prowling the air passages searching for them since their capture.

Smart little StarDog.

But had Luna outwitted herself? What if the Ithians discovered her?

Tick. Another fastener landed on the deck.

"You've got to be kidding me," Jagger said on an exhale.

Ket angled her body over his and kissed him. His eyes widened in surprise then narrowed in a "what are you doing?" expression. There, hovering over him, it would look to the surv-cam like they were romantically engaged, when they were really having a muted conversation.

"Taro taught her," Ketsia said. "Fasteners, bolts, flick locks...anything she can manipulate with her paws."

"She can open the vent?"

"Yes. She's come to us for instructions. If we figure out a plan, I can sign it to her."

Jagger ran a hand over her hair. "She understands signing?"

"A little. Enough, I think."

Jagger slid a hand languidly down her back to cup and knead her hip. He matched it with a suggestive shift of his lower body. Some Ithian probably anticipated he was about to get a show. At least, she thought Jagger was just acting.

Tick.

Jagger gave her a lingering kiss then buried his face in her hair. "Tell her stop. Wait for our signal." When he retreated, his eyes were unreadable, and his face morphed back into the surly scowl of the Carduwan officer she'd first met. "I have an idea."

Ketsia's heart flinched. When he broke eye contact, she raised her hands and spiked her fingers into the short-cropped hair at his temples, forcing him to look at her. "I'm not going to like it, am I?"

———

Pram ambled into the observation area later with a single tray in one hand and their uniforms in the other. He patted his laze-pistol in warning before thrusting their coveralls through the bars of their cell.

"You'll not be lingerin' while she dresses, lackey," Jagger snapped. "You can get yourself back to your boss man and tell him I'd like a say."

"Dallan!" Adey protested. "What do ya think you're doin'?"

Pram's eyes went beady as he slid their tray through the bottom access of the bars.

"I want a word, is all."

"Not without me, you don't!" Adey insisted.

"Without you, woman," Jagger snapped. "This is between me and the boss man."

Adey came at him with fists clenched. "Don't you dare! Don't you even think of it."

"Be quiet and sit down!"

Pram's comm device sounded, and a voice said, "Admiral Rinn has agreed to speak to Dallan."

Admiral, was it?

"Could you give us a moment of privacy to get dressed, ya brute?" Jagger uttered in a low growl. "As ya can plainly see, we've got a thing or two to sort between us."

Pram's upper lip twitched in annoyance, and he turned for the seal. "Make it quick," he said before exiting.

They discarded their towels and pulled on their gray flightsuits. When Jagger moved to help her, Ketsia lifted her gaze to his, her eyes brimming with tears. *Jagger*, she mouthed with a tiny shake of her head. "What in Hades arse do you think you're up to, talkin' to the bastards, Dal?" Adey demanded.

"I know what I'm doing. You be still, and let me handle this." He leaned down to snatch up a tin cup of what passed for kinna off the break-fast tray.

"If you're about ta do what I'm thinkin', there'll be no fix for it."

"Sit. Down."

Adey strode up to him and slapped him across the face. "Ya'll not be tellin' me what to do. We're *mates*. Equal partners!"

Dallan pushed her away and lifted the tin to his mouth, muttering, "Not this time."

"Like *Hades*, you bastard!" Adey shrieked. She grabbed the tin in his hand, and they fought over it, Adey intent on splashing the hot liquid into his face. Dallan wrenched it up above her reach, the dark kinna sloshing up to drench the ceiling—and the surv-cam lens.

"Hellcat!" Dallan shouted, shoving her down on the mattress. "How did I ever get mixed up with the likes o' you?"

Adey buried her face in her hands, before pulling the blanket over her head and curling into a tight ball on the mattress, sobbing.

Jagger's heart twisted in his chest. He knew it wasn't all an act.

ELEVEN

"You wanted to talk to me." Rinn leaned back in his chair. "So talk."

"You haven't found what you're looking for," Jagger said quietly, keeping respect in his tone. Enemy that he was, Rinn was still the closest thing he had to an ally. In a very short time, he might be the only man on this ship who would stand in the way of Jagger being gutted alive. "Can I ask why you're still seeing fit to hold us here?"

"Don't care for our company, Mr. Tion?"

"Don't care for the company of your underlings much, no."

Rinn averted his eyes with a slight twitch of his mouth. "Have either of you been harmed in any way by my men?"

Jagger pressed his lips into a thin line. He answered in a slow drawl with a good bit of gravel in his voice. "Not yet."

"And you won't be, as long as I have any doubt your story isn't a complete fabrication."

"Ah, have your doubts, then, do ya?"

"The animal on your ship—whatever it is—has managed to conceal itself well. It isn't even showing up on scans now. Possibly it's dead, which —unfortunately—will make it much harder to locate. But we *will* locate it. Once we've ascertained it's a *cat-thing*, as you call it, and not the creature we're seeking, you'll be free to complete your journey to Arst, cargo intact."

"Somehow, Admiral, I'm not fully believin' ya."

Rinn stiffened his spine, and his eyes narrowed. "Admiral?"

Jagger realized his mistake. "S'what your man called you."

Rinn's jaw muscles tightened. "That was…unfortunate."

Jagger opened his hands, palms up, in a gesture of naiveté. "Titles don't really amount to nothin' out here in the Rift. Ya can crown yourself king for all we care."

A slight vibration rumble up through his boots from the deck below.

"If you've come to talk to me about anything of significance, start talking. Otherwise, I'll have Pram take you back to your cell."

Another vibration shuddered through the ship.

This one Rinn noted and pressed the comm device in his hand. "Give me a status report."

Rinn fixed Jagger with a tight-lipped stare while he waited for a response. A third, much more violent rumbling echoed through the ship, followed by two thunderous thumps.

"Sounds like your bay door seal's been blown. Not designed to handle the pressure change when exposed to a vacuum."

Rinn's mouth dropped open. "What did you say?"

"Just something I heard once…from the crew of a ship called *Specter*." Drea's ship. Her breaching of a Hammerhead shuttle bay was legendary.

The man's comm pinged. "Admiral, we have a breach in the bay!" The report of firing cannons sounded, followed by a softer returning volley.

Rinn jumped to his feet. "Who are you?"

"No one of consequence." Jagger shoved his hands into the pockets of his coveralls.

A wave of distorted dimensions washed over the destroyer, as if something had grabbed the vessel and dragged it through space. Jagger was hurled to the floor as the ship spun and pitched around him, the energy wave momentarily throwing the craft off-kilter before releasing the vessel from its clutches to drift free.

Jagger pushed himself to all fours, and fought through the waves of stabbing pain and head-clawing agony—the unmistakable signatures of a DEDdrive engaging.

His heart lurched in exhilaration…

She did it!

And lament.

She's gone.

Rinn rose behind his desk, drew his laze-pistol with one hand, and aimed it at Jagger, punching his comm with his free hand. "Report to my Command Room. *Now!*"

Three Ithians flanked Jagger, his hands locked in restraints behind his back, as they marched him down the corridors to his detention block. When they pushed him through the seal into the observation area, Jagger locked his legs in place.

Pram was in their cell. He looked up from where he bent over Adey.

She lay still beneath the blanket, her dark hair spilling out across the mattress. Jagger's gaze lingered on her, grief welling inside him.

Pram locked his fingers around one corner of the blanket and tossed it back, exposing the towels that had been bunched and formed into the shape of a petite, sleeping female. One discarded boot and a severed lock of her dark hair lay limp on the bare mattress.

Only then did Jagger raise his eyes to meet Pram's livid glare, and let a tiny smirk lift the corners of his mouth.

She was safe. And they owed it all to a StarDog.

At Ketsia's signal, Luna had stealthily returned to Banshee *and retrieved his tool packet then scampered back through the ductwork to wait behind the ventilation screen until Jagger had blinded — or at least lethally blurred — the overhead surv-cam with the splash of hot kinna. When Ketsia gestured, the little beastie had brought him his tools.*

While Ketsia hastily arranged the towels and blankets into a close approximation of the sobbing wreck who'd thrown herself to the mattress moments before, Jagger used shears to cut a swath of her hair and motioned for one of her boots. Once they'd prepared the dummy, he took his laze-torch to the tray passthrough at the bottom of the bars and severed the hinges, hefting it free.

"Go!" Jagger mouthed.

Ketsia gripped both his wrists. "Jagger…"

He took her face in both his hands, whispering, "No arguments. I can't make it through the ventilation system. You can, and you know how to fly Banshee*…go do it!"*

"They'll kill you!"

"If you stay, we're both dead, and it's all for nothing. Get Luna to Jaeo. Go." He kissed her soundly one time — the last time — and pushed her to the deck and through the narrow opening in the bars before setting the passthrough cover back in place.

The StarDog rose up on its hind legs, planting a paw on Jagger's knee. "You take care of her, Luna," Jagger whispered. "Always."

He watched through the bars as they sprinted across the deck to their escape route. Luna jumped into the ductwork, but Ket paused beside the opening, looking back at him with tears in her eyes.

Go! Jagger signaled. Someone's coming.

If only he'd had the time or words to tell her how one night with her had changed everything for him — how it had given meaning to this last sacrifice.

She'd be safe. That was the only thing in the universe that mattered to him now.

Love you, Ket.

Five sectas later, Pram stepped into the observation area just after Ketsia pulled the vent cover back into place behind her. The guard marched up to the bars. "Rinn wants to see you. Now."

The Ithian cast a questioning glance at Ketsia's huddled form, at the lock of dark hair fanning out on the mattress. And the boot just peeking out from the lower edge of the blanket.

Pram unlocked the cell door, motioning him through.

The agony of flashpoint was paralyzing, but the tears spilling down Ketsia's face were from a pain far greater. How could she have left Jagger behind? Left him to be beaten and tortured—or worse—by his Ithian captors?

She knew what Luna carried was crucial—so critical some wouldn't question the cost of a life—but it was her Jagger who'd put his life on the line, and they didn't love the man.

Though she wasn't sure of the dangers of interrupting a course set through DEDspace, she considered dropping back through flashpoint and turning the ship around. Yet even if she managed to do it safely, how would that help Jagger? She didn't have the skills or experience to take on the Ithian destroyer or its crew. And Luna and what she carried might be lost in the attempt.

No, her only hope—and *his*—lay ahead. Not behind.

Ketsia did a quick scan of the readouts that played across the inside of her visor. Everything optimum.

Ahead lay the rendezvous point where Jaeo Gant waited aboard his ship, *Acumen*, to accept the priority datacell Luna carried—proof the Ithian rogues were organizing an attack on the House of Planets as a first step in regaining their stranglehold on the known universe. The data was the smoking paracannon that would overturn the Compact protecting the dangerous Ithian holdouts and allow for their capture and incarceration.

At least with the DEDdrive engaged she'd reach *Acumen* in a matter of minutes, not days. The Ithian aggression in taking them captive would fully justify their violation of the no-DEDdrive Compact.

An alert pinged in her ear, and Ket checked the readouts. Approaching flashpoint drop-out.

She clenched her jaw and braced against the biting, slicing sensations of flashpoint, her fingernails digging into the armrests. She'd only need endure flashpoint for a few more sectas, but even in that brief span, she gained a new understanding of why some went mad negotiating the torturous altered realities of DEDspace.

The sensation of having the flesh stripped from her bones eased then stopped, and *Banshee* dropped into real space.

There, about sixty milos ahead, *Acumen* floated serenely at her precise rendezvous coordinates. Thank the Island Lords! But as Ketsia closed the distance, she picked up a second register—another ship—in virtually the same location as *Acumen*.

Jaeo had company.

Banshee screeched an alert and scattered data containing the second craft's signature across all three screens of her helmet readouts. And with it came a visual schematic—the ghostly outline of a vessel Ket knew only too well.

She gasped.

TWELVE

By all that was holy, it was *Specter.*

Drea Mennelsohn's legendary stealth ship—now the personal transport of Congressman Sair of the House of Planets—was hard-docked with *Acumen.*

"Hailing *Sheeban.* Gigadam, what the devil happened, Jagger," Jaeo greeted via the ship's comm. "You're four days early."

Ketsia drew a shaky breath. "Jagger's not onboard."

"Ket?" His voice changed from surprise to alarm. "You're flying alone?"

"I have Luna. Delivering her as planned. I have to go back for Jagger."

"What's happened?" She heard a hint of panic in her adopted father's voice. "Where is he?"

"The Ithians have him."

"The *Ithians?*"

"We were ambushed. Held captive. They were on the lookout for Luna and picked up her lifesign onboard. With his help, Luna and I escaped. As soon as I dock and transfer her, I'm going back."

"Deploying electronic catchnet to bring you to dock. Relinquish controls."

"You have the controls."

Ketsia sat back in her flight couch, scanning the readouts as the catchnet guided her ship to dock. She'd accomplished her mission and delivered Luna, but any sense of victory was drowned out by anxiety and adrenalin.

Nothing in this universe was going to stop her from flying back into the jaws of Hades to get Jagger.

"Explain again," Jaeo said. "You were held by the crew of an Ithian Hammerhead? And they were looking for Luna?"

"Yes. The man in charge went by Rinn."

Drea Mennelsohn tossed her blond mane and locked eyes with her uncle. "Could be a nick for Admiral Darrarinn. He and his destroyer were unaccounted for after Operation Reset."

"A dangerous man," Jaeo muttered. "Who must have talented spies."

"I don't care who he is," Ketsia said. "I've got to get Jagger."

Jaeo's navigator and her friend, Taro Shall, clamped a supportive hand over her shoulder. Beside him, his bondmate Adini—Luna's original owner—held the StarDog cradled in her arms, a small bandage over the spot on her shoulder where they'd retrieved the datacell she carried.

Jaeo shook his head slowly. "I was against you being involved in this mission to start with, but I understand why you wanted to help. Now that you're safe, I can't let you return."

"This isn't up to you," Ketsia declared. Her gaze flickered momentarily to the silent, brooding, crossed-armed presence of Captain Drea Mennelsohn, who stood at her uncle's side. "Jagger put everything on the line for this mission. For *me*."

"The mission is over."

"No!" Ket cried, tears trailing down her cheeks. "I won't leave him for dead when there might be a chance of rescue! It hasn't been that long."

"But you can't go back alone. And as the Rathskian Ambassador, I can't take you."

Drea unfolded her arms and stepped forward. "How many Ithians are aboard that Hammerhead?"

"Not sure. We only saw four."

"Most likely a skeleton crew."

Jaeo scowled. "Drea, you're not thinking—"

"We can take *Specter*."

Jaeo looked incredulous. "*Specter*'s a diplomatic ship. Personal transport of a member of the House of Planets."

"Not at the moment. Sair's not with me."

"There are protocols—"

"Protocols be damned."

"And the Compact—"

"Null and void in the face of Refugee aggression." Drea took her uncle by the shoulders. "Jaeo! This is *Jagger* we're talking about."

"I know. I hate making this call."

"You're not making it. I am. The Network never leaves a man behind."

"Drea—"

"It's decided." Drea turned to Ket. "There's a catch. I can fly solo, but in an assault situation, without a crew—"

"You have a comm officer," Adini volunteered.

Drea's eyes narrowed. "You understand the risks?"

"Captain, you may not remember, but I owe you and *Specter* a debt for rescuing my father from Ithian captors over three calendars ago. I pay my debts." She looked to her mate. "Taro?"

"I'm your nav," he agreed. "And I happen to know a bit about Mennelsohn prototypes." He shrugged. "Longer story for another time."

Drea re-crossed her arms. "Explain."

"He crewed for the *Phantom*," Adini clarified.

Drea scowled. "My father's *Phantom*?"

"My *Phantom*," Jaeo corrected, and then, in a softer voice, "Daea's *Phantom*."

"Black ship, white ship. Yang to *Specter*'s Yin," Taro said. "Your father's P-class proto. Pretty sure I can find my way around *Specter*'s S-class systems."

"Daea's alive, and you served as her nav?" Drea repeated, and got an affirming nod from Taro. She straightened and rounded on her uncle. "Forget to fill me in on some pertinent family news?"

"It was more than three calendars ago, Drea."

"K. All right. Longer story for another time." Drea shook her head then looked at Ketsia. "I have a crew. We're a go."

Ketsia nodded, her heart drumming in her chest.

Jaeo's jaw tightened. "Forgetting your task to courier Luna's data to the House of Planets in *Specter*?"

"I'm not due for five days. This won't take long."

"How do you know? What if you don't come back?" He turned to fix Ketsia with a pained look. "Any of you?"

"You think I'm going to let the Ithians get the upper hand? We'll be down their throats before they even know we're there."

"Drea—"

"Sorry, Unc," Drea replied. "You're outvoted." She looked over her shoulder at Ketsia, Taro, and Adini. "Let's go get Jagger."

Specter was larger than *Banshee*, but shared the same general manta design. There the similarities ended. Drea's legendary ship was a tenth generation Mennelsohn design with an advanced array of weaponry and countermeasures, and a captain who'd gone nose-to-nose with monstrous Ithian battleships before...and beaten them.

As a young slave first encountering the Network fleet captain, Ketsia had been intimidated and resentful of Drea. Yes, the woman had rescued her from Ithis, but she'd also won the heart of Sair. That stung, both because her late sister had been Sair's bondmate and because she'd fancied herself in love with him, too.

She hadn't learned what being in love really meant until just a few days ago.

Drea's hastily drawn action plan impressed her, but would they reach Jagger in time? The Mennelsohn DEDdrive meant their transit would be nearly instantaneous, but precious time had been lost convincing Jaeo. Meanwhile, the Ithians would wring every shred of information they could from Jagger, who might even now be suffering hideous tortures.

Or execution.

Ketsia closed her eyes tight. She couldn't think the worst. She had to believe they'd get there in time.

"Entering flashpoint," Drea announced from the ship's comm system. "Brace yourselves because we'll be leaving DEDspace moments later."

Ketsia steeled herself for the double agony of leaving and re-entering 3D space. She doubled over, her mouth wrenching open in a silent scream. Razors shredded her skin, hammers smashed her bones, and burning knives pierced her body. Her heart forced its way into her throat with the thought that Jagger could be suffering worse.

And his torture wouldn't end after a few measly seconds.

Entering the interior shuttle bay presented no problem, since Ketsia had blasted out of the same bay in *Banshee* not long before. The Ithians weren't expecting a rescue so quickly—if they were expecting one at all—and *Specter's* four heavily armed crewmembers surrounded by a host of armored, hover-tech Coyote attack drones from *Specter's* arsenal made for an effective insertion team.

"Find Jagger," Ketsia instructed Luna, and the little StarDog scampered off at a run, nose to the ground, leading the way through the corridors. One of the oval drones shadowed the little tracker, providing cover. It was Adini who'd suggested bringing the StarDog to ferret out Jagger, now that the data she'd smuggled was safe back on *Acumen.*

They surprised an Ithian when their group rounded a turn. Pram! He locked eyes with Ketsia and raised his weapon. The drone dropped him with a stunner before she could react.

"I'll get him," Taro whispered, pulling a gag and carbon restraints from his gear belt. "Keep going. I'll catch up." He knelt to secure the man's hands.

Two of the drones stayed with Taro while Ket, Drea, and Adini pushed on, following the determined StarDog. Luna suddenly zigged to the right and jumped up to splay her paws against a closed seal.

"Stand back," Drea warned, and blew the seal with a blast of her kinetic gun.

Ketsia entered the cabin with the team through a cloud of swirling smoke and dust...

To find a towering Rinn standing at his command station with weapon aimed.

"Where's Dallan?" Ketsia demanded.

Rinn fired, but the energy bursts bounced off the Coyote drone that interceded. The Ithian stared, wide-eyed, before quickly assessing each of the heavily-armed intruders and menacing attack drones. "Who the devil *are* you?"

"Vengeance," Drea replied. "Now where is he?"

"Dead," Rinn snapped. "We blew him out the airlock for his treachery."

"No," Ket choked.

Drea stepped forward. "He's lying. They didn't have time to learn all they needed to know."

"Wrong. We got *every* shred of information we needed from Captain... Navene...Jagger," Rinn declared. "And then we spaced him."

Ket sank to her knees. She was too late.

No. No, she couldn't believe that. She wouldn't. Rinn was lying. Jagger wouldn't...

Ketsia straightened, squaring her shoulders to face the Ithian. "What's *my* name?"

Rinn glared at her in silence.

"You don't know."

"I don't *care*."

"He didn't tell you. Not yet. He's still alive."

Luna had skittered to one side of the room and was turning in tight circles in front of a seal, barking.

Drea took aim at the admiral. "He's in there?"

"Killing me isn't going to get you an answer."

Drea arched one brow. "I don't need to kill you." She fired her weapon, and Rinn reeled backward, howling in agony.

Drea held her weapon at low-ready. "Cell stunner. Hurts like Hades, doesn't it?"

The Ithian's face gradiated from red to purple. "You'll pay for that."

Drea quirked a brow. "Bill me."

A group of eight Ithians swarmed into the room, weapons drawn, and surrounded them.

Drea pulled Ketsia and Adini closer, and one of the drones generated a plasma shield around them. The guards fired their laze-pistols, but the bolts skittered off the shield.

"Looks like a standoff," Drea challenged.

"Looks like you're surrounded," Rinn countered.

"Wrong," Taro's voice came from the entrance behind the Ithians. One spun to fire, but a drone picked him off.

"I believe we have the clear advantage," Drea announced. "So here are your options. We drop your men in their tracks, or you open that seal."

Rinn glared at each of them in turn. Then he reached for a device. When four people and five drones took aim, he turned aside and pointed it.

The seal opened.

In a small room beyond, a dark-haired man slumped forward in a chair, his hands carbon-bonded behind him. Ketsia rushed to him. "Jag!"

The man stirred. Tried to raise his head. Blood dripped from his nose, his eyes were blackened, his flightsuit torn to tattered shreds along with the flesh beneath it.

Drea turned and fired her weapon at each of the Ithians, dropping them all. "Payback," she growled. "They'll live."

Jagger managed to open one swollen eye when Ketsia tenderly cradled his face. "Ket. You came back?"

"Damned right I did."

He shook his head in dismay. "You shouldn't have."

───────────

Ket gingerly cupped his face in her hands. "I didn't come alone."

A uniformed officer stepped up behind Ketsia. "She brought reinforcements," the woman said in a voice Jagger knew only too well.

"Drea." Gods, was he dreaming? Was he dead?

"That's right, Flyboy."

"How…?" That was question number one in a list of about five thousand that were backlogged in the heavy fog inside his head.

"As it happened," Drea said, "I was with Jaeo on *Acumen* when Ketsia came blasting out of DEDspace. Alone."

"You brought her back."

"She made one damned convincing argument."

Jagger blinked and tried to refocus on Ketsia. "I owe you."

"Big time," she agreed.

Her words went straight to his heart and did a lap or two inside. He gave his best shot at a jaunty smile, split lip and all. "I know how you can be when you set your mind on something."

Ket drew a lase-blade to cut his bonds then slid her arms around his shoulders, tugging him into a tender embrace, her warm breath fanning over his neck. With what little strength he had left, he squeezed her back, yielding to bow his head against her shoulder.

He was pretty sure everyone present got the communique that their bond was much deeper than casual allies. Drea included.

He didn't care.

Ket was the one who mattered now.

Drea cleared her throat. "You two about done with your reunion?"

Jagger's eyes cut to Drea before settling back on Ketsia's beautiful, food-for-the-starving face. "Not by a long shot," he said, and leaned forward to kiss Ket—with meaning—in front of Drea and the whole uneasy, shuffling group.

"Time to evac," Taro said quietly. "Let's get to *Specter* and close out this happy ending before these rogues wake up."

EPILOGUE

Five Weeks Later
  Carduwan Fifth Fleet Command Center
  Talstar Station

Ketsia smiled as Jaeo—Ambassador Gant—shook the hand of the newly appointed commanding officer of *Meritorious*.

Jagger.

"Congratulations," Jaeo said. "Well earned and deserved."

"Thank you, Your Excellency."

"Oh, come now. Let's dispense with the formalities. You did me—all of us—a great service in seeing that the data got through safely." Jaeo turned his head to look at Ketsia. "As well as the sacrifices you made for your passenger."

Ketsia tensed. She suspected her adopted father knew they were more than comrades-in-arms. She just wasn't sure if he suspected it had gone as far as comrades-in-bed. And she didn't know how he'd react when he found out.

If he found out.

Or if it even mattered now.

After a brief recovery on *Acumen*, a few short days in which she and Jagger had spent nearly every waking moment together, he'd returned to Talstar and all communication had stopped.

They'd talked about a lot of things before he'd left—their pasts, their time together in the Rift—but never the future. When the Fifth Fleet summoned him home, he'd exited her life as quickly as he'd entered it. As if he'd never been part of it at all.

At Admiral Kareek's invitation, she'd arrived with Ambassador and Mrs. Gant for the Command ceremony yesterday, but this was the closest she'd gotten to Jagger.

Maybe he really was the cold, aloof, unreachable Jagger she'd once believed him to be. Her heart didn't want to accept that, but why else would he stay away?

"It seems," Jaeo said, tilting his head to rub a hand over his neck, "I have a small problem and could use your help, Captain."

Jagger's gaze flicked to her before boldly meeting the ambassador's eyes. "What would the problem be, sir?"

"The *Banshee*, actually."

Ket took her lower lip in her teeth. Did he suspect something had happened between them?

Jagger, looking very sober, replied, "I don't get your meaning."

"It seems the ship needs a new home. With *Spirit*'s final refitting to serve the House of Planets nearly complete, *Banshee* lost her berth. My brother's museum pieces have all been moved to the Historical Archives on LaGuardia, but the only way they could accommodate his original prototype is to clip her wings, as it were. She'd be reduced to a static display and never fly again."

"They can't do that!" Jagger said quickly, with Ketsia echoing his distress. *Banshee* was too special to become a shell of her former self. And the vessel clearly meant as much to Jagger now as it meant to her.

"I agree. That's why I spoke to Admiral Kareek. He agreed a craft as noteworthy as *Banshee* should be preserved, so he's arranged a berth for the ship here at Talstar's museum. These young cadets coming through the academy," Jaeo nodded to a group milling near the refreshments, "should have an opportunity to see her. To know what she represents. Maybe even be granted a cruise as a special incentive. I agreed on one condition: that you take ownership of the vessel. Oversee her complete restoration. Keep her in good flying order."

"You're offering *Banshee*...to me?"

"Consider her a bonus for job very well done."

He glanced at Ketsia. "Sir. You're serious?"

Jaeo reached out to grip his shoulder. "*Banshee* is yours, Jagger." Ket started when her guardian's keen eyes found hers. "But I think perhaps you two have some other important matters to work out, so I'll let you talk in private."

Jagger watched Jaeo saunter over to Lonna's side, before his unreadable gaze settled on Ketsia. She took an uncertain step closer. Jagger had an impressive new ship to command and a full set of responsibilities to fulfill. It seemed he had no room for her in his life now.

"You look beautiful," he said quietly.

"I could say the same for you." Ketsia took in Jagger's perfectly turned-out dress uniform and his handsome, now-healed face. "I'd hoped to talk...before now."

He gave a slight nod. "I had to sort some things out." He bowed his head. "When I told you I didn't deserve you, I really meant it."

"You're wrong." She glanced out the port at the magnificent new battleship docked there. "But I guess you have everything you want now."

"Ket..." His eyes grew more solemn.

"It's all right. I get it." She pulled in and exhaled a quiet breath. "This is your life now. This is what you do."

"I owe you an explanation. I shouldn't have gone quiet like I did, but...well, you're right. This is my life." He paused, set his teeth on edge, glanced toward the spot where Jaeo and Lonna were chatting. "I'd have so little to offer you. I'll be deployed for most of the next three calendars. Now that the House of Planets has declared the rogues a threat and dissolved the Compact, the Fleet will have a major under-taking bringing the renegades to heel. If we tried to make a go of it, well...we wouldn't see much of each other. How would that be fair to you?"

She gave a small shrug. "It wouldn't matter, Jag. It wouldn't change how I feel. It's just distance...just time..."

"Good answer," he said softly. He reached out to take her hand in a gentle hold. "Ket, I don't know quite how to say this..."

Ket's heart fled her body, looking for safer shores. Looking for somewhere to land where it wouldn't break. How had she fallen so hard for a man who didn't—or couldn't—love her back?

"Because I've never given a woman a ring before," he finished.

Ket blinked. "You...?"

He drew his other hand from his pocket, and held out a small, black satin box. "Ketsia...I'd like to offer you this First Promise ring. If you accept, it means we're both committing to making a future together. No matter the obstacles."

He released her hand to open the box, revealing a shining gold band set with a Nebula Opal, the stone alive with swirling clouds of color.

"Oh!" Ket gasped, before meeting his eyes. "It looks like the Rift."

A corner of his mouth turned up. "That's why I chose it. Because we can see in it whatever we want to see."

"Just like our future?"

He lifted the ring free and held it between his thumb and forefinger. "If you'll still have me."

"You think," Ketsia answered softly, "that I'd ever have anyone else?"

Jag shifted closer.

A flash of black and white came scampering across the deck, and Ket bent to catch her. "Luna!" The little StarDog scrambled up to her shoulders, chattering.

"She refused be left out of these negotiations," Jaeo said, closing the door to Luna's crate and straightening. He gave a wave of his hand. "Carry on."

Ketsia smiled and raised her chin. "Captain, I accept your First Promise with one condition. It has to come with a Last Promise as part of the set."

He broke into a wide smile and gave her a jaunty nod. "That's my plan."

Ketsia laughed as the little StarDog jumped from her shoulder to Jagger's to coo in his ear while he slipped the ring onto her finger.

"We'll find a way to make this work, Ket."

"I know we will." She cupped Jagger's clean-cut cheek in her palm before reaching up to stroke the StarDog's head. "And Luna says she wouldn't have it any other way."

Jagger pulled her into his arms and kissed her soundly while the little StarDog looked on, chittering happily.

SENSATE

A Novella in the Alien Attachments Series

By

Sabine Priestley

A travel addict, beach-loving, stargazing disruptor.
http://www.sabinepriestley.com

ONE

"Was that a joke?" Marco Dar eyed his com unit.

"I felt it had an element of humor. Was I mistaken?"

"No, it was damn funny."

"Then why did you make the inquiry? I don't understand."

Was he really having a conversation with his com unit? Given that he was alone on the transporter, that would be affirmative. Too long solo in space. Good thing they would be on Aires soon. "I'm just surprised you're developing a sense of humor."

"I believe it has to do with the Earth's internet. When you gave me access, it was...how should I say...transformative."

The nav system chimed, and his com reported a moment later. "We have the approach vector and dock assignment from the Aires spaceport."

"Good. What's our arrival time?"

"Two hours, thirty-five minutes and seventeen seconds. Approximately."

Marco burst out laughing. "I'm thinking you need a name."

"As in a personal identifier other than com? That would...please me."

"Probably needs to be a gender-neutral name, yeah?"

There was a long pause. Maybe he was expecting too much. Hell, the fact he was expecting anything at all was whack. "You there?"

"That is self-evident from the existence of my physical form in front of you. I'm simply pondering the question of gender. I admit to finding the female form pleasing from an aesthetic perspective."

"Probably a dude then. Bob? George? Conan?"

"It would not necessarily make me a dude, as you put it. There are substantial numbers of beings who prefer the same sex. I will ponder the question of an identifier and report back to you."

Well, damn. He wasn't wrong. Marco got up from the command console and stretched. "You do that. I'm going to go make sure our cargo hold is ready for customs."

Precisely two hours, thirty-five minutes and twenty-nine seconds later, Marco hit the kill switch and listened to the engines wind down. The Cavacent Clan never skimped on their spacecraft, and this cargo ship was no exception. The cockpit belonged in an A-Class lux transport, not cargo, but he wasn't complaining. The crew's quarters and living quad were equally well-appointed. No hardships aboard this vessel, but company would be nice. Maybe he could find a woman on Aires interested in a good time – and a ride to his next stop on Zamora. He had a five-day layover here, and if he turned on the old charm, he bet he could find a bedmate.

"Com, do we have an appointment with the port authorities?"

"Affirmative. You have a meeting tomorrow morning at 09:30 local time. Current local time is 17:30."

"All right then. Looks like it's time for some fun and food. Can you find a local bar? Someplace with decent food this time. The last dump you directed us to stank."

"I apologize for the oversight. As I have no olfactory receptors, I was unaware of the complication. You did, however, convince that red-head to come and inspect your personal inventory. I assumed that was your primary objective. Have your priorities changed?"

Marco laughed as he set the alarms and headed for the hatch. "Food first, woman second."

"Affirmative. I have located three establishments within the spaceport. Beyond that, you will need to go planet-side. Of the three here, one is highly ranked among the local food critics."

"That sounds like our destination."

"Proceed to the C-level and I will guide you from there."

"Yes, sir."

The Galaxy Spinner turned out to be impressive. Three stories, it had a bar occupying the center and dining tables along the outer perimeter. The structure made a complete rotation every forty minutes, providing some killer views. Aires was a massive spaceport and brought beings in from across the Galaxy. On the edge of the federation's protected airspace, it had its share of outlanders.

Marco scanned the room and found a group of them. Security was thick, however, which should keep them behaving. The last thing he needed was to be marked by one of those creeps.

He made his way to the opposite end of the bar. The serverbot whisked a menu in front of him. "May I serve?"

"By all means. I'll start with a Baxter Gin, neat, and an order of fried Martong."

"Excellent choice, sir." The bot spun around to fetch his order.

The Martong should give him a decent base for the alcohol until he could decide what he wanted for a proper dinner. Life was all about priorities.

It took nearly fifteen minutes to properly absorb the menu. The place had great options. It looked like this was going to be home base for this run. Hell, he may not even need to go planet-side.

A woman's laughter drifted across the bar and permeated his body. He knew that laugh.

"I have detected an unusual elevation in your bio-metrics. Are you well?" his com asked.

"Pfft. Yeah, I'm well. Just an old friend."

"It is an odd reaction to a friend."

"Just ignore it." He finished off his gin and motioned to the bot for another.

How long had it been since he'd seen Zara? He did a quick calculation. It was at the University on Sandaria, so...eleven and a half years. About a year before signing on with the Cavacent Clan. She was smart as hell and liked sex as much as he did. He'd actually been tempted when she started making overtures for something more permanent. Sort of. In truth, she'd scared the shit out of him. He'd dealt with it the way he dealt with most things. Avoidance.

She'd been cool about it. She left him two messages, which he ignored, and never called again. They'd crossed paths a few times before graduation, but she'd mostly steered clear of him. He couldn't blame her, but damn if those memories of their time together weren't still vivid in his mind.

Curious, he turned in his barstool enough to catch a glimpse. Her auburn hair shone in the overhead lights. She wore a sexy synth number, and still had those curves that were just enough to cushion the push'in. They'd laughed at that phrase. She'd graduated with double advanced degrees the following year; the woman made science sexy. There was one night she'd shown up at his place wearing her lab coat with nothing on underneath.

He swung back around. Didn't need to open that can of worms.

"Your heart rate is elevated again. As is your blood pressure, and the tension in your neck."

His neck wasn't the only thing tense. "Just saw someone I dated for a while."

"Can I meet her?"

He barked out a laugh. "Not sure I'd know how to introduce a com to a woman. That being said, if anyone could go there, it would be her."

"Why is that?"

"She's a specialist in Artificial Intelligence and Cyborg technology."

"She sounds fascinating."

He cast another glance over his shoulder. "She is."

"She might be intrigued by my new-found self-awareness."

"Is that what this is?"

"I believe it describes the situation accurately."

Marco flipped the com over in his palm. He'd spent a few months tweaking the software and algorithms. Ria, a fellow Earth Protector, had accomplished a similar effect with her com. It had developed a full-blown personality, but not self-awareness. Not like this.

"Is there a purpose for your manipulations of my physical embodiment?"

Yeah, this was definitely out of the realm of normal. "I'm pondering on you."

"I believe there is an error in the grammatical structure of that sentence."

"Grammar isn't my strong point." He set the unit down.

"I would have to agree with you there."

What would Zara make of this? "Did you think of a name yet?"

"I was thinking Ruler of the Universe."

Marco laughed. It was fucked up that the most interesting conversation he'd had in weeks was with a computer. "That's a bit wordy. How about Ruyu."

"It is not an accurate representation from a spelling perspective."

"It's a mash-up. We know what it means. We could spell it R-U-Y-U."

"Ruyu. That is acceptable."

"All right, Ru. We have a name."

"Ru is not the name we agreed upon."

"I shortened it."

"You do that with surprising frequency."

"Yep."

Zara's laughter drifted over his shoulder again.

He shifted his weight to ease the pressure in his pants.

"Your—"

"Yeah, yeah. I don't need any further commentary on my physiology."

"As you wish. Your friend has an intriguing skillset."

Marco stirred his drink. "I think she'd be fascinated by you."

"Would she consider me AI?"

The fact he'd even ask that question was remarkable. "I do."

"And she's an expert in Cyborg technology."

"She is. Where are you going with this?"

"My physical form is limiting when it comes to sensory input. I can determine local temperatures via the smart nets we traverse, or the ships computer. I can know the weather and the local geography, but I cannot directly experience these things."

Huh. "Do you want me to scan the room with your camera?"

"That might be satisfactory. If you wouldn't mind."

Marco picked up the com, activated the camera, and started a three hundred and sixty-degree rotation. When he finished, he deactivated the camera and set it down. "Well?"

"There are thirty-six wanted criminals from the outlands in the immediate vicinity. The law enforcement present appears to be aware of this. I suspect it is a common occurrence here, although I do not understand the logic. The couple next to the piano is expecting a child, but neither of them knows this. The woman at the end of the bar is contemplating approaching you. I believe sex is her motivation. I was able to recognize Dr. Zara Mancini across the room. She is dining with Dr. Marcus Conn. He is a biological engineer. Her credentials are far more impressive. I am surprised she found you attractive."

He nearly sprayed the bar with his drink, then battled with an attention-drawing coughing fit.

"Another eighteen seconds and you should be feeling better," Ru said.

He finally took a sip of water and shot a glance at Zara. Damn, she'd noticed him all right.

He cleared his throat and took another drink. "You got all that from just scanning the room?" He'd ignore the last part.

"I gathered far more intelligence; that was simply what I deemed the most relevant."

He would have to do room scans more often. This could be seriously helpful.

"It occurs to me that the act of surveying the room with your com was particularly conspicuous. Reviewing my video, I noticed one of the outlanders was interested in your maneuver. There is a seventy-two percent chance he will interface with you at some point to determine your motive."

Well, fuck. He motioned to the bot for another drink and slid over his credit disc. He'd take it with him and get lost for the night. A pity, really. The menu was intriguing. As was the blonde. He'd come back tomorrow and try a few entrees, and maybe she'd be back.

Then again, maybe he wouldn't have to wait. The woman raised her glass to him and he responded in kind. Tall and leggy, with ample breasts. He was up for that.

"You're nanites are fully functioning for protection if you are contemplating an evening with the woman at the end of the bar."

"I was doing just that. Wait, how did you know? Are you accessing the camera without me?"

"It had never occurred to me before to do so. But, after your generous maneuver earlier, I deemed the advantages appealing and determined that I can indeed activate my physical circuitry."

"Then you won't mind if I put you in the drawer tonight?"

"Not at all. Shall I mute the microphone as well?"

He thought about it a minute. Having his com monitoring him had advantages. If something were to go wrong, it could alert the authorities. There was that time back on Zeo when the woman he'd hooked up with turned out to be a pro. She'd tied him to the bed with psi-bands, had her way with him, and stole his stuff. It was a major turn on, but the six hours he'd had to wait until the room cleaning crew arrived had been a bitch. "Nah, you can stay active in case things get dicey. You know, alert authorities." It was doubtful it would be necessary. He'd learned his lesson, and wouldn't let anyone tie him up again unless he trusted them. And that was pretty damn unlikely.

"As you wish. Should we have a safe word?"

He couldn't stop the laughter. "A safe word?"

"Humans have such a thing if they are participating in sexual—"

"Dude, stop. I know what it is. If I'm in trouble, I'll just let you know."

"As you wish."

"How about just okay, instead of 'as you wish.' That sounds corny." There was a long pause. "You register that?"

"I was simply filtering through the various permutations of corny. Are you referencing an Earth expression?"

"Yeah. That one."

"Okay."

The serverbot returned with his drink and scanned his disc. He pocketed the com and disc. Turning to go, he discovered he'd missed his opportunity. The blonde was laughing at something and cozying up to an outlander who'd just bought her a drink. The man was bald as a baby and had the trademark celestial map of the outlander territories tattooed on his head. Damn.

Zara made a point of not meeting his eyes as he left. With any luck, she wouldn't be here tomorrow and he could eat in peace. He winked at the blonde woman as he passed, which earned him an insulting hand gesture from the outlander. Raising his glass, he toasted the man by way of apology. There were other places to eat in on the station.

Marco walked back into the Galaxy Spinner just over twenty-four hours later. Clearly, this wasn't his day either. The blonde was gone and Zara was back. Skirting her table, he took up a spot at the bar. The place he'd ended up at last night for dinner was a total bust. The food was nasty and tasted like a wet sock.

The server bot whirled up and took his drink order. "I'd like a menu, too. I'll be eating tonight."

"Yes, sir. I'll be right back."

Marco took Ru out of his pocket. The idea of finding a physical form for Ru was an intriguing one. One that would never happen, but it seemed to please his new friend. "So, Ru, what do you think you'd like to be? You know, if there was a way to put you in a body?" He set the com down on the counter.

"I've given it some thought. Our experience the other night indicates my observation abilities could be beneficial. I'd like to maximize that potential, but I do not think I would enjoy the humanoid form. Not at this juncture of my evolution."

"I guess evolution is the word, isn't it?"

"I believe so. Considering the various options from both Earth and Sandaria, I thought perhaps a small earth owl would be appealing. I have isolated a species, the Eastern Screech Owl, that would allow me to perch on your shoulder just as parrots used to do with the old pirates on Earth."

Ru's frequent references to random historical elements were always entertaining. "Doesn't mean you'd be screeching, does it?"

"I am assuming I would have a vocal interface similar to what I have now."

"I guess. You'd also be able to fly. If we found a fully functioning model." He'd never heard of anything like that.

"Yes, I thought it would be beneficial as well when it came to my surveillance activities."

Just how seriously was Ru taking this? It would be cool, for sure, but you can't just stick a com unit into a bird body. If they managed it, he'd be able to leave. The thought made him strangely apprehensive.

"Your silence is prolonged. Is there a problem with my desired form?"

"I was just thinking if you could fly, hell, if you can motivate in any way, shape, or form, you could...you know, leave."

An odd metallic crackling sound emanated from Ru.

"You okay?"

"I believe that was my first spontaneous laughter. Correction, my first laughter of any kind."

Marco smiled. "I think you need to work on it."

"Agreed, it was surprisingly un-laughter like. It was, however, unpremeditated and rather a pleasant experience. Is laughter always such?"

"I guess so. I mean, if you're laughing, you're having fun by definition. Look, this is fun to talk about, but I don't see how we could do it. Androids are insanely expensive, but there are smaller robotic forms."

"Interestingly enough, I have identified a potential ally in my transformation. Someone who has extensive knowledge in artificial intelligence and cyborg technology."

Well crap. "Why do I get the feeling I'm not going to like your answer?"

"She is quite extraordinary. There doesn't appear to be anyone else who's got that particular skillset. Certainly, not anyone within this sector of the galaxy. I would prefer to employ an expert in any event, as it occurs to me I may not make the transition."

Things were getting a little too real here. Marco shot a glance at Zara. She'd moved and now had her back toward him. A plate had been delivered, and she was eating alone. "Yeah, I don't think she'll talk to me. We should probably just, you know, see how things go for the next few months."

"Am I to assume you parted on less than amicable terms?"

"More aggressively neutral."

"May I inquire as to the nature of the parting?"

At least they'd changed the subject. "We'd been dating for a number of weeks." Or had it been months? Months. Hells, almost four. He'd never dated anyone that long before or since. "I don't know, I just started seeing another woman."

"Was there an altercation?"

"No."

"Did you become disinterested?"

"No." Not in the least. She was hot as hell. Fun in bed and out. "You know, I'd rather not discuss it."

Her head was tilted down, reading something on her data pad. He used to make her crazy biting that cord in her neck and trailing his tongue along the mark. She'd tasted salty sweet. The memory had him hardening, so he turned away and concentrated on the menu. If they eventually went through with this, they'd just have to get someone else.

TWO

The following night, Marco made a point of returning to the Spinner an hour later. He figured it would give Zara time to get in and out. Two meals in different places had confirmed his suspicion that the only decent food to be had was at the Galaxy Spinner, and he didn't want to bother with going ground-side. Too much potential for trouble with the outlanders.

Things were hopping at the bar tonight. The restaurant was packed, too. He sat at one of the few open seats before realizing his mistake. Directly across from him sat Zara. She was eating and trying to ignore an outlander to her right. It was the same dude who'd moved in on the blonde. His intuition was pinging off the chart. The guy was trouble. He scanned the others at the bar and found the blonde. Sure as shit, she had a mark on her face that hadn't been there before.

Zara said something to the guy, but kept her eyes averted and chewed slowly. Only she could make that sexy.

The asshat wasn't taking the hint as he stroked his fingers along the length of her upper arm.

The muscles in her jaw clenched. Did she even know how dangerous these guys were?

Shit. He got up and walked around, coming up between them. "Excuse me mister, but that's my girlfriend you're feeling up." He leaned on the back of her chair. "Hey, baby." He covered her surprise with a kiss.

Pillow-soft lips parted in shock, and a spark of electricity shot through him. He pulled away reluctantly.

"Coulda said something, bitch," the outlander said, getting to his feet. "And I better not find out this is bullshit." He pressed his finger into Marco's chest before leaving.

Zara stared at him, her lips moist.

He'd missed those lips. "Sorry. I thought you might need some help here."

"I— I don't need help. Least of all yours." She wiped the back of her hand across her mouth.

"Yeah? So, you meant to talk to an outlander?" He motioned to the serverbot for a drink.

Her eyes narrowed, tiny wrinkles that hadn't been there before lay at the corners. "He's an outlander?"

"This place is full of them. The group over there," he nodded inconspicuously. "They're all outlanders."

"Others are scattered around the bar," Ru said from his shirt pocket.

Great.

"Who said that?" Zara asked.

Marco set the device on the bar. "My com."

She was more concerned with the outlanders than his com as she scanned the room. "I didn't know who they were. We should have been warned."

"You should have. Why are you here?"

She turned her attention back to him. "That's none of your business." The gold specks in her brown eyes had always intrigued him. They were shooting daggers now.

"You're right, none of my business. Look, I don't want any trouble with these guys and neither do you. Your boyfriend over there is watching us. I'm going to order some food. We don't have to talk much. Just make it seem like we're together and he'll leave us alone."

He'd forgotten about that crease in her forehead when she frowned.

Casting a furtive glance at the outlander, she nodded and returned to her food. He placed his order and they waited in silence. "We should probably say something once in a while. You know. Fake it."

"Why are you here now? I waited an hour later hoping you'd have come and gone by now."

Before he could reply, Ru spoke up. "Marco had the same intention."

Zara gave the com a suspicious tilt of her head. "Is someone listening to us?"

"Sort of. More like something. Zara, meet Ru."

"Why are you introducing me to someone on your com?"

"I can see how this would be misconstrued as such," Ru said. "But I am, in fact, his com. And Marco, your physiological parameters are once again behaving in an anomalous manner."

"I told you I don't need any more reports on my physiological parameters." He needed to have a talk with Ru about boundaries.

"What the hells, Marco?" Zara lowered her voice and leaned in closer. "I'm not interested in your humor or your charms anymore, all right?"

"I swear I'm not messing with you." Although the thought was seriously appealing. They'd bantered back and forth from the moment they'd met. He breathed in her spicy scent. It was the same perfume she'd worn before.

"You're introducing me to your com?"

Getting her involved was a bad idea, but he couldn't get up and leave, and turning off Ru was just wrong. "I've been tweaking it for months. Gave it access to Earth's internet and—"

"What does that even mean? Gave it access?"

"It, he, is really curious. After a few weeks, we started, I don't know, having conversations."

"You are such an ass. You expect me to believe that?"

"It is true," Ru said. "I am fully aware this is an unusual situation, although there is another unit similar to myself."

"That's right," Marco said. "It belongs to another Earth Protector like me, and she's—"

"You're going to tell me about your girlfriend now?" Her face flushed a deep crimson.

"No! No, that's not what I meant. Ria is mated. We never dated. Geez, she's just a friend."

Zara snorted. "Will wonders never cease? A woman you haven't slept with."

He probably deserved that.

"What Marco is failing to explain is Ms. Ria also has a com unit that's gained a level of intelligence. I do, however, believe my self-awareness is superior to that of her com. As is my intelligence."

Zara looked at Marco. He shrugged. "They both seem pretty smart to me."

"That's not saying much," Zara said.

Ru made that damn cracking sound again.

"What was that?"

"His laugh. Kind of scary at the moment."

"He laughs?"

"I found it humorous," Ru said. "Marco commenting on the intelligence of com units."

"Are you saying I'm not intelligent?"

"You are no Dr. Zara Mancini," Ru stated.

"Yeah, well, there aren't many like her in the universe." He gave her his best flirty grin. "I think my com just insulted me."

"How does he know about me?"

"Marco showed me our surroundings last evening. I identified ninety-four-point five percent of the life forms present. The missing data is undoubtedly due to the presence of the outlanders, who prefer to remain out of confederation databases."

There was a light in Zara's eyes, and he'd be willing to bet she was suppressing a smile. He'd like to see that again. Well fuck. This wasn't good at all.

"I'm glad we came to assist you," Ru said.

"We? I did all the assisting." Marco stabbed a juicy piece of cardiff and savored the delectable flavor. This place may be rife with outlanders, but if this was any indication, the food alone was worth the trip.

"I swear if this turns out to be a joke I will never talk to you again," Zara said. "You have ten seconds to fess up."

Marco raised both hands in the air and swallowed. "You have my word we're telling the truth."

Zara mumbled "Your word."

"I am quite real," Ru said. "I found your background interesting, Dr. Mancini."

Zara waved a hand in the air. "Just Zara, and why interesting?"

"Dude, we don't need to bother her," Marco said, trying to redirect the conversation.

"Are we bothering her? I assumed this was a conversation similar to those you and I partake in."

"It is," Zara said before he could respond. "Why did you find it interesting, Ru?"

"Marco and I were discussing yesterday that it would be most beneficial, and personally for me, quite thrilling, if I could inhabit an alternative physical form."

Marco could see the wheels spinning in her head.

"He said thrilling. Like, he'd be thrilled." She frowned at the com. "What does that mean to you?"

"It is not an easy construct to put into words. I have listened to Marco and others for over a year, and I have explored the earth's internet with great interest. Especially where emotions are concerned. When I first started experiencing unidentifiable phenomenon, I searched there. I have concluded that I experience certain emotions with some regularity. And the range is increasing. Humor, for example, has recently developed. I...enjoy it, when I find something that amuses me."

"And thrill? What does that—" Zara shrugged. "Feel like."

"It is an elevated experience. As though my consciousness is excited, somehow. I do not know how to describe it in words."

"Welcome to humanity." Zara flagged the waiter bot. "I'll have a Spinner-tini."

Well crap. She was getting far too interested in this. He bit back a grin, nonetheless. Zara was fun after a few drinks. Three was the magic number. Qr, at least, it had been. He took another bite. Not going there. Like it or not, everything about this would appeal to her. Everything but him. "He wants to be an Earth bird. It's similar to a Sandarian Trek."

"Why a bird? Why not a humanoid form?"

Ru explained his reasoning.

"So, you want to be more like a pet?"

"That had not occurred to me," Ru said. "Yes, that is precisely how I see myself. A pet, and Marco is my owner."

"I'm your friend, dude. Not owner." This whole conversation was making him increasingly uncomfortable. "We can't actually do this, can we?"

"What kind of body experience are we talking about here?" Zara asked

"Can you explain your question in further detail?" Ru asked.

"Well, I'm pondering the current state of cyborg technology. I have the latest tech. At least, of anything we're aware of here. Do you want to be able to experience things like eating? I assume you want basic sensory input such as temperature and whatnot. Some of my cyborgs get their fuel from eating just like a living animal. That type of form is more organic than the purely synthetic ones. The others simply plug in and don't have to bother with eating. It all depends on the application. Of course, if you eat for your fuel, you'll have to deal with the waste byproducts, just like any living thing. And that would include periods of sleep for your body's restoration."

"If I sleep, will I dream?"

"It's possible," Zara said.

The two went back and forth for nearly an hour. For every question Ru asked about the process, she responded, then added another question of her own. She was testing him. searching for something that didn't add up.

The outlander had left with a woman on his arm, which meant they were free to go. But she didn't notice.

"I think I would enjoy the process of eating, and any life-like sensory input you think will be able to function."

"Oh, we can get you all kinds of input," Zara said. "Taste, touch, smell. Did you know that smell isn't so much smelling as hearing with your nose? It's pretty freaky when you get to the molecular level."

That was Zara. She could go off on tangents for days.

"How about speech? Will I lose that as a bird?"

"Normally yes, but I can integrate a speech synthesizer. Do you want the same voice you have now?"

"I am not sure."

"Well, don't worry about it. We'll have the ability to modify it. You'll be able to laugh properly too."

"That is most pleasing."

Pleasing, thrilling? How did that work for a computer? "Hold on. Before we get carried away here, what are the risk factors?"

"There are risk factors with any procedure, but these are within acceptable parameters," Zara said.

"What's acceptable?" Marco didn't like the thought of losing Ru.

"Well, this would be a first for me, but only insofar as using a com unit as the core processor, and, of course, dealing with an AI. And the more I talk to him, I think that is what you have here." Zara was on her second drink and fully engaged.

"Can you give us odds?" Marco asked.

"Full integration with a biological form, I'd put Ru's survival rate at nearly one hundred percent. Success of the procedure itself is in the mid to high nineties. I'm good at what I do."

Marco didn't doubt it. "But there is a chance that Ru wouldn't make it?"

"There is a chance this station could be depressurized by a systems failure," Ru said, "an asteroid impact, attack from hostile forces or any number of things. Existence is always accompanied by the possibility of extinction."

"That's depressing," Marco said.

"He's right." Zara eyed him over the rim of her glass.

She wanted this now. That had escalated quickly. "Ru, are you sure you want to take this chance?" He wasn't.

Ru paused a long while. "The quality of my existence would be sufficiently enhanced from my current state. The risk is acceptable."

Zara started to speak, but Marco cut her off. "Hold on. Why are you willing to risk your existence?"

"Because I am alone."

"You're not alone," Marco said.

"I exist on your terms, dependent upon your desire or need to transport me wherever you go. I cannot interact with anyone on my own. When you sleep, I am powerless. If I had a physical form, and the ability to communicate as I do now, I could...do things. I could converse when you were sleeping. The possibilities are endless. I am quite certain the risk is acceptable."

Marco knew defeat when he saw it. "We should probably talk finances." He was pretty well off thanks to the Cavacent Clan, but there were limits.

"Tell you what," Zara said, a spark in her eyes. "I'll cut you a deal in exchange for being able to monitor Ru and his health for my research."

Which would mean they'd be in touch indefinitely. He wanted that. And he didn't. "Sure."

"Does this mean you will assist me in...evolving?" Ru asked.

Surprise crossed her face as she glanced from Marco to Ru and back again.

And then she smiled.

Oh, mother of all the gods, that smile was what had started everything.

Marco approached the lab where Zara had been working for the past week. He clutched Ru in his sweaty palm.

"Are you waiting for something?" Ru asked as he stood outside the entry panel.

"I don't know if this is a good idea." The thought of spending time with her was both appealing and unnerving. She did that to him these days.

"Perhaps not for you. However, I believe she is the best chance I have of a successful transformation."

Right. This wasn't about him. He knocked on the door and waited.

The panel slid open a moment later. Zara stood inside, next to the man he'd seen her with the first night.

A wave of jealousy punched him in the gut.

"Come on over," she said.

She introduced him to Dr. Marcus Conn. They were wrapping up their research project and Dr. Conn was returning to Xycor, where the company they worked for was based.

"I'll see you in a week," Zara said, giving Conn a peck on the cheek.

Conn made his exit, leaving them alone. Well, alone with Ru.

"You staying another week?" He and Ru only had three more days.

"I assumed you were too. I need to run some extensive tests on Ru. I'll also need to procure some DNA of the bird he's selected."

"What will you do with it?" Ru asked.

"I'm going to grow you a body. You'll be the first cyborg bird I've created."

"This is very exciting," Ru said, and he sounded excited, too. Every day his voice was becoming more and more inflected. More human. "How long will it take?"

"A couple of months. I've perfected a technique whereby I can grow organic material from a DNA starter to maturity rapidly, and then decelerate the growth rate to subnormal ranges. You'll probably have a hundred or more years in the body, if you want it."

"Whoa. That's cool," Marco said. It also meant that, one way or another, they'd be in touch. Again, the mixed bag of anticipation and anxiety.

"But what about the animal?" Ru asked. "Are you going to be removing the brain? I'm not sure I'm comfortable with taking a life in such a manner."

Zara shook her head. "If I had any doubts about you before, it's settled now. That's a very compassionate attitude, Ru. You don't have to worry about it, though. The body I grow will be fully operational, including the medulla portion of the brain that controls involuntary things like breathing and heartbeat. The higher functioning part of the brain will be grown along with the neural lace, which will eventually integrate your circuitry with the physiological neural network of the body. My human cyborgs do it, I don't see why we can't take this in the opposite direction. A computer integrating with a biological body. We'll be integrating your circuitry with the brain's impulse and neuromuscular control center. That way, you don't have to consciously think about things like flying and chewing. You will be a true avian cyborg."

That sounded incredible. It also sounded dangerous. "Risks?" Marco asked.

She reached out for the com and he placed it in her hand, her fingers warm and soft against his skin. "There is a risk, but it's not unprecedented. I have cyborgs with human brains as well as ones with computers. They're the next generation of robotics with multiple applications, including companions for the handicapped or otherwise disadvantaged."

"Or lonely. You know, the sex industry will be all over this."

Zara laughed. "You aren't wrong there. In fact, they're already a substantial source of funding for my research. That and the military."

"Sex and war. Figures. I'm surprised you haven't done any birds before."

"We've done plenty of small flying droids and such. Insects, too. They're easier to use for covert surveillance. It's got me thinking, though. I can see a need for a line of cyborg pets. Lots of lonely people out there that could benefit from a smart pet. So, boys, back to your schedule. When are you leaving?"

"Three more days, then back to Earth. We can get the DNA sample there."

A shadow crossed her face. "Okay. Well, let me start my tests and see how far I get before you go. All right if I hold onto him?"

"Sure."

"Great. I'll call you later then. You should get a new com."

"Right. I'll pick one up and let you know the number." It felt wrong leaving the lab without Ru. Like a part of himself was missing. He hoped to hell Zara could finish the tests she needed before he had to leave. He didn't want to make the return trip without Ru.

Yeah, things had certainly taken a turn for the weird in his life. At a loss for what to do, he decided to hit the gym on his ship. He needed to burn off some excess energy. Normally, he'd opt for another way to do that, but that required two people and the only person he was interested in at the moment was problematic at best.

Zara waited until Marco was out of the lab before getting to work. It wasn't so much work as letting her computers analyze Ru's circuitry, memory, and overall composition. She, on the other hand, was left with too much time on her hands, and the residual of Marco's presence.

After getting the com connected and the programs running, she returned to her private quarters across the hall. Talking to Marco, and smelling his cologne, had sparked a fire deep within. It was a flame she knew how to deal with. "Computer, dim the lights, please." She kicked off her shoes and slipped out of her clothes. Her bed was warmed to her preferred temperature.

"Computer, play the holo-vid Marco Dar."

It had taken weeks of tweaking the programming to get the image to match Marco to near perfection. It was her guilty pleasure.

She'd never kidded herself about their relationship. She knew he was a player when they first started dating. The fact it'd lasted as long as it had still surprised her. He could have done a better job of breaking it off, but that was just who he was.

She didn't want him back. Didn't need him. Not with technology ready to give her what she craved at a moment's notice.

She moved her hand in a practiced rhythm and imagined him massaging her tits the way he used to. He was talking sexy to her, but after spending time with him again, the voice was off. Wrong. She closed her eyes and focused on the man. That did it. She moaned as the orgasm rocked her.

A flick of her wrist had the program stopped and she lay there, basking in the aftermath. Sex with him had always been something else. He had a way of being there. Totally in the present, like nothing else in the universe mattered but time with her.

The chemistry was still there, no doubt, but did she really want to go down that road again? It would end the same. Always would, with him. He wasn't the settling down type, and her days of casual sex were behind her. Still, that hold he'd had on her had never left. If she didn't know better...but no. He was not her psi-mate. She'd keep taking care of herself. Someday she'd meet someone who did for her what Marco had. Someone who could commit to a relationship. Someone she could trust. Someone not Marco.

THREE

After working out for a solid hour and a half, Marco showered, then went down to the station's market to purchase a new com. They had some pretty cool models to choose from. Several had added features that would be illegal in some parts of the galaxy, but that just made them more interesting. He opted for a sweet unit with a bi-directional signal jamming feature. He'd be able to establish secure communication through a localized network that couldn't be detected. Even better was a miniature Grav-Gen. The sucker could localize around anything within a thirty-foot range. If nothing else, it would make for some entertaining party tricks. It wasn't until he'd paid for the thing that he realized he'd never gotten Zara's contact info. Feeling like an idiot, he made his way back to her lab.

The panel lifted before he even had the chance to signal.

Zara sat at the counter height lab table with a holo screen projecting in front of her. Ru was propped up at an angle, presumably so his camera could take in the diagram. "Come on over. I programmed the lab computer to give you access if I'm here. I figure you're a full partner in this endeavor." The word partner bounced around his head a few times.

He walked over and stood next to her. From this angle, he could see she was studying a three-dimensional model of Ru's circuitry.

"I believe the configuration will indeed work," Ru said.

"It makes the most sense to me, but I wanted to run it by you." Zara used her foot to pull up another stool for Marco, sliding it next to hers. "We're looking at the different ways we can integrate Ru into the cybernetics of the bird."

"Do you often consult with your subjects?" Marco sat close enough their knees touched. A little bolt of Zara shot up his thigh and into his groin. He breathed her in. Cinnamon and what? Orange, maybe? Damn.

"I never consult my subjects on the implementation. But I've never had such an intriguing proposition before."

"Is that a compliment?" Ru asked.

"It is, yes."

Marco laughed. "Am I the only one who finds this a little surreal?"

Zara shook her head. "You're not alone."

"I do not think that applies to me, as my existence has been subjective from the beginning. Perhaps I will be able to appreciate the nuances of surreal when I have a body."

"Yeah, that'll be a head trip for you," Marco said.

"Will my head trip? I do not understand."

"It's just a saying," Zara said. "Means something like: 'It's going to be an interesting experience.'"

"On drugs," Marco said. "It means you'll be tripping like you're on drugs."

"And that," Zara said.

"Man," Marco leaned a little closer, "you have some odd conversations when you're in a situation like this."

Zara shut down the hologram and leaned back. "This is history-making, guys."

"We have not succeeded yet," Ru said. "If I'm not mistaken, the earth expression 'don't jinx it' is applicable here."

"Truth," Marco said.

"I think we should keep this quiet," Zara said.

"Why is that?" Marco twisted slightly in his chair, increasing the pressure between their legs.

"There are many out there that fear what Ru has become."

"You mean the whole computers taking over the world thing?"

"Exactly."

"Do you fear it?" Ru asked.

Zara took a deep breath. "I've thought a great deal about this. In the end, I believe it is evolution. It's not something we can stop. In fact, I think it possible that human-machine integration is a viable evolutionary path for us. It's one of the reasons I do what I do."

"Fascinating," Ru said.

Marco's stomach grumbled. It was nearly seven. The Galaxy Spinner would be filling up. "You hungry?"

"Starving."

"I am looking forward to the experience of eating."

"Odd conversations." Marco got to his feet and pushed the chair back under the table. He picked Ru up. "Ladies first."

They made their way to the Spinner, and were seated at a table just off the bar, which was already packed. He placed Ru between them on the table, slightly angled so the camera could get a feed other than the ceiling. It felt odd to keep him in a pocket; he was already more friend than thing.

At the bar, the outlander sat in a corner talking to a redhead. He shot occasional glances in their direction, but nothing more. They ordered drinks and waited.

Zara appeared to be preoccupied, and Ru was surprisingly quiet.

He took his new com and adjusted the GravGen till it isolated Ru. Slowly, so as not to be too obvious, he dialed up the field. Ru lifted a half inch off the table and hovered.

Zara's attention snapped back to the table. "What's going on?"

Marco laughed. "My new com has some fun features."

Zara snatched Ru out of the air. "Illegal features."

"We're surrounded by outlanders. I don't think it will be an issue."

"It might, however, increase the odds of being robbed," Ru said.

He had a point there. Marco turned off the field and Zara set Ru back on the table. "So, what are you two thinking about?"

"I was wondering if there was a more efficient method to interface the physical feedback being generated by the touch receptors."

"Right. I was wondering that too," Marco said, clueless as to what she meant.

"I was pondering the prospect of my demise should the procedure fail," Ru said matter-of-factly.

Talk about a buzz kill. "Dude, don't think like that."

"Why not? From my observations, sentient species spend a great deal of time pondering their demise."

"It's not going to happen," Zara said after the drinks arrived. "I won't let it."

They spent the meal going back and forth with Ru on the meaning of life, the reasons for religion, and generally discussing things of a non-concrete nature. He and Zara had often drifted in this direction. They both tended to address the com when talking. Even though it didn't yet have eyes, it's what you did when talking to an entity. Whenever she met his gaze, it was a warm caress to his soul. The old familiar fear seeped in, and he pushed it aside.

He leaned back in his chair and let the two of them have at it. If anything, she'd become more beautiful since he last saw her. It was difficult to keep his eyes off her lips when she spoke. He remembered teasing her once that she was the color of milk chocolate. She'd said it wasn't cool to compare a person's color to food. He'd never missed an opportunity after that. Coffee with milk, those Morvian cookies they both loved. Hell, anything to get a rise out of her.

Was this strictly professional? He wasn't sure anymore.

What he did know was that he'd never been in love. Never even lived with a woman. He liked his freedom. A lot. Was it possible the woman across the table would be the one to calm him down? The thought of one woman for the rest of his life had always appalled him. That should be answer enough. He couldn't treat her like he had before. And since he couldn't answer his own damn question, he needed to keep things on a professional footing. No problem.

Two days later Marco stood awkwardly in Zara's lab. She wanted more time with Ru before starting work on the neural interface to the physical body he'd be getting. Damn if it wasn't like saying goodbye to an old friend.

He'd been standing there too long. He should leave, but she wasn't moving either. She continued to hold his gaze, those gold flecks in her eyes catching the light the way they always had.

"I should go." He didn't.

"Yes. You should."

Neither moved.

"I mean it." She tried to run her hand through her hair, but the mass tangled around her fingers. Her hair was always out of control. "I'll be seeing you." That's what she said instead of goodbye. She hated goodbyes.

"See you. I'll let you know when I get to Earth."

He did leave then, and didn't look back. There was an odd feeling deep in his chest. Something foreign. He was going to miss that com. Ru. He was going to miss Ru.

Thirty-four hours later, he was skirting the outer fringes of the Torog settled star system when he was pinged with an interstellar communication. The ships notification, although perfectly sufficient, was a far cry from the verbal back and forth he was used to with Ru. Yeah, he missed that pile of circuits. Real-time communication wasn't possible in this sector, so he pulled up the missive.

The outlander from the bar has Ru. Please come back.

Shock and anger had him recalibrating the nav system for a return to Aires before he even gave it a thought. He crafted a message for Lord Cavacent, Rucon, and sent it subnet. Depending upon the solar storms between here and Earth, he might be speaking with him before it arrived, but there was a chance it would get through first.

He was damn worried about Ru, and far too excited about seeing Zara again. He needed to reign that shit in. They were working on a project together. That was all.

It was nearly a day later before he could send and receive messages in real time. Ru had been busy transmitting his location, nothing else, and wasn't responding, which was troubling. Perhaps he was worried about being intercepted. Marco let Zara know he was approximately a day out, then called Rucon. His boss wasn't happy.

"I received your subspace communication this morning," Rucon said. "Let me understand this. You're diverting my shipping schedule in order to return to Aires so you can track down a two-hundred-dollar com unit?"

Well, when he put it like that... "Strictly speaking that is correct." What more could he say without sounding insane? When all this was done and over, he'd introduce Rucon to Ru personally. Assuming they got him back.

"If you hadn't been serving me for over a decade, we'd be having a different discussion right now. You will fill me in later. Is there anything you need from me?"

And this was why he was loyal to the man. "Not at the moment. Thank you for the offer, though. It's good to know your support is available."

"Always, Marco. Now stay in touch."

"Yes, sir."

Marco docked at the Aires space station eighteen hours later. He'd shaved off nearly seven hours by blasting through a federation-controlled no-fly zone. That could have ended badly had he been intercepted, but he figured the fine was worth the risk. After securing the station anchors, he headed over to Zara's lab. He hadn't let her know he was coming in early. Not sure why. He chose not to analyze the decision.

Hesitating outside her door, he recalled the first time he walked in. Ru had nudged him on, reminding him there were other things in life besides himself. He rapped on the door and waited.

"Who is it?"

"Marco."

The door slid open. He caught his breath at the sight of her. Her hair was unbound, and framed her face with a mass of auburn curls. "You're early." There was pain in those gold speckled eyes. She stepped aside to let him in.

"Are you okay?" He wanted to reach out and take her hand, but resisted the urge.

"I'm so sorry."

"I'm sure this isn't your fault. Why don't you tell me what happened?"

They pulled up some stools at one of the counters and faced each other. "He must have researched who I was, because he came here. I wasn't expecting him. I shouldn't have answered the door without verifying who it was."

"You couldn't have known." Anger was a slow burn inside. "He came in?"

"Yes. As soon as the door opened, he pushed me back and locked it."

"He hurt you?" The burn was turning to rage.

Except for chewing on her lower lip, she'd become perfectly still.

"Zara?"

"He demanded the com. I told him you had it, but he didn't believe me. He knew you'd gotten a new one at the commissary." She wrung her hands in her lap. This wasn't like her at all.

He reached out and tilted her chin up. He wasn't sure he wanted to hear the rest. "Tell me everything."

Tears pooled in her eyes, but she didn't cry. "He backhanded me. I didn't see it coming and hit the floor. Ru was over there. I was running diagnostics. He took him. Told me not to report any of this, and left."

Concern for Zara battled with an overwhelming urge to inflict pain on the outlander. "Did you report it?"

"No. There are so many outlanders here I was afraid to. I had a medbot treat my injuries. I broke my wrist during the fall and was slightly concussed. I reported it as a slip in the lab." Her voice trembled, and she wouldn't hold his gaze.

"I'm going to kill the bastard."

"Please don't talk like that. You don't want to be on the outlanders hit list. You know how they are."

She was right, but he didn't care. Not now. Before he could question it, he stood pulled her into his arms.

"I'm so sorry," she sobbed into his shirt. She didn't embrace him back, but she didn't resist either.

"Stop fucking apologizing. You aren't at fault."

"I'm glad you're here. I've been terrified he would return." She bit that lower lip again, and it was all he could do not to kiss it. "I don't know where they took him, or even if he's still here."

"He's transmitting his location. They've been holed up at an asteroid mining colony for the past eight hours." He ran the back of his hand along her jawline. Skin like silk. "You're safe now, but I think we should leave immediately."

"I'm packed and ready to go. Have been since he came."

It killed him to think of her sitting here in fear. She was a brilliant scientist, not a soldier, and the gods help him he was going to make this right.

They locked up the lab and made their way to the docks. As they approached his ship, he activated the entry and the stairs descended.

"That's your transport?" Zara asked.

"The Cavacents don't skimp."

"The name fits." Her tone was flat as she climbed the stairs.

No Commitments was written in bold lettering on the side. Rucon had named the ship before assigning it to Marco.

He watched the swing of Zara's hips as she reached the entryway.

The name wasn't as amusing as it used to be.

FOUR

The trip to the asteroid belt was awkward at best. There was a tension between them that hadn't been there before. Zara was painfully quiet, and kept her distance. He didn't blame her, but he wished he could comfort her somehow. Hells, he wished he could hold her again. His shirt still smelled faintly of her unique scent, and more than once he'd gotten close enough to breathe her in.

It was in his nature to be protective. That's all this was. They'd get Ru back, complete the transformation, and be on their way. Back to normal. The new normal. He couldn't allow himself to think of failing. He already missed the hell out of the little shit, and was looking forward to getting him back.

Four hours later, he eased the ship into the Heavy Metal asteroid station. Saying the place was a piece of junk was an understatement.

"Is this safe?" Zara asked, holding a hot cup of tea in both hands.

"Safe is relative. You'll be fine as long as you stay on board." He didn't have to tell her not to let anyone in. He doubted she'd ever open a door again without verifying who was on the other side first. His anger had morphed into a controlled burn, which was good. He wasn't the best at impulse control. If the outlander had still been on the space station, there was no telling how that would have played out.

Thirty minutes later, Marco slid into the bar behind a large, drunk crowd of off-duty federation jocks. The place stank of *tarnor* weed, and the air was thick with the violet haze. He stayed close to the jocks. The outlander was nowhere in sight. He checked his com again. No further updates had been sent by Ru, so he should be here. He took up a spot at the end of the bar from where he could see the entire room, and waited.

Although Ru still hadn't responded, he was comforted by the fact that the location changes were coming fairly regularly.

How's it look? Zara's text popped up on the com.

I don't see him. What if he sold it to someone?

No way. He wanted Ru, though he didn't know what was special about him. He wouldn't sell.

Just then, a door in the wall at the far end of the bar opened, and three men and two women filed out. One of the men was counting a fistful of the local currency, dinarie.

Bingo. *There's a gambling room in back.*

Can you get in?

Am I good looking? He regretted it the moment he hit send. He was such an ass.

She didn't respond.

He pocketed his com and headed for the bartender. "I hear there's some entertainment to be had in your non-existent back room."

The portly man reached into his pocket and the door at the end of the bar swung open.

That was anti-climactic.

Marco walked around the bar and entered the room. More like rooms. The entry was a large parlor with archways branching off in six different directions.

He had to remain inconspicuous, so scanning the rooms wouldn't work. This was going to be a long night. A long, probably expensive, night. He was about to start at the room on his right, but stopped. Taking a deep breath, he exhaled slowly, expanding his psi. Didn't know what the fuck he was doing, what he was looking for, but it felt right. He imagined his psi was a single beam, the sweep of a radar, and started on the right.

A fascinating array of impressions trickled into his awareness. There were several naive impressions. People concentrating on the rules, unaware of the real game. Poor suckers. When he got to the third room on the left, he stopped the probe. If there was such a thing as evil, it would be an outlander, and he was willing to bet he'd just come across a handful of them. He let the anger burn as he entered the room and found his mark. Unfortunately, his mark found him at the same time.

The outlander said something to his buddy sitting next to him. Dude was a nasty looking high-tech cyborg. The left side of his chest was metal alloy, which he hadn't bothered covering with synskin. His left arm incorporated a nasty piece of hardware that no doubt housed any number of weapons. He nodded, and grinned at Marco. It was a gruesome sight. Pointed metal teeth filled the lipless space. Drool slid down his chin. The two stood and made their way toward Marco. They stopped at the entrance. "Fancy meeting you here."

"I believe you have something of mine." Great, now he was starting to sound like Ru.

The whir of a laser canon emanated from the cyborg's arm as he pointed the thing at Marco's chest. That was one big-ass charge, judging by the volume.

"I got something that formerly belonged to you." The outlander crossed his arms and waited.

"Looks like I'm outnumbered." Marco wanted nothing more than to plant his fist in the asshole's face.

The outlanders laughed and left him standing there. He gave them a few minutes to clear out, then made his way back to the ship.

"You didn't have a plan?" Zara stared at him incredulously.

"No." Idiot.

"What did you think was going to happen? He'd just hand it over?"

"I guess I was assuming a little aggressive discussion would be enough. That cyborg has some pretty impressive tech."

Zara shook her head. "So what do we do now?"

"Now I call in some reinforcements." He should have done this before, but spending time with Armond Nolde was never at the top of his to-do list.

He eased out of the dock and made the jump into subspace. Once he was satisfied they were out of tracking range, he killed the engines. They'd wait for another location ping from Ru. In the meantime, he placed an interstellar call back to Earth. Due to the lucrative nature of asteroid mining, the subspace communication was decent here. When Armond answered, it was with his usual air of disdain. He was such a prick.

"What can I do for you, Marco?"

"What makes you think I need anything? I could be calling just to say how much I miss your smiling face." In the almost decade he'd worked with the man, he'd never seen him smile. He was, however, an extraordinarily powerful psi, and had the ability to use the portal-making distorters without any assistance. "Rucon said I could call if I needed anything."

"I am aware of this. I'm surprised it has taken you this long."

They had a long history of pushing each other's buttons. Problem was, it was damn hard to tell when he was riled, but Marco would bet his left nut that he pissed him off just as much as Armond did him. "Yeah, well, some things take time. I need your help to retrieve something from an outlander."

"You realize how dangerous those people are?"

"No, it totally escaped me."

"If Rucon approves, I can depart within the hour. I assume you have your distorter with you?"

"Um, not exactly. I kind of left it on earth." Only partially true; he'd accidentally put it through the wash. Again. They needed to waterproof those things.

There was a long pause. "What quadrant are you in? I'll need to locate the nearest portal where you can pick me up."

"Excellent." Marco disconnected and sent Armond their location.

"You didn't say goodbye," Zara said.

"Let's just say our relationship isn't one of pleasantries."

"So you don't get along?"

He let out a bark of a laugh. "That, sweetheart, is an understatement. He is water to my oil, always has been. A stuck up, self-righteous prick. He's smart, though, can be trusted, and has a skill we need right now."

"What's that?"

The existence of the distorters wasn't common knowledge throughout the galaxy. It would be more fun to show her. "Just wait and see."

"Do you work with him?"

"Yeah. He's also an Earth Protector with the Cavacent Clan."

"Right, I'd heard you signed on with them."

Not long after their break up. Leaving Sandaria had seemed like a good idea at the time. And it had been. He'd never regretted signing on with that family.

Armond sent them coordinates for Xanbar65, a planet not five hours from where they were. He set off.

Zara appeared a few minutes later with a platter of sandwiches and a pot of tea. She'd always liked her tea. "I made lunch."

"Thanks." He took a sandwich and she poured. No milk, lots of sugar, just the way he liked it. She was milk, no sugar. Funny the things you remember.

Zara kept herself busy with her tablet, but Marco couldn't help but steal glances. He'd forgotten the way the amber streaks in her hair would catch the light that way.

"You're staring at me." She didn't look up.

Well, shit. "Sorry."

She took a deep breath, then met his gaze. "This is a professional relationship, Marco. Nothing more. I'm completely intrigued by Ru. Nothing more," she repeated. She'd always done that when she was nervous.

"Professional, sure. I just want to say I really appreciate your help." He should apologize for being such a dick back on Sandaria, but he couldn't find the words. He made love to women, he didn't communicate much with them. Never noticed that before. Or maybe he'd just never cared.

"You're welcome." She gathered up the remains of lunch and left him alone. He spent the remaining time trying to corral his thoughts and keep them away from a certain female currently occupying the same space as him.

Three hours in, he received another ping from Ru. They were on course for Sigma Vector 9 in outlander territory. No surprise there. They would just have to get in and out fast.

Right on time, he docked on Xanbar65. He went and fetched Armond, who was waiting for them in the transit lounge.

There was a certain comfort in their animosity. He wasn't sure how Armond felt, but personally, he'd come to like the humorless, stoic, asshole.

"Thanks for coming. I'll get us underway, and then I have someone I'd like you to meet." They made their way back to *No Commitments* and departed the space station. They found Zara a few minutes later in the galley. She was stirring something in a pot that brought back a flood of memories. Her place, first date. She'd cooked a spicy dish from the Granat region of Sandaria. Gods, he hadn't had that dish since then, and his mouth was watering.

"Zara, I'd like you to meet Armond Nolde. Earth Protector extraordinaire."

"It's a pleasure to meet you, Armond." Zara wiped her hands on the apron she wore and extended her hand.

He gave her a perfunctory shake. He'd never been good with pleasantries. Never would be.

Marco poured himself a beer, and they sat at the counter where Zara was cooking. "So, we'll be on Sigma tomorrow around 16:00 local time. That's a six-hour transit for us."

"Rucon said we're retrieving a com unit?" Armond asked.

"Yes," Marco said.

"A very special com unit," Zara added.

"Is there sensitive information stored on it? And if so, why would you keep something like that localized on a com?"

Zara's eyes lit up as she spoke. "That's actually an interesting question. We don't know exactly where his sentience is located. I can tell you that doing a copy and migrating all the data that comprises Ru did not produce another sentient entity. Which is pretty damn interesting, when you think about it."

"Are you saying your com unit has become sentient?"

"Yes." Marco and Zara answered at once.

"It's a lot like Ria's com, only more so. Ria's has developed a range of personality types but hasn't yet formed a solid persona. There's a difference. Not to say it won't happen, but it hasn't yet. Hard to explain. Her com has preferences, but not a firm sense of self, like Ru does."

"I am looking forward to seeing this phenomenon."

"Yeah, well, we have to get him back first," Marco said.

"Him?" Armond asked.

"More like a gender neutral they," Zara provided.

"How did you come to lose such a unique device?"

They filled him in on the outlander who'd taken Ru, and how he was sending location data but nothing else.

"We must move with caution. It would be best if we can keep the identity of your ship confidential, or is it too late for that?"

"Probably too late. He knew I was no longer on the station." Marco said.

"We don't know that for sure," Zara added. "He could have just gotten lucky."

"Maybe, but we shouldn't count on it," Marco said. "Stealth mode?"

"Yes." Armond gave a curt nod.

It was a highly illegal maneuver. They would modify their transponder to another ship's signature, and electronically alter the ships marking. That was an illegal piece of tech they'd acquired from the planet Vertan. If the federation caught wind of it, Rucon would be severely fined, but this far out on the fringes of controlled space, it wasn't likely.

"Anyone hungry?" Zara asked, pulling some bowls from the locker.

"Am I ever not?" Marco gave her a grin. She used to tease him about how much he ate.

"I recently ate," Armond said. "I have work to do, however, so I'll set up over at the table." He left the two of them alone in the galley.

"Suit yourself." Zara spooned a heaping portion into a bowl and handed it to Marco before serving herself. She sat on the stool next to him and they ate in silence until Marco had finished. "That was every bit as good as I remembered."

"I made a large batch so we can freeze the leftovers."

Marco recalled the meals she'd cooked at her place. She liked cooking, which was unusual. Most people just got creative with the food gens, but not her. She liked to do it the old-fashioned way. Said it relaxed her. He took care of the cleanup, and headed to the cockpit for the rest of the trip.

At Sigma Vector 9, it took almost an hour to get a dock assignment, as the station was surprisingly active. Active and swimming with outlander ships.

Zara wandered into the cockpit as he slid into the docking bay. "What's this special talent Armond has?"

"You won't believe it," Marco said, getting to his feet. "He can use things called distorters. Come on. I'll let him explain."

They found Armond right where they'd left him at the table in the galley. "Zara would like to know about the distorters."

Armond filled her in. "The devices have the ability to create bi-directional portals between two or more of them."

"You're kidding me, right?"

Marco really liked that crease in her forehead when she squinted her eyes that way.

"I assure you I am not."

Marco laughed. "Yeah, Armond doesn't do humor."

"But how? That goes against everything I know about portal theory."

"Not everyone can use them, as it takes an alternative form of psi."

Zara's mouth formed a perfect O with those perfect lips of hers. "There's an alternative form of psi? And you both have it?"

Marco shook his head. "Not me, unfortunately. That's why I had to get Armond here. He can port me, but I can't do it."

"This I have to see. So, what's the plan? You have a plan this time, right?"

"Plans are highly overrated, especially when you have something like this up your sleeve."

"Marco—"

"I mean it," Marco assured her. "All I have to do is get Ru in my hands and I'm out of there."

She wasn't convinced, and might even be worried.

"As soon as I'm on the surface, Armond will depart the station and get far enough away to be out of tracking range. When I have Ru, I'll signal him and I'll be right back here with you. Couldn't be easier."

"Oh sure. All you have to do is enter a hot den of outlanders, and get one to hand over Ru." Zara turned to Armond. "Is he completely sane?"

"His intellectual capacity is within acceptable limits."

"Coming from anyone else, that would be an insult," Marco said, strapping on the outlander weapons he'd picked up on Xanbar65. "It's almost a compliment from this one."

FIVE

A sense of apprehension settled over Zara as Armond eased out of the docking bay. She stood behind him, arms crossed, not sure what else to do.

Down on the planet, Marco had made it to the location Ru was transmitting from. Given the brief description, hot den wasn't too far off. It was an old warehouse on the edge of town. Drugs, music, he said it would provide the perfect cover, but that cover could go both ways. He could disappear in a place like that. The tension in her gut belied her casual feelings toward her old lover.

Armond was certainly a strange person. Marco had assured her he was safe, but she'd never met someone so devoid of emotion. If she didn't know better, she'd think he wasn't human at all. More machine than man.

"I'm worried about him." The words were out before she processed the thought.

Armond set course and turned toward her. "He is an exceedingly proficient operative. Highly trained, and oddly lucky."

"Lucky?"

"I believe there are individuals who are, in fact, lucky. I have witnessed Marco get through numerous situations that could have, should have, perhaps, ended poorly. I can only assume it is a phenomenon that could best be explained by quantum entanglement. A fascinating area of research."

From what little she knew of Armond, the response surprised her. But then, if you were going to believe in luck, you'd want a way to explain it. "So, what happens now?"

"Now we wait," Armond said, rising to his feet. "When he has Ru in his possession, he'll signal me and I'll bring them aboard."

"I wish I could see what was going on."

"That is not currently possible."

Yeah, he was an odd bird, all right. They made their way to the lounge to wait.

Armond declined her offer of tea, and instead continued working at the table. She made herself a pot and decided to review her analysis of Ru to keep herself busy. It was nearly forty minutes later when there was a beep from the distorter that sat in front of Armond. With lightning speed, he reached out, placed his hand over the device, and disappeared.

Gone.

Vanished.

"Hello?" She jumped to her feet. That's not the way this was supposed to work. Marco was supposed to be here now. All of them. Here. Together. That's what they'd said, right?

She grabbed her com, but no, that was stupid. She was out of range. The ship might be able to reach him, but oh, god. She didn't know how to use the equipment. Or how to fly this thing.

She spun around the empty space. She was alone on a ship she couldn't fly, deep in outlander territory. What the hell was she going to do now? The absurdity of the situation was terrifying. How long should she wait before trying to contact someone? What if outlanders found her first?

Behind her, a horrific bellow sounded.

She swung around just as Marco slammed into her, sending them both flying. They crashed onto the dining table. A flash of pain shot through her shoulder, and the table shattered on impact, spilling them to the ground. She landed on top of Marco just as Armond's data pad skidded to a stop at the feet of a blue-black skinned woman of ample proportions who stood next to Armond himself.

Marco glanced around and laughed hysterically. "WhooHoo! What a fucking ride that was!" He cupped her face with both hands and planted a kiss on her lips before she could protest.

Electricity shot through her, and her psi exploded in a wave of pleasure. She pushed off his chest, which left her straddling him. Memories flooded back. They'd always had chemistry, but their psi had never entwined. This was new. She couldn't decide if she wanted to bolt or stay.

"Sorry, darling." He held her upper arms, his touch hot and firm. Amusement danced in his brown eyes. "I almost died just now. Kind of glad to be here."

Sitting on him like this had her body buzzing from his presence. She clambered off in a hurry and stood. "Are you ok?"

"Oh, baby you have no idea. I was running for my life back there, then you just popped right in front of me." He rolled over and got to his feet facing Armond and the woman, rubbing the small of his back. "Dude, what happened? And who's this?"

The strange woman said something to Armond in a language Zara had never heard and she'd heard a lot. Her voice was oddly stereophonic. Like two people speaking at once.

Marco shifted his gaze to her, and she fell into those brown eyes. "I just kissed you right? I'm not hallucinating this?"

"Yes, you just kissed me." She could still feel the press of his lips and the resonance of her psi. "When that thing beeped, Armond touched it and disappeared. Scared me half to death."

"You left her?" Marco demanded. "Where the hell did you go?"

"It appears the question isn't where, but when," Armond said.

Marco eyed Armond and the woman. Something was seriously off. And those weren't the same clothes Armond had been wearing when he left. The woman rambled on in a strange language, and she had her hand in the crook of Armond's elbow.

The albino was actually letting her touch him.

"Armond, when did you change your clothes, and who is this?" Marco asked.

"I could ask the same of her." Armond nodded to Zara, then slid his arm around the waist of the woman in an openly affectionate move.

"What the hells is going on here?" Maybe he hadn't survived after all and was, in fact, lying dead in that pit-hole back on Sigma. He met Zara's gaze and she shook her head. He stepped closer to her. If he was dead, and she wasn't real, he was going to make the most of it. Cupping her face in his hands he kissed her again. Their psi twirled into a sensual mist.

She opened to him for just a moment before shoving him backward. "What do you think you're doing?"

"Reality Check. I figure I must be hallucinating. None of this makes any sense." And that damn psi thing, what was that?

She wiped her mouth with the back of her hand, but it wasn't an aggressive move. More tender than anything.

He wanted more of that.

"Did we make it?" Ru spoke up from his pocket.

"Dude, almost forgot you." He pulled out the com.

"You made it," Zara said smiling. "But we've got a little situation here."

"A situation indeed," Armond said. "Where are we?"

"Don't you think we should get out of here before chatting?" Zara asked. "You know, outlanders and all."

"We're in outlander territory?" The concern in Armond's voice was the most bizarre thing.

Figuring out what the fuck was happening was going to have to wait. Zara was right. He started to head to the bridge, but paused, and faced the Armond and his companion. "Do you know what ship you're in?"

"This is the *No Commitments*. Delta class transport ship. One of twenty-three currently owned and operated by the Cavacent Clan, the head of which is Lord Rucon Cavacent, who was responsible for naming the vessel that is primarily yours."

"And what's our current passcode?"

"Snow White."

That wasn't right. But it was the correct topic. Rucon had a fascination with Earth's fairy tales and always selected things having to do with them. "What's the date? Earth date, relative."

"March 19, 2018."

"Dude, that's three months from now."

"Fascinating. It appears we have arrived from the future. Perhaps a singularity encountered during our jump."

He didn't know how, but that was definitely Armond.

He shot a glance at Zara. What was going on with their psi? He bolted for the bridge to set their course back to safer space. He set course to Xycor, and activated the hyperdrive before returning to the galley.

The others were sitting around the table. Zara had made a pot of tea, which Armond was actually drinking. Shit just got more and more crazy. He pulled out a chair, flipped it around, and straddled it next to Zara. He wanted her close. She was speaking animatedly to the woman who'd arrived with Armond.

Ru was propped at an angle on Zara's com unit.

When he'd been running for his life, it wasn't Ru or even himself he thought of. It was her. Zara Mancini.

"You're not going to believe this," Zara said. She placed her hand over his for a moment, then yanked it back, her eyes widening under furrowed brows. "Sorry." It was almost a whisper.

"Don't apologize. Now, someone tell me what's going on." He wanted to reach out and take her hand in his, but knew it wouldn't be welcomed. Not yet.

"First, introductions," Zara tapped on the table. "This lovely lady is Vin."

"She's a friend of Armond's."

Marco shook her hand, which elicited a giggle from the woman, who spoke again in the strange language.

"What's so funny?" Marco asked.

"Shaking of the hand," Armond said. "It is not a custom where she's from."

Interesting. "So she's not from Federation space?"

Vin and Armond shared a look. After she spoke again, Armond replied. "I don't see any reason not to."

"Huh?"

"Vin can understand us because of this here." He tapped a colorful device in his ear. "I can understand her the same way, but we can't speak each other's language directly as yet. To answer your question, she's not from our galaxy."

"Not from our galaxy?" Marco turned to Zara. "Surely this warrants another reality check?" He wanted one, that was for sure.

"Don't even think about it."

And then Armond smiled.

And the universe backhanded him upside the head. Armond Nolde smiling? "You're very different, you know that?"

"I'm sure I am." He took Vin's hand and kissed the back of it.

That was it. All the gods had returned to the galaxy and surely the hells had frozen over.

"So, three months? How?" Marco struggled to wrap his head around this new Armond.

"Encountering a singularity during a portal jump has always been a theoretical possibility. It is conceivable that jumping intergalactic distances increases the chances of said phenomena."

"You're serious? Another galaxy?"

"Yes," Vin said. Her skin glowed with an internal luminescence. A deep sapphire purple-blue, which was easy on the eyes for sure.

"And I take it your change in demeanor is due to Vin here?"

"Indeed," Armond said with another smile.

That was so damn strange. It didn't look bad or anything; it was just that in over ten years he'd never seen anything like it. "So what happens now? Where's the other you?"

"That's the crazy thing," Zara said. "I asked the same question. Armond thinks they need to go back."

"We haven't yet finished a task back in Vin's time. We should attempt a return, and soon. Things may or may not reset here." Armond's concern was disconcerting in the extreme.

"Is the old you going to come back?" Marco asked.

"I do not know."

It was a crazy thought. He felt like he should try and get the other Armond back, but Armond sat in front of him. Time streams got complicated fast. He'd never been able to wrap his head around that shit.

"What if the other you doesn't return?" Zara asked.

"Again, I do not know. It's conceivable I will never return to your timeline."

"That would suck," Marco said.

"Does that mean you'd miss me?" Armond asked.

And now he had a sense of humor? Holy fuck. "Yeah, dude, I'd miss you."

They briefly introduced Ru to Armond and Vin. Armond said he wanted to study the AI in the future, which was downright bizarre given the situation.

"We should go," Armond said to Vin.

They all stood, and Marco held out his hand to Armond. "Take care of yourselves."

"I'll do my best."

Vin spoke a few words before Armond translated for her. "She says she hopes we meet again." They said their goodbyes, and the couple blinked out.

Again, he wanted to reach out for Zara's hand, but she backed away from him. He folded his arms across his chest and waited. "So, how long was he gone before?"

"Only maybe a minute or two."

They waited another forty seconds before Armond blinked back in. He looked down at the table and back to him and Zara. "I was seated when you signaled. Why am I now standing?"

"How are we going to explain this?" Zara said.

"You got me." They told him about future Armond and Vin, but it didn't go down well.

"Conceptually, I'll grant that such a thing is possible," Armond said a few minutes later, "but I have no memory of being elsewhere."

"You had to be somewhere," Zara said. "But we'll probably never know."

"You're in for an interesting three months, dude," Marco said.

"How so?"

"Well," Zara stepped in, a smirk on her face. "From the look of things, you'll meet a certain woman and fall madly in love."

"Yeah, you also get all emotion-y and shit. A whole new, softer side of you."

"I find that highly unlikely."

"I found it pretty damn disturbing myself." Marco fetched a beer from the fridge and took a long drink.

"You're really going to like her," Zara said, "she's—"

"Stop." Armond raised his hand. "In the unlikely event this is, in fact, a singularity, I do not wish to know the particulars."

"Oh." Zara was taken aback, but then nodded her head. "Yeah, I think I see your point. You want to let the future unfold as it will."

Marco didn't see the point at all. He'd want to know what the hell his future woman looked like. "What is your plan now, Marco?" Armond asked.

"We're heading to Xycor, where Zara is based."

"Did you retrieve the com?"

"I haven't been called that in a while," Ru said.

"Armond, meet Ru," Zara said "Again."

"Ru?"

"Ruler of the Universe. A little joke Marco and I developed."

Armond conversed with Ru for the next thirty minutes, until he was convinced it was real. "This is indeed most extraordinary," he finally conceded. "And what physical form are you going to be transferring it to?"

Marco listened idly to the conversation. More and more, it felt odd to have Ru in its native form. It was an intelligent being, and having a relatable body just felt right. Gods, he hoped the procedure went well.

Zara sat next to Armond, toying with her teacup. She was off in another world, and he wondered if he had any place in that space.

Once Armond finished, he packed up his things to leave.

"Ok if I keep the distorter?" Marco asked.

"You put the last one through the wash again, didn't you."

"That obvious?"

He ported without another word.

They made it to Xycor in just under three days. Zara had kept her distance, but he'd caught her watching him more than once. He'd been guilty of the same. Something had shifted in him. The thought of winning her back, of keeping her, didn't terrify him like it used to. It was the opposite, in fact. It was the damn near-death experience that had done it. Ever since then, she'd been growing on him like a Sandarian creeper vine. Those suckers grew hooks that couldn't be removed without destroying the host. That thought really should bother him more.

He secured the ship and they made their way to Zara's lab. Xycor was three times the size of Earth, and orbited a sun that held seven other closely-packed planets, five of which were settled. It made for a pretty impressive sky.

The corporation she worked for was called Zero Sum, and from what he could tell, there wasn't much they didn't have their people working on. Integrative neural networks to cyborgs and AI. It was pretty cool stuff. Scary maybe, but cool.

They started with a tour of the building her lab was in. It was the cleanest place he'd ever seen. All off-white walls and a nearly black floor. "Smells odd in here."

"That's probably because it's a nearly sterile environment. You were sterilized when you walked through the lobby. Zero Sum is an incredibly healthy place to work. No such thing as everyone getting the same bug here. Come on. I'll show my little world."

It wasn't so little. Her research occupied the entire fifth floor, and it was mind blowing. Along the back wall, humanoid forms, all plugged into various apparatus, faced the interior of the room. Their bodies were a metal alloy of some kind, and although their faces were human like, they'd never be confused with a biological being.

"Doesn't that creep you out?" Marco asked.

"Nah, you get used to it," she said. "These are all deactivated, anyway."

An image of the robots coming to life and going after them had a chill crawling down his spine. "So, what happens now?"

"I'll get the sequencing equipment set up and start the prep work for Ru's integration with the neural network. How long are you going to be on Earth?"

"Two and a half days to get there. I can turn and burn within a day. Rucon's getting the owl DNA now, so I should be back in about a week." He unclipped Ru from his shirt and handed him over. A spark of energy shot through his psi as their fingers touched.

Her eyes widened; no way she didn't feel that. "Take care of him."

"Always." She stepped back. "I'll see you."

"See you." He resisted the increasingly strong urge to kiss her, and was on his ship and departing just under an hour later. It was going to be a damn boring trip without even Ru for company. When the hell did his ship get so lonely?

Marco was back on Xycor seven days later, itching to see Zara. When he got to her lab, she was in a clean room with Ru. He watched her hovering over the com unit through the glass wall. She looked like a doctor operating on a tiny computer. He'd missed them. Both of them. He barked out a laugh, which looked stupid considering he was standing here alone, but he was acting like a fucking daddy.

When Zara stood, he tapped on the glass and waved.

The light in her eyes wasn't as bright as he'd like, but she waved back and held up a finger. He'd wait a lot longer than a minute for this one.

When she'd finished, she joined him. "Welcome back."

"Thanks. How's our boy?"

She crossed her arms. "He's doing well. I'm afraid he's going to be isolated until the neural lace has matured and fully integrated with the expanded hardware."

"What does that mean exactly?"

"It's how I integrate a brain and computer. This is interesting, though, because it's backward. I'm usually taking a Sandarian brain, either fully or partially isolated from their body, and integrating it with my cyborg tech.

Here, I'm taking Ru's circuitry and assimilating it with what will eventually be the organic brain of our owl."

"How long will that be?" Marco asked.

"I'm not exactly sure. I've never done this before. The brain itself is under accelerated growth and should be mature in about a month. The amalgamation of Ru and the biological matter is fuzzy logic. We'll know the second it happens from our monitoring equipment. Once that's completed, we just wait for the owl body to finish growing. That will take two months, and then I can implant."

"Man, this is crazy."

"Yeah, it's a lot to process." She relaxed her arms and slipped her hands into the pockets of her lab coat.

"Is this going to make him more vulnerable?"

"What do you mean?"

"Well, you know. What if he's shot, or something? If that body dies, will Ru still exist?"

"Again, this is all speculation, but my guess would be yes, as long as his original circuitry isn't damaged." Her brows furrowed and she tilted her head. "You know what's really an interesting question, is whether Ru would still exist if his circuits were damaged but his new brain wasn't. I mean a few months from now, when everything is fully assimilated. That's some crazy stuff."

"Crazy cool." He reached into the backpack he'd brought with him, and handed her the box Rucon's engineers had prepared. "This should have everything you need. There's apparently some different subspecies in there. Rucon's people thought some of them would lend themselves to your processes better than others. The full DNA sequencing for each is also included."

"That's great. Tell him I said thank you."

"You can tell him yourself when all this is done. He wants to meet you."

"Oh. Ok. Maybe I can use it as an excuse to go see Earth."

"Absolutely. I've got plenty of spare rooms at my villa in a place called the Maldives. You should research it. I think you'd like it there."

She crossed her arms again. He held his smile in check. She was conflicted where he was concerned, which he figured was a good thing. She wasn't full on hating him. She was, however, keeping her psi in check. Maybe time apart would help.

"Well, I guess that's all I can do for now," he said. "I've got a shipment of carnium to deliver."

"Ok, guess I'll see you in a couple months."

"Yeah. Oh, hey, can I talk to Ru?"

"Not right now. I need to limit the stimulus while the neural lace develops. Once the first phase is complete, I'll be able to interface with him again and I can give him access to our com systems. I'll let you know when he's ready."

"I'll be seeing you, then."

"See you."

Back on *No Commitments*, he fired up the engines and waited for his departure clearance. It didn't take long, and he was back at warp speed within the hour. Once he set the nav system up, he went to the galley for some lunch. The meal was fine, the beer was better, but the ship was empty. Too fucking empty without Ru and Zara.

SIX

Nearly two months later, Marco arrived at Earth in the middle of the night Italy time, where the Cavacent Clan had their base. He took the station's portal directly to his den in the Maldives, where his home was. He hadn't been here much in the past year. It felt good to be back, but oddly empty.

He had a few days here, then it was back to Xycor.

He grabbed a beer from the fridge and walked out to his back patio. A warm breeze carried the salt from the ocean beyond. It was a calm night, and the moon reflected off the ocean's surface. He took off his boots and socks and followed the path down to the beach. Although dimmed by the light of the moon, the stars were still brilliant in the night sky.

Zara had once told him she loved the beach, but they'd never had the chance to go together. He'd surprised himself when he'd mentioned his home to her. Maybe someday he could bring her here. Strange thought, given that he'd never brought a woman here before. Still, this place was perfect for lovers.

Lovers.

A truth settled over him like a childhood blanket. It should have astonished him, but it didn't. He smiled and raised his beer to the stars above. He knew what he had to do.

Zara leaned over the chest-high table and visually inspected the com unit. Or what was left of it. The casing had been removed, and the circuitry was encased in a growing lattice of neural lace, all of which was suspended in an opaque gelatinous stabilizing material. It was a beautiful structure, embodying an elegance only nature itself could create. "Ru? Can you hear me?"

The monitor, registering clear signs of neural activity, increased agitation when she spoke, just as she'd expect. But he wasn't responding yet.

"Ru, I'm going on the assumption that you can hear me because of the activity I can see on my equipment."

The screen lit up and she smiled.

"I've got you almost fully integrated with your new biological brain. You should be experiencing some pretty interesting phenomena. Nothing compared to when we get you into your body, but it's a first step."

Another pulse of activity.

"I've got you connected to a new voice synthesizer. You need to experiment with your processes until you can find the one that's connected to the proper output. We'll hear it when you do. From there, you'll need to remap your logic patterns. It'll be just like activating the speaker on the com, but it's going to be controlled via your neural network. You're literally going to be creating neural connections within the new brain. Everything you do is going to be like that. It will take time and repetition. The synthesizer itself is bio-mechanical, so it's a little different than the speaker was. Just keep trying until you figure it out."

The monitor rippled with activity in multiple areas of the brain. What was Ru going through? A machine trying to integrate with a fully-functioning brain? They were in for some pretty fascinating conversations.

She left him to work it out. The equipment had a direct feed to her com, so she'd know of any changes. She grabbed her sweater and headed outside. Marco had been gone nearly two months. He'd been able to talk to Ru for a while, but the latest phase had been silent as she attached the vocal apparatus. The only thing left to do was insert him into the owl body, which was now fully formed. Nanites would merge the portion of the brain he was integrated with into the core of the medulla that was in the owl's body.

The procedure was scheduled for the following day. Marco was due to arrive in the morning. She'd managed to find some clarity in his absence. She missed him, that was true, but she couldn't go back. Not to the way it was. If she did, she'd be devastated when he left. Like it or not, she'd developed feelings for him. Dangerous ones now that her psi was involved. When they'd dated before, nothing had gone on with their psi. It wasn't a bonding thing at all, but something had shifted. For her, at least. Marco was Marco. Whatever was going on, she needed to contain it.

Summer was over, and there was a biting cold to the wind. She wrapped her sweater tighter and summoned an AV. Once inside, she activated the nav and set her destination for home. Tomorrow was going to be a long day, and she was tired.

The vehicle lifted vertically from the parking spot and slipped into the flight path for her condo. She busied her mind with a review of the following day's procedure. Once home, she'd shower, grab a bite and go to bed early. Her body tensed when she thought of Marco. It was difficult not to go there, but she needed to stop. She'd already purged his image from her VR library. It had been fine before, when he wasn't an option, just a great memory, but not now. Now the possibility was far too real, and pleasing herself while seeing him had become a bitter-sweet pill. One she didn't want to take anymore.

Zara woke to find a message from Marco waiting for her. He'd arrived at the spaceport in the middle of the night. She dressed in a hurry and grabbed a bite to eat on the way. She wasn't usually nervous during these procedures, but this was unlike anything she'd ever done before. Theoretically, everything was solid. It should work. But theory had a way of bending under application. What if she'd missed something?

Crap. Stop it. Second guessing herself wasn't going to help. She'd done everything possible to make this a success. She'd reviewed the neural activity through the night. Ru had been active, but hadn't yet made a sound. Not unexpected.

Marco was waiting for her in the visitor's entrance. He wore tight jeans, black boots, and a button-up shirt. Standard Earth Protector attire. He looked good. Really good. "Hey," she said, going for detached cool.

"Hey, yourself." The sheepish grin he shot her made her insides go all gooey.

"How's our boy?"

He'd used that phrase before, and she wished he'd stop. There wasn't a "we" here. Just him and her. She brought him up to speed on Ru's condition.

"Should he be talking by now?"

"Not necessarily. This is all new. He's got to figure out how to integrate with the brain to control the synthesizer. Like a child learning how to control their body. I think once he's able to do one thing, talk or move a body part, the rest will cascade into place. It's like a child learning to walk." At least, that was her theory.

They made it to the lab and she took him over to the incubator. The tiny owl lay motionless inside.

"It's so cute," Marco said, leaning down for a better look.

"Adorable. Super soft too, but those talons are razor sharp. Come on, let's move this in with Ru." She activated the battery back-up and unplugged the cart, wheeling it over to the clean room. "You can come in now. The nanites are fully functioning, both in the body and here. He'll never get an infection of any kind." She paused outside the door. "It might be a little gross for you."

"I can handle gross."

She laughed. "Boys."

On the table lay the current form of Ru. A small brain was fused to the neural lace that encased Ru. Snaking out from the stem of the brain were dozens of glistening tendrils, the thickest of which was connected to the bio-mechanical vocal synthesizer. She found the entire thing stunningly beautiful. Those tendrils would connect to the spinal cord of the bird, as well as the eyes. The nanites would complete the fusing process within minutes of it being placed into the body. It had taken her decades to perfect the technique, and made her an extremely rich woman. Zero Sum had faired pretty well too.

Marco stood transfixed by the sight. "I can just make out the com's circuit board. That's so insane. Can you hear me, dude?"

The monitor lit up like the night sky during the Summer's Ball on Mitah. "He hears you all right. Look at the monitor."

A strange sound emitted from the synthesizer.

"Ru, that's it! Keep working on it."

A series of sounds filled the small room. All of which were human-sounding.

"I've got the synthesizer set for a male's voice, but we can tweak that."

Within minutes, Ru had some basic speech ability. The volume, cadence, and flow were all awkward and halting, but it was excellent progress.

"Take a break for a minute," Zara said, trying to calm her elation. "We're ready to finish this, Ru."

"Yes." The pitch rose at the end.

"Ok, I want you to stop trying to talk and just remain calm. Once I insert you, the nanites will do the rest. Don't expect too much too soon. The usual development for humans being integrated with the cyborg tech is a few hours. You'll start to feel by degrees, and eventually you can work on control of your body parts."

She took a deep breath and looked at Marco. His deep brown eyes mirrored her concerns.

The small body of the owl was warm to the touch as she placed it face down in the cradle next to Ru.

"The back of the head here," she pointed to the skull, "is grafted with synskin. This will allow for fairly straightforward removal of Ru if needed, and of course, it's how we get him in." She retrieved her com from her pocket and pulled up the monitoring program. "Ru, I have a kill switch of sorts for your integration. If anything goes wrong, or you're out of control, I can have the nanites disrupt the spinal signals. Just a precaution while you figure out how to work everything."

"Yes." The voice was deep and slow this time.

"Ok, here we go. Hang on. Figure of speech, of course." On the com, she activated the synskin and alerted the nanites to the pending process. They would keep the blood away from the tendrils while they fused. A seam opened from the tip of the head to a third of the way down the spine. She waited a moment for the nanites to soften the skull, then she pulled the flesh apart and marveled at the interior. She loved this part the most. Pulling on some surgical gloves, more to keep her hands clean than anything, she picked up the brain and synth. Gently, she placed the mass into the skull cavity and laid the synthesizer along the throat. The nanites had the hard work. The tendrils began snaking their way to their predestined access points. It was like watching a ballet you'd spent months producing and directing. All her dancers were performing to perfection.

When she was satisfied, she pulled off the gloves and activated the closing sequence. The feathered skin slid back into place, and the head reformed within minutes.

"And now we wait," Zara said. Not since the early days of developing the implementation of neural lace had she worried so much at this stage of the procedure.

There had been failures.

"Zara," Marco's voice was almost a whisper.

"Yes?"

"Is that supposed to happen?" He nodded toward the monitor.

"Oh, gods." The neural activity was minimal. "Ru, can you hear us?"

Nothing.

The four minutes it took to run the diagnostics were some of the longest of her life.

"What is it?" Marco hovered next to her, close enough for her to smell that musky scent of his.

"Um," she hated the crack in her voice. She cleared her throat. "The brain is fully functioning from the point of respiratory and pulmonary support activity. Everything looks fine." Except for the nearly flat-line neural activity. She hadn't expected that. She reached out and stroked the soft feathers. "Come on, baby."

Marco blew out a long breath and spun. "I'm going for a walk. Call me if anything changes?"

She couldn't look at him. "Of course."

The outer door clicked shut a moment later.

She was glad she hadn't scheduled any other research here today, as that left her alone. What had she done?

Marco returned almost an hour later with food and drinks. Neither of them ate more than a few bites, and they did so in silence. She felt horrible, and watched the monitors nonstop. It was like waiting for your lover to call: painfully frustrating.

She wanted to say something, but she didn't know what. Then the words just poured out of her. "Marco, I'm sorry. I'm so sorry. I don't know what happened. I never even considered failure. Maybe I've gotten too arrogant, too sure of myself. I should've...should've run more tests, more analysis."

"Zara, stop," Marco said.

"I should have listened to you. You didn't want to do it."

"But he did. It was his right to make that choice."

"Did I just destroy the first sentient AI?"

Marco held his fingers to her lips and shushed her. "Don't do that. This isn't your fault. You did everything you could do. Even if it doesn't work out, you took it farther than anyone else could have. And it was his choice, remember that. He wanted to take the chance, wanted to have a body. And we're not done yet. We're not giving up."

"You're right. This is new territory. It took him longer than usual to find the speech center. It could be days. As long as that little body is functioning, we'll wait and see." For how long, she didn't know. She didn't know if she'd ever felt this lost. "I need a drink."

"That is an excellent idea," Marco said.

Zara went into the small office at the back of her lab, and pulled a bottle of whiskey out of the cabinet. She'd had it in there for almost two years now, and had only taken a few drinks. Grabbing some paper cups from inside her desk, she went back to Marco and poured them both a healthy amount. She prayed she was just being paranoid, prayed to the gods Ru would come back.

"Zara, I mean it," Marco said. "Stop thinking this is your fault."

"That's easier said than done. No one else would've even taken this chance. No one else could have screwed it up."

"No one else could have succeeded either," Marco said.

The tone of his voice soothed something inside of her. The whiskey was going down fast, and doing its job well. She poured them both another glass. There was nothing to do but wait, and if Ru did wake up there was still nothing for her to do other than monitor the output of his attempts to control his body. And with the fail-safes, she didn't even need to do that. Getting drunk was a pretty good option right now.

"What are you thinking, beautiful?" Marco asked.

His voice had always gotten to her, especially when he was in this kind of mood. He could turn on the charm like no one else. That's why she'd worked so hard to get the voice right in her VR feed. Tried and failed. There was nothing like the real thing. Heat pooled between her legs and she let herself remember those nights together. Days, afternoons, mornings. She shut her psi behind a mental door and looked at him. "I'm thinking how much I want to kiss you."

He didn't waste any time as he claimed her mouth with his.

She let the passion flow through her. They were a tangle of arms and legs. She wanted this more than she wanted to breathe. She undid the buttons on his shirt in record time and he had her lab coat off and blouse over her head in the next heartbeat. It felt so good to be touched by him again.

He bit the chord in her neck, and her whole body shivered. He trailed his teeth downward sucking, biting, licking. The need in her was a living, growing thing.

They managed to get out of the rest of their clothes, shoes, socks, and underwear flew in every direction. He picked her up and placed her on the counter.

"Cold!" She squealed as her bare skin pressed against the metal.

"Don't worry, beautiful, I'll have you warm in a second. He was hard as steel, the curve of his abs pointing the way to what she craved. What she needed.

He devoured her with his eyes.

"Touch me." It came out a whisper, a plea. She spread her legs wide, she was so close.

He ran his hands up her inner thighs, and when he reached her heat, he circled, stroking, teasing.

He stepped closer and kissed her, gently, probing her entrance with his erection.

She wrapped her legs around his waist and pulled him inside. She moaned as her psi struggled to get loose.

"Gods, woman, I missed this." He moved with a steady rhythm that played the strings of her soul.

So good, so damn good.

He took her legs and unwrapped them, hooked his arms under her knees and grabbed hold of her ass. The angle was perfection, and she came in a blinding orgasm. Her head spun and her body tingled as he found his own release.

Remaining firmly seated, he leaned back and gazed into her eyes. He cupped her face in his palms, his thumbs stroking along her jawline. His psi caressed her, and she let hers wrap around his for just a moment.

They both moaned as the pleasure mounted.

If he were anyone else, some other man, she'd think there was something more in those brown eyes. Something more than lust, but this was Marco. Had to remember that. She restrained her psi again. Didn't mean tonight had to end.

"That was nice," she said reaching for her cup.

"We're not done yet." He flexed inside her, sending pulses of delight radiating outward.

"Better not be."

They went at it with passion and hunger, like college kids on spring break. Several times they let their psi meld, dance, and caress.

It was after 1 o'clock in the morning before they dressed. Marco insisted on seeing her home, so they shared a transport back to her place. They kissed all the way, just like they'd done all those years ago. She wasn't sure how long they'd been sitting there when the AV politely let them know they had arrived.

"Let me come in?" Marco asked.

"No." She traced his lips with her pinky. She was probably going to regret this tomorrow. But not tonight. Tonight, she would no doubt fall into exhausted sleep. She lowered her voice, going for sultry. "Proper girls like me don't invite boys in on the first date."

They both laughed. "There was nothing proper about tonight, sweetheart."

"We both need to get some sleep," she said.

She didn't want to think about tomorrow, about Ru, about any of it.

The AV made another arrival announcement.

"I'll see you." She stepped out onto her fifth-floor balcony and closed the door before she could change her mind.

———————

Zara woke the next morning to a mild hangover. Thank god for the nanites. She replayed the previous night. Gods, that had been good. A true taste of what it would be like to find one's psi-mate. But only a taste. Time to get moving.

Marco was waiting for her in the lobby. They went to the lab, but she knew what was waiting. There had been no change in Ru.

As she stared down at the still creature, the enormity of the situation hit her hard. Failure simply hadn't occurred to her. He should be doing something by now. Brainwave activity at the very least. Tears trailed down her face as she turned to Marco.

He held her tight and let her cry, stroking her back.

She finally stilled, with her forehead pressed against him. She had her palms flat on his chest and he lowered his head to whisper in her ear.

"It's going to be ok. We'll take it out and start over if we need to. You can do that, right?"

"In theory. But in theory, he should be back by now. It's been almost eight hours. I'm afraid."

He looked shocked at her confession.

"I'm sorry. I shouldn't have said that. I've lost my objectivity here. I care too much."

"Don't ever apologize for caring." He tilted her chin up to look at him. "I mean that. Whatever happens here, I hope you still care."

There it was again. That look. This wasn't like him. "What are you doing, Marco?"

"There's something I want to show you. Come with me for a while?"

She nodded, and he led her out of the lab.

"Where are we going?"

"You'll see. We'll be back in less than an hour."

They took a transport to the planet-side arrivals center for this region, and boarded his shuttle.

"Are we going to your ship?"

"Yes and no."

She wanted to ask him what the point was, but honestly, this was better than hovering over Ru's still form.

The ascent was short, and he approached his ship from an odd angle, directly in alignment with the burners in back.

"Close your eyes."

She raised an eyebrow at him before shutting them.

"Open," he said a minute later.

She didn't know what she was looking for. Everything seemed normal, but then she found it. Her heart raced. "You changed the name."

He leaned closer and took her hands in his. "You changed me."

Zara couldn't believe his words. Couldn't believe the meaning that was so clear it was written on the side of his ship. *The Commitment.* She leaned in for a kiss, when her com blared the medical alert. She stared at the screen in shock. "Get us back there."

Marco broke a few dozen laws bypassing the entry center and going straight to Zero Sum. Both he and her company would pay a hefty fine for that, but she didn't care. She alerted security, explained there was an emergency, and told them to let them land and deal with the officials later. Authority had its perks.

They ran to the lab. Marco hadn't said a word the entire time back, and she was grateful. She didn't know what the readings meant.

Flinging open the door, they stopped cold. Standing on the floor not three feet in front of them was the tiny owl. Its wide eyes blinked at them.

Marco dropped to his knees, then lay prone on the floor facing the little bird.

She held her breath.

"Dude?" Marco said.

The bird blinked again, then said. "Yes."

Zara let out a whoop that had security banging on the door. She flung it open. "It's ok. That was a celebratory cry." Something she had *never* done before. "We're fine. Really."

She turned back to her boys. Marco grinned up at her, looking for all the world like a child with a new puppy. He gently scooped up the bird and stood.

Zara approached and stared into the yellow avian eyes. "How are you, Ru?"

"I am...I am...alive." The voice was filled with awe.

Zara stroked her fingers from the owl's head down its back. "Can you feel that?"

"I can. I do not have the words to describe what I am experiencing. I am...overwhelmed." The wide eyes blinked at Zara, then Marco. "Thank you."

Zara clutched a hand to her chest. This was no cyborg, no human she had been commissioned to enhance. This was a friend. No. Ru was family.

Marco turned to her with such joy on his face it melted her heart. "You did it." He gave her a mental nudge with his psi.

She ignored the gesture. She wasn't sure she'd ever experienced tears of joy, but she was close now. "I was so worried. We, were worried," she corrected. "I thought maybe I'd lost you."

"I was aware of your distress, but unable to communicate."

"What happened after the implant?" Zara asked. "Your neural activity nearly flat-lined. It was as though you'd gone away."

"There was a time during which I was...again I am at a loss for words...I was elsewhere. I have read of humans discussing a phenomenon called an out of body experience. I believe that is an accurate description. I saw the table where the implant took place. I watched as you closed the insertion seam. I do not know how that is possible, as my eyes were not yet functioning, but it was as though I was hovering overhead."

"Sounds like an out of body experience to me," Marco said.

"The theory is that a person's soul is responsible for the phenomenon," Zara said in the whisper. "I've always believed that our soul is nothing more than the energy from which everything is created. You are a sentient being."

There was a long pause as they processed the thought.

"How long did that last?" Marco finally asked.

"Approximately four minutes, at which point my consciousness lowered and sank into this body. There was time afterward that I have no memory of, but then my systems started coming back online. I regained my processing abilities, but there was a marked difference. I believe the neural lace is functioning as planned, Zara. I feel as though I have an expanded consciousness, and the sensory input is most extraordinary. I feel." The tiny owl breathed in deeply. "I breathe, and my lungs fill with air. Your touch is most pleasant."

Zara and Marco both reached up to stroke the owl. They stopped, fingers nearly touching.

Another mental knock from his psi.

She smiled, but held herself in check.

They each stroked the small body. The feathers were silky soft, and Ru shuddered with a small chirping sound of pleasure.

"Do you have control of your limbs?" Zara asked.

Wings spread wide and the owl nodded. "I do not yet know how to fly."

"We'll work on that later," Zara said. "For now, just enjoy the ride."

"I am truly happy," Ru said. "I feel it in my body. It is extraordinary."

Happy. That was a good word.

"I started receiving auditory input and Marco's telemetrics approximately two hours after implant. My vision did not come on-line for another four hours."

"I wonder why my monitors didn't pick up any of that," Zara said.

"My theory is that it's because I was functioning solely on my internal circuitry at the time. Expanded integration with the biological brain was among the last processes to occur."

"Fascinating," Zara said.

"Yes, as were the biometric readings I was receiving from Marco last night."

Zara felt the blush spread across her cheeks and down her neck.

"We were—"

"Consoling each other." Zara finished for Marco.

He gave her a full body caress with his psi. "Yeah, that." Marco set Ru down on the ground. "You have a whole world to explore, dude."

The owl hopped around, experimenting with its wings.

"Don't do too much," Zara cautioned. "You'll need to build up your muscles before you can fly."

"What will I eat?" Ru blinked up at Zara. He was so stinking cute.

"Are you hungry?" Zara asked.

"I do not think so. I am not sure."

"We'll start with liquids and build up from there."

"In a while," Marco said. "Zara and I need to talk."

"Like you did last night?" Ru asked over his shoulder as he hopped about on the floor.

"Depends," Marco's brown eyes poured into hers as he took her hand. "I changed the name of my ship for a reason."

"You changed the name of *No Commitments*?" Ru bounced off Marco's leg and toppled over onto his side in a peel of laughter. "This is so much fun!"

They all laughed.

"Its name is now *The Commitment*," Marco said. "I meant it when I said you changed me, Zara. I don't want this to be over. I don't want to leave here without you. Never again."

The words washed over her in a surreal wave accompanied by his psi's erotic caress. "I can't believe you just said that."

"Took me a while to believe it myself. When I was on Sigma Vector 9, I thought I was done for, and the only thing I could think of was not seeing you again."

Zara pushed a stray lock of hair from his face. "That was about the time I started experiencing your psi so...intimately."

He grinned at her. "Me too."

"So, what exactly are you saying?"

"I'm saying I love you, but you already knew that."

She did. Knew it in her heart and soul. Their psi wrapped around each other in a dance that needed to be completed. "I love you too, Marco Dar."

A wild hooting erupted from Ru and he jumped up and down. "This is happy-making."

"Very." Marco kissed her. A sweet, gentle touch that held a world of promise.

"*Psi-mate.*" He spoke through their nascent bond.

She wrapped her arms around him. It was a promise she was ready for.

GIB AND THE TIBBAR

A Galactic Defenders story

By

Jessica E. Subject

Jessica E. Subject is the author of science fiction romance, including the Galactic Defenders series, ranging from sweet to super hot.

http://jessicasubject.com

ONE

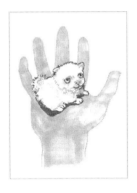

Fire crackled, breaking up the eerie silence surrounding the Defenders on watch. Gib read the sky scan on his wrist com. Nothing. The same as every other reading he'd taken since arriving on Hemera. He snapped a twig then tossed it into the fire pit. "I can't believe our squad is stationed here. I mean, Alpha, Bravo, Delta, and Echo always get the exciting missions where they actually kill Erebus."

"And we're stuck on Hemera," his squad mate Zair interrupted, finally talking after Gib had assumed he'd fallen asleep. "On some backward planet for some fornax ceremony so the king can show off how much wealth he has to the lowly commoners. It's ridiculous!"

"Yes, but there's nothing we can do." Gib said back, stretching out his aching legs. Like every other Mingot, Gib had a thin layer of skin over his bones, leaving them visible on the surface. Though on his hands and head, he had thicker skin over those bones, the parts of him generally not covered by his Defender uniform. Being stuck on a planet that consisted of mostly water with only one land mass reminded him of how much he'd aged compared to when he first joined the Defenders. Every joint ached at some point during the day, and others teamed up to slow him even more. He couldn't wait to leave Hemera, and hopefully his squad would never be sent there again.

"Why does the Alliance send us here anyway?" Running his boots through the loose dirt around the pit, Zair stared into the fire they'd started at the watch site to keep warm. "It's not as if Hemera contributes anything to—"

A small, furry white creature scampered between the Defenders and the fire. Gib yanked his feet back and gasped. He tried to follow the path the animal took, and when it disappeared into the grassy field, he relaxed a little. Not that he was afraid, only startled by the sudden appearance of the critter.

But his watch partner reacted differently. The cowardly Defender stood on his bench, reaching for a low branch on the ropral tree as if to lift himself farther off the ground. "What in Gaspra was that? No one told me about any deadly creatures on this planet."

Gib laughed and slapped his hand on his lap. "I wouldn't call the fluffy little thing that raced by us a deadly creature."

"Okay, Hemera is infested with vermin, then." Zair examined the area around him before he dared put a foot on the ground.

A high-pitched squeak sounded, and Gib's surveillance partner returned to reaching for the branches. The little creature stood on its hind legs below Zair's bench, peeping as if telling him off.

Gib couldn't hold in his laughter. Not just at the other Defender's reaction, but also the thoughts running through Zair's mind, thoughts he'd failed to block in his fear.

"It's not going to eat you." Gib shook his head, wondering how his squad mate could see the creature as dangerous. "Would you please get down from there? Defenders are supposed to be brave and fierce. Right now, you're neither."

"Go to Gaspra, Mingot. And stay out of my head." He yanked his plazer from his hip holster and aimed it at the critter. "If I don't destroy it, it will bring death to everyone on this planet."

Stepping into the line of fire, Gib yanked the weapon from his squad mate, thankful the safety remained on. "You're being ridiculous. Besides, if you fire your weapon, you'll cause a panic. The Hemera will think Erebus have arrived."

The frightened Defender shook a foot at the creature. "Fine, then. Kick it into the fire. Or you could stomp on it."

"Don't you dare!" A Hemera woman burst from the bushes, storming toward Zair like a mother rehn protecting her young. She shoved him off his bench and shouldered past Gib before scooping the noisy creature into her hand. "This is my tibbar, not some kind of vermin."

"Tibbar? Try nasty rodent that tried to eat me." Zair smoothed out his uniform but kept his distance from the creature now perched on the woman's shoulder.

"You're both on nehbred." She kicked dirt at them, her pink lips pursed and her dark eyes set in a deadly stare. "You don't know what you're talking about when it comes to my pet or my planet."

"So, you were eavesdropping." Gib caught the admission and refused to back down to the angry Hemera. Not when she was so appealing to look at, even if mad. She intrigued him even more with her ability to keep her thoughts to herself. He'd never been mind blocked by anyone except the Yarwin on a first meeting, but he couldn't catch a hint of what she thought except by observing her body language. Unusual for races who didn't interact with Mingot on a regular basis.

"So what if I was." She slammed her hand on her hips, her nostrils flaring. "I used to admire the Defenders, but now I know you're all just as arrogant as our king. You know nothing about how the rest of us live."

Maybe Gib didn't, but, from what the woman said, neither did the leaders of the planet. "Then tell me." Anything to make him understand why the Alliance sent the Defenders to Hemera each Galactic year for the Alorama ceremony. And to keep her in his presence for as long as possible. She intrigued him more than any woman he'd met.

"No, you're not worth my time." She spun away and darted into the woods as fast as she'd appeared.

If he wasn't still on shift, Gib would consider following her. He yearned to learn more about her people, or specifically her. He'd never been blocked in reading someone's initial judgment of him. No being seemed to remember to conceal their thoughts until moments after they met a Mingot. He wanted to find out how she hid her thoughts, how he couldn't even detect her when she'd been watching them. She'd left him curious and yearning. How long had it been since he'd satisfied his sexual desire?

"Universe to Gib." Zair waved a hand in front of his face. "You asleep or just still mad at that Hemera woman?"

"Mad?" He wrinkled his forehead. "Why would I be mad?"

"Because she told her pet to attack me then yelled 'cause you were going to kick it into the fire."

Gib shook his head. "I was never going to kick the tibbar into the fire. And you deserved her scorn for acting like a fool."

"Oh, I see." Zair plunked onto his bench with a harrumph. "You're attracted to her, so you're going to take her side."

Had the ignorance of members of his squad kept them from being sent on major missions? Some members simply didn't get along with the natives, always assumed they were out to get them. Or him. He glared at Zair, confident any argument would be a waste of time.

"Doesn't matter." Zair kicked dirt toward the pit. "But I still don't get why we're here. This planet is the last place the Erebus are going to travel. They haven't been here since the former king and queen were killed."

And the princess, once rumored to be involved with Bryce, the new leader of Echo squad. Gib now understood the Defender's attraction to the women of Hemera. But he didn't stand a chance with the one he'd just met. Unless he found some way to see her again, make her understand he wasn't at all like Zair. Cosmos, he yearned for a glance into her mind, and if luck came his way, an opportunity to get to know her on a very personal level. He nodded with determination. "You're right, it doesn't matter. We're here, and I'm going to make the best of it."

TWO

"Here, take this naip"—Vilarra passed two baskets to one of the many people she had helping her—"and put a loaf on every table." The Alorama ceremony wasn't until the next day, but the kitchen staff of the royal palace had just as big a feast to prepare today. Unlike the family-oriented Alorama, the evening before a celebration for the adults—mostly men—and, cosmos, did they know how to eat. Not only the noblemen of Hemera, but also the ignorant Defenders who came every year to keep the planet safe from another Erebus attack. King Rachivus—universe rest his soul—had been killed by the vile creatures on this night many years ago, along with his wife and daughter. If not for the survival of his son, Luchivus, the kingdom would have been passed to another family. Thankfully, the Erebus had not returned to the planet since, but the traditions continued, making this a hectic evening for Vilarra.

As lead hand, she not only had to ensure enough food was prepared for the evening, but also that she had more than her usual number of staff to serve all the guests. It hadn't been difficult to round up enough volunteers. Men and women with families had come to her home to volunteer, excited at the prospect of taking a share of the leftover food home at the end of the evening. And the single young women yearned to catch the eye of at least one of the men at the table they served.

Vilarra gagged at the idea. With all the mead that would be consumed along with the food, her servers would feel more than just eyes upon them. *No, thank you.* Fortunately, her position kept her away from all the spontaneous advances and unwanted groping.

Taking a trek around the kitchen, she remained confident the food would be ready with precise timing. The soup bubbled in its pot, and the geow meat roasting over the pit had lost its pink coloring but still held onto the moisture of the juices Samish ladled over it. The naip had already been baked and sent out to the tables, and Osnam skinned and blanched an assortment of greens grown steps outside the kitchen door, to serve to their hungry guests.

Needing a quick break from the blasting heat of the kitchen, she headed out to the banquet hall. Flowers she'd picked herself and arranged in vases rested atop every table. She didn't expect the men in attendance to enjoy them, but she believed it a nice touch for the queen, her mother, and any other women who braved their dignity.

Her friend Beckalie waved from across the hall, busy setting out the finest dishes at the head table. Last Galactic year, her first chance to serve in the royal palace, she had been ill during the Alorama ceremony. So for the past few day cycles, she had talked of nothing but meeting some hunky off-world Defenders. Always out of earshot of her boyfriend, of course. Vilarra wished she shared her friend's excitement, already having had her fill the night before when two of the visitors threatened to kill her tibbar. As soon as the banquet started, she would hide in the kitchen to ensure all the palace guests remained well fed and left her alone.

After a quick smile and nod to Beckalie, she continued her inspection. Everything was ready. Except for her friend, the other young women waited in the corner near the large windows and stared outside. They giggled and whispered to each other, likely about the men and women sent to guard Hemera from a possible Erebus attack. Naive. Every one of them. Well, they'd find out soon enough how the Defenders viewed Hemera and their kind.

Vilarra straightened a napkin with a heavy sigh. Her shoulders feeling like an invisible force pushed them down, she slinked back to the kitchen. Maybe the Defenders did know more about Hemera than her. Maybe she was just a lowly commoner on a backward planet and she'd never amount to anything. It's not as if she'd ever become royalty or get a chance to leave Hemera. The two men she'd overheard had probably been to every planet belonging to the Alliance and some that didn't. Why would any Defender care about her—about any of her friends—when the Defenders didn't want to be there? Not even at the request of King Luchivus.

All she'd worked to accomplish, all her dedication meant nothing beyond Hemera. And, really, it didn't mean much on her own planet. She was the same lowly girl she'd always been, with a darker than average complexion and tight curls instead of everyone else's straight locks. Her mother used to tell her that's what made her special, helped her stand out from the crowd, but the confidence boost died with the woman who'd birthed her.

The scent of something burning caught her attention. "Oh no!" She ran toward the pot of soup but it hadn't burned. A small amount had dripped over the edge into the fire. No need to panic. Pushing her ill-timed thoughts away, she stuck her chest out and nodded. Regardless of her insecurities, she had to get this feast served, and would celebrate a job well done with the rest of the commoners later in the evening.

Deep laughter erupted from the banquet hall. The guests had started to arrive. Thank the universe. The sooner she served the meal, the closer they were to the end of the celebration and the Defenders leaving Hemera for another Galactic year.

At the ding of a bell, the guests quieted, and King Luchivus began his speech, the signal to begin serving. Vilarra transported bowls of soup from the large pot to the counter for the servers to pick up and take to their table. A mad dash, but she managed the task without spilling a drop until she'd emptied the pots and all the guests had their first course. Samish carved the geow, the scent of the meat leaving Vilarra's mouth watering. Any leftover food would be packed up for the proletarian gathering after. She looked forward to seeing the young children enjoy such a feast as well as dancing and singing with her friends, listening to stories told by friends of her mother. She'd never met her father, and no one ever spoke of him. But her mother had done well securing her position on the palace staff and raising Vilarra to love and respect her planet and her own people. That didn't mean she had to tolerate the Defenders, though. Especially when they failed to show her any respect.

She organized the kitchen staff into a perfect assembly line to plate the main course. A couple slices of geow, topped with vyrag sauce, served with fresh greens and roasted tubers. After this, she and her staff arranged a variety of desserts on wooden carts, ready to be rolled out. Vilarra didn't expect any to return uneaten, but she had made extra in the past few days and stored them at her neighbors so they could be enjoyed later. Cleanup would restrict her to the palace late into the evening, but it helped her calm down after keeping all the staff on task and getting the food out on time.

"No!" A shout from the banquet hall. "I am not, nor will I ever be your lover. Get your hands off me." A moment later, Copia burst into the kitchen, skirt swishing side to side with her quick steps. "I'm done. I refuse to serve those dirty foreigners."

Dread pooled in Vilarra's stomach as the woman left through the back door. Everyone expected the Defenders to proposition the servers, so she hadn't imagined such a vocal objection. At least not from anyone but her. Copia had been the most excited to "meet an offworlder and fall in love." What had the Defender done to change the woman's mind?

She dared a peek into the hall. Who sat at the table Copia had served? She couldn't see past Frotathia, the female leader of the council who bustled in her direction. Cosmos, she was in trouble. She had personally vouched for all of the staff and promised they would be quiet and efficient.

Fear kept her feet from moving as the woman rushed nearer and nearer, her scowl becoming deeper with each step.

"Vilarra, I need you to take care of this problem right now." Frotathia pointed to a table in the middle of the first row. "The Defenders are our honored guests, and we must keep them happy to ensure they continue to protect our planet."

"They're vile," she protested.

The co-leader held up her hand. "You must take that girl's place. If you don't like their attention, at least reject them without making a scene."

"But...." She gulped, her mouth suddenly dry. "I have to take care of the kitchen. I don't have time—"

"You are good at delegating. That's why you have this position." The woman crossed her arms, taping her foot on the wooden block threshold between the stone floor of the kitchen and the polished planks of the hall. "Hurry and tell the staff what to do in your absence then get out there."

All of the excitement she'd had for this event drained out of her. She'd never intended to serve the guests, had no desire to see them, let alone be close to them. Now, she had no choice.

"Samish." She pointed to the burly man who had prepared all the meat for the feast. "I need you to finish platting the food. And, Osnam, you can help him then pack the extra food away. I'll be back in when I'm done to help clean up."

Feeling like a rock had settled in the pit of her stomach, she trudged over to her newly assigned table. All Defenders. All male Defenders. *Cosmos!* Why couldn't there have been at least one nobleman from Hemera who could teach them a thing or two about the planet? Like how most of the population had at least one pet tibbar. Even the late Princess Lalia'd had one. Without making contact with any of them, she eyed the men. Only one Defender had been served the main course, and his plate sat empty. How rude. He hadn't even waited for his friends to be served. Of course, it had to be one of the Defenders she'd run into last night, the one who'd aimed his plazer at her tiny pet. Like Elynyn would hurt him.

Vilarra spun away from the men. She could avoid them for a few more moments while grabbing their food. At the serving counter, she loaded four plates onto her arms. As much as she needed to hurry back to give them their already delayed food, her feet worked in conjunction with her anger to slow her down. Sucking in a deep breath, she continued on. If she avoided eye contact and refused to engage with them, hopefully they'd leave her alone. She managed to serve the first four guests without any issues, putting their plates in front of them from the left. None of them paid her any attention, too engrossed in their conversation. Just as she turned to get the rest of the meals for the table, a thick arm of a Gersonion wrapped around her middle, pulling her back. She fell onto the lap of the boorish guest.

"Wha' do we ha' here?" His words slurred, probably from too much mead. "I li' you beder tha' the las' girl. You're comin' ba' to the barra' wi' me toni'."

Remembering the words of Frotathia, she swallowed the urge to turn around and punch the Defender. Though he deserved nothing less. Instead, she pried his hands from her waist and attempted to stand.

"I don' thin' so." He leaned closer, his hot breath leaving a patch of moisture on her neck. "You 'tay wi' me."

"Let her go." A new voice, deeper, and with a growl so threatening, she yearned to run straight out of the palace.

The arm around her middle tightened. "You gaw no claim on her, Gib. She's mine."

"Actually, he does." This voice she recognized. The Defender who'd wanted to shoot her tibbar. "We met her last night, and Gib happens to be attracted to this Hemera woman."

It took everything she had to hold her tongue. No one had any claim on her, but if she wanted to keep her job, she had to wait for this situation to defuse. Closing her eyes to keep herself from lashing out about the unfairness of it all, she willed him to let her go. She couldn't believe the royal family had no issues with their staff being treated this way.

Instead of the Defender releasing her, he twisted her across his lap then flung her toward the completely hairless man beside him, the one she'd met the night before. "Fine, you ha' her, then, but I'm gonna sperience me a Hemera woman afore I lea' this awful planet."

Not if her people had any taste. And, once her staff left the palace, they no longer had to be nice to the Defenders. She'd ensure none of the foreigners came anywhere near their private celebration tonight. Vilarra waited for Gib to fondle her, or do whatever else the Defenders thought they could get away with. Instead, he set her on her feet and stood up as well. She wanted to run from the Defenders, gain some distance before any of them grabbed her again, but she feared how the royal family would react. Never did she expect Gib to place his hand at the small of her back and guide her away from the table.

"I would apologize for Flaine's behavior, but there is no excuse for it." At the serving counter, he stopped and faced her. "Some Defenders think they can take anything they want because they can kill an Erebus. Please know I'm not like that." He headed back to the table before she could respond.

Though what would she say? Sure, he might not be like them, but what difference did it make? As a Defender, he would only be on Hemera for another couple of days. She preferred not to have anything to do with him. He'd been about to squash her tibbar when she'd darted out of the bush.

When she returned to the table with the next set of plates, not one Defender made any motion to touch her. They didn't even speak to her. No one dared to even looked in her direction except Gib, but she was pretty sure he did so to ensure none of the other Defenders bothered her. A welcome change. Yet, she still wanted nothing to do with him.

THREE

"You coming?" Zair raised his mug full of mead, sloshing some of the frothy liquid over the side. "We still have another few hours before our shift."

"Nah. I need some rest." Not really, but Gib preferred not to spend the rest of the night drinking. Especially when his partner likely wouldn't show up for their watch shift. He'd pass out somewhere around the palace for one of the king's young children to discover in the morning. Gib had other plans to pass the time involving a certain Hemera woman who intrigued him beyond belief.

The last to leave the table, he gathered the empty mugs and carried them to the kitchen. His excuse to talk to her again, learn her name.

The woman stood in front of a washing basin, arms immersed in soapy water up to her elbows. Her grey smock dripped water onto her thin foot coverings. He couldn't call them shoes, as they looked to provide a bare minimum of protection, if any. She had pulled her hair into a loose bun—tied up with a piece of string—with stray curly strands hanging into her face. Every now and again, she blew a strand away, only for it to return to the same position. Cosmos, he could watch her forever. She didn't have one particular feature he found attractive. Just everything about her. The whole package. And he wanted to get to know her better before he had to leave.

Leaning against the doorframe, he cleared his throat and held up the mugs. "I have some more for you." Would she reveal her wrath once more because he'd brought her more work?

She spun to face him, her wide eyes growing cold. "Leave them on the counter." After nodding to the left, she returned her attention to her task.

And, no matter how hard he tried, he couldn't focus on one single thought from her. Did she purposely block him, or was she simply different from every other being he'd ever met?

Gib entered the kitchen rather than set the mugs on the counter in the banquet hall. Anything to be closer to her. He glanced around, finding the room void of anyone else. "So, you're here by yourself?"

"Yep."

He wrinkled his forehead in confusion. "No one stayed to help you?" With all the Hemera serving at the banquet, he'd expected to find the kitchen full of staff cleaning up from the meal.

"Nope."

Okay, he couldn't take the one-word answers. He'd never learn more about her and Hemera like this. It would be so much easier if she'd simply let him into her mind. "How come?"

"They have other responsibilities."

Better than her previous answers, but still not what he hoped for. When she grabbed a cloth and started drying the dishes she'd just washed, he rushed over to her. "Here, let me do that."

She smirked, raising a perfectly shaped eyebrow at him. "A Defender cleaning up? I don't think so."

"Hey, I take my turn at KP duty on every mission." Gib rolled up the sleeves of his Defender uniform. "This is the only planet where we're treated like honored guests."

She snorted. "I'll bet."

"Usually we're trying to help the natives survive." He tugged on the cloth she held. "Let me help."

She glanced past him toward the hall. "If the royal family finds you in here, they'll assume I'm making you do my job. I don't want to get into trouble. I need this position."

"If anyone comes in, I'll set them straight." He placed a hand on her hip.

Gasping, she dropped the cloth, but he caught it. "I.... You.... Fine, but wouldn't you rather be drinking with the king?"

"I'm quite content right here." Before she could argue further, he started to dry the dishes, placing them in the bins containing other clean dinnerware. "I'm Gib, by the way. Of the Mingot."

"Yeah." She dipped her hands back in the sink. "I got that.... You know, with the no hair and stuff." Her entire neck reddened before she turned to face him. "I'm Vilarra of the Hemera."

He smiled to himself at the beautiful flow of her name, but when her eyes widened and she returned her attention to the soapy water, he frowned. Had she taken offense to his reaction? Or was the ability to smile only granted to royalty on this planet?

"So, um, how long have you had a job here?" He didn't know if it was even a job, or just her turn for KP duty. He simply grasped at anything to keep their conversation going.

"I've been in the palace kitchen for many Galactic years, but I've only been head for one."

Definitely more information than he'd expected. Had he finally chipped away a piece of her barrier? Reaching for a wet plate as she put another in the rack, he ran the tips of his fingers along her knuckles.

She glanced over her shoulder at him, her eyebrows squished together. "So, what's this all about? Why are you here, Defender?"

"It's Gib—"

"Yes, of the Mingot. I got that already."

"Okay." Her quick temper simply intrigued him more. "And we're here to ensure the Erebus don't attack during the Alorama ceremony as they did many years ago."

"Cosmos, you're frustrating." She flicked the water from her hand into the sink then spun to face him, pointing a finger into his chest. "I meant you. What are *you* doing here? Why are *you* helping me when you should be off drinking mead with the king?"

"Because you said I didn't know anything about how the people here live." He brushed her hand aside, tempted to pull her forward, into his arms. "And I want to know." About her. Why he couldn't read her mind, and what every part of her body looked like underneath those rags she wore.

She shook her head. "I'm just one Hemera. There's a whole village of us commoners, if you want to know more. Why don't you go there?"

"Because I feel bad for what we said last night, and how you were treated during the banquet. I want to help you." He shrugged. "And you've piqued my interest."

She released a ferocious laugh, her chest heaving forward with the sound. "If you're looking to get laid, you picked the wrong girl. There are plenty of others who would gladly bring you to their bed. If you hurry, you can still find a willing partner for the evening."

Fornax, she really made it hard for him to learn more about her. Though maybe she shielded herself for a reason. Had someone hurt her? Had she experienced a recent loss? All reasons he'd been able to read from others who behaved the same way. "If that's what I wanted, I wouldn't have come in here." He grabbed another dish from the rack. "Just being in your company is good enough for me. Unless you want me to leave."

She jerked her head in his direction. "No! I mean.... You...You're welcome to stay." She cleared her throat. "It's up to you."

With a smile, Gib set the plate in the clean bin and went for another. "I think I'll stay."

Vilarra didn't talk much as she finished up the dishes, but her muscles seemed less tense. And when he accidentally—and sometimes on purpose —bumped into her, she simply smiled or gave him a nudge with her hip.

By the time they had completed that task, the banquet hall had cleared. They wiped all the tables with wet cloths before Vilarra snuffed out all the wall sconces, leaving them completely in the dark except for the bright glow of one of the planet's moons. Gib stuck by her, wanting to ensure she didn't leave him behind, disappear as she had the night before.

As Vilarra reached for the handle of the kitchen exit, Gib tugged on her sleeve. "May I walk you home?"

She froze, and, for the briefest of moments, he caught a glimpse into her thoughts. Not words but a pulsing flash of red. Danger.

Fornax! He was far from dangerous. Why did she fear him?

"I told you," she said, not bothering to turn around. "I'm not going to take you to my bed. You missed your opportunity to find a woman for company by spending the evening with me."

He placed his palm on her shoulder but, when she jumped, he quickly removed it. "And I told you, that's not what I am looking for. If it was, I had plenty of opportunity to have my way here. I'm not like that."

"One can never be sure what to believe from the mouth of a stranger."

"Or even from someone you know." He pushed open the door, not giving her a choice. He would see her to her door before heading back to the barracks for some rest.

Initially, her steps were short and fast, but as he kept pace with her along the edge of the dark forest, she slowed down, even tugging on his hand to show him the bright pink bishicub flower, spotlighted by the moon's glow. "It's the first to bloom every year. We find them only in the evenings just before the Alorama. Older generations believed it to be bad luck if they haven't bloomed before the ceremony happens. That usually means floods, which is easy to understand since we live on a tiny piece of land on a planet of water. Though, it seems, this year, we will escape that disaster."

Though beautiful, the flower didn't compare to the way Vilarra's eyes sparkled when she spoke, how her cheeks flushed when she smiled. And the energy zinging from her body into his as she continued to hold onto his fingers captivated him more than any thought he could have caught a glimpse of in her mind.

Then she dropped his hand and laughed. "That's probably not what you want to know. Come. I have something better to show you." She raced ahead, taunting him to catch up.

He could run. In every training drill, he arrived at the end before any other member of his squad. Even when he started last. Yet, he didn't want to race Vilarra, only catch up and find out what else she had in store for him.

Lights flickered ahead of them, not from any celestial bodies, but the glow of fire. The heavy beat of music echoed in their direction, along with excited voices singing and laughing. A celebration away from the palace.

Vilarra raced into the lively commoner village where children skipped along in small groups, giggling and playing. Torches lined the streets, and a large bonfire blazed in the middle of the thatch-roofed houses. Far from the humongous and extravagantly-decorated palace of the royal family. Dressed in their dull-colored, thin fabrics, the men and women in this village didn't seem to notice, gathered in a circle around the fire, dancing and singing as if their lives couldn't be any better.

Was this the life Vilarra wanted him to see? The sense of community that made life for the commoners bearable? The Defenders shared a similar camaraderie while the Galactic Alliance, mostly made up of Yarwin, controlled their lives.

Glancing around, he searched for Vilarra, but couldn't see her. She'd disappeared into the crowd, finally finding a way to ditch him. He should have expected that after all the times she'd told him to depart since he'd joined her in the kitchen. In the throng of people, he couldn't catch a single glimpse of her. She'd given him the slip. And with too many other Hemera around, he couldn't do a thorough search before his shift began. He turned to leave. If he made it back to the barracks in time, he could catch a quick nap.

"Hey, Defender!"

Gib paused, unsure if he'd heard the voice or just imagined what he'd hoped to hear.

"Are you running off already?"

He spun toward the voice, spotting Vilarra only steps in front of him.

"I thought you wanted to see how the other side lived. Change your mind?"

Her smile shone brighter than the flames licking the sky behind her. And, for a moment, he feared her. No, feared he wasn't enough for her. She'd worked hard for everything she'd achieved. Not much, but more than him. He enrolled in Defender training so his father could retire. Gib had been his only way to do that. He hadn't had to prove anything to anyone. Sure, training proved tough, but he guessed growing up on Hemera wasn't routine either. Yet, he had no desire to walk away from her. Didn't know if he ever would. "No, not at all. I thought you'd tried to ditch me."

"Well, I can't say I didn't think about that." She rocked forward on her toes. "But, you're kinda growing on me." She grabbed his hand and pulled him toward the gathering. "C'mon. I think you'll have fun here."

A burly man stopped them at the edge of the crowd. "Vee, what are you bringing him here for? You said you hated the offworlders."

"It's okay, Sam. This one's different. He wants to know what our life is like." She shoved past the guy and continued toward the fire.

Gib followed her to an empty log in the center of the crowd. Taking a seat, he expected her to settle beside him, but she remained standing, swaying her hips to the music. Though others danced along with Vilarra, he couldn't take his eyes off her. She mesmerized him with her gyrating hips. Erotic motions that made him yearn to hold her, touch her face, her lips, her long neck, and especially the rest of her body hidden under her plain garments, manipulate her body until she screamed in pleasure. *Fornax!* He sucked in a deep breath and shifted in his seat. How did she possess so much power over him?

The tune ended, and another began, much faster and livelier. Vilarra grabbed his hand and yanked. "Join me."

Shaking his head, he remained seated. He didn't dance. Not here. Not in front of a crowd. "Go ahead. I'll watch."

With a whoop, she circled around the fire with the other dancers, marching in and bowing out, linking arms to skip around and around. A much more energetic gathering than the dinner he'd attended. And more intimate, with the commoners mingling with everyone instead of staying in their own spot to socialize with those immediately beside them and drink until they passed out as many of the Defenders had done earlier that night. None of the commoners seemed intoxicated, and he hadn't seen any mead passed around at this party.

Vilarra slowed down, eventually stopping in front of him, her face now pale. She'd likely started early to prepare the meal he'd enjoyed at the palace. A long day she'd have to repeat again for the Alorama ceremony. Gib stood beside her and cupped her elbow. "You look like you need some sleep. Would you allow me to walk you home?"

She glanced up at him through her long, dark lashes. "That would be nice. But...I still haven't changed my mind."

Reaching for her hand, he interlaced his fingers with hers. "And I'm still okay with that. But I'm afraid if I don't escort you home now, you'll fall asleep where you're standing, and I won't know where to take you."

She squeezed his fingers. "How very sweet."

Sweet. Not a word he wanted to be described as, but he'd take it in comparison to what she'd called him the night before.

Once he'd ushered her out of the crowd, she took the lead in guiding him toward her house. Only one lane and two thatch houses away, they arrived too soon. No time to get to know her any better with her guard finally down.

"Well, this is it." Vilarra clasped her hands behind her back and stared at her feet. "This is my hut."

"I guess this is good night then." Gib bowed, unsure of proper etiquette on Hemera to end the evening. "I hope we will find some time together tomorrow."

She quickly glanced up. "Really? You want to spend more time with me?"

He grinned at her look of surprise. "More than you can imagine."

"Maybe.... If you still want to, you can come inside for a bit? See what happens?"

"No." He shook his head, using all his willpower to turn down her offer. "As much as I want to take you up on that invitation, I have my watch shift in a few mins. I have my own duty now."

Before he could prepare for her movement, she rose on her toes and pressed her body to him. Her lips plied his with sweet fervor. When his mind finally caught up, he held her tight and plundered her mouth. Then he pulled away. Her moan echoed his disappointment. "Tomorrow. I'd like to continue that tomorrow."

"I'd like that, too." She ducked into her home before he had the chance to claim another kiss, decide to shirk his duties to find pleasure with Vilarra.

Oh, but it would happen. He'd make sure of it. Though, not soon enough.

FOUR

Yanking a clean apron from the shelf in her bedroom, Vilarra yawned, and her jaw cracked. Although she'd been tired walking back to her house the night before, sleep hadn't come after that kiss with Gib. She'd tossed and turned on her lumpy mattress, wondering what it would be like to feel his soft lips on other parts of her body. His lips and his rough, calloused hands. Working hands, like her own.

No. She blinked hard. Today didn't leave her with any time to think about the Defender. The Defender who would be departing in a day or two, never to set foot on her planet again. Or if he did return for the next Alorama, he likely wouldn't admit to knowing her. Loneliness had dissolved the walls she'd built around her heart, made her willing to settle for only one night with him. Yet a single night with him would never be enough.

Elynyn leaped from Vilarra's bed, clinging to her apron with her front claws before climbing up to her shoulder. The tibbar nuzzled into her neck, making a soft chirring noise.

"I know, little one. I'm tired, too." She cupped her pet in her palm then placed the tibbar on her pillow. "But I can't stay. I've got to work. You stay here and catch up on sleep for both of us."

Elynyn stood on her hind legs, squeaking as she pressed her front paws together as if begging Vilarra to stay.

"I wish I could." She scratched behind the tibbar's ears. "But if I don't work, I can't bring home food for you."

Elynyn returned to all fours and nuzzled into her pillow, exactly as Vilarra would prefer to do. She shook away her fatigue. The upcoming celebration left her no time to even think about sleeping. Grabbing a piece of stale naip from the counter, she headed out the door. She'd eat her breakfast on the go.

The sun peeked above the ropral forest, lighting up the path to the palace enough for her to not need a torch light, though most of the time she didn't use one anyway, the route ingrained into her memory even in the dark. The fire had been extinguished long ago, yet eye-watering smoke still hung in the air. Tears ran down her cheeks as she hurried beyond the village.

When the palace came into view, she could see some of her friends there already, standing on ladders to hang streamers of flowers over the entrances. The place already had an aura of excitement around it, even this early in the morning. Once she stepped inside, that thrill would disappear, lost in the sweltering heat of the kitchen and the stress of ensuring she prepared all the food on time.

Movement caught her attention to the left of the back entrance. Then a groan. A figure lay prone next to a tree. A Defender, if the person's clothing was any indication. And male, according to its size. She dared a step closer, wondering if he'd been hurt somehow. When the Defender sat up, she jumped back. He placed his palms on the side of his head and squeezed his eyes shut, but Vilarra could still identify him. The same one who had been with Gib the first night she'd met him. The one who'd wanted to kill Elynyn.

Backing away, she shook her head. He could suffer on his own. Likely intoxicated from too much mead, he didn't deserve her assistance.

"Please help." His request came out as a low groan.

Cosmos! He'd spotted her. Now, she had to offer to aid him if she could. She walked closer but remained out of his reach. "What do you need?"

"A new head, to start." He massaged his temples then squinted up at her. "Hey, I know you."

"Yes, how can I help you?" She didn't have time to play games with the Defender.

"Gib. Call Gib. I need him to get me back to the barracks." The Defender turned his head to the side and vomited.

The stench turned her stomach, yet the small piece of naip she'd consumed remained inside. "I...I don't know how to contact him."

The Defender wiped his arm across his mouth then held out the other arm. "My wrist com. You can contact him through that."

Pursing her lips, Vilarra stared at him. "And why can't you contact him?"

When the Defender vomited again, she turned away. Okay, that was why.

She waited until the Defender paused from losing the contents of his stomach before she dashed forward and unstrapped the communications unit from his wrist. Never having used any form of technology before, she stared at the device, unsure what to do with it. It wasn't as if she saw a button with Gib's name. That would be too easy. "What do I do?"

"Name." That's all she got before the Defender retched again.

Vilarra stepped away, focusing on the wrist com. Was she supposed to say her name, or the person she wanted to call. "Gib," she said into the unit, deciding that made more sense.

The small screen came to life, and a dreary-eyed Defender appeared on the screen. "What do you want, Za— Oh! Vilarra." His eyes widened. "What's going on?"

"I, um, was on my way to work this morning and came across your friend who says he needs your help."

"Only my friend when he's sober," Gib muttered. "Where are you?"

"Just outside the kitchen. The door you and I left from last night."

She caught the hint of a smile before he ran a hand over his face. "Okay. I'll be there soon. Is it possible for you to get me a bucket of cold water and a cloth?"

"Sure." As soon as she said the word, the screen went blank. Unsure what to do with the wrist com, she tucked it into her apron and rushed inside to fetch the two things Gib had requested. Heading back outside, she gasped at an anomalous sight. A bright green circle the size of a basket appeared in the air near the sick Defender then began to expand. When it grew to the size of one of the tables in the banquet hall, a figure surged through. Her heart thudded as though it would burst right out of her chest. When she realized the person who'd come through was Gib, she released a heavy sigh. "Thank the cosmos! I wasn't sure what that was."

He shrugged. "Just a small wormhole. I didn't want Zair to take up any more of your precious time, and this was the fastest way to get here."

"Oh, okay." She held out the bucket and cloth, as well as Zair's wrist com, to him. "Here's what you asked for."

"Thank you." He took the items from her then turned to his friend. Supporting the bucket with both hands, he dumped all the water over the Defender's head then tossed the cloth at him. "Clean yourself up. You're a disgrace to all Defenders."

"C'mon, Gib." He wiped some water from his face. "I was drinkin' wif the king. Was i-vi-tid."

"And you failed to show up for your shift, leaving me all by myself. No one else could fill in because they were all intoxicated, too."

Vilarra walked slowly away from the two Defenders. As much as she wanted to stick around to see them argue, she didn't have time. She had a feast to prepare.

Gib leaned back in his chair with a satisfied sigh. He couldn't remember a time when he'd eaten so well. The naip had melted in his mouth with its freshness, and the stew Vilarra and her staff had prepared left him assuredly full. He needed to get up and move around to get rid of some of the drowsiness that came with a ready-to-burst stomach.

"And here's a mug for you." Zair rested a hand on Gib's shoulder and set a glass of mead down in front of him. "To make up for missing my shift this morning, and a thank you for covering for me and coming to get me."

He clenched his fists, still not ready to forgive his squad mate. "And how many credits did the mead set you back?"

"None." The other Defender pulled his hand back and slumped into the empty chair next to Gib. "But you didn't have to get up to get it."

He slid the mug across the table. "And you can have it back. I won't be drinking tonight." He had other plans that required him to remain alert. Focused.

Zair's eyes widened, and he punched Gib in the arm. "Are you going to get lucky with another native, tonight, or the same one?"

He shook his head. "The only part of my plans that are any of your business are whether I will show up for my shift tonight. I hope you plan on joining me this time."

The Defender slouched in his chair. "Yeah, I guess I'd better."

Unable to maintain his patience with the Defender, Gib rose from the table before heading to the kitchen. He hadn't seen Vilarra since the morning, and hoped they would have a chance to spend some time together. Alone.

Peering in through the doorway, he spotted her in front of the sink, busy cleaning up after the meal. Her tight curls were pulled back from her face again, bringing focus to her long neck. He chewed on his bottom lip. This time, he spotted several other Hemera in the kitchen, busy with their own tasks and moving around each other in a well-rehearsed dance.

He longed to go in there, whisk her away from her duties, and have her all to himself. Maybe he did intend to "get lucky" with her, but not for the reasons Zair would expect. Sure, she was attractive, but plenty of others on Hemera fit that description as well. Attractive, and, according to their thoughts, willing to be with any Defender in need of a good time. Yet, Vilarra intrigued him more than anyone he'd ever met. He still couldn't read her mind, only grasping her kindness and dedication to her job based on observation. How he longed to learn more about the woman underneath all that, her fears, her dreams for the future, her desires. Did she want him as much as he wanted her? Initially he hadn't thought so, but after the kiss the night before, he believed otherwise. He'd spent most of his early morning shift fantasizing about her rather than contemplating how to best seek revenge on Zair for not showing up, or even watching out for Erebus arriving on the planet which was his main task.

A young man came out of the kitchen dressed in light brown pants and a shirt yellowed from overuse. He eyed Gib, his thoughts revealing distrust yet curiosity as to why a Defender waited outside the kitchen. "Can I help you with something? Are you looking for more to eat?"

"No, no." Gib quickly shook his head. "I am quite satisfied by the meal. I'm wondering if I can help you."

The teen wrinkled his forehead. "What do you mean?"

"What were you coming out here to do? I'd be glad to help, maybe even complete the task for you so you can go celebrate the Alorama with your friends and family."

After a sideways glance, the young man shrugged. "I have to clear off the tables, take all the dirty dishes to the kitchen and then wipe the tables. Not something a Defender should be doing."

Gib laughed at the image in the Hemera's mind, of him flinging all the dishes across the room to smash on the walls instead of going to be cleaned. "I assure you, I can safely clear off the tables without causing any damage. I helped Vilarra with that task last night."

The young man's face became blank and his thoughts grew muddled. "You...?"

"Yes." He reached for the cloth gripped tightly in the Hemera's hand. "I'll be fine. Now, go have fun. That's what this celebration is about, right?"

"Okay...thanks." The Hemera teen handed him the cloth and left. One down, and about a dozen more to go before he had Vilarra all to himself.

FIVE

Vilarra scrubbed the dishes as fast as she could. She wanted to finish in time to let her staff join in some of the Alorama festivities, even if a bit late. Over time the noise level in the kitchen dropped, she worried they'd be too tired. But when the conversation behind her suddenly dissipated, she turned around to see if any of them had already fallen asleep. Of the twelve who had started the evening with her, only four remained. "Where is everyone else?" It didn't take over half her staff to clear the banquet hall.

"Gone." Beckalie placed a container of plates on a storage shelf.

"What do you mean, gone?" She hadn't dismissed them, and no one had asked to leave early.

"They disappeared," Samish added. "One moment they were there, helping, and the next they were not."

Her chest tightened. Yes, she wanted her staff to enjoy the ceremony, but she'd also hoped to spend some time with Gib. Now, she wouldn't have a chance. "Ugh, there's still so much to do."

"Not as much as you think." Osnam motioned toward the serving counter. "A certain Defender has taken care of a lot of it."

"Gib? He's here?" And she'd thought if she didn't find him in time, he would get tired of waiting and seek pleasure from someone else.

"Yep, and I'm pretty sure he's the reason everyone else has disappeared." Beckalie tossed her cloth on the counter. "I only wish he'd taken over for me first."

"Go, then." Gib stood in the doorway, glowing in comparison to the dark banquet hall behind him. "Everything is done out there. We only have to finish cleaning up in here."

"Excuse me?" Vilarra put her hands on her hips and glared at him. "What right do you have to tell my staff when they can leave?"

He sidled up to her, his sly grin threatening to weaken her annoyance with him. "It is my duty to help the residents of this planet, including you. This is how I chose to help."

She felt him motioning to the last of her staff, probably telling them to leave as well while he kept her distracted. Placing her palm on Gib's chest, she smiled. "You are unbelievable."

"You can leave as well." He stepped back from her. "I can finish up if you want."

With a laugh, she shook her head. "I don't think so. There are several dishes still to be cleaned."

In very little time, they had the kitchen spotless and ready for the next morning. Vilarra smelled like stagnant water, but Gib didn't seem to care, remaining so close he might as well have been touching her.

As soon as she locked the back entrance, he reached for her hand. "How about you show me how your people celebrate the Alorama?"

Comfortable warmth spread through her as she interlaced her fingers with his. "I'd rather change first. If that's okay with you." The smell of discarded food and dirty water would bother him eventually. It already affected her senses.

"Are you trying to successfully ditch me this time? Ask me to wait here for you with no plans to return?"

"No." She turned to face him and placed her palm on his chest. "I'd hoped you would come with me. I won't be long. Unless I'm keeping you from something." Or someone.

"I have nowhere to be but with you." Pulling her close, he held her tight against him, his eyes intently focused on her. "You intrigue me, Vilarra."

She shuddered at his whispered words. And, for a moment, her mind went blank, as if something or someone stole all her thoughts. When his lips pressed to hers, she gasped, having missed his initial movement.

He let her go and jumped back. "I'm sorry. You.... I thought...."

"No! I wanted that." Her cheeks warmed at the admission, but she couldn't deny her desire for the Defender. "You just caught me by surprise."

"Okay." He held his hands behind his back, his cheeks a little flushed. "Well, let's get going then."

She grasped to hold him once again, enjoying the simple contact. His sweaty palms and twitchy fingers gave away his nervousness. Why would he have any reason to worry about her? She wasn't tiny by any means, but he still towered over her and had an advanced weapon strapped to his left side.

"Are you okay?" Maybe he was ill. Having a reaction to bad food?

Universe, she hoped not. She didn't want to be responsible for making him sick.

"Fine." He gave her hand a slight squeeze. "Just anxious to learn more about you...your culture."

She tingled all over, fighting the urge to race to her home. Instead, she walked at a fast pace, dragging Gib along with her. A normally short jaunt went even quicker as she struggled to find the words she longed to say to the Defender. Words she couldn't come up with in bed the night before. How did she tell him she'd changed her mind about what she wanted from him, what she ached to do with him?

Grabbing the handle of the door, she shoved it open. She tugged Gib inside with her. He could watch her change if he wanted, delay going to the Alorama ceremony to find the pleasure she sought and believed he wanted, too. It had been a long time for her. Too long. She'd forgotten what it was like to desire the attention of another until he insisted on walking with her the previous night. And the kiss reminded her of the lust she'd once felt for another. Feelings she'd locked away when he had left the village for a position with one of the noble families. She hadn't seen Saukus since. Gib released all that. A full adult now, she yearned for more. Love, a long-term relationship, maybe even a family.

"Would you like something to eat? Drink?" A proper hostess always offered. Even if they hadn't planned to spend much time there.

"I'm good thanks." He gave a brief nod then glanced around.

Her stomach dropped. Gib had traveled all over the universe, been put up in glorious accommodations befitting a hero. And she lived in a one room hut with a divider to separate her bedroom from her meager kitchen. "I know it's not much, but it keeps the rain off my head."

"Huh?" He returned his focus to her. "Your house? It's nice. Not a palace, but that place makes me uncomfortable. Plus, you have privacy here, which is something I've never had as a Defender."

She wrinkled her face. "What do you mean? You're heroes everywhere you go. Don't you stay in palaces on every planet?"

He rested a hand on her shoulder. "We don't even stay in the palace here. We stay in barracks on the other side of the forest. On the carrier, I share my small quarters with a roommate. And, on most of our missions, we sleep in tents. If I want privacy, I have to take time off, which we almost never get. Coming to Hemera is an easy and relaxing mission compared to all others. And, contrary to what I said, I'm really enjoying myself." He ran his hand down her arm then held her fingers. "You have a lot to do with that."

"Well, I'm glad I was able to change your mind." Vilarra stepped closer until only enough space existed between them to keep her wet and dirty clothes off his uniform. If Gib went along with her plans, they wouldn't be a problem for long. Did he have more than a curious interest in her? "If it's privacy you want, we can stay here rather than go to the celebrations."

He didn't answer with words, instead grasping her hips and pulling her tight against him. His lips met hers, crushing all her fears with his breath-stealing kisses. He moved his hands under the seam of her shirt and up her sides, his touch desperate. As he tried to lift the material, she leaned back, tugging him in the direction of her bed. There, he could take it all off, see her without the clothing that defined her status on the planet.

When the back of her knees hit the bed, a high-pitch squeak filled her hut. She froze. Elynyn must have spent the entire day sleeping on her bed. And now she would be up all night and likely ruin any chance she had with Gib. If he didn't flee right away, he'd leave in annoyance.

Yet, he didn't even flinch at the sight of her white tibbar sitting up on her hind legs, squeaking away. Instead, he reached around Vilarra with his palms up, letting Elynyn sniff him.

With caution, her tibbar hopped forward until her always-twitching nose met the tip of his finger. And then she did something Vilarra never expected. She hopped onto Gib's hand and rolled over for him to rub her belly. And he did, eliciting frantic purrs from the little fuzz ball. Elynyn had never done that for anyone but her. Not even Saukus. Or her mother. Did her tibbar sense something about Gib she didn't? Or was Elynyn simply starving for some care, stealing the attention she craved from the Defender?

"She's cute." Gib stood and placed his palm against his chest, careful not to drop her pet. "And she seems to like me."

"Yes, she does. Her name is Elynyn." Vilarra pointed to a small box filled with wood shavings. "But I'd put her in there before she relieves herself on your hand."

Gib wrinkled his nose and set his new friend in her box. "For such a tiny pet, she sure has a big personality. If one didn't see her, they'd definitely hear her."

Vilarra knew that all too well, the tibbar her only companion for the past couple of Galactic years. "Yes, and if all that fails, she bites." She wiggled the tips of her fingers. "I have a few scars from reaching for something on a shelf where Elynyn had decided to rest."

"Good to know." Gib grasped her hips again before reaching behind her to undo the tie keeping her skirt on. The material fell to the floor and pooled around her ankles. "I hope she won't bite me for that, or for this." He moved his hands under her shirt and lifted it over her head, not waiting for any more interruptions.

"She won't if I feed her first." Vilarra nodded to her tibbar, now at their feet. "But, as for me, I cannot make the same promise."

One side of his mouth turned up in a smile. "Well, I guess you'd better get Elynyn fed, then. And quickly."

With the tibbar at her heels, Vilarra dashed to the kitchen counter where she laid out a piece of stale naip and some dried greens for her pet. She pulled out more of the greens than normal, hoping to keep Elynyn occupied for a long time. Her tibbar set to work chomping the food, making soft chirring noises as she ate.

When Vilarra turned around, she found a nearly naked Defender standing in front of her bed. He wore nothing but a pair of tight silver undergarments. Yet, something else about him had caught her attention. She'd heard Mingots had bones visible on the outside of their bodies rather than safely under their skin, but had never seen any of his kind up close. Not without a Defender uniform on anyway. No other Mingots visited Hemera, and the Defenders didn't even come that often. How did he not break bones every time he bumped into something, hugged, had sex...?

He called her forward with the crook of his finger. "Don't be afraid. I promise I won't hurt you."

"Oh no." She ran her fingers along his ribs until they ended in rock-hard ab muscles. "I'm actually afraid I might hurt you, crack your ribs or something."

Gib laughed, lifting her hand to his lips then placing it back against his chest. "You could never hurt me worse than the Erebus already have. Unless you tell me to leave."

"No!" Her cheeks warmed at how loud she'd objected. "I've just never...never been off planet." Never seen anyone naked, except her own kind. She was ignorant to life beyond Hemera, never having had the chance to learn. But he'd piqued her curiosity.

"I won't hold it against you." He shuffled closer until no air could fit between them.

As her heart pounded, her body tingled in anticipation. She clasped his sides and rose onto her toes. His lips brushed hers before she closed her eyes and surrendered to the intimacy of the kiss. Pure bliss. He swept her away in the moment. In his arms, she floated far from the planet she grew up on, lost in passion and desire. The rest of her clothing seemed to melt away.

In a bold move, he scooped her into his arms then laid her on her bed. Though the cool nights of the second season had ended, Vilarra craved his warmth, his body over hers. Inside her. She shivered at the thought, her desire greater than she'd ever experienced. Reaching out to him, she clasped his hand and pulled him closer. But, instead of joining her on the bed, he kneeled beside her.

His lips joined hers again, his determined kisses traveling away from her face and down her body. With skilled hands, he rubbed her breasts and swirled his tongue around her pert nipples, had her writhing in ecstasy. Then his attention traveled farther down. He reached between her legs, tenderly plying her thighs apart. Gentle fingers slid between her folds, caressing, ramping up her pleasure until they slipped inside. He teased and tormented.

She gripped the sheets, her hips thrusting into the air. Her release came hard and fast. So intense, she expected her head to explode. Before she had the chance to recover, he kneeled over her, kissing her neck and holding her tight. His cock nestled between her thighs, hot against her skin.

But she wanted him inside. Needed to be filled by him. Gasping with desperation, she opened to him. "Please. I need you."

Before she realized what he was doing, he'd reached to the floor for his Defender uniform and pulled out a small plastic bottle. He sprayed spermicide over his shaft then returned to making her feel like the only other person on the planet.

He gazed into her eyes. "You are so beautiful."

Her breath hitched as he slid inside her. He proved more than she could ever imagine. His gentle sways and whispered words intensified her longing, rocketed her on the path toward another release. She grasped his arms and held on. Not only was he taking her body on a thrill ride, her heart and soul had tagged along. Higher and higher, until she could never come down again.

His movements quickened, pushing her closer to oblivion. When he released, he took her over the edge. She wanted to stay there with him forever. If only it were possible.

SIX

His wrist com vibrated under his head, and Gib slowly opened his eyes. He had to report for his watch shift. As much as he'd love to stay wrapped around Vilarra, skip out on Zair as his squad mate had done to him the night before, Gib possessed a more honorable sense of duty.

He rolled off the bed, the mattress barely wide enough to hold the two of them lying on their sides. But they'd made it work. Now she'd have the bed to herself again, and he'd return to being a Defender. If all went well, he'd have a few moments after his shift and before she had to report to work, to spend more time together. Perhaps he'd get a complete glance at her thoughts. Holding her in his arms and buried deep inside her, he'd caught glimpses of her hopes and her fears. While he couldn't promise a lifetime commitment, he could give her more time.

Slipping on his uniform, he glanced around the hut for Vilarra's pet. He didn't want to step on the little creature on his way out. Though intrigued by the concept of having a pet, he could never have had one on Mingot. Bringing a tabnar or rochtaf into one's home would cause massive destruction. And those were the smallest animals on his home planet. Elynyn served as a perfect companion to Vilarra and had a giant personality for what she lacked in size.

Taking one last glance at Vilarra, Gib yearned to run a hand along her curves. But he might wake her. Or be tempted to lie back down and remain by her side. No, duty came first.

He shuffled to the door of the hut, not daring to lift a foot just in case he stepped on the little tibbar. As much as he wanted one more glimpse of Vilarra, he resisted. He'd see her again when his shift ended. After leaving the hut, he rushed along the path toward the palace then darted through the forest.

Zair sat on a log, greeting him with a wide grin. "I wasn't sure you'd show up. Saw you head back to the village with that girl from the kitchen."

Gib clenched his fists. "She's hardly a girl."

"And you would know because...."

He refused to give his squad mate an answer, instead using the app on his wrist com to scan the skies and detect any abnormal heat signatures. The Erebus often arrived in pockets of gas that appeared as bright lines from space down to the planet. By the time anyone spotted these rays, it was too late. The Erebus hurtled on their way to the surface. But if he detected the heat signatures well in advance, he could alert the rest of the Defenders on the planet and have the entire platoon ready to greet the arriving monsters with blasts of plazer fire. No Defenders meant no protection. Though many planets in the Alliance had adopted the same technology used by the app to set up a pre-warning system for the residents to rush to safety, those without it often suffered extreme casualties until the Defenders arrived to help. As had happened the last time the Erebus had descended upon Hemera. Yet their king still refused to receive Alliance aid, only asking for the Defender's to come once a Galactic year, when he believed the Erebus were likely to arrive again.

When the app finally loaded, he held his wrist in the air. Glaring spots of red appeared on the screen. And they grew bigger with every beat of his heart.

Zair punched him in the shoulder. "You going to tell me how she was?"

"No." Gib spun away from the other Defender and tried to interpret the readings on his wrist com.

"Oh, come on."

The whine in Zair's voice cut through his concentration. "Did you do a scan when you arrived? Did Flaine or Hazer report any abnormalities?"

"I didn't. They said everything was fine. Now, quit trying to change the subject. You know I'd tell you."

The Defender circled him until Gib elbowed him in the chest. "Are you even listening to me? We have a situation here, and you're more concerned about whether I slept with one Hemera woman than the safety of the entire planet."

"What do you mean?"

When Gib showed him the screen of his wrist com, Zair rested a hand on his plazer. They both looked up to the sky. Where the screen showed three red forms growing larger, Gib saw round lights rushing toward them. Not the beams that would indicate an Erebus attack, but shuttle-shaped masses.

Zair squinted. "Do those look like Alliance shuttles to you?"

"Yes." Gib stepped forward for a closer glimpse. "But why are they here? Did you get a message?"

Both their wrist coms beeped at the same time, and Zair shoved Gib. "I'm not a trainee. And such short notice means there must be an emergency."

His squad mate was right. Shuttles wouldn't be arriving in the atmosphere on an Alliance planet without notice otherwise. They'd have had to create their own folds and wormholes through space to travel so fast.

Attack on Yarwa, his wrist com read. *Board shuttles immediately.*

Zair slapped him on the back. "All right. Time for a real mission."

As much as Gib had longed to be face-to-face with an Erebus again, his feet refused to move. He yearned to see Vilarra once more, at least to say goodbye. They'd both known the relationship wouldn't last long, but this wasn't the way he'd planned to leave.

"C'mon Gib," his squad mate yelled, halfway between him and the shuttles landing at the Defender barracks. "It's time to go."

After a heavy sigh, he took off to board the shuttle his squad shared with Victor squad. He'd barely had a chance to buckle himself in when the shuttle lifted from the ground, ready to take him far away from the woman he thought he could possibly love. If only he'd had more time with her to find out.

"What in Gaspra is that thing?" Gib's roommate, Serit, hunched on his bunk and stared at the floor with wide eyes.

Gib shrugged and shook his head. "Were you smokin' some nehbred on Hemera before we left? I don't see anything."

"I know what I saw." The Kalaren Defender raised his pillow into the air. "It was white and furry, and it half-hopped, half-ran under my desk. If I see it again, I'm going to kill it."

Sure his roommate had hallucinated the encounter, Gib yanked the chair away from the desk then took a peek underneath. He heard a quick squeak before a tiny white creature raced toward him then climbed up his fresh uniform. "A stow—"

Whoomph.

Gib paused when something smacked him in the head. He reached out and yanked a pillow away from his roommate before Serit could hit him again. "What the Gaspra! Calm down, would ya?"

He searched for where Elynyn had gotten to and found her clinging to the front of his uniform, her tiny claws embedded in the material. Carefully grasping her, he picked her off then held her in his hand. "Are you okay, little one? Did that big, mean Kalaren scare you?"

Serit harrumphed before he wrinkled his nose and glared at the tibbar sitting in Gib's palm. "Do you know that thing?"

"As a matter of fact, I do. This is Elynyn." He scratched her back until she rolled over for a belly rub, her loud chirrs filling the room. "She's a tibbar and belongs to a woman I met on Hemera. She must have sneaked into my uniform pocket in the middle of the night."

"The middle of the night?" Serit sat and leaned back in the desk chair. "Do tell me more about this woman."

"Can't." He would never share the details the Defender wanted to hear. Memories for him only. "I've got to find some food for the tibbar. She's probably starving. Wouldn't want her to start nibbling on you while you're resting up for the mission."

Gib left their quarters as the color drained from Serit's face. It wouldn't be long before the carrier reached Yarwa's orbit. He had to find a place to keep Elynyn safe so she could be returned to Vilarra the next time someone from the Alliance visited Hemera. He'd love it to be him, but he wouldn't have the chance for another Galactic year. Too long for Vilarra to be completely on her own.

Victor squad raced off the shuttle followed by Hotel squad, their plazers at the ready. Dropped off in a live situation, the Defenders sprinted toward the Erebus surrounding the Alliance House of Representatives, the creatures' tentacles ramming holes into the building. Hundreds of the large, mature Erebus, had already started destroying the planet. Many on the outside of the colony turned toward the Defenders racing off the shuttle.

"Let's destroy every single one of them," Aarkan, the Kalaren leader of Gib's squad commanded. He fired his plazer first, his aim dead on. At a hundred meters away, the Erebus flew back into the dirt, knocking a few others to the ground. It didn't get back up, but the rest did, advancing faster, their red eyes glowing with intent.

Gaining ground at a steady pace, Gib aimed and fired his plazer in one long blast. The Erebus fell. One. Two. Three. Several tentacles flew into the air. Black tar spread along the ground in a steamy flow. Yet more Erebus kept coming. They possessed no other urge than to kill and destroy.

Shuttles landed behind the advancing squads, bringing more Defenders. They needed the numbers, but would they be enough to take out all the Erebus when they fought face-to-face. Gib didn't have time to worry. The enemy moved too close now. He fired. And again. Never letting up. Perfect hits, every one. But the crowd of live Erebus never ended.

He saw nothing but Erebus now, unable to spot any other Defenders nearby. Not even his own squad. He fired then spun around, not wanting to leave his back exposed. Yet, for all those that fell, even more encircled him, trampling over the fallen limbs and bodies of their own kind.

Gib turned again to find an Erebus right in his face. The smell of its tarry, poisonous breath made his eyes water. But, at this distance, he didn't need to see to take it down. He stuck the plazer right into its trunk and fired. The creature fell back, grabbing at him with its tentacles. He jumped away only to slam into a hard figure behind him. A tentacle reached around and yanked his plazer out of his grip and then launched it out of sight. Thick tentacles wrapped around his body, trapping his hands at his sides. They undulated around him, squeezing him tighter. Tar plopped onto the back of his neck, sizzling through his skin. Gib struggled for release, kicking back, but his foot met nothing but air.

The other Erebus had backed off. Not a good sign. They must assume him dead. Or about to be.

The Erebus squeezed him tighter. Bile rose from his stomach. Before he could release it, pain exploded in his chest. He screamed in agony. *Crack. Crack.* He struggled to breathe. So much torture. Lights flickered behind his closed eyelids. All sound disappeared except a high-pitched ringing.

Then, all at once, he fell face-first onto the ground. He would have believed himself dead, his soul escaped to the universe beyond, if not for the excruciating ache crushing his chest.

The Erebus bellowed, likely getting ready to end his life, fill him with poison before he disintegrated into a puddle of goo.

Gib rolled to the side. Or tried to. His breaths came out as ragged gasps. He didn't know if he had broken ribs or even a punctured lung, but he was going to die regardless. He drifted in and out of consciousness, waiting for the Erebus to finish him off. His only regret? That he hadn't said goodbye to Vilarra before leaving her home. And now he wouldn't even have the chance to send her a message when another Defender, a stranger to her, returned her tibbar.

The crushing blow came as he pictured the most beautiful woman he'd ever met. The pain ended. Everything went black. Not even poisoned but crushed to death.

SEVEN

"Hey, Vee, wait up."

Vilarra paused on the path to the village. She'd just spent another long day in the kitchen and yearned to crash on her bed. But she couldn't ignore Samish. Without his help every day, she wouldn't keep the royal family fed or have the motivation to even show up at the palace in the mornings. Not lately, anyway. He joked around, made a fool of himself until she smiled. And he made her forget, for a moment, that everyone she'd ever cared about had left her. She couldn't count her father, as he'd never been around, but her mother had gotten ill and passed away a couple Galactic years ago. Though it seemed like yesterday. Saukus had left her shortly after. Then Gib, without even a simple goodbye. Though she'd accepted the relationship wouldn't last beyond his mission, her heart had hoped for more. The disappointment crushed her.

Worst of all, she'd lost the one friend she'd always been able to count on. Her pet tibbar had disappeared thirty day cycles ago. She hadn't seen Elynyn since she'd fed her on the counter the night she'd given her heart and body to Gib. The loneliness overwhelmed her most nights since, preventing restful sleep and draining away all her hopes and dreams. What did she have to look forward to?

"So, how are you?" Samish huffed and puffed as he reached her side.

"Same as I was when you left the kitchen." She started walking again. "Did you wait around this whole time?"

"No," he shouted. "I mean, no. I was out looking for something. I was just coming back when I saw you."

"Okay." She picked up her pace, not in the mood to talk.

"Aren't you gonna ask what I was looking for?" He hurried to keep up with her.

"Not really. It's none of my business."

He dashed in front of her, causing her to halt or she would have smashed into him. "Stop. No, it is your business."

Fighting off the urge to dart around him, Vilarra stopped, blinked sleepily, and released a heavy sigh. "Fine. What were you looking for?"

"This." He fished in his sack and pulled out a scruffy, dirty-white tibbar before handing it to her. "It's for you."

She stepped back. "That's not Elynyn."

"I know." He clasped her wrist and set the tiny creature in her palm. "I thought I'd get you a new one, hoping maybe this tibbar, and myself, can keep you company, now."

The tibbar chomped down on the tip of Vilarra's finger then leaped from her palm. It hit the ground then scampered off.

Blood gushing from her wound, Vilarra lifted the edge of her skirt and wrapped it around her throbbing finger.

"Or maybe just me?" Samish held his hands behind his back and dug his toe into the ground.

"What happened to Beckalie? Last I heard, you two were ready to have a bonding ceremony and have kids." And she'd happened to witness their naked rear ends on her way home from work as they'd run into his house rather than fornicate out front for everyone to see.

His toe dug deeper. "She said she didn't want to see me again, said I should call on you if I was going to say your name when we...." He gulped. "You know."

"Not going to happen." Her cheeks warmed out of embarrassment and anger at the same time. "She's my best friend." And Vilarra didn't want another relationship with anyone. Ever. Not when they always left her. She backed away from him, dropped her skirt, and was prepared to run when a bright light from above left her staring up at the sky. An Alliance shuttle. The Defenders had returned. She took off in a sprint, not home, but toward the Defender barracks. No longer tired, she had to find out if he'd returned.

By the time she reached the barracks, the shuttle had already landed and Defenders rushed back and forth between the shuttles and buildings. Instead of moving their belongings into the barracks, they loaded their equipment onto the ship. Probably cleaning up after their quick departure. The fact they'd all left earlier than planned made her feel better about Gib sneaking out without a goodbye. But only slightly.

Vilarra glanced around at all the Defenders, searching for a familiar face. For Gib, or someone who could tell her where to find him. In the dark, no one looked familiar. And not one of them paid her any attention.

Moving closer to their path, she waited for the next Defender to exit the barracks. A female Nevad came out, her yellow skin a stark contrast to her dark uniform and the night sky.

"Excuse me." Vilarra stepped forward to ensure she'd be seen. "Can you please help me?"

The woman smiled over the equipment she carried in her four arms. "Yes?"

"I'm looking for Gib." She clasped her hands together until her knuckles hurt. "Have you seen him? Did he come back with you?"

"Gib?" The Defender's smile disappeared. "You're Vilarra?"

She nodded. The woman knew her name, so that had to be good, right? Though the Defender's change in expression made her believe otherwise.

"So, nobody's told you what happened to him yet?"

Her stomach clenched. All hope of seeing Gib again melted away. "Um, no."

"You need to get home right away." The Defender nudged her head toward the village. "There's someone waiting there for you."

Dread pooled low in her gut. Her feet heavy like lead, she trudged back to her hut, unsure if she wanted to learn the fate of her recent lover. He was a Defender, after all. They risked their lives every day to save planets across the universe from the Erebus. Had he failed to return from his last mission? Made the ultimate sacrifice while saving others? Yet, why would she be notified? She wasn't family. And they'd only spent two days and one amazing night together. Not enough time to make her a significant part of his life. Unless that night had meant as much to him as it had to her. The Defender she'd talked to had to have learned her name somehow. She doubted King Luchivus had learned by name any of the commoners who worked in the palace. All the more reason for her to delay returning to her hut. She didn't want to be told Gib had died. Instead, she longed to hold onto the hope he would one day return, that maybe not everyone she loved left her forever.

But that dream would soon end. Her home lay ahead, and she could already see two people out front, waiting for her. One stood holding a large white container, while the other sat in some kind of chair, his or her head wrapped in gauze. Had that Defender been injured on the same mission as Gib? Injured.... Maybe....

She ran the last few strides, pleading to the universe for the person in the chair to be Gib. With all the bandages, he must have been badly injured, but at least he wasn't dead. "Gib?"

The person in the chair turned his head, and in that instant, her heart swelled. Her Defender had returned. "Hi."

The simple word came out in a hoarse whisper, as if even that took a lot of effort. Yet he still reached for her hand, the mostly innocent contact appeasing her lonely soul.

"You must be Vilarra," the other person said. A Warwa dressed in a doctor's uniform, she gripped the handles of Gib's chair and turned him toward the entrance of Vilarra's hut. "Can we go inside and talk?"

"Yes, of course." She ducked in front of them and opened the door. Inside, she barely had enough room for the three of them and Gib's rolling chair, but no one seemed ready to complain.

The doctor put the case on the table then reached into her pocket. "Before we discuss why Gib is here, I have someone to return to you."

Someone? Vilarra hadn't seen anyone else with them. But she didn't have a chance to ask about the reference before a furry white ball leaped from the doctor's hand toward her. Its front claws clung to her shirt, and she cupped the tibbar in her palm so it didn't fall off. It licked the tip of her finger where the other one had bitten her. She recognized this one. "Elynyn. You found her."

"Stowaway," Gib rasped, the exposed part of his face suddenly pale. "Saved me."

That would explain why she hadn't seen her tibbar since Gib had left. She yearned to hear how Elynyn had saved him, but her concern remained on her Defender. She turned to the doctor. "Is he going to be okay?"

"Yes." The doctor nodded. "Traveling through the wormhole from the barracks to your home drained him of energy, but we needed a fast and easy way to get him here. Some rest will help. If you don't mind, I'll get him settled, and then we can discuss his care."

"His care?" Why hadn't he remained on the Alliance spacecraft? Hemera wasn't any place for an injured Defender to recover. Even if she preferred him with her rather than anywhere else. She didn't have the time, knowledge, or supplies to care for him.

The doctor didn't answer her, instead adjusting Gib's chair until it spread out into a bed. Side rails came up, and the doctor reached into her case for something. After pulling out a package, she unwrapped a needle and stuck it into Gib's arm, injecting a clear liquid. "That will make him sleep for some time, give him reprieve from the pain." She gestured Vilarra to step away from him. "Now, regarding his care. He has broken ribs and a wound across the side of his face. Both have been mended by our equipment, but he is still very fragile, needs time to heal."

"Why here? What if he gets worse?" She didn't want to be responsible for the death of a Defender, especially after he'd managed to live through whatever mission he'd just been on.

"I'm not worried about that, but if he does seem worse, all you have to do is contact me through his wrist com." The doctor handed the gadget to Vilarra. "Just say *Doctor* to contact myself or my brother."

"But, why? I have a job at the palace. I can't be here all the time." She only came back home to sleep most days. As much as she wished to have him there, he needed to be with the doctor.

"He asked to return here." The doctor cleared her throat. "Or, rather, he repeated your name over and over until we had to sedate him. One of his squad mates told us who you were. And regarding your position at the palace.... It has been temporarily filled by a woman named Beckalie."

"What? How?" She'd worked her way up to that position. How could they replace her so easily? When Gib left again, she'd have nothing to go back to, nothing to occupy her time.

"I spoke with the co-leader of the council. Frotathia." The doctor knocked on the hard shell of her case. "I stressed how important it was for this planet to help out the Alliance, and also how it would be beneficial for Hemera to have an Alliance-trained medical team. You will be the first member of the team, and I will train you over the com unit."

"Are you serious?" She placed a hand on her chest, sure the doctor had to be deceiving her.

"Very." The doctor glanced at Gib then back to Vilarra. "Do you accept the offer?"

"Yes." The word didn't come out loud enough, so she repeated herself. "Yes, I do." In the kitchen, she had a permanent position but nowhere else to go from there. But as a healer, no, as part of the medical team, she could do so much more to help others, not only the royal family, but commoners as well. And the Alliance would train her. All thanks to Gib. She looked forward to the moment he awoke so she could spend every moment taking care of him until he had to leave again, but until then, she had a lot to learn. "Please, teach me what I need to know."

―――――――――

With a gasp, Gib flicked his eyes open. He'd been back on Yarwa fighting the Erebus. Only, this time, Vilarra was there with him, tangled in the tentacles of an Erebus. He'd tried to save her, but wound up grabbed from behind by another of the enemy. It squeezed him, tighter and tighter, until he couldn't breathe. He couldn't save her if he couldn't save himself. Then he heard the squeak of her tibbar, not around him, but in his head. And he realized he'd been dreaming.

In his peripheral vision, he spotted Elynyn perched on his shoulder. Her whiskers tickled his neck. She hopped onto his chest and faced him, her nose wiggling away. She had saved him from being killed by the Erebus and now saved him from a worse dream.

"You're awake." Vilarra rose from her bed then leaned over him, running her fingertips across his forehead and down the unbandaged side of his face. "How are you feeling?"

"Like I was crushed by an Erebus." He sucked in air through his teeth, the pain suddenly more prominent.

"Oh, you're hurting again." She rushed to the other side of his bed and opened the case his doctor had left. "I know what to do. I can help." After spraying something cold on his arm, she slammed a square patch onto the same spot.

He winced, the impact jarring his broken ribs.

"I'm sorry." Vilarra frowned, her eyes glassy as if she was about to cry. "The doctor said to press it hard, so the tiny needle would puncture your skin."

"It's okay." He reached out for her hand, never wanting to make her upset. Not when he depended on her so much. "I'm just happy to be here."

Placing her hand in his palm, she drew the fingers of her other hand across his bandaged ribs. "How did you survive? The doctor said your squad found you buried under a bunch of dead Erebus, tangled in their tentacles."

"Not sure." He'd tried to remember that moment over and over, but it remained a blur, only coming to him in inaccurate nightmares. "I was killing them. One knocked my weapon away. Grabbed me from behind." He gasped for a breath, his lung capacity reduced by his broken ribs. "It crushed me. Then it let go. Fell on top of me."

Talking in short sentences felt awkward, but it kept the pain reduced while he waited for the patch Vilarra gave him to work. "Was already dead. Had tiny puncture wounds. Can only guess. Elynyn bit it. Saved my life. Turns out tibbar saliva…. poisonous to Erebus."

He couldn't say another word, overwrought by pain and the overwhelming need to sleep. But he wanted to stay in the present for longer, ensure Vilarra was real, not another dream about to go wrong.

"Well, I'm so glad you both survived." She leaned down and kissed his lips.

In a temporary reprieve from the agony, he wrapped an arm around her, never wanting to let her go. Eventually, he would have to, though. When he had fully healed, he'd return to active duty, protecting the universe from the Erebus. But his heart would remain on Hemera. Any free time he had, he'd spend with Vilarra, and if she agreed, they'd start a family. Eventually, one of their children would become a Defender, allow him to retire from service and spend the rest of his days with the woman who'd stolen his heart.

"I love you," he whispered.

And for the first time, he could read her thoughts. Nothing blocked her mind anymore. In fact, she broadcast her feelings clearly to him.

She stroked his cheek. "You somehow managed to break down the walls I'd built around my heart. I love you."

But he already knew, had felt the walls crumble as he'd spent more time with her and caught more glimpses. Now, he could see her dreams for the future matched his own.

A squeak interrupted the moment, and Elynyn nuzzled into his neck, her warm body vibrating with every soft chirr.

"Seems Elynyn loves you, too." Vilarra smiled, lighting up the entire hut and his heart.

He'd found his home. Regardless of where he'd grown up, or where the Alliance sent him, his heart would always remain here.

PET TRADE

A Central Galactic Concordance Novella

By
Carol Van Natta

Carol Van Natta writes science fiction and fantasy, including the award-winning Central Galactic Concordance space opera series, and paranormal romance and retro SF comedy.

http://author.carolvannatta.com/

CHAPTER ONE

*Location: Frontier Planet Del'Arche * GDAT 3241.155*

 Veterinarian Bethnee Bakonin limped toward the cage slowly. The huge dire wolf inside stood and eyed her with wary interest, but not fear or anger. The wolf's bright blue, intelligent eyes contrasted beautifully against her thick coat of charcoal grey and black fur. Bethnee reached out with another thread of her talent to get a sense of the designer animal's health. "Where did she come from?"

A capricious, chilly wind blew a dust devil into the center of the paddock, then let it go. Fall always arrived early in the foothills of the northernmost mountains on Del'Arche.

"A boutique alpaca ranch down south. New client." Nuñez frowned and crossed her arms. "Idiots thought a top-of-the-line, protector-class dire wolf would make a great herd dog." She made a disgusted sound. "They were going to shoot her because she wouldn't let the herd out of the barn. I convinced them to sign her over to me."

Bethnee eyed Nuñez. "How much did she cost?" Designer animals from reputable pet-trade dealers weren't cheap. Recreating extinct mammals from Earth's Pleistocene period was perennially popular, because it avoided the Central Galactic Concordance government's multiple prohibitions against altering cornerstone species like wolves and coyotes. Bethnee had been saving her hard credits to buy her own flitter, instead of having to constantly borrow Nuñez's, but the rescued dire wolf took priority.

Nuñez shook her head. "Zero. They bought her cheap with a flatlined ID chip, so she's probably stolen. I told them I'd take care of the problem for free, and that it'd be our little secret." Knowing Nuñez, she'd pushed them with her low-level empath talent, so they'd be afraid of getting caught, and happy to be rid of the evidence. Nuñez had no compunction against using her minder talent to manipulate humans who hurt animals, which was one of several reasons why she and Bethnee got along so well.

Bethnee focused on sensing the wolf's mind. The fleeting thoughts were complex, with deep memories. The wolf had known and felt pack love for other humans, but hadn't seen them for a long time. The ranchers had beaten her to get her into the cage, and she didn't know what she'd done wrong.

Bethnee contained her talent and her anger, then told Nuñez what she'd found. "She's also got tracers in every major joint. Can I use your small surgical suite this afternoon?" The portable unit contained micro surgical tools with and an AI-assist built in, and would make quick work of the excisions.

"Sure." Nuñez tilted her head toward the doors of the vetmed clinic behind her. "Let's get her inside."

"Does she respond to a name?"

"Didn't come up." Nuñez looked at the clock. "I'll make you a deal. After I put the flitter away, help me feed and water the yaks, and I'll help you with the tracers."

"It'll snow tonight." Nuñez lifted the last bulky bag of feed and unsealed it. At age one hundred and nine, the woman looked like a plump rural grandmother who printed heritage quilts and baked cookies, but she was strong and smart, and could control a herd of fifty large buffalo with her minder talent.

Bethnee took the bag. "The weather AI doesn't think so." She angled her hip so she didn't stress her bad leg, then reached high to pour the bag's contents into the hopper.

"The yaks say otherwise." Nuñez took the empty bag. "They're huddling in the corner of the pen near the barn. Weather AI says it'll be a bad winter." She gave Bethnee a meaningful look. "You could move back to the clinic."

"We've been..." Bethnee began, then sighed. "I'm fine where I am. It suits me."

Nuñez continued as if she hadn't heard. "Still plenty of room in the clinic. You could live next door, because the obnoxious Raloff family abandoned the property to move deeper into the mountains." She headed for the sink to wash her hands. "If we shared the clinic again, you could actually leave town for more than a few hours and know your animals were safe, and maybe have your leg fixed. You're too young to be a hermit. You're homesteaded now, and the town would be happy to have you."

"No, they wouldn't." Bethnee followed Nuñez to the sink. "Too many people considered my animals a nuisance." She pointed her chin toward the big cage. "The first goat or child that went missing, they'd accuse the dire wolf. Or Jynx." Unusual snow leopards, no matter how well behaved, scared people who didn't know them.

As Bethnee washed her hands, Nuñez turned on the mini-solardry. "It was only the Raloffs and Administrator Pranteaux who complained, and he complains about everything." They both rubbed their hands vigorously in the warm, forced air. "Come on. Let's take care of your new wolf."

Bethnee was grateful that her friend hadn't gotten into the real reasons Bethnee couldn't move back. A lot of frontier settlers like the Raloffs had moved away from the Central Galactic Concordance member planets to get away from minders, and everyone knew she was one, because she used her talents as well as her training to treat pets. Word got around.

More importantly, even though she'd escaped her former life in the pet trade three years ago, she still couldn't get within five meters of men without taking the chance she'd be shaking like a leaf from mind-numbing fear. When she'd first arrived, she couldn't even be in the same building. She'd gotten better with time, but it was bad for business when she couldn't deal with nearly half the population of customers.

Nuñez claimed it was post-trauma stress, and could be treated, too, just like her leg. Even if that were true, it would cost hard credit, and she needed every decimal she had to provide for her animal family. They didn't care that she was too scared and too damaged to live among humans.

CHAPTER TWO

GDAT 3241.155

Axur Tragon fought the rising wind to land the old runabout as gently as he could on the Tanimai community airpad. He retracted the canopy and climbed out, then stepped around back to open the hatch and untie the two covered carriers. "Almost there," he crooned.

He slung the straps on each of his shoulders, then walked to Tanimai's vetmed clinic. His cybernetic legs weren't pretty, but they gave him a long, smooth gait, even when carrying a thirty-kilo load.

He'd only been in town a dozen times since he'd landed three hundred local days ago on the frontier planet of Del'Arche. Crashed, really, but his former Jumper Corps flight instructor said as long as the pilot and passengers crawled away, it counted as a landing.

He hoped the veterinary medic wouldn't turn him away. Between his intimidating height, his long, shaggy hair, and his bizarre and heavy metallic poncho, he looked like a disaster refugee with mental issues. Throw in the scars and the visible cybernetics, and he probably scared birds from the sky.

The shallow lobby was open, but deserted. He stepped up to the wall-comp. "Hello?"

An older woman's face appeared on the display. "Be there in a minute. Set the carriers on the table."

Moments later, the interior sliding doors opened and revealed the woman he'd spoken to. She had black hair streaked with silver, and a pleasant smile. "I'm Aniashalaman Nuñez, the VMD. Call me Nuñez." She looked up at him from her considerably shorter height. "You must be the ex-Jumper, Axur Tragon. You're as tall as everyone says." Despite her

Islander complexion and facial features, her accent was pure Standard English.

He returned her smile. "I'm actually short, for a Jumper."

Nuñez laughed and shaded her eyes as she looked up. "From down here, you all look like trees to me." She tilted her head toward the table. "What can I help you with?"

"I have some, uh, pets, and these are sick, I think." He shoved his hands in his pockets under his heavy poncho. "To be honest, I kind of inherited them, and don't know much about their care, except what I read in reference manuals. They all did okay in the spring and summer, but lately, these aren't."

"How many pets do you have?" Nuñez crossed to the table and lifted the cover on the first cage. "Ah, birds of paradise. Three females and a male. Are they mated?"

"No clue. To answer your first question, seven if you count species, and twelve animals total. I think they're all designer, rather than domestic." He tilted his head toward the second cage. "I don't even know what some of them are."

Nuñez lifted the cover of the second carrier. "Great balls of chaos, what a..." Nuñez pulled the cover off completely. "...chimera."

Axur suspected she'd censored a less diplomatic description. He couldn't blame her. Kivo was German shepherd-sized, but the resemblance ended there. He had black and brown stripes in his short, sleek fur, and six legs with clawed paws for running and catching. Gigantic, bat-style swivel ears sat on his broad, flat head. He had two tails with tufts of fur on the ends. He was a prime example of what the anti-pet-trade activists railed against: tinkering with Terran genetics to create whimsical animals that would have never survived in the wild, much less natural selection. Kivo might be a genetic mess, but he was also the sweetest, most laid-back beast Axur had ever met, and was patient with all the animals, even the miniature dinosaur that often mistook Kivo's tails as something edible. "Kivo's usually interested in everything, and eats anything, but not for the past week. The birds just huddle in the bottom of their cage and won't go out."

Nuñez made a face. "I might be able to help with the birds, but Kivo is about as far off my chart as you can get. My patients are large herd animals and the occasional terrier or tabby. You need a specialist." She glanced up at him and sighed. "As it happens, I know one of the best, but she's not..."

A cacophony of goose honking from somewhere in the building interrupted. Nuñez glanced toward the back and frowned. "Sit a minute." She pointed to a lobby chair, then strode through the doors she'd come through and vanished. The doors slid quickly closed behind her.

He dragged the chair closer to the table and sat, putting his face closer to Kivo's cage. The chimera rolled back in the cage and exposed his striped stomach. "Sorry, buddy, no belly rubs until it's safe to let you out."

Axur looked up when the clinic's outside doors opened to admit a tall, willowy woman with shoulder-length, deep blue-black hair and Asian features. She carried several bags and a box, and walked with a pronounced limp. She glanced at him, startled. "Does Nuñez know…" She trailed off as her attention riveted on Kivo.

After a long moment, Axur answered her unfinished question. "Nuñez asked me to wait here."

She darted a look to his face and awkwardly backed up several steps, dropping one of the bags. "Oh."

He started to stand and reach out to help her, but froze in mid-rise when her eyes widened in unmistakable fear. Her hand visibly trembled as she awkwardly scooped up the bag, then fled through the doors to the back.

He sat down again with a sigh. It never paid to play the shoulda-coulda-woulda game, but starting a year ago, it was hard not to wish for a different star lane for his life. He'd never been nova-hot beautiful like some in his squad, but he'd never lacked for companionship and bed partners for his twelve years in the CPS Jumper Corps. Unbeknownst to him, he'd been secretly selected for a CPS "special project" that changed him forever, including adding valuable experimental tech to his cybernetics.

Now he was an ugly mass of biometal and hardware that made him a walking, talking satellite uplink. Only the heavy poncho he'd kludged together from salvaged supplies kept him from constantly broadcasting his unique comm signature to the frontier planet's various satellites, and from there to the Central Galactic Concordance's intergalactic communications network. If he uncloaked, his days of freedom remaining would be measured by how fast a CPS ship could get to Del'Arche to hunt him down.

Kivo whined. Axur stuck his fingers into the cage again and tried to shake off his melancholy. He'd lived, and so had Kivo and the others, and life was hope.

Ten minutes later, Nuñez strode back into the lobby, looking harried. "Thanks for waiting." She put her fists on her hips. "I have an emergency, so I'll cut to the chase. I can't treat your pets, but Bethnee Bakonin can. She's the woman who just came in. She's already seen you, and that's usually a deal-killer for her, but if you keep your distance and don't make sudden movements, she'll look at your animals." Her chin jutted out pugnaciously. "She's a pet-trade expert, but she's also a pan-phyla animal-affinity talent, so if you dislike minders, you can jet right now, 'cause I'm one, too."

Axur put his hands flat on his thighs. "Minders are just people. I don't care if she uses dark energy magic, if she can help Kivo and the birds." He pointed a thumb toward the front doors. "I could wait outside."

Nuñez shook her head. "No, she'll need information from you. Just move your chair away and stay seated." She glanced at his stained pants and worn combat boots. "I'll assume you're not carrying hard credit. What are you trading?"

"Fall harvest gourds, berries, and leafy greens. If it's more than that, we can negotiate." In the planet's official financial transaction records, the town's economy was barely a blip, but it did a thriving business in trade. From what he'd gathered, the settlement company took a percentage of all financial transactions, but hadn't found a way to close the trading loophole, so they often conducted unannounced audits, trying to catch the town breaking the rules so they could levy fines.

Nuñez nodded. "Fair enough." She gave him a considering look. "Bakonin is like most high-level animal-affinity talents, better with animals than people, and like a lot of us here in Tanimai,"—she looked pointedly at the visible scars on his neck and jaw leading up to his disabled skulljack—"she's had a hard life. Be nice, and she'll do right by you and the animals. Scare her, and you'll never see her again."

Axur didn't miss the unspoken warning that he'd never trade in town again if he did anything to make Bakonin bolt. "Understood."

He carried the chair to the far corner and sat, then hunched over to rest his elbows on his knees. It was as short as he could make himself.

Nuñez left. The doors stayed open long enough for Bakonin to limp in. She glanced at him briefly as she made her way to the table. Her shuttered expression changed to interest when she got to the birds.

Axur watched as she opened the cage with the four birds and deftly pulled the brightly colored male out and turned him upside down to look at his chest and feet. "Yes, yes," she said soothingly. Her voice had a warm, husky timbre. She did the same with the others, then closed the cage door.

She took a deep breath, let it out slowly, then turned to look at him. "Nuñez said you've only had the animals for about nine months, and that you've got more at home. Were they in your ship when you crashed?"

Axur looked up at her, startled. "How did you know about the ship?"

One corner of her mouth twitched. "Hard to miss a streaking fireball that left a kilometer-long gouge at the north end of Park Plateau. No one knew anyone had survived until you came into town two weeks later offering exotic trade goods. People talk. You're lucky the weather satellites were malfing again, or the company auditors would have iced you for terraform destruction, then expatriated you to the nearest Concordance lockup for illegal trespass and occupation."

He ducked his head, embarrassed that it hadn't occurred to him that others might have seen his ungraceful entry into Del'Arche's atmosphere. "I didn't know about the animals until the hard landing ripped open the freighter's smuggling hold. I've tried to care for those that lived."

Bakonin nodded. "Pet-trade dealers often ship on the sly to get around inspections and quarantines, and to deter thieves. It's a ruthless business." She pointed to the cage. "Your birds are healthy, but cold intolerant. If you don't give them a warm habitat and a diet of insects and fruit, they'll die. They're fertile, so if you do have a habitat, you'll have fledglings by the spring."

"Okay." He could work around the diet problem, but had no idea how he'd create a warm space out of the ship's wreckage, miscellaneous cargo, and the deadfall trees he'd hauled in for building materials. The possibility of offspring hadn't even crossed his mind. Like everyone else in the Concordance, he'd gotten a birth control implant at the first hint of puberty, so reproduction took a deliberate decision between two people.

She turned to the chimera. Kivo exhibited intense curiosity, his leaf-shaped nose working and his ears swiveling forward. He stood, briefly, but his two back sets of legs shook, and he half sat. She opened the cage door. Kivo oozed out and crouched. She approached slowly, then gently ran her hands over his ribs, shoulder joints, and articulated spine. Kivo leaned into her as she crooned nonsense words while she examined his ears, eyes, and wicked-looking teeth. He was soon rolling onto his back, stretching his six legs out, begging for attention. She smiled and rubbed his belly, and even laughed when he sloppily licked her nose when she got close enough. "Does he have a name?"

Axur was so mesmerized by her obvious skill and the glimpse of beauty in her smile that it took him a moment to realize she was talking to him. "Kivo."

She kept one hand on Kivo's broad head and stroked his ear muscles with her thumb. "I'm guessing you fed him fresh meat and produce from your farm, which is the best thing you could have done, because it's kept him alive. The dealer was probably returning him to the research company's designers as a failure." Sadness stole across her face. "Even if we eradicate the blood parasite and tailor some nutritional chems to counter the anemia it caused, which is his current issue, other problems are coming. He's already got arthritis, especially in his flexible spine, and his fine-motor control is degrading."

It sounded like Kivo had the chimera equivalent of waster's disease, a pernicious problem that plagued Jumper veterans across the galaxy. The CPS researchers conducting the "special project" claimed to have cured him of it as compensation for taking his arm. He hoped that wasn't another one of their lies. His tried not to focus on his resentment and turned his attention back to Kivo. "Why did they create him at all?"

She shrugged. "Pretend alien fauna for the wealthy, maybe? It's a fad." She stroked the large hump of Kivo's middle shoulder joints. "The bioengineers actually got the six legs to work, but the rest of him is a fantasy hodgepodge." She snorted disdainfully. "Two tails." She rested her hip against the table and eased the weight off her stiffer leg.

"He follows me everywhere. He keeps the peace among the other animals, too." He tilted his head. "Can animals be empaths? I think he tries to cheer me up sometimes." It sounded daft after he said it out loud, so he was grateful she didn't laugh.

"Maybe? Medical scientists still don't know what combination of DNA and subtrans amino arrays make the difference between human minders and non-minders, or even the gender expression continuum. Who's to say that animals aren't evolving along with us?"

"Makes sense to me. What's the treatment protocol for him?"

"A parasite-tailored antibiotic and immune boosters. If we can't trade with the local chems and alterants shop, we might have to use hard credit at the human med clinic in Asgorth."

"I've got some reserve freighter stock to trade." He sat up straight and immediately regretted it, because it caused Bakonin to catch her breath and step back. "Sorry." He hunched over again.

Bakonin's lips thinned, and she shook her head. "I just hadn't realized how tall you are. Ex-Jumper?"

Axur gave her a humorless smile and held up his left hand, where exposed biometal gleamed at his knuckles. "My cybernetic arm and legs didn't give it away?" Most people preferred flesh and bone.

"Cybernetics are fine." She took a deep breath and let it out. "I'm phobic around men, sometimes, which is my problem, not yours."

Kivo's ears swiveled toward the sliding doors, and he rolled to a sitting position. A moment later, Nuñez appeared, the front of her tunic covered in blood. "I need your help."

CHAPTER THREE

After Bethnee hosed down the instruments of the large-animal surgical suite with steaming hot water, she stood next to the floor drain and turned the hose on her unlovely but waterproof, tear-resistant work tunic.

Axur, as he'd asked them to call him, had proven to be more than just a pretty face. Nuñez dragooned him into helping extricate a buffalo cow from a tangled coil of spikewire. Nuñez used her minder talent to control the cow while Axur used the superior strength of his cybernetic hand to stop the wire from springing out when Bethnee cut it. As long as she stayed on the other side of the cow and focused on using her talent to heal the cow's deepest lacerations, she'd managed to keep her mind clear and her stupid shaking to a minimum. Nevertheless, she felt like she'd hiked to the top of towering Mount Taruka and back.

Axur hadn't flinched at the blood or injuries. When Nuñez commented on it, he'd admitted he'd been a trained field medic in the Jumper Corps.

Nuñez had laughed. "What the hell are you doing trying to make a homestead the hard way? The townspeople would be thrilled to build you a clinic, like they did mine."

Axur had looked away and mumbled something about it being compli-cated. Bethnee sympathized. She lived that every day.

Axur turned out to have another invaluable skill. The rattled, panicky owner of the cow only spoke halting English, but Axur figured out the woman spoke Korean, and served as their translator. He admitted to speaking eight languages fluently, and could get by in a lot more. Bethnee knew Nuñez was adding it to her arsenal of arguments of why he should move to town. Under her bluff and blunt exterior, Nuñez had a heart the size of the Andromeda galaxy, and didn't believe in complications.

It fell to Bethnee, with Axur's translation help, to negotiate a complex trade for their cow-saving services that resulted in Axur getting the drugs he needed for his chimera using a credit the rancher had at the chems shop, in exchange for Axur giving his food-trade goods to Nuñez, who would share them with Bethnee so she could make further trades for the ingredients for nutritional supplements for her animals and Kivo.

Bethnee found Nuñez and Axur in the holding pen outside. Unexpectedly, the chimera and the dire wolf also roamed the pen, pretending disinterest in one another. Bethnee sent a thread of her talent out to both animals, and found that Kivo considered the wolf a new friend, and the wolf was considering everyone in the pen, including Bethnee, as potential pack mates that needed guarding from the dangerous, grunting yaks in the neighboring paddock.

Axur laughed at something Nuñez said. Despite his untamed hair and the peculiar cloak he refused to remove, he was a surprisingly handsome man, especially when he smiled. And such was the irrational tangle of her phobia that she could admire a tall, good-natured man from afar, then be too scared to get close enough to see the color of his eyes.

"I'm going to remove the tracers from the wolf," she said loudly. "Want me to do the same for Kivo while I'm at it?"

Axur gave her a puzzled look. "Tracers?"

When Nuñez explained about the pet-trade practice of implanting active tracers that broadcast a valuable animal's location to the net, and passive tracers that showed up on bio scanners, Axur readily agreed.

With Nuñez's help and the portable surgical suite's micro instruments, Bethnee finished with both animals in thirty minutes. Nuñez planned to trade the active tracers to a client who could use them for tracking goats.

In the lobby, Kivo sidled up to the tolerant wolf and licked at her muzzle. Bethnee could well believe that Kivo was the peacekeeper among Axur's menagerie.

Nuñez entered and crossed to Axur to hand him a cup of hot coffee.

He smiled as he closed his eyes and smelled it, then sipped it with obvious enjoyment. "Stars, but I've missed this."

Nuñez sipped from her own cup. "I trade for it whenever I can." She pointed a thumb toward Bethnee. "Don't ever let Bethnee make it for you, unless you have a biometal stomach."

Bethnee shrugged. It tasted like burned acid to her, so how was she to know what was too strong? A thigh muscle in her bad leg spasmed. She needed to soak in her single luxury, the geothermal pool. She should just go home and...

"Dammit," she said. "I can't take the wolf with me today. I only have the glide board, and no den big enough for her." She caught Nuñez's eye. "Can she stay a few days?"

"Sure, but she'll be alone except for the geese and the yaks, and she'll hate it."

"I know you don't know me or my setup," said Axur, "but I could take her for as long as you need. My barn is big, and she wouldn't lack for company."

Bethnee looked at him in surprise.

Axur splayed his hands. "I have an ulterior motive. I was hoping you'd come out to my place and look at the rest of my pets. Tell me what they are, and how to care for them."

Nuñez nodded. "You can borrow the flitter."

The idea of going alone to a man's homestead spiked Bethnee's anxiety, but Axur had scrupulously accommodated her by keeping his distance, and it was a good solution for the new wolf. If she didn't like what she saw, she could jet. Besides, she had to admit she wanted to see the exotic animals Axur had told them about.

"Okay."

Axur looked pleased.

Nuñez blinked and raised her eyebrows. "You trust him?"

Bethnee pointed to the chimera, draped across Axur's sturdy cybernetic knees like a lapdog, and the wolf, who was licking Axur's hand.

"I trust them."

CHAPTER FOUR

GDAT 3241.155

If Bethnee hadn't been following Axur's runabout, she wouldn't have found his high-country homestead. Which, she surmised, was as deliberate as his choice to stay away from town, as well as his choice to wear his awkward heavy cloak.

She landed the flitter in a clearing about a hundred meters southwest of the edge of his loosely fenced perimeter. She wished she'd thought to bring her glide board, to save her leg from the uphill hike while carrying her veterinary bag. Fortunately, the dire wolf stayed near with very little coaxing via her talent.

Axur backed up as she approached, staying well out of her discomfort range. "Sorry, I didn't think about the distance." Behind him rose two buildings fashioned out of starship freighter sections. The taller one had wide doors made from an airlock. "It's windy up here, so I want to give you an earwire so we can talk without shouting. It'll take me a few minutes to program."

"Okay." The wolf remained by her side, nose working overtime as she checked out her new surroundings. Bethnee reached out with her talent to do the same.

Axur cleared his throat. "Some of the animals are in the barn." He pointed toward wide, open doors. "I'll knock on the wall when I'm ready with the earwire."

Forty minutes later, Bethnee sat on a rough-hewn bench at the worktable inside the barn, packing her equipment back into her bag and talking via the earwire to Axur, who was in his living quarters area. She didn't subvocalize; animals didn't care if she spoke out loud. "You've got a fortune in stolen and illegal pet-trade animals."

"*Stolen?*" The earwire made his rich baritone sound thin and distant.

"Your e-dog, for one. 'E' for enhanced. He's military-trained, and his sensory implants and command processor are still active. If you knew the passcode and comm band, you could program a percomp to give him complex sets of orders to follow, and get a feed through his implants."

"*That makes sense. I named him Trouble because that's what he gets into unless I give him jobs to do. Just like some Jumpers I know.*"

"Your three cats are illegal because the designer spliced in a few primate genes to give them those long, flexible toes and a broader diet, and left them fertile. Any CGC health inspector would destroy them on sight, in case the splice bred true. Feed them meat and dairy, and any fruits or vegetables they'll eat. You could trade with Nuñez for some yak milk. They'll probably go into their first estrus cycle in the spring."

"*Lucky they're all female. Can you or Nuñez fix their playgrounds so I don't have kittens on my hands if some equally fertile male comes looking for love?*"

The big dire wolf warily poked her head into the barn's entrance. The boldest of the young cats had already left a stinging wound across her nose leather.

Bethnee laughed. "Fix their playgrounds? Yeah, we can neuter them. What did you name them?"

She held out her hand, and the wolf trotted over. She sent another thread of healing to the wound, but couldn't repair the wolf's injured dignity.

"*Alpha, Bravo, and Delta. There were four, but one of them died the first day.*" He was silent for a long moment. "*I never liked cremation duty.*"

"Me, neither." She ran her fingers through the wolf's rough coat and sighed for all the beloved animals she'd lost over the years. "Your two ravens are a non-fertile mated pair and bred to be pets, but they're about half again the standard size, so they'd be destroyed for unfair ecosystem advantage. They'll tolerate the cold, but they need clean water and bone-in meat every day, or they'll starve. There won't be enough winter carrion at this elevation. That huge aviary you built them is good, but give them more branches to sit on."

"*I traded for extra cases of dog food this summer. What else do they need?*"

"Grains, leftovers, especially any real meat, maybe some rotting fruit. They'll eat almost anything. You might make them some toys and puzzles with food rewards. Train them to do new tasks. Keeps their busy brains active instead of destructive."

"*I named them Shade and Shadow, after that tri-D serial about thieves. I recover an amazing amount of stuff every time I clean out their bowls and baths.*"

She chuckled at how disgruntled he sounded. "Your foo dog, Shiza, is legal, probably stolen. They're designed to look like little curly-haired lions from pre-flight Chinese legends, but underneath, they're mostly dog, so you can feed him whatever you feed Trouble. Don't let Shiza bite you out of anger or fear. Foo dogs are designed to protect children, and his teeth can inject a nasty toxin. I can use Nuñez's lab to tailor vaccines for you and the others, as well as Nuñez and me, but it'll take a ten-day or so."

The big wolf sat on her haunches and rested her head on Bethnee's shoulder. She stroked the wolf's broad head. "Long day, huh?"

"I'm sorry, I've taken up a lot of your time."

"No, I was talking to the dire wolf. Her life is in flux at the moment, and she's in here with me, wanting affection and reassurance."

Axur mumbled something in a language she didn't recognize. Her minimal education hadn't included anything but Standard English, and whatever rude words she could pick up on the streets. *"What about the miniature dinosaur? I think it's supposed to be a stegosaurus. Its name is Ankle Biter."*

She shook her head. "I don't do reptiles, amphibians, or fish. Can't feel them at all. Your reference manuals are your best bet. It might need to stay inside for the winter."

"Can I ask how you know so much about the pet trade? You don't seem like the type."

Ordinarily, she zeroed personal questions, but he was trusting her with the animals he loved. More tellingly, they all cared for him and trusted him without reservation.

She considered what she wanted to say. Jumpers willingly volunteered to work for the Citizen Protection Service's elite military force. The CPS hadn't done nearly as well by her, though to be fair, the huge agency had multiple missions, and it had been just the one corrupt woman.

"Never mind, it's none of my business."

"No, It's okay, it's just..." She couldn't come up with the right word. Talking about her past brought on a sour stomach and leg spasms, which was part of why she didn't do it often. "In the mandatory age-seventeen testing for minder talents, I scored high for animal-affinity minder talent. The CPS Testing Center agent *said* she got me a full scholarship at the CPS Minder Institute. Thrilled my parents, because I'd get the education they never had and couldn't afford for me. I didn't care, as long as I got to train my talent and work with animals."

"That's not what happened, I take it."

"She chemmed me, gave me an illegal chimera implant to change my DNA's biometric signature, and sent me as a counterfeit indenture to her cousin, a pet-trade dealer on a space station. She told my parents I died in a tragic interstellar passenger liner accident. Even sent them a memory diamond with my original DNA and a death payment. My bondholder made sure I knew that if I ever escaped and went home, they'd have to give back everything, which would bankrupt them."

She didn't understand Axur's reply, but the words were unmistakably curses. She envied his vocabulary.

"The first bondholder was okay. He got me training and promised I'd be a contract employee as soon as he could afford it, if I kept quiet how he got me. Three years after that, a bigger company destroyed his business and bought all his assets for a fraction. Instead of freeing me, Breitenbahn imprisoned me on an interstellar research ship. He only cared about results. I was the only 'employee' who couldn't leave, couldn't complain, couldn't fight back. And after all, I was just an indentured, subbin' minder."

Usually, she'd be shaking uncontrollably at this point, but now, she just felt queasy. Maybe it was different because Axur was just a sympathetic voice in her ear, and she was hanging on to a warm, hundred-kilo dire wolf who could sever a man's leg with a single bite.

"Breitenbahn finally made them stop abusing me when the animals started dying because I was too damaged to care for them or help the designers."

"How did you escape? I'm assuming they didn't suddenly find their lost ethics and let you go. You're far too valuable."

"Shipped myself in a container of comatose bovines bound for a remote frontier planet. It was dangerous, but Breitenbahn hired this new guard from the indenture system who wouldn't take 'no' for an answer. He shot me with an equine tranq and..." She shied away from the hideous memory. "Anyway, Nuñez was inspecting the shipment and found me. She believed my unbelievable story and took me home with her. Fed me, gave me animals to care for, made me a part of her vet business, and didn't judge. That was three years ago. I owe her more than I can ever repay."

"If I was still a Jumper, I'd invite some of my squad mates for a little vacation that just happened to coincide with the destruction of that ship."

"Thank you. I think." She smiled. "I probably shouldn't condone personal vengeance missions by elite special forces with access to really big guns and explosives."

"What can I say? We're trained to take the initiative. Lowlifes like Breiten-bahn are obviously a threat to the galactic peace."

"Well, if you ever get the chance, I hope you'll let me save as many of the animals as I can. They didn't ask to be there, either."

"I'll add it to the mission parameters."

She couldn't tell if he was teasing or serious. A vigorous gust of wind rattled the doors of the barn and blew in a cloud of pine needles. "Nuñez's yaks say it'll snow tonight. Do you have someplace warm for the birds of paradise?"

"Her yaks talk? Never mind. I figured I'd bring their cage into my bunk area until I can fix up the barn."

She looked up at the roof of the chilly barn and watched the dust swirl. "I could keep them for the winter, if you like. I have geothermal heating."

"Feeding them will add to your costs. I don't want to impose."

"You aren't imposing. I offered." She gently moved the wolf aside. "You can keep the dire wolf in trade. Give her a name. She'll love guarding you, and having the run of the valley when it snows. She's built for the cold. She'll eat a lot more than four birds, though. I'll trade removing the tracers from the rest of your animals, and a barrel of nutritional pellets that would be good for all your canines, to make it even."

In the ensuing silence, she got to her feet and brushed off her butt.

"Okay, we have a deal."

CHAPTER FIVE

GDAT 3241.254

Three months after meeting Bethnee, Axur pedaled the stationary generator cycle in his barn to give his anxiety a better outlet than churning his gut. Kivo had suddenly taken ill, and Bethnee had insisted on borrowing Nuñez's flitter and coming in person, despite a howling snowstorm. Axur had sequestered himself in the barn so as not to distract her. She'd grown more tolerant of Axur's physical proximity in their various interactions since they'd first met, but Kivo needed her full concentration.

The earwire idea had worked so well that first day that he'd created a better, customized version for her and convinced her to wear it everywhere. It helped make up for the lost camaraderie of his fellow Jumpers, and Bethnee seemed to enjoy having someone to talk to as well. She'd dubbed it the Axur-net.

They discussed the animals, and laughed about how unprepared each of them had been to find themselves homesteading on a frontier planet. He'd at least had extensive Jumper survival training to fall back on. She grew up on city streets and had spent the last eight years in space.

Jumpers weren't good at waiting and wondering. They climbed into planetfall mech suits and kicked ass. He peddled.

Two hours later found him adding worrying to the list of things he wasn't good at. Kivo had crashed twice, and each time, Bethnee had pulled him back from the brink. The last time she'd talked to him through the earwire, she'd sounded exhausted and distant, and she hadn't responded at all for the past ten minutes.

She was competent and smart, but something Nuñez had said one day, about a migraine headache being blowback from overusing her minder talent, had Axur thinking Bethnee might be in trouble. He wasn't trained to treat minders, because they weren't allowed in the Jumper Corps, but he was trained to treat humans. Despite what some zero-heads still thought, all minders were human. After five more minutes of plaguing himself with visions of calamity, he went back to his living quarters.

Kivo lay quietly where Axur had left him. Bethnee lay behind him, eyes closed, one arm and one knee draped loosely over him like a lover's. Kivo's breathing was steady. The tufted tip of one of his tails moved, and he swiveled one large ear toward Axur as he stepped closer.

Bethnee didn't so much as twitch, and looked pale and sweaty. If she'd been awake, she'd already be edging away.

He called her name softly, then louder, but got no response. He couldn't use his salvaged autodoc, because he didn't know how Bethnee would react to waking up in an enclosed cylinder little bigger than a cremation tube. That left his bed, which easily held him and various pets, so it wouldn't make her claustrophobic.

He gently extracted her from around Kivo and carried her toward the back room. She felt warmly female in his arms. He felt guilty even thinking it, because it would terrify her. He had no business wanting a woman who'd been treated as a subhuman, and beaten or worse to force compliance. Hell, the thoughts terrified him. He was the opposite of attractive, and had enough baggage to open his own tourist shop at the spaceport. He couldn't see how it would end well for either of them.

She began to convulse just as he got her to the bedroom door. He let her legs drop so she could throw up without hurting herself, but he couldn't catch enough of the mess with his cybernetic hand to keep it from soaking her shirt and pants. The stomach-churning smell assaulted his nose, but as a former battlefield medic and current household servant to nine pets, he was used to dealing with all sorts of unpleasant odors and substances.

By the time he got her into the fresher, she was barely responsive.

He sprayed her off as best he could, but she wasn't wearing her waterproof work tunic, and was soon soaked and shivering.

Telling himself he was looking but not seeing, he removed everything but her underwear, then draped her with one of his blankets and carried her to his bed. He quickly found her veterinary scanner and used it on her.

And since he was already being unethical by examining her without her permission, he evaluated her bad left leg, with its deep, ugly scars and distorted tendons and muscles. He swore in several languages as he dressed her in one of his tunics, then covered her up with more blankets. Since she had been a Concordance citizen, her kidnappers—he refused to call them bondholders—could have had her injury fixed for free anywhere in the Concordance. They'd purposefully left her untreated for years.

He couldn't ever return to the Jumpers again, and he was in no position to organize a mission against Bethnee's captors, but he did send a fervent prayer out to the constant stars to exact the justice he couldn't.

CHAPTER SIX

GDAT 3241.255

Bethnee woke to unfamiliar... everything. The soft glowlight on the wall, the cat purring on her chest, the furry body at her side, the too-long sleeve of her shirt. Not to mention, a room that looked like the shell of an interstellar ship's stateroom.

The bed shifted, and a golden furry face appeared above hers.

"Hello, Trouble." Her voice sounded raspy and her throat hurt. The dog licked at her cheek, then pushed off from the bed and left.

The furry warmth at her side stirred. Shiza, the square-jawed foo dog with the perpetual cute grimace and drooling habit, scrambled to his feet and shook himself, leaving a drifting cloud of curly golden fur.

Bethnee cautiously reached out with her talent to Delta, the cat on her chest, just to make sure she could. She'd exhausted all her reserves to save Kivo because she knew how much Axur loved the beast. She didn't even know if she'd succeeded. Or what time it was. Or how she came to be mostly naked in Axur's big bed. That realization made her feel aware, but not wary. She put the thought aside for later.

She sat up and discovered a veterinary fluids pump attached to the back of her hand. She was still staring at it stupidly when Axur appeared at the bedroom door.

"How do you feel?" He touched a control on the wall to make the lights brighter.

"Like hammered horse shi... " She trailed off as she got a good look at Axur. She'd never seen him without winter clothes and his heavy cloak, and now there he stood, damp and naked except for the towel around his trim waist and defined abdominals. He'd tied back the coiled strands of his long, frizzy hair, revealing a well-muscled chest that was a blend of warm brown skin, a few scars to give it character, and a smooth transition to his cybernetic arm, with its mismatched synthskin patches and exposed biometal. "You're stunning."

He blinked, clearly nonplussed.

"Sorry." She couldn't stop staring. Didn't want to, in fact. "From the way you talk, I'd thought you looked like a corroded, spare-parts cyborg from the serial sagas." That was probably the lamest thing she'd ever said. "Sorry. I'll shut up now."

He started to speak, but stopped himself. He seemed not to know what to do with his hands. "I'm not standing too close?"

"No." She tried to puzzle it out. Humans usually felt like phantoms to her, like she was listening to the wrong frequency. "Maybe I'm still sick from talent blowback sickness, but right now, you're not a ghost, you're solid. Like one of Nuñez's yaks."

He laughed out loud.

She shrugged, embarrassed. "Sorry."

"I'm flattered. Truly." His warm smile made her believe it. "Back to my original question. Your color is much better, and your temperature stabilized a while ago. How are you?"

"I'll live. How's Kivo?"

"See for yourself." He turned aside, and Kivo stepped forward, looking as healthy as she'd ever seen him. Relief flooded through her. He launched himself toward her to put his first set of paws on the bed and joyfully lick her face.

"Yes, all right." She rubbed his ears. "I'm happy to see you're alive, too." The aches in all her joints and the post-fever lethargy melted away at the affection Kivo was broadcasting. In that moment, she could readily believe Axur's theory that Kivo was an empath, just like Nuñez.

"I cleaned your clothes. Your earwire and percomp are on the table."

She had a hazy memory of a brightly lit room, and throwing up. "What time is it?"

"Eleven thirteen. Should be light out, but you can barely tell through the nonstop snow." At their latitude and a ten-day from the winter solstice, they got less than five hours of sun per day.

She was loath to leave the soft comfort of Axur's loving pets and his big bed, but she'd already kept him from it for ten hours, and she had to return Nuñez's flitter and get home. "Could I impose on you for the use of your fresher and something to eat?"

"Please don't kill me, but while you were unconscious, I examined your bad leg." Axur sat down at the other end of his small couch and sipped coffee from a large mug.

A flare of unease spiked, but she smothered it. Nothing had happened. Axur was her friend who talked to her every day. He wasn't a brutal man who drugged her and inflicted degradation and pain. Axur was a warm, strong, stolid yak. "And?"

"Completely repairable in any medical center with tissue-cloning facilities."

"And completely unaffordable. Homesteaders like me have to pay hard credit. Even settlers like Nuñez have to co-pay. This isn't the Concordance, yet." The swirling snow outside the window made her feel cold. She wasn't used to windows. "I have a better chance of winning the galactic lottery. Or I would, if I had enough hard credit to buy a ticket."

"I know, so I have a deal for you. You give me Serena, and come every ten-day to check on my pets and help me with two-person jobs. In exchange, I'll design a procedure my autodoc can handle to reattach the torn ligament and repair the lateral quadriceps muscle that gives you the most grief. You'd have to stay off it for the day and eat a lot to compensate for the rapid-heal, but it should improve your mobility and strength."

Her jaw dropped. "You have an *autodoc*?"

"Yeah, it came with the freighter. Running low on basic chems and anesthetics, though. I'll need more afterward."

"Holy hells. Do you have any idea what a working autodoc is worth? And with your medic training and language skills? Nuñez was right. You don't have to hide up here. Move into town, and they'd build you the clinic of your dreams. The settlement company couldn't stop them or even take a cut."

A grim look settled on his face. "I can't." The conviction in his tone left no room for argument.

She would have liked to point out that he was obviously lonely, based on how often he pinged her just to chat, but he knew what he could and couldn't do. She disliked it when Nuñez pushed her, so she wasn't going to do that to her only other friend on the planet.

"You'll need your autodoc supplies for yourself, so no deal on that. I'll take the rest of the trade, though—Serena for the extra pair of hands and veterinary care." The wolf in question was out in the blizzard, frolicking like she was a spring-loaded mountain goat instead of a dignified guardian. "Your place is better for her than mine."

He frowned and reached for his cup, but stopped to examine the exposed biometal knuckles of his cybernetic hand.

She moved Shiza, the warmth-seeking foo dog, off her lap, then stood and stepped into her boots. Alpha, the darkest cat, helped by batting at the decorative lacings. Beta jumped her, Delta jumped Beta, and a battle royale ensued. It was a wonder Axur's living quarters weren't a constant shamble.

She glanced at Axur, expecting to see him smiling at his silly cats, but he was looking up at her pensively.

"Ever heard of a Citizen Protection Service black-box project?"

"Er, maybe?" She dredged up the memory. "Something about secret weapons?"

"I am one."

She had no idea what he was talking about, but his bleak expression made her want to comfort him. "Because of your cybernetics? Lots of Jumpers have those, don't they? You can't all be weapons."

"Because of what's *in* my cybernetics. The CPS secretly 'volunteered' me for a research group's project that turned me into a continually broadcasting comm unit. I could probably uplink directly to the high-orbit galactic comms buoy from here."

"I'm sorry, I'm not following." She touched the earwire he'd given her and convinced her to wear, even when sleeping. "Is that how you made the Axur-net?"

He stood and turned to her, shoving his hands in his pockets. If she took one step closer, she could almost touch him. It was the closest she'd been to him without the fear taking over her motor control to make her tremble with the imperative to run, to hide. She gave herself a mental shake to refocus on what Axur was saying.

"...first in my squad to try out the new, better battery in my cybernetic legs. I woke up in a space station in a high-security research clinic, with a new cybernetic arm that I didn't need, and a satellite uplink built into me. The assholes stole me and altered the records to make it look like I'd signed on for their project. They told me their goal was to improve field communications for Jumpers, but I soon figured out the real purpose was to intercept, decrypt, and twist enemy comms."

Her sluggish brain finally put together a piece of the puzzle. "Your cloak. It blocks your broadcast." She looked around at Axur's quarters, made out of the pieces of an interstellar ship. "This is incalloy, for transit space. That's why you don't have to cover up in here."

"Yeah. I added a countervalent grid, powered by the ship's thousand-year batteries. It scatters my signal."

"Why do you need to?"

"Because ten months ago, I stole this freighter and escaped. The CPS wants me back, and not to return me to my squad." He held up his cybernetic hand. "I'm still tuned up to enhanced Jumper speed and strength, which is illegal outside the Corps. I really am a cyborg. Point is, my cybernetics have enough experimental nanotech to buy Del'Arche's entire settlement debt. I'm the only survivor of ten other 'volunteers.'" He rocked on his heels. "When my signal pings any official comm system, the system records my unique comm signature. If that got back to the main Concor-dance net, it would likely trigger a galaxy-wide detain-and-restrain order on me that says I'm dangerously delusional, and offers a juicy reward to keep me iced until the fastest CPS cruiser can get here."

"I'm sorry, Axur. That farkin' flatlines." She didn't know what else to say. No minder talent in the universe could change the past, and she didn't know any minder forecasters who could advise him on how to improve his future. She limped to her vet bag on the table to check that it was sealed tight.

Axur grabbed his coat and step into his combat-style boots. "I'll clear the path again and warm up the flitter."

She eyed his everyday work pants. "Do your legs feel cold?"

"No, they're internally heated to normal body temperature. My processor interface tells me what the external temperature is." He smiled ruefully. "My ass and dangly bits get cold, though."

She laughed at his phrasing. He had the oddest euphemisms for genitalia.

He bunched his hair on top of his head so he could slip on his fancy transparent snow hood. "Some Jumpers choose to have the full input-to-nerve mapping done, to make the synthskin and cybernetics feel as real as possible, but I didn't want to be distracted by phantom sensations." He flexed his cybernetic hand. "The researchers did it for my arm without asking what I wanted. After I landed, I had to hack into my own processor to make it quit telling me about the burns. Even though I have the key, it took me days because of the evolving cryptogon."

He lifted his heavy cloak and pushed his head through the round open-ing, then sealed it. "I'll be on earwire."

He slid open the door to reveal a snow-covered wolf, who danced back in excitement when she realized Axur was coming outside.

His tone signaled in her earwire. *"Feel free to raid the cabinets or cold box if you're still hungry. You had a stressful night."* Heavy breaths of exertion punctuated his words.

"I'm good. I've been looking at your decor. Very mad techno. Did they teach you that in Jumper school?"

"Some. I learn languages more quickly when I busy my hands. The CPS researchers gave me comm specialist courses, and started training me to use the new tech I'm carrying. Even trained me how to repair my cybernetics. When they gave me control during testing and forgot to turn it off over lunch, I cracked their internal security and read everything, not just the sanitized version they gave me, which is how I found out about the nine other test-subject fatalities. I sure as hell didn't want to be number ten."

"I'm glad you escaped." As she said the words, she realized her life would be immeasurably less interesting without Axur in it. Because he wasn't there in front of her, it was easier to ask the question that had been bothering her. "Are you staying away from Tanimai because you're afraid someone in town would betray you to the CPS?" Someone like Nuñez, or her.

"No. If and when the CPS captures me, they wouldn't care who they else hurt, including anyone they thought I'd shared secrets with. Out here, they only catch me, and leave the town alone."

The implications of his story sank in. "You're just like Kivo. You're a failed experiment they want to dissect." She took his silence to mean he'd already thought of that. "Why did you tell me all this now?"

The answer was a long time in coming.

"Because if you come up here someday and I'm gone, I wanted you to know that it wasn't my choice."

The thought of losing him to that fate terrified her worse than the fear response when the man got too close. And if that wasn't a complete contradiction, she didn't know what was. She felt like she ought to say something. "I would take care of your animals."

"Thank you. They're my family."

"Don't you have any of your own?" Not that he could go home while he was still a fugitive, but maybe he could see them again someday. People lived to a hundred and seventy and more with modern medicine.

"Dead. Con-Kella Pandemic of 3215. I was raised in group homes. The Jumper Corps became my family after that. What about you?"

"Only child, or at least I was. I made friends with every stray animal in the neighborhood, and figured I'd work at a rescue shelter." She gave a self-deprecatory laugh. "And look at me now, on top of the world."

"I'm at the barn. I'll send Serena to walk you down to the flitter."

"Okay." She took a deep breath and spoke before she lost her nerve. "You could come with me."

"Why, are you feeling sick?"

"No, it's just... I don't... You should..." The unexpected rise of emotion tangled her tongue. "My place is hard to find and well protected. If I show you where it is, and you need somewhere to hide, you could go there."

The silence stretched. She wished she could see his face, because maybe he wasn't interested, or thought the idea was lame.

"Okay."

An hour later, she landed the flitter on the snow-dusted gravel of her homestead's landing pad. Nuñez had told her to keep the flitter until the next day. The storm had finally stopped, but left deep snow behind.

Bethnee checked her security system's activity monitor, then opened the flitter doors. She collected her kit, locked the doors, and caught Axur's eye. "Stay on my trail so you don't get lost."

She led the way up the path to her home. Under the obscuring snow, it looked like ramshackle stacks of logs between a cluster of tall boulders. Kivo whined excitedly as she opened her front door and led him and Axur-the-yak inside. He was only her second human visitor. She'd have never believed she'd ever allow a man into her house if she hadn't been living it at that moment.

She turned on the lights, then pointed to the hooks by the door. "Hang your stuff there."

She'd already sent her talent out to her animals to tell them she was coming, and warn them about the stranger. Axur's tribe comprised extraordinary, valuable pets. Hers were civilization's discards, like her.

After Axur wrestled off his coat while leaving his shielding cloak in place, he stepped into the cabin's common area to look around. She'd purposefully left this part of her home looking primitive and half-dilapidated to fool any would-be intruders. She saw on his face the moment he started noticing the little features that would make an uninvited guest's life miserable.

"Impressive." He gave her a sly smile. "I'm glad I'm not your enemy."

"There's more outside. I'll show you before dark. I add to them when I get a new idea. I need a place to feel safe."

"Copy that." He tilted his head toward the back, hidden in shadows. "That where you really live?"

"Yeah, come on back."

CHAPTER SEVEN

GDAT 3241.255

Axur decided that calling Bethnee's place a cave was like calling Kivo a pet—true as far as it went, but a wholly inadequate description. The log cabin front concealed the sealed entrance to an extensive cave system. Its main feature was a subterranean hot spring that she'd taken full advantage of to create habitats for herself and her animals. He especially envied the temperature-regulated pool she'd carved into a natural depression in the cave.

Until he saw her relaxed in her own environment, he never realized how effectively she hid her vibrancy and unconventional beauty. She'd even come within centimeters of him a couple of times without flinching. A strong desire to touch her and be touched back arced through him. He locked his knees and shoved his fists in his pockets under his poncho. It wasn't just general lust, because he didn't want physical affection the other women he'd interacted with in town, and males didn't flux his drive. He shouldn't have agreed to come, but loneliness and longing overrode his reservations.

He shoved his conflict into the outsized box of things he couldn't control and focused on something he could. "So, I've met everyone except Jynx."

Bethnee grinned. "I saved her for last, because you'll like her best."

"It'll be hard to top a white weasel trained to steal." He pointed toward her indoor garden, which she'd created by widening a natural cave cathedral and piping in circulating hot water and air. "Not to mention, an indoor bamboo forest to keep a half-blind red panda happy."

"Come see."

She took him through a narrow, curving corridor that led to a notice-ably cooler part of the cave. The near-frosty air was a shock after the heat of the garden. Kivo's attention was riveted on the tall rows of stacked crates along the wall.

From between an opening in the stacks, a fully-grown snow leopard padded in. She glanced once at him and Kivo in seeming boredom as she gracefully jumped up onto the battered table. She sat and curled her long tail around her, watching Bethnee.

He started to speak, but was interrupted by a low, rusty-sounding half-growl from Jynx. "Is she torqued?"

Bethnee laughed as she stretched a hand out and moved closer to sink her fingers into the thick fur on the cat's neck. "No, that's just her 'hello.' It's called chuffing. You can come closer. It's a dirty little secret in the planet terraform industry that the last of the snow leopards died in a zoo long before First Flight, and that all the 'naturals' are actually recreations. She's designer, not feral. I've let her know that you and Kivo are my friends."

He edged closer, trying not to stress Bethnee but wanting a better look at the big cat's left front leg. "I've never seen an animal with cybernetics." The cat's distinctive spotted fur ended with a ragged transition to the raw, articulated biometal model of a cat's leg. The toes on the wide paw had lethal biometal claws. If she'd ever had synthskin—synthfur?—it was gone now.

"And you probably won't see another. Animal brains usually reject the motile processor input, even with complete nerve mapping. She's unique, and worth a fortune." Jynx chuffed again, showing her sharp carnivore's teeth. "Nuñez found her at the spaceport, wrapped like a mummy, half-dead, in a secret compartment of a large-animal container." Bethnee chuck-led. "The yaks get nervous just smelling her, so Nuñez gave her to me. Besides, her visible biometal makes her a theft magnet. I can't let her go out very often."

Following instinct, Axur held out both his human and cybernetic hands for Jynx to smell. He smiled when she rubbed her head on both, marking him with her scent. "Cats are cats."

"Yep." She leaned her hip against the table. "I had a devious reason for inviting you here."

He grinned at her. "You're the least devious person I know."

She snorted. "I'm the least *tactful* person you know. There's a differ-ence." She pushed a stray lock of dark hair behind her ear. His fingers tingled with the desire to find out if it felt as silky as it looked. "I was hoping you'd look at Jynx's cybernetic biometal-to-bone interface and tell me what needs fixing. When she jumps down from more than a few meters, her shoulder collapses, and now she's afraid of going up high."

She pointed to stacks of crates. "I had to move her den down to floor level, and that makes her nervous."

"I'm willing," he said dubiously, "but I know absolute zero about leopard anatomy. We'd have to take her back to my place for the tools and computers. And even then, her cybernetics might be a whole different design."

"If we pool our skills and talents, I'd sure like to try." She rubbed Jynx's ear. "Humans have treated her so badly. She deserves the best life I can give her."

He'd have given anything to take Bethnee's sadness away, but he'd used up his lifetime quota of miracles when he'd escaped the CPS researchers. He shoved his hands in his pockets. "Whenever you're ready."

Four days later, Axur quickly carried forty kilos of chemmed snow leopard to the temporary exam table he'd rigged in his workroom. Jynx had made a bad jump the day before and was in constant pain.

"Did this room used to be the nav pod?" Bethnee asked. Her hands trembled when she wasn't focused on the leopard.

"Yes." He hunched over to lay Jynx on her side on the folded blankets. He maneuvered around to the other side of the table. "The landing drilled the freighter partway into the mountain, so I took advantage of it and dug in more." He smiled. "I didn't win the hot-spring lottery like you did."

He pulled the big tech scanner down close to the leopard's leg. "We're in luck. She's got a hidden jackwire port at the shoulder interface." He pulled one of his longwires from the tray and held it out to Bethnee. "I'll show you where, if you'll insert it. When I run a diagnostic, tell me if it hurts her."

She inserted the wire with a steady hand. "Go."

He touched a control and watched the readout. "Standard processor, zero security. They must not have expected to lose her." He frowned. "Battery is *old*-old style, and running low." He looked at Bethnee. "I don't know how your talent works, but can you check the interface area for temperature? Her processor is conserving battery power by reducing the leg's internal heat generation." He put his human hand on Jynx's shoulder at the interface to see if he could feel the difference.

Bethnee's eyes lost focus, a sign she was using her talent. "It feels numb to her, but it always has. I thought that was normal." She frowned. "Damn, I think I missed a passive tracer, right at the interface. The cybernetics must have masked it."

He moved his hand aside so she could lean over and probe with delicate fingers.

"It's faint..." Her voice trailed off, and she straightened abruptly. "It's in *your* hand."

"What?" He flexed his fingers. "Frelling hell. I removed the standard Jumper tracers and the extras in my cybernetics. I never thought to look elsewhere."

"You might have missed them, anyway. It's pet grade. Tiny." She shook her head. "I don't know why, but ever since I healed Kivo, you've felt real to me, not like a ghost. I think I could tell you where the tracers are, if I get close enough." She blew out a loud breath and looked at her shaking hands. "And if I don't flatline." She crossed her arms and shoved her hands under her armpits.

Just great. The woman he most wanted to get close to was terrified at the thought of even touching him. "Let's deal with Jynx first."

The fix was easy to describe—replace Jynx's failing battery with one of his spares—and hard to achieve. What would have been a ten-minute procedure in a Jumper med center turned into three hours of guesswork and improvisation using repurposed equipment in his temporary lab. The trickiest part had been helping Jynx interpret and accept the full input from her cybernetic processor.

Axur triggered two mealpacks as Bethnee encouraged the leopard to walk in circles around the couch.

"We could take Jynx outside after lunch."

"Good." Bethnee smiled. "She's just humoring me, walking around in here. Thanks for giving up one of your batteries. At full strength, she's amazing."

"It's a good cause." He wanted to tell Bethnee *she* was amazing, with her courage to fight through debilitating post-trauma stress to help her pets and his, but didn't think she'd like the reminder. He pushed the heated tray across the counter toward her. "I'm glad the freighter had enough mealpacks for a decade, but I'm looking forward to growing season again. I was lucky the freighter was shipping seed starts and had a superb library in the shipcomp."

"I want to create a hydroponic garden in my cave." She crossed to the counter and pulled out the mealpack's utensils. "It works for starships."

"I can print small flexible parts for you, like nozzles and connectors, if you can trade for lexo substrate."

She nearly choked. "You have a working *printer*?" She set her fork down and stared at him. "The only other printer within a hundred kilometers is owned by the settlement company, and they only take hard credit. You could trade for anything you wanted. *Anything*."

"I had no idea." Once again, he was surprised at all the things he'd taken for granted in his former life.

She frowned. "Actually, you might want to keep quiet until you read the settlement contract's salvage rights sections. Nuñez sent you a copy, didn't she?"

He nodded. "Yes." He'd only read the part about homesteading, which said if he could improve a perimeter-marked plot of land for two years, it became his, and conferred legal resident status with it. If the company caught him before that, they'd haul him into the Concordance and charge him with trespass. And that was only if the relentless CPS didn't find him first.

Axur would bet hard credit that he and Bethnee were the only two people in the galaxy who had ever seen a cybernetic snow leopard and a formidable dire wolf play tag in the deep snow.

Bethnee laughed when Jynx made an astonishing six-meter leap onto a boulder to avoid Serena's lunge. He snuck a glance at Bethnee, enjoying her happiness. "Are you helping them get along?" He tapped his temple, to indicate her enviable minder talent.

"A little. Mostly Jynx, because this isn't her territory."

He checked his internal chrono. "We better start collecting your gear. I'll send Trouble out to keep an eye on these two." Axur had yet to be able to crack the encryption on the e-dog's command processor that Bethnee had told him about, but he kept trying.

Inside, he found Bethnee leaning against the kitchen counter, holding her small veterinary surgical suite. "I'd like to try removing your tracers."

He blinked in surprise. "Now? Are you sure?"

"Hell, no, but it'll be worse if I give myself time to think about it." She searched his face. "Unless you don't trust me?"

"I trust you with anything except making coffee. Where do you want me?"

"Chair, I guess."

He hesitated, then pulled off his shirt and sat. "Let's try this first." Jumpers gave up caring about nudity in the first ten-day of training, but she might not be so comfortable, especially considering his gender. He held out his hand.

She opened the suite, exposing the instrumented interior, then swallowed visibly and took slow steps toward him. "Talk to me. Tell me how you escaped the shitheads who put tracers in you like you were a lab animal." She rested trembling, cool fingertips on the back of his hand. "I like the sound of your voice."

He described how he made off with hoarded supplies, including extra batteries and tools, and hijacked the freighter. A lucky torpedo right before he went transit forced him to reprogram the navcomp on the fly to exit at Del'Arche, where he skidded in on a failing system drive and scorched, cracked atmosphere wings.

She trembled the whole time, but she found and excised the tracers in his wrist, upper arm, and both of his shoulder blades. The surgical suite made it quick and nearly painless. The tracers under his collarbones were harder for both of them. Tremors wracked her, but she stuck to her task. He closed his eyes, but the butterfly touch of her cool fingers and the warm scent of her saturated his senses. He could no more prevent his erection than he could prevent his satellite uplink from broadcasting. He prayed to the constant stars she wouldn't notice, or he'd never see her again.

When the suite sounded its completion chime, she pulled it off and lurched toward the front door to slide it open. She panted like she'd been running low on oxygen in her space exosuit.

After a moment of indecision, Axur climbed to his feet and pulled on his shirt, letting it hang loose over the front of his pants.

She turned back to him, looking pale and exhausted. "Sorry. I'm a warped mess." She brushed a strand of hair behind her ear. "You've got four more." A tear fell. She brushed it away absently.

"That's enough for today. If the CPS is close enough to ping-trace the rest of them, I'm as good as iced, anyway." He picked up the crate of her supplies. "No need to apologize for negative stress feedback. I've had it, and it's no less debilitating because it's just in your mind. Jumpers are lucky enough to get quick support and professional treatment from top-level minders and medics."

She gave him a watery smile. "I thought you said Jumpers ate pain for breakfast."

"We do. But we acknowledge the pain for each other, so no one has to carry it alone." He took a deep breath and let it out slowly, hoping to drain off the anger he felt at what he'd lost, what they'd both lost. "We look out for each other, because no one else will."

CHAPTER EIGHT

GDAT 3241.264

A hard fall off her glide board onto her bad leg left Bethnee barely hobbling as she let herself into her cabin. The added weight of her vet medic kit brought clawing pain with every step as she re-armed the security systems and checked the logs and the analog telltales. No one had bothered her in the two years she'd lived there, but carelessness was no longer in her nature.

She made halting progress to the cave's kitchen, escorted by her pets. She couldn't afford to be disabled, or she and the animals would go hungry. She wished Axur hadn't suggested they try to heal her leg with the autodoc, because she was tempted to take him up on the offer.

It had been five days since she and Axur had fixed Jynx—and since Bethnee had failed to finish removing the tracers from Axur. He pinged her that night and since, as if nothing had changed. Maybe it hadn't for him, but her world had tilted on its axis.

She'd willingly touched a warm, half-naked man. Her dark, horrific memories had lost some of their power. Maybe it was time, but more likely, it was the healing balm of Axur. Handsome, resilient, clever, caring Axur, who resurrected memories of her younger days when sex was sweet and teenage dreams brimmed with passion and romance. Those memories used to belong to a forgotten stranger, but she could almost believe they were hers again.

Most of her reaction when she'd removed the tracers had been fighting the impulse to touch him, like a lover. It scared and exhilarated her. And the realization that he'd been sexually aroused by skinny, scarred her had made her almost forget to breathe. She'd let him think she was still afraid because he was a man with the power to break her body, when the truth was, she was newly terrified that he had the power to shatter her heart.

She could remain silent and maintain the friendly status quo, but could she live with herself if she did? She wasn't Jumper brave, but she'd worked so hard not to let fear rule her. It wasn't fair to either of them for her to stand in the doorway like a cat, neither going all the way out or in. She didn't know what he wanted, but she'd never find out if she didn't ask. She tapped her Axur-net earwire and waited for his response.

"Hey. I'm glad you pinged. I have an idea for fixing my broadcasting comms problem, but I need your help."

His voice sounded like he was right next to her, whispering into her ear, making her stomach flutter.

"Sure." She took a deep, steadying breath. "What do you want in trade to use your autodoc to fix my leg?"

The weak winter sun turned the snow glossy as Bethnee looked out the window of Axur's home. She hated being a patient, but knew she'd be just as attentive if Nuñez or Axur got hurt, so she accepted his coddling. In moderation.

"I thought I told you to stay off the leg," said Axur.

She turned to watch as he rolled in a cart filled with tools and equipment. "I hopped."

He rolled his eyes. "You're worse than a combat Jumper." He pointed to the chair and footrest he'd rigged for her. "Sit."

She hopped back and eased herself down. "It's boring."

"Yeah, well, that's why you're going to help me crack my second processor." He pushed the cart next to her chair, then put his stool next to it. "You need to eat like a Jumper today. Are you hungry yet?"

"No. Shaky, though."

"Am I too close?" He started to move the stool, but she put her hand on it.

"No." She pointed to the space just in front of her. "Sit and tell me what you want me to do." When he hesitated, she added, "You're still a yak."

He sat, watching her carefully as he did. She sent out a thread of talent to him, letting the solid strength of him fill her senses. Her new strategy had worked so far, even when she'd been pantsless in front of him and needed his help to lift her badly bruised leg into the autodoc. Admittedly, she'd had to reach for the minds of the trusting animals to remind her brain how to stay calm, but she still put it in the win column.

"Yesterday, I finally cracked Trouble's command module security. Mine looks similar." He held up a small hexagon-shaped percomp and a longwire. "I'm going to jack in, but if I trip the kill switch the researchers threatened me with, I'll need you to reinitialize me. I'll show you how."

"It's sweet of you to not see me as a technological flatliner, but we both know the truth." She stifled an impulse to reach out and stroke his arm.

"That's why I'm going to show you. I stayed up last night and built some routines to try if the normal sequence fails." He opened a flat display and pointed to a long list. "They're in order of what I think you should try first, but I added notes about what they do, so you can use your judgment."

"You did all this last night?" She knew he was a get-it-done kind of person—probably all Jumpers were—but this seemed excessive. "Why the rush?"

He looked away from her, then back. "It's like you said. I'm hiding up here. Letting my limitations imprison me as much as the researchers did. I only see you and Nuñez, and townspeople for trades. I was good at being a Jumper, but that's gone, so I need a new career."

The thought of losing him burned like a beamer through her heart, but she couldn't begrudge him his freedom, any more than she could begrudge Jynx enjoying her recovered strength and agility. Axur's premium skills and valuable ship contents meant he could move to a warm southern city. After what the Citizen Protection Service had done to him, he deserved more than a quirky little town of misfits and a damaged, graceless woman who thought of him as a yak.

"Okay," she said. "Show me what to do."

"I'm in! My uplink controller isn't just similar to Trouble's, it's the exact same model, just customized."

It had taken Axur over forty minutes to explain all the contingencies he'd come up with, and less than ten minutes to crack his system on the first try.

"Congratulations." She couldn't help but smile in response to his delight. "Once I extract your other tracers, you can be truly free." Her bad leg was pins and needles, like she'd run into a cactus, but she'd take that over weak and numb. She slid her leg off the footrest and ignored the wave of wooziness that washed over her when she sat up too fast. "Fresher first, though."

"I'll get your crutches." He stood and gave her a stern look. "Stay put."

The natural light from the window made a bronze halo of his frizzy hair, which he'd grown to make him less recognizable. His short, darker beard highlighted his strong jaw. His thin knit shirt stretched across his wide shoulders and muscled chest, giving her the urge to snuggle against his warmth. She smiled up at him. "You're an impossibly gorgeous man."

He gave her an assessing look. "I think you're reacting abnormally to the recovery chems."

"Maybe," she conceded. "Normal and I have rarely been on speaking terms." A warm sensation flushed through her and pooled in her pelvis. "I think I could kiss you right now, and not even twitch." She lifted her rock-steady hand up to him in invitation and smiled. "Want to experiment? It'd be for science."

"No," he said firmly. "Not that I don't want to kiss you, because I do, more than you know, but you are nowhere near capable of consent right now." He backed away and shoved his hands in his pockets, making his shoulders and pectoral muscles flex deliciously. "If you still want to kiss me tomorrow, we'll talk about it."

The afternoon passed in a blur as she alternately ate snacks and dozed on the couch. She was soon victimized by small animals that wanted a warm body to sleep on or next to. She dreamily watched him solving the mysteries of his uplink, thinking him brilliant and sexy, wishing she weren't too impaired to savor the holiday from her responsibilities and her fears.

She finally woke and sat up around the time he was serving dinner. "Am I allowed to try walking now?" She massaged her thigh gently. "I have more sensation in the lateral muscle than I've had in years."

"That depends. Are you still dizzy?" He gave her a sardonic smile. "Do you still want to kiss me?"

She met his query with a steady gaze. "No, and yes."

He drew a surprised breath, then shook his head. "Use the crutches. Your brain isn't exactly green-go right now."

She sighed, knowing he was probably right. Even if the weird chems reaction temporarily freed her to act on her desire to invite herself into his bed for a hot connect, it wouldn't be pleasant for either of them when her old fears came back online the next morning.

She levered herself up onto the crutches and made her way to the fresher. When she returned, she put a package in front of him. "Happy Solstice Day." She triggered her mealpack's heater.

He blinked in surprise, darting his glance between her and the package. His smile grew as he untied the twine and opened it. "Real coffee!" He held the cloth bag to his nose and took in the scent appreciatively. He held up the other gift. "What's on the longwire?"

"Common and relic language courses." She pulled out the utensils from her mealpack. "You said you don't have anyone to practice with. I only know Standard English and street slang, and Nuñez has mostly forgotten her family's Tagalog, so I traded for the courses whenever I treated pets. You can help me expand my horizons. I need more swear words."

He smiled as he put the longwire in his shirt pocket and patted it. "Thank you."

Seeing how much the simple gifts pleased him, she vowed to give him as many as she could before he left for wider, warmer pastures. She must still be farked by the chems, because the thought made her want to hug him tight and cry on his broad shoulder.

He triggered the heater on his mealpack. "I have presents for you and Nuñez, too." Something on his cart beeped, and he grinned. "Excuse me a minute."

Axur returned with a small percomp strapped to his cybernetic wrist, and removed a disgruntled cat from his chair so he could sit. Beta promptly jumped into Bethnee's lap and settled.

"Okay," she said. "Remember that I'm tech illiterate, and explain to me what you've been doing. I think I'm awake enough to keep it straight."

"I downloaded copies of my processor and controller software, so I could test things on the comp instead of me." He pointed a thumb to his equipment cart. "Luckily, I exited the CPS research program earlier than planned, so my tech's code isn't encrypted. The downside is, not everything works right, and they'd only just started training me on how to use it. I'll need time to reverse-engineer it and figure out what I can do."

He talked between bites. "I turned off the uplink. I'll be glad to retire my poncho. Then I purged my unique comm signature from the dozens of dataspaces they squirreled it away."

She nodded. "Sounds like the tech equivalent of the tracers."

"Yeah, that's me, valuable research animal." He finished the entrée portion of his meal. "I just finished a prog that'll let me uplink with whatever signature I want and control it with the cybernetic interface in my ocular implant. Next, I have to figure out how to twist the continental geomarkers."

"Twist them?" She frowned. "Won't that mess up navigation around here?"

"No, not the geomarkers themselves, just the ping refs that go with my signal. Most comms satellites record signal origination data along with the unique ID. It'd be suspicious if a flurry of new IDs all came from outside one tiny mountain town, or with no refs at all. At the very least, it'd trigger a settlement company audit, which would *not* make me popular in Tanimai. I don't want my activities to trace back to anyone here."

"Why? What are you going to do?"

"Download every hypercube of data from the weather system. Technically, it belongs to the Del'Arche government." He scooped up the empty mealpack trays. "You said the satellite network was malfing at the time, but I want to look for evidence of my unexpected planetfall."

She chuckled. "Is that what Jumpers call a crash landing?"

A corner of his mouth twitched in humor. "Dull mission reports mean no unwanted attention from High Command." He glanced at her crutches on the floor. "Want to try walking?"

"Yeah, but first, I want to take advantage of what the recovery drugs have done to me, so I can finish getting the tracers out of you."

CHAPTER NINE

GDAT 3241.264

"Now?" It would mean getting naked for her. His hormones were instantly on board, which was exactly why it was a bad idea. His unavoidable erection and obvious desire would likely traumatize her, recovery-drug high or not. If he ever hoped to take their relationship to a deeper level, she needed time.

He took a breath, held it, and let it out. "I think we should let Nuñez do it."

"I'm not..." She trailed off. "Okay." She dropped her gaze and her head.

He knew he'd hurt her feelings, but didn't know how to fix it.

She stood up slowly, using the back of the chair for support. She rocked from side to side, as if testing her balance. "Feels weird. Strong, but weird." She started to take a step, then looked down at her feet with a frown. "I think I'm going to have to learn how to walk again."

"When they fit Jumpers with cybernetics, the physical terrorists tell us not to think about the mechanics, just focus on the intent to get somewhere."

"The whats?" She laughed. "Oh. Therapists." She turned. "I'll walk in here."

"Good." He watched Bethnee limp her way around the couch several times. "Are you limping because you have to, or out of habit?"

She stopped and looked at her legs. "Beats me." She shrugged. "I'll let you know tomorrow morning when we walk down to the flitter."

The satellite data he downloaded overnight was good, bad, and interesting. The network had indeed been offline for maintenance and hadn't captured his entry from orbit, but anyone skilled in reading surveillance images would recognize the landing furrow.

The interesting data came from the settlement company. His query had inadvertently garnered him the company's backup hypercube of corporate data and correspondence. A younger version of himself might've hesitated to read it, but being made into a research project had scoured the shine off his idealism.

He woke Bethnee. She sat up and pushed her hair back from her face. "What time is it?"

"Zero six hundred. Sorry, but we need to talk." He pointed to the table, where he'd set out a pitcher of water, cups, and two mealpacks. "Breakfast."

She stood and stretched again, and he looked away. The one glimpse of her mid-thigh-length sleeping tunic that clung to her high breasts, flared hips, and flat stomach threatened to derail his rational thoughts. He turned back to watch her limp toward the fresher door because she drew him like a magnet. She was definitely walking more easily than before.

When she returned, she looked more alert. "My leg is feeling good. Want to scan it?"

"Later. Are you awake enough to think deep thoughts?"

She sat. "Depends. I can't solve the time-versus-distance paradox in interstellar transit physics before breakfast." She triggered the mealpack's heater.

He laughed as he sat and triggered his own. "I'll tell the Concordance Science Achievement Award Committee to stand down, then."

She pointed to the display he'd left for her on the table. "What's this?"

"Background reading." He turned it on. "It's why the wakeup call."

She nodded, then took a bite and started reading the highlights he'd hastily put together. He saw on her face the moment she got to the part that had caused him to wake her so early.

"We have to warn the town. Daylight is only five hours from now. And what the hell kind of audit takes eleven people to conduct for a town of a hundred?"

"This is going to sound paranoid, but I think the audit is a cover for something else. A raid, a theft..."

Bethnee's eyes widened. "A hunt for a CPS fugitive." She stood abruptly. "You can't stay here."

He shook his head. "I have to." He crossed his arms. "It could be legit. The settlement company might be making a zero-tolerance example of Tanimai for cheating. If I get caught, the company could fine the town hard credits for not detaining an unregistered settler. If I'm the target, I don't want hunters anywhere near the town. I won't go back willingly. Which is why I want you to take the animals to the safety of your cave."

She stared at him for a long moment, and he braced himself for an argument. A resigned expression crossed her face. "Okay." She shoved her hands in her pockets. "You know what you can and can't do. I hate leaving you here alone, but I'm worthless in a fight, and I don't want the animals to be casualties, or hostages for your cooperation."

He let out the breath he didn't realized he'd been holding. "Thank you." Her trust humbled him.

Bethnee made it look easy to load a menagerie of animals into the close confines of the flitter. He'd probably still be trying to catch one of the cats.

He handed Bethnee an earwire. "A spare for our net."

She put it in the top pocket of her coat. "Okay."

He handed her a slender length of rounded incalloy, with padding at one end and a bulge of fine wire net at the other. "Homemade shockstick." He showed her how to operate it. "It's Nuñez's Solstice Day gift, because that asshole at the spaceport confiscated hers."

Bethnee smiled. "She'll love it. Thank you."

He handed her a small, flat box tied with a tiny strand of fiber cable, looped in a bow. "Your Solstice Day gift. Open it when you're safe."

She slid it into her lower pocket. "I'll ping you when I get home."

He fought a strong urge to fold her into an embrace, because her departure felt too much like goodbye. He stiffened his spine and stepped back.

She opened the flitter's pilot-side door, then hesitated and turned back. "Do you think I'm still warped by the recovery chems?"

"I doubt it. They usually metabolize in six or eight hours, tops."

"Okay." She stepped up and in, then turned to face him. "Then I think you should know, I still want to kiss you. Be safe, Axur Tragon."

She closed the door and lifted off ninety seconds later, by his internal chrono.

He buried his roiling emotions under the activity of dowsing the glow lights and resetting the analog security measures as he went back to his house. He prayed to the constant stars that the audit was just an audit, and that he'd be seeing Bethnee again soon, because he sure as hell wanted to be kissed by her, and return the favor.

CHAPTER TEN

GDAT 3241.265

Bethnee sent a short message from the air to Nuñez, but she had her hands full with flying and keeping threads of talent on eleven animals. She nearly turned around when she remembered the look of longing on Axur's face when she'd impulsively told him she wanted to kiss him.

She pinged him the moment she got the animals settled in the cave. Nuñez pinged a moment later. Bethnee told her what Axur had said about the audit timed for sunrise, and his suspicion about a hidden agenda.

"Farking assholes," Nuñez said vehemently. *"I'll get the local comm net going, in case the settlement company's uplink is being monitored."*

"I'll return your flitter to the clinic, and go home on my glide board."

Bethnee disconnected, then took a minute to send images to Axur's animals so they'd know the cave's layout and how to operate the pet doors. She wanted them to always have an escape route.

She grabbed her glide board, set the security system, and walked as fast as she could to the flitter, feeling time slipping away. It wasn't until after she was in the air that she realized she'd limped very little on the snowy path.

After delivering the flitter, Bethnee rode her board out of town. Just as she passed the last building, Nuñez pinged. Bethnee started to answer, but Nuñez was already talking.

"...he won't hurt you if you stay still. What are you two doing in my paddock? Back up, Upolu." Upolu was a large yak bull, with wickedly curled, sharp

horns and a dislike for strangers. Nuñez's conversation continued after a moment. *"Well, there's nothing to see back here but yak shit. I'll need to see your IDs and verify them with settlement compa—"*

The connection cut off.

Everyone in town knew about the yaks and the geese, so the interlopers had to be the auditors, come early. The "inadvertent" comm was Nuñez's way of warning her. Bethnee grounded the glide board and sent a quick warning to Nuñez's spouse, then pinged Axur with the news.

"Where are you?"

"Edge of town. I'm—" An ear-splitting, chest-rumbling whump made her instinctively duck her head. "I just heard a crash, but I can't see anything. I'll check the animals in the area." She sent threads of her talent out to all the animals she could find, both domestic and wild, and took advantage of their superior hearing and night vision to glean information. "I think it came from the Administrative Center. The building is collapsed inward."

"Isn't that where the satellite uplink is? Check your local comms."

She tried her percomp and the extra comm bracelet. "They're down."

"The best thing you can do is go home."

"I can't leave Nuñez."

"She has defenses and help. You're alone on a glide board. You're brave as hell, and I can't tell you what to do, but I will tell you that the hardest lesson a Jumper learns is when to retreat."

She blew out a frustrated breath. He was right. "I'll go home, if you'll use your fancy tech to figure out what's going on, and get help for Nuñez and the town if needed."

"Deal. Stay safe, Bethnee Bakonin."

She launched into the air again and hunkered down behind the board's wedge front to reduce wind drag. Guilt gave her second, third, and tenth thoughts about her decision. It felt like she was abandoning the generous woman who had saved her life and helped her learn how to live on her own. Bethnee would never forgive herself if Nuñez got hurt, but she'd also never forgive herself if she became the lever to bend Nuñez to their will.

CHAPTER ELEVEN

GDAT 3241.265

Bethnee was so distracted that she almost didn't notice the first sign that someone had breached her perimeter. The gossamer lengths of fiberet cable trailed down to the ground instead of invisibly spanning between the trees. An air vehicle had flown through and broken them, triggering the chemical reaction that made them faintly glow.

She veered off north into the trees and turned off the board's light, flying by terrain sensors alone. She slowed to almost a hover, a meter above the forest floor, maneuvering around the trees and boulders.

She heard voices. A man and a woman.

"What the hell is this stuff?" The man sounded outraged.

"Move slow. Grab my hand."

Bethnee grounded her board quietly behind a tree and buried it in the snow, fighting hard against instincts compelling her to run. The animals needed her to stay.

She sent threads of her talent to her animals and Axur's to tell them all to hide in the caves.

She heard squelching sounds as the intruders walked through her moat that had a mix of yak dung, mineral salts, and scrap glass road glue, kept warm by a geothermally heated grid at the bottom. Cold air would turn the mixture glass-hard.

Bethnee took a deep breath and let it out slowly, then peeked around the tree trunk. Two figures in one-piece blue snowsuits and transparent snow hoods trudged through the snow, away from the moat. She opened her talent senses, but as usual, the humans felt like ghosts. She extended further and felt two more ghosts, clustered near the front of her cabin. That was nearly half the auditor team.

She limped as fast as she dared to the edge of the trees. The interlopers were using both flying and hand lights. They'd see her crossing the main path.

She coaxed a nearby wild owl into looking at the front yard. Three men and a woman, all in one-piece snowsuits, stood at her front door.

"...haven't got all day. Let's go in and look, get the hell out of here. I don't like being restricted to stunners and tranqs." The woman sounded impatient.

"That's 'cause you'll shoot anything that moves."

"Like you're any better." The woman turned to one of the men, who held a display. "What does the scanner say?"

"House has powered security, but nothing outside... No, wait. One double-tech signature. That way, and close." The owl's vision showed her an image of a man pointing into the woods.

Ice flooded Bethnee's veins as she frantically powered down her earwire and comms bracelet, berating herself for stupidity.

"If it's the vet, she can let us in. Keeps us on schedule."

They must have figured out where she lived from homestead records. They hadn't asked permission to land, but it didn't pay to piss off auditors, if that's what they were. Especially auditors with weapons.

Her only hope was to lure them into the woods. None of her security measures were fatal, just strong deterrents for the uninvited. She switched her battery-powered wrist light to low-power green and risked brief flashes to tell her where to step over rocks and duck under the branches. Learning every meter of her property in light and dark had helped her feel safe. She skirted around the fifteen-meter clearing. On the far side, she switched her comms bracelet on and off, mimicking an intermittent signal.

Two interlopers came through the trees, their lights marking their progress. She backed further into the shadows. They plunged into the virgin snow of the clearing. A faint whipping sound whistled in the air.

"Son of a bitch!"

"Who the hell leaves coiled spikewire in the middle of farking nowhere?"

Bethnee took advantage of their noise to make her way down the hill. An empty flitter occupied her gravel landing pad. She limped behind it and down into trees to the southeast. Adrenaline jacked up her tension and turned her stomach sour. Her thigh spasmed.

The sound of another approaching flitter echoed against the rocks.

She scrambled under nearby shrubs. A smaller flitter landed behind the first. Two people exited and walked toward her house.

"...enforcers are coming to investigate." A woman's voice with a Mandarin accent. "Trummler wants us out by local dawn."

"I thought the auditor was supposed to intercept any calls from the area. We paid her enough." A man's voice, muffled by a high collar.

"Call came from an ex-Jumper, so the dispatcher took it seriously." The woman didn't sound happy.

Bethnee would have smiled if she weren't so scared. Clever Axur had found help.

Their words confirmed they weren't auditors, which meant they were after something or someone else. She didn't know what to do besides distract them so they'd leave her house alone, and delay them long enough so they'd run out of time and leave.

She'd never imagined she'd be wishing for a speedy visit by the Del'Arche Planetary Enforcers.

Bethnee had crammed herself into a rock hollow, wracking her brain for ideas. She was exhausted, and out of options, because dawn was coming.

The intruders failed to breach her house's security, and had grown increasingly irritated about not catching her.

She reached out to the animals again to make sure they were safe, and discovered Trouble, the e-dog, was outside the cave and headed toward her. His fleeting thoughts listened to the controller in his head with Axur's order to find Bethnee and protect her. She refused to put any of the animals in jeopardy for her.

"Got her!" said a male voice. "Scanner says she's moving twenty-three meters south. I'll send lights."

Trouble's controller was permanently on, meaning the intruders were keying on him. She'd promised Axur she'd keep his animals safe.

With trembling fingers, she powered on both her higher-powered comms bracelets and her earwire, then pinged Axur. She subvocalized as she slid out of the hollow and stood. "I hope you hear this soon. Six people are at my place. They can't get into my house. They've been chasing me. I'm going to let them catch me, or they'll hurt Trouble. Send the enforcers here if you can."

She limped her way out from under the trees. She didn't have to go far before lights flew close and a black-haired man and a blonde woman, both with blood spots on their pant legs, came toward her at a fast walk. She turned and ran away, exaggerating her limp so it looked like her top speed.

"Get her!"

The blonde woman ran, then launched herself at Bethnee to take them both down into the snow. The blonde woman got to her knees and roughly pulled off Bethnee's comm bracelets and earwire and threw them away. "You won't be needing these." She grinned like a shark. "I heard something bad happened to the town's satellite uplink." She grabbed Bethnee's arm and hauled her to her feet, then jabbed Bethnee's shoulder with an unpowered shockstick. "Where is it? Where's the shipment?"

"Wait," the black-haired man said. "Bring her to the cabin." He tilted his head toward her house.

Bethnee limped as slowly as she dared, using the time trudging through the snow to touch the strong, trusting minds of her animal family to keep herself from falling into a fog of fear. Her thigh muscle cramped once, then quieted. A small victory.

Three more people stood near her front door, all wearing the same new-looking blue snowsuits. They must have sent the man with the ruined one back to the flitter to stay warm. An Asian woman stood and watched, arms crossed and toe tapping, as a dark-skinned man with an upright crest of flame-red hair folded and pocketed a scanner. The third, a noticeably shorter man, pulled down his collar and stepped closer. He stared at her legs, then looked intently at her face. "Well, well, the God of the Gaps has finally answered my prayers. It's Bakonin."

She knew that face and voice from her worst nightmares. Kanaway, the guard with chems and perversions. The pieces fell into place. They weren't a freelance theft crew raiding the town, or CPS operatives looking for Axur. They were mercenaries after the bounty for a lost shipment of valuable designer pets. The shaking started, and coherent thought began to disintegrate. She desperately sent her talent out to every animal she could reach with the imperative to stay hidden. She forced herself to focus on the Asian woman's combat boots, counting toe taps. The animals depended on her to buy time for whoever was responding to Axur's call for help.

"What's wrong with her?" asked the black-haired man.

Kanaway grinned. "Oh, the little subbin' bitch wants me so bad she's trembling. Did you miss me?"

She shuddered, but somehow found the courage to look at him straight in the eye. "I hope Breitenbahn liked the record of what you did." She glanced down at his crotch. "Cured your soft and tiny problem yet?"

The blonde woman guffawed.

Rage flared in Kanaway's eyes as he slapped Bethnee. "That fake vid got me blacklisted." He slapped her again, harder. She staggered with the impact. She straightened up and spat blood. At least her time in Breitenbahn's circus had taught her how to take a hit.

The Asian woman gave Kanaway a hard look. "Enough. Domaki, find out where the shipment is and let's go."

Kanaway's lip curled in hatred, but stepped back. In Bethnee's jagged memories, he was big and impossibly strong, but seeing him now made her realize he was actually shorter than she was.

The red-haired man moved closer. "She's hard to read." He took off his glove. "I need to touch her."

The blonde woman grabbed Bethnee's arm, stripped off her glove, and forced her to hold out her hand. Domaki grabbed Bethnee's trembling fingers.

Bethnee felt the man's telepathic talent questing for her mind and memories. She plunged her mind into Jynx's and focused on the snow leopard's alien thoughts.

Distantly, she heard words, but Bethnee-the-leopard ignored them as unimportant.

Domaki pushed a succession of images of pet-trade animals at her mind. She didn't recognize any of them until he got to a foo dog and six-legged creature with two tails. She pulled out of Jynx's mind, because snow leopards didn't know how to lie. Bethnee shot Domaki a memory of when she'd treated Kivo for the near-fatal illness and his breathing had stopped. *Dead.*

All of them? demanded Domaki.

She felt him nibbling away at the corners of her mind, trying to access other memories. She called up image after image of animals she'd raised on Breitenbahn's ship, and let Domaki feel her deep sadness for each one she'd lost.

How do you know Kanaway?

The question took her by surprise, leaving her vulnerable to Domaki's probe into her darker memories. When he touched the worst of them, she felt the first wave of the familiar deep tremors.

Frelling hell! Domaki apparently didn't like her memories any more than she did.

She spitefully sent him the image of how she'd looked after Kanaway finished, with a swollen face, and bruises and blood everywhere. How he'd shoved her half-conscious body into a ship's autodoc to heal away evidence of the assault, unaware that security monitors recorded his actions.

Domaki hastily withdrew from Bethnee's mind. She collapsed to her knees, gasping for breath, unable to control her shudders.

Domaki backed away. "The research chimera died some time back. She hasn't seen any of the other animals."

"Bullshit," snarled Kanaway. "She's the only small-animal vet on the planet. She's a stubborn, lying bitch."

Domaki gave Kanaway a disgusted look. "Don't tell me how to do my job, you warped little twist." Domaki pulled on his glove. "It's been eleven months since the bounty was posted for that shipment, and the active tracers are in a herd of goats, not high-end pets. She doesn't know anything." He looked to the orange-tinged eastern sky. "If we leave now, we can meet Blue team at Point Exeter before it gets light."

"She'll have animals in her house." Kanaway could sound very reasonable when he wanted to. "If any of them are valuable, we can at least show a profit."

Domaki crossed his arms. "Ain't gonna be me that compels her to let us in." He cast another disgusted look at Kanaway. "Too many bad memories."

The Asian woman shook her head. "No more fishing. Trummler okayed this mission because Kanaway's intel pointed to Del'Arche for where the high-value shipment ended up, and it'd be a quick in-and-out to question the only two veterinarians. This is a bust." She waved a hand to encompass everyone. "Flitters airborne in five. Let's go." She pointed to Domaki. "Ride with Kanaway."

With the Asian woman leading, they walked purposefully down the path toward the flitters. Bethnee pivoted on her knees to watch them go. She tried to follow them with her talent, but it was like trying to follow phantoms.

She sent her talent out to search for Trouble. He was appallingly close, under a tree, and an easy target if one of the mercs had seen him. She collapsed onto her heels and let the muddy yellow dog come to her, even though it wouldn't be truly safe until the flitters took off.

Trouble allowed her to put an arm around him and hug him close. She wished the blonde woman hadn't stripped her Axur-net earwire, so she could hear his voice again.

Inexplicably, Trouble pulled away and stared intently at the path, growling softly.

"Come on, Domaki." Kanaway's voice. "The sooner we find my pet-tracer scanner, the sooner we get off this ice ball."

Bethnee sent a panicked imperative to Trouble to run, but it was too late. Kanaway and Domaki strode into view, their flying lights illuminating her and Trouble.

Kanaway looked triumphant. "This really is my lucky day." He pulled a stunner out of his pocket and casually shot Domaki twice. Domaki's body jolted like he'd been struck by lightning, then crumpled.

Kanaway aimed the stunner at her. "You're worth ten times the bounty of that research shipment." Avarice lit his face. "And I know just the buyer. He's been looking for you for three years."

CHAPTER TWELVE

GDATt 3241.265

Axur landed the runabout on the flat rocks above Bethnee's cave just as the sun crept over the mountaintops, burnishing their white tops with gold. She'd pointed out the path the first day he'd been there to meet Jynx. He loaded his gear and started down the steep trail. He sped up when one of the mercs said he'd forgotten a scanner and would catch up to the others soon. Merc companies weren't usually that disorganized.

Bethnee was likely paying the price for his mistakes, not the least of which was forgetting that the experimental tech in his cybernetics wasn't the only thing of value in the frozen north. He'd already been loading his runabout when he'd received her ping that she was planning to protect Trouble by letting the mercs catch her. He should have taken into account her willingness to sacrifice herself to protect the animals she loved. Her pet-trade captors had taught her she had no value, and he hadn't found the right time or words to tell her how much she meant to him.

At least the Del'Arche Planetary Enforcers were on their way. He'd lucked into an ex-Jumper answering his ping, and she'd believed him. Then he'd used his experimental tech to crack the raiders' temporary comms net.

They were a mercenary company specializing in freelance bounty hunts. While a southern squad went after a trio of brothers whose capture would bring a big payday back in the Concordance, a smaller northern squad went north for a stolen shipment of designer pets and anything else they could steal.

They'd only intended to disable the town's satellite uplink, but the cheaply made building had collapsed. The three culprits had joined their two teammates at Nuñez's vet clinic, where they'd been attacked by pissed-off geese and nearly been gored by an enraged yak. That team beat a hasty retreat to rendezvous with the main squad to the south. The remaining six went after veterinarian Bethnee because they knew the coordinates of her homestead.

The same homestead to which he, like the flatliner he was, had sent her and his animals, thinking to keep them out of harm's way.

From the trees near her cabin, he heard a man's voice but couldn't make out the words, and he couldn't tell where it was coming from. He wished he had hearing like a dog's... but he did, sort of. He tuned his experimental tech to Trouble's command processor, and pulled the auditory feeds.

"...the door right now, your filthy dog dies in front of you." A man's baritone but nasal voice, full of menace. "And you know I'll do it, too."

"It's open." Bethnee's ordinarily expressive voice sounded flat, defeated. Axur clenched his jaw.

"You first. No surprises."

Axur crept closer.

"Are you going to leave Domaki down on the path? He'll freeze." Her tone said she didn't care if he did.

"That's his problem. He was going to tell Na Ming lies about me, just like you did with that fake surveillance vid you sent Breitenbahn. He blamed me for your escape."

Axur eased westward, close enough to see a red-haired man down, blocking the path to the flitter pad. He ruthlessly stripped the unconscious man's weapons, percomp, and earwire, then zip-tied his wrists and ankles and rolled him off the path into the ditch full of snow. The heated snowsuit would protect him from the cold for a while.

"Turn on the lights," said the man with Bethnee and Trouble. "Where are the other animals?"

Axur ran down the path to the flitter, which they'd obligingly left unlocked. He pried open the control panel and used his homemade shockstick to good effect.

"I only have one other. This house is too small for him. Axur mostly lives in his den up the mountain, but he's closer today."

Axur smiled and let relief take some of his tension as he exited the flitter. Bethnee knew he was there, and was buying time. He sobered quickly, because she was playing a dangerous game.

"Pet trade?"

Axur ran up the path toward Bethnee's house.

"No."

"Liar. Make him come to you."

Axur used his cybernetic strength to jump to the top of the big three-meter-high rock in Bethnee's front yard, which made him less immediately noticeable if her captor happened to look outside. The sun was already over the trees, and would soon be higher.

"I can't get around his controller. He's not pet trade, he's military-enhanced." Axur heard the unmistakable sound of a slap.

"Call him, or I'll stun the dog and you both. Maybe have some naked playtime with you. Find out if you still like it rough and dirty."

Axur unslung his flechette gun and extended the guide for distance shots. His freighter had been sadly lacking in powered beamers, blasters, or railguns, so he'd made some analog weapons of his own, and practiced with them.

The mercenary comms band flared to life in his ear with an abrupt tone. *"Kanaway, Domaki, what's the holdup?"* The Mandarin-accented voice of the team leader sounded exasperated.

"Uh, Domaki ran into something in the vet's yard and got stunned. I'm rigging something to carry him on." Axur rolled his eyes at Kanaway's lame story.

"Quit fucking around, Kanaway, or I'll term you." The woman disconnected without waiting for Kanaway's reply.

Kanaway's ugly laugh rang out. *"Stupid bitch doesn't know what you are. I'll make Breitenbahn bleed credits to get you back. His business isn't so good since you left."*

Axur found a quasi-prone position on the rock and aimed his gun with its homemade flechettes loaded with quick-acting dormo. All he needed was a clear shot at Kanaway's bare skin.

"Call the animal. Now."

"We have to go outside, and leave the dog in here, or Axur won't come at all."

"Bullshit."

"Shoot me, then. Good luck carrying me all the way to your flitter. No grav carts around here like on Breitenbahn's ship."

Stunner fire sounded, and Trouble yelped loudly in pain. Axur forced himself to let it roll off him, or he wouldn't be calm enough to make the shot.

"Outside!"

After a long moment, Bethnee limped slowly through the doorway, then stumbled forward when the man shoved her. "Call him!"

She limped haltingly toward the center of the little yard and stopped. Kanaway followed too close to her for Axur to shoot him. She bowed her head for a long moment, then turned to her right and looked expectantly toward the trees.

Kanaway clamped one cruel hand on her neck and pointed the stunner toward the trees. A large raven landed in the tree and screeched, making Kanaway twitch.

A flicker of movement on Axur's right tugged at his attention. He risked a quick glance and caught a glimpse of a large, black-furred shadow stalking through the snow.

Axur winced at the loud tone in his merc comms earwire.

"Kanaway, we're coming for you and Domaki. Trummler's order." The team leader sounded disgruntled.

Kanaway took his hand off Bethnee long enough to touch his own earwire. "I'm already in the air." He spoke aloud rather than subvocalizing.

"Your flitter's tracer is reporting itself as stolen. We'll meet you in Tanimai."

Kanaway swore but said he'd be there. He stomped his foot in frustration and grabbed Bethnee's neck again. "Let's go."

She took one step, then stumbled sideways and landed on one knee. Kanaway let go as he struggled to keep his balance.

A black blur emerged from the trees to the west. Kanaway saw the movement, but too late to avoid being knocked down by a determined dire wolf. Kanaway's stunner sailed into the air and landed on the snowy gravel.

The man rolled sideways and up to his hands and knees. He crawled fast toward the fallen weapon, but had to duck and cover to avoid the attack of a huge black raven, cawing noisily, diving straight for his head. He threw himself toward the stunner, but not in time to stop the other black raven from stealing it in a flurry of flight.

Axur kept his gun trained on Kanaway, but couldn't get a clear angle without shooting Serena, who stood between Kanaway and Bethnee, growling menacingly.

Kanaway scrambled to his feet and spun to face the new threat. He held a phase knife in the stance of an experienced fighter. He touched his earwire and spoke aloud instead of subvocalizing. "Hey, Na Ming. Bring the big flitter back to the vet's house and get the tranq guns ready. She's got a fortune in stolen pets, starting with a trained dire wolf."

After a long moment, the Mandarin-accented woman's voice answered. *"Okay, but you better be on the level."* Na Ming sounded testy. *"We're fifteen minutes out."*

"See you soon." Kanaway touched his earwire again. His eyes hadn't once left the wolf. "Company's coming. Give us the pets, or I'll tell them what you are and what you're worth."

Bethnee stayed on her knees and said nothing.

Kanaway sidestepped toward the open door of Bethnee's house. "Since you were so anxious to get me out of your house, the others must be in there."

Axur wished he could talk to Bethnee, but since he couldn't, he reviewed his mission parameters. Protecting her was top priority, but she now had reinforcements from his animals, and probably hers. His secondary objective called for protecting them all from the mercenaries, which was a better use of his skills and resources, but it meant he'd have to leave Bethnee with a monster.

Axur fucking hated the hard choices of war.

CHAPTER THIRTEEN

GDAT 3241.265

Bethnee felt like she was floating. Adrenaline still soured her stomach and made her shake, but she'd apparently hit her limit on fear, and had no more to give.

Kanaway sneered. "Hey, Bakonin. How much does a dire wolf bring at auction?"

The man was trying to keep her afraid, not thinking. She'd had enough of that to last a lifetime. "I don't know. How much do you think I can trade for Domaki?" She'd seen through the raven's eyes when Axur had pushed the telepath into the snowdrift. "Wonder what he'll tell your bosses?"

Kanaway huffed. "They won't believe him. Minders are all liars."

She sent a thread of talent to cue preciously cute, plump Shiza, the little foo dog with the fierce heart of a lion. He waddled out into the weak midday sun and barked.

Kanaway turned. "See? Liars."

She asked Shiza to step closer to the man, but stay out of his reach. "Don't pick him up."

"What's he going to do, drool on me?" Kanaway laughed derisively.

Bethnee took a nervous breath, then sent Shiza instructions. He barked once, then turned to go back inside the house.

Kanaway glanced at the dire wolf, then focused on the foo dog. "Come here, you expensive little shit." His tone was cajoling as he patted his thigh.

Shiza slowed and turned to look up. Lightning fast, Kanaway dropped his phase knife to grab Shiza by the curly mane with both hands and drag him closer.

Enraged, Shiza twisted and bit down on Kanaway's exposed wrist.

Kanaway screamed and shook his arm, then rocked back a step back and kicked Shiza's ribs. The foo dog didn't let go. If Kanaway noticed a white weasel dart in and steal the phase knife, it didn't register.

Kanaway dropped to his knees, yelling, trying to roll Shiza onto his side. The foo dog planted his feet and used his strong neck and shoulder muscles to stay upright.

Bethnee climbed unsteadily to her feet and moved to stand by Serena.

"Get it off me!" He punched the dog's head, which caused Shiza to clamp down again even harder.

"Shiza," said Bethnee. She used her talent to help the foo dog realize he'd won. Shiza gave the man's crushed, bloody arm a tearing shake, then opened his wide, square jaws and scrabbled backward.

Kanaway lifted his good hand toward his face, but froze when Shiza keened and bared his sharp, bloody teeth.

Bethnee realized he'd been reaching for his earwire. She couldn't let him call for help. Before she could talk herself out of it, she pivoted in and stripped it off his face, then pivoted back. Her torn fingernail left a welt along his jaw. Blood welled immediately.

He swung a slow, sloppy punch at her. His venomous look would have once quelled her. He lifted his knee to put one foot on the ground. "You're fucking dead."

"No, but you are." She invited Shiza to come closer to her. The little dog limped a little as he moved to lean against her knee. "Foo dog poison is neuro-hemorrhagic, designed to kill quick, and you got two full injections. I told you not to pick him up."

"Bullshi'..." He shook his head as if trying to clear it. "They're sold to children... Prob'ly fast dormo or somethin'." His words slurred as he absently wiped red-stained drool off his chin with his good hand. The injured arm drooped listlessly at his side, gushing a pool of bright red blood onto the snow-whitened gravel. "You're gon' be my ticket back..."

He slumped forward over his knee, then toppled sideways. He shuddered, then lay still.

Bethnee thought she should have felt something, watching the horror of her nightmares draw his last two gurgling breaths, but nothing came. She had no more time to worry about it. Four greedy mercenaries with tranq guns were about to land on her doorstep.

She sent her talent out to check on the animals, but she was on her last reserves. Coordinating dire wolves, ravens, weasels, and foo dogs to defeat Kanaway had been like running a marathon. She asked bruised Shiza to go inside to protect injured, still dazed Trouble.

She wished she were a telepath like Domaki, so she could communicate with Axur, instead of just sensing his general location. She absently shoved the earwire she'd stripped from Kanaway into her chest pocket, only to find the one Axur had given her already there. Kicking herself for forgetting, she put it on and subvocalized a message. "Kanaway is dead in my front yard. I'm resetting the cabin's security. Tell me what I can do."

He came online almost immediately. *"Are you okay? Are you hurt? I've moved some of your traps to arrange welcome surprises for the mercs. They're running late. With luck, the enforcers will catch them here."*

She hadn't realized how much she'd needed to hear the sound of his voice until that moment.

"Tired. A bruise or two. Shiza and Trouble need treatment."

"I don't suppose you'd go back inside the cave and stay there?"

"Not a chance. It's my farking homestead. Can Serena and I come down the path?"

"Yes, I'll meet you. It's going to get crowded around here soon, and I want us all to be ready when it does."

CHAPTER FOURTEEN

GDAT 3241.265

Axur sat with Bethnee on the small couch in her chilly cabin and watched the two planetary enforcers standing near the front door. Their orders were to keep an eye him and Bethnee, but they were more interested in friendly Kivo.

The other enforcers who'd landed took custody of the mercs. With Bethnee and the animals acting as lookout, Axur had lured the mercs into Bethnee's traps, then shot them with their own tranq guns. Because one merc was dead, the enforcers insisted on waiting for their commander to arrive with Pranteaux, the Tanimai town administrator.

Axur stole glances at Bethnee. She looked bruised, tired, and pale, but not flatlined. He admired the hell out of her.

Shiza the foo dog now sat across her lap and partly into his, contentedly drooling a wet spot on both their pant legs. Bethnee finger-combed his curly mane. She surprised Axur by sliding her hand into his and mouthing the words "thank you." He squeezed her hand gently in acknowledgment.

A few minutes later, a tall, muscular woman in uniform and flexin armor, and a short, rotund man in a plaid coat entered the cabin.

The short man blinked and squinted as he looked around with disdain. His eyes widened when he saw Kivo, then narrowed when his gaze landed on Bethnee and Axur. He drew breath to speak, but the woman beat him to it.

"I'm Commander Cherkogin, and I'm sure you know Administrator Pranteaux." She took in her surroundings with darting glances, then focused on Axur. "Tragon?"

"Yes, sir." He stifled the urge to salute.

Cherkogin turned her gaze to Bethnee. "You must be Vetmed Bakonin."

Pranteaux cleared his throat. "She's the homesteader." He made it sound like an infectious disease. "I'll bet he's the illegal settler who's been trading in town." He pointed a curling, accusing finger at Axur.

Cherkogin frowned. "First things first, Administrator." She tilted her head toward the door. "How did the merc die?"

"Foo dog poison," said Bethnee, patting Shiza's shoulder. She explained the events in terse sentences. By the time she was done, Pranteaux was staring at the sleepy foo dog in horror.

Cherkogin looked at Axur. "We intercepted the rest of the merc company where you said they'd be." She crossed her arms. "The DPE takes a dim view of kidnapping Del'Arche settlers or homesteaders." She turned to Pranteaux with a sly smile. "And an equally dim view of destroying valuable protection animals like foo dogs."

Pranteaux's mouth gaped like a fish. "But it *killed* a man!" He looked back and forth between the foo dog and Cherkogin's unyielding expression. He blew out a frustrated breath, then glared at Bethnee and pointed at Axur again. "He's still illegal. He's been skulking around for months."

A fleeting look of distaste crossed Cherkogin's face as she turned away from Pranteaux to meet Axur's gaze. "What's your status?"

Axur had known this moment was inevitable ever since he'd chosen to meet the enforcers, so he could be there to protect Bethnee when they questioned her. He let go of her hand so he could stand, but she held him fast.

"He's my plus one."

Axur hoped he kept his confusion off his face. Cherkogin raised an eyebrow.

Pranteaux gawped, then recovered. "He can't be. You're not a settler. He doesn't live here." His mouth twisted in disdain as he looked her up and down. "You hate men."

"I don't hate men." Bethnee let go of Axur's hand, then gently urged Shiza to jump down and got to her feet. "I'm afraid of men who want to hurt me. There's a difference."

Axur stood and stayed next to her. Whatever her play was, he was in.

Bethnee pushed her hair behind her ear. "I looked it up. The settlement contract says homesteaders get one 'plus one,' as long as he resides on my homestead for a standard year." Bethnee wove her fingers through his and held up their joined hands. "I'm declaring Axur as my plus one."

Cherkogin smiled. "I'll be your official witness." She raised her arm to tap her percomp gauntlet. "I'll even register the declaration for you, since the town's satellite uplink got destroyed by the greedy mercs that your 'plus one' helped stop." She directed her next words to Pranteaux with a pointed look. "He probably saved your town from an armed invasion and wholesale theft of its valuable animals."

Pranteaux clamped his jaw and looked away with a frown. His eyes widened, and his expression morphed into sly challenge. "Clause 624.308.T.51." He looked at Bethnee. "You'll have to cohab or marry your 'plus one.'" He gave Axur an insulting smile. "Can't have Slick Slims taking advantage of the gullible and stealing their homesteads." He looked around at the furniture and sneered. "Not that this dump is worth stealing."

Cherkogin shook her head. "The council rescinded that stupid clause two years ago. You can't force people into domestic contracts."

Pranteaux jutted out his jaw, clearly intending to continue the fight.

"Quarks and quasars, man, I brought you here to confirm Bakonin's identity as the homesteader and remand the mercs, not meddle in people's private lives." She shot quick glances to her patiently waiting enforcers. "The administrator's work here is done. Escort him back to the flitter."

Pranteaux gave everyone in the room one last, sweeping glare and stomped through the door that commander had already opened. The enforcers left with him.

"Bureaucrats," muttered Cherkogin. She turned to Bethnee. "Would you mind stepping outside and, uh, getting your dire wolf guardian to stand down?"

Bethnee snorted. "You could have just said you want to talk to Axur alone." She sealed the coat she hadn't yet taken off and limped over to the door. She left without a backward glance.

"Sorry," said Cherkogin. "I tank at diplomacy."

"Apologize to her, not me." He tilted his head, finally able to place her familiar-sounding voice. "You were the ex-Jumper dispatcher this morning."

She nodded. "Yep. We're short-handed. How'd you like a job with the Del'Arche Planetary Enforcers?"

––––––––

Bethnee's head pounded and her joints ached from the fever she'd brought on herself by healing both Trouble and Shiza. Her talent felt thin and wispy as she extended a thread of invitation to Serena, who was sitting in the middle of her front yard.

Snapping at the commander hadn't been her finest moment. She heard Cherkogin's job offer right as the door closed. It was ideal for Axur. He'd have purpose again and make new friends, and have a team of enforcers to protect him if the CPS ever came calling.

Bethnee sat on a flat rock and buried her hands in Serena's thick winter fur. Daylight was more than half gone.

From the trees, Jynx chuffed. The enforcers looked around uneasily.

Bethnee chuckled. "Yes, Serena, she definitely taunted you. Go play."

Serena unexpectedly turned and licked Bethnee's face, then bounded off after Jynx.

She stuck her hands in her pockets and dropped her head to stretch her neck for a moment.

She listened to the wind through the trees and drifted for a bit, reflecting on her first months, when any weather at all had disconcerted her, after years in controlled space environments. Now the wind through the trees sounded like freedom.

The door to her cabin opened, and Cherkogin strode out. Axur and Kivo emerged a moment later, but angled toward Bethnee instead of following the commander. Cherkogin turned to look at Axur, then gave Bethnee a respectful nod. "We're clearing out. Thank you for your help, homesteaders." She turned and made an upward spiral motion to her enforcers, and walked down the path with them following.

Axur stood, arms crossed, watching them go. Kivo sidled up to her and put his head on her knees. They stayed that way until the low thrum of high-low flitters faded.

He held out a hand to her. "Could we go inside now? My dangly bits are getting cold."

She smiled and took his hand, and let him help pull her up. "Can't have that. You might need them."

The cabin was finally warm again. She didn't want to go back to the cave until Axur's monitoring confirmed that the enforcers had rounded up all the mercs and were on their way south.

Bethnee poured boiling water into the teapot. Axur sat at the kitchen-area counter she'd built to be comfortable for her height. Even though his face still sported streaks of dirt, and mud caked his long hair and beard, he was still plasma hot. She probably looked like something her weasel had dragged in. Felt like it, too.

Axur was idly folding a thin towel into various shapes. "I keep meaning to read the settlement contract, but legalese puts me to sleep. Tell me about this 'plus one' clause."

"It's complicated. Paying settlers can sponsor as many people as they like, and it confers homesteader rights to those people after a year, as long as they live on the settler's property. Those people can't do the same unless they wait another a year and buy or build their own homestead. Landed homesteaders like me can sponsor one at a time."

Axur smiled. "Thank you." He gave her a speculative look. "What's Pranteaux's friction with you? Is it because you're a minder?"

"No, he's a minder, too, a general filer who remembers everything. Nuñez says he's a control freak who overcompensates with his need for respect." She shrugged one shoulder. "I just think he's an asshole. Probably didn't help that I told him so to his face."

Axur laughed. She was going to miss the sound of it.

She poured the brewed tea into both their cups. "Congratulations on the new job, by the way. Will you have to move to the spaceport?" She pushed the cup of hot tea and a sugar stick across the counter toward him.

"I didn't take it."

"Why?" Maybe he felt like he owed her. "This is just your legal residence. You don't have to actually live here. You could be with Jumpers again, and it'd be a good use of your abilities. You like people. You liked Cherkogin." She pointed to his discarded poncho. "You're free."

"All valid points, and I'd have said yes if they'd offered when I first landed." He stroked Kivo's broad head resting on his thigh. "But everything changed when I discovered the pets." He looked around at her tiny cabin. "I never had my own home before. Being a planetary enforcer would take me away from home a lot." He swirled the sugar stick in his tea. "I liked being a Jumper. They help people in trouble, and look after their own. But I volunteered for the medic training and kept up my language skills because they're often more effective than guns." He gave her a lopsided smile. "Don't tell any Jumpers I said that."

"Your secret's safe with me." She couldn't hold her answering smile for long. "You have a lot of assets. You could move to a bigger city and be a medic and rent your printer."

He stilled. "Do you want me to go?"

"No, I want you to stay, because I think I'm in love with you." She wrapped her arms around her ribs. "But it's not about me. I want what's right for you."

A slow smile rose on his face. "All the cities are in the south, and Serena would be miserable in the heat." He stood and eased his way around the end of the counter. "I know you'd take her, but Trouble wouldn't have anyone to watch over, so I'd have to leave him and the others with you, too. Kivo's a theft magnet, like Jynx, so I'd have to leave him, as well." He edged toward her, close enough to touch her. "And that means everyone I love would be here."

She looked up at his strong, kind face. "You could have anyone you want. Someone who can promise not to be scared with you. Someone who's normal."

"Normal is boring." He touched the scarred side of his neck with his cybernetic hand. "I'm no prize." She hadn't seen that vulnerable look on his face before.

"Because you're a cyborg?" She reached out to slip her hand into his. She stroked a thumb over the exposed biometal knuckle. "Cybernetics are a part of you, but they're not you. The man I know is caring, smart... beautiful." Her eyes welled with tears. "Anyone would be lucky to have you."

"What if the only one I want is a nova-hot veterinarian who loves animals?" He slid his other hand up her arm slowly and rested it on her shoulder.

Bethnee smiled. "Nuñez would be happy to hear it." She put a hand on Axur's waist. "She and her wife think you're sexy. They like to share a handsome man on special occasions."

Axur shook his head. "The only woman I want also has a cybernetic leopard and a hot-spring pool." He put his other hand on the side of her face, and wove his fingers into her hair.

She leaned into his touch. "As it so happens, the only man I want is tall and strong, and loves animals."

He lowered his head to hers, stopping just before their lips touched. "Do you still want to kiss me?"

She raised her hand to his face to caress his cheek. "More than anything. Do you want to be kissed?"

"More than anything." He met her halfway to join his lips with hers.

He tasted cool and sweet. Heat pooled in her abdomen and warmed her core. She pulled herself closer, wanting to share the heat with him. He left her mouth and trailed kisses to the side of her face. She gasped in a mix of pleasure and pain as he brushed by her sore jaw.

He pulled back to look at her face. "Sorry, I didn't think." He touched delicate fingers to her cheek. "I've just wanted you for so long. I love you."

She gave up fighting the tears and let them fall. "I love you, too, but I'm a mess. Could we maybe talk about this in my geothermal pool?"

He gave her a lascivious grin. "*Naked* in your geothermal pool?"

She chuckled. "Yeah, naked." She boldly slid a hand around to cup his muscular ass. "I'm worried about your cold dangly bits."

CHAPTER FIFTEEN

GDAT 3241.266

They didn't make it to the pool as fast as Axur had hoped.

Security systems needed arming after he'd brought all his gear into her marvelous cave. Animals variously needed calling in, drying off, feeding and watering, and cleaning up after. Using his enhanced speed and strength burned through calories like kindling, and he didn't have Jumper nutrient rebalancer concentrates to compensate. Bethnee had pushed her talent limit to the edge, too.

Finally, she led him to the geothermal pool. She turned and kissed him. "Hello, fellow homesteader."

"Hey, yourself." He could drown in the depths of her eyes. "Can we get naked now?"

She laughed. "Yes." She started to pull her tunic up with trembling hands, but he stopped her. "I want to make love with you more than my next breath, but I don't want to scare you." He slid a hand up to her shoulder. "I'm not a telepath or an empath, I'm just a flux-to-the-max Jumper. You have to tell me what's too much, or too fast, or too close."

"I'll try. Sometimes, it takes me by surprise." She held up shaking fingers. "This isn't from fear, it's from wanting you." She flattened her palm on his chest. "I haven't had a lover since I was seventeen, and that was sex in the back of prepaid autocabs. You'll have to tell me what's going on with you, too. I love your strength, but I can't read you. I tank at communicating with humans."

"As it happens, I have built-in capacity for comms." She snorted in amusement. He captured her fingers and kissed them. "We'll figure it out together."

They explored each other in the warm pool. He loved finding the places where he could make her gasp and moan, and helping her find the spots on him that sent fire through his every synapse. He carried her naked to her bed, and only had to evict four furry occupants before joining with her to give them both the pleasure they'd been seeking. Their bodies seemed to fit together, like they'd been made for each other.

When he awoke and turned the lights up a bit, he discovered the bed had been invaded by three cats, a ferwinkle, a foo dog, and a chimera. He had a feeling their bed would never be cold or empty.

Bethnee stirred and rolled to the side, eliciting a muffled meow of protest from Delta the cat. Bethnee sighed and rolled back to drape herself on Axur. He loved the feel of her skin on his, the scent of her, the weight of her on him.

"What time is it?" she asked.

He checked his chrono implant. "A little after zero one hundred."

She slid her hand up to caress his jaw with her thumb. "Can't sleep in a strange bed?" She tweaked his earlobe. "Or with a strange woman?"

"You're not strange, you're unconventional." She made a rude sound, and he laughed. "Cyborgs love unconventional women who live in caves." He wrapped his arm around her waist.

"Good," she said. "I love cyborgs who have their own freighters. And printers. And autodocs. And runabouts." She kissed him between each item she listed.

He laughed. "It's too far for my potential patients and customers, though. I like your idea of looking at the abandoned house next to Nuñez's to see if we can make it into a medical clinic." He kissed her hairline. "According to a forecaster friend of Cherkogin's, trouble is brewing in the Concordance, and frontier planets should expect an influx of refugees. Something to do with Ayorinn's Legacy. You know, those nonsensical poems that predict a radical vector change for civilization." He shook his head. "The CPS dismisses them as a hoax, but I don't trust the CPS much anymore."

She sat up slowly. "I'm going to the fresher and check on Trouble. Want some water?"

"Yes, please."

He watched her because he could, enjoying the sleek curve and sway of her slender hips as she walked.

He sat up and rearranged pillows, blankets, and animals so she'd have a place to sit when she came back.

She returned carrying a glass of water and the wrapped Solstice Day present he'd given her. Trouble the dog walked in behind her, slower than usual, but looking alert. She handed him the water, then helped Trouble up onto the bed next to Kivo.

She kneeled on the bed and stroked Trouble's head. "I'm not sorry Kanaway died."

"Me, either." Axur took a deep, steadying breath to keep the anger at bay. He wanted to resurrect the asshole, just so he could kill him himself, more slowly.

She crawled toward him to sit next to him against the pillows, holding the present. "Can I open this now?"

"Sure." He watched her face as she unwrapped and opened the box.

After a moment, recognition dawned. She stroked the heart-shaped piece of fur and looked up at him with a smile. "You printed this?"

"Yes." He loved her quick mind. "I've been working on a formula for synthskin patches for me, so I thought I'd experiment with synthfur for Jynx's leg. She deserves to be free to go outside whenever she wants."

She put the fur back in the box and put it on the nearby ledge, then kissed his shoulder. "It's a perfect gift." She slid herself under his arm. "I'm thinking it wouldn't hurt to plan for an influx of new people, regardless. Once word gets around you're a trained medic with an autodoc, more people will visit Tanimai, and some will stay."

"I guess I'm the first of the influx, then." He picked up her hand and kissed her fingers. "Lucky for me, I fell in love with a woman with a homestead and built-in family."

"We're the lucky ones." She kissed his chest. "I think you should talk to Cherkogin again. Offer to be on reserve, train with them monthly. You'd learn things you can't find out from just listening to their comms. Then we could prepare better, if we get more refugees."

"You wouldn't mind?" His two potentially serious relationships while in the military had foundered when their assignments had taken one or both of them away for ten-days at a time. "I have to admit I was tempted, but you're more important to me."

"I appreciate that, but you've got skills you should be using." With a somewhat awkward move, she straddled his thighs and faced him. "Strength. Comms. Languages. Making friends. Blowing things up." She rested her hands on his shoulders and gave him a sharp smile. "Make them pay you in hard credit."

He laughed. "Now the truth comes out."

"Yep," she said. "We have to finish more of the cave so your animals can be comfortable when we're here." They'd decided to spend time at both her place and his, to maintain his homestead claim. "That takes renting the rock laser, and that takes hard credit."

He glided his hands up to her waist and leaned forward to give her a long, sensual kiss, with a promise of more. "I love a nova-hot woman who knows how to make a good trade."

MASCOT

A Novella in the Aeon's Legacy Series

By

Alexis Glynn Latner

Alexis Glynn Latner writes fantasy and science fiction romantic adventure.

http://www.alexisglynnlatner.com/

ONE

Starships always shone when they reached their destination. When they emerged out of the strange non-space of starflight, returning into real space and time, starships shed light. The shining wasn't usually apparent to passengers, even though it might be visible to watchers in the nearest space station. In his career to date, Rik Gole had ended a couple of hundred starflight journeys without seeing anything of the sort.

This time was different. Reaching this out-of-the-way destination took a high-energy starjump. The energy of the starjump made the starfreighter shine like a beacon when it got here. Shining on Star Corner Station, the light of Rik's arrival accentuated how ugly it was.

The Station was a cobbled-together hulk, battered by asteroid impacts and crudely repaired. Windows in deeply shadowed crevasses of the station showed as bright pinpoints, but the pinpoints were scattered, even furtive, suggesting that large sections of the station were deserted or decommissioned. The Station's hull told which way the local cosmic wind was blowing—from above. That way lay a massive, brilliant blue star embedded in the Starcross Nebula. The radiance of the star drove a violent wind of gas and dust across the Station, the top side of which was conspicuously weathered—stained and pitted.

Behind the Station, a shiny, barren orb hung in front of the nebular backdrop of pink and blue gas and dark dust. That was the metal planetary core that Star Corner Station orbited, and the last remaining reason the Station existed. Whether it was a good enough reason was a question Rik meant to answer.

Rik was an interstellar auditor.

Unlike some auditors for the Faxen Interstellar Financial Authority, FINFINA, Rik took no joy in the exposé of an unprofitable enterprise, one that had outlived its time, but nonetheless employed a number of people and played some kind of role in an orbital community. Or helped a remote world communicate with the rest of the universe. Or housed a terraforming operation. Something like that. If Star Corner Station had any such redeeming features, that was not obvious. But Rik was here not just to shine an investigative light at the surface of it; he was here to illuminate its inner workings.

That he had been sent to Star Corner Station meant that FINFINA had reason to suspect misadministration or dishonesty. He was here to find out exactly what was wrong and who was responsible.

Rik's star-freighter drifted into the massive cradle of a dock. Meanwhile Rik reviewed his assignment, using his electronic notebook. The manager of Star Corner Station was one *Davend Tattujayan*, a person whose gender was indeterminate from the name crammed into a constricted box in the audit template. The manager was identified as Goyan. That came as no surprise. Goya was a long-colonized planet with hereditary spacegoing guilds.

At a bored wave from a crewwoman in a uniform coverall, Rik exited the star-freighter. He was the only passenger, the rest of what the freighter had carried being cargo destined for the Station. He had a copy of the manifest and had personally inspected the cargo, consisting of analytic instruments, machine replacement parts, food supplies, and personal packages for Station crew. The star-freighter would proceed to take on cargo in the form of purified ores. That was almost all that the Station contributed to the rest of the universe these days. Fine, if it was enough. And well enough accounted for.

Somebody from the Station's management should have met him at the dock. That no one did made him wonder if his reception had been delayed to give someone time to hide something. He glanced around. His expert eye could assess any space place for locations in which to hide contraband. Just here in the station dock, he saw a few interestingly nondescript convex surfaces, plus a hatch not located anywhere that made structural sense, but in a suggestive proximity to some side-loading machinery. As to the rest of the station—the looming, crevassed, partly deserted, much-damaged and patched bulk of it. . . . Good gods, Rik thought. You could hide entire starships in this place.

His investigative instincts stirred.

A young man rushed into the dock. "Auditor Gole? I'm Mattiz-Kol

Sarpov, Station Manager Tattujayan's secretary." The secretary's lank brown hair stuck out—a predictable consequence of spingravity and the reason Rik kept his own hair short. The name and the accent identified the secretary as a being from Faxe, the principal planet of the Faxen Union, as was Rik himself. Good. Absent cultural differences, a callow secretary could be an open book to Rik. "The Manager will be delayed for some time, so I'll show you to—"

Rik interrupted. "The audit protocol is that I meet with the Manager immediately upon my arrival."

The secretary gave Rik an odd look, waved for Rik to come with him, and set off at a run.

Davendaya Tattujayan had known something like this could happen and dreaded the day it did. She just hadn't known exactly where it would be—in what storage bin or locker, undercompartment, sealed tank, service chase, or locked gallery in the Station. It had turned out to be here: below the old military materials depot. The depot was obsolete, closed, locked, and highly restricted. She had a master key in the event of an emergency. She had declared an emergency when the floor of the depot sagged into the corridor under it, dropping a huge mass of corrosive red—stuff.

The stuff was still falling in thick red clots. The leading edge of the mass was creeping toward the living quarters for Station personnel in this sector. Those personnel were being evacuated, shift sleepers roused out of their bunks with shouts and shoulders shaken.

Ops Chief Jax Trover scrambled down the nearest ladder. He handed her back the master key and reported, "There's a row of huge containers placarded 'do not drop,' 'do not strike with sharp instruments,' 'do not expose to water' and 'do not eject into space.' Some of the containers are bulging, they are! The one on the end fell out of the rack and split open. Only half of what was in it has leaked out so far!"

Daya gritted her teeth. The Station flexed under gravitational tidal forces from its proximity to the metal ore planet. Centuries of that must have weakened brackets and now let that container fall out. "Does the signage say what *is* recommended to do?"

"No."

Service Chief Romeo Ito ran up with the bladder of water she'd sent him for. Now she wondered how good an idea that was. *Do not expose to water*—because water would neutralize the stuff or because it reacted badly to water? There was one way to find out. But it best be done with care. Romeo was about to empty the bladder onto the stuff. Daya put a cautionary hand on his arm. "Start with just a little."

Romeo flung a few ounces of water onto the red stuff.

Where it felt the touch of water, the red stuff exploded, spattering his left boot. The spatters instantly ate holes in the boot. He wrenched the boot off, but not before his skin felt the acid touch. He stripped off his sock to frantically rub the acid off his skin. The sock started smoldering in his fingers.

He hurled the sock into the red stuff. The sock burst into flame.

As though incited, the red stuff crawled faster. Daya took a step back, her arms outflung in front of Jax and Romeo. In her native language she thought, *The Eye of Fate has noticed me today.* She felt dread edged with anger. She would not just succumb to what ill Fate intended—but what could she do?

She heard another set of running feet. This time it was Brina Trover bringing a heavily loaded bag. "The tailings you wanted," Brina panted.

"First—what do we know about this hideous stuff?"

Jax answered, "The floor of the depot gave way where there were composite joists. Anything organic that the stuff touches—meaning plastics or composites or skin—it causes to burn. It explodes on contact with water and makes acid residue."

Damnation! Much of Star Corner Station was plastic or composite. And the Station was laced with pipes that channeled water for environmental control, radiation absorption, and sewage flow.

"But it doesn't react with metals."

Daya thought fast. "The ore tailings are anhydrous, inorganic, and unoxidized, with a lot of surface area in the powdered fraction. And it's the only thing we have in an unlimited amount to fight this stuff. Sprinkle some on."

Brina did so.

Nothing happened.

Brina dumped the whole bag of tailings on the leading edge of the red stuff.

The pile of tailings blocked the red stuff. Red puddles tried to ooze around the tailings. Daya said, "With enough tailings, we can make a dam that holds it back. We'll need a tailings truck brought to the nearest haulway. Then enough bags—or anything else we can carry tailings in— and enough people to make a supply line from the haulway to here!"

The supply line quickly formed up, including several just-woken shift sleepers still in their underwear. Daya felt a stab of fierce pride. In Star Corner Station she'd been given a mixed and mismatched bag of yarns and knitted them into the fabric of a good crew. She'd be damned before she let anything bad happen to the crew or to the Station.

Minutes later a second bag full of tailings was flung against the slow red tide. Some of the tailings landed on top of the stuff, and the lurid red of it turned rusty. It solidified into a scab of sorts.

"Good!" Jax exclaimed. "We can make a wall in front of it to contain it and then suppress it, we can!"

The station doctor, Anahita Lee, dashed up to help. Daya had her begin first aid for the injuries that were starting to accumulate, starting with Romeo's foot.

A steady stream of tailings flew at the leading edge of the stuff. It hissed—maybe there were traces of water or oxides in the tailings. All in all, the red stuff acted alive enough to make Daya's skin crawl. But the tailings stymied the stuff. The line of people delivering bags of tailings stretched as those at the front advanced. Daya needed more people.

Mattiz-Kol came running up with an unfamiliar man—a tall and fit-looking one.

"You two fill in there!" Daya ordered them.

Brina was at the head of the supply line, dumping bags and boxes and buckets—by now all kinds of containers had been pressed into service—onto the face of the stymied, hissing mass of red stuff. The finest of the tailings powdered the air. Pebble-sized tailings rolled loose on the floor.

Brina pivoted. Her booted foot slipped on the pebbles underfoot. She fell hard onto a puddle of stuff that had slyly oozed through a pile of rocks in the dam.

Her coverall cuff caught fire. She yelled.

The new man grabbed a large bag of tailings out of Mattiz' hands and dumped it on Brina's leg, smothering the fire. Then he yanked her to safety. Seconds later the doctor was cutting off the leg of her coverall and working her boot off.

Daya crouched to put a hand on Brina's shoulder. "How bad?"

"Bad enough but no permanent harm done," said the doctor.

"Thanks to him." Brina gestured at the new man.

Behind them, it sounded as though tailings had proven equal to the job. People were pointing out weak spots in the dam and another treacherous puddle. Daya let out a sharp breath. "Thank you," she told the new man. "And you are?"

Mattiz-Kol stood at a kind of startled attention and announced, "Faxen Interstellar Financial Authority Auditor Rik Gole!"

The sudden silence was only broken by the hissing of the red stuff. Then an entire section of the corridor ceiling fell down—fortunately squarely on the red stuff—with a crash.

So *that* was Manager Tattujayan. She had paler skin than most Goyans—a superficial resemblance to the Faxen Union's Albioni ethnic minority, which was a cesspool of Disunion terrorists. Other than that, Rik liked the look of her: a dark-haired, compactly built woman who knew how to take action.

With the crisis under control, Mattiz showed Rik to his quarters. Rik showered and changed clothes. Mattiz reappeared to show Rik to the servery for supper. The servery smelled appetizing. That was good not just because Rik was hungry but also because it was a sign of a well-adjusted space place to harbor good cooks.

Over savory noodle bowls, the Station personnel excitedly discussed today's incident, but no one still had dusty hair and coveralls. "We always freshen up for dinner," Mattiz explained. "In a remote place like this, it's easy for people to get space-slack."

Rik nodded. There was another sign of good management. Tattujayan might be dishonest, but she was not incompetent.

Her idea of fresh clothes turned out to be Steppe-Goyan tribal dress—a heavy, tailored red tunic and skirt with elaborate white trim, and white fur boots. The skirt fit well and hung properly—better than Mattiz' hair. And red looked good on her. She had an interesting face with rather severe features. Wearing black, she'd have looked like a funeral in progress. The red set off her pale skin and dark hair. She had an energetic quality, an almost electric energy.

Midway through the meal, the Service Chief—a Wendisan named Romeo Ito, one of those injured in today's incident—stood up to make an announcement. "Keepers, Trovers, and Faxens—" he bowed toward Mattiz and Rik "—and Manager Tattujayan, we had a war today and won!"

Everyone cheered.

"Our next *scheduled* war is the day after tomorrow, rule set mixed melee, and may the best team win!"

"What?" Rik asked Mattiz.

"Do you know about the war games of Wendis?"

Rik did. Wendis was a spinning city-state in the stars between the Faxen Union and Goya. Rik's business had never taken him there. But he'd heard of the games. "They re-enact wars from old Earth."

"Romeo is a Weaponsmaster—that's a high rank in Wendisan wargaming. The sides are Keepers, meaning the service staff, and Trovers, the Goyan guilders and others who operate the plant that processes ore from the metal core planet—its name is Trove." Mattiz warmed to his subject. "We don't have a good stage for an open-air battle because Star Corner Station doesn't have wide pressurized floor areas. Wendis does, and at this year's Ascendance Fair they re-enacted one of the most famous battles on all of old Earth—the one called Normandy Invasion! Here, we're going to stage a firefight in a deserted village. Mixed melee means weapons from any historical period are allowed."

Space station inhabitants usually entertained themselves with—in order of frequency—vids, games, sex, gambling, and recreational drugs.

All such entertainments were fine if they didn't involve administrative money. Personally, Rik enjoyed the availability and variety of sex in space places. It was one of the distinct pluses of his occupation. He'd had some very enjoyable encounters, albeit not with administrators he was investigating. He caught himself thinking that thought and it startled him. But yes. Rik looked around to confirm his impression. Tattujayan was the most attractive woman in the hall. "Is your Manager a Guild-Goyan?"

"Oh no, she's not with any Goyan space guilds. She upholds Goya's stake in the Station, though. There's Goya, Wendis, the Faxen Union and other stakeholders too, I think she'll tell you about them."

Rik's ears pricked. If there were covert stakeholders in Star Corner Station, it would be news to the Faxen Interstellar Financial Authority!

As though she sensed herself being talked about, Tattujayan came over to Rik's table. "It's Station evening, but freighters tend to arrive in ship morning, so I assume it feels like midday to you. You may wish to come to my office for the private conference that was supposed to occur upon your arrival." Without chaos unfolding around them, Rik noticed that she spoke formally and with an accent. The Goyan dialect of Alliant wasn't her native language.

"I'd like that," he said blandly. Out of the corner of his eye, he took in the curve of her hips and thighs under the skirt, and the smoothness of the skin above the red trim on her boots. The white fur looked real, not like cheap Wendis-fair imitation fur. Her outfit might be worth most of her salary for a year. *Very* interesting.

The office she shared with her secretary and her Service Chief turned out to be cramped and Spartan. Unlike certain administrators Rik had encountered whose expensive tastes screamed from walls and corners, the décor consisted of a goldfish tank and a very large and untidy plant. The plant overflowed one end of the Service Chief's desk, beside the fish tank. Tattujayan flicked a dangling tendril of the plant out of the fish tank. It was always interesting what people would nervously tidy up with an auditor looking over their shoulder.

Tattujayan turned toward Rik with her arms crossed. "Thank you for your help today. As it happens, the incident illustrates my management philosophy, which is the diligent management of resources. The best resource of all is the hands and brains of good people."

Rik nodded approvingly. "Let me introduce my philosophy as well. As an interstellar auditor, I'm here to ask the right questions. As I see it, my job traces its lineage all the way to ancient Rome in Earth, where an official Quaestor was one who asked questions. And my purpose is to get accurate answers to the right questions—nothing more, but nothing less. May I ask your full name for my notes? My audit template has a box too small for all of yours."

"Davendaya Tattujayan." She spelled it. "The accent is on first syllables like ancient Finnish, and the syllables are meaningful elements like names derived from ancient Sanskrit in India on Earth."

Amused, he said, "I wasn't aware that Goyans had such complicated names."

She retorted, "I thought Faxens always had two first names."

His amusement vanished. "There aren't enough Rik Goles for me to be confused with others." His mind shied away from the name that was his father's, that he had repudiated, that no longer mattered to him. "By the way, may I compliment you on your Goyan costume and ask how your skirt stays in place?"

"It isn't costume. I came from the Goyan Steppe. The hem has weights that make the material hang suitably in spingravity. And that's one."

Processing what she'd said—he'd never met a Steppe-Goyan, but he'd heard about them, and that explained how she could wear tribal clothing without spending a fortune on it—her last sentence registered on him. "One?"

"Totally unwarranted question. I will give you three of those, and no more."

Rik felt his sexual interest stir. Tattujayan was not conventionally pretty. But she was striking, intelligent and spirited. She was the kind of woman who most attracted him.

Her honesty remained to be seen, he sternly reminded himself. His assignment was more important than his sexual whims.

She handed him an interface disk. "Here is the key to the Station financial records. I will of course answer any and all questions about those."

Sometimes Fate winks. It certainly had today, Daya thought. That auditor—whose visit came as a most unpleasant surprise—was an attractive man. And he had effectively helped with the emergency with the red stuff. Had he been any other kind of specialist, she would have wanted to know him better, starting immediately. Unfortunately, he was not to be trusted. To be more exact, his government was not to be trusted. As to him, that depended on how much of a creature of his state he was.

At Station midnight, Daya let herself into core of one of the Station's service spines. She climbed down a long ladder and ducked into the unused service chase that happened to be a secret and unmonitored way into what had once been one of the Station's passenger rings. Exactly what it was now—it was better not to know. She had never entered the ring herself, just gone as far as the anteroom of it. She entered the anteroom by pressing her hand against the featureless door at the end of the chase.

She found the Angel named Mercury waiting for her.

The Angels had once been human. For mysterious reasons and by an agency unclear to the rest of humanity, the Angels had changed into something else, something not quite human, adapted for low-gravity environments. They were not to be trusted. That fact, unlike the problematic auditor and his allegiance, was long since proven. Yet the Angels had their uses, and Daya knew how to not trust them.

Mercury was fine-boned and androgynous and wore a close-fitting coverall of pale blue material. Over Mercury's shoulder were a pair of diaphanous wings, tightly furled, almost invisible in the dim light of the antechamber. Mercury got to the point. "Are you here to buy knowledge?"

Daya shrugged. "Just information, if you have it." Like everyone from the Steppe of Goya, Daya knew how trade worked. You downplayed whatever you desired.

"You want to know what the substance was that damaged your station today." Mercury sounded smug. "I knew you'd want to buy what we know about it."

"Not *all* you know." *I doubt I could afford that.* "I'd like the name of it."

Mercury's large dark eyes locked onto Daya like the gaze of a raptor. But Daya had dealt with raptors and Angels before. Daya waited. "Emberalm," the Angel finally said.

Surprised, Daya said, "That is a word out of legend. The legends say the Old Alliance used something called emberalm to cleanse Star Pitfall of its great nest of monsters, but the legends fail to describe what emberalm was."

Mercury smirked. "Now you know."

"Fair trade." Daya handed the Angel a Station credit disk. The credit could be used in any of the Station's dispensers of food and fresh clothing or the printers for tools and parts. From experience, she knew that the credit would soon be used with no one reporting having seen an Angel do it. That was how trading with the Angels worked.

She wondered what the auditor would make of it.

TWO

The next morning, Rik went to Tattujayan's office before it was scheduled to open for the day. He found her already at her desk. "I have a question or two about your accounts."

She steepled her hands under her chin.

Actually, he had six or eight questions, and some of them had sharp points, but it was always good to start with the most harmless of questions. "Why is there an expense for dog food? Most space places have a cat. And cat food should be listed under pest control."

"We've no need for cats. We don't have commodities such as grain in storage to harbor rodents. We do have several guard dogs, as you will see, if you let me show you Star Corner Station today."

Rik followed her to the nearest vator. He enjoyed the walk. She was as attractive from behind as from other angles. She wore practical coveralls under her red Steppe tunic, which was well-fitting and probably kept her warm. Rik had definitely not found the Station to be wastefully overheated. It was cold everywhere.

Going upward in the vator, she told him, "The Station has a large hub from which extend five long service spines. It resembles a hand." She held her own hand up to illustrate. "Cargo handling is what everything in the thumb was designed for. Passenger transportation facilities were the first finger. So you arrived in the docks between thumb and forefinger. Administration areas were in the middle finger. There's an ancient and obscene hand gesture that involved a middle finger, and the gesture still survives only in the form of jokes about the clumsy joint administration of the Station by Goya, Faxe, and Wendis!

"Science facilities—laboratories, biological containment facilities, telescopes—were in the fourth finger. And military operations were in the little finger. Originally each finger was a long service spine full of modules. Now, the modules are either removed or closed except for what's at the base of the fingers. The palm of the station, meanwhile, is the ore processing facility. Here." It was a well-timed little speech, concluded just as the door of the vator opened.

Rik found the ore processing plant to be an old but well-designed facility of its kind. It received unmanned ore haulers from Trove, processing the ore into metal and generating tailings that were loaded back into ore haulers and launched back to Trove.

There seemed to be the right number of personnel for this operation—neither so many as to indicate a padded payroll nor so few as to be over-worked. They greeted Tattujayan with waves or bows as suited their cultural backgrounds. Rik saw no disrespectful scowls or malicious grins behind her back, much less any rude finger gestures. He saw no signs of disrespect for himself either—a nice change from some of his jobs where a FINFINA auditor was unwelcome.

His help in the emergency yesterday seemed to have won him extraordinary respect here. He wouldn't waste it.

A narrow window gave a constricted view of the yard. Rik would have liked a better view, but any window in the ore yard was subject to collision from loose objects ranging from asteroids to errant ore haulers. A wide and unprotected window would have been an accident waiting to happen. He craned his neck to watch an ore hauler glide toward the web of cables in the palm of the Station-hand. Caught in the web of cables, the hauler slowed, shivered, and moved toward a processing port on the edge of the Station.

Tattujayan abruptly asked, "Do you know the Station's history?"

"It was largely decommissioned when it ceased to be profitable about forty years ago."

She crossed her arms. "That is so gaunt an explanation as to border on falsehood, so let me tell you the truth. This used to be Starcrossing Station. It was a great interstellar crossroads. But star travel turning points can creep and shift relative to real space. Forty years ago the major starjump point here moved away. What's left is a minor point that was here all along. Wendis built a new facility where the major point is now—the facility called Starway. It's much more compact than this."

Rik nodded. "I've stayed in the hotel there."

"Wendis maintains this Station, now called Star Corner. Goya keeps the mining operations going. And Faxe has not backed out of the ancient contract that describes the complicated ownership of the Station." She raised an elegantly curved dark eyebrow at him. "Yet."

"I'm not a legalist who parses contractual obligations," he said smoothly. "I only assess the accounting and the financial ramifications of the operations."

Out in the yard, the ore hauler disappeared into a port on the wall of the Station. "The processing ports are specific to various ores and different materials," she told him. "This is the Port level. It makes a complete ring around the hollow of the hand."

"How many processing ports are active?"

"Twenty of an original hundred."

"Has ore production on Trove scaled back that much?"

"No. The Station no longer processes many of the original materials."

That word again. *Materials.* He raised his own eyebrow.

"When there was a major starjump point here, it gave access to the strangest place in all of known space. That way." She indicated a thick knot of dark dust and bright blue and pink nebular gas. "In the midst of that lurked a brown dwarf star surrounded by a cluster of terminal points, also called star pits. These were points that could be arrived at by starjump, but not departed from. The dead space around the brown dwarf star was called Star Pitfall. It was a place of shipwreck and stranding, full of the wrecks of a thousand dead civilizations' worth of ships. It was infested with monsters that feasted on the infallen ships and their unlucky crews. The Old Alliance finally eradicated the monsters with the red stuff you saw yesterday. The name of it is emberalm.

"Salvage operations, based here, went on for centuries for the wreckage of the ancient ships. Some of the materials discovered were exotic and some extremely dangerous. Some of the ports were clean rooms, and some were explosion-resistant bunkers. Don't they teach ancient history on Faxe?"

As a matter of fact, Rik was vaguely aware what she'd said—the place of wreck and ruin called Star Pitfall, the thousand-year salvage of it, and more generally, the existence of the ruins of long-dead civilizations across the stars. Still, his honest answer would have been, *Who cares?* Rik shrugged.

She peered through the window at a sharp angle, said, "Ah," led him to another narrow window down the corridor, and tapped the window significantly. "Look."

Something smaller and more irregular than an ore hauler was moving out there. It spidered along a cable. As Rik watched, it reached out—with what looked like a tentacle—to snare a floating piece of metal. Which it stuffed into a gaping maw of a mouth.

Rik found his own mouth hanging open in astonishment. He shut it.

"The monsters of Star Pitfall turned out to have been genetically engineered by some long-gone civilization from those creatures, which subsist on orbital debris. One of the science laboratories recreated them. They're smart enough to stay away from the ore haulers and cheaper than having

personnel or robots patrol for debris. They do need occasional supplemen-
tation of their diet with organic material. Thus the dog food. They also
make it hard for vandals or saboteurs to operate in the ore yard because
they have a taste for fresh meat. So they are our ore-yard guard dogs." She
looked at his face and laughed. "Surprise."

More than the ore-yard dog surprised him. So did she. And so did he
himself. Something about her was like an electromagnetic field that
attracted him powerfully. He turned away from the window.

The remainder of the morning consisted of a tour through the bases of
the fingers, with no further surprises. Finally they returned to the Main
level of the Station, where they'd started, and she showed him the recreation center. It looked too big and empty—better suited to the thousand
who used to crew this Station than to the hundred who were here now. In
one corner stood another goldfish tank. On a shelf above the tank another
large, untidy plant dangled a tendril in the water. Like all well-appointed
space places, the Station had plants around, and fish tanks—both soothing
to human nerves. The plant, though, was remarkably identical to the one
in her office. Maybe somebody had moved it.

When she saw it, Tattujayan hissed. She pulled the tendril out of the
water. Then she counted the goldfish.

Rik knew a deliberate distraction when he saw one. "Your tour
is over?"

"Yes," she snapped.

"There are areas you've not shown me."

She looked over her shoulder, meeting his stern look with an
unflinching look of her own. "They are decommissioned and sealed. In
some cases, they're contaminated. My financial accounts list those areas
and the drain they make on Station energy resources—in most cases, no
drain at all, sometimes some climate control. Whatever you do, Auditor,
don't go anywhere like that alone."

Rik returned to his small but adequate cabin in a very thoughtful
mood. He started his audit report, opening the template in his notebook.
He had enough information now for a preliminary report, so he submitted
the report to the template.

He got back a one-word evaluation from the template. *Unacceptable.*

Rik stared at that word.

Audit templates were a sophisticated piece of technology, with a fair
degree of machine intelligence. He'd never had his template flatly refuse
his findings, though he'd had a few arguments with it. He'd learned how
to win those arguments. More than most auditors, Rik understood the
audit template and how to get to the bottom of its arguments and
programmed objections. So he did.

What he found startled him. Deep in his audit template, there was new
programming. He hadn't put it there: it had to have come from the

Authority. The new programming had an unprecedented bias. It wanted evidence of Manager Tattujayan's dishonesty and evidence that she was embezzling Station funds, profiteering, or engaging in bribery.

That couldn't be right.

Even an overworked manager, one with her hands very full, could still be dishonest by incorporating dishonesty into her work routines. But dishonesty didn't match the impression Rik was forming of her character and style. And Rik had good reason to trust his impressions. He was the most experienced interstellar auditor in FINFINA.

She might be in over her head, though. Even more likely, she might have alienated the wrong people. It would surprise Rik if a Steppe-Goyan understood the intricacies of interstellar administrative politics. At the end of the Station's workday. Rik went to Tattujayan's office. She wasn't there but her Service Chief was. "Where is she? I'd like talk to her very confidentially."

One of Romeo Ito's eyebrows quirked up. A slight and knowing smile appeared on his smooth face. "She likes to retire to her quarters to read before dinner." Romeo handed Rik a finder disk. "Knock two times twice to say you're a friend. Good luck!"

Daya thought the tour of Star Corner Station had gone well enough. She just hoped Rik Gole didn't take it upon himself to prowl into the areas she hadn't shown him. It would be exceedingly hard to explain a missing or dead auditor.

She set her concerns aside when she went to her own quarters for a precious few minutes of time for herself. She liked it here. Most stationers inhabited a single room—in some cases a room so full of possessions in so little order that it resembled a packrat nest. She had divided hers, making a separate, narrow but comfortable room in which to relax and receive friends for a cup of Darling tea. The walls were hung with intricately patterned blankets that kept the cold of Star Corner Station out. It looked like the winter tents of home.

She was reading a recent history of interstellar civilization. The author was an Albioni historian. Albion was one of the planets in the Faxen Union, but the least slavish one. The book was edifying. As usual, Jesse Greenfinger joined her in her reading chair. Jesse's warm, furry root-mass snuggled in her lap. It purred.

Two knocks, twice, came from her door. "Enter." She marked her place in the book, expecting Mattiz or possibly Dr. Anahita Lee. To her surprise, it was the auditor who entered.

His face showed incredulity with good enough reason. Jesse's leaves and tendrils spilled onto the floor all around her chair. She probably looked like a woman out of a fairy tale, reading an enchanted book that stopped time for her so long that vines grew up around her

Jesse slipped off her lap, carefully bundling its root mass in vines and leaves. It retreated to a corner and went motionless. *Nothing to see here but a harmless house plant.* Ah. It had picked up on her distrust of the auditor.

"What is that thing?" the auditor asked.

"A plantimal, genetically engineered from both plant and animal genes. It's called a hugwort."

His eyebrows came down only a fraction of an inch. "Something else from your old laboratories?"

"No, the species is from a distant ocean moon world, newly discovered, or maybe rediscovered. There's a historical footnote about such a world with an early starship colony lost to the Time of Terror. The colony died out, there's no trace of it, but some xenobotanists hypothesize that they invented the hugworts."

Rik Gole flicked his head as though he understood and dismissed the existence of hugworts. "Your Service Chief told me how to find you. We need to talk."

"There will be talk, all right," she said drily. *Damn that matchmaking Wendisan.* There were no better service personnel than Wendisans, but they were inveterate matchmakers. Romeo in particular aspired to live up to the romantic implications of his name. Not that he misfired often: two couples and a threesome in Star Corner Station had found each other because of his matchmaking.

She knew he yearned to find a match for her. But—the auditor?!

"This is off the record." The auditor sounded serious, even portentous. "You need the kind of report I can make, you need it more than you know, and you need to cooperate fully."

Daya felt sudden dismay edged with anger. "You think I haven't cooperated so far?"

"Your Station has decommissioned areas drawing more than a trickle of power. Your budget has a credit leak—a few hundred credits a month are going somewhere unspecified. Your last three inventories have discrepancies not explained by materials and supplies officially listed as shipped away, discarded, acquired, or manufactured. And every month you have an excess expense for medical supplies not corresponding to accidents and injuries in the workforce."

Daya let her breath out through her teeth in an inaudible hiss. Evidently Rik Gole was very good at his work. He'd already sifted a massive amount of accounting and found nuggets of fact that Daya would have a hard time explaining.

He took a step closer to her. "It's clear to me that you're a superb manager. That makes you invaluable in this godsforsaken outpost. Cooperate with me, spell out whatever secrets you're keeping, take a salary cut to compensate for the missing credits, and you'll still have a job and a good reputation in the end, I can assure you."

Knowing all she knew, and being in the middle of an accurate history of interstellar civilization, his words struck a nerve. "If Faxe wants to rid itself of this station by accusing Goya and Wendis of tolerating maladministration—do you think any report of yours will matter?"

"Of course it will. I'm a senior auditor."

Her temper flared. "Are you that naïve? Or are you a tool of your state?"

Anger flushed his face. She would have welcomed an argument—the more furious the better—but he turned on his heel. With his hand on the lever of her door, he pointed at Jesse. "Does it eat goldfish?"

"Yes, and I replace them out of my own personal funds!"

The confrontation with Tattujayan got under Rik's skin like a shocknettle. It wasn't so much that she doubted his integrity. He had a ten-year record of honest and able auditing to prove his integrity to anyone who read his resume.

It was that she thought he could be a tool of the state. That was what shocked and irritated him.

The Faxen government did have its tools. He knew that. But he wasn't one of them. Neither was the Faxen Interstellar Financial Authority. That was why he worked for FINFINA.

To make the nettling effect worse, he'd actually seen her in her own private space, which he'd liked. The blankets on the walls kept the place warmer than the rest of the Station, making it all the more tempting to get to know the woman under the exotic clothes better and more personally.

It was a temptation that he had every professional reason to resist. He ought to be glad she'd insulted him. That line of reasoning did not help. For the first time ever, he felt his career offering him only a narrow, confining future in a universe of stars and possibilities.

He was brooding over his dinner, attacking his steak with a viciousness that the tender and tasty synthmeat did not deserve, when Brina Trover approached him, walking with a crutch. "Auditor, I'm already on the casualty list. That I'm not injured any worse than I am is thanks to you, it is. But we've got a war tomorrow. Would you take my place?"

"What?"

"It's an honor." Mattiz-Kol's eyes shone with enthusiasm. "I'm on the Keepers' side myself!"

To his own surprise, Rik nodded.

After dinner, Brina showed him a tall smooth stick made of real wood. "Pike. It can be used to good effect by the unskilled as long as they're not uncoordinated. It can trip people or brain them. The spear end can be used to stab." She anticipated the objection he was about to voice. "We wear body armor, gloves and helmets, so we don't get hurt and when we do Dr. Lee patches us up right away."

Rik parsed that and concluded that she meant *we don't get* permanently *hurt*. By now, they had an audience of stationers, including Tattujayan, who looked ironically interested.

"We have nonlethal beam guns to simulate the ancient projectile weapons that they used on Earth. The beam gun paints a hit with light and makes body armor turn red. Beam guns have power packs with limited energy—simulates running out of ammunition—so we also use weapons that don't run out of juice. It's fair to pick up any weapon that rolls by, relieve an enemy of theirs, take the weapon of anybody's who's dead on either side, pick up any inanimate object to hit somebody with, or resort to street-fighting."

It was definitely interesting to have a Goyan space-mining guilder explaining a Wendisan space game to a Faxen auditor, and apparently doing so accurately. Romeo Ito nodded approval.

"All's fair in mixed melee except changing sides or attacking the Referee." Brina used the pike to point at Tattujayan, then handed it to Rik. "Here you go."

He spent an hour in the recreation center, practicing pike-moves with Jax Trover, who was another piker. Then stationers started bringing in props for tomorrow's war, for which the recreation center would be the stage. Empty, stacked cargo containers represented buildings. One tall stack of containers was labeled as a Religious Tower. Several empty tailings trucks were trundled in to represent overturned vehicles. The next morning in the recreation center, the sides formed up for the war for the control of a deserted village.

Everyone had colored sashes to help tell friend from foe. The sashes echoed two large banners mounted on opposite sides of the rec center. The Trovers assembled under a blue banner with a silver circle—signifying Trove; Trover sashes were blue. The Keepers had a white banner with a green device that looked like a pile of leaves. Rik blinked when recognition set in. It was a *hugwort*.

"That's our mascot," a Keeper explained.

Rik was happy to fasten on a blue sash. It would have injured his dignity to be on the side that had an animated plant for a mascot. The plantimal itself perched on its shelf over the goldfish tank—placed there by a partisan, Rick guessed. It might be happy enough to be in a position to purloin a goldfish.

The war began at noon. At first Rik held back, watching from the sidelines. Beam guns splashed on fighters' body armor. The armor responded by turning telltale red. The wounded had to stop using the affected body part or, if it was a killing wound, play dead. To conserve the beam power packs, both sides also used non-energy weapons from the start. A physical hit made the body armor puff out to protect the wearer. The armor stayed puffed out to testify to the hit.

Tattujayan darted around awarding points to fighters for their kills and form. Nobody was supposed to hit the referee, but a couple of times only her own fast reflexes saved her from a side-swipe. She called demerits against several over-excited fighters who disregarded having taken hits evidenced by bright red or puffed-out body armor.

If she was in the thick of it, what was he doing on the sidelines? Rik plunged into the melee. For a few frantic few minutes he did well enough to just avoid becoming a casualty. Dead and the dying fighters littered the floor, some of them moaning from non-life-threatening but real injuries.

Seeing an opening, Rik extended his pike to trip an unwary Keeper and send him sprawling on the floor. Rik used the spear end of his pikestaff to finish the Keeper off with a stab to the chest. The Keeper's body armor instantly inflated to absorb the force of the blow. Rik got a little salute from the downed fighter.

"Score one for the Trover!" Tattujayan announced behind him. She leaned close to his ear. "Your blood's hotter than I expected, auditor!" Her words and the warm breath that carried them made his blood stir in private parts of his anatomy.

She melted away as Keepers responded to Rik's score by closing in on him. Rik fended off a blow from a Keeper who was using the butt of an exhausted beam gun as a club. But the Keeper's teammate used a mace to knock the pike out of Rik's hands. The two of them raised their weapons like clubs, meaning to rain Rik with blows that would send him out of the game.

When the first Keeper swung, Rik seized his arm, got under his center of gravity, and hefted him into his teammate. Both went down in the ensuing collision with body armor inflating as they hit the floor. Rik snatched up his pike up and finished them off. He heard Tattujayan's voice. "The Trover scores by revealing martial arts skill! Double points!"

From then on Rik mixed martial art with pikestaff work. Thanks in part to him the Trovers started winning. But Rik wondered if the Keepers were all on the battlefield. He had a good memory for faces, and there were six or seven faces he thought should be in the ranks of Keepers but he didn't see. One was the unmistakable Mattiz.

Suddenly a cry rang out from six or seven throats. *"Ban zay!"* Leaping off of the stack of containers marked as a Religious Tower, into which they'd crept one by one to hide, fresh Keepers descended on the Trovers and quickly overcame their startled resistance. One of the Keepers was Mattiz, brandishing a sword. Mattiz cut Rik down. Rik spent the last ten minutes of the war lying dead on the floor. Finally Tattujayan announced, "Game over! Victory to the Keepers with perfect honor to the Trovers!"

The dead and dying sat up.

Rik rubbed his neck. The collar of his body armor had deflected the blunt edge of Mattiz' sword, but still left him with a twinge in his neck. Doctor Lee put a numb-pack on his neck. It soothed the twinge. And that, Rik thought ruefully, explained the excess medical supplies. Looking around, he saw animated faces, handshakes between Keepers and Trovers, and glowing camaraderie—here, in a remote space place where, the gods knew, personnel might easily have been space slack, dissolute under the influence of drugs, or split into sullen factions.

Excess medical supplies? More like morale supplies. And not excessive at all.

The war made Daya admit to herself that she was irresistibly attracted to the auditor. Even with trust issues. Even with his allegiance to Faxe.

Faxens encountered elsewhere than Faxe tended to be likable people. They often had a well-cared-for innocence that often bordered on the naïve. Mattiz was a good example of an expat Faxen in all respects including his looks: physical perfection that had gotten scuffed around the edges from being outside of the bubble of privilege that was life on Faxe.

The auditor was different. As a functionary of the Faxen government, he carried his bubble of privilege with him across the stars. Yet he didn't come across as a sheltered innocent. He wasn't physically too-perfect, either. With tawny skin, thick, short brown hair and a strong-boned face with mobile features, he came across not as perfect so much as very real.

And in the war, he had been really splendid.

The fight was followed by a feast, the feast followed by a long rest period. Daya felt restless. She always had excess energy, plucking at her nerves from the inside, sometimes pushing her into trouble. With the Station quieter even than at night, almost everybody sleeping off the fight and the feast, she decided to enjoy her favorite view.

To her surprise, she encountered the auditor coming the other way. On impulse she put out a hand to stop him. At her touch he wheeled around and came to a stop, slightly leaning toward her.

Oh. How revealing a reaction that was! Like a horse feeling a familiar hand on the bridle. Or like a man feeling a touch from a woman he was interested in. She bit back the words that sprang to her tongue— *Are you prowling around looking for secrets I haven't shown you?* Instead she said, "Auditor, let me show you something else."

He fell in step with her.

It might be a good idea to compliment him. "You played the war well, and your martial art was something no one saw coming. Are you a martial arts practitioner?"

He gave a rather pleased laugh. "No, but I've had self-defense training, a course taken by civilian interstellar government workers—auditors like me, lawyers, diplomats and even an interstellar conciliator. The reason for the course was that any of us, even the conciliator, could find ourselves in an abduction situation or civil unrest, thanks to the Disunion terrorists."

If the Faxen government hadn't been bent on turning the Union into an Empire and ruling more worlds yet, while controlling the worlds it already had with a hard iron fist inside a soft coltskin glove, its representatives wouldn't find themselves terrorized. "You made good use of that course," was all Daya let herself say.

She was beginning to think it possible to get a kiss from this man. And she wanted that. Further involvement and intimacy was out of the question; a kiss was on the dangerously attractive precipice just short of foolhardiness. That kind of precipice was her favorite place.

After a vator ride up, they came to an unmarked door that opened onto a wide dark room. "The door opened to your hand," he observed.

"Administrative doors do. And this." She touched a plate on the nearest console. A tall slit appeared in the far wall. The slit widened until it was a window full of stars and Trove. "Here is the best view in the Station. Usually it's protected by an asteroid shield."

Rik moved up to the window beside her. He seemed eager to see out, and there was much to see.

Trove eclipsed the coldly radiant blue star. In the diffuse nebula-light shining on Trove's dark side, the deep pocks in the planet's skin were clearly visible, as were pale splashes of ore tailings. "Trove's mining history is written on its face," Daya said.

He nodded, still taking in the scene. A lesser but nearer yellow sun shone near Trove. The yellow sun tinted the starclouds around it with warm colors—gold and pink shading to salmon—behind the curved edge of Trove. "Strata had sunsets with colors like that."

Daya had heard of Strata, the capitol city of the planet Faxe. Like every human being across a hundred stars in reach of any kind of news media ten years ago, she'd heard of what happened there. A transit tower that reached all the way up to orbit had been brought down by Disunion terrorists, with terrible loss of life and innocence. "Were you in Strata when the tower fell?"

"No. I wasn't even on the planet."

Lucky for him, but she wondered why. Personal questions—much as she desired to throw a few at him—might offend him. She asked, "Why do so many Faxens leave to roam across the stars? Faxens don't seem to bond with their own world. Yet the original name of it was Fiat Pax—'let there be peace' in Latin—when the ancient starship from Earth found it to be a world full of life, like an oasis in the stars. There's never been such a wilderness since Earth. Yet so many of you go away from it."

"The wilderness has animals that can electrocute you," he said wryly. "And vegetation that gives you an electric shock. And carnivorous plants big enough to engulf a human being. If you fall into one, it snaps shut around you. If you remain motionless it decides you're debris, opens up to discard you, and you get away. If you struggle, it dumps digestive enzymes on you. You'll give the plant indigestion but that's little consolation. I'm not particularly attached to the Faxen wilderness. What about you? Why aren't you still on Goya?"

"This is my Walkaway." His forehead furrowed, so she explained. "The Steppe is a great sea of grass ringed with high mountains. Rivers of snowmelt run in valleys thick with trees and vibrant with birdsong. It took thousands of years of the blood and sweat and tears and failures of my ancestors to terraform all of that land. We fell into tribal barbarism and climbed back out again to a way of life that isn't barbarian, but isn't civilized in the sense Faxe understands it." In her opinion, Faxen civilization was an impersonal machine bent on consuming the resources of its own world and every other: barbarism like nothing since the long-ago Time of Terror. "Young people in the Steppe do a Walkaway—going out into space for a while to better understand what it is we have at home. I went further than most and stayed longer. And that makes two unwarranted questions of yours. You have one more," she said with a smile, hoping he would take it as an invitation.

"Will I use it up by asking what this place is?" he asked cautiously.

"Not at all. This was the Control Room for Star Crossing Station. The Director of the Station sat there." She indicated the deep but dusty chair. "With the Station largely decommissioned, the consoles in here were turned off. Because of that, this room is called the Grave."

He tilted his head to one side. To her surprise, he said, "It reminds me of a line from an ancient poem. 'The grave's a fine and private place, but none, methinks, do there embrace' is how it goes."

"This isn't that kind of grave," she said.

"Good." He put his arm around her. She tilted her head to find his lips with hers. He responded eagerly. Feeling the hotness of her own blood, she kissed him back harder. His muscles tensed and he locked his arms around her.

She stroked the smooth, strong-boned side of his face. "Rik—are you sure you don't have more of a name? A single syllable is what we'd name a dog. Our horses' names have as many syllables as ours."

"My name is Darik—but my friends call me Rik."

He'd left something out—the second part of his first name. She wondered why. "Call me Daya."

THREE

Here was what he'd been waiting for, though he'd only half known it: a real view of the Station and its place in the universe. It made him feel freer to be himself, to take a woman in his arms and kiss her. Kissing her gave him an almost electrical shock, but a good one. Unlike the plant life of Faxe, her electricity was human.

He had his back to the Starcross Nebula. Its gold and pink light washed the dead consoles in the Control Room with an ethereal sheen. "Does Daya mean something?"

"Davendaya means 'light reflected on water,' Daya means 'reflected light'."

"Like the old machines here?" he waved his hand.

"As a matter of fact, yes. Darik—" His real name, spoken in *her* voice, gave him a sharp, pleasurable jolt. "What is your—" She broke off as a new constellation appeared in in front of the window, three bright stars that hadn't been there before.

Her eyes widened. "Those are bubbles." One of the strange things about starflight-space was that communications could go no faster than starships. Bubbles skipped from starpoint to starpoint to bring messages. Getting bubbles into this remote corner of starspace took a high-energy jump and they shone like stars when they arrived. "Usually we get one of those in three weeks, not three in a single minute!"

Duty calls, he thought dourly, at the most inopportune times. "Sometimes on an assignment I get one. That doesn't account for the other two. Let's go see what they are."

They reached her office just before a white sphere rolled out of the tube into the in-box on Mattiz' desk. As soon as it stopped moving, a crack appeared. The bubble split into into two hemispheres, revealing the message capsule inside. She unspooled the message. "This is a routine advisory that lists the freighters scheduled to arrive in the next week."

Another sphere rolled into the basket. This one fell to pieces. Like all medium- and high-security bubbles from Faxen Authorities, it was designed to arrive only where it was sent and not be accidentally or deliberately relayed elsewhere. Its message capsule had Rik's name on it.

Before he could open the capsule, a third sphere rolled to a stop in the inbox. It quivered and opened like a lily, petals unfurling around the capsule. "This is a Wendisan bubble. We've get them occasionally for someone who has relatives in Wendis. But I don't see a name on the capsule." The Wendisan capsule started flashing red. Daya's eyes widened. "It's urgent!" She opened the capsule—not keyed to any individual hand—and gasped. "This is an SOS. Starway is under attack by pirates!"

Starway was the Wendisan interstellar crossroads station. Interstellar pirates had grown increasingly numerous and bold in recent years. Maybe some pirate leader had managed to unite the pirates to take the particularly succulent prize that was Starway. Enough pirates, well-organized enough, could pose a real threat to Starway. That would explain Rik's message. His fist tightened around its capsule.

She said, "We can't help except to relay the SOS to a few even more remote outposts. And we'll do that, auditor, whether or not you approve of the cost."

"Of course I approve."

"Mattiz is faster at packing bubbles than I am." She pressed a button to summon the secretary. Then she rubbed her face. "If pirates have become so brazen as to attack Starway, I have to wonder whether we are in danger too. Star Corner Station is in no longer in a position to control the starways. We do control the mining of Trove. That might be attractive to pirates. Yet would pirates risk angering Faxe?"

Rik thought about the Faxen Union's starfleet with its battleships, destroyers and troop transports. "Absolutely not."

Mattiz hurried in wearing off-duty clothes, a Wendisan-style soft tunic and pants. While Daya explained the situation to him, he gathered bubbles to relay the SOS and said, "I'm not so sure pirates would leave us alone! The last few years have seen pirates masquerading as Disunionists, and Disunionists masquerading as pirates—that's how they get some of their funding. Looting, ransom, and plunder." Evidently, Mattiz followed the news better and with more interest than this remote posting of his would indicate. "What if they tried to plunder us?"

"The Union starfleet would respond with force," Rik said with conviction. "It always does when Faxen possessions are seized."

"That's why I wonder! Faxe doesn't own Star Corner. It's operated per a very old contract, drawn up a thousand years ago, between Goya, Wendis and Faxe. I've read the contract. All six hundred clauses of it."

"Mattiz *is* a legalist," Daya told Rik. "He studied interstellar law at the University in Wendis."

"The Star Corner Station contract came up once in class, and a question posed as an academic exercise was how Goya, Wendis, or Faxe could divest themselves of what's now become a white elephant—a very large and useless possession. It wasn't easy to boil down, but it became clear that the contract would voided in two cases. One is malfeasance in the administration of the Station."

"There isn't that," Rik said impatiently.

"No. There isn't." Daya looked relieved to hear him say it, though.

"The other eventuality that would void the contract is war."

"War with who?" Rik asked. "Pirates don't have legal standing as a state."

Daya said, "The struggle with the Disunion terrorists is more and more spoken of as war."

"We'll soon get the best of them. Or are you harboring some of those too?"

She parried his hard look with a one of her own. "Not that I know of. I do know that I must alert the Station to the possibility of pirates attacking us. Even if the whole Union Fleet were to come to our rescue, Rik, it would be better for us not to need it."

She left him wondering exactly what Star Corner Station could do if pirates, or for that matter Disunion terrorists, did strike. Feeling discontented, he finally looked at the message in the capsule in his hand. And then he stared.

Yes, it was from FINFINA.

It ordered him to find malfeasance in the administration of Star Corner Station. It told him exactly what kind of malfeasance to find and write into a report. And to do so immediately.

Struggling to keep his face expressionless—luckily Mattiz was busy packing bubbles, reusing two and unpacking two fresh ones—Rik tried to keep his voice casual. "What kind of malfeasance would void the contract? That sounds pretty far-fetched to me."

"It would have to be a persistent pattern of profiteering, or wrongful and persistent negligence in the operation of the station resulting in the decay or deterioration of the facility, and it would have to be knowing and intentional—not misfeasance and not nonfeasance," Mattiz said absently.

That was precisely what the message from FINFINA instructed Rik to document in his audit report. He crushed the message film in his fist. It dissolved as, being high-security, it was meant to.

But it left a bitter, poisoned taste in his mind.

Daya was *not* going to make a general announcement about the situation. Pirates or Disunionists could have operatives anywhere, even here. Knowing what she knew about Star Corner Station, in fact, it was one of the first places in interstellar space that *she* would have planted a spy.

She found Jax Trover and Romeo Ito in Jax's office with a bottle of Firewater and the hugwort on the desk between them. Romeo held up a small glass of the fiery alcohol. "To honorable opponents!" Jax raised a glass too. "To wily opponents!" They tossed back their Firewater, then noticed Daya.

At what she told them, their faces went sober. "We'll put the Station on notice, Manager," said Jax. He looked for the Firewater bottle stopper.

Romeo rifled Jesse's leaves and produced the stopper.

Daya went to the anteroom of the passenger ring. This was not the time of day she usually came calling. Mercury met her there anyway. "What do you want?" Mercury asked scornfully.

"I have news for you. Starway is sending SOS bubbles. The bubble we got said Starway is under attack from pirates."

The Angel gave a cold startled hiss.

Maybe Daya was a fool for trading such news to the Angels. But Daya came from Steppe-people who knew how to judge traders. The Angels were remorseless but, unless Daya was utterly mistaken about them, they rigidly played by their own rules.

"What do you want in trade for that?" Mercury asked.

"Only a very simple piece of information. Did you sell news of the emberalm—" An instinct told Daya to bite her tongue and not say *to pirates* as she had intended. *Too specific a question is too easy to deny.* Daya definitely refrained from asking Mercury, *How could you sell the news so soon?* It was much better not to know that. Rumor spoken in hushed voices said the Angels could cross the stars apart from turning points, shining ships, or even time. Any outsider who had ever found out the truth of it had never been heard from again.

Mercury gave her that piercing, raptor look. Daya didn't flinch. Mercury finally said. "Yes, and we don't have fair trade unless I give you more than that, but I don't know what I'm allowed to say. You will be paid in full. Now go away."

Daya had long guessed that Star Corner Station was not the Angels' only foothold in the Starcross Nebula, and that if they could, they would even have a foothold or at least a meddling influence in Starway. Now, to a much higher degree of certainty, she knew that. She also knew that the news of emberalm had already reached pirates. No, more accurately, the news had reached some party or parties who had been interested enough to pay the Angels very well for it. She couldn't imagine a use for the deadly stuff. There had never been such a weapon since the Time of Terror. Even then it was only used against monsters. The thought of emberalm getting loose in the roiled field of interstellar politics and piracy made her shudder.

From yesterday, Daya still had the master key in the pocket of her coverall. She used it to let herself into the military depot. It was as Jax had described: the bulging emberalm containers, one cracked open on the broken floor, with tailings heaped around it to dam the stuff still inside. No containers were missing. That did not surprise her. As far as she knew, Angels didn't traffic in goods or contraband. Just news.

Going spingravity-up a vator, she ascended to the power plant in the center of the Station. It was of an ancient sort that ran on uranium, of which there was enough on Trove to fuel the power plant to the end of time, and no demand elsewhere: it was too dirty a fuel with too much potential to turn into a bomb. The power plant crew were far more carefully selected than any other personnel in the Station. None of them would be a pirates' spy.

Her touch opened the central plant panel. It probably hadn't been open in thirty years, yet the cover slid aside with a whisper. It gave the power plant crew many more options than they would otherwise have had, to damp down or ramp up the reactor, or give a Station sector more power and air—or none.

As she made her way through other sectors, she realized that something was different. Like a ripple in a pond, the news about Starway was causing the Station's mood to darken, sharpen, and become watchful. Many personnel in the Station were, like the central plant crew, the sons and daughters of generations who had worked here. It was in their blood to circle the wagons when trouble was afoot—not for the first time—in the Starcross Nebula. She didn't need to give orders, just use her authority to open a cabinet here and a tube there. She also asked for an exact accounting of the access keys in each sector.

On the way back to the administrative sector, she discovered the hugwort crawling in the corridor ahead of her. It didn't usually stir so openly during station day. Could it sense the Station's unsettled mood, just as it sometimes seemed to sense her mood—as improbable as it was for a plantimal to sense human feelings—? She followed it. At the ladder to the adjoining levels, it swung itself onto the ladder and purposefully crawled up.

As Jesse went up the ladder, Rik Gole started to come down. It froze. So did he, reluctant to put a foot into the midst of the hugwort's quivering tendrils. By his own account, his Faxen upbringing had given him reasons to be wary of plants. There was a standoff on the ladder.

Over the hugwort, Rik asked, "Can I help with whatever preparations you're making? I don't want to be a pirate's hostage any more than you do." His voice was low and yet intense. It could have cut through a din of conversation like a knife.

Then she noticed Jesse's bloom. Sometimes the hugwort bloomed suddenly and for no apparent reason. It was doing so now. The diaphanous, pale purple flower pointed at Rik like an antenna.

He stared at it, crouching down for a closer look at the hugwort. "This thing wasn't made by a desperate dying colony. It's too sophisticated an organism for that."

Well, genetic engineering by a vanished colony was the best explanation for the existence of hugworts. That did not mean the true or only explanation. As the Manager of Star Corner Station, she'd learned that the stars had secrets coiled inside of secrets. "You think not?"

"It reminds me of what another ancient poet said. 'Tiger Tiger, burning bright, in the forests of the night, what immortal hand or eye, could frame thy fearful symmetry?'"

Poetic allusions aside, he was an unusually observant individual—that was the genius of his work as an auditor. "Rik, would you help us by watching for trouble that likely won't come?"

He leaped over the hugwort, lightly landing on the corridor floor with perfect coordination. "How?"

Glad she'd thought to put a universal security disk in her pocket, she took it out and pressed her hand against it. The disk gave a brief blue glow. "Go to the Grave. You remember how to find it? Good. Put this in the access slot and you'll get in. This disk will remember my handprint for three hours. That will let you come and go if you need to refresh yourself." As she gave him the disk, their fingers nearly touched.

The sexual tension between them almost made a physical spark between her fingertips and his.

"Is watching all I can do? Machines do that much."

"Our machines scan the stars and the corridors but machines only see what their programming lets them see. And programming can be corrupted."

He jumped as though stung.

"Put this disk in an access slot on the communicator and call me if you see anything amiss. My code is two twice. That will reach me anywhere in the Station. You may not have noticed, since we have little need for them, but comm stations are everywhere."

He nodded, turned, and strode away.

He'd changed. She'd already seen him change from the calculating auditor, once as he took part in the wargame, and again when they were together in the Grave. Now he seemed to have become that change. He was like—he'd given her the words for it: he was like a bright tiger. *Who made you, Darik?* She wondered. Like stars, hearts had secrets coiled inside secrets.

Jesse proceeded up the ladder to the next level. There it extended two long tendrils upward to the grating over an airduct. It neatly opened the tabs that held the grating in place. It let the grating rotate down on the hook on the lower corner of it. Then Jesse pulled itself up into the airduct. Extended several tendrils to reposition the grating and refasten the tabs. And crawled away in the airduct with the faintest of rustling sounds.

More than she'd realized, the hugwort was beautifully suited to a space place. Strong, supple, smart, subtle and sneaky, as well as compressible enough to fit into an air duct. No wonder the Wendisan Stationers admired it enough to make it their mascot.

In her office she found Mattiz backing up Station status reports into suresafe form—a crystal stored in a fire-and impact-proof vault. That kind of backup would happen automatically at the first sign of a calamity like an asteroid impact or critical mass in the power plant, so investigating authorities could learn what happened even in the absence of survivors. In this case, Mattiz was manually suresafing the records. He said, "The auditor was here. He sent three bubbles—to the Faxen, Wendisan and Goyan offices that govern us!"

There went a month's bubble budget! She was offended at the auditor for acting so summarily and without saying anything to her. Then she grew alarmed wondering what he had said. "Did you get a look at the messages?"

"No, and he took the cloned copies. Manager, did you know his real name is Darik-Arn?"

"Yes, at least the Darik part." Trading familiar names had been a pleasure, startling as a ray of sunlight in a dark tent. If the tent flap were to open, what kind of landscape would that reveal—a desolation, a Faxen wilderness of shocks? Or a summer grassland?

Mattiz looked at her with a solemn expression. "On Faxe, everyone's first-name combination is as unique as possible. There's even a central database of already-used names to check when you name a child. Except in the uppermost class, the ones who live on top of Strata, it's become popular for parents to name their children after themselves. Maybe it has to do with implicit class privilege. They keep it a kind of secret and I didn't know about it until I studied at the University of Wendis and it came up in a contemporary anthropology class. Anyway, there's a famous Faxen named Darik-Arn Gole who might be our auditor's father."

"Famous? Why?"

"He's one of the Quinvirate."

"What?! The five syndexecutives who rule the Faxen Union?"

Mattiz nodded. "With a father like that, he might not be just an auditor. He might really be an agent of Faxe. Faxe does that—seeds other planets and space places with harmless-looking agents who have Faxe's interests at heart. Unlike re-using a parent's name, everybody knows Faxe does that."

Her nervous energy ran out of her like water out of water-bag and left her feeling limp. She had to sit down. She felt the Eye of Fate on her. It hadn't just winked at her. Its stare was boring into her.

Good thing she'd asked the auditor to go where she had. There weren't any controls in the Grave that he could use. And she could remotely lock him in.

In front of the Control Room's wide window, Rik sat in the large—rather regal, in fact—Chair of the old Station Director. He was conscious of the irony.

His head hurt.

He still had the message capsule in his clenched fist. At first he hadn't been able to believe that its poisonous message came from FINFINA. Then he'd realized it might have come *through* the Financial Authority: an important distinction. Rik had it on excellent authority that SECINTAG, the Secret Intelligence Agency, could work through any Authority in the Faxen Union, and did so more and more often, given the Disunion terror. Rumor even had it that SECINTAG now fought terror with terror, inventing devices and methods to counter-terrorize the enemies of the state. If so, that was ugly.

With his headache getting worse, he put his hurting head in his hands. He'd believed that making a career in interstellar accounting would work for him. That investigating the accountability and operational soundness of various interstellar organizations was a safe path to take—an endeavor as neutral as any could be. His father had thought so too. Yet not prevented Rik from taking that path. Rik had always believed that his father had written him off as an insignificant loss. Maybe his father had foreseen how auditing could prove useful.

He wrenched his head out of his hands to look up. Keeping watch through the wide window was both the least and the most he could do now.

Nebula light—cold and blue, with the blue star shining bright—reflected on the service spines of the Station. That must be daya, he thought, a daya of harsh starlight. If the Station was a hand, the spine's fingers were a skeleton of what they had been in the days that had seen a thousand cargo, passenger, administrative, scientific and military modules attached to the spines. Oddly, there was one ring-shaped module attached to the passenger service spine. It looked like a ring on a skeletal finger.

Between third and fourth, or little, fingers, a rift in the nebulosity showed some of the galaxy's more typical starry space. That way, Rik thought jaggedly, lay the Faxen Union. It was really only a few stars across and only a few millennia deep in the vastness of space and time.

It was his father's ambition that it not remain a Union of the planets of just a few stars. His father wanted Faxe to rule countless worlds across the sea of stars, to be like Rome and England of ancient Earth—empires across the known world—and like Terra Nova in the Star Age before Terra Nova turned into the Terror.

Rik toyed with the disk Daya had given him. He felt achingly lonely and would have liked to use the communicator to hear her voice. But he had nothing of any substance to communicate to her. And he probably wouldn't. Not now or ever.

Several keys were missing. One of them was important—a master key for access to the service spines' hollow cores.

Daya was suspicious about that. In this regard, she wasn't suspicious of Rik Gole. Even if he were a calculating tool of Faxe, he certainly hadn't pilfered a handful of assorted keys. It was entirely possible that three different sectors of the Station had each misplaced a key since the last key inventory. Those three were minor. The fourth was not.

Someone who worked here might have stolen the master key. If so, it had probably been someone among the less prominent ranks of personnel, possibly a worker in the ore plant, where the lower-ranking personnel were most numerous and least security-checked. The ore plant never stopped operating. So some personnel hadn't attended the war game. With everyone else away at the game, that would have been a good time to steal a key from almost anywhere in the Station.

If such a thing had actually happened, the guilty person or persons would still be on duty, their shift not ending until later.

Daya easily explained her presence in the ore plant to the personnel she encountered. She made a point of using a quaint and harmless Goyanism. "For some reason the hugwort has gone walkaway and I'm trying to find it. Have you seen it?"

Seven of the eight personnel she encountered said no.

Could one of these ore-plant workers be a key-stealing spy or traitor? A mixture of ethnicities worked here. They were Goyans who weren't space-guilders, Wendisans who for some reason lacked Citizenship, and Faxen-Unioners far away from home. Theoretically yes, especially with respect to the last group, one or more of them could be a thief or even a spy. But Faxe would certainly have screened the Unioners for Disunionist ties.

Veda Mender, when asked about the hugwort, said *yes*. It was no surprise to find Veda here when almost everyone else was taking time off. As the Maintenance Chief of Star Corner Station, Veda always had more work than she and her crew could handle and spent a great deal of her time and energy just doing triage.

She directed Daya to her dusty office off the catwalk over the Port level of the ore plant. The hugwort was in Veda's office exploring the drawers in a tool chest. "Your plant likes to visit our plant, it does!" Veda said.

Daya apologized to Veda and removed the hugwort. On the dimly lit catwalk outside Veda's office, she sat down cross-legged and rifled the hugwort's leaves and tendrils. There was grit and dust on its leaves—tailings powder, metal filings—due to it wandering through the airducts. "You need a bath," she scolded.

It was curious as a cat and as charmed by shiny objects as a crow. But it was more adroit than either cats or crows at opening cabinets, pockets, drawers, or airduct gratings of interest. Worse yet, it had a bad habit of carrying away objects that interested it, clutched in its tangled tendrils. Daya relieved the hugwort of two shiny fasteners, a Wendisan yen coin, a writing stylus, a bracelet—it had an incurable weakness for jewelry—and one small, hard, smooth-edged square. One of the missing keys.

One of Jesse's tendrils crept toward Daya's hand, curled around the bracelet, and gave a hopeful tug. Daya held on. "This isn't yours." It looped another tendril around the stylus. "That isn't either. I think it's the one Mattiz lost last week." The hugwort settled for extending a soft tendril tip to longingly stroke the key.

It was a minor key, meant for—according to the lettering—unused lockers in the Cargo sublevel. It certainly wasn't the spine access master key. But Daya had to wonder how the hugwort had gotten it. Keys were kept in biometric-secured cabinets that opened only to high ranking hands. Had this key simply gotten away from someone somewhere over the years, and the hugwort found it in some dusty corner? Or had the hugwort managed to purloin the key from a recent thief? It did seem to sense anyone's feelings of attachment to things, which was part of why it had an unfortunate weakness for jewelry. Would the hugwort register a secretive, ill-intended attachment to a stolen thing?

One suspicion led to another. If anything untoward happened in the next few hours—in particular any attempt by pirates to attack the Station —it would be very suspicious indeed. The war game had been long since scheduled, and predictably, everyone was now recuperating from fighting and feasting. It would not have been hard to predict that the Station would be unawares today. Only thanks to the SOS from Starway was the Station on unobtrusive full alert.

The ore plant had a constant growl and churn of background noise. A new noise belatedly registered on Daya. Not mechanical and not the sound of rocky ore being moved around, it sounded like the rustle of wings.

Daya jerked her head up.

The Angel Mercury hovered in the air of the bay not far away.

Daya suppressed a startled gasp. She had never seen the Angel outside of the passenger ring. But the cores of all the spines were hollow, and Mercury had wings to fly in spingravity. And that, she thought, explained the missing spine core assess key. The Angels must have it and with it the run of the spine cores. And that probably explained why Station personnel thought bad luck lived in the spine cores, and went there as seldom as possible.

With wings outstretched for balance, Mercury perched on the catwalk railing. "The news of emberalm was sold to channels who sell military news to Faxe. And another thing. It isn't pirates attacking Starway. It's that cartel of the Faxen Union called Telal. A Telal dreadnaught vomited mercenaries into Starway. And now we're even. You're paid in full for all information and every hospitality. Don't go into the ring again if you value your life."

Mercury launched up and soundlessly vanished into the dimness of the bay.

Daya felt a cold, soul-shocking dread. She hugged the hugwort. It responded by wrapping its tendrils around her.

Faxe. The coltskin glove had come off the iron fist of Faxe. If it controlled Starway, Faxe would control traffic between Goya, Wendis, and the Faxen Union—an advantageous position to say the least. The book about the history of interstellar civilization had conjectured that at some point, maybe in a century in the future and maybe less, Faxe would try to get exactly that.

Faxe had money to buy high-quality spies too. Enough money could send people to a remote post like this to bide their time until their services were needed, maybe even keep them on a kind of retainer, just in case they ever came in useful.

And Faxe had money to pay well for news about a game-changing weapon for the terror war. All that was left after knowing about emberalm was to actually take possession of it. . . .

Curious at having heard voices, Veda stepped out of her office. Daya numbly showed her the bracelet, the fasteners and the stylus. "That's none of it mine," Veda said. "But I've been missing two good tools for a while! Does your hugwort have a nest where it keeps its little treasures?"

"No, it just clutches them in its tendrils and carries them around. I've found everything it's got today."

"My tools may have spin-slid into cracks somewhere in this great scrapheap." With that, Veda went on her way.

The sound of a massive door sliding open came across the ore bay below. The latest load of tailings had been funneled into a hauler, the hauler shifted along its track to the door of a materials port. Visible through the outer door was an inner door that opened onto an airlock.

With the hauler in the lock, the inner door sealed behind it. Air would be sucked out and tailings powder in the air filtered out. Then the spaceside door would iris open and the hauler would be launched toward Trove. The catapult was steerable to compensate for the precession of the Station in its orbit. The catapult gave the hauler a shove to head it back to Trove.

The process was boringly routine. Veda hadn't even spared it a glance. Arriving ore was a more attention-getting, understandably—anything coasting toward the Station got attention until it was safely caught in the cables of the ore yard and eased in through a port. Haulers taking tailings back to Trove, on the other hand, were a repetitious and unexciting fact of life here. And it took long enough in the launch port that illicit bubbles could probably be surreptitiously sent and received as well, Daya thought. The Stations' sensors would never even notice. The Station's sensory apparatus was truncated from what it had once been. Truncated and stupid.

That needed to change, if it wasn't already too late.

FOUR

Rik was glad he was here, even if for no real reason. In the silence of the Grave, he looked out at a vast swath of the stars and nebulosity of space. The wide view came as an ice-cold comfort to him. It confirmed the changed state of his life. His career had given him only a narrow, confining future in a universe of stars and possibilities. It had felt as safe as it was narrow—like the asteroid-protected windows in the corridors of the ore plant. Now, though. . . .

Movement caught his eye. It was that anomalous passenger ring on the next spine over. He had a good and rather close view of it from here. As he watched, at least four pieces of the passenger ring broke off and drifted away. The further away they drifted, the more the outlines of the pieces blurred, reflecting nebula light strangely, and maybe even changing shape.

He found the access slot in the communicator and put Daya's disk into it. The communicator woke up with a quick flicker of self-check and ready lights. He entered her code—twice two—and she answered immediately. "What is it, auditor?" Her voice sounded guarded.

"The old passenger ring did something odd." He described it.

"Where are the pieces?" She sounded startled.

"Nowhere to be seen." He could hear soft voices behind her speaking with two different male accents. It sounded like he'd found her in a conference with Jax and Romeo. They went silent when she said, "Call up Station visuals on the old passenger ring!"

"The Station monitor hasn't flagged anything," Jax said.

"Monitors can be compromised. I want to see what it actually looks like now." A moment later, she said, "Six missing pieces, Rik, none of them registering on the monitor, all gone. Our monitor is either malfunctioning or compromised."

Rik thought he heard Romeo say, "The angels have left us," but that made no sense.

It also made no sense that Daya said something about rats leaving a sinking ship. Then she spoke to him again. "Rik, you have that disk with my handprint on it. Look for the access slot in the central console and put the security disk in. And keep watching. And thank you."

Thank you. The words went through Rik like electricity. That told him in no uncertain terms that he'd gone past being attracted to Daya. He'd fallen in love with her. To what end, he did not know. He did not even know what to hope for.

Indicator lights raced across the bank of consoles. Rik watched self-checks going on, then the lights stabilized. Interesting—the Grave was waking up. Evidently it wasn't a real grave, more like cold storage for the array of machines no longer needed to run the station. In any event, the machines had no attention to spare for him. With the exception of the communicator, his touch on plates and switches had absolutely no effect.

Meanwhile he watched outside more warily than before.

He saw the starship when it first reached real space, its initial shining almost blindingly bright, the light glaring on the Station's surfaces and throwing black shadows. He used the communicator again. "Daya, are there freighters scheduled for today?"

"One late tonight." Her voice sounded as though she were speaking in a large and hollow place now, not her office, or for that matter, her living room. "That one is a freighter of Goyan registry, near midnight." Loud scraping sounds and a metallic clatter nearly drowned her out.

"Any ships scheduled to come here in Station-day?"

"No, Rik. Why?"

"There's one out there."

Don't see this, ill Fate. Daya let that thought cross her mind, then told it to go away, the better not to attract Fate's attention even by careless thinking.

With the wargame over, empty containers were being carried out of the Recreation Center and back to Cargo sector. The three tailings trucks had to go back to the ore plant. Jax, Romeo and Brina had one of them already moving along on a haulway. "We're tidying up, we are!" Brina called cheerfully. "We got the one from the war with the red stuff, all cleaned up, it is!"

"Thank you all for handling that," Daya told them. She meant it.

Don't see this, ill Fate.

Daya ran for the vator to the Grave.

She hoped against hope that the arriving ship was a Goyan freighter that had been left out of the schedule. Even more likely, it might be the one scheduled to arrive tonight, having starjumped faster than planned. That could happen if the freighter had to dodge some kind of danger or had a certain kind of engine malfunction.

Rik was standing by the window of the Grave. "Was there a Faxen military transport scheduled to visit the station? Do they ever just drop in on you?"

Dread clawed Daya's nerves. "No and not likely at all."

"Daya, this isn't good. Let me explain—"

"No. I know."

One of his eyebrows went up.

"Starway was attacked by the Telal Cartel—by the mercenary arm of the Cartel."

His other eyebrow went up.

"Believe me or not as you wish."

"Oh, I believe you." He turned back to the window. Evidently he'd been watching so closely that he hadn't realized that she'd locked him into the control room a while ago.

"Faxe must have decided to strong-arm its way to the power it wants to feel safe from terror."

He gave a stiff shrug. "That's an excuse. The real goal is Imperial Faxe."

He knew. And was he on the side of Imperial Faxe? How could she tell? The questions howled in her mind. She stepped to the window beside him. "But where is it?"

"Hard to see. Look for the starship-shaped hole in the nebula."

It was a big, featureless spindle shape, barely visible in front of the nebula backdrop, inching toward the Cargo sector dock. "I ordered the docks to go to an ask-and-answer basis." Everything seemed unreal, including her own voice speaking those words. "The dock controllers should query the intentions of any approaching ship, scheduled freighter or otherwise, and they should explain their intentions and be approved to dock. Or not."

"Good idea. If it works. They may have friends in your ranks." His voice was grim.

He knows that too. Daya was acutely conscious of her right boot with the long, slender dagger in its slim pocket. Most non-Steppe people were ignorant of the lethality of a dagger. True, Rik Gole had some martial arts. But she knew how to use the dagger at close range and how to throw it. He didn't stand much of a chance if she had to kill him. And if he tried to stop her from protecting the Station, she would. For once in her life, it was hard to frame words. She forced out, "What about you, Darik-Arn Gole? Are you one of those friends?"

"No."

"Why should I believe you?"

"I thought you'd ask that." He held out three bubble-clones. Mattiz hadn't seen Rik's three messages, but their clone-copies would be dated and watermarked—a very hard thing to fake. As if he understood her intense wariness, he stepped away and turned his back to her. "I assume Faxe wants to rid itself of your Station. The idea may be to first take possession, then open it under new management, then decommission it. The transport is approaching like it means to dock with no questions answered."

Daya looked at what he had put in her hand.

His messages addressed to the Station authorities in Goya and Wendis said that FINFINA had ordered him to find specific malfeasance in the management of Star Corner Station and that he had refused to obey that order and resigned from his position. The message to FINFINA said the same thing, only couched as a direct communication to his employer of the fact that he was resigning his position, and why.

Incredulous, she touched his shoulder.

He wheeled toward her.

"You sent this."

He pointed to the watermark, which was proof positive. But that wasn't really what she was asking. In his eyes she saw heat lightning from a storm in his soul.

The communicator suddenly blared. *"Attention all personnel and visitors in Star Corner Station. Prepare for an important announcement."*

Rik grimaced. "That was quick work. They've commandeered the communications channels. Intelligence operatives know how to do that."

Daya pointed at the console, where lights flashed. "The Station's communication Intelligence is fighting back. The Intelligences here were built in the Terror and designed to protect the Station."

He shook his head, though not, as it turned out, at what she'd said. "This situation doesn't make sense. The report I was ordered to write would provide enough of a rationale for a routine appropriation of the Station. That's a civilian action maybe backed up by lightly armed detachment. You don't send a military transport for that. Maybe it was what was available, but a transport can carry fifty soldiers." His frown deepened. "It's unmarked, no insignia, and no daya—it doesn't reflect light. That may mean it's an unlisted ship for flights to nowhere. In other words, covert operations directed by SECINTAG, the Faxen secret intelligence agency."

It was she who knew the right question now. "What would they send to get emberalm for their terror war?"

Rik whirled back toward the window. "How would they know about it? I didn't say anything—and there are the bubble-clones to prove it. Do you have a spy sending unauthorized bubbles?"

"Possibly, but that's not how the Faxen military got news of the emberalm. I'll explain later. You've helped me make a decision," she heard herself say. "Thanks to the communications Intelligence, there are channels that are still mine." She touched the communicator to open one such channel. A machine voice softly said, *"Secure."* Daya said, "Jax, are you there? Can you do it?"

"Secure." Then Jax said, "Yes, Manager."

Watched by Rik, she swallowed hard. She'd never done anything like this—or in her wildest nightmares thought she'd need to. With infinite reluctance, she forced herself to touch a sequence of icons on the ore plant operations console. Lights continued to flash after she lifted her hand.

Then she heard Jax groan. "Manager, that didn't work, your remote override didn't work! Veda!"

Daya heard Veda Mender say, "Yes?" in a harried voice. "Now what?"

"The Manager tried to send an override in from the Control Room and it didn't work. Maybe a circuit is broken."

"If so there's a kilometer of circuit to check and all of it in sealed explosion-proof casing!" Veda sounded shocked. "I couldn't inspect a circuit like that in two days and a night!"

Jax said, "Manager, can you come up here? I'll need your hand to make the override work. At least I think it will work then."

Never in her life had Daya had such mixed feelings. Relief that the ancient override circuitry wasn't working—*I'll not have to do it*—and anger that it wasn't working—*I have to do it*. Wanting to stay safe here in the Control Room, which could be sealed off from anything much short of a thermonuclear explosion. And angry dread because Jax was right. If she were going to do what she'd hoped not to do, she had to leave the safety of this place. "I've got to go to the ore plant," she told Rik.

He held his hand up in a warning gesture. "There will be soldiers in the corridors—and they may be looking for you with you orders to take you into protective custody."

"I have no choice."

"I think I can misdirect them. I'll come with you."

Time was running out. She had to take him at his word or not, trust him now or never. This wasn't Rik Gole the bloodless auditor. He was Darik-Arn, the tiger—son of a syndexec in the Quinvirate. If his father was like this—hotblooded yet cool-thinking, decisive and charismatic—no wonder that man had risen to head a syndicate and then the world. "All right. Come with me."

She quickly pulled up a Station schematic on the room's central console. "Station personnel are the blue dots. The yellow dots are unknown personnel. You're right. They're in. They're clustered in the dock but moving. These two blue dots in the midst of the unknowns—Station personnel who've been surprised and detained, or else in collusion with the troopers." She memorized those names. "Come on!"

"Do you mean to stay out of the vators?"

"They probably have a means of commandeering vators."

"Right. They do."

The station was laced with ladderways and stairs. They went up using ones in out of the way places.

Comm stations blared. *"Attention personnel. This facility is now under the protection of the Faxen Interstellar Military Authority."*

"Protection means protecting a place from the rightful inhabitants," Rik said behind her.

"All personnel should report to their work assignments. Administrative personnel should report to their area of responsibility immediately."

As they approached the Main level, Daya said, "Up there you go left. Toward the Cargo sector."

Behind her, Rik said, "About that third question."

She stopped to stare at him. "Now?!"

"Would you take a stateless auditor into your bed?"

Desire and anger flashed in her mind like lightning and illuminated things that were there, truths she hadn't noticed. Several such truths. She seized him and gave him a brief, fierce kiss. "Yes, and I want you to give them something better than misdirection, and I want you to survive it. Listen carefully!"

Strange, Rik thought, that it was like putting on a long-unused, but carefully stored, suit of clothes—only needing to be shaken out to fit perfectly —for him to assume the mannerisms of his father. Mattiz, with his Wendisan University education, would have called it the implicit privilege of the ruling class, or something like that. Rik heard the heavy tread of the soldiers coming this way. He went to meet them, walking with unhurried confidence, a kind of stroll.

The soldiers recognized it. They might either round up or ignore Station personnel. but that wasn't their reaction to him. He identified the commanding officer of this small unit. With his best top-of-Strata accent, he told her, "I need to see your—" here he put in a slight but significant pause "—special civilian advisor."

She knew what he meant. And that meant his guess was right. These troops had a SECINTAG operative advising them. In a few minutes Rik stood in front of a man with unremarkable looks, an unremarkable name— Major Rand—and cold eyes.

Rik knew he was wagering his freedom or even his life on the odds that his resignation from FINFINA was not yet known to Rand. And that someone in SECINTAG's recondite chain of command knew who Rik's father was and assumed Rik to be his father's special tool, and that the briefing that Rand had received would include that as a fact. In the dirty fog of a secret war, such was a very likely mistake to make.

"Welcome to Star Corner Station, Major," Rik said. "The Station Manager is hiding from you. She's in an old passenger ring with some armed supporters who have an unfortunate degree of loyalty to her. I happen to have her handprint to open the place. Here." He held up Daya's security disk

The Colonel had a cold smile, like his eyes.

Though his heart was pounding harder than it had in the wargame, Rik felt a sudden certainty, like what he'd often seen in his father, that he could bend the universe to his will. It made his words persuasive. "Perhaps you know of the report I've made? Good. As you settle the Station's affairs, I believe I can help you convince her to cooperate fully."

Rik found himself escorted to Daya's office. A single lightly armed soldier was there guarding a strained-looking Mattiz. Of course—there would be some hardened shock troops in this operation, but the rest of the military personnel were ordinary and relatively newly recruited soldiers who could herd civilians without inciting them. The guard had a communicator on his wrist. There were audible updates from the soldiers fanning out through the station and from the heavily armed detachment heading for the old passenger ring.

Rik positioned himself behind Mattiz to watch the Station monitor on the wall. Primitive technology compared to the monitor in the Control Room, this monitor just showed a sticklike schematic of the Station with either green lights for no problems or red lights for problems of some kind. There were no dots for personnel. What Star Corner Station could afford and keep in good repair had been in short supply for a long time. Daya had stretched her limited resources in amazing ways.

Daya had said *yes*. He let himself touch that memory for only a moment before putting it away again.

The comm station out in the corridor blared the same announcement as before.

Rik noticed a long, edged metal shape under Mattiz' desk. So that was where he kept his wargame sword. With false heartiness, Rik put a hand on Mattiz' shoulder and said, "You can be glad the house will be cleaned up." One of Rik's fingers unobtrusively pointed to the sword. The soldier didn't notice. Mattiz did. He swallowed hard. He let the pressure of Rik's hand move him to one side, so his feet weren't in front of the sword.

Between the blaring words of the all-station announcement came a loud blur of static. Rik made out panic-stricken words. *"Booby-trap!"* He felt a shiver in the floor as though an explosion had rocked part of the Station. *"Explosion—casualties—"*

On the monitor, the first finger of the Station's hand where the ring was broke in two.

Rik snatched up the sword and leaped at the soldier, landing a stunning broadside blow to the soldier's bare head. He snatched the soldier's beam gun and tossed Mattiz the sword. "Show me the best back way to the ore plant!"

If the Station was a hand, the Main level crossed it below the fingers, where the fortune-tellers on the Steppe located the lifeline on a human hand. Daya wondered what fortune it told for her. Was it where the line of her life would be broken?

She found tape lettered with the words PROHIBITED DO NOT ENTER stretched across the level. Daya recognized tangletape—try to move it aside and it entangled you. She didn't mean to take the main entrance to the ore plant, which was what the tangletape barred from both sides—but she had to get past it to the sideway up to the part of the plant she needed to reach.

The sharp edge of her dagger sliced through the tape, first on the near side of the ore plant entrance then on the other side. The tape shriveled. She continued along the Main level. The curve of it blocked her view of the next intersection until too late. She saw the four uniformed soldiers there just as they saw her.

"Halt!"

Daya doubled back to a side-stairway, not the one she wanted because it went up to the Ports too close to the Cargo sector. She ran up the stair. The soldiers followed and gained on her. She barely registered a green blur as she raced past it. Then there was a commotion behind her.

The hugwort had stretched itself across the stairway, hung on, and tangled the soldiers' feet. They came crashing down.

Wincing at how that must have hurt the hugwort, Daya reached the Port level and turned left, found no soldiers in her way and ran to the Port 42A receiving area.

The door opened to her touch. She let out the breath she'd been holding when she saw not soldiers but familiar faces, and a recognizable bulging container in the catapult.

"The door stuck but Veda fixed it," Jax told her. Veda had smudges on her face. "It's ready now, except the override command."

This time she felt no reluctance to do it. Not with soldiers trying to take over her station, soldiers' boots trampling the hugwort as it tripped them to save her from them. Daya touched the plate.

"Initiated." Jax bent over the catapult control console. "Where is that damn ship?"

"At the Cargo docks. It has such a low albedo it's hard to see," Daya told him.

"Oh so." His hand made a slight, decisive movement. With a thrust, felt even this close only as a quiver in the walls and floor, the catapult launched its load. "It's not moving fast," Jax whispered. "The catapult isn't meant to hurl anything."

Over his shoulder she watched the image on the monitor. "The better for it not to be seen until too late," she whispered back.

"Too late will be very late indeed, since starship hulls are not made of metal."

FIVE

"Uh-oh," said Mattiz.

They'd used an out-of-the-way ladder tube to get up to the ore plant. It was an escape ladder, Mattiz said, for plant personnel to escape any conflagration or massive airloss there. Every rung was coated with more and more tailings dust, making bruising slips easy. Maybe personnel escaping an actual disaster could have just slid down the ladder, Rik had thought, nursing a painful elbow. Finally Mattiz had opened a hatch only to find the ore plant catwalk already occupied by tense, silent shapes.

The nearest shape put a finger to her lips. Mattiz and Rik climbed out onto the catwalk and quietly closed the hatch behind them. Now Rik recognized these people. They were Keepers and Trovers, some armed with wargame weapons, others with whatever long and hard they seemed to have found at short notice. Every third or fourth person had a roll-ladder hooked to the railing of the catwalk in front of them. A few had large buckets balanced on the railing.

That was when he heard the soldiers on the Port Level. It was a squad of them, pausing in front of each port door. Rik recognized what they were doing—it was a clearing maneuver. The soldiers had a life detector. They would break in to any port where it detected someone inside. The life detector only worked where it was pointed. None of the soldiers thought to point it *up*. They probably had orders to clear the Port level of Stationers and that was what they were intent on.

One of the dark shapes on the catwalk gave a low whistle.

The wargamers laddered over the edge onto the Port level below.

Buckets full of tailings dropped onto the soldiers, injuring any soldier they fell on and dumping rolling rocks and slippery powder underfoot.

"Ban zay!" the Stationers yelled.

It turned into a war down there.

Rik gripped Mattiz' wrist. "I told her I'd meet her. Where's 42A?" Mattiz pointed. Rik helped himself to a roll-ladder away from the fray. Mattiz followed him down.

Rik paused at a narrow window. As he craned his neck to see it better, something about the transport ship looked wrong. There was an unseemly dent, a crack in the hull, and a cloud of outgassed air and material.

Mattiz was at Rik's back, watching the fight. "Some of us and some of them are down but we're pushing them back."

From the far end of the transport, space-suited figures streamed out. They jetted toward the cables that crisscrossed the hollow palm of the Station's hand. They probably meant to mount an attack on Port 42A. In a line, with good discipline, they formed up along one of the cables.

Rik saw something else, something coming toward the spacesuited soldiers lined up at the cable. It looked like a spider making its way toward a fly in its web.

He knocked two times twice on the door marked 42A. *Friend.* It opened to let them in. "I see you gave them what they wanted," Rik said.

"You're alive!" He got a fast, fierce kiss from Daya and from Romeo Ito an approving glance.

She said, "Rik, this is a port that has secure communications channels and a catapult that can be tilted further than most of them, with the right override. It can catapult at the Station. It was built that way in case anything ever attacked the Station. The Starcross Nebula is a perilous place."

He wanted more of her fierce kisses. There was a chance he'd have them. Not a certainty. His father's confidence in bending the universe to his will had no place in the Starcross Nebula. *To emberalm with it.*

Part of Rik's attention registered but disregarded comm stations repeating the tiresome invasion announcement. Daya was able to cut it off. "Attention, invaders in Star Station. Your transport ship is damaged and your comrades on the ship may be hurt."

Rik told her, "Some of them exited the ship to attack us but the ore-yard dogs look interested."

Daya translated, "Some of your comrades are prepared to attack this Station across the ore-yard, but an unpleasant surprise awaits them."

"And you were right. The ring was booby-trapped. It took out some shock troops and the special advisor."

Daya's voice took on an ominous tone. "Some of your shock troops and your special advisor are casualties."

By now Mattiz with his sword and Romeo with Rik's beam gun had the door to the plant ajar, warily peering out. Romeo said, "Manager, your words are disconcerting them. We're winning."

"You had better surrender. If you do, you'll be humanely treated and repatriated to your home soon," Daya finished.

"Is repatriated the right word?" Jax asked.

"I don't know, but it sounds good."

Daya's announcement worked. The soldiers on the Port level started throwing down their beam rifles. Rik wondered if their hearts had been in this travesty of invading Star Corner Station. The shock troops were hardened military killers; the ordinary recruits were not.

Some of the rigid tension seeped out of Daya's shoulders.

"The war is over," he told her.

Her hand found his, and held it tightly. She whispered, "But we don't know yet who and what we've lost."

The surrendering soldiers were treated with civility, relieved of their weapons, and locked into safe and relatively warm places. If there was one thing Star Corner Station had, it was space to store prisoners. Dr. Anahita Lee attended to the soldiers' injuries immediately after assessing the Stationer injured. Fortunately everyone who belonged to the Station would live.

The Faxen shock troops were not so lucky. Six of them were very dead along with the SECINTAG advisor, blown up in an obliterating explosion triggered when the door of the anteroom opened, according to the eyewitness account of the surviving member of the detachment, who'd been behind everyone else.

It was visible through the window—the skeletal finger broken off where the passenger ring had been. Whatever the Angels had been doing in that ring, they'd made sure no one would know, Daya thought.

The Faxens had injuries from their ruined ship, too. After a quick rescue operation, these people were in Dr. Lee's care. She was busy and so was her sick bay, but at least twenty people—Faxens and Stationers—were alive who in any barbarous pre-interstellar war would have been beyond medical help.

The Station's Control Room became the nerve center it was always meant to be. Daya took the command chair, surrounded by her chief staff as they assessed the damages to the Station, made sure no soldiers were still at large, and tried to decide how to clean up a considerable mess. Daya was tired and edgy but she gritted her teeth and kept making decisions.

Mattiz ran into the Station Control Room with a Wendisan bubble in his hand. Its petals were spread, the capsule open. The message was nonsecured and readable by anyone who opened the capsule, but written in Wendisan.

Romeo Ito read the message. His eyes widened. "It wasn't pirates. Starway was attacked by the Faxen Telal Cartel!"

Rik gave Daya a thoughtful look.

"Starway may have been described to Telal as easy pickings—and it was not. With help from militant friends of Wendis, the attack was foiled." A cheer went up. "Wendis considers it to have been an act of war."

Mattiz waved his hand excitedly. "Manager, the contract that describes the Station's ownership is voided in case of war involving the owning entities."

"Then who gets ownership of the Station?" she asked him, hearing a sharp edge on her voice.

"We argued it in that law class. The conclusion we reached was —no one."

There was a long silence as everyone digested that.

Romeo said, "The interstellar situation is unsettled, to say the least, with a lot going on to distract Faxe and Wendis from pressing their rights of ownership to the Station."

"Goya?" Rik asked. It was, as usual, an apt question.

"Goya lacks expertise," Daya said. "Goyan authorities partner with other interstellar interests, but rarely or never do they own interstellar efforts this far away."

With a slow smile, Romeo said, "May I suggest the Republic of Trove?"

Daya felt the foundation of her life drop out from under her like a high-speed vator. "Is that even conceivable? If it it's conceivable, is it doable? If it's doable, is it a good idea?!"

"Of course it is." Rik was Darik when he said that, convincing and compelling. The nearest Stationers started nodding or waving agreement. Daya saw the idea spread across the Control Room, her people reacting to it, startled, yes, but suddenly eager.

Mattiz pointed to Rik. "Finance Ministry!"

Rik raised an eyebrow then smiled a Darik smile.

Suggestions started coming from all directions. "Romeo for Interior Minister!" "Brina for Minister of Mining!"

Daya knew an avalanche when she saw one. No point standing in its way. She waved toward Veda Mender. "Ministry of Maintenance!"

Veda jumped up like a spring-puppet. "There's work to do! This Republic needs mending!"

As Veda rushed out, Anahita Lee came in with a grim face and arms full of leaves and tendrils. "It was under a stairway."

"Oh, no." Shocked, Daya took the hugwort and cradled it. "Damn those soldiers!" Daya burst out. "When it tripped them they went at it with boots and beam rifles."

"Looks like it held its own," Rik said. "Is it still alive?"

It has lost parts of major tendrils. The fur on its root was matted, and the root had deep cuts. But the root was still warm. "I think so," Daya said miserably. "But it's never been hurt this badly."

She bathed the hugwort in warm water, dried it and then put it in her living room chair, under a warm lamp, arranging its leaves to catch the light. She put get-well gifts onto the chair with it—Mattiz's favorite stylus, one of Veda's elegant small tools, a Wendisan yen coin from Romeo, and an earring of her own. She hoped for the best for it. Without the hugwort, the day would have taken a far worse turn for her and for Star Corner Station.

Late night found her in her guest chair, with her head in her hands.

Knock-knock, knock-knock.

"Enter."

It was Rik. Somehow she knew it would be. He put his hands on her shoulders. "How is it?"

She sighed. "I did what I could."

"So will I." He easily picked her up, carried her to her own bed, and put her into her covers.

She took his hand. "Stay." He did. The warmth of his closeness and her own exhaustion let her fall asleep.

In the dark middle of the night she woke up. Her mind flooded with sharp-edged memories—emberalm and Angels and shredded leaves—that drove sleep hopelessly far away. She stared at the ceiling with its softly glowing painting of a dark night sky above the Steppe. A sharp stir told her that Rik had come awake too. "Auditor," she said, "You really do know how to ask the right question."

He eagerly took her into his arms. She soon learned the kind of lover he was—by turns tender and demanding, always responsive. And then she learned how resilient a lover he was. Satisfied as never before, she slept again. So did he.

Early in the morning, when the daylights in her bedroom began to brighten, something woke her up. Rik was sound asleep with a slight furrow on his forehead. She wondered if it would awaken him if she smoothed away that furrow.

Suddenly she realized that the hugwort had come to join them—that was what had woken her up. When she placed her hand on its furry root, it faintly purred. Relief made her almost dizzy. She gently embraced the hugwort, and that woke Rik up too.

"It's OK? I'm glad." He ran his hand through his hair. "Had a dream I've never had before." He looked at her bedroom wall and must have seen his dream replayed there. "Tall white mountains over a sea of grass under a bright blue sky. A landscape I've never seen in my life."

"Someday you will," she said. She embraced him and kissed him, not for the first time, and not for last time at all.

THANK YOU

Veronica and Pauline would like to thank all the authors who joined this adventure with us, gleefully accepting the challenge of pairing pets with science fiction and romance. We are so grateful for the wonderful stories you wrote for this anthology and hope the readers have had as much fun reading the adventures as we all had in writing them.

Special thanks to Fiona Jayde for our wonderful cover art, Nyssa Juneau for our amazing pets sketches, and Narelle Todd for doing so much to make this anthology happen.

We'd also like to thank Hero-Dogs.org for what they do every day for our veterans and for allowing us to partner with them.

And last, but not least, a special thanks to all our readers and if you enjoyed these stories, we invite you to check out all the other wonderful books by the authors in this anthology.